THOMAS MANN

THE MAGIC MOUNTAIN

Thomas Mann was born in Germany in 1875. He was awarded the Nobel Prize for Literature in 1929 and left Germany for good in 1933. Among his major novels are *Buddenbrooks* (1901), *The Magic Mountain* (1924), the tetralogy *Joseph and His Brothers* (1933, 1934, 1936, 1943), and *Doctor Faustus* (1948). He is equally well known for his short stories and essays. Thomas Mann died in 1955.

About the Translator

John E. Woods is the distinguished translator of many books—most notably Arno Schmidt's *Evening Edged in Gold,* for which he won both the American Book Award for translation and the PEN Translation Prize in 1981; Patrick Süskind's *Perfume,* for which he again won the PEN Translation Prize in 1987; Mr. Süskind's *The Pigeon* and *Mr. Summer's Story;* Dorris Dörrie's *Love, Pain, and the Whole Damn Thing* and *What Do You Want from Me?;* Libuše Moníková's *The Façade;* and, most recently, Thomas Mann's *Buddenbrooks.* Mr. Woods lives in San Diego.

INTERNATIONAL

BOOKS BY **THOMAS MANN,**

AVAILABLE FROM VINTAGE

Buddenbrooks
The Magic Mountain
Death in Venice and Seven Other Stories
Doctor Faustus
Confessions of Felix Krull, Confidence Man

THE MAGIC MOUNTAIN

THE MAGIC MOUNTAIN

A Novel

THOMAS MANN

Translated from the German
by John E. Woods

VINTAGE INTERNATIONAL

VINTAGE BOOKS   A DIVISION OF RANDOM HOUSE, INC.   NEW YORK

FIRST VINTAGE INTERNATIONAL EDITION, NOVEMBER 1996

Copyright © 1995 by Alfred A. Knopf, Inc.

All rights reserved under International and Pan-American Copyright
Conventions. Published in the United States by Vintage Books, a division
of Random House, Inc., New York, and simultaneously in Canada by
Random House of Canada Limited, Toronto. Originally published in hardcover
by Alfred A. Knopf, Inc., New York, in 1995.

The Library of Congress has cataloged
the Knopf edition as follows:
Mann, Thomas, 1875–1955.
[Zauberberg. English]
The magic mountain : a novel / Thomas Mann ;
translated from the German by John E. Woods.
p.   cm.
ISBN 0-679-44183-2
I. Woods, John E. (John Edwin).   II. Title.
PT2625.A44Z32   1995
833'.912—dc20   94-42885
CIP
Vintage ISBN: 0-679-77287-1

Random House Web address: http://www.randomhouse.com/

Printed in the United States of America
20 19 18

CONTENTS

Foreword   ·   ix

I

Arrival   3
Room 34   10
In the Restaurant   13

2

The Baptismal Bowl/Grandfather in His Two Forms   18
At the Tienappels'/Hans Castorp's Moral State   28

3

The Shadow of Respectability   36
Breakfast   39
Teasing/Viaticum/Interrupted Merriment   45
Satana   54
Clarity of Mind   63
One Word Too Many   68
But of Course—a Female!   72

Herr Albin   76
Satana Makes Shameful Suggestions   79

4

A Necessary Purchase   91
Excursus on the Sense of Time   100
He Tries Out His Conversational French   103
Politically Suspect   108
Hippe   113
Analysis   122
Doubts and Considerations   128
Table Talk   132
Growing Anxiety/Two Grandfathers and a Twilight Boat Ride   138
The Thermometer   158

5

Eternal Soup and Sudden Clarity   180
"My God, I See It!"   201
Freedom   216
Mercury's Moods   222
Encyclopedia   233
Humaniora   247
Research   263
Danse Macabre   281
Walpurgis Night   316

6

Changes   339
Someone Else   362
The City of God and Evil Deliverance   380
An Outburst of Temper/Something Very Embarrassing   405
An Attack Repulsed   417

Operationes Spirituales   432
Snow   460
A Good Soldier   489

7

A Stroll by the Shore   531
Mynheer Peeperkorn   538
Vingt et un   ,   546
Mynheer Peeperkorn (Continued)   564
Mynheer Peeperkorn (Conclusion)   604
The Great Stupor   616
Fullness of Harmony   626
Highly Questionable   644
The Great Petulance   672
The Thunderbolt   696

FOREWORD

T HE STORY OF Hans Castorp that we intend to tell here—not for his sake (for the reader will come to know him as a perfectly ordinary, if engaging young man), but for the sake of the story itself, which seems to us to be very much worth telling (although in Hans Castorp's favor it should be noted that it is *his* story, and that not every story happens to everybody)—is a story that took place long ago, and is, so to speak, covered with the patina of history and must necessarily be told with verbs whose tense is that of the deepest past.

Nor is that detrimental to our story, indeed it may well work to its advantage; for stories, as histories, must be past, and the further past, one might say, the better for them as stories and for the storyteller, that conjurer who murmurs in past tenses. But the problem with our story, as also with many people nowadays and, indeed, not the least with those who tell stories, is this: it is much older than its years, its datedness is not to be measured in days, nor the burden of age weighing upon it to be counted by orbits around the sun; in a word, it does not actually owe its pastness to *time*—an assertion that is itself intended as a passing reference, an allusion, to the problematic and uniquely double nature of that mysterious element.

But let us not intentionally obscure a clear state of affairs: the extraordinary pastness of our story results from its having taken place *before* a certain turning point, on the far side of a rift that has cut deeply through our lives and consciousness. It takes place, or, to avoid any present tense whatever, it took place back then, long ago, in the old days of the world before the Great War, with whose beginning so many things began whose beginnings, it seems, have not yet ceased. It took place before the war, then, though not long before. But is not the pastness of a story that much more profound, more complete, more like a fairy tale, the tighter it fits up against the "before"? And it may well be that our story, by its very nature, has a few other things in common with fairy tales, too.

We shall tell it at length, in precise and thorough detail—for when was a story short on diversion or long on boredom simply because of the time and space required for the telling? Unafraid of the odium of appearing too meticulous, we are much more inclined to the view that only thoroughness can be truly entertaining.

And so this storyteller will not be finished telling our Hans's story in only a moment or two. The seven days in one week will not suffice, nor will seven months. It will be best for him if he is not all too clear about the number of earthly days that will pass as the tale weaves its web about him. For God's sake, surely it cannot be as long as seven years!

And with that, we begin.

THE MAGIC MOUNTAIN

Arrival

AN ORDINARY YOUNG MAN was on his way from his hometown of Hamburg to Davos-Platz in the canton of Graubünden. It was the height of summer, and he planned to stay for three weeks.

It is a long trip, however, from Hamburg to those elevations—too long, really, for so short a visit. The journey leads through many a landscape, uphill and down, descends from the high plain of southern Germany to the shores of Swabia's sea, and proceeds by boat across its skipping waves, passing over abysses once thought unfathomable.

From there the path, which until now has followed grand, direct routes, turns choppy. There are stopovers and formalities. At Rorschach, a town in Swiss territory, you reboard a train that takes you only as far as Landquart, a small station in the Alps, where you must change trains again. After standing for a while in the wind, gazing at a rather uncharming landscape, you climb aboard a narrow-gauge train, and the moment the small, but uncommonly sturdy engine pulls out, the real adventure begins, a steep and dogged ascent that will never end, it seems. The station at Landquart lies at a relatively low altitude; but now your route takes you on a wild ride up into real mountains, along tracks that squeeze their way between walls of rock.

Hans Castorp—that is the young man's name—found himself alone in a small compartment upholstered in gray; with him he had an alligator valise, a present from his uncle and foster father—Consul Tienappel, since we are naming names here—a rolled-up plaid blanket, and his winter coat, swinging on its hook. The window was open beside him, but the afternoon was turning cooler and cooler, and, being the coddled scion of the family, he turned up the silk-lined collar of his fashionably loose summer overcoat. On the seat beside him lay a paperbound book entitled *Ocean Steamships*, which he had perused from time to time earlier on his trip, but which now lay neglected, the cover dirtied by soot drifting in with the steam of the heavily puffing locomotive.

Two days of travel separate this young man (and young he is, with few firm roots in life) from his everyday world, especially from what he called his duties, interests, worries, and prospects—separate him far more than he had dreamed possible as he rode to the station in a hansom cab. Space, as it rolls and tumbles away between him and his native soil, proves to have powers normally ascribed only to time; from hour to hour, space brings about changes very like those time produces, yet surpassing them in certain ways. Space, like time, gives birth to forgetfulness, but does so by removing an individual from all relationships and placing him in a free and pristine state—indeed, in but a moment it can turn a pedant and philistine into something like a vagabond. Time, they say, is water from the river Lethe, but alien air is a similar drink; and if its effects are less profound, it works all the more quickly.

And Hans Castorp experienced much the same thing. He had not planned to take this trip particularly seriously, to become deeply involved in it. His intention had been, rather, to put it behind him quickly, simply because that was how things had to be, to return quite the same person he had been at departure, and to pick up his life again where he had been forced to leave it lying for the moment. Only yesterday he had been totally caught up in his normal train of thought, preoccupied with what had just occurred, his exams, and with what was about to occur, his joining the firm of Tunder and Wilms (dockyards, machine works, and boilers), and looking well beyond these next three weeks with as much impatience as his nature allowed. But now it seemed to him that present circumstances demanded his full attention and that it was inappropriate to shrug them off. Being lifted like this into regions whose air he had never breathed before and whose sparse and meager conditions were, as he well knew, both unfamiliar and peculiar—it all began to excite him, to fill him with a certain anxiety. Home and a settled life not only lay far behind, but also, and more importantly, they lay fathoms below him, and he was still climbing. Hovering between home and the unknown ahead, he asked himself how he would do up there. Was it unwise and unhealthy, perhaps, for him, born only a few feet above sea level and accustomed to breathing that air, to be suddenly transported to such extreme regions without spending at least a few days someplace in between? He wished he had already reached his goal, because once you were up there, he thought, you lived just as people did everywhere, instead of having the climb constantly remind you of how unsuitable these precincts were. He looked out—the train was winding through a narrow pass; you could see the forward cars and the laboring engine, emitting great straggling tatters of brown, green, and black smoke. Water roared in the deep ravine on his right; dark pines on his left struggled up between boulders toward a stony gray sky. There were pitch-black tunnels, and when daylight returned, vast chasms were revealed, with a few villages far below. These views closed again, too, and were followed by new passes with patches of snow left in clefts and crevices. The train pulled into dingy little stations and backed out again on the same set of tracks, confusing your sense of direction until you no longer knew whether you were heading north or south. Magnificent vistas opened onto regions toward which they were slowly climbing, a world of ineffable, phantasma-goric Alpine peaks, soon lost again to awestruck eyes as the tracks took another curve. Hans Castorp thought about how he had left hardwood forests far below him, and songbirds, too, he presumed; and the idea that such things could cease, the sense of a world made poorer without them, brought on a slight attack of dizziness and nausea, and he covered his eyes with his hand for a second or two. This passed. He realized that their climb was coming to an end, that they had taken the crest. The train was now rolling more comfortably along the level floor of a valley.

It was almost eight o'clock, but still daylight. A lake appeared in the distant landscape; its surface was gray and from its shores black pine forests climbed the surrounding slopes, grew thinner toward the top, and gave way at last to bare, fog-enshrouded rock. They stopped at a little station, Davos-Dorf, as Hans Castorp learned when someone outside shouted the name—he would be at journey's end shortly. And suddenly, right beside him, he heard his cousin Joachim Ziemssen saying in an easygoing Hamburg voice, "Hello there. This is where you get off." And when he looked out, there on the platform below his window stood Joachim, wearing a brown ulster but no hat of any sort, and looking healthier than ever. He laughed and said again, "Come on, get off, don't be shy!"

"But I'm not there yet," Hans Castorp said, dumbfounded, keeping his seat.

"Sure you are. This is Davos-Dorf. The sanatorium's closer from here. I've got a carriage. Hand me your things."

And with a laugh that betrayed his confusion and excitement at having arrived and seeing his cousin again, Hans Castorp lifted out his valise and winter coat, his plaid blanket roll plus cane and umbrella, and finally

Ocean Steamships. Then he ran along the narrow corridor and jumped down onto the platform for a proper and more or less personal greeting, though this was done without any exuberance, as is fitting between people who are cool and reserved by custom. Strangely enough, they had always avoided calling one another by their first names, purely out of fear of showing too much warmth of emotion. And since they could not very well address one another by their last names, they confined themselves to the use of familiar pronouns—now a deeply rooted habit between the two cousins.

They quickly shook hands with some embarrassment—young Ziemssen never losing his military bearing—watched all the while by a man in livery with a braided cap, who then approached and asked Hans Castorp for his baggage ticket; this was the concierge of the International Sanatorium Berghof, and he proved quite willing to fetch the guest's large trunk from the station at Davos-Platz while the gentlemen themselves drove on ahead to dinner. The man had an obvious limp, and so the first thing that Hans Castorp asked Joachim Ziemssen was, "Is he a war veteran? Is that why he limps so badly?"

"Right! A war veteran," Joachim replied, somewhat sarcastically. "He's got it in the knee—or had it, that is, now that he's had his kneecap removed."

Hans Castorp mulled this over as rapidly as possible. "Oh, I see," he said, lifting his head and hastily looking back as they walked on. "But you're not going to try to tell me that you still have anything like that, are you? You look as if you've already received your commission and were just home from maneuvers." And he gave his cousin a sidelong glance.

Joachim was taller than he, with broader shoulders, the picture of youthful vigor, a man made for a uniform. He was very dark-haired, a type not all that uncommon in his blond hometown, and his naturally dark complexion was now tanned almost bronze. With his large black eyes and dark little moustache above full, finely chiseled lips, he would have been downright handsome, if his ears had not stood out so badly. For most of his life, they had been his one great sorrow, his only care. Now he had other worries. "You will be coming back down with me, won't you?" Hans Castorp went on. "I really see nothing standing in your way."

"Back down with you?" his cousin asked, turning to him with large eyes that had always had a gentle look, but that in the last five months had taken on a weary, indeed sad expression. "When do you mean?"

"Why, in three weeks."

"Oh, I see—you're already thinking about heading back home," Joachim replied. "Well, wait and see, you've only just arrived. Three weeks are almost nothing for us up here, of course, but for you, just here on a visit and planning to stay a grand total of three weeks, for you that's a long time. Acclimatize yourself first—and you'll learn that's not all that easy. Besides, the climate's not the only unusual thing about us. You'll see quite a few new sights here, just watch. And as for what you've said about me—well, I'm not in such fine feather as all that, my friend. 'Home in three weeks,' that's a notion from down below. I'm nicely tanned, of course, but that's mostly from the snow and doesn't mean much, as Behrens is always saying, and at my last regular checkup he said that it's fairly certain it will be another six months yet."

"Six months? Are you crazy?" Hans Castorp cried. They were taking their seats on the hard cushions of a yellow cabriolet that had stood waiting for them on the gravel apron in front of the station, itself not much more than a shed; and as the pair of bays began to pull, Hans Castorp spun around now in vexation. "Six months? You've already been here for almost that long! We don't have that much time in life!"

"Ah yes, time," Joachim said, nodding to himself several times, paying no attention to his cousin's honest indignation. "You wouldn't believe how fast and loose they play with people's time around here. Three weeks are the same as a day to them. You'll see. You have all that to learn," he said, and then he added, "A man changes a lot of his ideas here."

Hans Castorp gazed steadily at his profile. "But you really have made a splendid recovery," he said, shaking his head.

"Do you think so?" Joachim replied. "It's true, isn't it? I think so, too!" he said, sitting up taller against the cushioned back, but immediately slumping again a little to one side. "I am feeling better," he explained, "but I'm not yet entirely well, either. The upper left lobe, where the rattling used to be, there's only a little roughness there now, it's not so bad, but the lower lobe is still *very* rough, and there are also sounds in the second intercostal."

"How learned you've become," Hans Castorp said.

"Yes, a fine sort of learning, God knows. I would gladly have unlearned it all on active duty," Joachim retorted. "But I still have sputum," he said with a nonchalant, but somehow vehement shrug that did not suit him at all; and now he pulled something halfway out of the nearer side pocket of his ulster, showed it to his cousin, and put it away again at once—a curved, flattened bottle of bluish glass with a metal cap. "Most of us up here have one," he said. "We even have a name for it, a kind of nickname, a joke really. Having a look at the scenery, are you?"

And indeed that was what Hans Castorp was doing, and he exclaimed, "Magnificent!"

"You think so, do you?" Joachim asked.

They had first taken a street that was faced by an irregular pattern of buildings and ran along the railroad tracks, following the valley's axis, but then turned left and crossed the narrow tracks and a brook; and they were now trotting up a gently rising road in the direction of wooded slopes and a low, outcropping meadow where an elongated building stood, its façade turned to the southwest, topped by a copper cupola, and arrayed with so many balconies that, from a distance as the first lights of evening were being lit, it looked as pockmarked and porous as a sponge. Dusk was falling fast. A pale red sunset that had enlivened the generally overcast sky faded now, leaving nature under the transient sway of the lackluster, lifeless, and mournful light that immediately precedes nightfall. Lights were coming up in the long, meandering, populous valley, dotting its floor and the slopes on both sides—particularly on the swelling rise to the right, where buildings ascended a series of terraces. Paths led up the meadowed hills on their left, but were soon lost to sight in the dull black of pine forests. Behind them, the mountains in the more distant background, where the valley tapered to an end, were a sober slate blue. Now that the wind had picked up, the evening had turned noticeably cooler.

"No, to be quite frank, I don't find it that overwhelming," Hans Castorp said. "Where are the glaciers and snowcapped, towering peaks? Seems to me, the ones here aren't all that high."

"Oh, they're high all right," Joachim replied. "You can see the tree line almost everywhere, it's really quite clearly defined; the pines come to an end, then everything else—the end, then rocks, as you can see. And over there, to the right of the Schwarzhorn, on that jagged peak there, is a glacier for you—can you still see the blue? It's not that big, but it's a textbook glacier, the Scaletta Glacier. And there's Piz Michel and Tinzenhorn in that gap—you can't see them from here, but they're always snow-covered, year-round."

"Eternal snow," Hans Castorp said.

"Right, eternal, if you like. And they're all very high. But we're dreadfully high up ourselves, keep that in mind. Five thousand three hundred feet above sea level. So you don't notice the difference in height that much."

"Yes, it was quite a climb. Certainly had me scared, let me tell you. Five thousand three hundred feet. Why, that's over a mile high. I've never been this far up in my whole life." And in his curiosity, Hans Castorp took a deep breath, testing the alien air. It was fresh—that was all. It lacked odor, content, moisture, it went easily into the lungs and said nothing to the soul.

"Excellent!" he remarked politely.

"Yes, the air is famous. But the landscape is not showing itself to its best advantage this evening. It can look better, especially in the snow. But you soon get your fill of staring at it. Believe me, all of us up here have definitely had our fill of it," Joachim said, and his mouth wrenched in an expression of disgust that seemed both exaggerated and out of control—and once again it did not suit him.

"You're talking so strangely," Hans Castorp said.

"Strangely, am I?" Joachim asked, turning to his cousin and looking worried somehow.

"No, no, beg your pardon, it just seemed that way to me for a moment or so," Hans Castorp hastened to say. But what he really meant was that the phrase "us up here," which Joachim had used three or four times already, somehow made him feel anxious and queer.

"Our sanatorium lies at a higher altitude than the village, as you can see," Joachim continued. "A hundred fifty feet. The brochure says 'three hundred,' but it's only half that. The highest of the sanatoriums is Schatzalp, across the way, you can't see it now. They have to transport the bodies down by bobsled in the winter, because the roads are impassable."

"The bodies? Oh, I see. You don't say!" Hans Castorp cried. And suddenly he burst into laughter, a violent, overpowering laugh that shook his chest and twisted his face, stiffened by the cool wind, into a slightly painful grimace. "On bobsleds! And you can sit there and tell me that so calm and cool? You've become quite the cynic in the last five months."

"That's not cynical at all," Joachim replied with a shrug. "Why do you say that? It doesn't matter to the bodies. All the same, it may well be that we do get cynical up here. Behrens is an old cynic himself—a regular brick, by the way, an old fraternity man and a brilliant surgeon, you'll like him, seems to me. And then there's Krokowski, his assistant— a very savvy character. They make special note of his services in the brochure. He dissects the patients' psyches."

"He what? Dissects their psyches? That's disgusting!" Hans Castorp cried, and now hilarity got the better of him. He could no longer control it. Psychic dissection had finished the job, and he bent over and laughed so hard that the tears ran out from under the hand with which he had covered his eyes. Joachim laughed heartily, too—it seemed to do him good. And so the two young men were in fine good humor as they climbed down from their carriage, which had borne them at a slow trot up the steep loop of the driveway to the portal of the International Sanatorium Berghof.

Room 34

ON THEIR IMMEDIATE RIGHT, between the outer and inner doors, was the desk for the concierge, and a French-looking attendant, dressed in the same livery as the limping man at the train station, was sitting by the telephone reading newspapers; he came up to them and led them across the well-lit lobby, with public rooms opening off it on the left. Hans Castorp peered in as they passed, and discovered them empty. Where were the guests? he asked, and his cousin replied, "Taking their rest cure. I was excused from it today because I wanted to meet your train. Otherwise I'd be lying out on my balcony after my evening meal, too."

It would not have taken much for Hans Castorp to be seized by another fit of laughter. "What? You lie out on your balcony rain or shine, night or day?" he asked, his voice wavering on the edge.

"Yes, it's in the rules. From eight till ten. But come on, let's have a look at your room, and you can wash up."

They got on the elevator, the Frenchman operating the electric switches. As they glided upward, Hans Castorp dried his eyes.

"I'm exhausted, I've laughed so hard," he said, catching his breath through his mouth. "It's all these crazy things you've been telling me. The psychic dissection was just too much, I could have done without that. Besides, I'm a little weary from the trip, I suppose. Do your feet get cold so easily, too? And at the same time your face flushes—it's an unpleasant feeling. I assume we'll be eating soon? I think I'm getting hungry. Do they feed you properly up here?"

They passed soundlessly down the coconut runners of the narrow corridor. Cool light came from the milk-glass shades of lamps set in the ceiling. The walls were painted with a hard, glistening white enamel. A nurse in a white cap appeared from somewhere, a pince-nez set on her nose, its cord tucked behind one ear. She had the look of a Protestant nurse, of someone with no real devotion to her profession, but kept restless by curiosity and the burden of boredom. Some balloon-shaped objects had been set out in the corridor, beside two of the white-enameled doors— large, potbellied containers with short necks. Hans Castorp was going to ask their purpose, and just as quickly forgot the question.

"Here you are," Joachim said. "Number thirty-four. I'm on your right, and on your left is a Russian couple—they're rather slovenly, and loud, I must say, but there was nothing else we could do. Well, what do you say?"

There was a double door, with clothes hooks in the space between the two. Joachim had turned on the ceiling light, and its sharp luster revealed a room that was both cheerful and restful, with white, practical furniture; heavy, washable wallpaper, likewise white; a floor covered with spotless linoleum; and linen curtains, embroidered with a simple, cheerful pattern of modern design. The door to the balcony stood open to a glimpse of lights in the valley and the sound of distant dance music. Joachim had thoughtfully placed a few wildflowers in a small vase on the dresser—some yarrow and a couple of bluebells, in their second bloom this summer, that he had picked on the slopes.

"How kind of you," Hans Castorp said. "What a nice room. I'll have no trouble putting up here for a week or two."

"An American woman died here the day before yesterday," Joachim said. "Behrens told me he was sure it would be all over with her before you arrived, and that you could have the room. Her fiancé was with her, an English naval officer, but he didn't exactly keep a stiff upper lip. He kept coming out into the corridor to cry every few minutes, like a little boy. And then he'd rub his cheeks with cold cream because he'd just shaved and the tears stung. The evening before last, the American woman had two first-class hemorrhages, and that was that. But she's been gone since yesterday morning, and of course it was all thoroughly fumigated with formalin—they say it's very effective, you know."

Hans Castorp was listening to this narrative with edgy bemusement. He had rolled up his sleeves and was standing now at the large washbasin, its nickel taps sparkling under the electric light, but he cast no more than a fleeting glance at the bed's white metal frame and fresh sheets.

"Fumigated, that's spiffing," he said glibly and somewhat incongruously while he washed and dried his hands. "Yes, methyl aldehyde, even the toughest bacteria can't take that—H_2CO, but it does burn in your nose, doesn't it? It's obvious, of course, that strict cleanliness is essential." His accent, particularly his *st*'s, betrayed his Hamburg origins, whereas starting back in his student days, his cousin had adopted more standard pronunciation. Feeling much chattier now, he rambled on, "What I was going to say was . . . that naval officer probably used a safety razor, that's what I think, it's easier to cut yourself with those things than with a well-stropped straight razor, that's been my experience at least, so I alternate between the two. And, of course, salt water does smart on chafed skin, so he probably got in the habit of using cold cream while he was in the service, that doesn't seem at all peculiar to me." And he chatted away, telling about how he had packed two hundred Maria Mancinis—his cigars—in his trunk, but that getting through customs had been easy as pie. And then he extended greetings from various people back home.

"Don't they heat the rooms?" he suddenly exclaimed and ran over to put his hand on the radiator.

"No, they keep it rather cool," Joachim answered. "The weather would have to turn really bad before they would turn on the heat in August."

"August, August," Hans Castorp said. "But I'm freezing! I'm ab-so-lute-ly freezing, I mean my body is, although my face feels awfully flushed—here, feel it, it's burning up."

The suggestion that someone feel his face was not at all typical of Hans Castorp, and even he was embarrassed by it. Joachim did not acknowledge it, but merely said, "It's the air here, it doesn't mean anything. Behrens himself walks around with purple cheeks all day. Some people never get used to it. Well, come on now, or we'll not get anything to eat."

In the corridor they ran into the nurse again, who squinted with near-sighted curiosity as she watched them pass. They had reached the second floor, when Hans Castorp suddenly stopped in his tracks, mesmerized by a perfectly ghastly noise he heard coming from beyond a dogleg in the hall—not a loud noise, but so decidedly repulsive that Hans Castorp grimaced and stared wide-eyed at his cousin. It was a cough, apparently—a man's cough, but a cough unlike any that Hans Castorp had ever heard; indeed, compared to it, all other coughs with which he was familiar had been splendid, healthy expressions of life—a cough devoid of any zest for life or love, which didn't come in spasms, but sounded as if someone were stirring feebly in a terrible mush of decomposing organic material.

"Yes," Joachim said, "it looks bad. An Austrian aristocrat—you know, an elegant fellow, your born horseman. And now it's come to this. Although he's still up and about."

As they walked on, Hans Castorp remarked, referring to the horseman's cough, "You must realize that I've never heard anything like it, that it's all quite new to me, and that it does make an impression. There are so many kinds of coughs, dry ones, loose ones, and loose ones are healthier, people say, better than dry barks. Back in my youth"—he actually said "in my youth"—"I caught the croup, and it had me barking like a wolf, and everyone was happy when it loosened up, I still remember it quite well. But a cough like that—that's something new, to me at least—it's not even human. It's not dry, but you can't call it loose, either, there's no word for it. It's as if you were looking right down inside and could see it all—the mucus and the slime . . ."

"Well," Joachim said, "I hear it every day, so you don't need to describe it for me."

But Hans Castorp could not get the cough he had heard out of his mind and kept repeating that it was literally like looking down inside the horseman; and as they entered the restaurant, his eyes, weary from the trip, had taken on a glint of nervous excitement.

In the Restaurant

T HE RESTAURANT was well lit, elegant, and comfortable. It was to the right of the lobby, directly across from the social rooms, and was used, as Joachim explained, primarily for new arrivals or residents who either had missed a regularly scheduled meal or had visitors. But birthdays or imminent departures were celebrated there, too, as were favorable results of a general checkup. Things could get very lively in the restaurant on occasion, Joachim said; they even served champagne. There was no one there now except one lady, perhaps thirty years old, sitting alone and reading—humming to herself the whole time while drumming softly on the tabletop with the middle finger of her left hand. When the young gentlemen had seated themselves, she changed places, so that her back was to them now. She was standoffish, Joachim explained in a low voice, and always ate in the restaurant with just her book. Rumor had it that she had entered a tuberculosis sanatorium as a very young girl and had never lived in the outside world since.

"Well then, compared to her you're a mere novice with your five months, and still will be with a whole year to your credit," Hans Castorp said to his cousin; to which Joachim merely gave his new, uncharacteristic shrug and reached for the menu.

They had taken the raised table beside a window hung with cream-colored curtains—the nicest table in the room. They sat opposite one another, their faces illumined by an electric table lamp with a red shade. Hans Castorp clasped his freshly washed hands together and rubbed them in congenial expectation, a habit of his whenever he sat down to eat— perhaps because his forebears had prayed before every meal. They were waited on by a friendly girl in a black dress and white apron, whose large face glowed with robust health and who spoke in a guttural dialect. To his great amusement, Hans Castorp was instructed that waitresses here were called "dining attendants." They ordered a bottle of Gruaud Larose, which Hans Castorp sent back to be brought to room temperature. The food was excellent. There was asparagus soup, followed by stuffed toma-toes, a roast with several vegetables, an especially well done dessert, and a tray of cheese and fruit. Hans Castorp ate heartily, although with not quite the lively appetite he had expected. But he was accustomed to eating large meals—even when he wasn't hungry—purely out of self-respect.

Joachim did not do much credit to his meal. He had had enough of the cooking here, he said, everyone up here had, and it was customary to disparage the food, because when you had to sit up here forever and a day . . . But he did enjoy drinking, taking to the wine with something like abandon; and while carefully avoiding all sentiment-laden phrases, he repeatedly expressed his satisfaction that at last someone was here with whom it was possible to have a rational conversation.

"Yes, it's top-notch, your having come," he said, and there was feeling in his nonchalant voice. "And let me tell you it's quite an event for me. First of all, just the variety of it—I mean, it's an interruption, a break in the everlasting, endless monotony."

"But I would think time ought to pass quickly for you all," Hans Castorp suggested.

"Quickly and slowly, just as you like," Joachim replied. "What I'm trying to say is that it doesn't really pass at all, there is no time as such, and this is no life—no, that it's not," he said, shaking his head and reaching again for his glass.

Hans Castorp drank as well, although his face was burning like fire by now. But his body still seemed cold, and he felt a pleasurable and yet somehow annoying restlessness in his joints. Words tumbled out, he misspoke himself several times, but went right on with a dismissive wave of his hand. Joachim was likewise in a lively mood, and after the humming, drumming lady suddenly stood up and departed, their conversation turned even more candid and high-spirited. They gesticulated with their forks as they ate, tucked bites of food in their cheeks, looked important, laughed, nodded, shrugged, and went right on talking without even first swallowing their food properly. Joachim wanted to hear about Hamburg and brought the conversation around to plans for making the Elbe more navigable.

"Epoch-making!" Hans Castorp said. "An epoch-making development for our maritime commerce—simply not to be overestimated. We've added a line in our budget for an immediate payment of fifty million, and you can be sure that we know exactly what we're doing."

But then, despite the importance he attached to navigation on the Elbe, he at once abandoned the topic and demanded that Joachim tell him more about life "up here" and about the guests; which Joachim proved ready and willing to do, happy to open his heart and unburden himself. He had to repeat the part about the bodies being sent down by bobsled and once again asserted unequivocally that he knew it to be true. And when Hans Castorp was taken by another fit of laughter, Joachim joined in, seeming heartily to enjoy the opportunity, and then told more comic stories, just to add fuel to the general merriment. There was a lady who sat at his table, Frau Stöhr was her name, and quite ill by the way, the wife of a musician from Cannstatt—and she was the most illiterate person he had ever met. She said things like "decentfiction"—in all seriousness. And Krokowski, the assistant—she called him the "eighty camp." You had to sit there and swallow it, without a trace of a smile. And she was a gossip, besides, as were most people up here, by the by, and she claimed that another lady, Frau Iltis, carried a "stirletto" around with her. "She calls it a stirletto—isn't that capital!" And throwing themselves back in their chairs, half lying, half leaning, they laughed so hard that they shook until they both began to hiccough at almost the same time.

But every now and then, Joachim was reminded of his own fate and would turn gloomy. "Yes, here we sit laughing," he said with a pained expression, broken by occasional spasms of his diaphragm, "and yet there's no telling when I'll get out of here, because when Behrens says another six months, that's his low estimate, and you need to be prepared for even longer. But it is hard, you must admit. It's really sad, isn't it? I had already been accepted and would have taken my officer's exam next month. And here I am lounging about with a thermometer in my mouth and counting Frau Stöhr's illiterate howlers, and time is passing me by. A single year plays such an important role at our age, it brings so many changes and so much progress with it when you're living down below. And here I am stagnating like an old water hole—a stinking pond, and that's not too crude a comparison, either."

Strangely enough, Hans Castorp's only reply came as a question—did they serve porter here? And when Joachim looked at him in astonishment, he realized that his cousin was very near to falling asleep—was in fact already nodding.

"Why, you're asleep," Joachim said. "Come on, it's high time we went to bed, both of us."

"It's not time for anything," Hans Castorp said with a thick tongue. But he joined his cousin all the same, walking on stiff legs and bent so low that he looked like a man being dragged toward the floor by weariness. But as they moved across the now dimly lit lobby, he pulled himself together by sheer force of effort when he heard Joachim say, "That's Krokowski sitting there. I really must introduce you, I suppose."

Dr. Krokowski was sitting in the light, close to the fireplace, just inside the sliding door opening onto one of the social rooms. He was reading a newspaper, but stood up as the young men approached. Joachim, striking a military pose, said, "Might I introduce you, doctor, to my cousin Castorp? He's just arrived from Hamburg."

Dr. Krokowski greeted the new resident with a kind of jovial, rugged, and reassuring heartiness, as if to imply that in his presence any diffidence was quite superfluous and cheerful mutual trust the only appropriate response. He was about thirty-five years old, broad-shouldered, stout, considerably shorter than the two men across from him, so that he had to tip his head back to look them in the eye, and extraordinarily pale— there was almost a translucence, even phosphorescence, to his pallor, and it was enhanced by dark, glowing eyes, black eyebrows, and a rather long beard that already showed a few gray strands and ended in two diverging points. He wore a black, rather worn, double-breasted business suit and black open-worked shoes, almost sandals really, over gray woolen socks; Hans Castorp had seen a soft, floppy collar like that only once before— sported by a photographer in Danzig—and indeed it did lend something of the artist's studio to Dr. Krokowski's general appearance. As he shook the young man's hand, an effusive smile revealed yellowish teeth under his beard, and in a baritone voice betraying the drawl of a foreign accent, he said, "We bid you welcome, Herr Castorp. I do hope that you'll make yourself comfortable and soon feel right at home here with us. You have come as a patient, have you not—if you'll pardon the question?"

It was touching to see how Hans Castorp struggled to be polite and master his drowsiness. He was annoyed with himself for being in such bad shape, and with the leery self-consciousness of youth he detected traces of an indulgent smirk in the assistant director's reassuring smile. In answering, he said something about three weeks, mentioned his exams, and added that, thank God, he was perfectly healthy.

"You don't say!" Dr. Krokowski replied, thrusting his head forward at a derisive slant and smiling more broadly. "In that case you are a phenomenon of greatest medical interest. You see, I've never met a perfectly healthy person before. And what kind of exams were those, if you'll pardon the question?"

"I'm an engineer, doctor," Hans Castorp answered with modest dignity.

"Ah, an engineer." And Dr. Krokowski's smile receded, as it were, losing something of both its energy and warmth for a moment. "Bravo, my congratulations. And so you'll not be availing yourself here of any sort of medical attention, either physical or psychological?"

"No, no, thanks just the same," Hans Castorp said, almost stepping back.

With that, Dr. Krokowski broke into his triumphant smile again, and shaking the young man's hand once more, he exclaimed in a loud voice, "In that case, sleep well, Herr Castorp—in full enjoyment of your impeccable health. Sleep well, and I'm sure we'll see more of one another." And then he dismissed the young men and sat back down to his newspaper.

The elevator was no longer running, and so they used the stairs, climbing in silence, slightly bewildered by their meeting with Dr. Krokowski. Joachim accompanied Hans Castorp to room 34, where they found that the limping concierge had properly delivered the new guest's luggage; and they chatted for another fifteen minutes while Hans Castorp unpacked his nightclothes and toiletries after first lighting a thick, mild cigarette. He never had got around to a last cigar—which struck him as odd, quite unusual, really.

"He does have a distinguished look about him," he said, and the inhaled smoke tumbled out with the words. "He's pale as chalk. But as for his choice of footwear, it's really dreadful, I must say. Gray wool socks—and then those sandals. Was he offended there at the end?"

"He's a little sensitive," Joachim admitted. "You shouldn't have been so brusque about rejecting medical treatment, at least not the psychological part. He doesn't like for people to try to avoid it. He's not all that well disposed toward me, either, because I don't confide enough in him. But now and then I do tell him a dream, so that he'll have something to dissect."

"Then I really did rub him the wrong way just now," Hans Castorp said with annoyance, for it always upset him when he offended someone; and now weariness overcame him with renewed intensity as well.

"Good night," he said. "I'm ready to drop."

"I'll come by for you for breakfast at eight," Joachim said and left.

Hans Castorp hastily went through the motions of getting ready for bed. No sooner had he turned out the lamp on his nightstand than sleep overwhelmed him—but he started up again when he recalled that someone had died in that very bed only two nights before. "Not for the first time, either," he told himself, as if that might serve to reassure him. "It's just a deathbed, an ordinary deathbed." And he dozed off.

But as soon as he was asleep, he began to dream and kept on dreaming almost nonstop until morning. Most of the time he saw Joachim Ziemssen, in a strangely contorted position, riding down a steep slope on a bobsled. He was as phosphorescently pale as Dr. Krokowski, and up front sat the Austrian horseman, steering, although the face was very vague, like that of someone you've only heard cough. "It really doesn't matter to us—to us up here," the contorted Joachim said, and now it was he, and not the horseman, who was coughing in that ghastly, slimy way. And this made Hans Castorp weep bitterly, and he realized that he would have to run to the pharmacist to get himself some cold cream. But Frau Iltis was sitting beside the road, a roguish pucker on her face, and she was holding something in her hand that was supposed to be her "stirletto," but was really nothing more than a safety razor. That only made Hans Castorp laugh again, and so he was tossed back and forth by waves of emotion until the dawn came to the half-open balcony door and awakened him.

The Baptismal Bowl/
Grandfather in His Two Forms

Hans Castorp retained only faint recollections of his actual parental home; he had hardly known his father and mother. They had both dropped dead within the brief period between his fifth and seventh years of life. His mother had died first, quite unexpectedly, while awaiting the birth of a second child, of an arterial blockage caused by phlebitis, an embolism, Dr. Heidekind had called it, triggering instantaneous cardiac paralysis—she had been sitting up in bed, laughing, and it looked as if she simply toppled over in a fit of laughter, whereas in fact she did it because she was dead. It was not something that Hans Hermann Castorp, the father, found easy to understand, and since he had been very fond of his wife and was not the most robust man himself, he simply did not know how to get over it. From then on, his mind was muddled, his focus narrow; and in his befuddlement he made mistakes in his business, resulting in serious losses for the firm of Castorp and Son. While inspecting a harbor warehouse on a windy day the following spring, he caught pneumonia, and since, despite all the conscientious attention given him by Dr. Heidekind, his already agitated heart could not hold out against the high fever, he, too, was dead within five days. Escorted by a quite respectable number of his fellow citizens, he joined his wife in the Castorp family grave, a very beautiful plot in the cemetery of Saint Catherine's Church, with a view to the botanical gardens.

His own father, the senator, survived him, if only by a little, and during the brief period until his death—likewise caused by pneumonia, against which he struggled amid great agony, for unlike his son, Hans Lorenz

Castorp was a man rooted firmly in life, a tree hard to fell—during this brief period of a mere year and a half, then, the orphaned Hans Castorp lived in his grandfather's house, which had been built on a narrow lot on the Esplanade in the early years of the century just past. Its Nordic classical façade, painted a dreary, weather-beaten color, was adorned by pilasters at both sides of the front door, which was set in the center of the first floor and had five stairs leading up to it; the main level was topped off by two more stories, both with windows reaching to the floor and ornamented with wrought-iron grills.

The first floor was taken up exclusively by formal rooms, including the bright dining room—with its ornamental plaster and three windows hung with burgundy curtains and looking out on the little back garden— where during those eighteen months the grandfather and grandson dined together daily at four in the afternoon, served by old Fiete, who had rings in both ears, silver buttons on his swallowtail coat, and a batiste necktie exactly like the one worn by his master, in which, also in imitation of his master, he buried his clean-shaven chin, and whom the grandfather always addressed familiarly in Plattdeutsch, not for any comical effect (for he was a man without humor) but quite matter-of-factly, just as he did whenever he dealt with the commonfolk—warehouse workers, messengers, coachmen, or servants. Hans Castorp enjoyed listening to the dialect, and also enjoyed Fiete's answers, likewise in Plattdeutsch, delivered while serving from the left and bending around behind his master to speak into his right ear, out of which the senator heard considerably better than the left. The old man understood and nodded and went on eating, sitting very erect between the high mahogany back of his chair and the table, barely bending forward to his plate; and his grandson, seated opposite, would watch with silent, profound, and unconscious attention as his grandfather's hands—beautiful, white, gaunt, aged hands, with rounded, sharply tapered fingernails and a green signet ring on the right forefinger— arranged a bite of meat, vegetable, and potato on the tip of the fork with a few practiced motions and guided it to the mouth with just the least forward tip of the head. Hans Castorp looked down at his own still awkward hands and sensed stored within them the possibility that one day he would hold and use his knife and fork as adeptly as his grandfather.

It was quite a different matter whether he would ever be able to bury his chin in such a necktie, tied so that it filled the wide opening created by his grandfather's peculiarly shaped collar, whose pointed tips brushed the old man's cheeks. Because for that you would have to be as old as he was, and even in those days no one, far and wide, wore such collars and neckties, except him and his old Fiete. What a shame that was, because little Hans Castorp was delighted by the way his grandfather could rest his chin in the high, snow-white necktie; and even as an adult, the memory of it pleased him no end—there was something about it that found approval in the very depth of his soul.

When they were finished eating and had folded their napkins, rolling them up and pushing them through their silver rings—a procedure that Hans Castorp managed only with difficulty, because the napkins were as large as small tablecloths—the senator would rise from his chair while Fiete pulled it back and then walk, shuffling his feet as he went, to the "den" to fetch a cigar. Sometimes his grandson would follow him.

This "den" was the result of the dining room's having been designed with three windows, so that it extended across the full width of the house, thus leaving no space for three drawing rooms, as was usual with this style of house, but for only two, one of which, placed at right angles to the dining room, would have been disproportionately deep, with only one window to the street. This was why one quarter of its length had been partitioned off, forming the "den," a dim, narrow room lit by a skylight and furnished with only a few items: a whatnot stand for the senator's cigar cabinet, a card table with a drawer full of enticing objects— a deck of whist cards, game tokens, scorecards with little hinged stands, a slate and chalk styluses, paper cigar holders, and other things, too— and finally, set back in one corner, a rococo china cabinet made of rosewood, with yellow silk curtains pulled across the inside of its window-panes.

"Grampa," little Hans Castorp might say once they were in the den, raising himself up on tiptoe and stretching to reach the old man's ear, "please show me the baptismal bowl."

And his grandfather, who had already pushed back the long, soft flap of his frock coat and pulled a bundle of keys from his trouser pocket, now opened the china cabinet, from whose interior rose a fragrance the boy found both strange and pleasant. All sorts of objects that had fallen out of use, which made them all the more captivating, were kept inside: a pair of sinuous silver candlesticks; a broken barometer, its wooden case carved with figures; an album of daguerreotypes; a cedar chest for liqueurs; a little Turk in a bright silk costume, whose body was rigid to the touch but contained a mechanism that, though it had long since fallen into disrepair, had once enabled him to run across the table; a model of an old-fashioned ship; and way at the bottom, a rattrap no less. But from the middle shelf, the old man took a heavily tarnished, round silver bowl set on a silver plate and showed the boy both pieces, separating them and turning them both about in his hands, all the while reciting a story he had told many times before.

The bowl and the plate were not originally a set, as one could plainly see and as the boy was now instructed yet again; but they had been used together, his grandfather said, for around a hundred years now, ever since the bowl had been acquired. The bowl was beautiful, its lines simple and elegant, fashioned according to the austere taste of the early years of the last century. Smooth and massive, it rested on round feet, its interior lined with gold, though the yellow luster had faded with the years. The only ornamentation was an embossed wreath of roses and serrated leaves around its rim. As for the plate, one could read its much greater age right on its surface. There stood "1650" in ornate numbers, and framing the date were all sorts of curlicued engraved lines, done in the "modern fashion" of the period, bombastic and capricious arabesques and crests that were half stars, half flowers. The underside, however, was inscribed in a variety of ever-changing scripts with the names of those heads of the household who had been its owners over the course of time. There were seven names in all now, each rounded out with the date of inheritance, and the old man in the white necktie pointed with his ringed forefinger as he read off each of them to his grandson. His father's name was there, as was in fact his grandfather's, and his great-grandfather's; and now that syllable came doubled, tripled, and quadrupled from the storyteller's mouth; and the boy would lay his head to one side, his eyes fixed and full of thought, yet somehow dreamily thoughtless, his lips parted in drowsy devotion, and he would listen to the great-great-great-great—that somber sound of the crypt and buried time, which nevertheless both expressed a reverently preserved connection of his own life in the present to things now sunk deep beneath the earth and simultaneously had a curious effect on him: the same effect visible in the look on his face. The sound made him feel as if he were breathing the moldy, cool air of Saint Catherine's Church or the crypt in Saint Michael's, as if he could sense the gentle draft of places where as you walked, hat in hand, you fell into a certain reverential, forward rocking motion, your heels never touching the ground; and he also thought he could hear the remote, cloistered silence of those reverberating spaces. At the sound of those somber syllables, religious feelings got mixed up with a sense of death and history, and all of it together somehow left the boy with a pleasant sensation—indeed, it may well have been that it was solely for the sake of that sound, just to hear it and join in reciting it, that he had once again asked to be allowed to see the baptismal bowl.

Then his grandfather would put the basin back on its tray and let the boy look into its smooth, soft golden hollow, which began to shimmer as it caught the light falling from above.

"And it will soon be eight years now," he said, "since we held you over it and the water with which you were baptized trickled down into it. Lassen, the sexton from Saint Jacob's, poured it into the cupped hands of our good Pastor Bugenhagen, and then it ran down over your hair and into the bowl here. But we had warmed it first, so that you wouldn't be frightened and start crying, and you didn't, either, quite the contrary, you had been bawling beforehand, making it difficult for Bugenhagen to give his homily, but then came the water, and you fell silent, and that was out of respect for the holy sacrament, let us hope. And in a very few days now, it will be forty-four years since your dear departed father was the baby being baptized, and water ran down from his head into this same bowl. That happened here, in his parents' home, across the way in the drawing room, in front of the middle window, and it was old Pastor Hesekiel who baptized him, the same one who almost got himself shot by the French when he was a young man, for preaching against their looting and burning—he's been resting in the Lord for a long, long time now. But seventy-five years ago, it was me they baptized, that was in the drawing room, too, and they held my head over this same bowl sitting on its tray here, and the pastor spoke the same words that were spoken over you and your father, and warm, clear water ran down over my hair, too—there wasn't much more of it in those days than I have on my head now—and flowed into this golden basin."

The boy looked up at his grandfather's narrow gray head which was bent over the bowl again, just as it had been in that long-vanished hour he was talking about, and a familiar feeling stole over him—a strange, half-dreamy, half-scary sense of standing there and yet being tugged away at the same time, a kind of fluctuating permanence, that meant both a return to something and a dizzying, everlasting sameness, a feeling that he knew well from previous occasions and that he had been waiting for, hoping it would touch him again. It was partly for the sake of that feeling that he had contrived to have this abiding, mutable heirloom shown to him.

When considering it later, as a young man, he realized that the image of his grandfather was imprinted much more deeply, clearly, and significantly in his memory than that of his parents—and this may possibly have had its basis both in mutual sympathy and a special physical affinity, because the grandson did look like his grandfather, to the extent that a lad with down on his rosy cheeks can resemble a sallow and stiff septuagenarian. Probably the most significant factor, however, was that without question the old man had been the central figure in the family, its picturesque personality.

From the viewpoint of the outside world, time had made Hans Lorenz

Castorp's character and convictions obsolete long before his passing. He was a most Christian gentleman, a member of a Reformed parish, with strict traditional opinions, so stubborn an advocate of restricting qualifications for those who govern to the aristocracy that it was as if he were living in the fourteenth century, when, against the dogged resistance of the old free patricians, tradesmen had first begun to win seats and voices in the town council—in sum, a man who opposed anything new. His active years had come during decades of violent expansion and numerous upheavals, decades of progress at a forced march, all of which constantly demanded great public courage and sacrifice. But it had not been old Castorp's fault, God knows, that the modern spirit had enjoyed its celebrated, brilliant victories. He had held the customs of his forefathers and their old institutions in far higher regard than any expansion of the harbor at breakneck speed or the godless tomfooleries of a great city, had impeded and tempered wherever he could. And had it been up to him, the city administration nowadays would look just as old-fashioned and idyllic as his office had looked when he was in his prime.

And this was how the old man was viewed, both during his lifetime and after, by his fellow citizens; and even though little Hans Castorp understood nothing about the affairs of government, the perceptions gained by his own calm, alert child's eye were much the same—unspoken and therefore uncritical perceptions, though enthusiastic for all that, which when they later became conscious memories retained their exclusively positive stamp, immune to all discussion or analysis. As noted, mutual sympathy was at work here, the kind of family affection and affinity of personality that not infrequently leaps a generation. Children and grandchildren observe in order to admire, and they admire in order to learn and develop what heredity has stored within them.

Senator Castorp was tall and gaunt. The years had bent his back and neck, but he attempted to compensate for this by pressing against the curvature, which pulled down the corners of his mouth in a kind of painful dignity, while the lips, with no supporting teeth behind them, rested on bare gums—he wore his dentures only to eat—and this counterpressure, which presumably also helped him steady his head (because it had begun to shake of late), was probably what caused him to carry himself with an austere, forward tilt and to prop his chin in the way that so pleased little Hans.

He loved his snuff; he had a longish tortoiseshell box inlaid with gold, and snuff was also the reason he carried red handkerchiefs, the tip of one usually visible dangling from the back pocket of his frock coat. And although this harmless vice added a jaunty touch to his appearance, the ultimate effect was much more that of the license of old age, the kind of carelessness that age either consciously and merrily permits itself or brings with it, cloaked in dignified oblivion; in any case, it was the only such carelessness in his grandfather's appearance that little Hans Castorp's sharp eye ever observed. Both to the mind of the seven-year-old and in the memories of the adult, the everyday appearance of the old man was not what was essential and real about him. His essential reality was quite different, much more handsome and authentic than his everyday appearance. That reality, you see, was to be found in a painting—a life-size portrait that at one time had hung in the living room of Hans Castorp's parents and had been transported along with the boy to the house on the Esplanade, where it had been given a spot above the large red silk sofa in the parlor.

It showed Hans Lorenz Castorp in his official dress as a town councillor—the sober, even godly attire of citizens from a vanished century, a costume that later citizens, whether staid or dashing, had carried with them through the years, continuing to wear it on pompous occasions in order ceremoniously to make the past present, and the present past, and to proclaim the permanent continuity of all things and the venerable trustworthiness of their official signatures. There, large as life, Senator Castorp stood on a red-tiled floor, against a perspective of columns and Gothic arches. There he stood, his chin lowered, his mouth drawn down, his blue, thoughtful eyes, the bags heavy beneath them, directed into the distance; he was clad in a robelike black jacket, hanging open at the front, edged in fur along the hem and lapels, and reaching well below his knees. Emerging from under its wide, braid-trimmed, puffy sleeves was a second set of tight-fitting sleeves of simpler fabric, ending in lace cuffs that covered the hands to the knuckles. He had pulled black silk stockings over his skinny old-man's legs, and on his feet he wore shoes with silver buckles. Around his neck, however, lay a wide, starched, heavily pleated ruff, slanted forward, but sloping upward on both sides, beneath which, to top it all, could be seen a pleated batiste jabot and a vest. Under one arm he carried an old-fashioned, broad-brimmed hat that tapered to a point.

It was a splendid portrait, painted by a renowned artist, executed tastefully in the style—as suggested by its subject—of the old masters and awakening in the observer all sorts of images of the late Middle Ages in the Spanish Netherlands. Little Hans Castorp had often studied it, not with any artistic acumen of course, but with a certain more general, even penetrating understanding; and although he had only once seen his grandfather in real life in the fashion pictured there on canvas—just for a brief moment as part of a dignified procession into the town hall—he could not help, as we have said, regarding this pictorial presence as his authentic and real grandfather, seeing in the everyday one a temporary, imperfectly adapted improvisation, so to speak. From that perspective, the lapses and eccentricities in his everyday appearance were apparently mere imperfections, or inept adaptations, were the vestiges or hints of a pure and true nature that could not be totally eradicated. Granted, his stiff collar and high, white necktie were old-fashioned; but such a term could never be applied to that marvelous article of clothing—he meant the Spanish ruff—of which the former were merely present-day traces. And it was the same with the peculiar rounded top hat that his grandfather wore in public, which on some higher plane of reality corresponded to the broad-brimmed felt hat in the picture—or the long, pleated frock coat, whose genuine prototype little Hans Castorp found in the fur- and braid-trimmed robe.

And so when the day came to say farewell, in his heart of hearts little Hans Castorp was relieved to see his grandfather decked out in his authentic perfection. It was in the dining room, the same room where they had so often sat across the table from one another; in the middle of the room Hans Lorenz Castorp now lay in a silver-trimmed coffin, atop a bier surrounded and besieged with wreaths. He had battled pneumonia to the end, had battled long and obstinately, even though, to all appearances, he had accommodated himself only in part to contemporary life; but now here he lay in state—one could not be sure whether triumphant or vanquished, but in any case, with a stern, satisfied look on his face, though it was greatly changed, his nose looking pinched after his struggles; his lower body shrouded under a coverlet, on which lay a palm frond; his head propped up on the silk pillow so that his chin rested most handsomely in the indentation at the front of the ceremonial ruff. And in his hands—half hidden by lace cuffs, the fingers looking cold and inanimate despite their artificially natural pose—someone had placed an ivory cross, upon which his eyes, beneath their lowered lids, seemed to be fixed.

Hans Castorp had seen his grandfather several times in the early stages of his last illness, but then no more toward the end. He had been spared any sight of the struggle, which had taken place primarily at night, and had been touched by it only indirectly—the anxious atmosphere in the house, old Fiete's reddened eyes, the comings and goings of doctors. But from its outcome, which he now found displayed before him in the dining room, he gathered that his grandfather had now received solemn dispensation from his interim stage and had finally returned to the form appropriate to him—an event of which he could only approve, though old Fiete wept and constantly shook his head, even though Hans Castorp himself wept, just as he had wept at the sight of his unexpectedly deceased mother and, a short time later, of his father lying there equally serene and strange.

For this was now the third time within so few months and at such a young age that little Hans Castorp's mind and senses had been affected by death—his senses in particular. The sight of it, the impression it left, was no longer new to him, but really quite familiar, and just as on the first two occasions he had behaved responsibly and kept his composure—with no sign of nervous weakness, although much distressed, as is only natural—he did so now as well, but to an even greater degree. Unaware of the practical implications of these events on his life, or perhaps regarding them with childish indifference while trusting that the world would take care of him one way or the other, he betrayed a similarly childish reserve and businesslike attentiveness when viewing coffins, which on this third occasion took on nuances of precociousness, both in his emotional reaction and the look of knowledgeable experience on his face—it being unnecessary likewise to describe his natural reaction of being caught up in the frequent tearful outbursts of others. Within three or four months after his father died, he had forgotten death; now he remembered it, and all the impressions from before reemerged simultaneously—in every precise, piercing, and incomparable detail.

Analyzed and put into words, his feelings might have been expressed as follows: there was something religious, gripping, and sadly beautiful, which was to say, spiritual about death and at the same time something that was the direct opposite, something very material, physical, which one could not really describe as beautiful, or gripping, or religious, or even as sad. The religious, spiritual side was expressed by the pretentious lying-in-state, by the pomp of flowers and palm fronds—which he knew signified heavenly peace—and also, and more to the point, by the cross between the dead fingers of what had been his grandfather, by the blessings a copy of Thorvaldsen's Christ extended from the head of the coffin, and by two towering candelabra on either side, which on an occasion like this also took on an ecclesiastical character. The explicit and well-intended purpose of all these arrangements was apparently to show that Grandfather had now passed on forever to his authentic and true form. But they also served another purpose—one that little Hans Castorp likewise noted, if not admitting it to himself in so many words; in particular, the masses of flowers and more especially the very well represented tuberoses were there for a more sobering reason—and that was to gloss over the other side of death, the one that is neither beautiful nor sad, but almost indecent in its base physicality, to make people forget it or at least not be reminded of it.

It was this aspect of death that made his dead grandfather look so strange, not really like his grandfather at all, but like a life-size wax doll that death had slipped into the coffin in his place and for which this whole solemn show was being put on. The man who lay there, or better, *what* lay there, was not Grandfather himself, but a shell—which, as Hans Castorp knew, was not made of wax, but of its own material. It was just stuff, and that was what was indecent, and so not really even sad—no sadder than things that have to do with the body, and *only* with it, are sad. Little Hans Castorp gazed at the stuff out of which this life-size dead figure was made, at this waxy, yellow, smooth stuff with the consistency of cheese, gazed at the face and hands of what had been his grandfather. And just then a fly settled on the inert forehead and began to move its proboscis up and down. Old Fiete circumspectly shooed it off, though avoiding actually touching the forehead; a shadow of respectability darkened his face, as if he should not know, and did not want to know, what he was doing—an expression of propriety, which apparently was related to Grandfather's being only a body and nothing more. All the same, after a long, looping flight, the fly came to rest again on Grandfather's fingers, sitting up pertly very close to the ivory cross. And while all this was going on, Hans Castorp thought he could smell more clearly than before those faint, but very peculiar and persistent fumes that he knew from before, and which, to his shame, always reminded him of a school chum who suffered from an offensive affliction that made everyone avoid him, the same odor that the tuberose scent was supposed to cover up on the sly, but was unable to do, for all its lovely, austere richness.

He returned several times to stand by the body: one time all alone, except for old Fiete; a second time together with his great-uncle Tienappel, the wine merchant, and his two uncles James and Peter; and then a third time as well, when a group of workmen from the harbor in their Sunday best stood for a few moments beside the coffin to take leave of the former head of the house of Castorp and Son. Then came the funeral and a dining room full of people; dressed in his Spanish ruff, Pastor Bugenhagen from Saint Michael's, the man who had baptized Hans Castorp, performed the service, and afterward he spoke to little Hans Castorp in very friendly tones as they sat together in the coach, the one right behind the hearse and the first in a long, long procession. And with that, this part of Hans Castorp's life came to an end as well, and a very short time later he changed homes and neighborhoods—for the second time now in his young life.

At the Tienappels'/Hans Castorp's Moral State

THE CHANGE did not work to his detriment, because he moved in with Consul Tienappel, his legal guardian, and lacked for nothing—certainly not in any personal sense, or for that matter, as regarded the supervision of his larger interests, about which he still knew nothing. Consul Tienappel, an uncle of little Hans's late mother, acted as executor for the Castorp estate, putting the property up for sale, taking charge of liquidating the firm Castorp and Son, Imports and Exports, realizing from these transactions some four hundred thousand marks—Hans Castorp's inheritance, which the consul then invested in gilt-edged securities. At the beginning of each quarter, he deducted from the interest earned—without any prejudice to his sense of family ties—a commission of 2 percent.

Set well back from Harvestehuder Weg, the Tienappel home was fronted by a large garden; to the rear it looked out on a lawn where not the tiniest weed was permitted, a public promenade with roses, and beyond it, the river. Although he owned a fine coach, the consul walked to work in the old city every morning, just to get a little exercise, because he sometimes suffered from congestion of the blood in his head; and he returned home by the same route at five each evening, when, in most civilized fashion, the Tienappels sat down to dinner. He was a heavyset man who always dressed in the best English fabrics. His watery-blue eyes were bulgy behind gold-rimmed spectacles, he had a ruddy nose, a gray seaman's beard, and he wore a sparkling diamond on the stubby little finger of his left hand. His wife had been dead for years. He had two sons, Peter and James—the one in the navy and seldom at home, the other an employee in the family wine business and the designated heir of the firm. The house had been kept for many years now by Schalleen, the daughter of a goldsmith in Altona, who always wore white starched ruffles at her thick, cylindrical wrists. She was responsible for laying out an extensive cold buffet at breakfast and supper: shrimp and salmon, eel, goose breast and roast beef with tomato ketchup; she kept a vigilant eye on the extra servants hired when Consul Tienappel gave a formal dinner; and she was also the person who, as best she could, acted as a mother to little Hans Castorp.

He grew—despite miserable weather, despite wind and fog—grew up, one might say, in his yellow mackintosh, and on the whole was a quite cheerful lad. He was probably a little anemic from the start, or so Dr. Heidekind said, prescribing for him a nice daily glass of porter, to be drunk with his snack when he returned from school—a robust brew, as everyone knows, which Dr. Heidekind believed helped build the blood and which, however that might be, Hans Castorp discovered, much to his satisfaction, had a calming effect on his spirits and pleasantly assisted him in his proclivity to "doze"—as his Uncle Tienappel put it—when he would sit with his mouth slightly open, dreaming away without a single firm thought in his head. But otherwise he was a regular, healthy lad, a passable tennis-player and oarsman, although on summer evenings, instead of manning an oar, he preferred sitting on the terrace of the Uhlenhorst Boathouse, a refreshing drink in hand, listening to music and watching the boats as they drifted among the swans, their lights reflected in the bright, smooth water. And if you were to hear him talking—in his nonchalant, reasonable way, his voice a little hollow and monotone, with just a hint of Platt—or even if you just saw him there, so blondly correct, his hair nicely trimmed, his head with the stamp of something classic about it, his air cool and languid, suggesting an inherited, unconscious arrogance, then you could not doubt that this Hans Castorp was an honest, unadulterated product of the local soil, superbly at home in it—even he himself, had he ever actually considered the matter, would not have doubted it for a moment.

The atmosphere of the metropolitan seaport, the damp atmosphere of global shopkeeping and prosperity, had been the air of life itself for his forefathers, and with great gusto he breathed it now as a matter of course and found it profoundly satisfying. His nose took in the fumes of the harbor, of coal and tar, the pungent odors of the world's produce piled high, and his eyes watched the huge steam cranes on the docks—so calm, wise, and monumentally strong that they looked like hardworking elephants—as they transferred tons of sacks, bales, crates, barrels, and carboys from the bowels of idle seagoing vessels to railroad cars and sheds. He watched the merchants in yellow mackintoshes, like the one he himself was wearing, as they streamed at noon toward the exchange, where things could get quite fierce, as he well knew, and someone might very suddenly be motivated to hand out invitations to a grand dinner, in hopes of prolonging his credit. He watched—and this would later prove to be his special area of interest—the teeming dry docks, the towering, mammoth cadavers of ships that had sailed to Asia and Africa, but now lay braced on strutbeams thick as trees, looking monstrous and clumsy on dry land, their keels and screws naked, swarmed over by hosts of midget laborers—hammering, scouring, whitewashing. He gazed at the roofed-over slips, which were wrapped in webs of smoky fog and from which the ribs of ships under construction protruded, while engineers, blueprints and pump-charts in hand, gave orders to the workers. From boyhood on, these were all familiar sights to Hans Castorp, awakening in him a warm sense of belonging, a feeling that reached its zenith, perhaps, on those

occasions when he would join James Tienappel or his cousin Ziemssen—
Joachim Ziemssen—in the pavilion on the Alster for a Sunday breakfast
of warm rolls and smoked beef, washed down by a glass of old port, then
lean back in his chair and puff devotedly on his cigar. For in this he was
true to type: that he dearly and truly loved living well, and despite his
thin-blooded, refined appearance, he clung to the cruder pleasures of life
as a gluttonous baby clings to its mother's breast.

The upper class of this commercial and democratic city-state bequeaths
its children the burden of higher civilization, and Hans Castorp bore it
on his shoulders with a certain easy dignity. He was bathed spotless as a
baby, and he had his clothes made by a tailor who enjoyed the trust of
the young men in his circle. Schalleen took splendid care of his little
treasure of neatly monogrammed underwear and shirts, which were tucked
away in the English-style drawers of his wardrobe. Even when Hans
Castorp left home to study, he regularly sent his things home to be
laundered and mended—for it was his maxim that no one in the empire
except residents of Hamburg knew how to iron—and a badly creased cuff
on one of his pretty pastel shirts filled him with a terrible unease. Although
the shape of his hands was not particularly aristocratic, he took good care
of them, keeping the skin supple and setting them off with a simple
platinum band and his grandfather's signet ring; his teeth, which were
rather soft and subject to damage, had been repaired with gold inlays.

Both when standing and walking, he thrust his lower body forward
somewhat, which left the impression of a certain slackness; but his posture
at the dinner table was excellent. He would politely turn his erect upper
body toward his neighbor for small talk (always reasonable, with a hint
of Platt), would rest his elbows easily at his sides when cutting a piece of
fowl or deftly extracting the pink meat of a lobster claw with the appropriate utensils. When a meal was over, his first requirement was a finger
bowl of perfumed water, his second a Russian cigarette, on which he paid
no customs duties, since he had found a way to obtain them with a few
well-placed, casual bribes. This was a prelude to his cigar, a Maria Mancini,
a very tasty brand from Bremen—we shall come to speak about that
again—whose spicy toxins blended so satisfyingly with those of his coffee.
Hans Castorp kept his tobacco away from the deleterious effects of the
house's steam heat by storing it in the cellar, and every morning he would
descend to provide his cigar case with its daily ration. Only reluctantly
would he have eaten butter served in pats rather than in fluted little balls.

As is apparent, we are attempting to include anything that can be said in
Hans Castorp's favor, and we offer our judgments without exaggeration,
intending to make him no better or worse than he was. Hans Castorp

was neither a genius nor an idiot, and if we refrain from applying the word "mediocre" to him, we do so for reasons that have absolutely nothing to do with his intelligence and little or nothing to do with his prosaic personality, but rather out of deference to his fate, to which we are inclined to attribute a more general significance. He was bright enough to meet the demands of a modern secondary school without overtaxing himself; in fact, under no conceivable circumstances would he have been willing to do that, no matter what the goal—not so much out of fear that it might be painful as because he saw absolutely no reason why he should, or to put it better: no *unequivocal* reason. But perhaps that is why we do not call him mediocre—precisely because he felt that in some way or other such an unequivocal reason was lacking.

A human being lives out not only his personal life as an individual, but also, consciously or subconsciously, the lives of his epoch and contemporaries; and although he may regard the general and impersonal foundations of his existence as unequivocal givens and take them for granted, having as little intention of ever subjecting them to critique as our good Hans Castorp himself had, it is nevertheless quite possible that he senses his own moral well-being to be somehow impaired by the lack of critique. All sorts of personal goals, purposes, hopes, prospects may float before the eyes of a given individual, from which he may then glean the impulse for exerting himself for great deeds; if the impersonal world around him, however, if the times themselves, despite all their hustle and bustle, provide him with neither hopes nor prospects, if they secretly supply him with evidence that things are in fact hopeless, without prospect or remedy, if the times respond with hollow silence to every conscious or subconscious question, however it may be posed, about the ultimate, unequivocal meaning of all exertions and deeds that are more than exclusively personal—then it is almost inevitable, particularly if the person involved is a more honest sort, that the situation will have a crippling effect, which, following moral and spiritual paths, may even spread to that individual's physical and organic life. For a person to be disposed to more significant deeds that go beyond what is simply required of him—even when his own times may provide no satisfactory answer to the question of why—he needs either a rare, heroic personality that exists in a kind of moral isolation and immediacy, or one characterized by exceptionally robust vitality. Neither the former nor the latter was the case with Hans Castorp, and so he probably was mediocre after all, though in a very honorable sense of that word.

In saying this, we are speaking here of the young man's innermost state not only during his years in school, but also during the period that followed, when he had already chosen his profession. As to his career at school, he did indeed have to repeat a class or two. But for the most part, his background, his urbane manners, and ultimately a pretty, if rather dispassionate talent for mathematics helped him move ahead; and after receiving his report card in his freshman year, he concluded he would finish school—primarily, truth to tell, because that allowed him to extend a familiar, provisional, indecisive state of affairs and to win time for reflection as to what Hans Castorp would most like to do, because he was not even close to deciding that, not even as a senior, and when it finally was decided (to say *he* decided would be saying almost too much), he was quite aware that the decision could just as easily have been otherwise.

But this much was true—he had always taken great delight in ships. As a small boy he had filled his notebooks with penciled drawings of fishing cutters, vegetable barges, and five-masters. And when at age fifteen he had the chance to watch from a front-row seat as the *Hansa*, a new double-screw mail-steamer, was launched from the docks of Blohm and Voss, he painted a strikingly good watercolor of the trim ship, exact down to almost the last detail, which Consul Tienappel had hung in his private office. And he had so lovingly and deftly captured the transparent, glassy-green, rolling sea that someone had said to Consul Tienappel that the lad had talent and would make a good painter of seascapes—a pronouncement that the consul had no qualms repeating to his ward, because Hans Castorp simply laughed amiably at the idea and gave not a moment's thought to a life of eccentricity and starving for art.

"You don't have much," his Uncle Tienappel would remind him. "James and Peter will get the lion's share of my money, that is to say, it stays in the business and Peter will draw an annuity. What belongs to you is invested quite nicely and will yield a secure return. But it's no fun nowadays trying to live off interest unless one has at least five times as much as you have, and if you fancy living a nice life here in the city, like the one to which you're accustomed, then you'll have to earn a tidy sum yourself—take note of that, my boy."

Hans Castorp took note and looked around for a profession in which he could prove himself—both to himself and others. But he thought quite highly of his profession once he had chosen it—at the suggestion of old Wilms, of the firm of Tunder and Wilms, who said to Consul Tienappel over a game of whist one Sunday evening that Hans Castorp should study shipbuilding, that was the ticket, and join his firm, where he would certainly keep his eye on him. Although damned complicated and demanding, it was nevertheless an excellent, important, splendid profession and far preferable, given his peaceable nature at any rate, to that of his cousin Ziemssen, who was the son of his late mother's half sister and determined to become an officer. Joachim Ziemssen wasn't exactly strong in the lungs, of course, but that was precisely the reason why a profession in the open air, one that could hardly be said to involve serious brainwork or stress, was probably just the thing for him—as Hans Castorp had remarked rather patronizingly. For he had the greatest respect for work, although, for his part, he found that he did tire easily.

Which brings us back to our previous suggestion, which proposed that the damage inflicted by the times on someone's personal life can have a direct influence on that person's physical organism. How could Hans Castorp not have held work in high esteem? That would have been unnatural. As things stood, work had to be regarded as unconditionally the most estimable thing in the world—ultimately there was nothing one could esteem more, it was the principle by which one stood or fell, the absolute of the age, the answer, so to speak, to its own question. His respect for work was, in its way, religious and, so far as he knew, unquestioning. But it was another matter to love it. And as much as he respected it, he could not love it—for one simple reason: it did not agree with him. The exertion of hard work was a strain on his nerves, tiring him quickly, and he quite candidly admitted that he much preferred his leisure—when time passed easily, unencumbered by the leaden weight of toil, and lay open before you, instead of being divided into a series of hurdles that you had to grit your teeth and take. Strictly speaking, the contradictions in his attitude toward work needed to be resolved. If he had been able to believe at the foundations of his soul (there where he himself did not know what was what) that work has unconditional value, is a principle that answers its own question, might not both body and mind—first his mind, and through it, his body—have been more amenable to work and exhibited more stamina? Would that have set his mind at ease? Which brings us back to our previous question about his mediocrity or more-than-mediocrity, to which we do not wish to give a conclusive answer. For we do not see ourselves as Hans Castorp's eulogist and want to leave room for the suggestion that, for him, work was simply something that stood in the way of the unencumbered enjoyment of a Maria Mancini.

He was not attracted to military service himself. Something deep within him resisted the idea, and he knew how to avoid it. It may also be that Dr. Eberding, the staff surgeon, who was a regular on Harvestehuder Weg, had heard in casual conversation with Consul Tienappel that young Castorp, having just left for the university, would regard being forced to bear arms as a serious disruption in his studies.

His brain, which worked calmly and slowly—particularly since Hans Castorp retained the habit of drinking porter with his morning snack—gradually filled up with analytical geometry, differential equations, mechanics, projective geometry, and graphical statics. He calculated displacements—with full cargo and empty—stabilities, shifts in trim, and metacenters, though it was drudgery at times. His technical drawings, all the sketches of ribbing, waterlines, and full-length projections, were not quite as good as his watercolor depiction of the *Hansa* on the high sea, but when the abstract graphics required the sensual addition of a wash for shading or lively colors for various materials in a cross section, Hans Castorp proved more skillful than most.

When he came home on vacations—very neat, very well dressed, sporting a little reddish-blond moustache in the middle of his sleepy, young, patrician face, looking for all the world like a young man on his way to a respectable place in life—the people who concerned themselves with the affairs of the community, who kept themselves well informed about various families and the staffing of municipal offices (and that means most people in a self-governing city-state), his fellow citizens, then, looked him over and asked themselves what public role young Castorp might one day grow into. He had tradition behind him, his was a good, old name, and it was almost inevitable that someday he would have to be reckoned with as a political factor. By then he would be sitting in the assembly or on the committee of burghers, making laws, would hold an honorable post where he would participate in the concerns of government, as an administrator, perhaps as director of the finance or building committees. His voice would be listened to and his vote would count. People were curious about which party young Castorp would one day embrace. Appearances were deceiving, but he looked exactly like someone democrats would *not* be able to count on, and the resemblance to his grandfather was undeniable. Perhaps he would take after him, become a conservative, a brake on other elements. That was quite possible—but so was the opposite. For he was an engineer after all, a shipbuilder in the making, a man of global commerce and technology. So that it might well be that Hans Castorp would join up with the radicals, turn out to be a go-getter, a profane destroyer of old buildings and beautiful landscapes, as footloose as a Jew, as irreverent as an American, a man likely to prefer a ruthless break with venerable traditions to cautious development of natural resources, a man who would plunge the state into reckless experiments—that was conceivable, too. Was it in his blood to regard their Excellencies, the men for whom the sentries at the town hall presented arms, as elders who knew best—or would he be inclined to support the opposition in the assembly? His curious fellow citizens could find no answer to such questions in those blue eyes under their reddish-blond brows; and Hans Castorp, being an unwritten page, would probably have had no answer, either.

When he set out on the journey where we met him, he was twenty-three years old. He had four semesters of study at Danzig Polytechnic behind him, plus four more spent at technical colleges in Braunschweig and Karlsruhe, had recently put his first final exams behind him, passing them with no trouble, though without fanfare or drum roll, and was about to join the firm of Tunder and Wilms as an unsalaried engineer-in-training in order to gain practical experience on the docks. And at that point, his life took the following turn.

His exams had meant a long period of concentrated work, and upon returning home he looked paler than he ought—even given his general type. Dr. Heidekind scolded whenever he saw him and insisted on a change of air, and he meant a radical change. Norderney or Wyk on the island of Föhr, he said, would not do it this time, and if you were to ask him, what Hans Castorp needed was a few weeks in the Alps before going to work on the docks.

That was fine, Consul Tienappel told his nephew and ward, but then their paths would have to part for the summer, because wild horses couldn't drag him, Consul Tienappel, to the Alps. That was not for him, he required sensible barometric pressure or he would have another attack. Hans Castorp could go right ahead and take a trip to the Alps. Why not pay Joachim Ziemssen a visit?

That was a logical suggestion. Joachim Ziemssen was ill in fact—not ill like Hans Castorp, but really, dangerously ill, had even given them all quite a scare. He had always been susceptible to bronchitis and fevers, and then one day he actually coughed up red, and Joachim was shipped off posthaste to Davos—much to his great regret and dismay, because he was very close to seeing his ambition fulfilled. Bowing to the will of his family, he had first spent a couple of semesters studying law, but then, following an irresistible urge, he had changed horses and volunteered as an ensign, and had been accepted. And for the last five months he had been sitting in the International Sanatorium Berghof (Dr. Behrens, supervising physician), and was bored half to death, as he wrote in a postcard. And so if Hans Castorp was to treat himself to a little vacation before taking up his job with Tunder and Wilms, nothing could be more sensible than to provide his poor cousin with company up there in the mountains—it was the most pleasant solution for both parties.

It was the height of summer when he decided to take the trip—already the last week of July.

He planned to stay three weeks.

3

The Shadow of Respectability

H ANS CASTORP had been afraid he would oversleep, he had been so thoroughly exhausted, but he was up and about earlier than neces- sary and had plenty of time leisurely to pursue his usual, highly civilized morning routine—its chief utensils included a rubber basin, a wooden bowl of green, lavender-scented soap, and a straw-colored brush—and was able not only to tend to matters of personal hygiene but also to unpack and put his things away. And as he passed the silver-plated blade across the perfumed foam on his cheeks, he recalled his muddled dreams and smiled an indulgent smile at such nonsense, shaking his head with the superiority of a man shaving by the light of reasonable day. He did not feel all that well rested, but fresh enough to meet the morning.

He powdered his cheeks and slipped into his plaid undershorts and red morocco-leather slippers, and still drying his hands, he stepped out onto the balcony, which, although private, was connected to those adjoining and separated from them only by an opaque glass partition that extended almost to the railing. The morning was cool and cloudy. Long banks of fog lay motionless along the hills to both sides, while masses of clouds, white and gray, were draped on the more distant mountains. Patches and streaks of blue sky were visible here and there, and when a ray of sun broke through, the village in the valley below glistened white against the dark forests of pine on the slopes. Somewhere morning music was playing; presumably it came from the same hotel where the concert had been held the evening before. Muted chords of a chorale drifted toward him; a march followed after a brief pause. Hans Castorp loved music with all his heart, its effect being much like that of the porter he drank with his morning snack—profoundly calming, numbing, and "doze"-inducing—and he listened now with pleasure, his head tilted to one side, mouth open, eyes slightly bloodshot.

He looked down at the winding road they had followed up to the sanatorium the evening before. Short-stemmed, starlike gentians were blooming in the moist grass of the slope. A section of the level ground had been fenced in to form a garden with gravel paths, flowerbeds, and an artificial grotto beneath a stately silver fir. Next to a metal-roofed arcade, open to the south and filled with lounge chairs, stood a flagpole, painted reddish brown and displaying a banner that fluttered full now and then—a fantasy flag, green and white, with a snake-entwined caduceus, the symbol of healing, at its center.

A woman was walking in the garden, an older lady with a gloomy, even tragic look. Clad completely in black, with a black veil wound round her disheveled grayish-black hair, she wandered restlessly along the paths, keeping an even but quick pace, her knees slightly bent, her arms hanging stiffly at an angle in front of her. Her brow was creased by a frown, and her lowered, coal-black eyes, the skin beneath them forming drooping bags, were directed straight ahead. Her aging face, with its pale Mediterranean complexion and large, careworn mouth turned down at one corner, reminded Hans Castorp of a picture he had once seen of a famous tragedian; and it was eerie to watch how this pale woman dressed in black matched her long, somber strides, apparently without realizing it, to the rhythm of march music in the distance.

Hans Castorp gazed down at her in thoughtful sympathy, and it seemed as if her sad appearance darkened the morning sun. Simultaneously, however, he perceived something else, something audible, coming from the adjoining room on his left, the room with the Russian couple, so Joachim had said—noises that were likewise ill suited to this cheerful, fresh morning, that tainted it, making it seem sultry somehow. Hans Castorp remembered that he had heard the same sounds the night before, but had been too tired to pay them any attention. Giggles, gasps, grapplings—there was no disguising the indelicate nature of the sound, although in his kindheartedness the young man at first tried hard to give it a harmless interpretation. One could use other terms for his kindheartedness—an insipid phrase like "purity of soul," for instance, or a more serious and beautiful word like "modesty," or disparaging words such as "avoidance of the truth" and "hypocrisy," or even a phrase about "the mystic piety of shyness"—and Hans Castorp's reaction to the sounds from the adjoining room combined something of them all and was visible now as a shadow of respectability that darkened his face, as if he should not know and did not want to know anything about what he heard there. It was an expression of propriety—not exactly original, but one he was in the habit of assuming under certain circumstances.

And with this look on his face he returned to his room to avoid having to listen any longer to the proceedings, which despite the giggles sounded terribly serious, disconcertingly so. But the events on the far side of the wall were even more audible from his room. An apparent chase around the furniture, the crash of an upturned chair, a grab, an embrace, slaps and kisses—and then, of all things to accompany the invisible scene, a waltz was struck up in the distance, the tired melody of a popular ballad. Hans Castorp stood, towel in hand, and listened against his best intentions. And suddenly a blush rose up under his talcum, because what he had clearly seen coming had now arrived, and beyond any doubt, the game had turned bestial. "Good God in heaven!" he thought, turning away to finish dressing with as much noise as he could manage. "Well, they're married, for heaven's sake, that's as it should be at least. But in broad daylight, that is a bit much. And I'm almost certain that they disturbed the peace last night, too. After all, they are ill, that's why they're here, or one of them is at least, and a little self-control wouldn't be out of place. But of course," he realized angrily, "the real scandal is that the walls are so thin and that you can hear everything so clearly, and that's simply intolerable! Cheap construction, naturally, shamefully cheap! I wonder if I shall see these people later, or even be introduced to them? That would be most embarrassing." But now Hans Castorp realized to his amazement that the flush that had come to his freshly shaven cheeks had not subsided, or at least the warmth that had come with it was not about to depart—the same hot, dry face that had bothered him yesterday evening, and that had disappeared while he slept, was back now in full force. This did not make him feel any friendlier toward the married couple next door, indeed he pouted his lips and muttered something very disparaging about them; and now he made the mistake of splashing his face with water again to cool it, which only made matters worse. And so he was feeling cross and at loose ends when he heard his cousin knock on the wall and call out to him. His expression, as Joachim entered the room, was not that of a man refreshed by sleep and ready to greet the morning.

Breakfast

"Hello," Joachim said. "So that was your first night up here. Are you well satisfied?"

He was ready for a walk, dressed in sporty clothes and sturdy, tooled boots, his ulster flung over his arm, the outline of the flat bottle clearly visible in one pocket. He wasn't wearing a hat today, either.

"Thanks," Hans Castorp replied, "well enough. I'll not categorize it any further. I had some rather confused dreams. And the place has one shortcoming, you know, it's not soundproof—that is rather annoying. Who was the woman in black out in the garden?"

Joachim knew at once whom he meant.

"Ah, that's *Tous-les-deux*," he said. "That's what we all call her at least, because those are the only words you ever hear out of her. She's Mexican, you see, and knows not a word of German and almost no French, either, just a few scraps. She's been here with her eldest son for five weeks now, a perfectly hopeless case, who'll be making his exit soon enough—it's all through him, his whole body's poisoned with it, you could say, and at that stage it looks a lot like typhoid fever, Behrens says—gruesome for all involved, at any rate. And two weeks ago, now, her second son arrived up here, because he wanted to see his brother one last time—handsome young fellow, by the way, but then so is the other— both of them pretty as pictures, with those glowing eyes that drive the ladies crazy. Well, the younger one already had a little bit of a cough down below, but was otherwise in quite good shape. And no sooner does he arrive than he has a temperature—and I mean a high fever, a hundred and three right away—he takes to his bed, and if he ever gets up again, Behrens says, he'll have more luck than sense. But in any case, it was high time, and then some, for him to come up here. Yes, and since then the mother just wanders about, when she's not sitting with them, and the only thing she ever says to anyone she meets is: '*tous les deux!*' Because that's all she knows how to say, and there's no one here who understands Spanish."

"So that's her problem," Hans Castorp said. "I wonder if she'll say the same thing to me when I get to know her? That would be so strange— I mean, it would be comical and weird at the same time," he said, and his eyes took on yesterday's look—seemed too hot and heavy, as if he had been weeping for a long time, and shone with the same glint that the

Austrian horseman's novel cough had enkindled in them. In fact, he felt as if he had only just now reestablished a connection with yesterday, as if he were taking in the whole picture again, as it were, which had not really been the case since he awoke. He was ready, by the way, he declared, shaking a few drops of lavender water on his handkerchief so that he could dab at his brow and under his eyes. "If it's all right with you, we can go to breakfast—*tous les deux*," he added as a joke, in a burst of high spirits. Joachim cast him a gentle glance and smiled a curious smile—melancholy and slightly mocking, it seemed—but why, he kept to himself.

After making sure that he had cigars to smoke, Hans Castorp picked up his walking stick, coat, and hat—the last out of obstinacy, because he was all too definite in his own civilized habits to change them lightly and adopt strange new ones for a mere three weeks. And so they left, taking the stairs, and as they passed one door or another, Joachim would name its occupant—German names, but also all sorts of odd-sounding ones—adding brief remarks about the person's character and the severity of the case.

They also met people already returning from breakfast, and whenever Joachim said good morning to anyone, Hans Castorp would politely tip his hat. He was tense and nervous, like a young man about to introduce himself to a host of strangers, all the while plagued by the distinct feeling that his eyes and face are red—which was only partly true, because he was actually rather pale.

"Before I forget," he suddenly said rather impulsively, "you can go ahead and introduce me to the lady in the garden if we happen to meet her, I have no objections. She can repeat her '*tous les deux*' to me, it won't matter. I'm ready for it now and understand what it means and will know how to put on the proper face. But I don't want to make the acquaintance of the Russian couple, do you hear? I definitely don't want that. They are people devoid of all manners, and although I am going to have to live next door to them for three weeks because there was no other way to arrange things, I do not wish to know them. I am perfectly within my rights in expressly forbidding it."

"Fine," Joachim said. "Did they disturb you all that much? Yes, they are barbarians, so to speak—uncivilized, to put a word on it—I did warn you. He always comes to meals in a leather jacket—quite shabby, let me tell you. I'm amazed Behrens doesn't do something about it. And she's not all that well groomed herself, despite the plumed hat. But in any case, you needn't worry, they sit a good distance away, at the Bad Russian table—because there's also a Good Russian table, where the more refined Russians sit. So there's hardly any possibility you'd meet them, even if

you wanted to. It's not at all easy to make acquaintances here, if only
because there are so many foreigners among the guests. I personally have
got to know only a few myself in all my months here."

"Which of them is ill?" Hans Castorp asked. "He or she?"

"He is, I think. Yes, just him," Joachim said, obviously preoccupied.
They hung their coats on the stands outside the dining hall, and entered
it, a bright, low-vaulted room, where voices buzzed, dishes clattered, and
"dining attendants" scurried about with steaming pots of coffee.

There were seven tables in the dining hall, five placed lengthwise, only
two crosswise. The tables were large, with room for ten persons at each,
although not all the places had been set. They took only a few steps
diagonally across the room, and Hans Castorp found that he was already
at the place set for him, at the end of the middle table toward the front
of the room, halfway between the two crosswise tables. Standing erect
behind his chair, Hans Castorp bowed stiffly and cordially to his tablemates as Joachim formally introduced them, although he barely looked
at them, let alone made a conscious note of their names. The only face
and name he put together was Frau Stöhr, noticing her red face and oily,
ash-blond hair, and an expression of such willful ignorance that it was
easy to believe her guilty of howling gaffes. Then he sat down and noted
approvingly that early breakfast here was a serious meal.

There were pots of marmalade and honey, bowls of oatmeal and
creamed rice, plates of scrambled eggs and cold meats; they had been
generous with the butter. Someone lifted the glass bell from a soft Swiss
cheese and cut off a piece; what was more, a bowl of fruit, both fresh
and dried, stood in the middle of the table. A dining attendant in black
and white asked Hans Castorp what he wanted to drink—cocoa, coffee,
or tea? She was as small as a child, with an old, long face—a dwarf, he
realized with a shock. He looked at his cousin, who merely shrugged and
lifted an eyebrow as if to say, "Right, what else is new?" And so Hans
Castorp simply accepted the fact and, since it was a dwarf, asked for his
tea with special courtesy. He began with some creamed rice topped with
sugar and cinnamon, meanwhile letting his eyes wander over the other
items he intended to sample and across the seven tables of assembled
guests—Joachim's colleagues, his companions in misfortune, all with the
same illness deep inside, all chatting and breakfasting.

The room was done in the kind of modern decor that combines the
most efficient simplicity with just a dash of fantasy. It was not deep in
relation to its width, and on all four sides was a kind of passageway where
the sideboards stood and that opened as a series of arches onto the central
dining area. Its columns were paneled with a sandalwood finish, but only

partway up; the top of each was painted white, like the upper half of the walls and the ceiling, but colorfully trimmed with simple, cheerful stenciled stripes, which then continued along the broad arches of the low ceiling. The hall was also decorated with several shiny brass chandeliers, all electric, each a series of three stacked rings joined by delicate filigree, with bells of milk glass set like little moons on the lowest circle. There were four glass doors—two on the long wall opposite, opening onto a veranda outside; a third up front to the left, leading directly into the front lobby; and finally the one through which Hans Castorp had entered and that opened off a different hallway, because Joachim had not used the same set of stairs as the night before.

To his right was a homely creature in black, with a dull, flushed complexion and fuzzy cheeks; he took her to be a seamstress or dressmaker, chiefly because her breakfast consisted of nothing but coffee and buttered rolls—and for some reason he had always associated dressmakers with coffee and buttered rolls. On his left sat an English maiden lady—likewise well on in years, very ugly, with skinny, frigid fingers, who was drinking tea the color of blood and reading letters from home, written in a full, rounded hand. Next to her came Joachim, and then Frau Stöhr in a Scotch-plaid woolen blouse. She kept the balled fist of her left hand pressed to her cheek while she ate and took obvious pains to make a refined impression when she talked, primarily by pulling her upper lip back to expose her long, narrow, rabbitlike teeth. A young man with a sparse moustache and an expression on his face as if he had something foul-tasting in his mouth sat down next to her and ate his breakfast in total silence. Hans Castorp had already taken his seat when the fellow entered, his chin sunk against his chest as he walked, and took his place without a glance at anyone, showing by his demeanor that he absolutely did not wish to be introduced to the new guest. Perhaps he was too ill to value or see any point in mere formalities, or even to take any interest in his surroundings. Seated across from him, very briefly, was an extraordinarily gaunt, very blond young woman, who emptied a bottle of yogurt onto her plate, spooned down this dairy product, and promptly departed.

The table conversation was not exactly lively. Joachim chatted politely with Frau Stöhr, inquiring after her health and expressing gentlemanly regrets that it left something to be desired. She complained of her "listlessness." "I'm so listless," she said, drawling it out with the affectation of the uneducated. Her temperature had already been 99.2 degrees when she got up, and what would it be by afternoon? The dressmaker admitted to a temperature equally as high, but declared the effect was just the opposite with her, that she felt quite excitable, nervous and restless inside, as if some special, decisive event were about to happen, which was not the case at all, this being simply a physical excitation with no psychological basis. She was probably not a dressmaker after all, because she spoke correctly, almost pedantically. All the same, Hans Castorp found her excitability, or at least her discussion of it, somehow inappropriate, almost indecent for such a nondescript, insignificant creature. He asked them, first the dressmaker and then Frau Stöhr, how long they had been up here—the former had been a resident for five months, the latter for seven; he marshaled his English to ask his neighbor on the left what sort of tea that was she was drinking—rose-hip, he learned—and whether it tasted good, to which she responded almost stormily in the affirmative. He now gazed out across the room where people were coming and going: early breakfast was not a strictly communal affair.

He had been a little afraid of the dreadful effect all this might have on him, but found himself disappointed in that—the dining hall atmosphere was quite congenial, one had no sense of being in a place of misery. Well-tanned young people of both sexes entered humming a tune, spoke with the dining attendants, and weighed into breakfast with a robust appetite. There were more mature people as well, married couples, a whole family with children, including teenage boys, all speaking Russian. Almost all the women wore close-fitting jackets of wool or silk, called "sweaters," in white or bright colors, with shawl collars and side pockets; it looked very pretty when they just stood there chatting, both hands buried in their sweater pockets. Photographs were passed around at several tables—recent shots they had taken themselves, no doubt; at one table they were trading postage stamps. The talk was of the weather, of how one had slept and what one's "oral measurement" had been that morning. Most of them were cheerful—for no particular reason presumably, but simply because they had no immediate cares and were assembled in considerable numbers. A few people, to be sure, sat at the table with heads propped in their hands, staring straight ahead. People let them stare and paid them no attention.

Suddenly Hans Castorp flinched—he was annoyed and offended. A door, the one to his left that led to the lobby, had banged shut—someone had simply let it slam, or perhaps even slammed it intentionally, and that was a noise that Hans Castorp absolutely could not tolerate, he had always hated it. Perhaps it was a learned dislike, perhaps an inborn idiosyncrasy—whatever it was, he abhorred banging doors and could have slapped anyone guilty of slamming one within earshot. In this case, the door was divided into little glass panes, which only heightened the shock: it was a bang *and* a rattle. "Damn it," Hans Castorp thought angrily, "what kind of sloppiness is that?" Since the seamstress had said something to him at the same moment, he had no chance to determine who the malefactor was. But as he answered the seamstress, there were deep furrows between his blond eyebrows and his face was wrenched with distress.

Joachim asked whether the doctors had been through yet. Yes, they had been there once already, someone replied, but had left the dining hall at almost the same moment the cousins arrived. Then they might as well not wait, Joachim said. There would be an opportunity in the course of the day to make the introductions. But at the door they almost collided with Director Behrens, who came striding through it at high speed, followed by Dr. Krokowski.

"Whoops, heads up, gentlemen!" Behrens said. "That could have meant some badly trodden corns for all parties." He spoke with a strong Lower Saxon accent, chewing his words broadly. "So, *you're* the fellow," he said to Hans Castorp, after Joachim clicked his heels together and made the introductions. "Well, my pleasure." And he extended a hand as big as a shovel. He was a bony man, a good three heads taller than Dr. Krokowski, with a shock of white hair; his neck vertebrae stuck out, and his watery, bloodshot blue eyes protruded; he had a snub nose above a little short-cropped moustache, which sat slightly askew because his upper lip was turned up at one corner. What Joachim had said about his cheeks proved to be the absolute truth—they were purple, making his head look that much more colorful against his belted, white surgical smock, which fell just below the knees, revealing striped trousers and colossal feet in a pair of yellow, rather worn, laced boots. Dr. Krokowski was in professional uniform as well, except that his smock was more shirtlike, with elastic at the wrists, and of a black, shiny fabric that only emphasized his pallor. He played the role of the perfect assistant, taking no part whatever in the exchanged greetings—although the tense, critical way he held his mouth suggested that he found his subordinate position a little absurd.

"Cousins?" the director asked, gesturing with his hand, pointing now at one, now at the other, and looking down out of bloodshot blue eyes. "Well, is he going to march to the pipe and drum like you?" he asked Joachim, nodding his head toward Hans Castorp. "Ha, God forbid— right? I spotted it at once." And now he spoke directly to Hans Castorp: "There's something so civilian, so comfortable about you—no rattling sabers like our corporal here. You would be a better patient than he, I'd lay odds on that. I can tell right off whether someone will make a competent patient or not, because that takes talent, everything takes talent, and this Myrmidon here hasn't the least talent for it. For military drill, maybe, I can't say as to that, but none for being ill. He constantly wants to leave, can you believe it? Forever asking to leave, pesters and badgers me and simply can't wait to live a life of drudgery down below. What a zealot! Won't give us six months of his time. Even though we have such a lovely place here—you must admit, Ziemssen, it is lovely here, isn't it? Well, your good cousin will know better how to appreciate us, he'll be able to amuse himself. There's no shortage of ladies—we have the most adorable ladies here. Many of them quite picturesque—viewed externally, at least. But *you*'ll have to improve your color somewhat, too, otherwise the ladies will give you the cold shoulder. 'The golden tree of life is green,' true, but a green face is really not quite the thing. Totally anemic, of course," he said, and mechanically stepped up to Hans Castorp, extended two fingers, and pulled an eyelid down. "No doubt of it, totally anemic, just as I said. Do you know what? It was not all that stupid of you to leave your Hamburg to fend for itself for a while. A highly commendable institution, your Hamburg. Always sends us a nice contingent, what with its intoxicatingly damp meteorology. But if I might use this opportunity to give you some modest advice—quite *sine pecunia*, of course—as long as you're here with us, why don't you do just what your cousin does? In a case like yours, there's no wiser course than to live for a while as if it were a slight *tuberculosis pulmonum*, and build up your protein a little. It's very curious, you see, the way protein is metabolized up here. Although one's general metabolism increases, the body stores the protein. Well, and you slept well, did you, Ziemssen? Fine, fine. But now, do get on with your promenade! But no more than half an hour. And make sure you stick the old mercury cigar in your mouth afterward. And always jot down the results, right, Ziemssen? Conscientiously doing one's duty. I'll want to see your chart come Saturday. And your good cousin should measure, too. Measuring never hurts. Morning, gentlemen. Have a good time. Morning, morning . . ." And Dr. Krokowski joined him as he sailed off, swinging his arms, palms turned clear around to the back, tossing his question right and left as to whether people had slept well, which was universally answered in the affirmative.

Teasing/Viaticum/Interrupted Merriment

"VERY NICE MAN," Hans Castorp said as they walked out the front door, with a friendly nod to the limping concierge, who was sitting in his office sorting letters. The main door was on the southeast side of the large white building, whose middle section rose one story higher than the two wings and was crowned by a clock tower roofed with slate-colored sheet iron. Leaving the building by this exit, you did not approach the garden, but came out facing directly onto an open slope of mountain meadows, dotted with a few tallish firs and several low mountain pines that hugged the ground. The path they took—actually it was the only one available other than the main road that descended to the valley—led them gently up the rise to their left, past the rear of the sanatorium, where the kitchens and offices were located and steel garbage cans lined the railing beside the cellar stairs, and held to that direction for a good distance, then made a sharp hairpin to the right and began a steeper ascent up the sparsely wooded hill. It was a firm earthen path, reddish in color and a little damp, with boulders here and there along the edge. The cousins quickly learned that they were not alone on their walk. Guests who had finished breakfast shortly after them followed on their heels, and coming toward them were whole groups of people on their way back, stomping the way people tend to do walking downhill.

"Very nice man," Hans Castorp repeated. "Has such an easy way with words, it's fun just to listen to him. 'Mercury cigar' for 'thermometer' is really quite splendid, I caught on right away. But I'm going to light a real one now," he said, coming to a halt. "I can't stand it any longer. I've not had a decent smoke since yesterday noon. Excuse me a moment." And from a buff leather etui monogrammed in silver, he extracted one of his Maria Mancinis—a lovely specimen from the top of the box, flattened on just one side the way he especially liked it—trimmed the tip squarely with a small tool that hung from his watch chain, produced a flame from his pocket lighter, and after a bit of concentrated puffing managed to light the rather long, blunt-ended cigar. "There!" he said. "Now we can get on with our promenade, for all I care. Of course, being a zealot, you're not smoking these days, are you?"

"I've never smoked," Joachim replied. "Why should I start up here, of all places?"

"I don't understand," Hans Castorp said. "I don't understand how someone can not be a smoker—why it's like robbing oneself of the best part of life, so to speak, or at least of an absolutely first-rate pleasure. When I wake up I look forward to being able to smoke all day, and when I eat, I look forward to it again, in fact I can honestly say that I actually only eat so that I can smoke, although that's an exaggeration, of course. But a day without tobacco—that would be absolutely insipid, a dull, totally wasted day. And if some morning I had to tell myself: there's nothing left to smoke today, why I don't think I'd find courage to get up, I swear I'd stay in bed. You see, if a man has a cigar that burns well—

and obviously it can't have any breaks or draw badly, that's really terribly annoying—what I'm saying is, that if a man has a good cigar, then he's home safe, nothing, literally nothing, can happen to him. It's the same as when you're lying on the beach, because there you lie on the beach, you know? and you don't need anything else—no work, no other amusements. Thank God, people smoke all over the world, there's nowhere you could possibly end up, as far as I know, where tobacco's unknown. Even polar explorers lay in a good supply of smokes to get them over their hardships—that's always struck a sympathetic chord in me whenever I've read about it. Because things can go very badly—let's assume, for instance, that things would go miserably for me—but as long as I had my cigar, I'd carry on, that much I know, it could bring me through anything."

"All the same, it's a sign of a rather weak will," Joachim said, "to be so dependent on tobacco. Behrens is quite right—you're a civilian. He meant it more in praise, to be sure, but you are an incurable civilian, that's the point. And besides, you're healthy and can do what you like," he said, and a weary look came into his eyes.

"Yes, healthy except for anemia," Hans Castorp said. "That was a bit much, though, when he told me that I look green. But he's right, it's even obvious to me that in comparison to you folks up here I'm downright green—whereas I never really noticed it at home. And that really was very nice of him to just go ahead and offer some advice, quite *sine pecunia* as he put it. I'll be happy to do as he says, and I hereby resolve to adapt my habits to yours—what else can I do as long as I'm up here with all of you? And it can't hurt me, for heaven's sake, to build up my protein, although that does sound disgusting, you must admit."

Joachim coughed a couple of times as they walked—the climb was taxing for him, it seemed. When he started coughing a third time, he stopped and scowled. "Go on ahead," he said. Hans Castorp first hurried on without looking back. Then he slowed his pace and almost came to a stop, assuming that by now he had a considerable lead on Joachim. But he did not look back.

A party of guests of both sexes was coming toward him—he had noticed them moving along a level stretch of path about halfway up the slope, and now they were tramping downhill, moving directly toward him, and he could hear the babble of voices. There were six or seven people of various ages, from very young things to a few who were somewhat further along in years. Still thinking about Joachim, he tilted his head and looked them over. They were all bareheaded and tanned, the ladies in colorful sweaters, the gentlemen without overcoats for the most part, even without walking sticks—they looked as if they had just stepped out the door for a breath of air, hands in their pockets. Since walking downhill is not a matter of strenuous exertion but more a sport, where you brace your legs and apply the brakes to keep from tripping or running—nothing more than helping yourself fall, really—there was a kind of nimble frivolity to their gait, which spread even to their faces, until the whole effect might very well have made you want to join their party.

They were just ahead of him now, and Hans Castorp took a close look at their faces. They were not all tanned, two of the ladies were conspicuously pale: the one thin as a rail, with an ivory complexion; the other shorter and plump, her face blemished by moles and freckles. They all looked at him, all smiling the same cheeky smile. A tall young girl in a green sweater, her hair in untidy disarray and with doltish, half-closed eyes, brushed past Hans Castorp, so close that she almost touched him with her arm. And whistled—no, that was just too crazy! She whistled at him, but not with her mouth; her lips weren't puckered at all, were tightly closed in fact. The whistle came from inside, and all the while she stared at him, with her doltish, half-closed eyes. An extraordinarily unpleasant whistle, harsh, intense, and yet somehow hollow, an extended tone, emerging inexplicably from somewhere in her chest and falling off toward the end—it reminded him of the music you get from those inflatable rubber pigs you buy at a carnival, the way they wail mournfully when you squeeze the air out. And then she and the rest of her party had moved on.

Hans Castorp stood there aghast, staring straight ahead. Then he quickly turned around and decided that the horrid sound must have been a joke, a prearranged prank—that much at least was clear now, because as they moved off he saw their shoulders jiggling with laughter, and one stocky lad with thick lips, his hands stuck in his pants pockets, hitching his jacket up in a rather unbecoming way, blatantly turned to look back— and laughed. Joachim had caught up by now. He greeted the party in his usual chivalrous way, bowing and clicking his heels, almost standing at attention, and there was a gentle look in his eye as he joined his cousin.

"What sort of face is that you're making?" he asked.

"She whistled!" Hans Castorp answered. "She whistled from her stomach as she passed me by. Would you kindly explain that to me?"

"Oh," Joachim said, laughing dismissively. "Not from her stomach, what nonsense. That was the Kleefeld girl, Hermine Kleefeld, who can whistle with her pneumothorax."

"With her what?" Hans Castorp asked. He was terribly agitated, but he didn't quite know in what sense. Wavering between laughter and tears, he added, "You can't expect me to understand your jargon."

"Let's move on," Joachim said. "I can just as easily explain it while we walk. You look like you've struck root. As you might guess, it has to do with surgery, an operation that they perform up here. Behrens is quite an expert at it. When one lung has been badly ravaged, you see, but the other is healthy or relatively healthy, the infected one is relieved of its duties for a while, given a rest. Which means that they make an incision here, somewhere along the side here—I don't know precisely where they cut, but Behrens has it down perfectly. And then they let gas in, nitrogen, you see, and that way the caseated lobes of the lung are put out of commission. The gas doesn't last that long, of course, and has to be replaced twice a month or so—they more or less pump you up, that's how you have to picture it. And after they've done that for a year or so, if all goes well, the lung will have rested long enough to heal. Not always, of course, it's really rather risky business. But they say they've had some nice successes with their pneumothorax. All the people you just saw have had it done. Frau Iltis was with them—the one with the freckles—and Fräulein Levi, the skinny one, if you recall—she was confined to bed for a long time. They've formed a group—something like pneumothorax brings people together, naturally—and call themselves the 'Half-Lung Club,' that's the name everyone knows them by. But the pride of the club is Hermine Kleefeld, because she can whistle with her pneumothorax—it's her special talent, it's certainly not something everyone can do. Not that I can tell you how she manages it, she can't explain it clearly herself. But if she's been walking rapidly, then she can whistle from inside, and of course she uses it then to startle people, especially newly arrived patients. I presume, by the way, that she's wasting nitrogen by doing it, because she has to get a refill every week."

And Hans Castorp was laughing now; during Joachim's explanation, his agitation had resolved into mirth, and as he walked along, bent forward and shading his eyes with his hand, his shoulders were convulsed by his soft, rapid giggles.

"Has the club been registered?" he asked, though he found it hard to speak, and it sounded more like a whine or whimper from suppressed laughter. "Do they have bylaws? What a shame you're not a member, Joachim, because then they could include me as an honorary guest—or associate member. You should ask Behrens to put you temporarily out of commission. Maybe you'd be able to whistle, too, if you really set your mind to it, after all it must be something you can learn. That's the funniest thing I've ever heard in my life," he said, taking a deep breath. "You'll have to forgive me, really, for talking like this, but they were in a merry mood themselves, your pneumatic friends. Here they come walk-

ing up . . . and to think that it was the Half-Lung Club! 'Tweeet'
she whistles at me—what a harum-scarum! What absolute devil-may-
care. And I'm sure you can tell me just why they're so devil-may-care,
can't you?"

Joachim searched for an answer. "My God," he said, "they're so *free*.
I mean, they're young and time plays no role in their lives, and they may
very well die. Why should they go around with long faces? I sometimes
think that illness and death aren't really serious matters, that it's all more
like loafing around, and that, strictly speaking, things are serious only
down below in real life. I think maybe you'll come to understand that in
due time, after you've been up here with us a little longer."

"Certainly," Hans Castorp said, "I'm certain I shall. I'm already taking
a great deal of interest in all of you up here, and once one is interested,
why then understanding follows as a matter of course, doesn't it? But
what's wrong with me—this doesn't taste good," he said, looking at his
cigar. "I've been asking myself the whole time what was the matter, and
now I realize that my Maria is the problem. I swear to you, it tastes like
papier-mâché, exactly as if I had a terribly upset stomach. It's really quite
incredible! I did eat an unusually large breakfast, but that can't be the
reason, because when you eat a lot, it always tastes especially good at
first. Do you think it can be because I slept so restlessly? Perhaps that's
thrown me off track. No, I'm simply going to have to toss it away," he
said after trying once more. "Every puff is a disappointment; there's no
point in forcing it." He hesitated for a moment and then flicked the cigar
down the slope among the wet pines. "Do you know what I'm convinced
is to blame?" he asked. "I am thoroughly convinced that it has something
to do with this damned flushed face of mine—it's been bothering me
again ever since I got up. Damned if it doesn't feel as if I'm constantly
blushing in embarrassment. Was it the same with you, too, when you
first arrived?"

"Yes," Joachim said, "I felt rather strange, too, at first. Don't worry
about it. I told you, if you remember, that it's not all that easy to get
used to our life up here. But you'll soon be back on track. Look there,
that bench has a nice view. Let's sit down for a bit and then head home—
I need to take my rest cure."

They were now about a third of the way up the hill, but the path had
leveled out, heading now in the direction of Davos-Platz. From between
the tall firs and a few stunted ones bent by the wind, the view looked
down on the village, which lay white under a brighter sky. The rudely
fashioned bench on which they sat had its back to the steep slope. Water
fell in an open wooden trough beside them, gurgling and splashing on its
way to the valley.

Pointing with the tip of his alpenstock, Joachim set about teaching his cousin the names of the cloud-topped peaks that appeared to close off the valley to the south. But Hans Castorp was bent forward, glancing up only fleetingly while drawing figures in the sand with the silver-trimmed knob of his citified cane. And now he demanded to know other things.

"What I wanted to ask you—" he began. "The case in my room expired just before I arrived, you said. Have there been a lot of other deaths since you've been up here?"

"Several, certainly," Joachim replied. "But they deal with them discreetly, you see, so you don't hear about them, or only occasionally, later on. When someone dies it's kept a strict secret, out of consideration for the other patients, in particular the ladies, who might easily go to pieces. If someone dies right next door, you don't even notice it. The coffin is brought in early in the morning while you're still sleeping, and then the party in question is removed only at another more suitable time—during meals, for instance."

"Hmm," Hans Castorp said and went on drawing. "So that quite a bit is happening backstage."

"Yes, you can put it that way. But recently—it must have been, wait a moment—probably eight weeks ago—"

"Then you can't call it recently," an alert Hans Castorp remarked dryly.

"What? Well then, not so recently. You're so precise. I was just guessing at the date. But anyway, some time ago, I had a peek backstage myself, purely by accident, but it's as real as if it had happened today. It was the little Hujus girl, Barbara Hujus—she was Catholic—when they brought her the viaticum, the sacrament for the dying, you know, extreme unction. She was still up and about when I arrived here, and could be so playfully funny, so downright silly, a real teenager. But then it all went very fast, she couldn't get up anymore, lay bedridden just three rooms down from me, and her parents came, and so now the priest arrived, too. He came one afternoon, when everyone was at tea, with nobody in the halls. But you have to picture it—I had overslept, had fallen asleep during my rest cure and hadn't heard the gong and was a quarter hour late. And so at the decisive moment I happened not to be where everyone else was, but had wandered backstage, as you put it, and as I'm walking down the corridor, I see them coming toward me, in lace shirts, a cross leading the way, a gold cross with little lanterns, one of them carrying it up front like the glockenspiel in a Turkish-style military band."

"That's a poor comparison," Hans Castorp said rather sternly.

"It just seemed that way to me. It automatically reminded me of it. But now listen. They're coming toward me, left right left, double-time, three of them if I'm not mistaken, the man with the cross first, then the priest, spectacles perched on his nose, and then a boy with a censer. The priest was carrying the sacrament against his chest, it had a cover over it, and holding his head very devoutly to one side—it's their holy of holies, after all."

"That's precisely it," Hans Castorp said. "That's the reason why I was astounded when you said what you did about the glockenspiel."

"Yes, yes. But just wait, if you had been there, you wouldn't know what kind of face to put on, either, thinking back on it. It was like something you might see in a dream—"

"In what way?"

"Let me tell you. So there I am, asking myself how I ought to act under the circumstances. I didn't have a hat to take off—"

"You see!" Hans Castorp quickly interrupted yet again. "You see, a man should always wear a hat. I've noticed, of course, that you people up here never wear one. But you should, so that you can tip it whenever the occasion demands. But now what happened?"

"I stood back against the wall," Joachim said, "taking up a respectful pose, and made a little bow as they came even with me—it was right in front of the little Hujus girl's room, number twenty-eight. The priest was glad to see my response, I think, and returned my greeting very politely, doffing his cap. But by this time they have all come to a halt, and the altar boy with the censer knocks on the door, then lifts the latch, and lets his supervisor step ahead into the room. But now, just picture it, just imagine the terror I felt. The moment the priest sets a foot over the threshold, a hue and cry starts up inside, first a shriek like nothing you've ever heard, three or four times in a row, and then just screaming without a pause or break, like a mouth gaping wide open, I suppose, 'Ahhh—' and with such misery and terror and defiance in it that I can't describe it, and such ghastly pleading mixed in, too, and then all of a sudden it turns hollow and muffled, as if it has sunk down into the earth or is coming from a deep cellar."

Hans Castorp had turned abruptly to face his cousin. "And was that the Hujus girl?" he asked in exasperation. "But why 'from a deep cellar'?"

"She had crawled under her blanket," Joachim said. "Just imagine how I felt. The priest was standing just on the far side of the threshold, speaking soothing words—I can still see him—the way he constantly thrust his head forward and then jerked it back. The cross-bearer and the altar boy were stuck there at the door and couldn't get in. But I could see between them into the room. It's a room just like yours or mine, with the bed to the left of the door along one side, and there were people standing at its head, her family of course, her parents, directing comforting words down at the bed, where you could only see a formless mass, begging and protesting hideously and kicking its legs."

"Are you saying she was kicking with her legs?"

"For all she was worth. But it didn't help, she had to be given the sacrament of the dying. The pastor walked over to her and the other two stepped inside as well, and then the door was closed. But just before that, I saw the Hujus girl's head emerge for a mere second, her light blond hair, and her pale eyes, no color to them at all, gaping wide, staring at the priest—and then she ducked under the sheets again with a loud wail."

"And you're telling me only now?" Hans Castorp said after a pause. "I can't understand how you didn't bring it up yesterday evening. But, my God, she must have had a lot of strength left to fight back like that. That takes strength. You shouldn't send for a priest until they're very weak."

"But she was weak," Joachim replied. "Oh, there are lots of things I could tell you about; it's hard to know what to pick out first. She was already weak—it was fear that gave her so much strength. She was terribly frightened, because she realized she was going to die. She was just a young girl, so it is excusable, after all. But even grown men carry on like that sometimes, which is, of course, inexcusably weak-willed of them. Behrens knows how to deal with them, he can strike just the right tone for such cases."

"What sort of tone?" Hans Castorp asked with a scowl.

" 'Don't make such a fuss!' he says," Joachim replied. "At least that's what he said to one fellow recently—we heard about it from the head nurse who was present to help restrain the dying man. He was one of those types who makes a dreadful scene right at the end and absolutely refuses to die. And so Behrens simply dressed him down: 'Would you please not make such a fuss,' he said, and the patient quieted down at once and died quite peaceably."

Hans Castorp slapped his thigh with one hand, threw himself back against the bench, and stared at the sky.

"Listen here, that's weighty stuff," he cried. "Snaps his head off and says, 'Don't make such a fuss!' To a dying man. Weighty stuff. A dying man deserves a certain amount of respect. You can't just walk up to him so calm and cool and. . . . There's something holy about a dying man, as it were—in my opinion."

"I won't deny that," Joachim said. "But if he starts carrying on in such a weak-willed way . . ."

"No," Hans Castorp insisted with a ferocity not at all appropriate to the mild objection Joachim had offered. "I'll not let you talk me out of it. A dying man has something nobler about him than your average rascal strolling about, laughing and making money and stuffing his belly. It won't do." And his voice began to waver strangely. "It just won't do to walk up so calm and cool and . . ." But now his words were swallowed in a fit of laughter that suddenly overwhelmed him, the same laughter as yesterday, welling up from deep inside—convulsive, unbounded laughter, until he had to close his eyes for the tears.

"Psst," Joachim said suddenly. "Quiet!" he whispered and gave his cousin, still laughing uncontrollably, a silent poke in the ribs. Hans Castorp looked up through his tears.

A stranger was coming up the path on their left, a delicate man with brown hair and a black moustache twirled at the ends; he was wearing pastel checked trousers and exchanged a good-morning with Joachim as he came up to them—his greeting was precise and melodious. And now he stopped, striking a graceful pose in front of them by propping himself on his cane and crossing his ankles.

Satana

I T WOULD HAVE BEEN DIFFICULT to guess his age, but it surely had to be somewhere between thirty and forty, because, although the general impression was youthful, he was already silvering at the temples and his hair was thinning noticeably, receding toward the part in two wide arcs, making the brow even higher. His outfit—loose trousers in a pastel yellow check and a wide-lapelled, double-breasted coat that was made of something like petersham and hung much too long—was far from laying any claim to elegance. The edges of his rounded high collar were rough from frequent laundering, his black tie was threadbare, and he apparently didn't even bother with cuffs—Hans Castorp could tell from the limp way the coat sleeves draped around his wrists. All the same, he could definitely see that he had a gentleman before him—the refined expression on the stranger's face, his easy, even handsome pose left no doubt of that. This mixture of shabbiness and charm, plus the black eyes and a handlebar moustache, immediately reminded Hans Castorp of certain foreign musicians who would appear in his hometown at Christmastime and strike up a tune, then gaze up with velvet eyes and hold out their slouch hats to catch the coins you threw them from the window. "An organ-grinder!" he thought. And so he was not surprised by the name he now heard as

Joachim got up from the bench somewhat flustered and introduced him, "Castorp, my cousin—Herr Settembrini."

Hans Castorp had also stood up by way of greeting, traces of excess merriment still on his face. But the Italian politely remarked that he did not wish to disturb them and urged them to take their seats, whereas he remained standing in his becoming pose. He stood there, smiling and observing the cousins, particularly Hans Castorp, and the delicate line at one corner of his mouth, the mocking curl of the lip just below where his full moustache swept handsomely upward, had a peculiar effect—somehow it exhorted one to be alert and clearheaded, and in a flash so sobered the inebriated Hans Castorp that he felt ashamed of himself.

Settembrini said, "The gentlemen are in high spirits—and with good cause, good cause. A splendid morning! The sky is blue, the sun is smiling." And with an easy, felicitous wave of his arm he lifted his little, yellowish hand toward the heavens and simultaneously cast an oblique glance in the same upward direction. "One could in fact forget completely just where one is."

He spoke without any accent—at most one might have recognized him as a foreigner from the precision in the way he shaped his sounds. His lips took a certain delight in forming the words. It was a pleasure to listen to him. "And your journey, sir, to join us here was pleasant, I hope?" he asked, turning to Hans Castorp. "And is one already in possession of the verdict? I mean—has the gloomy ceremony of the first examination taken place yet?" Had he cared for an answer, he would have fallen silent and waited—for he had asked a question and Hans Castorp was about to reply. But the stranger went right on with his inquiries: "And did it go well? Given your hilarity"—he fell silent for a moment and the furrowed curl at the corner of his mouth deepened—"one could draw contradictory conclusions. How many months have our Minos and Rhadamanthus saddled you with?" The phrase "saddled you with" sounded particularly droll coming from him. "Shall I guess? Six? Or nine, right off? They're not stingy, you know . . ."

Hans Castorp laughed in surprise—meanwhile trying to recall who Minos and Rhadamanthus were, exactly. He answered, "How do you mean? No, you're mistaken, Herr Septem—"

"Settembrini," the Italian corrected him with particular verve, accompanied by a facetious bow.

"Herr Settembrini—beg your pardon. No, you are mistaken. I am not sick at all. I'm merely visiting my cousin Ziemssen for a few weeks and using the occasion for a little relaxation myself."

"Great Scott! You are not one of us? You are healthy, you are merely stopping over, as it were, like Odysseus in the realm of shades? How bold of you to descend into the depths, where the futile dead live on without their wits—"

"Into the depths, Herr Settembrini? But I beg your pardon—I climbed a good five thousand feet to join you up here."

"It only seemed that way to you. Upon my word—it was an illusion," the Italian said with a decisive gesture of one hand. "We are creatures who have fallen to great depths, are we not, lieutenant?" he asked, turning to Joachim, who took considerable delight in the title, but tried to hide the fact in a sober reply.

"We do become rather tedious, I suppose. But one can always pull oneself together again."

"Yes, I trust you shall; you're an upstanding fellow," Settembrini said. "Yes, yes, yes," he repeated, hissing the *s* all three times. Turning again to Hans Castorp, he clicked his tongue softly an equal number of times. "I see, I see, I see," he now said in another triplet of sharp *s*'s, gazing at the newcomer so steadily that his eyes took on a fixed, vacant look; but then life returned to them again and he went on, "You've joined us up here quite voluntarily so that we downsliders may enjoy the pleasure of your company for a while. Well, how lovely. And what sort of a time period do you have in mind? I mean that not as a subtle question—I am simply intrigued to know how long the sentence is when it is pronounced by oneself and not by Rhadamanthus."

"Three weeks," Hans Castorp said with a kind of breezy self-complacency, realizing he was the object of envy.

"*O Dio*, three weeks! Did you hear, lieutenant? Is there not something impertinent about saying: I'm coming here for three weeks and then moving on? We do not know the week as a unit of measurement, sir, if I may be permitted to instruct you. Our smallest unit of time is the month. We measure on a grand scale—it is one of the privileges of shades. We have others as well, all of equal quality. Might I ask what profession you pursue down below—or more correctly, for what profession you are preparing yourself? You see, our curiosity knows no bounds—we count curiosity among our privileges, too."

"Oh, no offense taken," Hans Castorp said, and provided the information.

"A shipbuilder—how marvelous!" Settembrini cried. "I assure you, I think that's marvelous, although my own talents lie in a different direction."

"Herr Settembrini is a literary man," Joachim said, explaining with some embarrassment. "He wrote the obituary of Carducci for the German papers—Carducci, you know." And he grew even more embarrassed when his cousin looked at him in amazement as if to say: "What do you know about Carducci? About as much as I do, I bet."

"That's right," the Italian said with a nod. "I had the honor of telling your countrymen about that great poet and freethinker once his life had drawn to a close. I knew him, I may even say that I was a disciple. I sat at his feet in Bologna. I have him to thank for whatever refinement and good cheer I call my own. But we were speaking of you—a shipbuilder? Do you know that you are visibly growing in stature right before my eyes? Suddenly there you sit, the representative of a whole world of labor and practical genius."

"But Herr Settembrini—I'm really only a student, I'm just beginning."

"To be sure, and the first step is always the most difficult. Indeed, all labor truly deserving of the name is difficult, is it not?"

"Devil knows that's right," Hans Castorp said, and it came from the heart.

Settembrini's eyebrows flew up. "And you even call upon the Devil," he said, "to support your opinions? Satan himself? Did you know that my great teacher once wrote a hymn to him?"

"Excuse me," Hans Castorp said, "to the Devil?"

"The Devil himself. It is even sung on certain festive occasions in my homeland. '*O salute, O Satana, O ribellione, O forza vindice della ragione*' . . . a splendid hymn! But that was most probably not the Devil you had in mind, because *he* is on excellent terms with labor. The one you mean, the Devil who considers labor an abomination because he fears it, is presumably the other one, of whom it is said one shouldn't give him an inch."

All this had a very strange effect on Hans Castorp. He did not understand Italian—and felt no more comfortable about the rest of it. There was a preachy flavor to it, although it was delivered in the light, bantering tone of small talk. He looked at his cousin—who simply lowered his eyes—and then said, "Ah, Herr Settembrini, you take my words all too literally. My reference to the Devil was merely a figure of speech, I assure you."

"Someone must show some wit," Settembrini said, gazing dolefully into the air. But then he grew animated again, brightened up, and charmingly brought the conversation around. "In any case, I am correct in concluding from your words that you have chosen a profession as demanding as it is honorable. My God, I am a humanist, a *homo humanus*, and understand nothing of such ingenious matters, however sincere my deep respect for them. But I can well imagine that the theoretical side of your profession demands a clear and keen mind and its practice no less than the whole man—is that not so?"

"It certainly is, yes, I can agree with you unconditionally there," Hans Castorp responded, instinctively attempting to speak with a little more eloquence. "Its demands are colossal nowadays—one dare not be all too aware of just how exacting or one might truly lose all heart. No, it is no fun. And when one's constitution is not all that strong—I am here only as a guest, true, but my constitution's not exactly the strongest, and I would be lying were I to claim that work suits me splendidly. Indeed it rather wears me down, I must say. Actually, I only feel really healthy when I am doing nothing at all."

"Now, for example?"

"Now? Oh, I'm still so new up here—a little confused, as you can well imagine."

"Ah—confused."

"Yes, I didn't sleep all that well, and then the first breakfast was really too sumptuous. I'm used to a good breakfast, but what we had today seemed to me a little too heavy, too 'rich,' as the English say. In short, I'm feeling somewhat uneasy, particularly since my cigar didn't seem to taste good this morning—just imagine! That almost never happens to me, really only when I'm seriously ill. And today it tastes like leather. I had to toss it away, there was no point in forcing it. Are you a smoker, if I may ask? No? Then you can't imagine what an annoyance, what a disappointment that is for someone like myself, who has smoked with such gusto from youth on."

"I am inexperienced in that area," Settembrini replied, "but find myself in rather good company in that lack of experience. A great many noble and prudent minds have detested tobacco smoke. Carducci did not love it, either. But you'll find sympathy from Rhadamanthus there. He is a devotee of your vice."

"Now, now—vice, Herr Settembrini . . ."

"Why not? One must apply truth and energy in naming things. It elevates and intensifies life. I have my vices, too."

"So Director Behrens is also an expert on cigars, I see. A charming man."

"You think so? Ah, and so you have already made his acquaintance?"

"Yes, just now, as we were leaving for our walk. It was almost a kind of consultation, but *sine pecunia*, you know. He immediately noticed that I am rather anemic. And suggested that I should adopt my cousin's style of life here—lie out on the balcony a great deal, even said I should measure my temperature, too."

"Is that right?" Settembrini exclaimed. "Excellent!" he cried into the air above him, throwing his head back and laughing. "How does that go in the opera of your greatest composer? 'I am the man who catches birds, am always merry, mark my words!' In short, that's very amusing. And you wish to follow his advice, do you? Indubitably. Why shouldn't you? A devil of a fellow, our Rhadamanthus. And truly 'always merry'— though at times it's a little forced. He tends to melancholy. His vice is not good for him—but otherwise, it would be no vice—tobacco only makes him melancholy. Which is why our venerable head nurse has taken charge of his supply and allows him only a small daily ration. It has been said that on occasion he succumbs to the temptation of stealing them, and then slips into melancholy. In a word, a confused soul. You do know our head nurse, do you not? No? But that is a mistake—you are in error not to seek out her acquaintance. From the house of the von Mylendonks, sir! She differs from the Medici Venus only in that where the goddess has a bosom, she wears a cross."

"Ha ha, excellent!" Hans Castorp laughed.

"Her given name is Adriatica."

"You don't say?" Hans Castorp exclaimed. "That is extraordinary— von Mylendonk and Adriatica, to boot. It sounds as if she ought to have been dead for centuries. It has an absolutely medieval ring."

"My good sir," Settembrini replied, "there is much here that has a 'medieval ring' to it, as you have chosen to express it. I for my part am convinced that our Rhadamanthus has made this fossil the chief supervisor of his palace of horrors simply out of a sense of artistic style. He is after all an artist—you did not know that? He paints in oils. And why not? It is not forbidden, you know—everyone is free to do as he chooses. Frau Adriatica tells anyone who will listen, and others as well, that toward the middle of the thirteenth century a Mylendonk was the abbess of a cloister in Bonn on the Rhine. She herself surely must have first seen the light of the world shortly thereafter."

"Ha ha ha. What a sarcastic man you are, Herr Settembrini."

"Sarcastic? You mean malicious. Yes, I am a little malicious," Settembrini said. "My great worry is that I have been condemned to waste my malice on such miserable objects. I hope that you have nothing against malice, my good engineer. In my eyes it is the brightest sword that reason has against the powers of darkness and ugliness. Malice, sir, is the spirit of criticism, and criticism marks the origin of progress and enlightenment." And all of a sudden he began to speak about Petrarch, whom he called the "Father of Modernity."

"We must return to our rest cure, however," Joachim said circumspectly.

The literary man, who had underscored all his words with charming

gestures, rounded his thoughts off now with a flourish in Joachim's direction and said, "Our lieutenant is pressing us into service. And so let us
depart. We are taking the same path—'to the right, which leads to the
walls of mightiest Dis.' Ah, Virgil, Virgil, gentlemen, he is unsurpassed.
I believe in progress, certainly. But Virgil had a command of epithets
beyond that of any modern poet." And as they made their way home,
he began to recite Latin verses with an Italian accent, but broke off when
he saw a young girl approaching—a daughter of the town, it appeared,
and not an especially pretty one—and switched with a smile to a philan-
derer's tune. "Tut, tut, tut," he clicked his tongue. "Ah, ah, ah! La, la,
la! Sweet young thing, won't you be mine? Ah, behold 'her flashing eye
in the slippery light,' " he quoted—God only knew from what—and
turned to blow a kiss at the embarrassed girl's back.

"What a windbag," Hans Castorp thought, and did not change his
mind when Settembrini moved on from this fit of flirtation and returned
to casting aspersions. His primary object was Director Behrens—he
sneered at the size of the man's feet and lingered over his title of *Hofrat*,
which had been bestowed on him by a prince suffering from tuberculosis
of the brain. The prince's scandalous behavior was still the talk of the
valley, but Rhadamanthus had simply winked an eye, both eyes—every
inch a *Hofrat*. Did the gentlemen know, by the way, that Behrens had
been the inventor of the summer season? Yes, he and he alone. Honor
to whom honor is due. In days past, only the most faithful of the faithful
had held out over the summer in this valley. But then "our humorist"
with his incorruptibly keen eye had realized that this unhappy state of
affairs was nothing less than the fruit of prejudice. He had set forth the
theory that, at least as far as *his* institution was concerned, the summer
cure was to be recommended no less than the winter, that it was especially
efficacious, indeed absolutely indispensable. And he had known how to
spread his theory among the public—among other methods, by writing
popular articles that he had then passed on to the press. And since then
business in summer was as lively as that in winter. "A genius!" Settembrini
said. "What in-tu-i-tion!" he said. And then he scoffed at the other sanatoriums in town and sarcastically praised the business acumen of their owners. There was Professor Kafka—every year, at the critical moment of
thaw, when a great many patients demanded to leave, Professor Kafka
would suddenly be called away for a week or so, promising to take care
of discharges on his return. But then he would stay away for six weeks
while the poor things waited—and, let it be noted, their bills increased.
Kafka had once been summoned to consult on a case in Fiume, but he
refused to depart before he had been assured of a fee of five thousand

Swiss francs, and that had taken a good two weeks. The day after the *celebrissimo*'s arrival, the patient had died. And as for Dr. Salzmann, he claimed that Professor Kafka did not keep his syringes sterile and infected his patients with other diseases. He glided on rubber soles, so Salzmann said, to keep the dying from hearing his approach. Whereas Kafka claimed that Salzmann demanded his patients drink "the vine's gladdening gift" in such quantities—likewise with a view to rounding off their bills—that people were dying like flies, and not of phthisis, but of cirrhosis.

And so he continued, while good-natured Hans Castorp laughed heartily at this torrent of glib slander. There was something curiously agreeable in the flow of the Italian's words, spoken as they were in pure and precise German, free of every trace of dialect. Each one emerged taut, neat, and brand-new from his mobile lips; he savored every educated, biting, nimble turn of phrase that he used, taking obvious, effusive, and exhilarating enjoyment even in grammatical inflections and conjugations, and seemed to have far too much clear presence of mind ever to misspeak himself.

"You have such a droll way of speaking, Herr Settembrini," Hans Castorp said. "It's so—lively. I don't really know how to put it."

"Graphic, perhaps?" the Italian responded, fanning himself with his handkerchief, although the air was actually rather cool. "That would be the word you're looking for. I have a graphic way of speaking, is what you want to say. But wait," he cried, "what do I see? Behold the judges of the dead out for a stroll! What a sight!"

The hikers already had the hairpin turn behind them. Whether it was Settembrini's conversation, the steepness of the path, or their not having left the sanatorium nearly so far behind them as Hans Castorp had thought—because a path always seems considerably longer when we first walk it than when we have come to know it—in any case, the return trip had taken a surprisingly short time. Settembrini was right: there were the two doctors striding across the open area at the back of the sanatorium— the director in his white smock leading the way, his head thrust forward, his hands rowing in the air; and in his wake, Dr. Krokowski, still in his black smock, looking about with an even more self-assured air, because clinical custom demanded he walk behind his supervisor as they made their rounds.

"Ah, Krokowski," Settembrini exclaimed. "There he goes, filled with all the secrets of our ladies. I beg you, please regard the delicate symbolism of his garb. He wears black to indicate that his particular specialty is the night. The man has but one thought in his head, and it is a filthy one. My good engineer, how is it that we have not yet spoken of the man? Have you made his acquaintance?"

Hans Castorp said he had.

"Well, then? I am beginning to surmise that you liked him as well."

"I really don't know, Herr Settembrini. I've only had the most fleeting introduction. And, then, I'm not all that rash about forming opinions. I look at people and think: So that's how you are? Well, fine."

"That's pure sluggishness," the Italian replied. "Form opinions! That's why nature gave you eyes and reason. You remarked that I speak maliciously, but if I have done so, then it was not without a pedagogic purpose. We humanists all have a pedagogic streak. Gentlemen, the historical connection between humanism and pedagogy only proves the psychological basis of that connection. One should not deny the humanist his position as an educator—indeed it cannot be denied to him, for he alone preserves the tradition of man's dignity and beauty. There came a time when he took over from the priest, who in murky and misanthropic eras of the past was permitted to arrogate the education of youth to himself. But since then, gentlemen, absolutely no other type of educator has ever emerged. Schools based on humanistic education—you may call me backward if you like, sir, but on principle and *in abstracto*, do understand me correctly, I beg you—I remain their firm supporter."

He was still arguing his case in the elevator and fell silent only when the cousins got off at last on the third floor. He rode it on up to the fourth, where, as Joachim explained, he had a small room with a view to the rear.

"He hasn't much money, I suppose?" Hans Castorp asked as they entered Joachim's room. It looked exactly like his own next door.

"No," Joachim said, "probably not. Or just enough so that he can pay for his stay here. His father was a literary type himself, you know, and I believe the grandfather was, too."

"Well, you see," Hans Castorp said. "Is he seriously ill, then?"

"It's not dangerous, as far as I know, but a stubborn case and it keeps recurring. He's had it for years and has left off and on, but always returns."

"Poor fellow. Especially since he seems to be such an enthusiast for work. He's certainly a fantastic talker, just slips easily from one topic to the other. He was really a little fresh with that girl, I was mortified there for a moment. But then what he said about human dignity, afterward, sounded so spiffing, like formal oratory. Do you often spend time with him?"

Clarity of Mind

BUT JOACHIM COULD PROVIDE only a garbled, impeded reply. A red leather case lined in velvet lay open on the table; from it he had extracted a little thermometer and stuck the end filled with mercury into his mouth. He held it tightly under his tongue so that the glass tube jutted up at an angle from one corner. Then he made himself comfortable, pulling on his house shoes and a tuniclike jacket, picked up a chart and a pencil from the table, plus a book of Russian grammar—he was learning Russian because, as he said, he hoped it would be of use in his career—and thus equipped, he stretched out on the balcony lounge chair, tossing the camel-hair blanket lightly over his feet.

He hardly needed it, because in the last quarter hour the layer of clouds had grown thinner and thinner, and the summer sun was breaking through—so warm and dazzling now that Joachim had to screen his face with a white canvas sunshade ingeniously fixed to one arm of the chair and adjustable to the angle of the glare. Hans Castorp praised the contraption. He wanted to wait until Joachim had finished measuring, and so in the meantime he watched how things were done, examined the fur-lined sleeping bag stored in one corner of the balcony—Joachim used it on cold days—and propping his elbows on the railing, gazed down into the garden, where the common lounging area had now filled up with recumbent patients—reading, writing, chatting. Only a small portion of the inside of the arcade, about five lounge chairs, was visible.

"And how long does that take?" Hans Castorp turned around to ask.

Joachim raised seven fingers.

"Seven minutes must be up by now."

Joachim shook his head. After a while he took the thermometer out of his mouth, looked at it, and said, "Yes, when you pay close attention to it—time, I mean—it goes very slowly. I truly like measuring my temperature four times a day, because it makes you notice what one minute, or even seven, actually means—especially since the seven days of a week hang so dreadfully heavy on your hands here."

"You said 'actually.' But 'actually' doesn't apply," Hans Castorp responded. He was sitting with one thigh hiked up on the railing; the whites of his eyes were bloodshot. "There is nothing 'actual' about time. If it seems long to you, then it is long, and if it seems to pass quickly, then it's short. But how long or how short it is in actuality, no one knows."

He was not at all used to philosophizing, and yet felt some urge to do so.

Joachim contested this. "Why is that? No. We do measure it. We have clocks and calendars, and when a month has passed, then it's passed—for you and me and everyone."

"But wait," Hans Castorp said, holding up a forefinger next to one bloodshot eye. "You said that a minute is as long as it seems to you while you're measuring your temperature, correct?"

"A minute is as long as . . . it *lasts,* as long as it takes a second hand to complete a circle."

"But how long that takes can vary greatly—according to how we feel it! And in point of fact . . . I repeat, in point of fact," Hans Castorp said, pressing his forefinger so firmly against his nose that its tip was folded to one side, "that's a matter of motion, of motion in space, correct? Wait, hear me out! And so we measure time with space. But that is the same thing as trying to measure space with time—the way uneducated people do. It's twenty hours from Hamburg to Davos—true, by train. But on foot, how far is it then? And in our minds—not even a second!"

"Listen here," Joachim said, "what's wrong with you? I think being up here with us is getting to you."

"Just be quiet. My mind is very clear today. So then, what is time?" Hans Castorp asked, bending the tip of his nose so forcefully to one side that it turned white and bloodless. "Will you please tell me that? We perceive space with our senses, with vision and touch. But what is the organ for our sense of time? Would you please tell me that? You see, you're stuck. But how are we ever going to measure something about which, precisely speaking, we know nothing at all—cannot list a single one of its properties. We say time passes. Fine, let it pass for all I care. But in order to measure it . . . no, wait! In order for it to be measurable, it would have to flow *evenly,* but where is it written that it does that? It doesn't do that for our conscious minds, we simply assume it does, just for the sake of convenience. And so all our measurements are merely conventions, if you please."

"Fine," Joachim said, "then it's probably also just a convention that my thermometer has risen four and a half lines above normal. And because of those four little lines I have to loaf around here and can't go on active duty—and that's a disgusting fact all to itself."

"Are you at ninety-nine point five?"

"It's already going back down." And Joachim entered it on his chart. "Yesterday evening it was almost a hundred point four—your arrival did that. Whenever anyone gets a visitor, his temperature goes up. But that's a good thing, really."

"And I'll go now," Hans Castorp said. "My head is full of all kinds of ideas about time—a whole complex of thoughts, let me tell you. But I don't want to get you worked up over them, not when your temperature's already too high. I'll keep it all in mind, and we can talk about it later then, after second breakfast perhaps. You will call me when it's time to eat? I'll go take my rest cure now, too—it can't hurt, thank goodness."

And with that he slipped past the glass divider across to his own balcony, where someone had placed an unfolded lounge chair and a table. He fetched his *Ocean Steamships* and his traveling blanket, a lovely plaid of dark reds and greens, and noticed that his room had been nicely tidied up. And now he stretched out.

But he soon had to put up his sunshade, the blazing glare was unbearable the moment you lay down. Still it was terribly pleasant just to lie there, Hans Castorp discovered at once to his delight—he could not remember ever having used a more comfortable lounge chair. The frame, a little old-fashioned in design—but that was only a stylish touch, really, since the chair was obviously new—was made of polished reddish-brown wood, and the mattress, covered with a soft cottonlike fabric, actually consisted of three thick cushions that reached from the foot of the chair up over the back. And then, attached to a string and slipped into an embroidered linen case was a roll for your neck, neither too firm nor too soft, and it simply worked wonders. Hans Castorp propped one elbow on the broad, smooth surface of the chair arm, and lay there blinking, not even bothering to entertain himself with *Ocean Steamships*. Seen through the arches of the balcony, the hard, barren landscape lay under the bright sun like a framed painting. Hans Castorp regarded it pensively. Suddenly it came to him—and he said aloud into the silence, "That was a dwarf who served us at breakfast."

"Shh," Joachim said. "You have to be quiet. Yes, a dwarf. So what?"

"Nothing. Just that we hadn't spoken about it."

And then he went on dreaming. It was already ten o'clock when he lay down. An hour passed. It was an ordinary hour, neither long nor short. And when it was over, a gong rang out in the building and across the garden—first distant, then nearer, then distant again.

"Breakfast," Joachim said, and you could hear him getting up.

Hans Castorp ended his rest cure for now, too, and went back into the room to get ready. The cousins met in the corridor and went downstairs.

Hans Castorp said, "Well, that felt marvelous just lying there. What sort of chairs are those? If they're for sale up here, I'll take one with me back to Hamburg, they're simply heavenly. Or do you think that Behrens has them made up according to his own specifications?"

Joachim did not know. They hung up their coats and for the second time today they entered the dining hall, where the meal was in full swing.

The room glistened with white from all the milk—a large glass at every place, a good pint of it at least.

"No," Hans Castorp said, taking his seat again at the end of the table between the seamstress and the Englishwoman and conscientiously unfolding his napkin—although he was still weighed down by his first breakfast. "No," he said, "God help me, but I do not drink milk, and certainly not now. Is there some porter, perhaps?" And he turned to ask this question politely and gently of the dwarf. There was no porter, unfortunately. But she promised him some Kulmbach beer, and indeed she brought it. It was thick and black, with a foamy brown head, and was an excellent substitute for porter. Hans Castorp drank thirstily from the tall pint glass. He ate cold cuts on toast. There was more oatmeal on the table and lots of butter and fruit again. He at least let his eyes pass over it all, since he was incapable of helping himself to any of it. And he observed the other guests, too—the crowd was beginning to sort itself out for him and individuals were emerging.

His own table was full, except for the seat at the head opposite him, which, as he was told, was reserved for the doctors. Because whenever their schedules allowed, the physicians took part in communal meals, but at a different table every time—and a place was kept free for them at the head of each one. Neither of them was present at the moment; word was that they were operating. The young man with the moustache entered again, his chin pressed to his chest, and sat down with a worried, self-absorbed look on his face. The very blond, gaunt young woman took her seat and spooned down her yogurt again, as if this were the only thing she ever ate. Next to her this time was a chipper little old lady, who spoke to the silent young man in a steady flow of Russian, to which his only reply was a worried expression and a nod of the head—and that same look on his face as if he had something foul-tasting in his mouth. Across from him, on the other side of the old lady, yet another young girl was seated—she was pretty, with a rosy complexion, prominent breasts, chestnut hair nicely coiffed and waved, round, brown, childlike eyes, and a little ruby on her pretty hand. She laughed a great deal and likewise spoke Russian, only Russian. Her name was Marusya, Hans Castorp heard someone say. He also happened to notice that Joachim would lower his eyes with a stern look whenever she laughed or spoke.

Settembrini came in by way of the side entrance, and twirling his moustache all the while, he strode to his seat, which was catercorner from Hans Castorp's. His tablemates broke into peals of laughter as he sat down—presumably he had made one of his malicious remarks. And Hans Castorp also recognized the members of the Half-Lung Club. Doltisheyed Hermine Kleefeld shoved her way to her table, over near one of the doors opening onto the veranda, and greeted the thick-lipped lad who had hitched his jacket up so unbecomingly. At the table set crosswise on his right sat Fräulein Levi with the ivory complexion and, next to her, plump, freckled Frau Iltis and a group of others whom Hans Castorp did not know.

"Those are your neighbors," Joachim said softly to his cousin and bent his head forward. Passing very close to Hans Castorp was a couple making for the last table on the right—the Bad Russian table, that was—where a family with an ugly boy was already seated, all of them wolfing down great mounds of oatmeal. The man was slightly built and had gray, hollow cheeks. He wore a brown leather jacket, and on his feet were boxy felt boots with clasp buckles. His wife, likewise small and slim, wore a hat with a bouncing feather and minced ahead on tiny, high-heeled boots of red Russia leather; around her neck was draped a shabby feather boa. Hans Castorp stared at the two of them with a tactlessness that was quite foreign to him and that even he found brutal—although what was really brutal about it was the sudden pleasure he took in it. His gaze was simultaneously blunt and piercing. And when at that same moment the glass door on his left slammed shut with a bang and a rattle, just as it had at first breakfast, he did not flinch as he had earlier that morning, but merely grimaced languidly. And just as he was about to turn his head to look in that direction, he suddenly found that it was simply too much trouble and not worth the effort. And so he did not determine this time, either, who it was that was so sloppy about the door.

The fact was that his breakfast beer, which normally had only a slightly befuddling effect on the young man, had completely stupefied and lamed him—it was as if he had been struck a blow across his brow. His eyelids were leaden; his tongue simply would not obey the simplest thoughts when he tried out of courtesy to chat with the Englishwoman; even shifting the direction of his eyes demanded a great struggle with himself. Added to all of which, the ghastly flush he had experienced yesterday had returned to his face in full force—his cheeks felt puffy from the heat, he was breathing heavily, his heart was pounding like a hammer wrapped in cloth. But despite it all, he was not suffering particularly—primarily because his head felt as if he had just taken two or three deep breaths of chloroform. Dr. Krokowski had appeared for breakfast and taken the seat opposite him at the head of the table; but, as if in a dream, he barely noticed the fact, although the doctor looked him in the eye, repeatedly and sharply, while carrying on a conversation in Russian with the ladies on his right, during which the younger ones—that is, Marusya with her rosy complexion and the gaunt yogurt-eater—kept their eyes cast down in meek embarrassment. It goes without saying that Hans Castorp kept his dignity, preferring to say not a word once his tongue had proved refractory and handling his knife and fork with special decorum. When his cousin nodded to him and stood up, he did the same; after bowing blindly to his tablemates, he followed Joachim, taking deliberate, careful steps as he went.

"When is the next rest cure?" he asked as they left the building. "That's the best thing here, as far as I can see. I wish I were lying in my splendid lounge chair again right now. Are we going to walk far?"

One Word Too Many

"No," Joachim said, "we don't dare go very far. Around this time I always take just a short walk down through Davos-Dorf and on into Platz, if I have time. You can window-shop and watch people and buy whatever you need. Not to worry, we'll lie down for an hour before dinner, and then again till four."

They walked down the drive in the sunshine and crossed the brook and the narrow-gauge tracks; the line of mountains above the valley's western slope rose directly ahead of them, and Joachim supplied their names: Little Schiahorn, the Green Towers, and Dorfberg. Across the way, a little distance up the hill, was the walled cemetery of Davos-Dorf— and Joachim pointed it out as well with his walking stick. And now they were on the main road, which was set one terrace-level above the valley floor.

One could not really call Dorf a village; at least, nothing except the name itself was left now. It had been devoured by the resort spreading relentlessly toward the entrance to the valley, and that part of the settlement called Davos-Dorf merged imperceptibly, without transition, into what was called Davos-Platz. Hotels and boardinghouses, all of them amply equipped with covered verandas, balconies, and rest-cure arcades, lay on both sides, as well as private homes with rooms for rent. Here and there new buildings were under construction, but sometimes the line of houses was broken by an open space that allowed a view of the valley's green meadows.

In his desire for his customary and cherished stimulant, Hans Castorp had lit another cigar; and, thanks apparently to the beer he had drunk and much to his indescribable satisfaction, now and then he was able to whiff something of the aroma he craved—but only rarely and faintly, to be sure. It was a strain on his nerves just to try to detect a hint of his usual enjoyment—and that repulsive leathery taste predominated. Unwilling to accommodate himself to such failure, he struggled for a while to find a pleasure that either was totally denied him or simply teased him with a distant inkling of itself, and finally out of weary disgust he tossed the cigar aside. Despite his dazed state, he felt courtesy demanded that he carry on a conversation, and for that purpose he tried to recall the excellent things he had wanted to say about "time" earlier. Except it turned out that he had forgotten every bit of the whole "complex"—not one single thought about time still resided in any corner of his brain. And so instead he began to speak about bodily functions, although in a rather strange fashion.

"When do you take your temperature again?" he asked. "After dinner? Yes, that's a good idea. The organism is at the height of its activity, so it would register then. For Behrens to demand that I ought to take mine, too—now listen, that was surely just meant as a joke. Why, Settembrini laughed his head off at the notion. There would be absolutely no point in it. I don't even own a thermometer."

"Well," Joachim said, "that's no problem whatever. You need only to buy one. There are thermometers for sale here everywhere, in almost any shop."

"But why should I? No, the rest cure, that's not a half-bad idea, and I'll probably go along with it. But keeping track of my temperature would be too much for a visitor, I'll leave that to the rest of you up here. If I only knew," Hans Castorp continued, pressing his hands to his breast like a man in love, "why my heart keeps pounding the whole time—it's so disconcerting. I've been thinking about it for quite a while now. Because, you see, your heart pounds when you're looking forward to some joyous event or if you're afraid—when your emotions are stirred up, isn't that right? But if your heart starts pounding all by itself, for no earthly reason, of its own accord, so to speak, I find that downright bizarre, if you see what I mean? It's as if the body were going off on its own and no longer had any connection to your soul, more or less like a dead body that is not really dead—even though there is no such thing—and goes on living a very active life, but all of its own accord. The hair and the nails keep on growing, and for that matter, in terms of the chemistry and physics, or so I've heard, it's a regular hustle and bustle there inside."

"What sort of an expression is that," Joachim reprimanded him discreetly. " 'A regular hustle and bustle!' " And perhaps he was revenging himself a little for the rebuke he had received earlier today for his "glockenspiel."

"But it's true! It is a regular hustle and bustle. Why are you so offended by that?" Hans Castorp asked. "And anyway, I only mentioned it incidentally. All I was trying to say is that it's bizarre and upsetting when the body goes off on its own accord, living with no connection to one's soul and putting on airs—like a heart pounding for no purpose whatever. One literally searches for some reason for it, some emotional stimulus, a feeling of joy or fear, that could justify it, so to speak—at least that's how it is with me, I can only speak for myself."

"Yes, yes," Joachim said with a sigh, "it's probably much like having a high fever. There's quite a hustle and bustle—to use your expression—going on in your body in that case, too, and it may well be that one automatically looks around for some emotional stimulus, as you put it, to provide at least a halfway reasonable explanation for all the hustle and bustle. But we're talking about such unpleasant things," he said in a quivering voice and then broke off. To which Hans Castorp merely gave a shrug—in perfect imitation of the shrug he had first seen Joachim give the evening before.

They walked along in silence for a while.

Then Joachim asked, "Well, how do you like the people here? I mean the ones at our table?"

Hans Castorp's face showed his indifference as he reviewed them in his mind. "Oh, Lord," he said, "they don't seem very interesting to me. There are more interesting people sitting at some of the other tables, I think, but maybe I'm just imagining that. Frau Stöhr should get her hair washed, it's so greasy. And little Mazurka, or whatever her name is, seems pretty silly to me. She keeps stuffing her handkerchief in her mouth because she's constantly giggling."

Joachim laughed out loud at the bungled name. " 'Mazurka'—that's splendid!" he cried. "Her name's Marusya, if you please—it's about the same as our Marie. Yes, she really is too enthusiastic," he said. "When she has every reason to be more sedate, because she's more than a little ill."

"You'd never know it," Hans Castorp said. "She's in such good shape. You'd never take her for someone with a weak chest." And he tried to catch his cousin's eye, but discovered that Joachim's tanned face looked all blotchy, the way tanned faces do when the blood rushes out of them, and that he had wrenched his mouth into a peculiar, woeful expression that gave Hans Castorp a vague fright and caused him immediately to change the subject. He asked about certain other people and tried to forget both Marusya and Joachim's expression—and was totally successful at it.

The Englishwoman with the rose-hip tea was named Miss Robinson.

The seamstress was not a seamstress, but a teacher at a public school for well-bred young ladies in Königsberg, and that was why she chose her words so precisely. Her name was Fräulein Engelhart. As for the chipper old lady, Joachim had never learned her name in all the time he had been there. In any case, she was the great-aunt of the yogurt-eating girl, and both were permanent residents of the sanatorium. The sickest person at the table was Dr. Blumenkohl, Leo Blumenkohl from Odessa—the young man with the moustache and the worried, self-absorbed look. He had been up here for years now.

They were now walking on a city sidewalk—it was immediately apparent that this was the main street of an international resort. The strolling tourists they met were mostly young people, the gentlemen in sport coats and without hats, the ladies in white skirts and also without hats. You heard Russian and English spoken; to both left and right were rows of shops with elegant displays in the windows. Hans Castorp's curiosity was now seriously battling his flushed exhaustion, and forcing his eyes to take it all in, he lingered awhile outside a men's clothing shore, just to make sure that his own wardrobe was up to snuff.

Then came a rotunda with a covered gallery where a little band was playing. This was the Kurhaus, the spa hotel. Several games were in progress on the tennis courts. Long-legged, clean-shaven young men wearing freshly pressed flannels and rubber-soled shoes had rolled up their shirtsleeves to play opposite tanned young ladies in white, who kept reaching boldly up toward the sun in order to hit the chalk-white ball out of the air. A kind of floury dust drifted over the well-kept courts. The cousins sat down on an unoccupied bench to watch and critique the play.

"You've not been playing up here, I take it?" Hans Castorp asked.

"I'm not allowed to," Joachim answered. "We have to rest, always lying at rest. Settembrini says we live horizontally—we're the horizontals, he says, it's another one of his rotten jokes. Those are healthy people playing there, or they're disobeying their doctors' orders. Anyway, they're not playing serious tennis—it's more for the outfits. And as far as not obeying orders goes, lots of forbidden games are played here— poker, you know, and *petits chevaux* in certain hotels. We can be discharged for playing that, they say it's the most unwholesome of all. But there are plenty of people who sneak past the guards in the evening and come down here to gamble. They say the prince who gave Behrens his title of *Hofrat* did it constantly."

Hans Castorp was hardly listening. His mouth was hanging open, because he couldn't breathe through his nose right, although he didn't

have a cold. He dimly noticed the disconcerting effect of his heart's pounding out of time to the music. And feeling confused and at odds with
himself, he was just dozing off when Joachim suggested they needed to
start back.

They covered the distance in almost total silence. Hans Castorp stumbled a few times on the level pavement, at which he merely shook his
head and smiled wistfully. The elevator operator who took them up to
their floor was the man with the limp. Exchanging a brief "till later,"
they parted outside room number 34. Hans Castorp steered his way across
the room and out to the balcony, where he let himself fall into his lounge
chair, just as he was, and without changing his position once, he fell into
a dull semistupor, broken now and then by the annoyance of his rapidly
beating heart.

But of Course—a Female!

H OW LONG THAT LASTED he didn't know. At the appropriate time,
the gong rang out. But, as Hans Castorp was aware, it was not the
call for dinner itself, merely the warning to get ready for it; and so he
lay there for a while until the metallic rumble swelled and fell away a
second time. When Joachim came through the room to fetch him, Hans
Castorp wanted to change first, but Joachim said it was too late and
wouldn't let him. He hated unpunctuality. How could you ever make
any progress and become healthy enough for military service again, he
said, if you were so weak-willed that you couldn't make it to meals on
time. He was right, of course, and Hans Castorp could only point out
that he wasn't the one who was sick, although he certainly was incredibly
sleepy. He just washed his hands quickly; and they walked down to the
dining hall, for the third time.

The guests were streaming in through both entrances. Some were even
coming through the veranda doors that stood open opposite, and soon
they were all sitting around the seven tables as if they had never left them.
That at least was Hans Castorp's impression, a purely dreamy, irrational
impression of course, which he could not get out of his befuddled brain for
the moment and which even gave him a certain pleasure—such pleasure, in
fact, that he tried to recapture it several times during the course of the
meal and, indeed, was able to recreate the illusion perfectly. The chipper
old lady was once again keeping up a steady stream of blurry Russian
directed diagonally toward Dr. Blumenkohl, who listened with a careworn

face. Her skinny grandniece finally ate something other than yogurt: the gooey cream of barley soup that the dining attendants had served in large plates—but only a few spoonfuls, and then she let it stand. Pretty Marusya kept pressing her little handkerchief, fragrant with orange perfume, to her mouth to stifle her giggles. Miss Robinson was reading the same letter in the same rounded hand that she had been reading that morning. Apparently she could speak not a word of German and did not wish to. Joachim struck a chivalrous pose and said something to her in English about the weather, to which, while still chewing, she gave a monosyllabic reply and then fell silent again. As for Frau Stöhr in her Scotch-plaid woolen blouse, she had had her checkup that morning and reported about it in her affected, uneducated way, drawing her upper lip back from her rabbitlike teeth. She complained of a rattle on the upper right, and her breathing was reduced just under her left shoulder blade, and the "boss" had told her she would have to stay another five months. In her unlettered fashion, she called Director Behrens the "boss." Moreover, she declared her outrage that the "boss" was not sitting at their table again today. The "retardation" schedule (she apparently meant "rotation") demanded that the "boss" should be sitting at their table for dinner today, whereas the "boss" was once again sitting at the table on their left (and indeed there sat Director Behrens, his gigantic hands folded in front of his plate). Though to be sure, that was also where fat Frau Salomon from Amsterdam was seated, and she came to dinner every day of the week in a low-cut dress, apparently quite to the "boss's" liking, although she, Frau Stöhr, could not understand it, because, after all, he could see however much of Frau Salomon he wanted at every checkup. A little later she told them in an excited whisper that yesterday evening the lights had been turned out in the upper common lounging area—the one on the roof—for purposes that Frau Stöhr described as "transparent." The "boss" had noticed it and gone into such a rage that you could hear him all over the building. But of course once again he had not located the guilty party, although one didn't have to have a university degree to guess that, of course, it had been Captain Miklosich from Bucharest, for whom it could never be dark enough when he was in the company of ladies—a man lacking in every refinement, although he did wear a corset, and who was no better than a beast of prey—yes, a beast of prey, Frau Stöhr repeated in a smothered whisper as beads of sweat appeared on her brow and upper lip. Why, all of Dorf and Platz, too, knew the nature of his relationship with Frau Wurmbrandt from Vienna, the general consul's wife—one could hardly call it *clandestine* anymore. It wasn't enough that the captain frequently paid morning visits to Frau Wurmbrandt in her room, with her still lying in bed, and stayed there the whole time she dressed, but last Tuesday he had not *left* Wurmbrandt's room until four o'clock the next morning—the nurse looking after Franz in room 19, the boy whose recent pneumothorax operation had turned out so badly, had run into him in the hall, and had been so embarrassed that she got her doors mixed up and found herself in the room of Prosecutor Paravant from Dortmund. And finally Frau Stöhr held forth at length about a "cosmological salon" down in town, where she bought her mouthwash. Joachim stared down at his plate.

The dinner was as splendidly prepared as it was lavish. Including the nourishing soup, it consisted of no fewer than six courses. The fish was followed by a superb roast with vegetables, which was followed by a salad, then roast fowl, a dumpling dessert in no way inferior to the one Hans had eaten the night before, and, finally, cheese and fruit. Each item was offered twice—and not without good effect. People filled their plates at all seven tables—they ate with the appetites of lions here in these vaulted spaces. Theirs was a hot hunger that it would have been a joy to observe, if its effect had not at the same time seemed somehow eerie, even repulsive. Not only the more lively among them displayed such hunger as they chatted and pelted one another with little pills of bread—no, but also the silent, gloomy ones, who between courses would put their heads in their hands and stare into space. At the next table on their left was an adolescent boy—still of school age, to judge by his appearance—whose coat sleeves were too short, and who wore thick, circular glasses; he chopped up everything heaped on his plate until it was a pasty hodgepodge, then bent over it and wolfed it down, now and then pushing his napkin up behind his glasses to dry his eyes—it was unclear whether this was to wipe away sweat or tears.

During this major meal of the day, two incidents occurred to attract Hans Castorp's attention, insofar as his condition allowed. First, the glass door slammed shut again—just as the fish course was being served. Hans Castorp flinched in irritation and told himself indignantly that this time he really must find out who the culprit was. He didn't merely think it— he was so in earnest that he spoke it out loud. "I have to know!" he whispered with exaggerated fervor, so that both Miss Robinson and the teacher glanced at him in amazement. And turning his whole upper body to the left, he opened his bloodshot eyes wide.

It was a lady who crossed the hall now, a young woman, a girl really, of only average height, in a white sweater and brightly colored skirt, with reddish-blond hair, which she wore in a simple braid wound up on her head. Hans Castorp saw only a little of her profile—almost nothing, in fact. In quite marvelous contrast to her noisy entrance, she walked soundlessly, with a peculiar slinking gait, her head thrust slightly forward, and proceeded to the farthest table on the left, set perpendicular to the veranda doors—the Good Russian table. As she walked she kept one hand in the pocket of her close-fitting wool jacket, while the other was busy at the back of her head, tucking and arranging her hair. Hans Castorp looked at that hand—he had a good eye and a fine critical sense for hands, and it was his habit always first to direct his gaze at them whenever he made a new acquaintance. The hand tucking up her hair was not particularly ladylike, not refined or well cared for, not in the way the ladies in young Hans Castorp's social circle cared for theirs. It was rather broad, with stubby fingers; there was something primitive and childish about it, rather like the hand of a schoolgirl. Her nails had clearly never seen a manicure, and had been trimmed carelessly—again, like a schoolgirl's; and the cuticles had a jagged look, almost as if she were guilty of the minor vice of nail-chewing. Hans Castorp only surmised all this, however, more than he actually saw it—she was really too far away. Her tablemates greeted the latecomer with nods; as she took her seat on the near side of the table—her back to the room and right beside Dr. Krokowski, who was presiding—she turned, her hand still at her hair, and looked back over her shoulder at the assembly. And Hans Castorp caught a fleeting glance of her broad cheekbones and narrow eyes—and at the sight, a vague memory of something or somebody brushed over him.

"But of course—a female!" Hans Castorp thought, and again muttered it so emphatically to himself that the teacher, Fräulein Engelhart, understood what he had said. The shriveled old maid smiled in sympathy.

"That is Madame Chauchat," she said. "She's so careless. A charming lady." And Fräulein Engelhart's fuzzy cheeks turned a shade rosier—which was the case, actually, whenever she opened her mouth.

"French?" Hans Castorp asked sternly.

"No, she's Russian," said the teacher. "Perhaps her husband is French, or of French extraction, I can't say for sure."

Still incensed, Hans Castorp asked if *that* was her husband there, and pointed to a gentleman with hunched shoulders sitting at the Good Russian table.

"Oh no, that isn't he," the teacher responded. "He's never been here even once, he's quite unknown to us."

"She should learn to close a door properly," Hans Castorp said. "She always lets it slam. It's really very impolite."

But since the teacher meekly accepted his rebuke as if she were the guilty party, nothing more was said about Madame Chauchat.

The second incident consisted of Dr. Blumenkohl's leaving the room—it was no more than that. Suddenly the slightly disgusted look on his face heightened and he gazed even more worriedly at some particular point in space. Then he slid his chair back in one decisive motion and left the room. At this juncture, however, Frau Stöhr displayed her poor upbringing in the most garish light, because—apparently out of some crude satisfaction that she was less ill than Blumenkohl—she accompanied his departure with a few half-sympathetic, half-contemptuous remarks. "The poor man," she said. "He's on his last legs. He's off to have a talk with his Blue Henry again." With a stubborn, obtuse look on her face, she uttered the grotesque term "Blue Henry" without the least hesitancy, and Hans Castorp felt an urge both to laugh and to shudder as she said it. Dr. Blumenkohl, by the way, returned after a few minutes, carrying himself in the same diffident fashion as when he left, took his seat again, and went on eating. He, too, ate a great deal, and with a worried, self-absorbed look on his face mutely took a second helping from each course.

Then dinner was over; but thanks to the capable service—and their dwarf in particular was marvelously fleet of foot—it had lasted only a little more than an hour. Breathing heavily and not rightly knowing how he had got there, Hans Castorp found himself lying in the splendid lounge chair on his balcony—because there was a rest cure between dinner and tea, the most important of the day, in fact, and rigorously enforced. He lay there between the opaque glass walls that separated him from Joachim on one side and the Russian couple on the other; his heart pounded as he dozed, and he drew air in through his mouth. When he used his handkerchief, he found red traces of blood, but he did not have the energy to think much about it, although he was easily inclined to worry about himself and tended by nature to play the hypochondriac. He had lit another Maria Mancini and smoked it to the end this time, despite the taste. Feeling dizzy, anxious, and dreamy, he thought how very strangely things were going for him up here. Two or three times he felt his chest shaken by suppressed laughter at the gruesome term that Frau Stöhr had used in her ignorance.

Herr Albin

DOWN IN THE GARDEN the fantasy flag with the caduceus lifted now and then in a light breeze. The sky had clouded over completely again. The sun was gone, and there was an almost inhospitable chill in the air. It appeared that the lounging arcade was crowded—the area below was filled with conversations and giggles.

"I beg you, Herr Albin, do put that knife away, put it in your pocket before there's an accident!" a high, wavering female voice fretted.

"My dear Herr Albin, spare our nerves and remove that dreadful lethal object from view!" a second voice chimed in.

And then a blond young man, sitting sideways on a lounge chair clear at the front, a cigarette dangling from his mouth, replied in a flippant voice, "Wouldn't think of it. You ladies will surely allow me to play with my knife a little. Yes, I'll grant, it's a particularly sharp knife. I bought it in Calcutta from a blind magician. He would swallow it, and then his boy would immediately dig it up some fifty paces away. Would you like to see it? It's much sharper than a razor. You only have to just touch the blade, and it goes right into the flesh as if it were butter. Wait a moment, let me show you up close." And Herr Albin stood up. General shrieks. "No, I think I'll go fetch my revolver," Herr Albin said. "That would interest you all more. A damn fine weapon. Packs quite a punch. I'll get it from my room."

"No, Herr Albin, don't. Herr Albin, don't do it!" several different voices wailed. But Herr Albin was already emerging from the arcade, heading for his room—very young, with a shambling gait, a rosy childlike face, and narrow sideburns at his ears.

"Herr Albin," a woman called after him, "you'd do better to get your coat—put it on as a favor to me. You lay bedridden with pneumonia for six weeks, and here you are sitting without an overcoat, without even a blanket, and smoking cigarettes. That's tempting Providence, Herr Albin, I swear it is."

But he only laughed derisively as he walked away, and within a few minutes he returned with his revolver. This aroused even more silly shrieks than before, and you could hear several ladies stumble as they tried to jump up from their chairs and got tangled in their blankets.

"Look how small and shiny it is," Herr Albin said, "but if I press right here—it will bite." New shrieks. "It's loaded with live ammunition, of course," Herr Albin continued. "There are six cartridges in this cylinder here, which moves ahead one chamber with every shot. And by the by, I don't keep this thing just for fun," he said, noticing that the effect was wearing off. He slipped the revolver back into his breast pocket, sat back down on his chair, crossed his legs, and lit another cigarette. "Definitely not just for fun," he repeated, pressing his lips together.

"But why? Why do you have it, then?" several trembling voices asked with foreboding. "How horrible!" one voice suddenly cried—and Herr Albin nodded.

"I see you're beginning to understand," he said. "And in fact, that is why I keep it handy," he went on lightly, after first inhaling and then exhaling a great quantity of smoke, despite his recent bout with pneumonia. "I keep it at the ready for the day when all this malarkey here gets too boring and I shall have the honor of paying my final regards. It really is very simple. I've studied the matter at some length, and I have a very clear idea about how best to pull it off." (Another shriek in response to the words "pull it off.") "The region of the heart is out of the question—it's rather awkward to aim there. And besides, I prefer snuffing out the conscious mind on the spot, and can do so by applying one of these pretty little foreign objects to this interesting organ . . ." And Herr Albin pointed with his index finger to his close-cropped blond head. "One aims here"—Herr Albin pulled the nickel-plated revolver from his pocket again and tapped the barrel against one temple—"here, just above the artery. Slick as a whistle, even without a mirror."

Several voices of pleading protest, including one sobbing violently: "Herr Albin, Herr Albin, put that revolver away, take it away from your temple, I can't even watch! Herr Albin, you're young, you'll get well again, you'll enjoy life again in a circle of friends who love you, I swear you will! Put on your coat now, lie down here and pull a blanket over you, it's time for your rest cure. And don't chase the bath attendant away again when he comes by and offers to rub you down with alcohol. And you must stop smoking, Herr Albin, do you hear? We implore you, for your own sake, for the sake of your young, precious life!"

But Herr Albin was implacable. "No, no," he said, "let me alone, everything's fine, thank you all very much. I have never refused a lady's request before now, but you'll see—there's no point in trying to sabotage fate. This is my third year here—and I'm fed up with it. I'm not going to play along anymore—can you blame me? Incurable, ladies. Just look at me—here I sit before you, an incurable case. The director himself hardly bothers to conceal the fact, not even for appearance' sake. You simply must grant me the license that results from my condition. It's much the same as in high school when you know you'll be held back—they don't bother to ask you questions, you don't bother to do any work. And now I've finally come to just such a pretty pass again. I don't need to do anything anymore, I'm no longer in the running—and I can laugh at the whole thing. Would you like some chocolate? Please, help yourselves. No, you won't exhaust my supply—I've got scads of chocolate up in my room. I have eight boxes of assorted fudges, five bars of Gala-Peter, and four pounds of Lindt nougats. The ladies of the sanatorium had them delivered to me while I was down with pneumonia."

From somewhere a bass voice rang out, demanding quiet. Herr Albin let out a brief laugh—a fluttery, ragged laugh. Then it grew quiet in the lounging area—as quiet as if a nightmare or a ghost had been routed. And any word spoken sounded strange in the silence. Hans Castorp listened until the last one had died away, and although he was not quite certain if Herr Albin was a phony or not, he could not help feeling a little envious of him nevertheless. That comparison taken from life at school had made an impression on him, because he had been held back in his sophomore year, and he could recall the somewhat ignominious, but humorous and pleasantly untidy state of affairs that he had enjoyed in the last quarter, once he had given up even trying and was able to laugh "at the whole thing." But since his thought processes were dull and confused, it is difficult to be very precise about them. On the whole, however, it seemed to him that although honor had its advantages, so, too, did disgrace, and that indeed the advantages of the latter were almost boundless. He tried putting himself in Herr Albin's shoes and imagining how it must be when one is finally free of all the pressures honor brings and one can endlessly enjoy the unbounded advantages of disgrace—and the young man was terrified by a sense of dissolute sweetness that set his heart pounding even faster for a while.

Satana Makes Shameful Suggestions

IN TIME he lost consciousness. His pocket watch said half past three when he was awakened by a conversation behind the glass partition on his left. Dr. Krokowski, who made his rounds at this hour without the director, was speaking in Russian with the rude married couple, inquiring, so it seemed, about the husband's state of health and checking his fever chart. But now he continued on his journey—not via the balcony, however, but by way of the hall, detouring around Hans Castorp's room and entering Joachim's through the door. Hans Castorp felt rather hurt that he had been circumvented and left lying there to his own devices—not that he felt any great need for a tête-à-tête with Dr. Krokowski. To be sure, he happened to be healthy, and so he wasn't included. Because as things stood with people up here, he thought, anyone who had the honor of being healthy didn't count and wasn't going to be asked any questions— and that annoyed young Castorp.

After spending two or three minutes with Joachim, Dr. Krokowski moved on down the row of balconies, and Hans Castorp heard his cousin say that they should get up now and get ready for their afternoon snack.

"Fine," he said and stood up. But he felt very dizzy from lying there so long, and the unrefreshing semisleep had left his face badly flushed again, although his body felt chilled all over—perhaps he had not been covered warmly enough.

He rinsed his eyes and washed his hands, combed his hair and set his clothes to rights. He joined Joachim in the corridor. "Did you hear that Herr Albin?" he asked as they descended the stairs.

"But of course," Joachim said. "The man should be disciplined. Disrupting the afternoon rest period with his chatter and getting the ladies so upset that he's set them all back for weeks. Gross insubordination. But who wants to play the informer? And besides, most people find that sort of talk entertaining."

"Do you really think it possible," Hans Castorp asked, "that he's serious about applying that foreign object, 'slick as a whistle,' as he puts it?"

"Oh, indeed," Joachim replied, "it's certainly not impossible. That sort of thing happens up here. Two months before I arrived, a student who had been here for a long time went for his checkup—and then hanged himself out in the woods. Everyone was talking about it my first few days here."

Hans Castorp's mouth gaped wide. "Well, I can't say that I'm feeling all that well here with you," he declared. "It's possible I'll not be able to stay on, that I'll have to leave—would you be offended?"

"Leave? What's got into you?" Joachim exclaimed. "Nonsense. You've only just arrived. How can you judge after only one day?"

"Good Lord, is this still just my first day? It seems to me as if I'd been up here with you all for a long, long time."

"Now don't start in theorizing about time again," Joachim said. "You had me all confused this morning."

"No, don't worry, I've forgotten it all," Hans Castorp replied. "The whole complex. And my mind isn't the least bit clear now, that's all over. . . . And so now it's time for tea."

"Yes, and then we'll walk up to that same bench from this morning."

"Good God—well, let's hope we don't run into Settembrini again. I'm incapable of taking part in another learned conversation today, let me tell you that ahead of time."

The dining hall offered every beverage one could imagine might be drunk at teatime. Miss Robinson once again drank her bloody-red rose-hip tea, and the grandniece was back to spooning yogurt. There were also milk, tea, coffee, hot chocolate, even bouillon; and guests on all sides, who had spent the last two hours resting after their heavy dinner, were busy spreading butter on large slices of raisin cake.

Hans Castorp had them bring him tea, and he dunked zwieback in it. He tried a little marmalade, too. He took a good look at the raisin cake, but the thought of eating any of it literally made him shudder. And once again—for the fourth time—he sat at his place in this hall with its simply but brightly decorated vaulted ceiling and its seven tables. A little later, around seven o'clock, he would sit there a fifth time—that would be for supper. And in the brief, worthless time in between, there was a walk to the bench up on the mountain slope, right next to the water trough—the path was teeming with patients, so that the cousins frequently had to greet people. Then it was back to the balcony for another rest cure—a fleeting, shallow hour and a half. Hans Castorp felt chilled and shivered badly.

He dressed painstakingly for supper, and, seated between Miss Robinson and the teacher, he ate julienne soup, pot roast with vegetables, and two pieces of a torte with layers of just about everything—macaroon, buttercream, chocolate, fruit jam, and marzipan—followed by a very good cheese and pumpernickel. He again ordered a bottle of Kulmbach beer to go with it. But he had drunk only half a glass when it became obvious to him that he belonged in bed. His head was buzzing, his eyelids were like lead, his heart beat like a little kettledrum, and to add to his agony, he took a notion that pretty Marusya, who was sitting bent forward, her face buried in the hand with the ruby ring, was laughing at *him*, even though he had taken considerable pains not to give her any reason to do so. Far in the distance, he could hear Frau Stöhr telling some story or making some claim that seemed so absolutely crazy that in his confusion he was not sure whether he had heard right or if what Frau Stöhr was saying had been transformed into nonsense inside his head. She was explaining that she knew how to prepare twenty-eight different sauces for fish—and she would stake her reputation on the fact, although her husband had warned her not to speak about it. "Don't say anything about it!" he had said. "No one will believe it, and even if they do, they'll simply find it ridiculous." All the same, she was quite willing to confess before one and all that she could prepare a total of twenty-eight different fish sauces. This was just too horrible for poor Hans Castorp; in his dismay, he pressed his hand to his brow and simply forgot that he had a bite of pumpernickel and cheddar in his mouth, ready to be chewed and swallowed. He still had it in his mouth when everyone stood up to leave.

They exited through the glass door on the left, that nuisance of a door that was always slamming shut and led directly into the front lobby. Almost all the guests went out this way, because it turned out that for an hour or so after supper people gathered informally in the lobby and the rooms opening off it. The majority of the patients stood about chatting in little groups. Two green folding tables had been set up for devotees of games—dominoes at the one, bridge at the other, although only young people were playing cards, among them Herr Albin and Hermine Kleefeld. In the first social room there were also a few optical gadgets for their amusement: the first, a stereoscopic viewer, through the lenses of which you stared at photographs you inserted into it—a Venetian gondolier for example, in all his bloodless and rigid substantiality; the second, a long, tubelike kaleidoscope that you put up to one eye, and by turning a little ring with one hand, you could conjure up a magical fluctuation of colorful stars and arabesques; and finally, a little rotating drum in which you placed a strip of cinematographic film and then looked through an opening on one side to watch a miller wrestle with a chimney sweep, a schoolmaster paddle a pupil, a tightrope-walker do somersaults, or a farmer and his wife dance a rustic waltz. Laying his chilled hands on his knees, Hans Castorp gazed into each of these apparatuses for a good while. He spent some time beside the bridge table, where the incurable Herr Albin, his mouth drooping at the corners, played his cards with a worldly nonchalance. Dr. Krokowski was sitting off in one corner, engaged in lively, cordial conversation with a semicircle of ladies, including Frau Stöhr, Frau Iltis, and Fräulein Levi. The occupants of the Good Russian table had withdrawn to a smaller adjoining salon that was set off from the game room by heavy curtains—they formed their own intimate clique. In addition to Madame Chauchat, this consisted of a blond-bearded, lackadaisical gentleman with a concave chest and pop-eyes; a very dark-skinned girl with an original, droll face, golden earrings, and a mop of frizzy hair; Dr. Blumenkohl, who had likewise joined them; and two hunch-shouldered youths. Madame Chauchat was wearing a blue dress with a white lace collar. The focus of the group, she was sitting on the sofa behind the round table at the far end of the small salon, her face turned toward the game room. Hans Castorp, who could not look at this ill-mannered woman without feeling some disapproval, thought to himself: "She reminds me of something, but I can't really say what." A tall man of about thirty and with thinning hair was sitting at a small brown piano, and he played the "Wedding March" from *A Midsummer Night's Dream*—three times in a row; and when a few of the ladies begged him, he first gazed deeply and silently into the eyes of each, one after the other, and started playing the melody yet a fourth time.

"Might I inquire how you are feeling, my good engineer," asked Settembrini, who had been strolling about among the guests, his hands in his pockets, and now came up to Hans Castorp. He was still wearing the same gray, petersham coat and pastel checked trousers. He smiled as he addressed him, and once again Hans Castorp felt sobered at the sight of that delicate, mocking curl of the lip under the sweep of the black moustache. All the same, he stared at the Italian with bloodshot eyes and a rather foolish, slack mouth.

"Oh, it's you," he said. "The gentleman from this morning's walk, whom we met up there on the bench . . . next to the water trough. Of course, I recognized you at once. Would you believe," he went on, although he was quite aware that he should not be saying this, "that at first glance this morning I took you for an organ-grinder? It was, of course, pure foolishness on my part," he added when he saw Settembrini look at him with a cool, searching eye. "Dreadful foolishness, to be sure. It's really totally inconceivable how of all things in the world I could have . . ."

"Please, don't trouble yourself over it—it doesn't matter," Settembrini responded, after first silently regarding the young man for another moment. "And how did you spend your day—the first one of your stay at our cozy resort here?"

"Thanks for asking. Quite as per regulation," Hans Castorp answered. "Primarily in the 'horizontal fashion,' as I've been told you like to put it."

Settembrini smiled. "It may be that I have described it that way on occasion," he said. "Well, and did you find it diverting to live horizontally?"

"Diverting and dull, both, just as you please," Hans Castorp replied. "It is at times hard to differentiate, you see. I certainly haven't been bored—there's all too much hustle and bustle up here among you for that. There are so many new and remarkable things to see and hear. And yet, on the other hand, it's as if I had been here not for just a day, but considerably longer—almost as if I had grown older and wiser, it seems to me."

"Wiser, as well?" Settembrini said and raised his eyebrows. "Might I be permitted a question: how old are you really?"

And of all things—Hans Castorp didn't know! For the moment at least, he didn't know how old he was, despite intense, indeed desperate attempts to collect his thoughts. And to win some time, he asked for the question to be repeated, and then he said: "Me . . . how old am I? I'm in my twenty-fourth year, of course. That is, I'll be twenty-four soon. Forgive me, I'm very tired," he said. " 'Tired' isn't the word for it. You know what it's like when you're dreaming and know that you're dreaming, and try to wake up, but can't? Well, that's just how I feel right now. I definitely have a fever, there's no other explanation. Would you believe it—my feet are cold all the way up to my knees. If you can put it that way, since knees aren't part of your feet, of course. You must excuse me—I'm absolutely groggy, but then that's no wonder, really, when first thing in the morning you get whistled at by a pneumothorax and afterward have to listen to that Herr Albin talking, and from the horizontal position, to boot. Just imagine—it's as if I can no longer trust my five senses, and I must say I find that bothers me more than a flushed face and cold feet. Tell me quite frankly—do you think it's possible that Frau Stöhr knows how to make twenty-eight sauces for fish? I don't mean whether she can actually make them—that's out of the question, I'm sure—but whether she really claimed she could while we were sitting at the table just now, or if I just imagined she did. That's all I want to know."

Settembrini stared at him. He hadn't seemed to listen; his eyes had "set" again, taking on that same fixed, vacant look. Just as he had earlier that morning, he repeated a threefold "yes, yes, yes" and "I see, I see, I see" with hissing, deliberately ironic *s*'s.

"Twenty-four, you say?" he then asked.

"No, twenty-eight," Hans Castorp said. "Twenty-eight sauces for fish. Not just sauces in general, but sauces specifically for fish—that's what's so monstrous about it."

"My good engineer," Settembrini said, angrily admonishing him, "pull yourself together and leave me out of such depraved nonsense. I don't know what you're talking about, and I don't want to know. In your twenty-fourth year, you say? Hmm . . . please permit me one more question, or if you will, a modest suggestion. Since your stay here appears not to be good for you—neither physically nor, if I am not mistaken, mentally—how would it be, if you were to forgo the pleasure of growing older here, in short, if you were to pack your things tonight and be on your way with one of the scheduled express trains tomorrow morning?"

"You mean I should leave?" Hans Castorp asked. "When I've only just arrived? But no, how can I possibly decide about that after only one day?"

And as he said it, quite by chance he caught a glimpse of Frau Chauchat in the next room, head-on—her narrow eyes and broad cheekbones. "What is it," he thought, "what or who is it that she reminds me of, for heaven's sake?" But try as he might, his weary brain could find no answer.

"Of course I'm not finding it all that easy to get acclimatized up here," he went on, "but that was to be expected. If I were to throw in the towel so soon, simply because I'll be a little confused and flushed for a few days—why I'd be ashamed of myself, I'd feel like a coward. And besides, it would be quite counter to reason—no, you must admit . . ."

He was suddenly speaking with great urgency, shifting his shoulders excitedly, as if hoping to convince the Italian to make a formal retraction of his suggestion.

"I salute reason," Settembrini replied. "And I salute courage as well, by the way. What you say sounds good, and it would be difficult to find any truly cogent objection. Because I, too, have seen some marvelous cases of acclimatization. There was Fräulein Kneifer just last year, Ottilie Kneifer, from a fine family, the daughter of a higher governmental official. She was here for about a year and a half, and became so splendidly accustomed to life up here that once she had been completely restored to health—and that does happen, people do get well up here sometimes— she refused to leave on any account. She fervently begged the director to be allowed to stay—she simply could not, would not return home. This was home to her, this was where she was happy. But there was such a press of people wanting to get in, and they needed her room. Her pleas proved in vain, and they insisted that they would have to dismiss her as healed. Ottilie came down with a high fever, let her chart just shoot up with a vengeance. Except that they found her out—by substituting a 'silent sister' for her usual thermometer. You don't yet know what that is—it's a thermometer without any markings, and the doctor checks it by laying a scale up against it and draws the chart himself. Ottilie, sir, had a temperature of ninety-eight point four. Ottilie had no fever. And so she went for a swim in the lake. It was only the beginning of May, still with frost at night, but the lake was no longer ice—a degree or two above freezing in fact. She stayed in the water for a good while, trying to catch her death of something—and with what success? She remained perfectly healthy. She left us in agony and despair, deaf to her parents' words of comfort. 'What is there for me down below?' she kept crying. 'This is my home!' I don't know what became of her. . . . But it seems you're not listening, are you, my good engineer? If I'm not quite mistaken, you're having difficulty staying on your feet. Lieutenant, do take your cousin here," he said, turning to Joachim, who had just arrived, "and put him to bed. He is a man who unites reason with courage, but he's a little indisposed this evening."

"No, really, I'm over it," Hans Castorp protested. "A silent sister, then, is merely a column of mercury without a scale. You see, I was paying complete attention." But all the same, he took the elevator up with Joachim and several other patients. The festivities were over for today, people were scattering to their balconies or the lounging areas for the evening rest cure. Hans Castorp followed Joachim to his room. The corridor floor with its coconut runners undulated gently under his feet, but he found it was not all that unpleasant a sensation. He sat down in Joachim's large flowered armchair—there was a chair like that in every room—and lit a Maria Mancini. It tasted like paste, like coal, like anything except what it should; nevertheless he continued to smoke it as he watched Joachim get ready for his rest cure, slipping into his tuniclike house jacket, putting an old overcoat on over that, and then taking the nightstand lamp and his Russian grammar with him out to the balcony, where he turned on the lamp, stuck his thermometer in his mouth, sat down, and began to wrap himself with amazing dexterity in two large camel-hair blankets that lay spread over the chair. Hans Castorp watched in frank admiration of how deftly he performed the task of throwing one blanket over the other—first the left side, flung lengthwise all the way up to under his armpit, then the bottom tucked over his feet, and then the right side, so that it finally built a smooth, regular package, with only head, shoulders, and arms sticking out.

"You do that very well," Hans Castorp said.

"It's a matter of practice," Joachim responded, holding the thermometer firmly between his teeth as he spoke. "You'll learn how, too. We'll definitely have to find a couple of blankets for you tomorrow. You'll be able to use them down below again, too. And they're an absolute necessity up here, especially since you don't have a fur-lined sleeping bag."

"Well, I'm not going to lie out on my balcony at night in any case," Hans Castorp declared. "I won't do that, let me tell you. That would seem really too strange. Everything has its limits. And there has to be some way for me to tell that I'm only a visitor up here among you all. I'll sit here for a while yet and smoke my cigar, just as usual. It tastes terrible, but I know it's good and that will have to suffice for me today. It's almost nine o'clock—well, not quite nine yet, sad to say. But once it's half past, that will be late enough for me to go to bed at something like a normal time."

He felt a chill and shivered—first once, then several times. Hans Castorp leapt up and ran over to the wall thermometer as if hoping to catch it *flagrante delicto*. It read fifty-two degrees Fahrenheit. He felt the pipes of the radiator; they were cold and dead. He muttered something incoherent, rambling on to the effect that even if it was August, it would be no disgrace to heat the place, because it wasn't a matter of the month, but of the temperature, and right now it was so low that he was freezing to death. But his face was burning. He sat back down, then stood up again, muttered a request to use the blanket from Joachim's bed, spread it over his legs, and went back to sitting—flushed, chilled, and tormenting himself with the disgusting taste of his cigar. A wave of misery swept over him— it seemed as if he had never felt this miserable in all his life. "This is wretched," he murmured. But suddenly, a curiously extravagant sense of joy and hope stirred within him, and he sat up, waiting to see if it would return. But it didn't; only the misery remained. Finally he stood up, tossed Joachim's blanket back on the bed, and with wrenched lips he muttered something that sounded like: "Good night. Don't freeze out there, and call me again for breakfast"—and staggered out to the corridor and into his room.

He hummed to himself while he undressed, but not out of any sense of cheer. Mechanically and without really paying attention, he went through the motions of the civilized ritual of getting ready for bed: poured pink mouthwash from a travel container into a glass and gargled discreetly, washed his hands with a fine, mild violet soap, and put on his long batiste nightshirt, the monogram HC embroidered on the breast pocket. Then he lay down and put out the light, letting his hot, muddled head fall back against the American woman's death-pillow.

He had been certain that he would sink into sleep at once, but it turned out he was wrong, and whereas he had barely been able to keep his eyes open before, they simply would not remain closed now, but kept fluttering open restlessly the moment he shut them. It was not his normal bedtime, he told himself, and then, of course, he had napped too often during the day. And someone was beating a carpet outside—which was less than probable and indeed not the case. It turned out that it was his heart that he heard pounding somewhere far in the distance outside—just as if someone were walloping a rug with a wicker carpet-beater.

It was not totally dark in his room yet; both Joachim and the couple from the Bad Russian table had taken lamps out onto their balconies, and light was coming in through his own open door. And as Hans Castorp lay there on his back, his eyes blinking open and shut, he was suddenly visited again by an impression—one of many he had experienced that day—an observation that he had tried on the spot to forget, out of both dismay and tact. It was the expression on Joachim's face when he had mentioned Marusya's physical attributes—that peculiar, woeful wrenching of Joachim's mouth and the blotchy pallor of his tanned cheeks. Hans Castorp understood now, saw through it, discerning its meaning in such a new, exhaustive, and intimate fashion that the carpet-beater outside doubled both in pace and intensity, almost drowning out the sounds of the evening concert in Platz—because there was a concert down at the hotel again. An insipid, symmetrically fashioned operetta melody echoed through the darkness, and Hans Castorp whistled along in a whisper (a whistle can be whispered, you know), while his chilled feet kept time under his feather comforter.

This was, of course, no way to fall asleep, and Hans Castorp now felt no inclination to do so, either. Now that he had such a new, vivid understanding of why Joachim had blushed, the whole world seemed new, and that sense of extravagant joy and hope stirred again deep within him. But he was still waiting for something else, too, although he did not really ask himself what it was. But when he heard his neighbors on the right and left ending their evening rest cure and returning to their rooms to exchange one horizontal position outside for another inside, he announced to himself his conviction that the barbaric married couple would be quiet. "I'll be able to fall peacefully asleep," he thought. "They'll be quiet this evening, at least I certainly expect them to be." But they weren't, and in all honesty Hans Castorp had not assumed they would be—to tell the truth, from his personal point of view, he would not have understood it if they had remained quiet. Nevertheless, he blurted out a monotone cry of furious amazement at what he now heard. "Scandalous!" he cried under his breath. "That's outrageous. Who would have thought it possible?" And periodically his lips returned to their whispered whistling of the operetta melody, which was still surging stubbornly in the distance.

Sleep did come later. But with it came dreams even more tortuous than those of the night before and from which several times he started up in fright or in pursuit of some strange fancy. He dreamed that he saw Director Behrens wandering along the paths of the garden, his knees slightly bent, his arms hanging stiffly at an angle in front of him, matching his slow and yet somehow bleak strides to the rhythm of march music in the distance. When the director came to a halt in front of Hans Castorp, he was wearing glasses with thick, circular lenses and was babbling nonsense. "Civilian, of course," he said and without asking permission extended two fingers of his gigantic hand and pulled down Hans Castorp's eyelid. "Respectable civilian, I could tell right off. But not without talent, certainly not without talent for raising his general metabolism. Won't be stingy about a few little years, a few spiffing years of service with us up here. But, whoops, gentlemen, do get on with your promenade!" he cried, sticking both enormous forefingers in his mouth and giving a whistle so euphonious that the teacher and Miss Robinson, both shrunk in size, came flying through the air from different directions and sat down on the director's shoulders, one to the right, one to the left, just as they sat on either side of Hans Castorp in the dining hall. And then the director went hopping away, all the while pushing his napkin up behind his glasses to dry his eyes—it was unclear whether this was to wipe away sweat or tears.

And now as he dreamed on, it seemed to him that he was in the same schoolyard where he had spent his recesses for so many years, and he was just about to borrow a drawing pencil from Madame Chauchat, who also happened to be present. She gave him a reddish one, about half the normal length, in a silver holder, but at the same time she warned Hans Castorp in a pleasantly husky voice that he definitely had to give it back to her after class, and looked at him with her narrow, bluish-gray-green eyes set above broad cheekbones, and he tore himself out of his dream—because he had it now and wanted to hold on to it: the person and situation that she had so vividly reminded him of. He quickly made sure he would remember it the next morning, because he could feel sleep and dreams enfolding him again; and he soon realized that he was trying to get away from Dr. Krokowski, who was lying in ambush for him in hope of subjecting his psyche to dissection, which aroused in Hans Castorp wild, truly mad terror. His foot was injured and he limped as he fled from the doctor down along the balconies, squeezing past the glass partitions, and he took a possibly fatal leap down into the garden and in his distress tried to climb the reddish-brown flagpole—and woke up in a sweat just as his pursuer grabbed him by the trouser leg.

But no sooner had he calmed down and dozed off again than his situation took on a new shape. He was trying with his shoulder to push Settembrini off balance, as he stood there smiling that refined, dry, ironic smile, just below where his full moustache swept handsomely upward—and it was the smile that offended Hans Castorp. "You bother me," he heard himself saying quite clearly. "Go away! You're only an organ-grinder, and you are in my way here." Except that Settembrini would not budge, and Hans Castorp was still standing there trying to think what to do next, when quite unexpectedly he had a brilliant insight into what time actually is—nothing less than a silent sister, a column of mercury without a scale, for the purpose of keeping people from cheating. And he awoke definitely intending to share his discovery with his cousin Joachim the next morning.

The night passed amid several such adventures and discoveries, and even Hermine Kleefeld played a nebulous role, as did Herr Albin and Captain Miklosich, who carried Frau Stöhr away in his jaws, only to have Prosecutor Paravant run him through with a spear. But there was one dream that Hans Castorp dreamed twice that night, and it was exactly the same both times. It came the second time toward morning. He was sitting in the dining hall with its seven tables when the glass door banged shut louder than ever, and in came Madame Chauchat, wearing her white sweater, one hand in her pocket, the other at the back of her head. Instead of proceeding to the Good Russian table, the ill-mannered woman walked soundlessly up to Hans Castorp and silently extended her hand for him to kiss—not the back, but the palm. And Hans Castorp kissed her hand—her unrefined, slightly broad hand with its stubby fingers and jagged cuticles. And once again he felt sweeping through him, from head to foot, that sense of dissolute sweetness that had risen up inside him when he had tried out what it must be like to be free of the pressures of honor and to enjoy the unbounded advantages of disgrace—and he experienced that sweetness again in his dream, except that it was overwhelmingly sweeter.

4

A Necessary Purchase

"IS YOUR SUMMER OVER NOW?" was the ironic question Hans Castorp posed to his cousin on his third day.

The weather had taken a terrible turn for the worse.

His second day as a visiting guest up here had been a glorious summer day. The sky shone deep blue above the spear-shaped tops of the pines, the town glistened brightly in the heat of the valley floor, and the cheerful, serene sound of bells filled the air as cows wandered the slopes and grazed on short, sun-warmed Alpine grass. Even at early breakfast, the ladies had been wearing sheer washable blouses, some with open-worked sleeves, which did not suit them all equally well. It looked particularly bad, for example, on Frau Stöhr, whose arms were too spongy—diaphanous clothes were simply not for her. And, each in his own way, the gentlemen of the sanatorium had likewise made allowances for the fine weather: some appeared in jackets of luster wool, some in linen suits, and Joachim Ziemssen had worn ivory flannels and a blue sport jacket, a combination that lent him the perfect military look. As for Settembrini, he had in fact repeatedly remarked on his intention to change his suit. "Damn!" he had said as he joined the cousins for a stroll down into town after lunch. "That sun is hot. It appears I shall have to don lighter apparel." But although he expressed himself elegantly, he went right on wearing his checked trousers and long petersham coat with the wide lapels—presumably that was the full extent of his wardrobe.

On the third day, however, it was as if nature had taken a tumble— everything was turned upside down. Hans Castorp did not believe his own eyes. It was just after dinner and they had all been lying in the rest cure for twenty minutes or so, when the sun abruptly hid itself, ugly peat-brown clouds moved in from over the ridges to the southeast, and a wind bearing cold, alien air that went to your bones and seemed to have come from unknown regions of ice suddenly swept down through the valley, setting the temperature plunging and inaugurating a whole new regimen.

"Snow," Joachim's voice said from behind the glass partition.

"What do you mean, 'snow'?" Hans Castorp asked in response. "You're not trying to tell me that it's going to snow now?"

"I certainly am," Joachim replied. "We know that wind. Once it starts, there'll be sleigh rides."

"Nonsense!" Hans Castorp said. "If I'm not mistaken this is still the beginning of August."

But as a man well versed in local conditions, Joachim turned out to be right—for within a few minutes, amid repeated claps of thunder, a powerful snowstorm set in, with flurries so heavy that everything seemed veiled in white mist and both town and valley were lost to sight.

It continued snowing all afternoon. The central heating was turned on, and while Joachim put his fur-lined sleeping bag to good use and held to the regimen of rest cure, Hans Castorp took refuge in his room; he dragged a chair over to the warm radiator and, shaking his head, peered out into the monstrous state of affairs. It was no longer snowing the next morning; but although the thermometer outside registered a few degrees above freezing, there was still a foot of snow and a perfect winter landscape lay spread out before Hans Castorp's astonished eyes. They had turned off the heat again. The temperature in his room was forty-five degrees.

"Is your summer over now?" Hans Castorp asked his cousin with bitter irony.

"There's no telling," Joachim replied matter-of-factly. "God willing, there'll be some lovely summer days yet. That's still quite possible, even in September. But the main thing is that the seasons here are not all that different from one another, you see. They get all mixed up, so to speak, and pay no attention to the calendar. In winter the sun is often so strong that you sweat and take off your jacket when you're out for a walk, and in summer—well, you've just seen how summer can be here sometimes. And then there's the snow—it mixes everything higgledy-piggledy. There's snow in January, but almost as much in May, and it can snow in August, too, as you've noticed. On the whole, you can say there's not a month when it doesn't snow—that's the one rule a man can hold on to. In short, there are winter days and summer days, spring and autumn days, but no real seasons, we don't actually have those up here."

"What a pretty mess," Hans Castorp said. Dressed in his winter overcoat and galoshes, he was walking down into town with his cousin to buy some blankets for his rest cure, because it was obvious that in this weather his old plaid one would not suffice. He even briefly considered whether he ought not to buy a sleeping bag, but backed off from that—indeed felt somewhat frightened by the idea.

"No, no," he said, "we'll just stick to blankets. I'll find some use for them again down below—people have blankets everywhere. There's nothing so special or sensational about blankets. But a fur-lined sleeping bag is much too distinctive—you see what I mean? I'd feel as if I were planning to make myself at home here for good, as if I'd become one of you, so to speak. So then, I'll not say anything more about it, except that there would be absolutely no point in my buying a sleeping bag for just these few weeks."

Joachim agreed, and so they found a lovely, well-stocked shop in the English quarter, where they purchased two camel-hair blankets like the ones Joachim had—extra long and wide, in a natural beige fabric that was delightfully soft to the touch. They left orders for them to be delivered to the sanatorium at once: International Sanatorium Berghof, Room 34. Hans Castorp intended to put them to use for the first time that afternoon.

This occurred, of course, after second breakfast, because that was the only opportunity the schedule offered for going down into town. It was raining now, and the snow on the streets had turned to slush that splashed up on them. On the way home, they caught up with Settembrini, who was also headed for the sanatorium; although bareheaded, he was carrying an umbrella. The Italian looked yellow somehow, and was evidently in an elegiac mood. In exquisite, perfectly enunciated words, he deplored the cold and damp, which were a bitter affliction for him. If only they would heat the rooms. But their wretched overseers let the fire go out the moment it stopped snowing—an idiotic rule that mocked all reason. And when Hans Castorp objected that he assumed a lowered room temperature was part of the regimen for the cure and presumably a way of keeping the patients from getting too spoiled, Settembrini responded with fierce scorn. Ah yes, indeed. The cure regimen—the exalted and inviolable rules. Hans Castorp had indeed adopted the right tone in speaking of them—that of religious submission. It was, however, striking—in the best sense of the word—that precisely those rules that corresponded exactly to their overseers' economic interests enjoyed unconditional veneration, whereas rules for which said correspondence was less applicable were more likely to be winked at. And while the cousins laughed, Settembrini moved on from the topic of the warmth for which he so yearned, to the subject of his deceased father.

"My father," he said, protracting the words with relish, "was such a refined man, sensitive equally in body and soul! How he loved his warm little study in winter, loved it with all his heart, and demanded that the temperature be kept at a constant seventy-seven degrees, by means of a little stove that glowed warm and red. And on cold damp days, or those on which the biting tramontana was blowing, one would enter the room from the hallway of his cottage—and warmth draped itself about one's shoulders like a soft cape, and one's eyes filled with happy tears. His study was crammed full with books and manuscripts, rarest treasures among them; there he stood dressed in his blue flannel dressing gown, behind a little lectern, and amid all those intellectual riches, he abandoned himself to literature. A short, slight man, a good head shorter even than I, just imagine! With great tufts of gray hair at his temples—and with a long, finely chiseled nose. What a scholar of Romance letters, gentlemen. One of the finest of the age, a master of our tongue, few could match him, and a stylist in Latin, the like of which there is none today, a *uomo letterato* to warm Boccaccio's heart. Learned men came from far and wide to consult with him, from Haparanda and from Kraków, expressly to visit Padua, our town, and pay their respects—and were received with cordial dignity. He was likewise a poet of distinction, who in his leisure hours penned narratives in the most elegant Tuscan prose—a virtuoso in the *idioma gentile*," Settembrini said, rocking his head back and forth and taking utmost pleasure in letting the native syllables melt on his tongue. "He designed his little garden after Virgil's models," he continued, "and his words were robust and beautiful. But it had to be warm, warm in his study, otherwise he would shiver and could weep tears of rage if anyone allowed him to freeze. And now just imagine, my good engineer, and you my fine lieutenant, what I, the son of such a father, must suffer in this damnable and barbaric place, where my body shivers with cold at the height of summer, even as my soul is constantly tortured by debasing sights. Ah, it is hard, surrounded by such creatures. Our director, the *Hofrat*, a buffoon, an imp of Satan. And Krokowski"—and Settembrini pretended the name was a tongue twister—"Krokowski, our shameless father confessor, who hates me because my dignity as a man will not permit me to subject myself to his monkish excesses. And then at my table—the society in which I am forced to dine! To my right sits a brewer from Halle, Magnus is his name, with a moustache like a wisp of straw. 'You can forget the literature,' he says. 'What's in it for me? Beautiful characters. What am I supposed to do with beautiful characters? I'm a practical man, and beautiful characters almost never occur in real life.' That's his notion of literature. Beautiful characters . . . O Mother of God! His wife sits across from him, sits there and wastes away, losing protein and sinking deeper and deeper into dim-wittedness. It is a filthy, wretched state of affairs . . ."

Without exchanging a word or a sign, Joachim and Hans Castorp were in complete agreement about this little speech: they found it petulant and unsettlingly seditious—but entertaining as well, of course, indeed edifying in its brazen rebelliousness. Hans Castorp laughed genially at the "wisp of straw," and at the bit about "beautiful characters," too, or rather, at the droll, despondent way Settembrini related it.

And then he said, "Good Lord, yes, it is a rather mixed society at our establishment here. One cannot choose one's tablemates—goodness knows what that would lead to. There's a lady like that at our table, too—Frau Stöhr, I presume you know her, don't you? She's gruesomely ignorant, I must say, and sometimes one doesn't know where to look when she's babbling on like that. And she complains constantly about her temperature, and that she's so listless, and unfortunately it's probably a rather serious case. That is so strange—sick and stupid. I don't know whether I'm putting it quite right, but it seems to me very peculiar for someone to be stupid and sick besides, and when the two are joined it's surely the most pitiful thing in the world. One absolutely doesn't know what sort of face to put on, because for someone who's ill one wants to express a certain seriousness and deference, doesn't one? Illness has something more or less venerable about it, if I may put it that way. But when stupidity keeps coming up with things like 'eighty camp' and 'cosmological salon' and other such gaffes, one truly no longer knows whether to laugh or cry. What a dilemma for our human emotions—and so sad that I can't even begin to express it. I mean, there's no rhyme or reason to it—they don't belong together, one is not used to picturing them together. One assumes stupid people must be healthy and vulgar, and that illness must ennoble people and make them wise and special. At least that's what one normally thinks, is it not? I've probably said more than I can defend," he concluded. "It was merely because we just happened to stumble on the subject . . ." And he was completely muddled now.

Joachim, too, was somewhat embarrassed. Settembrini said nothing, just raised his eyebrows, which left the impression that he was waiting out of politeness for the end of the speech. In reality, he was simply allowing Hans Castorp to lose his train of thought completely, before he answered.

"*Sapristi*, my good engineer," he said now, "you exhibit philosophical talents that I would never have expected of you. According to your theory, you would have to be less healthy than you give the appearance of being, since you apparently possess an intellect. Permit me to observe, however, that I cannot follow your deductions, that I reject them, indeed, that I stand in positive opposition to them. I am, as you see, a little impatient in matters intellectual and would prefer to be denounced as a pedant rather than to leave uncontested views I consider to be as deserving of refutation as those that you have formulated here."

"But, Herr Settembrini . . ."

"Per-mit me, please, to continue. I know what you wish to say. You wish to say that you did not mean to be taken so seriously, that the view you have advocated is not yours per se, but rather merely one possible view out of many hovering in the air, as it were, which you then seized upon in order to have an irresponsible go at it. It is characteristic of your years to eschew manly resolve in favor of temporary experimentation with all sorts of standpoints. *Placet experiri*," he said, pronouncing the *c* of *placet* with the soft Italian *ch*. "A fine maxim. But what disconcerts me is simply that your experiment has taken precisely the direction it has. I doubt this is purely accidental. I fear the presence of a tendency that threatens to become an indelible trait of character unless one opposes it head-on. Which is why I feel it my duty to correct you. You suggested that the combination of sickness and stupidity is the most pitiful thing in the world. I will grant you that much. I, too, prefer a clever invalid to a consumptive idiot. But my protest begins at the point where you regard the conjunction of illness and stupidity as a kind of stylistic blunder, as an aberration of taste on the part of nature and a 'dilemma for our human emotions'—as you chose to express it. At the point where, or so it appears, you consider illness to be so elegant or—as you put it—so 'venerable' that there is absolutely 'no rhyme or reason' why it and stupidity should belong together. Those, too, are your words. In that case, no! Illness is definitely not elegant, and certainly not venerable—such a view is itself a sickness, or leads to it. Perhaps I can best arouse your abhorrence of that idea by telling you that it is outdated and ugly. It comes from an era of superstitious contrition, when the idea of humanity was demeaned and distorted into a caricature, a fearful era, when harmony and health were considered suspicious and devilish, whereas infirmity in those days was as good as a passport to heaven. Reason and enlightenment, however, have banished those shadows, which once lay encamped in the human soul—not entirely, however, for even today the battle is still being waged. That battle, however, is called work, sir, earthly labor, work for the earth, for the honor and interests of humankind. And steeled by each new day in battle, the powers of reason and enlightenment will liberate the human race entirely and lead it forth on paths of progress and civilization toward an ever brighter, milder, and purer light."

"Damnation," Hans Castorp thought, both bewildered and abashed, "that was a regular aria! How did I provoke that? Although it all seems a little dry to me. And what is this fixation he has about work? He's always going on about work, although it really does not fit all that well here." And aloud he said, "Very fine, Herr Settembrini. Definitely worth listening to—the way you put it. It could not be expressed more . . . more graphically, I mean."

"Backsliding," Settembrini began again, lifting his umbrella high to avoid the head of a passerby, "intellectual backsliding, a return to the views of that dark, tormented age—and believe me, my good engineer, that is itself a sickness, a sickness that has been abundantly researched and for which science has provided various names—one from the language of aesthetics and psychology, another from that of politics, both of them academic terms of no consequence, which you may happily eschew. But since in the life of the mind all things cohere and one idea emanates from another, since one cannot give the Devil an inch but that he takes a mile, and you along with it—and since, on the other hand, a sound principle can give rise only to sound results, no matter with which sound principle one may begin—for all such reasons, then, imprint this on your minds: illness is very far from being something so elegant, so venerable that it may not be associated with stupidity, even in passing. Illness is, rather, a *debasement*—indeed, a painful debasement of humanity, injurious to the very concept itself. And although one may tend and nurse illness in the individual case, to honor it intellectually is an *aberration*—imprint that on your minds!—an aberration and the beginning of all intellectual aberrations. The woman of whom you made mention—pardon me for choosing not to recall her name—Frau Stöhr, yes, thank you—in brief, it is this ridiculous woman herself, and not her case, it seems to me, that presents our human emotions with a dilemma, as you put it. Sick and stupid—in God's name, that is misery itself. The matter is quite simple— we are left only with pity and shrugs. The dilemma begins, sir, the real *tragedy* begins where nature has been cruel enough to break the harmony of the personality—or to make it impossible from the very start—by joining a noble and life-affirming mind to a body unfit for life. Do you know Leopardi, my good engineer? Or you perhaps, lieutenant? An unhappy poet of my country, a hunchbacked, sickly man with a soul—a large soul originally, but one forever humbled by the misery of his body and dragged to the lower depths of irony, a soul that could produce laments to rend the heart. Just listen—"

And Settembrini began to recite in Italian, letting the lovely syllables melt on his tongue, rocking his head back and forth, even closing his eyes now and then, oblivious to the fact that his companions understood not a word. It was evident that he did it to savor both his own powers of memory and the words themselves—and to show them off to his audience.

Finally he said, "But you do not understand. You hear, and yet you do not comprehend the painful meaning. As a cripple—gentlemen, you must grasp the situation in its entirety—Leopardi lacked the love of a woman, and that in fact was what made him incapable of preventing his soul from being stunted. Fame and virtue lost their luster for him, he viewed nature as evil—and she *is* evil, stupid and evil, I agree with him there—and he despaired, horrible to say, he despaired of science and progress. That is tragedy, my good engineer. That is your 'dilemma for our human emotions.' It is not the woman at your table—I refuse to tax my memory for her name. Do not speak to me of some 'spiritual redemption' that may result from illness—for God's sake, do not speak of it. A soul without a body is as inhuman and horrible as a body without a soul— whereby the first is the rare exception and the latter the rule. Normally it is the body that grows unchecked, usurping all importance, all life to itself, emancipating itself in the most loathsome fashion. A human being who lives as an invalid is *only* a body, and that is the most inhuman of debasements—in most cases, he is no better than a cadaver. . . ."

"That's funny," Joachim said, bending forward to look at his cousin, who was walking on the other side of Settembrini. "You said something very similar quite recently, too."

"I did?" Hans Castorp said. "Yes, it may well be that something similar ran through my mind."

Settembrini was silent as they strode on for a few paces. Then he said, "All the better, gentlemen. All the better, if that is so. Far be it from me to lecture you with some sort of original philosophy—that is not my calling. If for his part our good engineer has already voiced analogous opinions, that only confirms my surmise that, like so many talented young men, he is playing the intellectual dilettante, temporarily experimenting with possible points of view. The talented young man is no blank page, but is rather a page where everything has already been written, so to speak, in appealing inks, the good with the bad. And it is the educator's task explicitly to foster the true—and by appropriate practical persuasion forever to eradicate the false when it tries to emerge. The gentlemen have been shopping?" he asked, adopting a lighter tone.

"No, not really," Hans Castorp said, "that is . . ."

"We bought a couple of blankets for my cousin," Joachim replied casually.

"For the rest cure, what with this miserable cold weather. I am supposed to join in for these few weeks," Hans Castorp said with a laugh, looking down at the ground.

"Ah, blankets, rest cure," Settembrini said. "Yes, yes, yes. I see, I see, I see. Indeed: *placet experiri!*" he repeated, pronouncing it with his Italian *c*; and now he took his leave, for they had arrived at the sanatorium, where they were greeted by the limping concierge. Once they were in the lobby, Settembrini turned off into one of the social rooms to read the papers before dinner, as he said. He apparently intended to play hooky from the second rest cure.

"Heaven help us!" Hans Castorp said, as he took his place beside Joachim in the elevator. "That's your true pedagogue—he himself said not long ago that he had a pedagogic streak. You have to be awfully careful not to say one word too many, otherwise you'll get an extensive lecture. But it is worth listening to, just the way he speaks, how each word leaps from his mouth so round and appetizing—listening to him always reminds me of fresh hot buns."

Joachim laughed. "You'd better not tell him that. I'm sure he'd be disappointed to learn you're thinking of hot buns when he's lecturing."

"Do you think so? Well, I'm not so certain about that. I always have the impression that what is really important to him is not the lecture itself—perhaps that's only secondary—but more especially the speaking of it, the way he lets his words roll and bounce, like little rubber balls. And that he isn't at all displeased, in fact, if you pay attention to that, too. Magnus the brewer is certainly a little silly with his 'beautiful characters,' but Settembrini should have said what literature is actually about. I didn't want to ask for fear of leaving myself wide open. I don't really understand much more about it myself, and I've never met a literary man before. But if it's not a matter of beautiful characters, then evidently it's a matter of beautiful words, that's my impression when I'm around Settembrini. And what a vocabulary! He's not the least embarrassed to use words like 'virtue'—I mean, really! That word has never passed my lips once in all my life—even in Latin class we always just translated *virtus* as 'bravery.' It made me wince deep inside, let me tell you. And besides, it makes me a little nervous the way he squawks about the cold and Behrens and Frau Magnus, who's losing protein—about almost everything in fact. He's a professional naysayer, that much was clear to me right off. He hacks away at everything around him, and I can't help it—that always makes things rather untidy and disorderly."

"You could say that," Joachim said, musing. "But then again, there's a kind of pride about him, with no hint of anything disorderly, quite the contrary. He's a man with a lot of self-respect, or better, respect for people in general, and I like that about him, there's something decent about that, as I see it."

"You're right," Hans Castorp said. "There's even something *rigorous* about him. It often makes you quite uneasy because you feel, let's call it, controlled—controlled, that's not a bad word for it. Would you believe that I had the definite feeling that he didn't approve of my having bought those blankets for the rest cure, was against it and ridiculed it somehow?"

"No," Joachim replied in composed surprise. "How could that be? I really can't imagine it." And then he headed off for his rest cure, lock, stock, and thermometer, while Hans Castorp began to wash and change for dinner—it was less than an hour away.

Excursus on the Sense of Time

WHEN THEY CAME BACK UP from their meal, the package of blankets was lying on a chair in Hans Castorp's room, and he made use of them that day for the first time. Joachim, as the expert, gave him lessons in the art of wrapping oneself the way they all did it up here, something every novice had to learn right off. You spread the blankets, first one, then the other, over the frame of the lounge chair, but so that a long piece was left dangling to the floor at the foot. Then you sat down and began to wrap the top one around you, first flinging it lengthwise all the way up to under the armpit, then tucking the bottom up over the feet—and for that you had to sit up, bend forward, and grab the fold with both hands—and finally tugging the other side over, making sure that the double foot-tuck fit tight against both sides to form the smoothest and most regular package possible. And then you followed the same procedure with the second blanket—but it was more difficult to handle, and as a bungling beginner Hans Castorp groaned quite a bit while he bent forward and reached out to practice the moves as he was taught them. Only a very few old veterans, Joachim said, were able to fling both blankets around them at once in three deft motions, but that was a rare and coveted skill, which demanded not only years of practice, but also a natural predisposition. And Hans Castorp had to laugh at that word as he leaned back with aching muscles.

Joachim did not understand what was so funny and gazed at him uncertainly, but then joined in the laughter. "So then," he said—as Hans Castorp, exhausted from all these gymnastics, lay there a solid, unbroken cylinder, the pliant roll tucked behind his neck—"it could be five below now and it wouldn't matter." And then he ducked behind the glass partition to wrap himself up as well.

Hans Castorp doubted what he had said about five below, because he was definitely freezing, and he kept shivering as he gazed through the wooden arches into the damp, trickling drizzle out there, which seemed to threaten to turn to snow again at any moment. How strange, too, that despite the wet, his cheeks still felt so hot and dry, as if he were sitting in an overheated room. And he felt absurdly frazzled from the practice session with his blankets—in fact, when he now looked down at *Ocean Steamships*, it lay trembling in his hands. He was not so terribly healthy after all—totally anemic, just as Director Behrens had said, and that was probably why he tended to chill so easily. These unpleasant sensations, however, were counterbalanced by the comfortable position furnished by the lounge chair and its almost mysterious properties, which Hans Castorp found difficult to analyze but which had found his highest approval from the very first and had stood the test again and again. Whether it was the texture of the cushions, the perfect slant of the back support, the proper height and width of the armrests, or simply the practical consistency of the neck roll—whatever it was, nothing could possibly have offered more humane benefits for a body at rest than this splendid lounge chair. And so Hans Castorp's heart was filled with contentment at the thought that before him lay two empty, safely serene hours: the main rest cure, sacred to the rules of the house. Although he was only a visiting guest up here, he, too, found it to be a very suitable arrangement. For he was a patient man by nature, who could spend long hours doing nothing in particular and loved, as we recall, his leisure time, with no numbing activity to demolish, banish, or overwhelm it. At four there would be afternoon tea with cake and preserves, followed by a little exercise outdoors, and then he would come back up here to rest in the lounge chair again, with supper at seven—which, like all the meals, brought with it certain sights and tensions that he looked forward to—and afterward a peep or two into the stereoscopic viewer, the kaleidoscopic tube, or the cinematographic drum. Hans Castorp had the daily schedule down pat, though it would perhaps be too much to say that he had now "settled in," as the expression goes.

Ultimately, there is something odd about settling in somewhere new—about the perhaps laborious process of getting used to new surroundings and fitting in, a task we undertake almost for its own sake and with the definite intention of abandoning the place again as soon as it is accomplished, or shortly thereafter, and returning to our previous state. We insert that sort of thing into the mainstream of our lives as a kind of interruption or interlude, for the purpose of "recreation," which is to say: a refreshing, revitalizing exercise of the organism, because it was in immediate danger of overindulging itself in the uninterrupted monotony of daily life, of languishing and growing indifferent. And what is the cause of the enervation and apathy that arise when the rules of life are not abrogated from time to time? It is not so much the physical and mental exhaustion and abrasion that come with the challenges of life (for these, in fact, simple rest would be the best medicine); the cause is, rather, something psychological, our very sense of time itself—which, if it flows with uninterrupted regularity, threatens to elude us and which is so closely related to and bound up with our sense of life that the one sense cannot be weakened without the second's experiencing pain and injury. A great many false ideas have been spread about the nature of boredom. It is generally believed that by filling time with things new and interesting, we can make it "pass," by which we mean "shorten" it; monotony and emptiness, however, are said to weigh down and hinder its passage. This is not true under all conditions. Emptiness and monotony may stretch a moment or even an hour and make it "boring," but they can likewise abbreviate and dissolve large, indeed the largest units of time, until they seem nothing at all. Conversely, rich and interesting events are capable of filling time, until hours, even days, are shortened and speed past on wings; whereas on a larger scale, interest lends the passage of time breadth, solidity, and weight, so that years rich in events pass much more slowly than do paltry, bare, featherweight years that are blown before the wind and are gone. What people call boredom is actually an abnormal compression of time caused by monotony—uninterrupted uniformity can shrink large spaces of time until the heart falters, terrified to death. When one day is like every other, then all days are like one, and perfect homogeneity would make the longest life seem very short, as if it had flown by in a twinkling. Habit arises when our sense of time falls asleep, or at least, grows dull; and if the years of youth are experienced slowly, while the later years of life hurtle past at an ever-increasing speed, it must be habit that causes it. We know full well that the insertion of new habits or the changing of old ones is the only way to preserve life, to renew our sense of time, to rejuvenate, intensify, and retard our experience of time—and thereby renew our sense of life itself. That is the reason for every change of scenery and air, for a trip to the shore: the experience of a variety of refreshing episodes. The first few days in a new place have a youthful swing to them, a kind of sturdy, long stride—that lasts for about six to eight days. Then, to the extent that we "settle in," the gradual shortening becomes noticeable. Whoever clings to life, or better, wants to cling to life, may realize to his horror that the days have begun to grow light again and are scurrying past; and the last week—of, let us say, four—is uncanny in its fleeting transience. To be sure, this refreshment of our sense of time extends beyond the interlude; its effect is noticeable again when we return to our daily routine. The first few days at home after a change of scene are likewise experienced in a new, broad, more youthful fashion—but only a very few, for we are quicker to grow accustomed to the old rules than to their abrogation. And if our sense of time has grown weary with age or was never all that strongly developed—a sign of an inborn lack of vitality—it very soon falls asleep again, and within twenty-four hours it is as if we were never gone and our journey were merely last night's dream.

These remarks are inserted here only because young Hans Castorp had something similar in mind when, after a few days, he said to his cousin (while gazing at him with bloodshot eyes), "I've always found it odd, still do, how time seems to go slowly in a strange place at first. What I mean is, of course there's no question of my being bored here, quite the contrary—I can assure you that I'm amusing myself royally. But when I look back, retrospectively as it were—you know what I mean?—it seems as if I've been up here for who knows how long already, and that it's been an eternity since I first arrived and didn't quite understand right off that I actually had, until you said, 'This is where you get off!'—do you remember? It has absolutely nothing to do with reason or with measurements of time—it's purely a matter of feeling. Of course it would be absurd to say, 'It's as if I'd been here two months already'—that would be pure nonsense. All I really can say is 'a very long time.' "

"Yes," Joachim replied, a thermometer in his mouth, "it's good for me, too. Since you've been here, I feel as if I have you to hold on to, so to speak." And Hans Castorp laughed at the way Joachim said this so straight-out, without any explanation.

He Tries Out His Conversational French

No, he had not actually settled in yet, neither in terms of his intimacy with life here in all its peculiarities—an intimacy it would be impossible to gain in so few days, or as he told himself (and admitted quite candidly to Joachim), in three weeks, sad to say—nor as regarded the adaptation of his organism to the very peculiar atmospheric conditions found among "the people up here," because it seemed to him that his physical adjustment was proceeding only painfully, very painfully, if indeed at all.

The normal day was carefully organized and neatly divided into its constituent parts; one quickly fell in with the routine and learned to move with its turning gears. In the framework of a week or larger units of time, however, there were certain recurring deviations that made their appearance little by little—one variation might appear, for instance, only after another had already repeated itself. And even in terms of the objects and faces that made up the details of a day, Hans Castorp had to learn at every step to take a closer, less casual look at accustomed facts and faces and assimilate new things with youthful receptivity.

Those balloon-shaped containers with short necks, for example, which were set out beside the doors in the corridor and which had caught his eye on the evening of his arrival—Joachim explained about them when he asked. They held pure oxygen, for six francs the demijohn, and the stimulating gas was provided to dying patients in order to help preserve their energies and rouse them one last time—it was sipped through a rubber hose. And behind the doors where these potbellied containers stood lay the dying or the *moribundi*, as Director Behrens called them one day, when Hans Castorp chanced to meet him on the second floor— just as the purple-cheeked director in his white smock came rowing down the corridor. They walked down to the next floor together.

"Well, my innocent bystander," Behrens said, "what are you up to, have we found favor in your searching eyes? We are honored, we are honored. Yes, our summer season's quite the thing, of very good parent- age. It cost me a pretty penny to puff it a bit, too. But what a shame, really, that you don't want to stay through the winter with us—want to spend a mere eight weeks, I've heard, correct? Oh, three? But that's just dropping by, not even worth taking off your hat and coat. Well, just as you like. But it really is a shame that you'll not be spending the winter, because the crème de la crème"—he made a joke of his outrageous pronun- ciation—"the international creme de la crème down in Platz doesn't arrive until winter, and you really must see them, just for educational purposes. Split your sides, watching these lads leaping about on planks tied to their feet. And the ladies—Lord, Lord, the ladies! Regular birds of paradise, I tell you, and eminently amorous. Well, now I have to attend to my *moribundus*," he said, "in room twenty-seven here. Last stage, you know. Exit up center. He's downed five dozen fiascoes between yesterday and today, the guzzler. But he will probably be joining his ancestors by noon. Well, my dear Reuter," he said, stepping into the room, "how would it be if we crack another bottle . . ." His words were lost behind the door as he closed it. But for a moment Hans Castorp could see across the room to a waxen profile against pillows, a young man with a sparse goatee, who slowly rolled his very large eyes toward the door.

This was the first *moribundus* that Hans Castorp had ever seen in his life, inasmuch as both his parents and his grandfather had died behind his back, so to speak. What dignity in the way the young man laid his head against the pillows, his goatee jutting upward. What meaning in the gaze of those huge eyes as he turned them slowly toward the door. Returning to the stairway now, still absorbed in that fleeting glimpse, Hans Castorp instinctively tried to make the same large, meaningful, and deliberate eyes as those of the dying man; and it was with that look that he greeted a lady who had emerged from a door behind him and caught up with him now at the head of the stairs. He did not realize at once that it was Madame Chauchat. She smiled wanly at the eyes he was making, put a hand to the braid at the back of her head, and preceded him down the stairs—soundlessly, supplely, her head thrust slightly forward.

HE MADE ALMOST no new acquaintances in those first days, and not for some time afterward, either. On the whole, the daily routine was not conducive to it. Reserved by nature in any case, Hans Castorp felt that he was merely a visitor here, an "innocent bystander," as Director Behrens had put it, and so for the most part he was quite content with Joachim's conversation and company. To be sure, the nurse on their corridor kept craning her neck as they passed, until Joachim, who had stopped to chat with her on occasion before, introduced her to his cousin. The cord of her pince-nez tucked behind her ear, she spoke with an affectation that was absolutely excruciating, and from up close, one had the impression of a woman whose reason had long suffered the tortures of boredom. It was very difficult to get away from her, because she displayed an almost pathological fear of a conversation's drawing to a close; and as soon as the young men assumed an air of wanting to move on, she would cling to them with hasty words and looks and a desperate little smile, until they took pity on her and stood there a while longer. She spoke at great length about her papa, the lawyer, and her cousin, the doctor—apparently to cast herself in a favorable light and to indicate that she came from the educated strata of society. As for the patient she tended behind the closed door there, he was the son of a doll-manufacturer in Coburg, Rotbein was the name—and recently it had spread to young Fritz's intestines as well. That made things hard for everyone involved, as she was sure the gentlemen could well understand, particularly hard if one came from an academic household and possessed the sensitivities of the upper classes. One dared not turn one's back for a moment. And recently, if the gentlemen could believe it, when she returned from having gone out for just a moment, merely to purchase some tooth powder, she found her patient sitting up in bed, with a glass of dark, heavy beer, a salami, a piece of coarse rye bread, and a pickle, all spread out before him. His relatives had sent him these homey delicacies to help him build up some strength. But the next day, of course, he had been more dead than alive. He was hastening his own demise. And that would in fact be a release, but only for him, not for her—Sister Berta was her name, by the way, or more accurately, Alfreda Schildknecht—because *she* would only move on then to another patient in a more or less advanced stage of the illness, here or at some other sanatorium. Such were her prospects, and no others would ever open before her.

Yes, Hans Castorp said, her profession was certainly difficult, but it did have its satisfactions, or so he would presume.

Certainly, she replied, there were satisfactions, although it was very difficult.

Well, their best wishes for Herr Rotbein. And the cousins made to go.

But she clung to them with words and looks, and her exertions, as she tried to hold on to the young men for just a while longer, were so pitiful to watch that it would have been cruel not to grant her a little more time. "He's sleeping," she said. "He doesn't need me. I stepped into the hall for just a few minutes." And she began to complain about Director Behrens and the tone of voice he used with her—all too offhand, considering her background. She much preferred Dr. Krokowski—she found him so full of soul. Then she came back around to her papa and her cousin. Her brain would yield nothing more. In vain she grappled to find something to hold the cousins still longer, and as they started to go, she suddenly made another running leap at them, raising her voice almost to a shriek— they escaped and went their way. But the nurse gazed after them for a long time, her body bent forward, her eyes following them as if she hoped to suck them back to her. Then she heaved a great sigh and returned to her patient in his room.

The only other person whom Hans Castorp met during these first days was the pale lady in black, the Mexican woman, whom he had seen in the garden and who was known as *Tous-les-deux*. And indeed it came to pass that he himself heard her lips form the mournful phrase that had become her nickname. But since he was now prepared for it, he maintained his demeanor and afterward found he was quite satisfied with his behavior. The cousins met her at the front door as they stepped out after early breakfast for their morning constitutional. Veiled in a black cashmere scarf, her knees slightly bent, she was strolling aimlessly in long, restless strides; and her aging face, with its large, careworn mouth, shimmered dull white against the black veil she had wound around her silver-streaked hair and tied beneath her chin. Joachim, bareheaded as usual, greeted her with a bow, and she looked up and slowly acknowledged him while the long creases deepened on her narrow brow. Noticing a new face, she stopped, and gently nodding her head, she waited for the young men to approach, because she apparently felt it necessary to learn whether the stranger knew of her fate and to accept his condolences. Joachim presented his cousin. From under her mantilla she extended a hand to the visitor— a skinny, yellowish, heavily veined hand, adorned with rings—and went on looking at him and nodding.

Then it happened: *"Tous les dé, monsieur,"* she said. *"Tous les dé vous savez . . ."*

"Je le sais, madame," Hans Castorp replied in a muted voice. *"Et je le regrette beaucoup."*

The drooping bags of skin under her jet-black eyes were larger and heavier than any he had ever seen. A faint, wilted odor came from her. A mild, grave warmth stole over his heart.

"Merci," she said with a clanking accent that stood in strange contrast to her fragility, and one corner of her large mouth drooped tragically low. Then she pulled her hand back up under the mantilla, nodded, and turned to take up her wanderings again.

As they walked on, Hans Castorp said, "You see, it didn't bother me at all. I managed very nicely with her. I can handle people like that very nicely in general. I believe I have a natural understanding of how to deal with them—don't you think so, too? I even think that on the whole I get along with sad people better than with happy ones—God only knows why, perhaps because I am an orphan and lost my parents so early on. But when people are serious and sad or if death is involved, it doesn't really depress or embarrass me. Instead, I feel in my element somehow, or at least better than when things are just chugging right along—I'm less good at that. I was thinking only recently that it's really foolish the way the local ladies carry on about death and things connected with it, that everyone is so skittish, protecting them and making sure the last rites are brought while they're downstairs eating. No, phooey! That's silly. Don't you love to look at coffins? I've always enjoyed looking at one now and then. I think of a coffin as an absolutely lovely piece of furniture, even when it's empty, and if there's someone lying in it, it's really quite sublime in my eyes. There's something so edifying about funerals—I've sometimes thought that when we need a little spiritual uplift, we should attend funerals rather than church. People wear their best black clothes and take their hats off and gaze at the coffin and seem so serious and devout—and

no one dares make bad jokes, the way they normally do. I really do like
it for people to be a little more devout once in a while. Sometimes I've
asked myself if I shouldn't have been a pastor—in some ways I don't
think I would have made a bad one. . . . I hope there weren't any mistakes
in my French when I answered—were there?"

"No," Joachim said. " *'Je le regrette beaucoup'* was quite correct as
far as that goes."

Politically Suspect

D EVIATIONS from the normal schedule occurred regularly. First of
all, there was Sunday—a Sunday with a band concert on the terrace,
offered every fourteen days as a way of marking the passage of two weeks;
and it was in the middle of week number two when Hans Castorp entered
from the outside world. He had arrived on a Tuesday and so it was his
fifth day, an almost springlike day after the bizarre turn in the weather
that had thrown them back into winter—mild, yet fresh, with tidy clouds
in a bright blue sky and a sun shining gently on the slopes and valley,
which now had returned to their proper summer green, because the recent
snowfall had been doomed to melt quickly.

It was clear that everyone took pains to dignify and honor Sunday;
both management and residents supported one another in the effort. There
was crumb cake at early breakfast, and beside each setting was a little vase
with a few flowers, wild mountain pinks and even Alpine roses, which
the gentlemen then took as boutonnieres. Prosecutor Paravant went so
far as to don a black swallowtail coat with a dotted vest, and the ladies'
attire had a diaphanous and festive look. Frau Chauchat appeared at breakfast in a flowing open-sleeved lace peignoir, and stood there at attention—
having first slammed the glass door—and charmingly presented herself,
as it were, to the dining hall, before proceeding in her slinking gait to her
table; and her attire suited her so splendidly that Hans Castorp's neighbor,
the teacher from Königsberg, expressed her unequivocal enthusiasm. Even
the barbaric couple from the Bad Russian table gave the Sabbath its
due, the male portion having exchanged leather jacket and felt boots for
a kind of short frock coat and leather shoes; whereas *she* still wore her
shabby boa, but beneath it was a green silk blouse with a ruffled collar.
Hans Castorp scowled as he spotted the two of them, and blushed—
something he tended to do often here.

Immediately after breakfast, the concert began out on the terrace; all sorts of brass and woodwinds had gathered there, and alternating lively and slow pieces, they played almost until the midday meal. The rest cure was not strictly enforced during the concert. True, some people did enjoy sweet melodies from their balconies, and three or four of the chairs in the arcade were occupied; but the majority of the guests sat at little white tables placed out on the covered porch, although frivolous and fashionable society, for whom sitting on chairs was apparently too respectable, took up a position on the stone steps leading down to the garden and gave free rein to merriment—youthful patients of both sexes, most of whose faces or names Hans Castorp knew by now. Hermine Kleefeld was part of the group, as was Herr Albin, who passed around a large flowered box of chocolates from which all the others ate, whereas he did not touch them, but instead assumed a paternal air and smoked gold-tipped cigarettes. Also in the party were the thick-lipped lad from the Half-Lung Club; Fräulein Levi, looking as thin and ivory-skinned as ever; an ash-blond young man who answered to the name of Rasmussen and dangled his hands chest-high, like fins at the end of limp wrists; Frau Salomon from Amsterdam, a lady of ample proportions, who was dressed in red and had joined the young people; the tall gentleman with the thinning hair who could play selections from *A Midsummer Night's Dream* and who now sat behind her, his arms hugging pointed knees, his gloomy eyes fixed on the brown hair at the nape of her neck; a red-haired young lady from Greece; another girl of unknown origin with the face of a tapir; the gluttonous adolescent with the thick, circular glasses; another fifteen- or sixteen-year-old boy, who squinted through a monocle and at every cough put his little finger, its long nail shaped very much like a saltcellar spoon, to his lips—a first-class ass, it would seem; and several others.

The boy with the fingernail, Joachim explained in a low voice, had been only very slightly ill on arrival, with no temperature—his being sent up was more a precautionary measure by his father, a physician—and had been advised by the director that he would have to stay about three months. And now, after three months, with a temperature between 100 and 100.4 degrees, he was seriously ill. But he led such a reckless life that he deserved to have his ears boxed.

The cousins had a table to themselves, off to one side from the others, because Hans Castorp wanted to smoke a cigar with the dark beer he had brought out with him from breakfast—and from time to time the cigar even tasted rather good. Dazed from the beer and the music, which as always made him lay his head a little to one side with his mouth hanging open, he looked with bloodshot eyes out at the resort life around him. It came to him that all these people were subject to an inner decay that would be halted only with great difficulty and that most of them were slightly feverish, but the realization did not bother him at all—on the contrary, there was a certain special intensity and intellectual charm to the whole scene. People sat at their tables drinking sodas; someone was taking photographs down on the steps. Others were trading stamps. The red-haired young lady from Greece had been sketching Herr Rasmussen on her pad, but she refused to show him the picture now, and with a broad smile that revealed her gap teeth, she kept turning from side to side, and it was a long time before he managed to grab the pad away from her. Hermine Kleefeld sat on the steps, her eyes half-closed, and beat time to the music with a rolled-up newspaper, and simultaneously she let Herr Albin pin a little bouquet of wildflowers to her blouse. The thick-lipped lad, sitting at Frau Salomon's feet, turned his head around, gazed up at her, and chatted away, while the pianist with the thinning hair stared resolutely at the nape of her neck.

The doctors arrived and mingled among the hotel guests—Director Behrens in his white smock, Dr. Krokowski in his black. They walked along the rows of tables, the director dispensing a casual, witty remark to almost everyone, so that a wake of mirth rippled behind him. They now moved down to the young people, where the females, with wagging heads and sidelong glances, flocked around Dr. Krokowski. In honor of the Sabbath, the director showed the gentlemen a little stunt with his lace boots: placing one huge foot on a higher step, he undid the laces, then gathered them with a special grip in one hand, and without help of the other, crisscrossed them through the hooks so deftly that everyone stood there amazed—and several lads tried the trick out themselves, with no success.

Later Settembrini appeared on the terrace. He emerged from the dining hall, stopped, and leaned on his cane; dressed today as well in his petersham coat and pale yellow trousers, he first looked about with a refined, alert, and critical air and then approached the cousins' table with a cry of "Ah, bravo!"

He asked permission to join them. "Beer, tobacco, and music," he said. "Behold the Fatherland. I see you're caught up in the patriotic mood, my good engineer. I'm happy to see you in your element. Permit me, please, to take some part in your harmonious state."

Hans Castorp ordered his facial expression—had, in fact, already done so the moment he spotted the Italian. He said, "You're late for the concert, Herr Settembrini. It will soon be over, I fear. Don't you enjoy listening to music?"

"Not when I'm ordered to do so," Settembrini replied. "Not if it's decreed by the day of the week. Not when it has a pharmaceutical odor and is prescribed from on high for reasons of health. I have some little regard for my freedom or what is left to us of our freedom and human dignity. On such occasions I am merely a visitor, much as you play the full-time visitor. I drop by for fifteen minutes and then go my way. It gives me the illusion of independence. I'm not saying it is anything more than an illusion, but who can object if it gives me a certain satisfaction? It's quite different with your cousin. For him it is a duty. You do regard this as one of your duties here, am I not right, lieutenant? Oh, I know, you've learned the trick of keeping your pride, even in slavery. A puzzling trick. Not everyone in Europe knows how to pull it off. Music? You asked if I consider myself a fancier of music, did you not? Well, when you say 'fancier' " (actually, Hans Castorp did not recall putting it that way) "that's not a bad word for it—it has a hint of delicate frivolity. So then, fine, I'll accept your term. Yes, I am a fancier of music—which is not to say that I particularly revere it—not, for instance, as I love and revere the written word, the bearer of the human intellect, the tool, the shining plow of progress. Music . . . there is something only semi-articulate about it, something dubious, irresponsible, indifferent. You will object, I presume, that it can also be quite clear. But nature can be clear as well—a brook can be clear, but what good does that do us? It is not true clarity, but a dreamy, empty clarity that demands nothing of us, a clarity without consequences, and therefore dangerous, because it seduces us to take our ease beside it. But, if you like, let music assume its most high-minded pose. Fine! And then our emotions are inflamed. And yet the real point should be to inflame our reason. Music, it would appear, is movement for its own sake—although I suspect it of quietism. Let me overstate my case: my distaste for music is political."

At this point Hans Castorp could not help slapping his knee and exclaiming that he had never heard anything like that in all his life.

"Please consider it, nevertheless," Settembrini said with a smile. "Music is invaluable as the ultimate means for awakening our zeal, a power that draws the mind trained for its effects forward and upward. But literature must precede it. By itself, music cannot draw the world forward. By itself, music is dangerous. And for you in particular, my good engineer, it is absolutely dangerous. I read that at once from your face as I arrived just now."

Hans Castorp laughed. "Ah, you mustn't even look at my face, Herr Settembrini. You can't imagine how your air up here plays havoc with me. I find it much more difficult to get acclimatized than I thought I would."

"I'm afraid you're deluding yourself."

"No, what do you mean? Damn if I'm not more tired and flushed than I've ever been."

"It seems to me, however, that we should be grateful to the management for these concerts," Joachim said circumspectly. "You are viewing the matter from a higher standpoint, Herr Settembrini, as a writer, so to speak, and I would not want to contradict you there. It seems to me, however, that we should be grateful for this bit of music here. I am not particularly musical myself, and there's nothing remarkable about the pieces as such—neither classical nor modern—especially the way they're playing them, merely a little band music. But it is an enjoyable change. It fills a few hours up so nice and properly, I think. It divides them up and gives some content to each, so that there's something to them after all—whereas normally the hours and days and weeks hang so awfully heavy on one's hands. Such an unpretentious concert piece lasts perhaps seven minutes, am I correct? And each piece is something all to itself, has a beginning and an end, stands out in contrast to the rest, and that is what keeps them, in some sense, from being swallowed up in the general routine. And, besides, each is then divided up into several parts itself—into melodic phrases, and those by the rhythm itself—so that something's always going on and every moment takes on a certain meaning that a person can hold on to, whereas otherwise—I don't know if I'm putting it right, but . . ."

"Bravo!" Settembrini cried. "Bravo, lieutenant. You have described very nicely an indubitably moral element in the nature of music: to wit, that by its peculiar and lively means of measurement, it lends an awareness, both intellectual and precious, to the flow of time. Music awakens time, awakens us to our finest enjoyment of time. Music awakens—and in that sense it is moral. Art is moral, in that it awakens. But what if it were to do the opposite? If it were to numb us, put us asleep, counteract all activity and progress? And music can do that as well. It knows all too well the effect that opiates have. A devilish effect, gentlemen. Opiates are the Devil's tool, for they create dullness, rigidity, stagnation, slavish inertia. There is something dubious about music, gentlemen. I maintain that music is ambiguous by its very nature. I am not going too far when I declare it to be politically suspect."

He went on speaking in these terms for a while, and Hans Castorp listened, too, but was unable to follow the argument very well—not only because of his weariness, but also because he was distracted by the conviviality among the flighty young people down on the steps. Was he seeing right—or what was that exactly? The girl with the face of a tapir was busy sewing on a button at the knee of the knickerbockers worn by the boy with the monocle. But she was panting hot and hard because of her asthma, and all the while he coughed and held his saltcellar-spoon fingernail to his lips. They were ill, both of them—all the same, it certainly showed what peculiar social customs young people had up here. The band was playing a polka.

Hippe

AND SO SUNDAYS stood out—including the afternoons, which were marked by carriage rides undertaken by various groups of guests. After tea, several pairs of horses trotted up the loop of the drive, pulling carriages that stopped outside the front door for those who had ordered them—mainly Russians, particularly Russian ladies.

"Russians love to go for rides," Joachim told Hans Castorp as they stood together at the front door and amused themselves by watching people depart. "And now they'll ride to Clavadel or to the lake or to Flüela Valley or Klosters, those are the usual destinations. We could take a ride ourselves sometime while you're here, if you like. But I think you've probably got enough to do for right now just getting settled in, and don't need any adventures."

Hans Castorp agreed. He had a cigarette in his mouth and his hands in his trouser pockets. He watched as the chipper little old Russian lady and her skinny niece took their seats in the carriage and were joined by two other ladies—Marusya and Madame Chauchat. The latter was wearing a light duster, belted across the back, but no hat. She sat down next to the old woman at the front, with the two young girls on the backseat. All four were in a merry mood and their mouths worked ceaselessly at their soft, rather boneless language. They talked and laughed about the difficulty of fitting under the blanket, about the wooden box of Russian candies, wrapped in paper and bedded in cotton, which the great-aunt had brought along as provisions and now offered around. Hans Castorp was pleased to discover that he could pick out Frau Chauchat's opaque voice. As always when he set eyes on this careless woman, he was reminded of the resemblance that he had been trying to recall for some time now and that had flashed across his dream. Marusya's laugh, however, the sight of her round, brown eyes, blinking childishly out over the handkerchief with which she covered her mouth, and her full, prominent chest—said to be more than a little ill on the inside—reminded him of something else that had shaken him when he had noticed it recently, and so without turning his head, he glanced cautiously toward Joachim. No, thank God, Joachim's face wasn't turning blotchy as it had that day, and his lips were

not in their woeful grimace. But he was watching Marusya—and in a
pose, with a look in his eyes, that could not possibly be called military,
but rather so gloomy and self-absorbed that one would have to term it
downright civilian. He pulled himself together, all the same, and quickly
peered at Hans Castorp, who just had time to pull his own eyes away
and gaze off vaguely into the air. As he did, he felt his heart pounding—
for no reason, all of its own accord, as it had taken to doing up here.

In other respects Sunday offered nothing out of the ordinary, apart
perhaps from the meals, which, since they could hardly be more sumptuous, were at least marked by a refinement in the cuisine. (Dinner included
a *chaudfroid* of chicken, garnished with shrimps and halved cherries; ices
with pastries in little baskets of spun sugar; even fresh pineapple.) After
drinking his beer that evening, Hans Castorp felt more exhausted, chilled,
and torpid than on any day thus far; he said good night to his cousin a
little before nine, quickly slipped in under his comforter, pulling it up
over his chin, and fell dead asleep.

But the very next day, his first Monday up here as a visitor, brought
another standard deviation from the routine—and that was one of the
lectures Dr. Krokowski gave in the dining hall every two weeks before
the entire German-speaking, nonmoribund, adult population of the Berghof. As Hans Castorp learned from his cousin, this was one of a series
of popular-scientific talks presented under the general title "Love as a
Force Conducive to Illness." This instructive entertainment took place
after second breakfast, and, as Joachim likewise informed him, it was not
permitted, or was at the very least frowned upon, for anyone to absent
himself—and it was therefore considered an amazing license that Settembrini, who surely was fluent in German as few others were, not only had
never attended these lectures, but also vilified them at length. As for Hans
Castorp, he had decided at once that he would attend—primarily out of
courtesy, but also out of undisguised curiosity. Before the lecture, however, he did something quite perverse and ill advised: he took the notion
of going for an extended walk all by himself, which turned out bad beyond
all expectation.

"Now listen"—these had been his first words when Joachim came into
his room that morning—"I have decided that things can't go on like this. I
have had my fill of horizontal living—it's as if my blood were practically
falling asleep. Needless to say, it is quite another matter for you—you're a
patient here, and I have no intention of corrupting you. But if you don't
mind, I want to take a real walk this morning right after breakfast, a couple
of hours of just walking out into the wide world wherever the path leads.
I'll stick a little something in my pocket for a snack, and I'll be on my own.
And then we'll see if I'm not a new man when I get back."

"Fine," Joachim said, realizing that his cousin was quite serious about following through on his plan. "But don't overdo it—that's my advice. It's not the same up here as at home. And make sure you're back in time for the lecture."

In reality, there were other reasons beyond the purely physical that had put this idea into young Hans Castorp's head. It seemed to him that his difficulties in acclimatizing himself had less to do with his flushed face, or the bad taste he usually had in his mouth, or the pounding of his heart, and more with things like the activities of the Russian couple next door, the table talk of someone as sick and stupid as Frau Stöhr, the Austrian horseman's flabby cough that he heard every day in the corridor, Herr Albin's opinions, the impression left on him by the social customs of sickly adolescents, the expression on Joachim's face when he looked at Marusya, and all sorts of similar matters he had observed. He thought it could only do him good to break the grip of the Berghof for once, to breathe deep of the open air, to get some real exercise, and if one was going to be exhausted of an evening, at least to know the reason why. And so after breakfast, he boldly took his departure from Joachim—who dutifully started out on his measured promenade up to the bench beside the water trough—and swinging his walking stick, he now marched off down the main road on his own.

It was almost half past eight on a cool, cloudy morning. As he had planned, Hans Castorp breathed deeply of fresh, light, early-morning air that went so easily into the lungs and had neither odor nor moisture nor content, that evoked no memories. He crossed the brook and the narrow-gauge tracks, came out on the main road with its irregular pattern of buildings, and left it almost at once for a meadow path, which ran on level ground for only a short while and then led up the slope on his right at a rather steep angle. Hans Castorp enjoyed the climb; his chest expanded, he pushed his hat back from his brow with his cane, and when from a good height he looked back around and saw in the distance the surface of the lake his train had passed on arrival, he began to sing.

He sang the kind of songs he knew—sentimental folk melodies, the ones you find in the handbooks of sport and business clubs, including one that contained the lines:

> The bards do praise both love and wine,
> Yet virtue still more often—

and he hummed them softly at first, but soon was singing at the top of his voice. It was a brash baritone, but he found it lovely today, and his own singing inspired him more and more. If he started in too high a key, then he would sing falsetto, and he found that lovely, too. When memory failed him, he made do by singing the melody to nonsense syllables and words, tossing them off into the air with the splendid back-rolled *r* and well-rounded vowels of opera singers, and at last moved on simply to fantasizing both text and music and accompanying these vocalizations with theatrical gestures. But since it is quite an exertion to both climb and sing, he soon found he was short of breath—and it kept getting shorter. But out of idealism and love for the beauty of song, he ignored his distress and, despite frequent sighs, gave it all he had, until finally he sank down at the base of a thick pine tree—totally out of breath and gasping, half-blind, with only bright patterns dancing before his eyes, his pulse skittering. After such exaltation, his sudden reward was radical gloom, a hangover that bordered on despair.

Once his nerves had settled a bit again, he got up to continue his walk, but his neck was twitching so violently that, young though he was, his head was wobbling just as old Hans Lorenz Castorp's once had done. The phenomenon suddenly awakened in him warm memories of his late grandfather, and instead of finding it repulsive, he took a certain pleasure in imitating the venerable chin-propping method that the old man himself had used to control his shaking head and that had so delighted Hans Castorp as a boy.

He kept climbing along the serpentine path. The sound of cowbells drew him on and he found the herd, too; they were grazing near a wooden hut, whose roof was weighed down with stones. Two bearded men were coming toward him, axes on their shoulders, but then, not all that far from him, they took leave of one another. "Well, fare thee well and much obliged," the one said to the other in a deep, guttural voice; he now switched his axe to his other shoulder and began to stride down toward the valley, his steps cracking loudly as he forged a path through the pines. It had sounded so strange there in this lonely, remote place, that "fare thee well and much obliged," like words in a dream brushing past Hans Castorp's senses, numbed by climbing and singing. He spoke the words softly to himself, trying to imitate the guttural and sober rustic dialect of these mountain men; and he kept climbing for some distance beyond the hut, determined to reach the tree line. But one glance at his watch, and he gave up that plan.

He followed a path—level at first and then descending—that led around to the left in the direction of town. A forest of tall pines swallowed him, and wandering through it now, he even began to sing a little again, although more prudently—but as he descended his knees shook still more unsettlingly than before. When he emerged from the woods, he was astonished by the splendid view opening up before him—an intimate, closed landscape, like some magnificent, peaceful painting.

From the slope on his right, a mountain stream swept along a flat, stony bed, then rushed foaming over terraced boulders in its path, and finally flowed more serenely toward the valley, crossed at that point by a picturesque wooden bridge with simple railings. The ground about was blue with bell-like flowers of a lushly growing shrub. Dour spruces, symmetrical and gigantic, stood solitary and in small groups along the bottom of the gorge and farther up the slopes. One of them, rooted in the steep bank of the brook, jutted across the view at a bizarre angle. The murmur of isolation reigned above this beautiful, remote spot. Hans Castorp spied a bench on the far side of the brook.

He crossed the wooden bridge and sat down to enjoy the sight of the falling water and rushing foam, to listen to its idyllic chatter, a monotone filled with interior variety. Hans Castorp loved the purl of water as much as he loved music, perhaps even more. But he had no sooner made himself comfortable than his nose began to bleed—so suddenly that he was unable to keep his suit from being stained a little. The flow of blood was strong and persistent and kept him occupied for a good half hour, forcing him to run back and forth between the bench and the brook, rinsing out his handkerchief, sniffing water to rinse his nostrils, then lying down flat on the planks again, the wet cloth over his nose. There he lay quietly until the bleeding finally stopped—his hands clasped behind his head, his knees drawn up, his eyes closed, his ears filled with the rushing of the water. It was not that he felt sick, but rather that the profuse bloodletting soothed him and left him in a state of strangely reduced vitality; he would exhale, and for a long time feel no need to take in new air, but simply lie there, his inert body calmly letting his heart run through a series of beats, until at last he would lazily take another shallow breath.

And he found himself transported to an earlier stage of life, one which only a few nights before had served as the basis for a dream filled with more recent impressions. And as he was pulled back into the then and there, time and space were abrogated—so intensely, so totally, that one might have thought a lifeless body lay there on the bench beside the torrent, while the real Hans Castorp was moving about in an earlier time, in different surroundings, confronted by a situation that, for all its simplicity, he found both fraught with risk and filled with intoxication.

He was thirteen years old, a seventh-grader in short pants, and he was standing in the schoolyard talking with another boy about his age, but from a different class—a conversation that Hans Castorp had initiated more or less arbitrarily and that delighted him no end, although it would be a short one, given the limited scope offered by the physical object under discussion. It was during recess between the last two periods of the day for Hans Castorp's class—between history and drawing. The schoolyard—paved with red bricks and cut off from the street by a high shingled wall with two entrance gates—was filled with pupils, some walking back and forth in little rows, some standing in groups, some leaning or half sitting against the tiled abutments of the school building. There was a babel of voices. Supervising these activities was a teacher in a slouch hat, who now bit into a ham sandwich.

The boy that Hans Castorp was talking to was named Hippe, Pribislav Hippe—and the remarkable thing was that the *r* in his first name was pronounced like an *sh:* he called himself "Pshibislav." And that outlandish name did not fit badly with his looks, which were not ordinary at all, indeed were decidedly foreign. Hippe, the son of a high-school history teacher—and so a notorious model student—was already a grade ahead of Hans Castorp, although he was not much older. He came from Mecklenburg, and to judge from appearances, he was obviously the product of an ancient mixing of races, the blending of Germanic blood with Slavic-Wendish, or vice versa. He was blond, and his hair was kept trimmed close to his round head. But his eyes, bluish-gray or grayish-blue eyes (a rather indefinite and equivocal color, much like that of distant mountains) had a curious, narrow, and, if you looked closely, slightly slanted shape, and right below them were prominent, strong, distinctive cheekbones—features not at all ill proportioned in his case, but really quite pleasing, although they sufficed for his schoolmates to award him the nickname of "the Kirghiz." Hippe, by the way, already wore long trousers, plus a blue jacket, gathered at the back and buttoning up to the collar, where a few flakes of dandruff usually lay scattered.

The thing was that Hans Castorp had had his eye on young Pribislav for a long time, had chosen him from among all the boys in the bustling schoolyard, those he knew and those he didn't know, had been interested in him, had followed him with his glances—should one say, admired him?—in any case, observed him with ever-growing sympathy. Even when walking to and from school, he looked forward to spotting him among the other boys, to watching him talk and laugh, to picking out his voice from a good distance—that husky, opaque, slightly gruff voice. Granted, there was no sufficient reason for this sympathy—particularly if one disregarded such things as his heathen name, his status as a model pupil (which, indeed, could have played no role whatever), or those Kirghiz eyes, which from time to time, in certain sidelong glances, when gazing at nothing in particular, could darken, almost melt, to a veiled dusky look—but whatever the reason, Hans Castorp did not worry about the intellectual or emotional basis of his reaction, or even what name he would give it if he had to. It could not be called friendship, because he didn't really "know" Hippe. But from the start, there was not the least reason to give it a name; the furthest thing from his mind was ever to talk about the matter—that would have been most unlike him and he felt no need to do so. Besides, to give it a name would have meant, if not to judge it, at least to define it, to classify it as one of life's familiar, common-place items, whereas Hans Castorp was thoroughly convinced at some subconscious level that anything so personal should always be shielded from definition and classification.

But with or without a reason for them, these feelings, though far from having a name or being shared, were so powerful that Hans Castorp carried them silently about with him for almost a year—approximately a year, since it was impossible to fix their beginnings exactly—which at least spoke for the loyalty and steadfastness of his character, particularly when one thinks what a huge chunk of time a year is at that age. Unfortunately, there is normally some sort of moral judgment involved in identifying traits of character, whether for the purpose of praise or censure, even though every such trait has its two sides. Hans Castorp's "loyalty" (in which he did not take any particular pride, by the way) consisted—and no value judgment is intended—of a certain stodginess, slowness, and stubbornness of spirit, a sustaining mood that caused him to regard conditions and relationships of long-standing attachment to be that much more valuable the longer they lasted. He also tended to believe in the infinite duration of the state and mood in which he happened to find himself at a given moment, cherished it for just that reason and was not eager for change. And so his heart had become accustomed to this mute, distant relationship with Pribislav Hippe, and he considered it a fundamental, permanent fixture in his life. He loved the surges of emotion that came with it, the tension of whether he would meet him on a given day, whether Pribislav would pass close by him, perhaps even look at him, loved the silent, tender satisfaction that his secret bestowed upon him, loved even the disappointments it sometimes brought, the greatest of which was when Pribislav was "absent"—and then the schoolyard was desolate, the day lacked every spice, but enduring hope remained.

And so things continued for a year, until that adventurous high-point; and another year passed as well—the result of Hans Castorp's abiding loyalty. And then it was all over—without his ever noticing the loosening and breaking of the bonds that tied him to Pribislav Hippe, any more than he had noticed their strengthening. Pribislav left the school and the city, too, when his father was transferred. But Hans Castorp barely noticed, he had already forgotten him by then. One might say that the figure of this "Kirghiz" emerged imperceptibly out of the fog and into his life, slowly taking on clarity and palpability, until the moment when he was most near, most physically present, there in the schoolyard, stood there in the foreground for a while, and then gradually receded and vanished again into the fog, without even the pain of farewell.

But Hans Castorp now found himself transported back to that moment, to that risky, adventurous moment when he had had a conversation, a real conversation with Pribislav Hippe. And this is how it had come about. Drawing class was next, and Hans Castorp noticed that he did not have his drawing pencil with him. All his classmates needed theirs; but he had acquaintances here and there among the boys in other classes whom he could have approached for a pencil. But the boy he knew best, he discovered, was Pribislav—he felt closest to him, he was the one with whom he had spent so many silent hours. And on a joyful impulse of his whole being, he decided to seize the opportunity—he even called it an opportunity—and ask Pribislav for a pencil. He wasn't even aware what an odd thing this was for him to do, since he really didn't know Pribislav—or maybe he simply did not care, blinded as he was by some peculiar recklessness. And so there he stood in the tumult of the brick schoolyard, face to face with Pribislav Hippe. And he said, "Excuse me, could you lend me a pencil?"

And Pribislav looked at him out of Kirghiz eyes set above prominent cheekbones and in his pleasantly husky voice and without any astonishment—or at least without betraying any astonishment—he said, "Glad to. But be sure to give it back to me after class." And he pulled a pencil from his pocket, in a silver-plated holder with a ring you had to push up to make the reddish pencil emerge from its metal casing. As he explained its simple mechanism, both their heads bent down over it.

"And don't break it," he added.

What made him say that? As if Hans Castorp intended to treat it carelessly—or worse, *not* give it back at all.

Then they looked at one another and smiled, and since there was nothing more to say, they turned away, first shoulders, then backs, and walked off.

That was all. But Hans Castorp had never been happier in all his life than during that drawing class as he sketched with Pribislav Hippe's pencil—and before him lay the prospect of returning it to its owner in person, which came as a simple, natural part of the bargain. He even took the liberty of sharpening the pencil a little, and he kept three or four of the red-lacquered shavings in the drawer of his desk for a year or two—anyone who might have seen them would never have guessed their significance. The return of the pencil, moreover, took the simplest form possible;

but that was just what Hans Castorp intended, indeed he took a special pride in it—after all, he was more than a little spoiled and blasé after his long, intimate relationship with Hippe.

"There," he said. "Thanks."

And Pribislav said nothing at all, simply gave the mechanism a quick check and shoved the holder into his pocket.

And they never spoke another word—but just that one time, it really did happen, thanks to Hans Castorp's enterprising spirit.

He opened his eyes wide, confused by the depth of his trance. "I suppose I was dreaming," he thought. "Yes, that was Pribislav. I haven't thought of him in a long time. What ever became of those shavings? The desk is up in the attic at Uncle Tienappel's. They must still be in that same little drawer, clear at the back on the left. I never removed them. Didn't even pay them enough attention to throw them out. It was Pribislav, it was him all over. I never would have thought that I'd see him so clearly again. And he looked so strangely like her—that woman up here. Is that why I've been so intrigued by her? Or maybe that's why I was suddenly so interested in *him*. What nonsense. What a lot of nonsense. I've got to be on my way, and I mean right now." But he lay there a while longer, pondering and remembering. Then he sat up. "Well, fare thee well and much obliged!" he said out loud, and tears came to his eyes even as he smiled. And with that he stood up to go, and just as quickly sat back down, hat and cane in hand, forced to admit that his knees couldn't support him. "Whoops," he thought, "I don't think that's going to work. And I'm supposed to be at the lecture in the dining hall at eleven on the dot. A long walk up here can be lovely, but it has its drawbacks, too, it seems. Yes, indeed—but I can't stay here. It's just that I'm a little stiff from lying down; it will get better once I'm moving." And he tried to get to his feet again—and making a concerted effort to pull himself together, he succeeded.

But it was a miserable walk home, especially after such an optimistic start. He repeatedly had to stop to rest—the blood would suddenly drain from his face, cold sweat would break out on his brow, and his irregular heartbeat made it hard to breathe. He wearily struggled down the serpentine path, finally reaching the valley close to the spa hotel in Platz; he now realized all too clearly that he would never be able to manage the long walk back to the Berghof on his own; and since there was no tram and he didn't see any carriages for hire, he asked the driver of a delivery wagon headed for Dorf with a load of empty boxes to let him climb aboard. Back to back with the driver, his legs dangling over the side of the wagon, half-asleep as he swayed and nodded with each jolt, he rode along, the object of the amazed sympathy of passersby. He got off at the railroad crossing, offered some money without bothering to look if it was too much or too little, and lurched headlong up the loop of the drive.

"*Dépêchez-vous, monsieur!*" the French doorman said. "*La conférence de Monsieur Krokowski vient de commencer.*"

And Hans Castorp tossed his hat and cane on the hallstand—and carefully, cautiously, his tongue between his teeth, he squeezed his way past the glass door, only just ajar, and entered the dining hall, where the residents were sitting in rows of chairs. To his right, at the narrow end of the room, Dr. Krokowski stood in his frock coat, behind a cloth-covered table, graced by a carafe of water—he was already speaking.

Analysis

LUCKILY there was a corner seat available near the door. He sidled down into it and put on a face as if he had been there all along. The audience was listening attentively to Dr. Krokowski's every word and paid Hans Castorp barely any notice. And that was a good thing, because he looked dreadful. His face was as pale as linen and his suit was blood-stained, so that he looked like a murderer fresh from his awful deed. The lady in front of him did turn her head as he sat down, studying him with her narrow eyes. It was Madame Chauchat, he realized with something like indignation. What a hell of a thing to have happen! Wasn't he ever going to be able to calm down? He had thought that, having arrived at his goal, he could sit there quietly and recover a little, and now he had to have her right in front of his nose—a coincidence that might possibly have pleased him under other circumstances, but what good did it do him in his weary, frazzled state? It only made new demands of his heart, and he would be preoccupied and tense all through the lecture. She had looked at him with eyes exactly like Pribislav's, staring into his face and at the bloodstains—a rather impolite, brazen stare, by the way, that matched the manners of a woman who slammed doors. What awful posture she had! Not like the women in Hans Castorp's social circle at home, who sat straight-backed at the table and turned only their heads to speak with pursed lips to gentlemen on either side. Frau Chauchat sat in a limp slouch, her back rounded, her shoulders drooping forward, and at the same time she thrust her head out so that her neck bones were visible above the collar line of her white blouse. Pribislav had held his head like that, too; but he had been a model student and led a life full of honors (although that had not been the reason why Hans Castorp had borrowed a pencil from him)—whereas it was all too clear that Frau Chauchat's careless posture, her door-slamming, and her brazen stares were bound up with her illness, that in fact they were all expressions of that same license young Herr Albin had praised, the advantages of which, if not honorable, were at least almost endless.

As he gazed at Frau Chauchat's limp back, Hans Castorp's thoughts grew jumbled, ceased being thoughts, became daydreams into which Dr. Krokowski's drawling baritone and gently rolled *r* drifted from some great distance. But the stillness in the room, the profound, spellbound attention displayed all around him, had its own effect and literally roused him from his doze. He looked about—next to him sat the pianist with thinning hair, arms crossed, head thrown back, mouth hanging open as he listened. Fräulein Engelhart, the teacher, a little farther down the row, had eager eyes and downy red spots on both cheeks, a flush that Hans Castorp discovered on other ladies' cheeks as well when he looked more closely— even Frau Salomon there, next to Herr Albin, and the wife of Magnus the brewer, the woman who was losing protein. Frau Stöhr, sitting just a little behind him, had an expression on her face revealing such ignorant ecstasy that it was pitiful to behold, while Fräulein Levi of the ivory complexion sat leaning back in her chair with half-closed eyes and hands resting palms-up in her lap—and one would have taken her for a corpse if her chest had not risen and fallen with such striking regularity, although Hans Castorp thought she looked more like a mechanically driven wax figure he had once seen in a sideshow. Several people held their hands cupped to their ears; others merely held their hands up halfway, suggesting that the strain of concentration had frozen them in that pose. Prosecutor Paravant, a tanned, primally robust man, or so he appeared, first flicked at his ear with his forefinger to hear better, then pulled it forward to catch the flow of Dr. Krokowski's words.

And what was Dr. Krokowski talking about? What train of thought was he pursuing? Hans Castorp gathered his wits to try to catch up, but did not succeed right away, since he had not heard the beginning and then had missed still more of it while contemplating Frau Chauchat's rounded back. The subject was a force, the force . . . ah yes, the subject was the force of love. But of course, the same topic as in the title of the lecture series—what should Dr. Krokowski be talking about if not his specialty? It was indeed rather odd to hear a lecture about love, since the lectures he usually attended were about things like gear transmissions in ships. How did one go about discussing such a delicate subject, something of such a private nature, here in broad daylight, before an audience of both ladies and gentlemen? Dr. Krokowski discussed it by using a hybrid terminology, a blend of poetical and academic styles, all of it uncompromisingly scientific, but in an ornate, lilting tone, which seemed rather unsuitable to Hans Castorp, but which perhaps accounted for the flush on the ladies' cheeks and the way the gentlemen kept flicking their ears. In particular, the orator constantly used the word "love" in a gently irresolute sense, so that one was never quite sure whether he meant its sanctified or more passionate and fleshly forms—leaving one feeling slightly nauseated and seasick. Never in his life had Hans Castorp heard this word spoken so many times in a row as he did here and now; indeed, when he thought about it, it seemed to him as if he had never spoken it himself before or heard it pass anyone else's lips. He might have been mistaken—but at least he did not think such frequent repetition did the word any good, either. On the contrary, this slippery syllable with its lingual and labial consonants and scanty vowel in the middle really began to disgust him after a while, conjuring up for him somehow images of watery milk—something whitish-blue and insipid, particularly when compared with all the robust fodder that Dr. Krokowski was serving up. Because this much was clear, that if one went about it the way he did, one could say some very stiff things without driving people from the room. It was not enough for him to speak in tactful, intoxicating tones about matters that, although generally well known, are usually left under a veil of silence. He destroyed illusions, he was merciless in giving knowledge the honor it was due, he left no room for tender faith in the dignity of silver hair or in the angelic purity of little children. Along with his frock coat, by the way, he wore his soft, floppy collar and his sandals over gray socks, which gave the impression of some fundamental idealism, although Hans Castorp found the look rather startling. Supporting his arguments with all kinds of examples and anecdotes from the books and loose pages that lay on the table before him, even reciting poetry a few times, Dr. Krokowski discussed love's frightening forms—bizarre, agonized, eerie mutations of its symptoms and omnipotence. Of all our natural instincts, he said, it was the most unstable and exposed, fundamentally prone to confusion and perversion—and no one should be surprised at that. Because there was nothing simple about this powerful instinct. It was by its very nature composed of many elements, and however legitimate this instinct was when regarded as a whole, each of its constituent elements was a perversion. But since, and quite rightly so, Dr. Krokowski continued, one ought not conclude that the whole was itself a perversion simply because its parts were, one was therefore compelled to enlist the legitimacy of the whole, if not its whole legitimacy, and apply it to each of the perverse parts. Logic demanded it, and he begged his listeners to keep that in mind. There were counteracting and corrective psychic factors, wholesome and ordering instincts—one might almost call them bourgeois—under whose compensating and modifying effects perverse components were fused to a consistent and useful whole; and this was, all in all, a common and welcome process, whose consequences, however (as Dr. Krokowski rather superciliously remarked), were of no importance to the physician or thinker. But in other cases that process might not succeed— would not, indeed could not, succeed—and who could say, Dr. Krokowski asked, if those psyches were not perhaps the more noble, the more precious? In such a case, to be precise, the two clusters of forces, both those of the love instinct and the impulses hostile to it, among which shame and disgust were to be noted in particular, exhibited tensions and passions that exceeded all normal bourgeois bounds; and the ensuing battle between these two forces, which was now carried out in the depths of the soul, prevented wayward instincts from being restrained, steadied, and civilized in the manner necessary for a normal, harmonious, and appropriate love life. And how did it end, this clash between the forces of chastity and love—for those were indeed the forces involved? It ended to all appearances with the triumph of chastity. Fear, conventionality, aversion born of modesty, the quivering longing for purity—all these repressed love, held it chained in darkness, at best giving in only partially to its wild demands, but certainly never permitting them a conscious, active existence in all their variety and vigor. Except that chastity only apparently triumphed, its victory was a Pyrrhic victory, because the demands of love could not be fettered, or coerced; suppressed love was not dead, it continued to live on in the dark, secret depths, straining for fulfillment—and broke the bands of chastity and reappeared, though in transmuted, unrecognizable form. And in what form or mask did suppressed and unsanctioned love reappear? Dr. Krokowski looked up and down the rows as he asked this question, as if seriously expecting an answer from his listeners. But no, he would have to provide the answer himself, though he had already provided so many. No one else knew the answer, but he would be sure to know this, too—you could see it just by looking at him. With his glowing eyes, his waxen pallor, his black beard, and those monastic sandals over gray woolen socks, he seemed to symbolize in his person the battle between chastity and passion about which he had been speaking. At least this was Hans Castorp's impression, as he sat there expectantly waiting, along with all the others, to learn in what form unsanctioned love would reappear. The women were barely breathing. Prosecutor Paravant quickly gave his ear another flick, to make sure that it would be open and receptive. And Dr. Krokowski said: In the form of illness! Any symptom of illness was a masked form of love in action, and illness was merely transformed love.

And so now they knew, even if not all of them were able fully to appreciate the knowledge. A sigh went through the room, and Prosecutor Paravant nodded his weighty approval while Dr. Krokowski continued to elaborate his thesis. For his part, Hans Castorp lowered his head to think about what he had heard and to explore whether he really understood it. But being unpracticed in such discursive reasoning and anything but intellectually alert after his unsalutary walk, he was easily diverted, and was in fact diverted almost immediately by the round back in front of him and by the arm extending from it, which lifted and reached back, so that the hand—now right before Hans Castorp's eyes—could tuck at the braid of hair.

It was almost suffocating to have that hand so close to his eyes—you had to look at it, whether you wanted to or not, to study its inherent humanness and all its defects, as if you were holding a magnifying glass to it. No, it had nothing at all aristocratic about it, this stubby, school-girlish hand with the carelessly trimmed nails—you couldn't be certain whether the knuckles toward the tips were even clean, and the cuticles were gnawed, there could no longer be any doubt about that. Hans Castorp grimaced, but his eyes remained fixed on Madame Chauchat's hand, and a vague, halfhearted recollection passed through his mind of something Dr. Krokowski had said about corrective bourgeois forces that counteracted love. . . . But this arm was more beautiful, this arm bent gently behind the head—and was barely clad, because the fabric of the sleeve was thinner than that of the blouse, the flimsiest gossamer, which lent the arm just a hint of delicate illusion, making it even prettier than it probably would have been without any covering. It was both tender and full at the same time—and cool, one could only presume. There could be no question whatever of any counteracting bourgeois forces.

Hans Castorp began to daydream, his eyes directed at Frau Chauchat's arm. The way women dressed! They displayed this or that portion of their necks and breasts, lent their arms a radiant illusion with transparent gossamer. They did it all over the world, just to arouse our ardent desires. My God, but life was beautiful! And one of the things that made it so beautiful was that women dressed so enticingly, simply as a matter of course. It was second nature to them, and such a universally accepted practice that you hardly even thought about it, just accepted it unconsciously, without further ado. But if you wanted truly to enjoy life, Hans Castorp told himself, you really should keep the custom in mind and never forget how exhilarating and, ultimately, almost magical it was. Granted, there was a very definite reason why women were allowed to dress in that exhilarating, magical way, without at the same time offending propriety. It all had to do with the next generation, the propagation of the human species, yes indeed. But what happened when the woman was sick deep inside, so that she was not at all suited for motherhood—what then? Was there any point in her wearing gossamer sleeves so that men would be curious about her body—about her diseased body? There was obviously *no* point in that whatever, and it ought to be considered improper, to be forbidden. Because for a man to be interested in a sick woman was certainly no more reasonable than . . . well, than for Hans Castorp to have pursued his silent interest in Pribislav Hippe back then. A stupid comparison, a rather embarrassing memory. But it had just come to him, insinuating itself all on its own. His daydreams broke off at that point, primarily because his attention was directed again to Dr. Krokowski, whose voice had risen noticeably now. And in fact, as he stood there behind the table, arms spread wide, head tilted to one side, he looked— despite his frock coat—almost like Jesus on the cross!

It turned out that Dr. Krokowski concluded his lecture with a grand advertisement for psychic dissection—he spread his arms wide, and invited them to come unto him. Come unto me, he said, though not exactly in those words, all ye that labor and are heavy laden! And he left no doubt of his certainty that they all, without exception, labored and were heavy laden. He spoke of hidden suffering, of shame and affliction, of the redemptive effects of analysis; he praised the effects of light piercing the dark unconscious, explained that illness could be transformed again into conscious emotion, admonished them to trust, promised recovery. Then he let his arms fall, set his head erect again, gathered up the printed materials that he had used for his lecture, and holding the bundle against his shoulder with his left hand like an ordinary schoolteacher, he exited into the lobby, head held high.

They all stood up, pushed back their chairs, and began slowly to move toward the same door through which the doctor had left the dining hall. As they gathered in concentric circles from all sides, it was as if they were thronging after him—hesitant, without a will of their own, and yet in dazed unanimity, like a swarm of rats behind the Pied Piper. Hans Castorp stood stock-still in midcurrent, his hand on the back of his chair. "I am only a visitor here," he thought. "I'm healthy and all this has nothing to do with me, thank God. I won't even be here for the next lecture." He watched Frau Chauchat leave—slinking, her head thrust forward. "Does she let herself be dissected, too?" he asked himself, and his heart began to pound. He did not even notice Joachim working his way through the chairs toward him, and he flinched when his cousin spoke to him.

"You arrived at the last moment," Joachim said. "Did you go very far? How was it?"

"Oh, nice," Hans Castorp replied. "But I did walk rather far. And I must admit it did me less good than I expected. It was perhaps a little too soon for it, or maybe just the wrong idea altogether. I'll not be doing it again right away."

Joachim did not ask him whether he had liked the lecture, and Hans Castorp said nothing about it, either. As if by tacit agreement, neither of them ever mentioned the lecture again.

Doubts and Considerations

TUESDAY CAME. Our hero had been up here for seven days now, and when he returned from his constitutional that morning, he found a bill totaling up the charges for his first week—a tidy commercial document in a green envelope, with an exquisite picture of the Berghof at the top of the page and excerpts from the brochure arranged attractively in a narrow column along the left margin, where italicized mention was also made of "psychological therapy by the most modern methods." The list itself, done in elegant calligraphy, came to almost exactly 180 francs, which was broken down into 8 francs a day for room, 12 francs a day for board and medical treatment, plus separate entries of 20 francs "entrance fee," and 10 francs for "disinfection of the room," with the final total rounded out by smaller fees for laundry, beer, and the wine he had drunk at his first supper here.

Hans Castorp saw nothing to complain about when he and Joachim checked the addition. "True, I make no use of medical treatment," he said, "but that's my business. It's included in the daily rate, and I can't ask them to deduct it. How could they do that? They've overcharged for the disinfection—they couldn't possibly have gone through ten francs worth of H_2CO to smoke out the American woman. But on the whole, I must say I find the rates reasonable—not really expensive, considering what they offer." And so before second breakfast, they went down to the management office to take care of the bill.

"Management" was on the ground floor: after crossing the lobby and following the hallway past the cloakroom, kitchen, and housekeeping, you could not miss it, especially given the porcelain sign on the door.

Hans Castorp's interest was aroused by the glimpse it offered him into the business side of the establishment. It was a normal, small office where a woman was busy at a typewriter, and three male employees stood bent over lecterns, while in the adjoining room a gentleman with the imposing look of a department head or manager sat working at a freestanding, barrel-like desk and cast his clients a glance just over the top of his glasses, measuring them with cold, practical eyes. While their business was being taken care of—payment made with a large bill, change returned, a receipt written out—they both took on that serious, modest, silent, even subservient look by which young Germans show that their respect for authority applies to all offices, to any room where records are kept and services rendered; but once they were outside and were heading off to breakfast—and later on that day, too—they chatted about the general setup of the Berghof, with Joachim, as the older, more knowledgeable resident, answering his cousin's questions.

Director Behrens was neither the owner nor the proprietor of the sanatorium—although one might get that impression. Above and behind him stood invisible forces, made manifest only to a certain degree in the management office: a board of directors, a joint-stock company—and the stock would not be a bad thing to have, because according to Joachim's trustworthy assertions, juicy dividends were distributed annually to the shareholders, despite the high salaries paid the doctors and some very liberal business practices. The director, then, was not an independent man, but merely an agent, a functionary, an associate of those higher powers—though, of course, the highest and supreme associate here, the soul of the place, the determining factor for the whole organization, including the management office. As the supervising physician, to be sure, he stood far aloof from anything to do with the commercial side of the operation. He came from somewhere in northwestern Germany; and it was general knowledge that he had fallen into the position years ago quite by accident and without any planning on his part. He had been brought here by his wife, whose remains had long since been given over to the cemetery in Davos-Dorf—the picturesque graveyard above the village, on the right-hand slope, toward the entrance of the valley. She had been a very charming woman, if a little cross-eyed and gaunt, to judge from photos you found scattered about the director's official residence, not to mention oil portraits of her that were hung on the walls—painted by his own amateur hand. After she had presented him with two children, a son and a daughter, they had brought her up to this valley, her body already frail and feverish, and within a few months that body had wasted away entirely. People said that Behrens, who idolized her, had been so over-

then, and had in fact been there once already during Joachim's stay; and he told how it had been such a thrill for the ladies of the sanatorium—temperatures rose, little jealousies erupted into spats and skirmishes in the public lounging area, and a press of patients had appeared for Dr. Krokowski's private consultations.

The assistant director had a private consulting room, which, like the general examination room, the laboratory, the operating room, and the X-ray room, was located in the well-lit basement of the building. We have called it a basement, but although the stone stairway leading down to it from the ground floor did indeed create the impression of a descent into a basement, this was almost entirely an illusion, the reasons for which were, first, that the ground floor sat rather high, and second, that the whole edifice had been built on a steep, mountainous slope, so that the "basement" rooms faced the front and looked out onto the garden and the valley—a state of affairs countered and negated, as it were, by the effect of the stairway. You had the sense you were descending below ground level, but in fact, once downstairs, you were right back on ground level again, or at most a foot or two below it—an effect that delighted Hans Castorp when he discovered it for the first time that afternoon as he accompanied his cousin "down" to those regions, where Joachim was scheduled to have himself weighed by the bath attendant. It was a realm where clinical brightness and cleanliness held sway, everything done in white on white, the doors glistening with white enamel—even the one to Dr. Krokowski's reception room, to which one of the learned man's calling cards had been tacked and which lay two steps lower than the hallway itself, so that the room behind the open door looked rather like a suite. This door was just to the right of the stairway, at the near end of the hall, and Hans Castorp kept his eye on it as he paced up and down the corridor, waiting for Joachim. He saw someone come out, too, a lady who had arrived only recently and whose name he did not know—a small, dainty woman, with curls across her forehead and golden earrings. Gathering her skirts in one hand, she bent low as she took those two steps, and with her other small, heavily ringed hand, she pressed a handkerchief to her mouth—above it, her large, pale, distraught eyes stared at nothing. Still hunched over, she hurried toward the stairway with mincing steps that made her petticoats rustle, stopped suddenly as if pondering something, then began to mince her way up the steps, and vanished up the stairwell—still hunched over, her handkerchief still at her lips.

Behind her, where the door had opened, it was much darker than in the white hallway—the clinical brightness of these lower rooms apparently did not penetrate that far; Hans Castorp noted that murky twilight, deep dusk, reigned in Dr. Krokowski's analytical chamber.

Table Talk

WHEN HE SAT DOWN to meals in the bright dining hall, young Hans Castorp found to his embarrassment that he was still subject to the grandfatherly tremor he had first noticed on his long, solitary walk. It would start up again with amazing regularity at almost every meal—it was impossible to stop and hard to hide. The venerable chin-propped-against-chest method offered no permanent solution, and so he looked for other ways to disguise his weakness—for instance, he kept his head in motion as much as possible, turning it to the right and left when conversing, or if he was guiding his soupspoon to his mouth, he would press his left forearm firmly against the table to stabilize himself, and he would even put both elbows on the table and prop his chin in his hand between courses, although he considered that boorish and permissible, at best, in the dissolute company of the sick. But it was all an annoyance, and it would not have taken much for him to have given up meals entirely in disgust, although he had come to value them for the sights and tensions associated with them.

But the fact was—and Hans Castorp knew it only too well—that this deplorable phenomenon with which he was struggling was not merely of organic origin, was not attributable solely to the local air or the strain of adjusting to it, but was also the expression of an inner excitement and was bound up intimately with those same sights and tensions.

Madame Chauchat almost always came late for meals, and until she arrived Hans Castorp would sit there with fidgeting feet, waiting for the glass door to slam, a sound that inevitably accompanied her entrance; and he knew that he would flinch and his face would suddenly feel cold— and that is what happened almost every time. At first he would whip his head around indignantly each time and with angry eyes follow the late-comer to her place at the Good Russian table, even scold her under his breath, rebuking her between his teeth with a cry of outraged protest. But he had given that up, and now he would bend his head farther over his plate, even bite his lips sometimes, or intentionally and elaborately turn to look the other way; because it seemed to him that he no longer had a right to be angry and was not really free to censure her, but that he was an accessory to the offense and answerable for it to the others— in short, he was ashamed. It would be less than precise to say that he was ashamed for Frau Chauchat; rather, he felt personally ashamed in front of all these people. He could have spared himself that, by the way, because no one in the dining hall cared about either Frau Chauchat's vice or Hans Castorp's embarrassment for her—except, perhaps, Fräulein Engelhart, the schoolteacher on his right.

This pitiful creature had understood from Hans Castorp's sensitivity about slamming doors that a certain emotional bond was developing between her young tablemate and the Russian woman, and what was more, that the nature of such a bond was less important than that it existed at all, and finally, that his pretended indifference—and given his lack of talent or experience as an actor, he was very poor at pretending—did not diminish but rather strengthened that bond, was a sign that it had moved to a higher plane. Having given up all hopes and pretensions for herself, Fräulein Engelhart was constantly breaking into raptures about Frau Chauchat; and the remarkable thing was that although Hans Castorp recognized and saw through her rabble-rousing—if not at once, then at least over time—and was indeed disgusted by it, he proved no less willing to allow her to influence him and egg him on.

"Bang!" the old maid said. "That's *her!* You don't even have to look up to make sure who just came in. Of course, there she goes—and what a charming way she has about her—like a kitten slinking to its bowl of milk. I wish you could change seats with me so you could observe her as easily and effortlessly as I can. I do understand that you don't always want to turn your head to watch. God only knows what she might think if she noticed. Now she's greeting her table. You really should have a look, it's so refreshing to watch her. When she talks and smiles the way she's doing now, a little dimple shows in one cheek—but not always, only when she wants it to. Yes, she's a darling woman, a spoiled creature, that's why she's so careless. We all love people like that, whether we want to or not, because when they annoy us with their carelessness, the annoyance becomes just one more reason for being fond of them. What fun it is to be annoyed at people and yet have no choice but to love them."

The teacher whispered all this behind her hand to keep others from hearing. Her flushed, downy spinster's cheeks suggested a temperature above normal, and her titillating remarks stirred Hans Castorp's blood. A certain lack of self-reliance created in him the need to hear confirmed from a third party that Madame Chauchat was indeed an enchanting woman, and the young man also wanted others to encourage him to give himself over to his feelings, when both his reason and conscience were offering unsettling resistance.

These conversations, however, were much less fruitful when it came to facts, because, for the life of her, Fräulein Engelhart knew little or nothing about Frau Chauchat, no more than was general knowledge in the sanatorium; she did not know her, could not claim even to have any acquaintance in common with her. The only thing that could possibly increase her standing in Hans Castorp's eyes was that she herself was from Königsberg, a city not all that far from the Russian border, and so could manage a little broken Russian—very meager attributes indeed; all the same, Hans Castorp was prepared to regard them as some kind of extended personal connection to Frau Chauchat.

"She doesn't wear a ring," he said. "I don't see a wedding ring. Why is that? She is a married woman, you said, did you not?"

The teacher felt so responsible for representing Frau Chauchat to Hans Castorp that his question embarrassed her—as if she had been driven into a corner and would have to talk her way out of it. "You mustn't take that all too seriously," she said. "She is married, most assuredly. There can be no doubt about that. She does not use the title of Madame merely for the greater respect that comes with it, as is common, for instance, among young foreign ladies once they are a little older, but as we all know, she really does have a husband somewhere in Russia—it's common knowledge here. She has a maiden name, a Russian one, not French, something ending in -avov or -ukov, I did hear it somewhere but I've forgotten it. If you'd like I could find out for you. There are surely several people here who know the name. A ring? No, she doesn't wear one, I have noticed that myself. Good heavens, perhaps it doesn't become her, perhaps it makes her hand too broad. Or she finds it rather bourgeois to wear a wedding ring, just a plain gold band—all she'd need then is a little basket for her keys. No, she's certainly too liberal for that. I know it well—Russian women are by their very nature so very free and liberal. And besides, there's something so cold, so disillusioning about a ring— it is a symbol of a woman's dependence, it seems to me; it makes a woman seem practically a nun, turns her into a wallflower, a touch-me-not. I'm not at all surprised that Frau Chauchat has no use for it. Such a charming woman, at the very peak of her beauty. I presume she has neither reason nor desire to remind every gentleman to whom she gives her hand of her marital bonds."

"Good God, how she does go on," Hans Castorp thought, staring in alarm into her eyes, but she returned his gaze with a kind of defiant, savage awkwardness. Then both of them fell silent for a while to recover. Hans Castorp ate, meanwhile suppressing the tremor of his head. At last he said, "And what about her husband? Doesn't he care about her at all? Doesn't he ever visit her up here? What does he do, actually?"

"Civil servant. An administrator for the Russian government, in some remote province, Daghestan, you know, it's somewhere far to the east, beyond the Caucasus—he was transferred out there. No, I told you already, he's never been seen up here once. And she's been here now for three months this time."

"So this is not her first time here?"

"Oh no, this is her third time already. And in between she's somewhere else, at other places like this. It's just the other way around—*she* visits *him* now and again, not often, once a year for a little while. They live separate lives, one might say, and she visits him now and again."

"Well, after all, she is ill."

"Certainly, that she is. But not all *that* ill. Not so seriously ill that she would have to live in sanatoriums, separated from her husband. There must be other reasons beyond that. People here generally assume there are. Perhaps she doesn't like it out there in Daghestan beyond the Caucasus, in such a savage, remote region—there really would be nothing so surprising about that. But it must be at least partly the husband's fault if she doesn't like being with him. He has a French name, true, but he is a Russian official, and believe me, those are coarse people. I even saw one once— he had iron-gray whiskers and such a red face. It's terribly easy to bribe them, and then they are all given to *vodka*, Russian schnapps, you know. For the sake of propriety they'll order a little something to eat, a couple of marinated mushrooms or a piece of sturgeon, and chase it down with drink, quite to excess. And that's what they call a snack."

"You blame it all on him," Hans Castorp said. "But we really don't know if it might not be her fault that they don't get along together. One must be fair. I just have to look at her—and then there's the unmannerly way she slams doors, too—I certainly don't imagine she's an angel. Please don't take offense, but I simply would not trust her out of my sight. But then you're not without bias in the matter. You sit there up to your ears in prejudice in her favor."

That is how he worked it sometimes. With a cunning that was actually foreign to him, he pretended that Fräulein Engelhart's enthusiasm for Frau Chauchat was not in reality what he very well knew it to be, but that her enthusiasm was some neutral, droll fact that he, Hans Castorp, as an uninvolved party standing off at a cool, amused distance, could use to tease the old maid. And since he was certain that his accomplice would accept this audacious distortion and go along with it, it was not a risky tactic at all.

"Good morning," he said. "Did you rest well? You did dream about lovely Minka, your Russian miss, didn't you? No, look at you blush at the mere mention of her. You're terribly infatuated, don't try to deny it."

And the teacher, who had indeed blushed and was now bent deep over her cup, whispered out of the left corner of her mouth, "Shame, shame, Herr Castorp. It isn't at all nice of you to embarrass me with your insinuations. Everyone has already noticed that it's her we're talking about and that you're saying things to make me blush."

What a strange game these two tablemates were playing. Both of them knew that their lies had double and triple twists—that Hans Castorp teased the teacher just so he could talk about Frau Chauchat, but that at the same time he took unwholesome delight in flirting with the old maid; and that for her part, she welcomed all this: first, because it allowed her to play the matchmaker, and second, because she probably had become smitten with Frau Chauchat, if only to please the young man, and finally, because she took some kind of wretched pleasure in being teased and made to blush. They both knew this about themselves and each other, and they also knew that each of them knew this about themselves and one another—and that it was all tangled and squalid. But although Hans Castorp was usually repelled by tangled and squalid affairs and even felt repelled in this instance as well, he continued to splash about in these murky waters, taking consolation in the certainty that he was here only on a visit and would soon be leaving. Affecting a businesslike tone, he offered his expert opinion about the appearance of this "careless" woman, that she looked decidedly younger and prettier in full face than in profile, that her eyes were set too far apart, that her posture left a great deal to be desired, although he did have to admit that her arms were beautiful and "softly formed." And as he was saying all this, he attempted to hide his wobbling head—and all the while he was not only aware that the teacher had spotted his futile attempts to do so, but he also realized to his profound disgust that she, too, suffered from the same tremor.

It was also a purely political tactic, a bit of unnatural cunning, that he had called Frau Chauchat "lovely Minka," since it allowed him to continue: "I call her 'Minka,' although I don't know what her real name is, actually. I mean her first name. As infatuated as you undeniably are, you must surely know her first name."

The teacher thought hard. "Now wait, I do know it," she said. "Or I did know it. Isn't her name Tatyana? No, that wasn't it, and not Natasha, either. Natasha Chauchat? No, that's not what I heard her called. Wait, I have it. Her name's Avdotya. Or something of that sort. Because she's definitely not named Katyenka or Ninotchka. It has simply slipped my mind. But I can easily ascertain it for you, if that's of some consequence to you."

And the very next day she knew the name. She told him over dinner, just as the glass door banged shut. Frau Chauchat's first name was Clavdia.

Hans Castorp did not understand right away. He had her repeat the name and spell it for him before he actually grasped it. Then he pronounced it a few times himself, all the while looking over at Frau Chauchat with his bloodshot eyes, trying it out on her, so to speak.

"Clavdia," he said, "yes, that's very likely it, the name suits her very well." He made no secret of his delight at having acquired this intimate knowledge, and from now on he spoke only of "Clavdia" when he meant Frau Chauchat. "Your Clavdia is rolling her bread up into little pills, I just noticed. Not very refined, I'd say."

"It all depends who's doing it," the teacher responded. "It's very becoming for Clavdia."

Yes, the meals in the dining hall with its seven tables held the greatest fascination for Hans Castorp. He regretted the end of each, but his consolation was that very soon, in two or two and a half hours, he would be sitting there again—and once he sat down it would be as if he had never stood up. What happened in the meantime? Nothing. A brief walk up to the water trough or to the English quarter, a little rest in his lounge chair. Those were no serious interruptions, no obstacles worth taking seriously. It would have been different had it been work, some worry or trouble, that interposed itself—his mind could not have overlooked or bridged that sort of thing quite so easily. But such was not the case in the cleverly and pleasantly regimented life of the Berghof. When he stood up from one communal meal, Hans Castorp was already delighting in the next—insofar as "delighting" was the right word, and not too cheery, simple, light, or common a word for the anticipation bound up with being together again with a lady as ill as Frau Clavdia Chauchat. It is possible that the reader may be inclined to see only such expressions, that is, cheery and common ones, as fitting and proper for the emotional life of a person like Hans Castorp; but we would like to remind the reader that as a young man of reason and conscience he could not simply "delight" in watching and being near Frau Chauchat; and since we must know, we can unequivocally state that had this word been suggested to him, he would have shrugged and cast it aside.

Indeed, he was getting to be very particular about how he did express himself—a characteristic well worth noting. As he walked around, his cheeks flushed with dry fever, he hummed to himself, sang to himself, because in his present state he was sensitive to all things musical. He hummed a little song that he had heard sung in a light soprano voice, who knew where or when, at some party or charity concert, and that had turned up now in his memory, a gentle bit of nonsense that began:

> How oft it thrills me just to hear
> You say some simple word,

and he was about to add:

> That spoken from your lips, my dear,
> Does leave my heart so stirred!

and suddenly he shrugged and said, "Ridiculous!" and cast aside the delicate little song as tasteless and insipidly sentimental—rejecting it, however, with a certain austere melancholy. Some young man who had "given his heart," as they say, given it calmly, legitimately, and with a promising view to the future, to a healthy little goose down there in the flatlands—such a young man might have found satisfaction and taken pleasure in such a heartfelt song, abandoning himself to his legitimate, promising, reasonable, and ultimately cheerful emotions. When applied to him and his relationship with Madame Chauchat, however—and the word "relationship" must be credited to Hans Castorp, we refuse any responsibility for it—such verses were most decidedly inappropriate. Lying in his lounge chair, he found himself moved to pronounce upon them an aesthetic verdict of "Silly!"—and broke off now, turning up his nose, although he knew of nothing more suitable to replace them with.

He did take satisfaction in one thing, however, as he lay there listening to his heart, his physical heart, pounding rapidly and audibly in the stillness—the stillness that was prescribed by house rules and reigned over the entire Berghof during the main rest cure of the day. His heart was pounding insistently, urgently, the way it had done almost constantly ever since he had arrived here; and yet of late that did not upset Hans Castorp as it had the first few days. One could no longer say that it thudded on its own accord, for no reason, and without any connection to his soul. There was a connection now, or at least it would not have been difficult to establish one—a justifiable emotion could easily be assigned to his body's overwrought activity. Hans Castorp needed only to think of Frau Chauchat—and he did think of her—and his heart had a suitable emotion to make it pound.

Growing Anxiety/Two Grandfathers and a Twilight Boat Ride

THE WEATHER was vile—in that regard Hans Castorp had no luck with his short vacation in these climes. It wasn't snowing, exactly, but it had been raining heavily for days; ugly, thick fog filled the valley, where thunderstorms raged and rolled in knotty reverberations—absurdly superfluous, really, considering it was so cold that the heat had been turned on in the dining hall.

"What a shame," Joachim said. "I had thought we would have breakfast up on Schatzalp or wherever at least once. But it looks as if it's not to be. Let's hope your last week will be better."

But Hans Castorp replied, "No matter. I'm not itching for another excursion. My first didn't turn out all that well. It does me more good just to live each day as it comes, without much variety. That's for those who spend years up here. But with my three weeks, what do I need variety for?"

And that was how it was—he kept himself occupied, felt his days were full enough as things stood. Whatever hopes he might have were just as easily fulfilled or disappointed here as on some Schatzalp or other. It wasn't boredom that bothered him; on the contrary, he began to fear that the end of his stay was winging its way toward him. His second week was passing quickly now; two-thirds of his time would soon be gone, and once the last third began, he would have to start thinking of packing. For Hans Castorp, the initial refreshment of his sense of time was long since past; the days began to fly now, and yet each one of them was stretched by renewed expectations and swollen with silent, private experiences. Yes, time is a puzzling thing, there is something about it that is hard to explain.

Is it necessary to spell out those private experiences, which both weighed down Hans Castorp's days and gave them wings? But everyone knows them: flimsy, tender, perfectly normal experiences that would have taken the same course even in a more reasonable and promising situation, where the sentimental little song about "how oft it thrills me" would have been more applicable.

It was impossible for Madame Chauchat not to notice at least something of the threads strung between a certain table and her own; and it was definitely part of Hans Castorp's uninhibited plan that she should notice something, indeed as much as possible. We call his plan uninhibited, because he was fully aware of just how irrational his situation was. But then, anyone in his condition, or incipient condition, will want the other side to be aware of it, even if there is no reason or common sense in doing so. That is how we humans are.

After Frau Chauchat had turned toward his table two or three times at meals, drawn either quite by chance or by some magnetic effect, and each time found her eyes met by Hans Castorp's, she looked his way a fourth time on purpose—and met his eyes again. The fifth time, she did not catch him looking at her; he was not on guard at just that moment. And yet he immediately felt she was looking at him and turned his gaze so eagerly to her that she smiled and glanced away. Her smile filled him with apprehension and delight. If it meant she thought him childish, she was mistaken. But he definitely had to refine his tactics. And so at the sixth opportunity, when he felt, sensed, knew somewhere deep within, that she was looking his way, he pretended to stare with emphatic distaste at a pimply lady who had stepped up to his table to chat with the great-aunt; he held his eyes fixed on her for a good two or three minutes, never yielding until he was certain that the Kirghiz eyes across the way had given up—a strange bit of playacting that Frau Chauchat could easily have seen through, indeed was meant to see through, so that Hans Castorp's refinement and self-control would give her pause. But something happens now: in a break between courses, Frau Chauchat turns around nonchalantly to survey the room. Hans Castorp has been on guard. Their eyes meet. And as they look at each other—the sick woman peering at him with vague mockery, Hans Castorp staring back fiercely, even clenching his teeth as he holds firm—her napkin begins to slip from her lap to the floor. With an anxious start, she reaches for it; he, too, is unnerved, is pulled up halfway from his chair, and is about to dash blindly across eight yards and around an intervening table to come to her aid, as if it would be a catastrophe for her napkin to touch the ground. She manages to grab it just before it reaches the stone tiles. But in that stretched and bent position and still holding the napkin by one corner, she scowls, evidently annoyed at her unreasonable little burst of panic, for which she apparently blames him. Now she glances his way again, notices his wide eyes and the way he is poised to leap—and she turns away with a smile.

The event left Hans Castorp triumphant, absolutely exuberant. But it came not without its setback, because Madame Chauchat did not turn his way even once for two whole days, for ten long meals—indeed, refrained from her custom of "presenting" herself to her audience as she entered the dining hall. That was hard. But since such acts of omission were without doubt committed for his sake, there was clearly a connection between the two of them now, even if it had taken a negative form; and that would have to suffice.

He had come to realize that Joachim had been quite right when he said that it was not all that easy to make acquaintances here, except for tablemates. During the one brief hour after supper—and sometimes that shrank to a mere twenty minutes—when there was some regular social interchange, without exception Madame Chauchat would take her seat at the back of the little salon, an area reserved apparently for the Good Russian table, where she was joined by the gentleman with the concave chest, the droll frizzy-haired girl, silent Dr. Blumenkohl, and the two hunch-shouldered youths. And Joachim was always trying to urge an early departure so as not to cut short his evening rest cure, as he said, and perhaps for other reasons of regimen, which he did not go into but which Hans Castorp guessed and respected. We accused Hans Castorp before of being uninhibited, but whatever the aim of his desires, a social acquaintance with Frau Chauchat was not what he had in mind, and he was in fundamental agreement with those circumstances that worked against it. The vague, tense connection that his looks and actions had established between him and the Russian woman was of an extrasocial nature, entailing no obligations, indeed intended not to entail them. From his standpoint, a considerable amount of social distance suited their connection, but the fact that thoughts of "Clavdia" set his heart pounding was certainly not a sufficient reason for a grandson of Hans Lorenz Castorp to have his firmly held convictions shaken. In reality—that is, in any sense beyond this secret connection with her—he could not possibly have anything to do with a strange woman who lived her life at various resorts, separated from her husband and yet never wearing a wedding ring, who had bad posture, slammed doors behind her, rolled her bread into little pills, and doubtless chewed her fingernails; deep chasms separated her existence from his, and he could never have defended her against criticisms that he himself acknowledged. Quite understandably, Hans Castorp was a man without any personal arrogance; but an arrogance of a more general and traditional sort was written on his face and in the drowsy look in his eyes. It was the source of the sense of superiority that he could not and would not throw off when considering Frau Chauchat's character and person. Strangely enough, it was the day he heard Frau Chauchat speak German that this general sense of superiority became especially vivid, that he was perhaps even conscious of it for the first time. It was after a meal, she was standing in the dining room with both hands in the pockets of her sweater, trying to carry on a conversation with another patient, an acquaintance from the lounging arcade presumably, struggling in a most charming way, as Hans Castorp could hear, to speak German; and he suddenly discovered a pride in his own mother tongue that he had never known before—and, simultaneously, an urge to sacrifice that pride to the enchantment that filled him at the sound of her winsomely bungled, broken stammering.

In a word, Hans Castorp saw his silent relationship to this one careless person among all the others up here as a vacation adventure, which had no claim before the court of reason—or of his own reasonable conscience—and that was primarily because Frau Chauchat was sick, listless, feverish, and worm-eaten deep inside, a condition that was closely bound up with the dubious nature of her whole being and that itself contributed strongly to Hans Castorp's sense of caution and need to keep his distance. No, it never entered his mind to seek out a real acquaintanceship. As for the rest, it would all be over with no consequences, for better or worse, in another week and a half, when he would enter training with Tunder and Wilms.

For the present, however, he found himself beginning to see the emotions, tensions, satisfactions, and disappointments growing from his tender relationship to this patient as the true purpose and meaning of his vacation, to live entirely for them and allow his mood to be dependent on their success. Conditions here were most beneficial for encouraging him, because people lived together in a restricted area and followed a rigid schedule mandatory for all. Granted, Frau Chauchat's room was on a different floor—the second—from his own, and she took her rest cures, as Hans Castorp learned from Fräulein Engelhart, in the general lounging area located on the roof, the same one where Captain Miklosich had turned off the lights recently. But the possibility, indeed inevitability, of meeting her presented itself at each of the day's five meals and on countless other routine occasions from morning till evening. And Hans Castorp thought that was marvelous—as was also the fact that life here had no cares or worries to block the view. At the same time, however, there was something suffocating about being locked up in a box together with auspicious chance.

And yet he did help things along a bit, by putting his mind to the task and figuring out how best to improve his luck. Since Frau Chauchat normally arrived late for meals, he made a point of being late himself, so that he could meet her on the way. He dawdled in his room and wasn't ready when Joachim came by to fetch him, told his cousin to go on ahead, said he would catch up. Following the advice of instinct, he would wait the few moments he thought necessary and then hurry down to the second floor; but instead of continuing down the same set of stairs, he would follow the corridor almost to the far end, to a second stairway, which was very close to a door he had come to know quite well—room 7. And at every step of the way along this hall connecting the two sets of stairs, there was a chance that one particular door might open at any moment— and so it did, on repeated occasions, slamming shut behind Frau Chauchat, who would emerge soundlessly and glide soundlessly toward the stairs. She might precede him, tucking her hair with her hand, or Hans Castorp might precede her, and then he would feel her eyes on his back, which made his legs cramp and caused pins and needles up and down his spine. But playing the role to the hilt, he would pretend not to know she was even there, as if he led his life in solitary, stout independence. He would bury his hands in his coat pockets and roll his shoulders pointlessly or clear his throat noisily while pounding his chest with his fist—all to proclaim his indifference.

On two occasions he carried this bit of roguery even further. After taking his seat at the table, he patted himself with both hands and said in dismayed annoyance, "I knew it—I've forgotten my handkerchief. That means I'll have to go back upstairs again." Which he did—just so that he and "Clavdia" could meet *head-on*, which was something quite different, more dangerous and more intensely alluring than when she walked before or behind him. The first time he tried this maneuver, she measured him with her eyes, from top to bottom, quite brazenly and without the least embarrassment, while still some distance off; but as she drew nearer she turned her face away indifferently and walked right by him. He could not give the results of this meeting a very high rating. The second time, however, she looked directly at him, and not just from a distance; she looked at him the whole time, gazed firmly at him during the entire encounter, scowling just a little, and as they passed one another, she turned her head toward him—and his blood ran cold. Not that we should pity him—he had not wanted it any other way and had arranged the whole affair himself. But this meeting had a powerful effect as it was happening—and afterward, too, because only when it was all over did he see quite clearly how it had been. Never had he observed Frau Chauchat's face so close up, with every detail plainly visible: he could have counted every strand of reddish-blond hair—each with a slight metallic sheen— that had come free from the simple braid wound around her head. Only a few handbreadths separated his face from hers, its features so extraordinary and yet familiar to him for so long now—and that face spoke to him like nothing in the world. It was both foreign and full of character (but then, only things foreign to us always seem to have character), an exotic and mysterious look of the North, demanding you probe further, for its features and proportions were not easily fathomed. Probably the most distinctive characteristic was the prominent, high cheekbones: they pushed against her unusually wide-set eyes, flattening and lifting them at a subtle slant, and at the same time they were the reason for the soft concavity of her cheeks, which was, then, the direct cause for the slightly voluptuous pout to her lips. And then there were the eyes themselves, those narrow and absolutely magical (or so they seemed to Hans Castorp), Kirghiz-shaped eyes, bluish-gray or grayish-blue like distant mountains, which from time to time, in certain sidelong glances, when gazing at nothing in particular, could darken, almost melt, to a veiled dusky look—Clavdia's eyes, which had examined him brazenly and somewhat sternly from close up, and which in shape, color, and expression so amazingly and frighteningly resembled those of Pribislav Hippe. "Resembled" was not the right word—they were the same eyes; and the breadth of the upper half of the face, the flattened nose, everything, including the flush of the white skin, the healthy color of the cheeks—which in Frau Chauchat's case only feigned health and as with all the people up here was merely the superficial by-product of rest cures in the open air—it was all exactly like Pribislav, who had looked no different when they had passed one another in the schoolyard.

It was thrilling in every sense of the word. Hans Castorp was inspired by this meeting, and at the same time he sensed something like a growing anxiety, much like that suffocating feeling of being locked up in a box together with auspicious chance; what was more, the fact that the long-forgotten Pribislav had reappeared up here as Frau Chauchat and had looked at him with Kirghiz eyes made him feel as if he were locked up together with something inevitable and inescapable—an inescapability that both cheered and alarmed him. It filled him with hope; and at the same time an eerie, even threatening sense of helplessness stole over young Hans Castorp, setting in motion a vague, instinctual groping, a search for help—one might say he was looking about deep inside himself for advice and support. He thought of various people, one after the other, hoping the mere thought of them might prove beneficial somehow.

There was Joachim, good, upright Joachim there at his side, whose eyes had taken on such a sad expression in these last months, and who at times would shrug in that dismissive, vehement way he had never, ever done before—Joachim with his Blue Henry in his pocket, as Frau Stöhr liked to call the item, with that willfully shameless look on her face that shocked Hans Castorp every time. There was honest Joachim, then, who pestered and badgered Director Behrens so that he could return to the "plains," to the "flatlands"—as people up here called the world of the healthy with a gentle, but clear trace of contempt—and take up the military duties he so longed for. And both to do that and to save time (which people simply wasted up here), he had from the first been as conscientious as possible in doing his rest-cure duty—doing it, no doubt, in order to recuperate as soon as possible, but as Hans Castorp sometimes thought he could sense, doing it just a little for the sake of the cure itself, which ultimately was a sort of service like any other, since doing one's duty was doing one's duty. And so each evening, after perhaps fifteen minutes, Joachim would propose that they leave the social gathering for their rest cure; which was fine, since his military scruples made up somewhat for Hans Castorp's civilian attitudes, for he would probably have preferred to linger there, for no good reason and with no prospects, except a view to the little Russian salon. But Joachim was so insistent about cutting the party short that there had to be another, unspoken reason—one that Hans Castorp had come to understand only too well ever since he had realized the precise meaning of Joachim's blotchy pallor and the peculiar, woeful way he wrenched his mouth at certain moments. Because Marusya, laughter-loving Marusya, with the little ruby on her pretty finger, her orange-blossom perfume, and her prominent, worm-eaten chest, was usually present at the gathering as well; and Hans Castorp understood that it was this circumstance that drove Joachim away, precisely because it held such a strong, terrible attraction for him. Was Joachim "locked up" here, too? Was it even more narrow and suffocating for him than for Hans Castorp himself? Marusya, after all, with her little orange-scented handkerchief, sat down at the same table with them five times a day. In any case, Joachim was much too preoccupied with himself to have been of any real inner help to Hans Castorp. His flight from the festivities each evening seemed honorable enough, but the effect was anything but calming; and then, too, there were certain moments when it seemed as if Joachim's good example at doing one's rest-cure duty—and even his expert introduction to its procedures—had a dubious side as well.

Hans Castorp had not been up here for two weeks, but it seemed much longer to him, and the Berghof's daily schedule, which Joachim observed so dutifully, had begun to take on the stamp of sacred, axiomatic inviolability in his eyes as well, so that when viewed from up here, life in the flatlands below seemed strange and perverse. He had already gained great proficiency in manipulating his two blankets to form a smooth, regular package, turning himself into a veritable mummy for his cold-weather rest cures. It would not be long before he would be as skilled as Joachim in the art of wrapping them around himself in the prescribed fashion, and the thought that no one in the plains down there knew anything about the rules of the art seemed almost amazing. Yes, that was peculiar—but at the same time Hans Castorp was astonished that he found it peculiar, and the uneasy feeling that had sent him searching for advice and support rose up inside him again.

He was forced to think of Director Behrens, of the advice he had given him *sine pecunia* to live the life of a patient and even keep track of his temperature—and of Settembrini, who had thrown back his head and laughed out loud at the advice and then quoted something from *The Magic Flute*. So he gave thinking about these two men a try, just to see if that would do him any good. Director Behrens was a man whose hair had turned white, he could have been Hans Castorp's father. He was in charge of the sanatorium, its highest authority—and Hans Castorp's heart felt a restive longing for paternal authority. And yet try as he would, he found he could not regard the director with a child's trust. The man had buried his wife here, the grief of it had even made him rather odd for a while, and then he had stayed on, both because he felt bound to her grave and because he had become slightly infected himself. But was he over it now? Was he healthy and single-mindedly bent on making others healthy so that they could quickly return to the flatlands and take up their duties there? His cheeks were always purple, and without doubt he looked as if he had a fever. But that might be an illusion, his color could be the result of the air up here. Hans Castorp himself had felt a dry flush, day in, day out, without having a fever—at least as far as he could judge without a thermometer. True, when you listened to the director talk you might sometimes think he had a temperature—there was something not quite right about the way he spoke, it sounded so brash and jovial and easygoing, but there was also something strange about it, something over-wrought, especially when you considered those purplish cheeks and watery eyes, which looked as if he were still weeping for his wife. Hans Castorp remembered what Settembrini had said about the director's "melancholy" and tendency to "vice," even calling him a "confused soul." That might have been malice or hot air; but nevertheless he did not feel particularly fortified by the thought of Director Behrens.

And then, of course, there was Settembrini himself—naysayer, windbag, and *homo humanus*, as he called himself—who had rebuked him with a lot of taut words for calling sickness and stupidity a contradiction and a dilemma for human emotions. What about him? Was it beneficial to think of him? Hans Castorp recalled quite well how in several of the exceedingly vivid dreams that filled his nights up here, he had been annoyed by the Italian's delicate, dry smile, the mocking curl of the lip just below where the full moustache swept handsomely upward, how he had berated him as an organ-grinder because he was in the way up here. But that had been a dream, and the waking Hans Castorp was a different man, less uninhibited than in his dreams. Things might be different awake; maybe in looking for inner support he would do well to give Settembrini's novel nature a try—rebellious and critical, though sentimental and bombastic, too. He had called himself a pedagogue, after all; apparently he wanted to exert some influence; and young Hans Castorp craved to be influenced; but, of course, that did not mean he was going to let Settembrini run his affairs—or that he was going to pack his bags and leave early as the fellow had recently suggested in all seriousness.

"*Placet experiri*," he said to himself with a smile, because he understood that much Latin at least, without having to call himself a *homo humanus*. And so he turned an eye to Settembrini and reviewed eagerly, but cautiously and attentively, too, all the things the man had favored him with at their various encounters—on regular constitutionals to the bench on the mountain slope, or when they happened to meet on the way down to Platz, or on other occasions, too, as when, for example, Settembrini would be the first to get up after a meal, stroll through the dining hall with its seven tables, and, contrary to all customs and usages, stop to visit awhile with the cousins at their table. He would stand there in his checked trousers, a toothpick between his lips, assume his graceful pose with his ankles crossed, and chatter away, gesticulating now and then with the toothpick. Or he would pull up a chair and sit down at one corner, either between Hans Castorp and the teacher or between Hans Castorp and Miss Robinson, and watch his new tablemates consume a dessert he had apparently turned down.

"I beg admission to this noble circle," he would say, shaking both cousins' hands and including all the others in his bow. "It's my beer-brewer yonder—not to mention the depressing sight of Madame Beer-brewer. But as for Herr Magnus himself—he has just delivered a lecture on ethnic psychology. Would you like to hear? 'Our beloved Germany is one huge barracks, granted. But a great deal of hard work went into it, and I would not trade our sturdy honesty for the fine manners of other nations. What good are fine manners if I'm being cheated up one side and down the other?' In that sort of style. I'm at the breaking point. And then across from me sits a poor creature with graveyard blossoms on her cheeks, an old maid from Transylvania, who goes on endlessly about her 'brother-in-law,' a gentleman whom no one knows, nor wishes to know. In short, I could not take any more—I bolted."

"And so hastily vacated the primroses," Frau Stöhr said. "It's easy to see why."

"Precisely," Settembrini cried. "The primroses! I see there's quite a different wind blowing here—no doubt of it, I've found the right shop. And so I hastily vacated them—what a way you have with words, Frau Stöhr! Might I presume to inquire as to the state of your health?"

Frau Stöhr's affectations were dreadful to behold. "Good God," she said, "it's always the same, as the gentleman knows himself. One takes two steps forward and three back—and when one has served one's five months, the boss comes and adds another six to your sentence. Ah, the tortures of Tantalus. You push and push, and you think you've reached the top of the hill . . ."

"Oh, how prettily you express it. You've finally put a little variety into poor Tantalus's life. You've let him roll the famous marble boulder for a change. I call that genuine kindness. But what is this I've heard, madam, about mysterious things happening to you? There are stories about a *doppelgänger* and astral bodies. I would never have believed such things until now, but what I hear you've experienced quite perplexes me. . . ."

"It seems the gentleman is trying to reticule me."

"Most assuredly not—I wouldn't think of it! But please, first set my mind at rest about a certain dark side of your life, and then we can talk about reticules. I was taking a little walk yesterday evening between nine-thirty and ten, and I happened to glance up along the balconies, and the electric lamp on yours was glimmering in the darkness. You were, therefore, taking your rest cure, just as duty, reason, and regulation demand. 'There our lovely patient lies,' I said to myself, 'faithfully observing the rules so that she may return speedily to the arms of Herr Stöhr.' But what did I hear a few minutes ago? That at the same hour you were seen at the *cinematographo*"—Herr Settembrini accented the word on its fourth syllable—"at the *cinematographo* in the arcade of the Kurhaus, and afterward as well in the pastry shop, over dessert wine and some sort of meringues, and indeed . . ."

Frau Stöhr wiggled her shoulders and tittered into her napkin, poked an elbow in the ribs of both Joachim Ziemssen and silent Dr. Blumenkohl, gave a sly, intimate wink—all varied displays of her asinine smugness. In order to deceive the authorities, she was in the habit of putting her nightstand lamp out on her balcony each evening, then stealing away to amuse herself in the English quarter down in town. Meanwhile, her husband waited for her in Cannstatt. Nor was she the only patient who engaged in this practice.

"And indeed," Settembrini continued, "you partook of these meringues in the company of a gentleman. And of whom? Of Captain Miklosich from Bucharest. I have been assured that he wears a corset, but good God, that is of little or no consequence here. I implore you, madam— where were you? There must be two of you! Or at the least, you fell asleep and while the earthly part of your nature held its solitary rest cure, the spiritual part was making merry in the company of Captain Miklosich over foamy meringues."

Frau Stöhr wriggled and squirmed as if someone were tickling her.

"One really cannot say whether one might not prefer it the other way around," Settembrini said, "so that you could have enjoyed your meringues alone and taken your rest cure with Captain Miklosich."

"Tee-hee-hee . . ."

"Have the ladies and gentlemen heard what happened the day before yesterday?" he asked out of the blue. "Someone was snatched away—by the Devil, or to be more accurate, his mother, an energetic lady. I rather liked her. It was young Schneermann, Anton Schneermann, who sat up there at the same table with Mademoiselle Kleefeld. As you see, his chair is empty. It will soon be occupied again, I'm not worried about that, but

Anton is gone on the wings of the storm, like a shot! before he knew what hit him. He had been here a year and a half—and was only sixteen himself. And another six months had just been added. And what happens? I don't know who passed the word on, but at any rate Madame Schneermann got wind that her little son was leading a life *in Baccho et ceteris.* She shows up here quite unannounced, a matron three heads taller than I, white-haired and hot-tempered, doesn't say a word, but gives our Herr Anton a few quick boxes on the ear, grabs him by the collar, and sets him on the train. 'If he's going to the dogs,' says she, 'he can just as well do it down below.' And home they go."

Everyone within earshot began to laugh, because Herr Settembrini had a droll way of telling stories. For all his mocking and criticizing of the social life of people up here, he kept up with the latest gossip. He knew the names and more or less the general circumstances of every new arrival; he could report that yesterday somebody or other had undergone a rib resection and had it on best authority that beginning in autumn no one with a temperature above 101.3 degrees would be admitted. The night before, or so he said, the little dog kept by Madame Kapatsoulias from Mytilene had sat on the emergency button on her nightstand, which resulted in considerable commotion and tumult, particularly since Madame Kapatsoulias was not alone, but in the company of Judge Düstmund from Friedrichshafen. Even Dr. Blumenkohl had to laugh at the story. Pretty Marusya almost choked on her orange-scented handkerchief, and Frau Stöhr began to shriek, holding both hands to her left breast.

But Lodovico Settembrini spoke, too, about himself and his origins when he was alone with the cousins—during walks or at the evening gatherings or after the noonday meal when a large majority of patients had already left the dining hall and the three gentlemen remained seated at one end of the table for a while as dining attendants cleared dishes and Hans Castorp smoked a Maria Mancini, which by the third week had regained some of its flavor. Cautious, attentive, puzzled, but willing to let himself be influenced, he listened to the Italian's tales, which opened up a strange and very new world for him.

Settembrini spoke about his grandfather, who had been a lawyer in Milan, but above all a great patriot, playing a considerable role as a political agitator, orator, and contributor to various periodicals—he, too, a naysayer like his grandson, though one who went about it all in grander, bolder style. For whereas Lodovico, as he himself reported with bitterness, found himself restricted to deriding life and manners at the International Sanatorium Berghof, to offering his sardonic criticism and protesting in the name of beautiful, vigorous humanity, his grandfather had given governments trouble, had conspired against Austria and the Holy Alliance, which in those days held his dismembered fatherland in the grip of darkest bondage, and had been a zealous member of certain secret societies that had spread throughout Italy—a Carbonaro, as Settembrini suddenly declared, lowering his voice, as if it were still dangerous even now to speak the word. In short—at least as he was presented to the cousins in the tales of his grandson—this Giuseppe Settembrini was a shadowy, passionate, and incendiary figure, a ringleader of conspiracy; and despite the polite pains they took to show their respect, they did not quite succeed in banishing from their faces an expression of apprehension and aversion, indeed of outright disgust. True, things were different then—the stories they heard now were from long ago, almost a century past; it was history, and from history, at least ancient history, they had learned in theory about the type of person presented here—a man of courage, uncompromising in his hatred of tyrants and consumed by the fire of liberty—though they had never thought they would come into such direct human contact with one. And then, too, this grandfather's seditious conspiracy, or so they were told, had been bound up with the love of his fatherland, which he hoped to see free and united—indeed, his subversive activities were the fruit and outcome of that honorable affection; and however strange this mixture of rebellion and patriotism might seem to both cousins (accustomed as they were to equating patriotic feelings with preservation of the established order), they did have to admit in private that as things had stood back then, rebellion might very well have been commensurate with civic virtue and sober loyalty with idle unconcern about matters of public order.

But Settembrini's grandfather had been not only an Italian patriot, but also a fellow citizen and brother-in-arms with all peoples thirsting for freedom. For after the failure of a certain plot to overthrow the state in Turin, in which he had been involved both in word and deed, he very narrowly escaped Prince Metternich's hirelings and spent the years of his banishment fighting and bleeding for a constitution in Spain and the independence of the Hellenic peoples. It was in Greece that Settembrini's father had first seen the light of the world—which probably explained why he was such a great humanist and lover of classical antiquity—born, by the way, of a mother with German blood, a girl whom Giuseppe had married in Switzerland and taken along with him throughout the course of his adventures. Later, after ten years of exile, he was able to return to his native land and work as a lawyer in Milan, but that in no way prevented him from continuing to call—with voice and pen, in verse and prose— for the freedom and unity of his country, to draft revolutionary programs with passionate autocratic élan and to proclaim in a lucid style that liberated peoples must unite and forge their universal happiness. Grandson Settembrini mentioned one detail that made a special impression on young Hans Castorp: Grandfather Giuseppe had worn only black when appearing among his fellow citizens, because, as he said, he was in mourning for Italy, his fatherland, which languished in misery and bondage. As had been the case with several items in the story, this piece of information reminded Hans Castorp of his own grandfather, who likewise had worn black all the years his grandson had known him, although for reasons profoundly different from those of this grandfather here; Hans Castorp thought now of those old-fashioned clothes, the makeshift adaptation by which Hans Lorenz Castorp's true nature, belonging to a time long past, had indicated its dislike of the present, until in death he had solemnly returned to the form appropriate to him—in Spanish ruff. Those had indeed been two spectacularly different grandfathers! And as Hans Castorp thought about it, he closed his eyes tight and shook his head cautiously, which could just as easily have been taken as an expression of admiration for Giuseppe Settembrini as of dismay and rejection. And he honestly did attempt not to judge what was alien to him, but simply to define and compare. He was back in the "den" and saw Hans Lorenz's narrow head bent down over the pale golden circle of the baptismal bowl, · that abiding, mutable heirloom; and he saw him round his lips to form the syllable "great," that pious, somber sound that reminded you of places where as you walked you fell into a reverential, forward rocking motion. And he saw Giuseppe Settembrini—the tricolor in one hand, a swinging saber in the other, black eyes turned heavenward to seal his vow—at the head of a troop of revolutionaries storming the phalanx of despotism. Each had his beauty and honor, he thought, trying all the harder to be fair because he knew his own personal or partly personal biases. Grandfather Settembrini had struggled for political rights—but his own grandfather, or at least his ancestors, had originally possessed all those rights, which over the course of four centuries the rabble had wrested from them by force and slogans. And so they had both worn black, the grandfather in the North and the one in the South, and both for the purpose of drawing a strict line between themselves and the evil present. But the one had done so to show his reverence for the past and to honor death, to which his whole being already belonged; the other, in contrast, had done so out of rebellion and a belief in irreverent progress. "Yes, those were two worlds, two opposing points of the compass," Hans Castorp thought, and as Herr Settembrini went on talking, he stood there halfway between them, so to speak, casting a critical eye first on the one and then the other; and it seemed to him that he had experienced all this once before. He remembered a lonely boat ride on a lake in Holstein several years before—in late summer, at twilight. It had been around seven o'clock, the sun had set, an almost full moon had already risen above the wooded shore to the east. And for ten minutes, while Hans Castorp rowed across the still water, it all became a baffling, dreamlike scene. Bright daylight reigned in the west—glassy, cool, definitive light; but if he turned his head, he found himself gazing into utterly magical moonlit night draped in a web of mist. This strange condition was held in balance for almost a quarter of an hour before it tipped in favor of night and the moon, and all the while Hans Castorp's dazzled and bewildered eyes moved in serene amazement between one landscape and luminary and the other, from day to night and out of night back into day. It all came back to him now.

Given the kind of life lawyer Settembrini had led and all his extensive activities, he could not have been a great scholar of the law, or so Hans Castorp thought. But the universal principle of the law had inspired him from infancy on, or so his grandson would have them believe; and although Hans Castorp was not feeling all that clearheaded as his organism strained to deal with one of the Berghof's six-course meals, he struggled to understand what Settembrini might mean by calling this principle "the source of freedom and progress." As for the latter concept, until now Hans Castorp had understood it as something like the improvement of hoists and cranes during the nineteenth century; and he discovered that Herr Settembrini had no low opinion himself of such things, nor had his grandfather for that matter. Indeed, the Italian paid high tribute to his listeners' fatherland for two inventions: gunpowder, which had turned feudalism's suits of armor into junk, and the printing press, which had made possible the democratic propagation of ideas, or rather, the propagation of democratic ideas. And so in that regard, and insofar as the past was concerned, he had praise for Germany, although to be fair he thought his own nation should be given the palm for having unfurled the banner of enlightenment, culture, and freedom while other nations had still lain sleeping in superstition and bondage. But although he paid due honor to technology and transportation, Hans Castorp's own field of labor—as he had, for instance, on that first day beside the bench up on the slope—he seemed to do so not for the sake of those forces themselves, but rather for their significance in helping humankind reach moral perfection, for, as he explained, he happily ascribed such significance to them. As technology brought nature increasingly under its control, he said, by creating new lines of communication—developing networks of roads and telegraph lines—and by triumphing over climatic conditions, it was also proving to be the most dependable means by which to bring nations closer together, furthering their knowledge of one another, paving the way for people-to-people exchanges, destroying prejudices, and leading at last to the universal brotherhood of nations. The human race had come out of darkness, fear, and hate, but now it was moving forward and upward along a shining road toward a final state of understanding, inner illumination, goodness, and happiness—and technology was the most useful vehicle for traveling that road. But as he spoke, he brought together, in a *single* breath, categories that until now Hans Castorp had been accustomed to think of as widely divergent. "Technology and morality," he said. And then he actually spoke about the Savior of the Christians, who had first revealed the principle of equality and brotherhood; the propagation of that same principle had been considerably advanced by the printing press, and finally the great French Revolution had raised it to the status of law. But in fact, it all sounded most decidedly confused to Hans Castorp, though for reasons not quite apparent to him and despite Herr Settembrini's having put it in clear and taut words. Once, only once, just at the beginning of the prime of his life, the Italian said, had his grandfather rejoiced with all his heart—in the days of the July Revolution in Paris. He had publicly proclaimed that all men would one day place those three days in Paris alongside the six days of Creation. And at that a flabbergasted Hans Castorp could not help banging his hand on the table. For someone to place three days in the summer of 1830, during which the Parisians had written a new constitution for themselves, alongside the six in which the Lord God had divided the waters of the firmament and created great lights in the heavens and the flowers, trees, fish, birds, and life itself— that really seemed a bit much. And afterward, when he was alone with his cousin Joachim, he expressly let it be known that he found it more than a bit much, indeed absolutely offensive.

But he was willing to let himself be influenced, in the sense that it was pleasant to experiment, and so he reined in the protests that piety and good taste would have raised against the Settembrinian order of things and decided that what seemed blasphemous to him might be termed bold and what he found in bad taste might, at least in those days and under those conditions, be considered the excesses of a high-minded and noble nature—as, for example, when Grandfather Settembrini called barricades the "people's throne" or declared it necessary to "consecrate the citizen's pike on the altar of humanity."

Hans Castorp knew why he listened to Herr Settembrini, not in so many words, but he knew. It was partly out of a sense of duty—but it was also the irresponsibility of the vacationer and visitor who does not wish to harden himself against new impressions and takes things as they come, well aware that tomorrow or the day after he will spread his wings and return to his accustomed routine. But conscience—or more precisely, the qualms of a conscience uneasy for some reason—demanded that he listen to the Italian, whether he was sitting there with one leg crossed over the other, puffing on his Maria Mancini, or all three of them were on their way back from the English quarter, climbing the hill to the Berghof.

According to the outline Settembrini presented, two principles were locked in combat for the world: might and right, tyranny and freedom, superstition and knowledge, the law of obduracy and the law of ferment, change, and progress. One could call the first the Asiatic principle, the other the European, for Europe was the continent of rebellion, critique, and transforming action, whereas the continent to the east embodied inertia and inactivity. There was no doubt which of these two forces would gain the victory—that of enlightenment, of reasoned advancement toward perfection. Because human progress was always gathering up new nations in the course of its brilliant advance, conquering new continents—indeed all of Europe itself—and had even started to press on into Asia. Yet there was much to be done before total victory, and great and noble efforts would have to be made by those to whom the light had been passed on, if that day were ever to come when monarchies and religions would at last collapse in those European nations that, truth to tell, had experienced neither an eighteenth century nor a 1789. But that day would come, Settembrini said, smiling delicately beneath his moustache—it would come, if not on the feet of doves, then on the pinions of eagles, and would burst as the dawn of universal brotherhood under the emblem of reason, science, and justice; it would bring about a new Holy Alliance of bourgeois democracies, the shining antithesis of that thrice-infamous alliance of princes and ministers whom Grandfather Giuseppe had declared his personal enemies—in a word, the Republic of the World. But to achieve this goal, it was necessary above all to strike at the Asiatic principle of bondage and obduracy at its vital center point, at the very nerve of resistance—in Vienna. One must deal a fatal blow to Austria and crush her, first to avenge past wrongs and second to open the way for the rule of justice and happiness on earth.

This final twist to the melodious torrent of Settembrini's argument did not interest Hans Castorp at all. He did not like it, in fact, and every time it reappeared he found it embarrassing, as if it were some testy personal or nationalistic prejudice—not to mention the reaction of Joachim Ziemssen, who would refuse to listen whenever the Italian started down that road, would scowl and look away, sometimes diverting the conversation or reminding them that the duties of the rest cure called. Indeed, Hans Castorp did not feel he was required to pay any regard to such aberrations, evidently they lay beyond the limits set by an uneasy conscience demanding that he at least try to be influenced—and its demands were indeed audible, so audible that whenever Herr Settembrini would sit down with them or join them in the open air, he would ask the Italian to expand on his ideas.

These ideas, both as ideals and efforts of the will, Settembrini remarked, had been handed down as a tradition in his family. Three generations had dedicated their lives and intellects to them—grandfather, father, and son, each in his own fashion, the father no less than Grandfather Giuseppe, though unlike him, he had not been a political agitator and freedom-fighter, but a quiet and gentle scholar, a humanist at his desk. But what was humanism? Love of humankind, nothing more, and so it, too, was political, it, too, was a rebellion against everything that had soiled and degraded the ideal of humanity. Humanism had been accused of exaggerating the importance of form; but it cultivated beautiful form purely for the sake of the dignity of man—in brilliant antithesis to the Middle Ages, which had sunk not only into misanthropy and superstition, but also into ignominious formlessness. From the very first, his father had fought for the cause of humanity, for earthly interests, for freedom of thought and the pursuit of happiness, and had firmly believed that we can leave heaven to the birds. Prometheus! He had been the first humanist and was identical with *Satana*, whom Carducci had apostrophized in his hymn. Oh, good God, if only the cousins could have come to Bologna and heard that old enemy of the Church taunting and inveighing against the Christian sensitivities of the Romantics. Against Manzoni's *Sacred Hymns*. Against the shadowy moonshine of the *Romanticismo*, which he had compared to "Luna, that pallid nun of heaven." *Per Bacco*, what an exquisite delight it had been! If only they could have also heard Carducci's interpretation of Dante—celebrating him as a citizen of a great city, who had defended the revolutionary and reforming spirit of human enterprise against asceticism and all denial of the world. Because it had not been the sickly and mystagogic Beatrice whom the poet had honored in his poem with the title of "*donna gentile e pietosa*," but rather his wife, the embodiment of this-worldly knowledge and practical, lifelong labor.

And so now Hans Castorp had heard a thing or two about Dante, and from the best of sources. Given the fact that it came from a windbag, he did not trust the information entirely, but it was worth hearing about how Dante had been a quick-witted citizen of a great city. And it was likewise worthwhile listening to Settembrini talk about himself, declaring that he, the grandson Lodovico, had united the propensities of his two immediate forebears—the political bent of his grandfather and the humanistic bent of his father—by becoming a man of letters, a free-lance writer. For literature was nothing other than the union of humanism and politics, which could come about all the more easily since humanism was already politics and politics already humanism. Hans Castorp pricked up his ears at this and took pains to understand it, because he had reason to hope that he would now be able to grasp the nature of Magnus the brewer's crass ignorance and learn in what way literature was something totally different from "beautiful characters." And had the cousins ever heard of a Signore Brunetto, Settembrini asked, Brunetto Latini, who had become the town clerk of Florence around 1250, and had written a book on virtue and vice? He was the great master who had first given the Florentines their polish and taught them both how to speak and the fine art of guiding their republic by the rules of politics.

"There you have it, gentlemen!" Settembrini cried. "There you have it!" And he spoke now about the "Word," about the cult of the Word, about eloquence, which he called the triumph of humanity. Because the Word was the glory of humankind, and it alone gave dignity to life. Not just humanism, but humanity itself, man's dignity and self-respect—they were inseparable from the Word, from literature. ("You see," Hans Castorp said later to his cousin, "you see? Literature is a matter of beautiful words. I saw that right off.") And politics were bound up with literature, too—or rather they were derived from the oneness of humanity and literature. For the beautiful Word gave birth to the beautiful deed.

"Two hundred years ago," Settembrini said, "you had a poet in your own country, a fine old confabulator, who set great store by beautiful handwriting, because he said it leads to a beautiful style. He should have taken that one step further and said that a beautiful style leads to beautiful actions." Writing beautifully was almost synonymous with thinking beautifully, and from there it was not far to acting beautifully. All moral conduct and all moral perfection emanated from the spirit of literature, from the spirit of human dignity, which simultaneously was also the spirit of humanity and of politics. Yes, they were all one and the same force, one and the same idea, and could be summarized in a *single* word. And what was that word? Well, it consisted of familiar syllables, but the cousins had probably never truly grasped their meaning and majesty. And that word was—civilization! And as Settembrini released the word from his lips, he thrust his small yellow right hand into the air, as if proposing a toast.

Young Hans Castorp found all this well worth listening to—not that he was obliged to, of course, it was more an experiment—but in any case, well worth listening to, and he said as much to Joachim Ziemssen, who had just stuck a thermometer in his mouth and so could only mumble a reply and then became too involved in reading the numbers and entering them on his chart to be able to comment on Settembrini's views. Hans Castorp, as we have said, took note of them in his kindhearted way and he opened himself to them as a way of testing them—from which it became particularly clear that the waking Hans Castorp was a very different person from the fatuously dreaming Hans Castorp, who had called Settembrini an "organ-grinder" to his face and tried with all his might to push him out of the way because he was "bothering" him. Awake, however, he listened to him politely and attentively and tried to be fair, compensating for or suppressing feelings that he felt rising in opposition to his mentor's opinions and characterizations. For it cannot be denied that opposition was stirring in his soul—both the sort that had always been there naturally from the start and the sort that arose specifically from the present situation, partly from indirect observation, partly from personal experience among these people up here.

What a piece of work is a man, and how easily conscience betrays him. He listens to the voice of duty—and what he hears is the license of passion. And out of a sense of duty to be fair and balanced, Hans Castorp listened to Herr Settembrini. With the best of intentions he tested the man's views on reason, the world republic, and beautiful style—and was prepared to be influenced by them. And each time, he found it all the more permissible afterward to let his thoughts and dreams run free in another direction, in the *opposite* direction. To put our suspicions and true understanding of the matter into words—he had probably listened to Herr Settembrini for one purpose only: to be given carte blanche by his conscience, a license it had been unwilling to grant him at first. And what or who stood on the opposing side of patriotism, the dignity of man, and beautiful literature—the side toward which Hans Castorp believed he should direct his thoughts and deeds? There stood . . . Clavdia Chauchat—listless, worm-eaten, Kirghiz-eyed; and whenever Hans Castorp thought of her (although "thought" is an all-too-inhibited word for describing how he turned inwardly toward her), it seemed to him that he was sitting again in that boat on the lake in Holstein and gazing with dazzled and bewildered eyes out of glassy daylight across to the eastern sky and the moonlit night draped in a web of mist.

The Thermometer

HANS CASTORP'S WEEK here ran from Tuesday to Tuesday, because it was on a Tuesday that he had arrived. A few days had passed since he had gone down to the office and paid his bill for the second week—the modest weekly sum of 160 francs. And it was modest and fair to his mind, even if you disregarded the priceless benefits of his stay— which were not on the bill because they were priceless; but then neither were certain other entertainments, which could very well have been calcu- lated, the band concerts every two weeks, for example, or Dr. Kro- kowski's lectures. The bill was solely for room and board, for the basic services of the hotel—comfortable lodging and five prodigious meals.

"It's not so much, it's rather cheap. You can't complain they're over- charging," the visitor said to the long-term guest. "You need around six hundred fifty francs a month for room and board, and that's with medical treatment included. Fine. Let's assume you give out about thirty francs a month in tips—if you're a decent fellow and like to see friendly faces. That makes six hundred eighty. Fine. And now you'll say that there are other fees and expenses. You have to lay out money for drinks, toiletries, cigars, an occasional excursion, a carriage ride if you like, and now and then a bill for the cobbler or tailor. Fine, but even with all that included, try as you will, you'll still be under a thousand francs a month. That's not even eight hundred marks! Which adds up to less than ten thousand marks a year. It certainly can't be more than that. That's all it costs you."

"First-rate mental arithmetic," Joachim said. "I didn't know you were so good at it. And how generous of you to figure up the charges by the year, too—you've definitely learned a thing or two up here. But your figures are on the high side, you know. I don't smoke cigars, and I hope I won't need to have any suits made for me up here, thanks all the same."

"So that was still too high," Hans Castorp said, slightly confused. And no matter how it had come about that he had included cigars and new suits in his cousin's bill, as far as the nimble mental arithmetic went, that was nothing more than intentional deception about his natural talents. Because as in everything else, Hans Castorp was somewhat slow and uninspired at that, too; and his quick reckoning in this case was not ad lib, but the result of preparation, with paper and pencil in fact, carried out one evening when he had been taking his rest cure (because he had begun taking it in the evenings now, too, since everyone else did). On a sudden inspiration, he had got up out of his splendid lounge chair and gone back into the room for what he needed to do the figuring. And he had determined that his cousin, or rather, anyone just in general would need, all things considered, twelve thousand francs a year here. Just for the fun of it, he had pointed out to himself that his own funds were more than adequate for a life up here, seeing as he was a man with an annual income of eighteen to nineteen thousand francs.

And so three days had passed since the bill for his second week had been taken care of with a thank-you and a receipt—which is the same thing as saying that he was now in the middle of the third and last week of his scheduled stay up here. On the coming Sunday he would be present for another of the regular fortnightly band concerts, and on Monday he would likewise attend another of Dr. Krokowski's fortnightly lectures—or so he said to himself and to Joachim. On Tuesday or Wednesday, however, he would depart, and leave Joachim behind alone, poor Joachim, for whom Rhadamanthus had decreed who-knew-how-many more months and whose gentle black eyes dimmed with melancholy every time Hans Castorp made a passing reference to his approaching departure. Yes, good Lord, where had his vacation gone! It had flowed past, sped past, vanished—and one could not rightly say just how. After all, they had intended to spend twenty-one days together—quite a number really, too many to take them all in at once at the beginning. And suddenly there were only three or four paltry days left, a remnant hardly worth considering, though given some weight by the two upcoming periodical deviations in the daily routine, but already filled with thoughts of packing and farewell. Three weeks were as good as nothing up here—they had all told him that right off. The smallest unit of time here was the month, Settembrini had said, and since Hans Castorp's stay came in under that, it was not really a stay at all—he was merely dropping by, as Director Behrens had put it. He wondered if the increase in one's general metabolism here made three weeks seem no more than a moment or two. Such a velocity of life was some consolation for Joachim in light of the five months that still awaited him—if five would in fact be the end of it. But they should have paid more careful attention to time during those three weeks, the way you did measuring your temperature, when the prescribed seven minutes became a significant period of time. Hans Castorp felt sincerely sorry for his cousin—you could read in his eyes his sadness at the impending loss of a human companion—but he pitied him most when he thought about how the poor fellow would have to stay on here without him, whereas he would be living down in the flatlands, hard at work in the service of transportation technology, which brought nations closer together. There were moments when he felt the pity as a burning pain in his chest, felt it so intensely that now and again he seriously doubted he would be able to bring himself to leave Joachim here alone. And so pity became at times a searing pain, and that was probably the reason why, all on his own, he spoke less and less about his departure. It was Joachim who would bring the conversation around to it once in a while. Given his natural tact and delicacy, Hans Castorp seemed not to want to think of it until the very last moment.

"Well, at least we can hope," Joachim said, "that you've recuperated here with us and will feel refreshed once you're back down."

"Yes, and I'll give everyone your greetings," Hans Castorp replied, "and tell them that you'll follow in five months at the most. Recuperated? You're asking if *I*'m feeling better after these few days, is that it? I would certainly like to think so. A certain amount of relaxation probably comes just by itself even after a short time. Although there were a lot of novel things to experience up here, novel in every regard, very exciting, but also very taxing to both mind and body. I don't have the feeling that I've quite got used to it all yet and acclimatized myself, although that would be a precondition for any real recuperation. Maria is back to her old self, thank God, she's been tasting good for several days now. But from time to time my handkerchief shows a little red when I use it, and it doesn't look as if I'm going to be rid of either this damn flushed face or this silly pounding in my heart before I leave. No, no, you can't really say I've acclimatized myself, but how could anyone in such a short time? It takes longer to get acclimatized here, to get used to all these new impressions. It's only then that you can begin to recuperate and build up protein. And that's a shame, because it was definitely a mistake for me not to have arranged for a longer stay—more time certainly would have been available. I feel as if once I'm back home in the flatlands I'm going to have to recuperate from my recuperation and sleep for three weeks, that's how run-down I feel sometimes. And then to top it all there's this catarrh I've caught."

Indeed, it did look more and more as if Hans Castorp would be returning to the flatlands with a first-class case of the sniffles. He had caught a cold, presumably from lying outside in the rest cure—the evening rest cure, to carry the presumption further, in which he had been participating for about a week now, despite the cold, damp weather, which did not look as if it would improve before his departure—although he had learned that it was simply not recognized as such, that the notion of bad weather had no right to exist up here, that no one paid it any attention or feared it; and with the docility of youth, with its ability to adapt to the ideas and customs of almost any environment in which it may find itself, Hans Castorp had begun to make this indifference his own. Even when it was raining cats and dogs, you were not allowed to assume that it made the air any less dry. And it probably wasn't in fact, because it left his head feeling just as hot as before, as if he were sitting in an overheated room or had drunk too much wine. And however cold it got—and it did get very cold—there was no point in his taking refuge in the room, because as long as it wasn't snowing, there was no heat, so that it was no more comfortable for him to sit in his room than to put on a winter overcoat, artfully wrap himself in his two good camel-hair blankets, and lie out on the balcony. On the contrary, it was better out there, incomparably more comfortable, by any criterion the most agreeable state of affairs that Hans Castorp could remember ever having tried out—a judgment from which he could not be dissuaded by some writer and Carbonaro who made malicious remarks with snide connotations about the "horizontal life." In particular, he found evenings there agreeable—the little lamp glowing on the table beside him, a Maria between his lips and tasting good once more, he would wrap himself in his blankets and savor the advantages offered by this style of lounge chair, though they were difficult to describe exactly. The tip of his nose froze, of course, and he had to hold his book (it was still *Ocean Steamships*) in terribly numbed, chapped hands, but he could gaze out through the arches of the balcony to the valley, which was adorned with scattered lights that clustered brightly here and there and from which almost every evening, for at least an hour, music came drifting his way, pleasantly muted, familiar melodic airs: fragments of operas, selections from *Carmen*, *Il Trovatore*, or *Der Freischütz*; well-constructed, smooth waltzes as well as marches to which you could jauntily rock your head back and forth; and cheerful mazurkas, too. Mazurkas? Marusya was her name, the girl with the little ruby ring—and in the next balcony, behind the thick milk-glass partition, lay Joachim. Now and then Hans Castorp would exchange a word or two with him, though discreetly, out of consideration for other "horizontals." Life was just as good for Joachim out on his balcony as it was for Hans Castorp—although he was unmusical and unable to enjoy the evening concerts as much. What a shame—instead of listening, he was probably reading his Russian grammar. Hans Castorp, however, left *Ocean Steamships* lying on his blanket and listened with ardent interest to the music, gazing with contentment into the transparent depths of its structure and taking such genuine delight and inspiration in each melodic invention that he felt nothing but hostility when he occasionally recalled Settembrini's opinions about music, annoying statements, such as how music was politically suspect—

which was no better than Grandfather Giuseppe's slogan about the July Revolution and the six days of Creation.

Joachim, then, did not participate in these musical pleasures, and the spicy diversion of smoking was likewise alien to him; but otherwise he, too, lay there on his balcony—safe, secure, content. The day was over, everything was over for now; one could be sure that nothing more would happen—no more upsets, no more unreasonable demands on the musculature of the heart. And at the same time one could be sure that such would also be the case come *tomorrow,* when, given the favorable probabilities of narrow space and regular schedules, everything would begin all over again. This double sense of security and safety left Hans Castorp feeling very cozy and, together with the music and the rediscovered flavor of his Maria, made his evening rest cure a truly delightful state of affairs.

This, however, did not prevent the visitor, a frail novice at all this, from catching a very bad cold while outside in his rest cure—if that was where he caught it. A bad case of the sniffles appeared to be in the making. He felt it as a pressure in his sinuses; his throat and uvula were sore and scratchy; air didn't pass normally through the channel prescribed by nature, but was impeded, and its steady cold draft unleashed fits of coughing; overnight his voice had taken on the hollow timbre of a whiskey bass; and as he told it, he had not slept a wink—he had kept starting up from his pillow because of the stifling dryness in his throat.

"Very annoying," Joachim said, "almost embarrassing, really. You should know that colds are not *reçus* here. It is denied that they exist, they do not occur—the air is officially much too dry here. And you won't have much success as a patient if you go to Behrens with a cold. But it's different with you, after all, you have a right to catch cold. It would be good if we could fend off your catarrh somehow—there are the methods practiced in the flatlands. But here—well, I doubt if they'll be interested up here. It's better not to get sick here, no one pays you any attention. It's a well-known fact, but you're learning it at the end of your stay. When I arrived there was a lady here who kept one hand pressed to her ear for a whole week, complaining of the pain, and finally Behrens took a look at it. 'You can set your mind at ease,' he said, 'it's not tubercular.' And that was that. Yes, we'll have to see what can be done. I'll mention it to the bath attendant tomorrow morning when he comes for my massage. That's the usual official channel—he'll pass it on, and perhaps we can do something for you then."

That was Joachim's advice; and official channels worked. Hans Castorp had no sooner returned from his morning constitutional on Friday than there was a knock at his door, and he was given the opportunity of making the acquaintance of Fräulein von Mylendonk, or Head Nurse Mylendonk, as she was titled. Until now he had seen this evidently very busy woman only from afar—leaving one sickroom and crossing the corridor to a room opposite. Or he had caught a fleeting glimpse of her in the dining hall, or heard her squawky voice. But now she was paying him a personal visit; drawn here by his catarrh, she gave a bony, sharp rap on his door and entered almost before he could say "come in," although at the threshold she leaned back to make sure she had the right room number.

"Thirty-four," she croaked at full voice. "Right. Well, man alive, *on me dit, que vous avez pris froid, ich höre, Sie sind erkältet, vy, kazhetsya, prostudilis'*, I hear you have caught a cold. Which language do you prefer? German, I see. Ah, young Ziemssen's visitor, I see. I should be in the operating room. There's a gentleman who's to be chloroformed, and he's gone and eaten bean salad—if I didn't keep my eyes open . . . And, man alive, you claim you've caught a cold here with us, do you?"

Hans Castorp was taken aback by the old noblewoman's manner of speech. She seemed to dismiss her own words as she spoke—her head moving about in a restless, looping roll, her nose lifted in the air, searching, like some caged beast of prey. Her freckled right hand was closed in a loose fist, the thumb sticking upward, and by keeping it in constant motion, twisting her wrist back and forth, she seemed to say, "Quick, quick, quick! Don't listen to what I'm saying, but speak up so I can be on my way." She was a woman in her forties, with a stunted, shapeless figure under a white, belted clinical smock. A garnet cross dangled at her chest, and sparse tufts of reddish hair stuck out from under her nurse's cap. Her watery-blue, bloodshot eyes wandered unsteadily, and to make matters worse, one had a sty in a very advanced stage; the nose was turned up, the mouth froglike, the lower lip protruding at an angle and moving like a shovel as she spoke. Hans Castorp gazed at her meanwhile with all the modest, patient, and gullible kindness native to him.

"What sort of a cold is it, eh?" the head nurse asked now, trying to fix her eyes in a piercing stare—but did not succeed, since they began to wander. "We don't like these colds. Do you catch cold often? Hasn't your cousin caught a lot of colds, too? How old are you? Twenty-four? Not an easy age. And so you've come up here and caught a cold? Good man alive, one should not speak of 'colds' here—that's twiddle-twaddle from down below." The word "twiddle-twaddle" sounded ghastly and bizarre when she spoke it, with her lower lip shoveling away. "You have the loveliest catarrh of the upper respiratory tract, I will admit, one can see it in your eyes." And she made another of her odd attempts to stare directly at him, without any real success. "But catarrhs are not colds, they come from an infection to which one is already susceptible, and the only question is whether what we have here is an innocent infection or one that is less innocent, all the rest is twiddle-twaddle." (There was that gruesome "twiddle-twaddle" again.) "It is of course possible that you tend to be more susceptible to the harmless type," she said and seemed to look at him with the well-advanced sty—he was not sure how she managed that. "Here we have a harmless antiseptic. It may do you some good." And from the black leather bag that hung from her belt she pulled out a little box and put it on the table. It was Formamint. "Though you do look rather hectic, too—as if you had a fever." And she would not release him from her gaze, although her eyes kept ranging off a little to one side. "Have you measured your temperature?"

He said he had not.

"And why not?" she asked, letting her protruding lower lip dangle in the air.

He had no reply. The good fellow was still young enough that he could respond with the silence of a schoolboy who doesn't know the answer and so just sits there mutely on his bench.

"Don't you ever measure it?"

"Oh certainly, Nurse Mylendonk. When I have a fever."

"Man alive, the point of taking one's temperature is to find out *if* one has a fever. And you are of the opinion that you have none, is that it?"

"I don't really know, Nurse Mylendonk. It's hard to tell the difference. I've been both a little chilled and flushed since my arrival up here."

"Aha! And where is your thermometer?"

"I don't have one here with me, Nurse Mylendonk. Why should I? I'm here just as a visitor. I'm healthy."

"Twiddle-twaddle! Did you call me because you're healthy?"

"No," he said with a polite laugh, "but because I've caught a little—"

"Cold. We've seen colds like that here often enough. Here—" she said and rummaged in her bag again, pulling out two longish leather cases, one black, one red, which she also laid on the table now. "This one costs three francs fifty, and this one five francs. You'll do better to take the one for five, of course. It will last a lifetime if you take proper care of it."

He picked up the red case with a smile and opened it. The glass instrument lay bedded like a precious gem in its red velvet cushion, the indentation exactly matched to its form. The full degrees were marked in red, the tenths in black. The numbers were red; the lower, tapered end was filled with lustrous, glistening mercury. The column stood at a cool lowpoint, well below normal animal warmth.

Hans Castorp knew what he owed himself and his social station. "I'll take this one," he said, without giving the other so much as a glance. "The one for five francs. May I use it now?"

"That settles that!" the head nurse squawked. "Never be niggardly when it comes to important procurements. No hurry—it will be on your bill. Give it to me, we need to shrink him down to nothing, all the way down—like this." And she took the thermometer out of his hand, thrusting it at the air several times and driving the mercury down even further, below ninety-five degrees. "He'll climb back up, wander right up the column, old Mercury will," she said. "Here is your purchase. You do know, don't you, how we do things up here? We put it under our pretty tongue, for seven minutes, four times a day, and keep our lips nicely tucked around it. Adieu! Good man alive, my best wishes for good results." And she was out of the room.

Hans Castorp bowed as she left and stood now beside the table, staring at the door through which she had vanished—and at the apparatus she had left behind. "So that was Head Nurse von Mylendonk," he thought. "Settembrini doesn't like her, and there is something disagreeable about her, it's true. The sty is not pretty, although I don't suppose she always has one. But why does she keep saying 'man alive,' as if she were addressing me? It's so odd, so slangy. And now she's sold me a thermometer—always has a couple in her bag. They're for sale here everywhere, in all the shops, even those you wouldn't expect to carry them. Joachim said so. But I didn't have to go to the trouble, it simply fell right into my lap."

He took the instrument from its case, examined it and walked restlessly with it back and forth in the room a few times. His heart was beating fast and strong. He looked out through the open door to the balcony, then moved in the direction of the hall door, with the idea of looking in on Joachim, but then gave that up and stood there again beside the table. He now cleared his throat to see just how hollow his voice sounded. He then coughed. "Yes, I do need to see if I have a little fever with my cold," he said and quickly stuck the thermometer in his mouth, the mercury tip under his tongue, the glass tube jutting up at an angle from one corner, his lips tucked tightly around it to keep air out. Then he looked at his wristwatch—it was 9:36. And he began to wait for seven minutes to pass.

"Not one second too many," he thought, "or too few. You can depend on me, whether up or down. They won't need to exchange mine for a silent sister, like that girl Settembrini was talking about . . . Ottilie Kneifer." And he walked around the room, keeping the thermometer clamped tightly under his tongue.

Time crept by—seven minutes seemed endless. Only two and a half had passed when he looked at his watch again, worried that he might have missed the precise moment. He did a thousand things, picked up objects, put them back down, walked out onto the balcony, but not so that his cousin could notice, looked at the landscape of this Alpine valley, his eyes now more than familiar with its shapes and forms—its peaks, ridges, and cliffs; in the background on his left, though somewhat closer, was the jutting Brämenbühl, whose crest fell abruptly toward town and whose flank was thickly covered with coarse grasses; there were the mountain formations on his right, whose names he also knew by now; and then to the south was the Alteinwand, which from here looked as if it closed off the valley. He looked down at the paths and flowerbeds of the level gardens, the grotto, the silver fir, listened to whispers drifting up from the lounging area, where people were taking their rest cure—and turned back into the room, where he tried to correct the way the instrument sat in his mouth. Stretching his arm to free his wrist from its sleeve, he brought his forearm up to his eyes. With much trouble and effort—as if he were shoving, pushing, kicking them—he had got rid of six minutes. But now, standing there in the middle of the room, he fell to daydreaming and let his thoughts wander, and the one remaining minute scurried away on little cat's feet, until another motion of his arm told him that the minute had secretly escaped and that it was a little late now. Almost a third of the next had passed before he grabbed the thermometer from his mouth, telling himself that it did not really matter, would not alter the results, could not hurt anything—and he stared down at it now with confusion in his eyes.

He was not immediately the wiser. The sheen of the mercury blended with the refraction of the light in the elliptical glass tube; the column seemed now to reach clear to the top, now not to be present at all. He held the instrument close to his eyes, turned it back and forth—and could make out nothing. Finally, after a lucky turn, the image became clear; he held it tightly and hastily applied his intellect to the task. And indeed Mercury had stretched himself, very robustly. The column had risen rather high, it stood several tenths above the limit of normal body temperature. Hans Castorp had a temperature of 99.7 degrees.

Between nine-thirty and ten, in the middle of the morning, his body temperature was 99.7 degrees—that was too high, it was a fever, the result of an infection to which he had been susceptible. And now the question was: what sort of infection? At 99.7 degrees—Joachim's wasn't any higher than that, nor was anyone else's, who wasn't bedridden, terribly ill, or moribund. Not young Kleefeld with her pneumothorax . . . nor Madame Chauchat. In his case, of course, it surely wasn't anything like that—just the usual fever that went with the sniffles, people would have said down below. But there was no way to differentiate it precisely, to keep the kinds of fever apart. Hans Castorp doubted that the fever had only appeared just now in conjunction with his cold; and he truly regretted not having consulted Mercury before this, right at the beginning, when the director had suggested it to him. It had been very sensible advice, that was apparent now, and Settembrini had been wrong to throw his head back and laugh so scornfully—Settembrini with his republic and his beautiful style. Hans Castorp despised the Italian's republic and his beautiful style; but he also went on examining the thermometer reading, which he lost several times in the glare, and then recovered after twisting and turning the instrument. It still said 99.7 degrees—and in the middle of the morning.

He was terribly agitated. He paced the room a few times, still holding the thermometer—horizontally, so as to not disturb the reading by some vertical shake. He then laid it as carefully as possible on the rim of his washstand and decided for now to put on his overcoat and finish his rest cure. He sat down, flung his blankets around him—just as he had learned, from both sides, from below, one after the other, with a skilled hand now—and lay still as he waited for the hour of second breakfast and Joachim's arrival. Now and then he smiled, and it was as if he were smiling at someone. Now and then his chest gave an uneasy heave, and then he would have to cough his bronchial cough.

When the eleven o'clock gong sounded, Joachim came by to fetch him for second breakfast and found him still lying there.

"Well?" he asked, stepping up beside the lounge chair.

Hans Castorp stared straight ahead in silence for a while. Then by way of reply, he said, "Yes, the latest is that I have a little temperature."

"What do you mean?" Joachim asked. "Do you feel feverish?"

Hans Castorp again waited awhile before answering, but then at last he said with a certain lethargy, "I've felt feverish for a long time now, my friend—almost the whole time. It's no longer a matter of a subjective feeling now, but of precise evidence. I measured it."

"You took your temperature? With what?" Joachim cried, stunned.

"With a thermometer, of course," Hans Castorp replied, not without a mixture of severity and scorn. "The head nurse sold me one. Why she keeps saying 'man alive,' I really don't know. It's very slangy. But she did sell me a first-rate thermometer with utmost dispatch, and if you want to check for yourself what it read, you'll find it in there on my washstand. It's only slightly elevated."

Joachim did an about-face and walked back into the room. When he returned, he said tentatively, "Yes, it reads ninety-nine point six."

"Then it's gone down a little," Hans Castorp responded quickly. "It was point seven."

"You can't really call that just slightly elevated, not in the middle of the morning," Joachim said. "Now isn't this a nice mess," he said, standing beside his recumbent cousin the way one stands beside a nice mess, his hands on his hips, his head lowered. "You need to be in bed."

Hans Castorp had his answer at the ready. "I don't see," he said, "why I should go to bed with ninety-nine point seven, when you and a lot of other people with temperatures that are no lower are running about just as you please here."

"But that's a totally different matter," Joachim said. "Yours is acute, but harmless. It's the fever that goes with a cold."

"First," Hans Castorp replied, dividing his response into a first and second, "I don't understand why someone with a harmless fever—we'll assume there is such a thing—with a harmless fever, then, has to stay in bed, but not in the opposite case. And second, I'm telling you that my cold has not made me hotter than I already was. My position remains," he concluded, "that ninety-nine point seven is ninety-nine point seven. And if you can run around with that, so can I."

"But I had to lie in bed for four weeks when I first arrived," Joachim objected. "And they let me get up again only when it became clear that my temperature wasn't going away with bed rest."

Hans Castorp smiled. "So what?" he asked. "I thought yours was an entirely different problem, was it not? It seems to me you're getting tangled up in contradictions. First you differentiate the two cases, then equate them. That's just twiddle-twaddle."

Joachim turned on his heels, and when he turned back to his cousin his tanned face was visibly a shade darker. "No," he said, "I am not equating them—you're the muddlehead. I'm simply saying that you've caught a wretched cold—I can hear it in your voice—and you should go to bed, so that you can be over it sooner, especially since you want to go home next week. But if you don't want to—I mean, if you don't want to lie in bed, then you don't have to. I'm not going to make rules for you. At any rate, we have to go to breakfast now. Come on, we're late."

"Fine, let's go!" Hans Castorp said, tossing his blankets aside. He went back into the room to run a brush through his hair; as he did, Joachim took another look at the thermometer on the washstand—and Hans Castorp watched him from a distance. They left, not saying a word, and took their places in the dining hall, which, as always at this hour, glistened white from all the milk.

When the dwarf brought Hans Castorp his Kulmbach beer, he refused it with some seriousness. He would rather not drink beer today—wanted nothing at all, thanks, at most a little water. This caused a general stir. What was this? What innovations were these? Why no beer?—He had a slight temperature, Hans Castorp remarked casually—ninety-nine point seven, insignificant.

And now they wagged their forefingers, cautioning him—it was all very curious. They began to tease him, laying heads to one side, winking, and putting fingers up to their ears, as if these were racy, risqué revelations about someone who had played the innocent until now. "Now, now, my friend," the teacher said, laughing as she chided him, her downy cheeks turning red. "What pretty goings-on—sowing his oats. Just wait and see."

"My, my, my," Frau Stöhr said, admonishing him with a stubby red finger waved in the vicinity of her nose. "So Mr. Visitor has a little temp himself. Look at you—what a fine fellow you turn out to be, quite the gay blade."

And when the news reached the great-aunt at the other end of the table, even she made a sly joke of chiding him; pretty Marusya, who had paid him barely any attention before now, bent forward to look at him, her orange-scented handkerchief pressed to her lips, and reprimanded him with her brown, round eyes. And Dr. Blumenkohl, too, who heard of it now from Frau Stöhr, could not help joining in the general reaction— not that he looked directly at Hans Castorp. Only Miss Robinson, closed off to the world as always, appeared indifferent. Joachim behaved with perfect propriety and kept his eyes lowered.

Hans Castorp, flattered by so much teasing, felt that modesty required him to demur. "No, no," he said, "you're mistaken, my case is the most harmless imaginable. I have the sniffles. As you can see: my eyes are watery, my chest is congested, I coughed half the night away—that's quite unpleasant enough."

But they would not accept his explanations. They laughed, they waved this off, they cried: "Yes, yes, yes. No fibbing, no excuses, we know all about sniffles and fever, know all about it." And then all of a sudden they demanded that Hans Castorp immediately make an appointment to be examined. His news had animated them; the conversation at their breakfast table was livelier than at any of the other six.

Frau Stöhr in particular became wildly talkative, and her willful face, its cheeks lined with tiny wrinkles, turned scarlet above her ruffled collar. She expatiated on the pleasures of coughing—yes, there was something perfectly delightful and enjoyable about a tickle in the depths of your chest, that got worse and worse until you reached down deep for it, squeezing and pressing to let it have its way. Sneezing was just as much fun—the way you felt it swelling up with a vengeance inside you, until it became irresistible and you breathed in and out in one great frenzy, gave yourself over to the bliss of it, your face drunk with pleasure—you could forget the whole world in one blessed eruption. But sometimes they came in twos and threes, one right after the other. Those were the pleasures in life that didn't cost a cent—it was the same, for example, with scratching your chilblains in the spring, when they itched so deliciously—and you scratched away fervently and brutally until you drew blood, just for the mad pleasure of it. And if you happened to see yourself in the mirror, there was a little demon looking back at you.

Obtuse Frau Stöhr went on and on in this way with ghastly thoroughness until the brief, if ample meal was over. The cousins now stepped out for their second walk that morning, a stroll down to Davos-Platz—Joachim was lost in thought the whole way. Hans Castorp groaned with the agony of his cold, and his rusty chest wheezed.

On the way home Joachim said, "Let me make a suggestion. Today is Friday—I have my monthly checkup tomorrow morning after dinner. It's not a complete physical, but Behrens pounds around a little on you and has Krokowski jot down some notes. You could come along and ask him to use the occasion for a quick listen to you. It's really absurd—if you were at home, you would send for Heidekind. And here, with two specialists in the house, you run around and don't know what to think, unsure how deep the problem sits, and whether it might not be better to take to your bed."

"Fine," Hans Castorp said. "Whatever you think. Of course I can do that. And I'd find it interesting to be present at a checkup, too."

And so they came to an understanding; and as chance would have it, upon their arrival at the sanatorium they ran into Director Behrens himself and took the opportunity to present their request on the spot.

Behrens was just emerging from the portico—tall, with protruding neck vertebrae, a bowler shoved to the back of his head, a cigar in his mouth, purple-cheeked and pop-eyed; he was at full swing in his daily routine, about to attend to his private practice and make calls in town, having just been on the job in the operating room, as he declared.

"Greetings, gentlemen!" he said. "Out hoofing it, I see? Having a grand time out there in the big, wide world? I've just come from a lopsided duel with knives and bone saws—great stuff, rib resections. Used to be that a good fifty percent of them would be left on the operating table. We've got it down better now, but it still happens often enough that we have to pack our bags *mortis causa*. Well, the fellow today knew how to take a joke, and he put up a good fight for a while. Crazy sight, a human thorax that isn't one anymore. Mushy spots, you know, quite unseemly, a slight fuzziness of the ideal, so to speak. Well, and how about you? How are your admirable constitutions doing? Life really is more festive as a twosome, don't you think, Ziemssen, you sly old dog? But why the tears, my good excursionist?" he said, turning now to Hans Castorp. "Tears are not allowed in public here. The rules of the house forbid it. Why, everybody would be in tears if we let them."

"It's sniffles, Director Behrens," Hans Castorp replied. "I don't know how it could have happened, but I've caught a nasty cold. I've got a cough, too, and a lot of congestion here in the chest."

"Really? I would suggest you consult a doctor."

They both laughed, and clicking his heels, Joachim responded, "We were just about to do that, Director Behrens. I have my checkup tomorrow, and we wanted to ask if you would be so kind as to fit my cousin in at the same time. We're concerned whether he will be well enough to travel on Tuesday."

"N. s. s. t. d.!" Behrens said. "No sooner said than done. With pleasure. Should have done it long ago. Once you're up here, you might as well take advantage of the place. But, of course, we didn't want to seem pushy about it. So there'll be two of you tomorrow, right after you've put on the feed bag."

"Because I do have a little fever, too," Hans Castorp added.

"You don't say!" Behrens exclaimed. "And I suppose you think that's news to me, do you? Do you think I don't have eyes in my head?" And he pointed with one massive forefinger at his own two bloodshot, watery, protruding blue eyes. "How high is it, then?"

Hans Castorp modestly supplied the numbers.

"In the morning? Hmm, not bad. Not at all untalented for a beginner. Well, then, you can fall in, two by two, tomorrow. It will be an honor. And now, do go in and savor your taking of nourishment." And with knees slightly bent and rowing with his hands, he began to trudge downhill, a trail of cigar smoke billowing behind him.

"Well, it's all arranged just as you wanted," Hans Castorp said. "We couldn't have struck it luckier, and so now I have an appointment. He probably won't be able to do anything more for me than prescribe some licorice syrup or a tea for my cough, but all the same it's nice to have a little medical advice when you feel as bad as I do. But why does he always rattle on in that overenergetic, peppy sort of way?" he said. "At first I rather liked it, but after being here awhile, I can't say I enjoy it. 'Savor your taking of nourishment!'—what sort of gibberish is that? You can say 'enjoy your meal,' or even '*bon appétit*' has a nice ring to it when you're sitting down to your daily bread. But 'taking of nourishment' is basic physiology, and to tell someone to 'savor' it is pure sarcasm. I don't like to see him smoking, either, it makes me uneasy somehow, because I know it's not good for him and makes him melancholy. Settembrini says his merriment is forced, and Settembrini has a critical eye, is a man who forms his own opinions, one must grant him that much. I should perhaps form my opinions more, and not take everything just as it comes—he's right about that. But sometimes a person begins with opinions and judgments and valid criticism, but then things creep in that have nothing to do with forming opinions, and then it's all over with strict logic, and what you end up with is an absurd world republic and beautiful style." And he continued to mutter on, although he did not appear quite sure what it was he meant to say.

His cousin merely gave him a sidelong glance and said, "Till later." Each then went to his room and sat out on his balcony.

"How high?" Joachim asked in a low voice after a while, although he had not actually seen Hans Castorp consult his thermometer.

And Hans Castorp replied nonchalantly, "Nothing new."

In actuality, no sooner had he entered his room than he had picked up his recent fragile purchase from the washstand, given it a few vertical shakes to erase the 99.7, which had served its purpose now, and with the glass cigar in his mouth had taken to his rest cure like an old hand. But despite his rather soaring expectations and although he held the instrument under his tongue for a full eight minutes, Mercury stretched himself again just to 99.7, but no farther—which was indeed a fever, but no higher than it had been earlier that morning. After dinner, the little column rose to 99.9, but that evening, when the patient was very tired after all the excitement and novelty of the day, it held at 99.5, and by the next morning was even down to 98.6, only to return by noon to the high of the previous day. And that was how things stood as the hour neared for the day's main meal and, once it was over, his appointed rendezvous.

Hans Castorp remembered later that at dinner that day Madame Chauchat had worn a golden yellow sweater with large buttons and pockets trimmed with braid—a new sweater, or new at least to Hans Castorp, as he watched her make her entrance, late as always, and, just as he had come to expect, stand there at attention, facing the dining hall for a moment. Then, as she did five times every day, she had glided to her table, taken her seat in a soft, fluid motion, and begun to eat, while chatting with her neighbors. And as always Hans Castorp had glanced past Settembrini—who sat with his back to him at one end of the intervening crosswise table—to get a view of the Good Russian table; this time, however, he had paid particular notice to the way her head moved as she spoke, to the arch of her neck and the limp posture of her back. As for Frau Chauchat, she had not turned to look around the dining hall even once during the entire meal. But when they had all finished dessert, and the tall clock, a pendulum and chain affair at the far end of the room on the right, struck two, it had happened—much to Hans Castorp's puzzlement and shock. For as the clock struck, once, then twice, the charming patient had slowly turned her head, and a little of her upper body, too, to gaze plainly and openly over her shoulder at Hans Castorp's table—and not just at the table in general, no, quite unmistakably and very personally at *him*, a smile playing on her closed lips and in her narrow Pribislav eyes, as if to say: "Well? It's time. Are you going to go, Hans?" (Because when only the eyes speak, things become quite informal, although her mouth had never even once said "Herr Castorp.") The incident had confused and shocked Hans Castorp to the depths of his soul; he had barely been able to believe his eyes and had first gaped in stupefaction at Frau Chauchat's face, and then, raising his gaze above her brow and hair, had stared into space. Had she known that he had made an appointment for an examination at two o'clock? It had certainly looked that way. And yet that seemed quite as unlikely as her knowing that he had just asked himself, not a minute before, whether he should not have Joachim tell the director that his cold was already better and that he now thought the examination superfluous—a new plan whose advantages had withered beneath her inquisitive smile and that had suddenly become disgustingly boring. Barely a second later, Joachim had placed his rolled-up napkin on the table, signaled with raised eyebrows, bowed to the others, and left the table—and Hans Castorp, still sensing both eyes and smile directed at him, had followed his cousin out. His step was firm, his mind was reeling.

They had not spoken to one another about the day's plan since yesterday morning, and even now walked on by tacit agreement. Joachim was in a hurry—he was already late for his appointment, and Director Behrens insisted on punctuality. The way led from the dining hall, along the ground-floor corridor, past "management," and down the freshly waxed linoleum stairs to the "basement." Joachim knocked on a door directly opposite the stairway—a porcelain sign declared it to be the entrance to the consulting room.

"*Come* in!" Behrens called, with a strong emphasis on the first word. He was standing in the middle of the room; he had on his smock and in his right hand he held a stethoscope—which he patted now against his thigh.

"Chop-chop!" he said, directing his pop-eyes at the wall clock. "*Un poco più presto, Signori.* We're not here exclusively to serve you, good sirs."

At the double desk beside the window sat Dr. Krokowski, looking pale against his shiny black smock—elbows propped on the desktop, a pen in one hand, the other buried in his beard. There were papers spread out before him, the patient's records presumably, and as the two men entered, he looked up at them with the dulled expression of a distinguished personage who is there merely to assist.

"Well, hand over your report card," the director said in reply to Joachim's apologies. He accepted the temperature chart and looked it over while his patient quickly undressed above the waist and hung his garments on a clothes stand next to the door. No one paid attention to Hans Castorp. He stood there awhile, watching, but then sat down in an old-fashioned easy chair that had tassels on the arms and was placed next to a table with a carafe of water. Along the walls were bookcases filled with broad-spined medical works and bundles of records. There was no other furniture apart from a chaise longue, which could be cranked up or down and was covered with white oilcloth, except for a paper towel laid over the headrest.

"Point seven, point nine, point eight," Behrens said, paging through the week's chart, where Joachim had faithfully recorded the results of the measurements he took five times a day. "Still on the lambent side, my good Ziemssen, can't exactly say you've gotten any sturdier of late." ("Of late" meant in the last four weeks.) "Still toxic, still toxic," he said. "Well, it doesn't happen from one day to the next—we're not sorcerers here, you know."

Joachim nodded and gave a shrug of his bare shoulders, although he might have protested that he hadn't arrived up here only the day before.

"And how is that little twinge in the right hilum, where it always sounds a little aggravated? Better? Well, come here. Let's give you a few polite thumps." And the auscultation began.

Spreading his legs, leaning back slightly, and wedging his stethoscope under one arm, Director Behrens first tapped high up on Joachim's right shoulder, flicking his right hand at the wrist so that the massive middle finger worked as a hammer, while the left hand provided support. Then he moved below the shoulder blade and thumped down the side of the middle and lower ribs; Joachim, well trained in all this, now lifted an arm and let him tap just below the armpit. And then the whole procedure was repeated on the left side; and having finished with that, the director ordered, " 'Bout face!" so that he could thump away at the chest. He tapped just below the neck at the collarbone, tapped above and below the breasts, first on the right, then the left. And when he had pounded to his satisfaction, he moved on to listening; putting one end of his stethoscope to his ear and placing the other end against Joachim's chest and back, he now shifted it everywhere he had already tapped. Meanwhile, Joachim was required to alternate between deep breaths and coughs, which appeared to tax him a great deal, because he was soon out of breath and tears came to his eyes. Director Behrens, however, reported to his assistant at the desk everything he heard there inside, speaking in curt, prescribed terminology, so that Hans Castorp could not help being reminded of the procedure at the tailor's, when a well-dressed gentleman takes your measurements for a suit, laying the tape measure in a traditional sequence here and there across your torso and along your limbs, and then dictates the resulting numbers to his assistant, who sits there bent over pen and paper. "Shallow . . . diminished," Director Behrens dictated. "Vesicular," he said, then once more, "vesicular"—that was good, evidently. "Rough," he said and made a face. "*Very* rough . . . rattle." And Dr. Krokowski entered it all like the tailor's helper recording numbers.

Tilting his head forward and to one side, Hans Castorp followed the whole procedure, but was soon lost in thought as he regarded Joachim's upper body, the way the ribs—thank God he still had all his ribs—rose under the taut skin while the stomach fell with each breath he took. It was a slender, yellowish-brown, youthful torso, with black hair at the breastbone and along the still powerful arms, one of which was encircled at the wrist by a gold bracelet. "A gymnast's arms," Hans Castorp thought. "He always did enjoy gymnastics, whereas I didn't care much for them, and that was all part of his wanting to become a soldier. He always was concerned about his body, much more than I, or at least in a different way than I, because I was always the civilian, and more interested in a nice warm bath and good food and drink, when what he wanted were challenges and exploits. And now his body has stepped to the fore, but in a totally different way, declaring its independence and putting on airs—by means of illness. He's lambent, still toxic, and doesn't seem to get any sturdier, no matter how much he wants to be a soldier in the flatlands. Look at him, a perfect adult male, an absolute Apollo Belvedere, to a T. But inside, Joachim is ill, and outside he's too warm—because of illness. Illness makes people even more physical, turns them into only a body." And he was so taken aback by the thought that he rapidly shifted his searching glance from Joachim's naked upper torso to his eyes, to his large, black, gentle eyes, with tears in them from all the forced coughs and deep breaths of the examination. Those eyes were gazing mournfully now beyond his audience, into space.

But Director Behrens had finished. "Well, that's fine, Ziemssen," he said. "Everything's in as good shape as can be expected. By next time"—that would be in four weeks—"it's sure to have improved a little all over."

"How long, Director Behrens, sir, do you think—"

"Are you trying to push me again? You can't bully recruits about in your lambent condition. I told you six months the other day—and you can count from then if you like. But that's the minimum. Life's not all that bad here, after all—and a little courtesy is in order. We're not a prison ship, you know. We're not a Siberian salt mine. Or are you trying to say that we resemble anything of that sort? So, that's fine, Ziemssen. Dismissed! Next—whoever feels up to it," he shouted, staring into the air. And extending one long arm, he handed his stethoscope to Dr. Krokowski, who stood up and grabbed it, so that he could perform his own little assistant's post-examination on Joachim.

Hans Castorp had sprung to his feet as well, and with his eyes fixed on the director, who stood there lost in thought—legs spread, mouth open—he began quickly to get ready himself. He was in too much of a hurry and had trouble getting out of his dotted, French-cuffed shirt, which he slipped over his head. And there he stood—white, blond, and narrow-chested—opposite Director Behrens. His figure certainly looked more civilian than Joachim Ziemssen's.

But the director, still lost in thought, let him stand there. Dr. Krokowski had sat back down and Joachim had begun to get dressed again, when Behrens finally decided to take some notice of the person who "felt up to it."

"Ah yes, it's *your* turn now!" he said; grabbing Hans Castorp's upper arm with one massive hand, he shoved him into place and gave him a sharp look. But he did not look directly at his face, the way you look at another human being, but at his body. He spun him around, the way you spin an object around, and examined his back as well. "Hmm," he said. "Well, let's have a look at what you're up to." And he took up his thumping again.

He pounded everywhere, just as he had with Joachim Ziemssen, but kept coming back to certain spots. For a good while he alternated tapping a spot near the left collarbone and one a little below it, comparing.

"Hear that?" he called across to Dr. Krokowski. And Dr. Krokowski, sitting five paces away at the desk, showed he had heard by lowering his head—pressing his chin against his chest so earnestly that the tips of his beard curled to points on each side.

"Breathe deep! Cough!" the director commanded, stethoscope in hand once more; and Hans Castorp worked hard, for perhaps a good eight or ten minutes, while the director listened. He said not a word, but placed the stethoscope here and there and in particular repeatedly listened to the two places where he had lingered when tapping. Then he wedged his instrument under his arm, crossed his hands behind his back, and stared at a spot on the floor between himself and Hans Castorp.

"Yes, Castorp," he said—and this was the first time he had ever addressed the young man simply by his last name—"just as I thought, the situation looks rather *praeter-propter*. I can admit to you now that I haven't liked your looks from the start, not since the first time I had the undeserved honor of making your acquaintance—and was pretty sure of my guess that you were secretly one of the locals, and would finally come to appreciate the fact yourself, as has many a man before you, who came up here just for the fun of it, looked around with his nose in the air, and one fine day discovered he would do well—indeed, mark my words, would do more than *well*—to remain on here, for reasons having nothing to do with the seductions of mere curiosity, for a rather more extended stay."

Hans Castorp had turned pale, and Joachim, who had been buttoning his suspenders, stopped right where he was and listened.

"You have a fine, sympathetic cousin there," the director went on, nodding in Joachim's direction and rolling back and forth between the balls of his feet and his heels, "of whom we hope someday soon to say that he *was* ill at one time, but even when that day comes, he will still *have been* ill—your fine cousin will. And that, as the philosophers say, casts a certain *a priori* light on your own situation, my good Castorp."

"But he's only a half cousin, Director Behrens."

"Now, now, you're not going to disown your own cousin, are you? Half or whatever, he is still a blood relation. On which side, actually?"

"On my mother's side, sir. He's the son of my mother's half—"

"And your dear mother is enjoying life, I hope?"

"No, she's dead. She died when I was still small."

"Of what?"

"Of a blood clot, sir."

"A blood clot? Well, it was long ago in any case. And your good father?"

"He died of pneumonia," Hans Castorp said. "And so did my grandfather," he thought to add.

"I see, him too? Well, enough of your forebears. As for yourself—you've always been rather anemic, am I right? But don't really tire all that easily from physical or mental labor? Oh, you do? And your heart pounds sometimes? Has only started that of late? Fine. In addition there is apparently an active proclivity for catarrh in the upper respiratory system. Did you know that you were ill once before?"

"Me?"

"Yes—I do mean you. Can you hear the difference?" And the director tapped again, alternating between a spot high on the left side of the chest and one a little lower.

"It sounds a bit more hollow there," Hans Castorp said.

"Very good. You should become a specialist. That is what we call a muffled tone, and muffled tones come from old infections where calcification has set in, a kind of scarring, if you will. You are an old patient, Castorp, but we'll not lay the blame on anyone for your not having known that before. Early diagnosis is difficult—particularly for my good colleagues in the flatlands. I certainly don't claim that we have finer ears up here, although our special training does contribute something. But the air helps us to hear better, you see—the thin, dry air up here."

"Of course, certainly it does," Hans Castorp said.

"Fine, Castorp. And now listen to me, young man, I am about to utter several golden words. Please understand me now—if it were nothing more than muffled tones and scars on your Aeolus's bellows there, merely some calcified foreign matter, then I would send you packing to rejoin your lares and penates, and not worry one whit more about you. You do understand that, don't you? But as things stand and on the basis of my examination, and seeing that you are already here—it would not pay for you to return home, Hans Castorp. Because you would be back to see us in very short order."

Hans Castorp felt the blood rush to his heart again—it began to pound. Joachim just stood there, his hands resting on the back buttons, his eyes on the floor.

"Because apart from the muffled tones," the director said, "you have some roughness at the upper left, which is almost a rattle and doubtless comes from a fresh area. I would not yet call it a focus for softening tissue, but it is certainly a moist spot. And if you were to continue your life just as before down below, my good man, the whole pulmonary lobe would go, willy-nilly, to the devil."

Hans Castorp stood there stock-still, though his mouth twitched strangely and his heart hammered visibly against his ribs. He glanced across to Joachim and then back to the director's face—with its purple cheeks, blue pop-eyes, and little skewed moustache.

"We find objective confirmation for this," Behrens continued, "in your temperature: ninety-nine point seven at ten in the morning, which more or less matches our acoustic observations."

"I just assumed," Hans Castorp said, "the fever came from my catarrh."

"And the catarrh?" the director retorted. "Where does it come from? Let me tell you something, Castorp, and pay close attention now—you certainly have sufficient gray matter for that, as far as I can see. First and foremost: there's the air up here. It's good for fighting off illness, wouldn't you say? And you'd be right. But it is also good *for* illness, you see, because it first enhances it, creates a revolution in the body, causes latent illness to erupt, and your catarrh—no offense intended—is just such an eruption. I don't know if you were already febrile down in the plains, but in any case you had a fever your very first day here, and not because of any catarrh—that, at least, is my opinion."

"Yes," Hans Castorp said, "yes, I truly believe that, too."

"You felt tipsy right off, I presume," the director said to prove the point. "That comes from soluble toxins released by the bacteria; they have an intoxicating effect on the central nervous system, you see—which gives you those flushed cheeks. And so first off, Castorp, we're going to stick you in bed; we'll see if we can't get you sobered up with a few weeks of bed rest. And then we shall see what we shall see. We'll take a pretty interior snapshot of you—it's always fun to get a look at what's happening inside your own body. But let me tell you right off: a case like yours is not healed just like that. We don't promote ourselves with a lot of publicity about miracle cures. I knew at once that you'd be a better patient than visitor, with more talent for being ill than our brigadier general here, who tries to slip away the moment his fever goes down a tenth or two. As if 'At ease!' weren't just as good a command as 'Attention!' A citizen's first duty is to stay calm, and impatience never helps anything. And so I do insist that you not disappoint me, Castorp, or prove me wrong about my knowledge of human nature. And now, forward march!—off to the stall with you both!"

And the consultation was over, and Director Behrens sat down at his desk—a busy man like him had to make good use of what little time he had before the next examination by taking care of paperwork. Dr. Krokowski, however, stood up and strode over to Hans Castorp; tilting his head to one side and smiling so pithily that it revealed the yellow teeth under his beard, he placed one hand on the young man's shoulder and with the other offered a hearty handshake.

5

Eternal Soup and Sudden Clarity

AND NOW we have a new phenomenon—about which the narrator would do well to express his own amazement, if only to prevent his readers from being all too amazed on their own. The fact is, the account of the first three weeks of Hans Castorp's stay with "the people up here" (twenty-one days at the height of summer, to which, by all calculation, it was supposed to have been limited) has consumed quantities of space and time that correspond only too well to what the author himself expected, and indeed half confessed; the coverage of the next three weeks of the visit, however, will require about as many lines—or words, or even seconds—as the first three weeks required pages, quires, hours, and working days. We can see it coming—we'll have those three weeks behind us and laid to rest in no time.

That may well cause amazement—and yet it is perfectly in order and corresponds to the laws of how stories are told and listened to. Because both good order and the laws of narrative require that our experience of time should seem long or short, should expand or shrink, in the same way it does for the hero of our story, for young Hans Castorp, who quite unexpectedly has found himself impounded by fate. It may also be useful to prepare the reader for other wonders and phenomena that are connected with the mystery of time and that we shall encounter while in his company—quite apart from this striking instance. But for now it is enough for us to remind everyone how quickly a number of days, indeed a great number, can pass when one spends them as a patient in bed. It is always the same day—it just keeps repeating itself. Although since it is always the same day, it is surely not correct to speak of "repetition." One should speak of monotony, of an abiding now, of eternalness. Someone brings you your midday soup, the same soup they brought you yesterday and will bring again tomorrow. And in that moment it comes over you—you don't know why or how, but you feel dizzy watching them bring in the soup. The tenses of verbs become confused, they blend and what is now revealed to you as the true tense of all existence is the "inelastic present," the tense in which they bring you soup for all eternity. But one can't speak of boredom, because boredom comes with the passing of time— and that would be a paradox in relation to eternity. And we want to avoid paradoxes, particularly if we are to live with our hero.

Hans Castorp had been confined to his bed since Saturday evening, by order of Director Behrens, the highest authority in this world in which we are encapsulated. There he lay, his monogram on the breast pocket of his nightshirt, his hands clasped behind his head, in his clean, white bed—the American woman's deathbed and probably that of many others as well—staring up at the ceiling with his ordinary blue eyes, watery now from a cold, considering this strange state of affairs. Which does not mean that if he had not had a cold, his gaze would have been clear and unequivocal, because that was not how things looked on the inside—and however ordinary he might be on the inside, things in there were also very murky, confused, uncertain, and only half-sincere. And as he lay there, one moment the wild laughter of triumph would convulse him, rising up from somewhere deep within, and his heart would stop, aching with an expansive joy and hope he had never known before; and the next moment, he would turn pale with fear and alarm, and the pulsing of his conscience became his heart banging against his ribs in a rapid, fickle rhythm.

Joachim had left him in peace the first day and avoided any long conversation. He stepped cautiously into the sickroom a few times, nodded to his cousin lying there, and out of courtesy asked if there was anything he needed. And he found it that much easier to acknowledge and respect Hans Castorp's aversion to any discussion, because he shared it, and indeed considered his own situation even more embarrassing than his cousin's.

But on return from his solitary Sunday-morning constitutional, he could no longer put off consulting his cousin about things that demanded immediate attention. Taking a position beside his bed, he heaved a sigh and said, "Yes, well, it's no use. We have to do something. They're expecting you at home."

"Not yet," Hans Castorp replied.

"No, but within a few days—Wednesday or Thursday."

"Oh," Hans Castorp said, "they're not expecting me on any particular day. They have other things to do besides waiting for me and counting the days till I return. I'll arrive when I arrive, and Uncle Tienappel will say, 'So here you are!' And Uncle James will say, 'Well, have a good time?' And if I don't arrive just yet, it will be a good while before they even notice, you can be sure of that. Though it goes without saying that in due time they will have to be notified."

"You can imagine," Joachim said with another sigh, "how unpleasant the whole affair is for me. What's going to happen now? Of course I feel more or less responsible. You come up here to visit me, and I introduce you to life up here, and now here you sit, and no one knows when you'll be able to get away again and start your career. You must realize how terribly embarrassing this is for me."

"I beg your pardon," Hans Castorp said, his hands still clasped behind his head. "What are you getting in such a stew about? That's simply nonsense. Did I come up here to visit you? Yes, that too. But the primary reason, after all, was to take a vacation, on orders of Dr. Heidekind. Well, and now it turns out that I needed a vacation a lot more than he or any of us dreamed I did. I'm surely not the first person who thought he was just dropping by for a visit, and then had things turn out differently. Just think of *Tous-les-deux*'s second son, and how it turned out very differently for him, too. I don't know whether he's even still alive, perhaps they removed the body during a meal one day. I really am surprised to learn that I'm a little ill, but I'll just have to get used to being a patient here, to actually being one of you, instead of merely the visitor I've been until now. But, then again, I'm not that surprised, either, because I've never really felt all that splendidly healthy, and when I think of how both my parents died young—then where was such splendid health supposed to come from? That you've got a little problem yourself—although it's as good as cured now—why, none of us has ever pretended otherwise. So it may well be that it runs in the family a little—Behrens at least dropped a hint to that effect. At any rate, I've been lying here since yesterday asking myself just how I've always felt about it all, what my attitudes are, you know, about the whole thing, about life and its demands. I've always been rather serious by nature, with a certain aversion to anything loud or robust. We were speaking about the same thing here not long ago, about how I've sometimes almost wished I had become a clergyman, what with my interest in sad, edifying things—you know, like a black funeral pall with a silver cross and R.I.P. on it. *Resquiescat in pace*—that's the loveliest phrase, and I find it personally much more appealing than something rowdy like 'he's a jolly good fellow.' It all comes, I think, from my having a little problem myself and having understood something about illness from the start—which has all become apparent now. But since that's how things have turned out, I can only say it was a lucky thing I came up here and got myself examined. You don't have to reproach yourself for anything. You heard him say yourself that if I had stayed down below and continued my life just as before, it's quite possible my whole pulmonary lobe would have gone, willy-nilly, to the devil."

"You can't be sure of that!" Joachim said. "And that's just it—that you can't be sure at all. He claims you had some spots before that no one paid any attention to and they healed by themselves, so that all you have left are a few unimportant muffled tones. The same thing might have happened with this moist spot you've got now if you hadn't happened to come up to visit me—you just can't be sure."

"No, you can't be sure of anything," Hans Castorp replied. "Which is precisely why no one has any right to assume the worst—about how long I'll have to stay on here at your spa, for instance. You say that no one knows when I'll get away and start work on the docks, but you say it from the pessimistic point of view. And that, I think, is premature, precisely because you can't be sure. Behrens mentioned no dates—he's a prudent fellow and doesn't want to play the fortune-teller. And I haven't even had my picture taken with X-rays yet, and only that will give us an objective view of the facts. Who knows whether anything worth mentioning will even show up, or whether I won't have rid myself of my fever by then and can bid you all adieu. I'm for not playing this thing up too soon, so that we end up crying wolf back home. It will be enough if we write a letter—I can write it myself with my fountain pen if I prop myself up a little—and tell them I've got a bad cold and a fever, that I'm staying in bed and won't be traveling just yet. And then we shall see what we shall see."

"Fine," Joachim said, "that's what we'll do for now. And the rest of it can wait, too."

"What rest of it?"

"Well, just stop and think! You arrived here with a steamer trunk packed for a three-week stay. You'll need underwear, shirts, winter clothes, and some other footwear. And finally, you'll need to have more money sent, too."

"*If*," Hans Castorp said, "*if* I need it."

"Good, let's wait and see," Joachim said and began to pace the room. "But we ought not—no, we cannot allow ourselves to have any illusions. I've been here too long not to know what's what. Once Behrens says that you have a rough spot, almost a rattle . . . But, of course, of course, we can wait and see."

And that was how they left things for now. The regular schedule, with its weekly and fortnightly deviations, took its course. Even in his present situation Hans Castorp participated in it all—if not by direct enjoyment, then at least through the reports Joachim gave him when he visited and sat down on the edge of the bed for fifteen minutes.

His Sunday breakfast tea tray was decorated with a little vase of flowers, and they had not forgotten to send along some of the pastries served in the dining hall on Sundays. Later in the morning, things turned lively in the garden and on the terrace. With a fanfare of trumpets and screechy clarinets the fortnightly Sunday concert began, for which Joachim had joined his cousin in his room, taking a seat out on the balcony to listen. Hans Castorp sat half propped up in bed, his head tilted to one side and a blurry look of fond devotion in his eyes, and he listened now to the harmonies drifting in through the open balcony door—though not without a mental shrug at the thought of Settembrini's babblings about music being "politically suspect."

But, as we have noted, when it came to the rest of the day's sights and events, he had Joachim provide him a report; he asked him about the festive outfits that had been brought out for Sunday, the lace peignoirs and such (although it had turned too cold for lace peignoirs); about whether there had been any afternoon carriage rides (there had indeed— the entire Half-Lung Club had left on an excursion to Clavadel). On Monday, when Joachim looked in on him on his way back from Dr. Krokowski's lecture and before his afternoon rest cure, Hans Castorp demanded to hear everything that had been said. Joachim proved rather closemouthed and reluctant to report on the lecture—but then, the two of them had not said much about the previous one, either. Nevertheless, Hans Castorp insisted on hearing details.

"Here I lie, paying full price," he said, "and I want to get something out of what is offered, too." He recalled his independent walk on Monday two weeks before and that it had not done him much good; he even expressed a rather definite conjecture that it had created a revolution in his body and caused his silent, latent illness to erupt.

"And the way the people up here talk," he exclaimed, "the common people, I mean. It sounds so dignified and solemn, almost like poetry sometimes. 'Fare thee well and much obliged!' " he repeated, imitating the woodsman. "I heard that up in the forest, I'll never forget it as long as I live. That sort of thing gets caught up with other impressions and memories, you know, and just keeps ringing in your ears till the day you die. And so Krokowski spoke about 'love' again, did he?" he asked, grimacing as he said the word.

"But of course," Joachim said. "What else? It is his topic, after all."

"What did he have to say about it today?"

"Oh, nothing special. You know yourself from last time the way he puts things."

"But what new ideas did he treat us to?"

"Nothing new, really . . . yes, well, he was selling basic chemistry today," Joachim reluctantly and patronizingly reported. It was all about a kind of poisoning, about the organism poisoning itself, which, Dr. Krokowski had said, was the result of the decomposition of a certain, still-unidentified substance present throughout the body; the by-products of that decomposition had an intoxicating effect on certain centers in the spinal cord, not all that different from what happens when other poisons, such as morphine or cocaine, are introduced into the body.

"So that's what causes flushed cheeks," Hans Castorp said. "Think of it, that's something worth learning. The things that man knows! He's a regular fountain of information. Just wait, someday soon he'll identify that substance present throughout the body, and he'll manufacture those by-products himself, the ones with the intoxicating effect on the spinal cord. He can really get folk tipsy, then. It may well be that people knew the trick of it at one time. Listening to him makes you think there's something to those stories about love potions and the other stuff they talk about in old sagas. Are you going now?"

"Yes," Joachim said, "I really have to take my rest cure. The curve on my chart has been rising since yesterday. This problem of yours has definitely had its effect on me after all."

And so Sunday, and Monday, passed. And the evening and the morning were the third day of Hans Castorp's stay in the "stall," a weekday with nothing to distinguish it—a Tuesday, the day of his arrival. He had been here for three weeks, and so he felt compelled to write a letter home and inform his uncle, however superficially for now, of how things stood. His pillows stuffed behind his back, he wrote on sanatorium stationery about how his scheduled departure had been delayed. He was lying in bed with a fever and a cold, which Director Behrens, being the overconscientious doctor he was, had evidently refused to take all that lightly and instead saw within the larger context of his—the letter-writer's—general constitution. At their very first meeting, in fact, the supervising physician had found him very anemic, and in consequence of all this, it now appeared that the length of stay that he—Hans Castorp—had originally planned could no longer be regarded as sufficient. Further details as soon as possible. "Just right," Hans Castorp thought, "not one word too many, and yet it takes care of things for a while, no matter what." The letter was handed to the porter, who avoided the postal detour of a mailbox, and took it down to meet the next scheduled train.

This done, our adventurer felt he had put things in general good order and his mind was at ease; and although tormented by the cough and stuffy head of a cold, he lived each day as it came—each normal day, its established sameness divided into little segments, neither diverting nor boring, and always the same. Each morning there would be a robust knock on his door, and the bath attendant would enter, a sinewy fellow named Turnherr, with rolled-up sleeves and heavily veined forearms. In a gurgling voice with a serious impediment, he would address Hans Castorp—as he did all the patients—by his room number and then proceed to rub him down with alcohol. Not long after he left, Joachim would appear, already dressed by then, to say good morning and ask his cousin about his seven o'clock temperature and inform him of his own. While Joachim was eating his breakfast downstairs, Hans Castorp would sit up, pillows stuffed behind his back, and do the same, with the healthy appetite that a change in life can bring—and would be disturbed hardly at all by the bustling, businesslike invasion of the doctors, who by this time had passed through the dining hall and were now making their rounds, moving at double time through the rooms of the bedridden and moribund. His mouth full of jam, he would announce that he had slept "quite well" and gaze across the rim of his cup at the director, who was standing in the center of the room, one fist braced against the table, hastily scanning the temperature chart; he would respond in a calm, drawling voice as they wished him good morning and departed. He would light a cigarette, and before he had even realized that Joachim was gone, here would come his cousin, already back from his morning constitutional. They would chat about one thing or another, and the time until second breakfast, which Joachim faithfully used for a rest cure, was so brief that even a downright dimwit or lamebrain could not have managed to be bored, whereas it gave Hans Castorp an opportunity to feast on his impressions of the first three weeks up here and to meditate on his current situation and what it perhaps might lead to—so that he had almost no use for the two thick illustrated magazines from the sanatorium library that lay on his nightstand.

It was the same with the time required for Joachim's second walk, this time down to Davos-Platz—another easy hour. He would look in again on Hans Castorp and, standing or sitting beside the sickbed for a moment, tell him about whatever he had happened to notice on his walk, then leave to take his noon rest cure. And how long was that? Again, just a brief hour. No sooner had you clasped your hands behind your head to gaze at the ceiling and pursue some passing thought than the gong sounded for those who were not bedridden or moribund to get ready for the day's main meal.

Joachim would leave, and the "midday soup" would arrive—soup was the simplified, symbolic name for what came. Because Hans Castorp was not on a restricted diet—why should he have been? A restricted diet, short commons, would hardly have been appropriate to his condition. There he lay, paying full price, and what they brought him at this hour of fixed eternity was "midday soup," the six-course Berghof dinner in all its splendor, with nothing missing—a hearty meal six days a week, a sumptuous showpiece, a gala banquet, prepared by a trained European chef in the sanatorium's deluxe hotel kitchen. The dining attendant whose job it was to care for bedridden patients would bring it to him, a series of tasty dishes arranged under domed nickel covers. She would shove over the bed table, which was now part of the furniture, a marvel of one-legged equilibrium, adjust it across his bed in front of him, and Hans Castorp would dine from it like the tailor's son who dined from a magic table.

And no sooner had he finished eating than Joachim would return; and then it would be almost two-thirty before he left for his balcony and the silence of the main rest cure settled over the Berghof. Not quite two-thirty, perhaps; to be precise, it was more like a quarter past. But such extra quarter hours left over from nice, round whole ones don't really count, they are simply swallowed up along the way—at least that is what happens wherever time is managed on a grand scale, on long journeys, for instance, or on train rides that last for hours, or in similar situations when life is emptiness and waiting and all activity is reduced to whiling time away and putting it behind you. A quarter past two—that's as good as half past; and half past two is the same as half till three, for heaven's sake. Those thirty minutes can be regarded as a prologue to the full hour from three till four and that takes care of them. That is how it's done under such circumstances. And so, in the end, the main rest cure was actually reduced to a mere hour—which in turn was abbreviated, contracted, and given an apostrophe, as it were. And the apostrophe was Dr. Krokowski.

Yes, Dr. Krokowski no longer circumvented Hans Castorp when he made his independent afternoon rounds. Hans Castorp counted now. He was no longer an interval or hiatus, he was a patient; he, too, was questioned, instead of being left lying there to his own devices, as he had been every day until now—much to his slight and secret annoyance. It was on

Monday that Dr. Krokowski had first materialized in his room—we say "materialized," because that is the best word for the strange, almost terrifying impression it had made on Hans Castorp, no matter how hard he tried to shake it that day. He had been lying there dozing for fifteen minutes or half an hour, when he was startled awake by the sudden realization that the assistant was in his room, striding toward him, having entered not by way of the door, but from outside. He had not used the corridor, but had moved along the balconies, and had come in now through the open balcony door, creating the impression that he had materialized out of thin air. At any rate, there he had stood beside Hans Castorp's bed—black and pale, broad-shouldered, stout, the hour's apostrophe—and visible under his two-pronged beard had been a manly smile and yellowish teeth.

"You seem surprised to see me, Herr Castorp," he had said in his gentle baritone; his consciously affected, drawling accent had an exotic, palatalized r—not a rolled r, but simply a single tap of the tongue just behind the upper front teeth. "I am merely fulfilling a pleasant duty in stopping by to see how you are doing. Your association with us has entered a new phase—overnight our guest has become a comrade." (The word "comrade" had made Hans Castorp feel rather uneasy.) "Who would have thought it!" Dr. Krokowski had joked in a comradely voice. "Who would have thought that evening when I first had the pleasure of greeting you, and you responded to my mistaken view—it was a mistake at the time—by declaring that you were perfectly healthy. I think I expressed something of my doubts at the time, but I assure you that I did not mean this. I do not wish to represent myself as more perspicacious than I am. I certainly wasn't thinking at the time of a moist spot, my intentions were quite different, more general, more philosophical. I was articulating my doubts that the words 'human being' and 'perfect health' could ever be made to rhyme. And even today, despite what happened at your examination, from my viewpoint—which is different from that of my distinguished supervisor—this moist spot here"—and he had lightly touched Hans Castorp's shoulder with the tip of one finger—"cannot be regarded as the primary object of interest. It is merely a secondary phenomenon. Organic factors are always secondary."

And Hans Castorp had flinched.

"So in my eyes at least, your catarrh is merely a tertiary phenomenon," Dr. Krokowski had added very nonchalantly. "How is that cold, by the way? I'm certain bed rest will soon take care of it. Have you been measuring your temperature today?" And at that point the assistant's visit had taken on the character of a rather harmless inspection, which continued to be the case in the following days and weeks. Dr. Krokowski would enter by way of the balcony at a quarter till four or a little earlier, greet the recumbent patient in his cheerful, manly way, make a few very elementary medical inquiries, bring the conversation around briefly to more personal topics, and make a comradely joke or two. And although these visits never failed to have a certain dubious aura about them, one can eventually become accustomed to dubious things—if they remain within limits. And Hans Castorp soon found he had no objections to Dr. Krokowski's regular "materializations." They simply belonged to the fixed schedule of a normal day, and ended the main rest cure with an apostrophe.

And so by the time the assistant stepped back out onto the balcony, it was four o'clock—which meant late, late afternoon. Suddenly and before you even realized it, it was late afternoon, which would deepen now seamlessly into oncoming evening. And by the time tea had been taken, both in the dining room below and in room 34, it was very close to five o'clock; and by the time Joachim had returned from his third obligatory walk and had dropped in on his cousin again, it was so close to six o'clock that, once you rounded it off a little, the time left in the rest cure until supper was reduced to just one hour—and it was child's play to drive such paltry forces of opposing time from the field of battle, particularly if you had thoughts in your head and an *orbis pictus* on the nightstand.

Joachim would look in before leaving for supper. His own tray would be brought in. The valley would long since have filled with shadows, and while Hans Castorp ate, it would grow discernibly darker in the white room. When he had finished, he would sit there propped up against his pillows, his empty dishes and his magic table before him, and gaze out into the quickly falling dusk—today's dusk, which was hardly distinguishable from yesterday's, or the dusk of the day before yesterday, or of a week ago. There was evening—and there had just been morning. The day, chopped into little pieces by all these synthetic diversions, had in fact crumbled in his hands, and turned to dust—and he would notice it now, either in cheerful amazement or, at worst, with a little pensiveness, since to shudder at the thought would have been inappropriate to his young years. It seemed to him that he was simply gazing, "on and on."

One day, ten or twelve days perhaps after Hans Castorp had taken to his bed, there was a knock on his door at that same hour—that is to say, just before Joachim was due to return from supper and the evening social. And in response to Hans Castorp's tentative "come in," Lodovico Settembrini appeared on the threshold. All of a sudden the room was dazzlingly bright—because the visitor's first gesture upon opening the door had been to switch on the ceiling lamp, and in a flash the room was overflowing with a sudden clarity that was reflected off the white of the ceiling and furniture.

The Italian was the only person among the sanatorium's residents about whom Hans Castorp had expressly asked during this period. All the same, every time Joachim sat or stood beside his cousin's bed for ten minutes or so—and that happened ten times a day at least—he would report about all the little events and anomalies in the institution's daily life, and if Hans Castorp had questions they were always of a more general, impersonal nature. Despite his isolation, his curiosity did not go beyond asking if new guests had arrived or any familiar faces had departed; and he seemed content to learn that only the former was the case. There was one newcomer, a young man with a greenish, sunken face, and he had been given a place at the table to the cousins' right, between Levi of the ivory skin and Frau Iltis. Well, Hans Castorp could wait to see him with his own eyes. And so no one had left? Joachim replied curtly in the negative, his eyes lowered. But he had to answer the same question several times, every other day really, and finally, with some impatience in his voice, he tried to settle the issue once and for all, declaring that as far as he knew no one was planning to depart—people didn't normally leave here that abruptly.

But as for Settembrini, Hans Castorp had expressly asked about him, demanding to know what he had "to say about it." —About what? — "Why, that I'm lying here, presumably ill."

And, in fact, Settembrini had responded, although very briefly. On the day Hans Castorp vanished, he had approached Joachim and asked where their visitor might be, obviously expecting to be told that Hans Castorp had departed. And in reply to Joachim's account, he had uttered just two words in Italian. The first was, "*Ecco!*" the second, "*Poveretto!*"— meaning "There you are!" and "Poor fellow!"—you did not have to understand any more Italian than these young men to grasp the meaning of those two words.

"But why '*poveretto*'?" Hans Castorp had asked. "Here he sits with his literature, made up of equal parts of humanism and politics, but he can't do much by way of improving the more mundane issues in life. He shouldn't be so arrogant about pitying me. I'll be back down in the flatlands before he is."

And now here stood Herr Settembrini in the abruptly illuminated room. Bracing himself on an elbow to turn toward the door and blinking into the light, Hans Castorp recognized him now, and blushed. As always, Settembrini was wearing his heavy coat with the wide lapels, a frayed turndown collar, and checked trousers. He had come directly from supper and, as was his habit, had a wooden toothpick between his lips. Under the handsome upward sweep of his moustache, the corners of his mouth were drawn into the familiar, delicate, dry, critical smile.

"Good evening, my good engineer. Do the rules allow my looking in on you? If so, we needed some light for it—please forgive my arbitrarily taking care of the matter," he said, waving one small hand toward the ceiling lamp. "You are engaged in deep contemplation—I certainly don't mean to disturb you. An inclination to ponder matters would be quite understandable in your situation, and there's always your cousin if you wish to chat. You see, I am perfectly aware of just how superfluous I am. All the same, one lives in such close proximity, one senses a mutual regard, man to man, a certain sympathy, a sympathy of both the mind and the heart. It is almost a week now since we last saw one another. I had indeed begun to suspect that you had departed when I saw your place vacant down in the refectory. The lieutenant set me to rights—hmm, or should we say, set me to what was wrong, if that does not sound impolite. In short, how are you doing? What are you doing? How do you feel? Not all too depressed, I hope?"

"It's you, Herr Settembrini. How kind of you. Ha, ha—'refectory'? Another one of your jokes. Please, have a chair. You're not disturbing me in the least. I've been lying here musing—and musing is probably an exaggeration. I was simply too lazy to turn on the light. Thanks so much, I'm feeling almost normal, subjectively at least. My cold is almost gone, thanks to the bed rest, but it's apparently only a secondary phenomenon, or so I've been told. My temperature still is not quite what it should be—sometimes ninety-nine point five, sometimes ninety-nine point nine. That hasn't changed in the past few days."

"You've been measuring regularly, have you?"

"Yes, six times a day, just like all of you up here. Ha, ha—excuse me for laughing, I was just thinking about your calling our dining hall a refectory. That's what they call it in a monastery, is it not? There really is some resemblance—I've never been in a monastery, but I can imagine it's much like here. And I can rattle off the litany of the 'rule' and observe it quite faithfully."

"Like a pious monk. One might say you've ended your novitiate and have taken your vows. My solemn congratulations. You're already calling it 'our dining hall,' yourself. By the way—not that I wish to cast any aspersions on your masculinity—but you almost remind me more of a young nun than a monk, one of those innocent young brides of Christ, her hair newly shorn, with great martyr's eyes. Whenever I happened to notice those sacrificial lambs, it was never without . . . without a certain flood of sentimentality. Ah, yes, yes, your good cousin has told me all about it. And so at the last moment you let them examine you."

"Because I was feverish. What would you have me do about such a cold, Herr Settembrini? I would have consulted our family doctor down in the plains. And up here, with two specialists, where information comes from the horse's mouth, so to speak—it would have been strange if . . ."

"Quite so, quite so. And you had been measuring your temperature, too, before anyone instructed you to do so. Although that was suggested to you right from the start. Nurse Mylendonk slipped you a thermometer, am I right?"

"Slipped me one? Since I needed it, I bought one from her."

"I understand. Purely a business transaction. And how many months has the director saddled you with? Good God, I asked you that same question once before. Do you remember? You had just recently arrived. You were very cocky with your answers that day."

"I certainly do remember, Herr Settembrini. I've had a great many new experiences since then, but I can remember it as if it were yesterday. You were so amusing, even that first day. You turned Director Behrens into one of the judges of hell—Radames? No, wait, that's somebody else."

"Rhadamanthus? It's possible I might have called him that in passing. I don't always remember everything that may burst from my lips."

"Rhadamanthus, right! Minos and Rhadamanthus! And you even spoke to us about Carducci that first day . . ."

"If you will pardon me, my friend, we shall leave *him* out of this. *His* name sounds all too strange coming from you at the moment."

"Fine with me," Hans Castorp laughed. "But you have taught me a great deal about him, you know. Yes, back then I hadn't the vaguest, and I told you that I had come for three weeks. How could I have known any different? And Fräulein Kleefeld had just whistled hello to me with her pneumothorax, and I was a little taken aback. Although I felt feverish from the start, too—because the air here is good not only for *fighting off* illness, but it's also good *for* it, sometimes bringing it to eruption. Which is probably necessary in the end, if there's to be any healing."

"An alluring hypothesis. Did Director Behrens also tell you about a certain Russian woman whom we had here for five months last year— no, wait, the year before last? No? He should have. A delightful lady, of German heritage, married, a young mother. She came from somewhere in the Baltic region, anemic, lymphatic, there were perhaps more serious problems as well. Well, she spends a month here and complains of feeling very ill. Just be patient! A second month passes, and she continues to maintain that she's not getting better, but worse. She is told that the doctor, and the doctor alone, can tell how she is *doing*; she can merely tell him how she is *feeling*—and that doesn't matter much. They are satisfied with her lung. Fine, she says nothing, she continues her rest cure and loses weight with every week. She faints during her four-month checkup. That's of no concern, Behrens says; they are really quite satisfied with her lung. But when by month five she can no longer walk, she writes her husband back by the Baltic, and Behrens receives a letter from him—the envelope is marked "personal" and "urgent" in a vigorous hand, I saw it myself. Yes, Behrens says now with a shrug, it has begun to look as if the climate here does not agree with her. The woman was beside herself. They should have told her that before, she cried, she had felt it all along, and now they had ruined her health entirely! We can only hope that she regained her strength once she joined her husband again by the Baltic."

"Excellent. What a way you have with stories, Herr Settembrini—every word is absolutely graphic! I've laughed quietly many a time at your story about the girl who went for a swim in the lake and then was given a silent sister. Yes, the things that happen here. Always something new. My own case is still quite uncertain, by the way. The director claims he has found a little something wrong with me. There are some old spots, where I was sick once before without ever knowing it, I heard those myself when he tapped, and now he says he can hear a fresh one—ha, 'fresh' sounds quite peculiar in that context. But so far it's merely a matter of acoustical observation, and we won't have any real diagnostic certainty until I'm on my feet again and they X-ray me and take an interior snapshot. Then we'll know for sure."

"Do you think so? Did you know photographic plates often show spots that are assumed to be cavities when they are mere shadows, and that sometimes when something *is* there, it doesn't show *any spots* at all? *Madonna*, the photographic plate! There was a young numismatist here who was feverish; and since he was feverish one could clearly make out cavities on his photographic plate. They even claimed to have heard them! He was treated for phthisis—and died. The autopsy revealed there was nothing wrong with his lungs and that he had died of some coccus infection or other."

"Now, listen here, Herr Settembrini, you're already talking about autopsies. I don't think I'm that far along just yet."

"My good engineer, you are a wag."

"And you are a dyed-in-the-wool critic and skeptic, if I do say so! You don't even believe in exact science. Does *your* plate show spots?"

"Yes, it shows a few."

"And you really are ill, aren't you?"

"Yes, unfortunately I am rather ill," Herr Settembrini replied and hung his head. There was a pause, broken by his cough. Hans Castorp looked up from his bed at his guest, whom he had reduced to silence. With two very simple questions, it seemed, he had dumbfounded him, refuted every possible argument, even the world republic and beautiful style. For his part, he did nothing to start up the conversation again.

After a while Herr Settembrini sat up with a smile. "But tell me now, my good engineer," he said, "how has your family taken the news?"

"Which news do you mean? About the delay in my departure? Ah yes, my family. My family at home consists of three uncles—a great-uncle and his two sons, who are more like cousins to me. I have no other family than that, since I was orphaned very early. Taken the news? They really don't know all that much yet. When I first had to take to my bed, I wrote them that I had a bad cold and could not travel. And yesterday, since it has been a little while now, I wrote again and said that in treating my catarrh Director Behrens had become interested in the state of my lungs and insisted I extend my stay until we could achieve some clarity about that. They will have taken it all quite calmly."

"And your new position? You spoke of a course of practical activity on which you intended to embark shortly."

"Yes, as an unsalaried engineer-in-training. I asked them to excuse me from my duties on the dock for now. You mustn't suppose they are in any despair about it. They can get along without a trainee for as long as necessary."

"Fine, fine. So that from that side, everything is in order. Composure up and down the line. People are generally detached in your native land, are they not? Although they can be energetic, too!"

"Oh yes, energetic, too, very energetic," Hans Castorp said. From a distance now, he examined life in his homeland and found that his interlocutor had characterized it correctly. "Detached and energetic, you're probably right there."

"Well," Herr Settembrini continued, "should you remain somewhat longer, I have no doubt we shall all make your good uncle's acquaintance—I mean your great-uncle's. He's certain to come up and check on your situation."

"Out of the question!" Hans Castorp cried. "Under no circumstances! Wild horses couldn't get him here. My uncle is very apoplectic, you see— stout, hardly any neck. No, he requires sensible barometric pressure. He would do worse here than the Russian lady from the Baltic region. He'd be in an awful mess."

"What a disappointment. Apoplectic, you say? What good are detachment and energy in that case? Your good uncle is a rich man, I take it? And you are rich, too, aren't you? People are generally rich where you come from."

Hans Castorp smiled at Herr Settembrini's literary generalization and from his bed he looked again into the distance, to the world at home from which he was now removed. He thought back, trying to judge impersonally, and found that distance helped him to do so.

"Some people are rich, yes," he answered now, "and some are not. And if not—so much the worse. And me? I'm no millionaire, but what I have is well invested. I'm independent, have enough to live. But let's leave me out of it. If you had said one *has* to be rich back there—I would have agreed with you. Because let us assume you are *not* rich, or stop being rich—you are in a sorry state! 'Him? Does he still have some money left?' they ask. Those are their very words, and that's the face they make. I've heard those words often enough, and I realize now that they are engrained in my mind. And so they must have struck me as rather strange even though I was used to hearing them—otherwise they would not be engrained in my mind. Don't you think? No, I don't suppose that as a *homo humanus* you would feel at home with us. Even for someone like me whose home it is, it all seems rather crude sometimes—though I must add I've never personally had to suffer under it. If someone doesn't make sure that the best, most expensive wines are served at his dinners, people simply don't go, and his daughters end up old maids. That's how people are. As I lie here now and look at it all from a distance, it does seem crude to me. What were the terms you used—detached and . . . And energetic! Fine, but what does that really mean? That means hard, cold. And what does hard and cold mean? It means cruel. The air down there is cruel, ruthless. Lying here and watching from a distance, it almost makes me shudder."

Settembrini listened, nodding. He nodded again when Hans Castorp finished his critical remarks for now and fell silent. Then he heaved a sigh and said, "I will not attempt to gloss over the specific forms life's natural cruelty takes in your society. Be that as it may—the charge of cruelty is a rather sentimental charge. You would hardly have been able to make it there among your own people, for fear of looking ridiculous even to yourself. You have rightly left the making of that charge to life's shirkers. For you to make it now is proof of a certain alienation that I would not like to see take root. Because a man who gets used to making that charge can very easily be lost to life, to the form of life for which he was born. Do you know what that means, my good engineer: 'to be lost to life'? I know, I do indeed. I see it here every day. Within six months at the least, every young person who comes up here (and they are almost all young) has nothing in his head but flirting and taking his temperature. And within a year at the most, he will never be able to take hold of any other sort of life, but will find any other life 'cruel'—or better, flawed and ignorant. You love stories—let me supply you with one. Let me tell you about a young man, someone's husband and son, who was here for eleven months, whom I got to know. He was a little older than you, I believe—several years older in fact. He improved and was released on probation. He returned home and was received with open arms by his family—not just uncles, but a mother and a wife. He lay around the whole day with a thermometer in his mouth and paid no attention to anything else. 'You don't understand,' he said. 'You have to have lived up there to know how things really are. You people down here lack the basic concepts.' It finally came to the point where his mother declared, 'Go back up. There's no living with you here.' And he came back up. He returned to his 'home.' You do know, don't you, that people call this 'home' once they've lived up here? He was a total stranger to his young wife, she likewise lacked the 'basic concepts'—and decided not to join him. She realized he would stay on and find a lady friend at 'home' whose 'basic concepts' agreed with his own."

Hans Castorp had apparently been only half listening. He went on staring at the incandescent clarity of his white room, as if gazing into the distance beyond. His laugh came a little late now and he said, "He called it home, did he? That's really rather sentimental, as you put it. Yes, you do know an endless number of stories. I was still considering what we were saying about hardness and cruelty. I've been mulling over the same thing in one form or another for the last few days. You see, a person probably needs a rather thick skin to be in perfect natural agreement with the way people think down there in the flatlands, asking questions like 'Does he still have some money left?' and making those faces they make. I never found it all that natural, even if I'm not a *homo humanus*. It has always struck me that way, although I've only noticed it just now, after the fact. Maybe my own unconscious tendency to illness had something to do with my finding it unnatural. I heard those old spots myself, and now Behrens has evidently found a fresh minor problem. It was something of a surprise, I suppose, and yet I really wasn't all that astonished, either. I've never felt all that robust, actually; and besides, both my parents died so young—I was orphaned twice as a child, you know."

Herr Settembrini coordinated head, shoulders, and hands in a serene, polite gesture to illustrate his question: Yes, well? And what of it?

"You're a writer," Hans Castorp said, "a literary man. You really should be able to understand and appreciate how under such circumstances a person might not be so tough-minded or find it perfectly natural for people to be so cruel—normal people, you know, who stroll about and laugh and make money and stuff their bellies. I don't know if I'm expressing myself . . ."

Settembrini bowed. "You wish to say," he explained, "that early and repeated contacts with death give rise to a basic mind-set against the cruelties and crudities of life as it is thoughtlessly lived out in the world. Or, let us say, it makes one aware of and sensitive to its cynicism."

"Precisely," Hans Castorp exclaimed with genuine enthusiasm. "You've put it perfectly, dotted the i and crossed the t, Herr Settembrini. Contacts with death! I know that as a man of letters you . . ."

Laying his head to one side and closing his eyes, Settembrini held out a hand toward him in a very beautiful and gentle gesture of restraint, a plea to be heard further. He held this pose for several seconds, long after Hans Castorp had fallen silent to wait somewhat awkwardly for what was to come. Finally he opened his black eyes—those organ-grinder eyes—and said, "Permit me, permit me, my good engineer, to tell you something, to lay it upon your heart. The only healthy and noble and indeed, let me expressly point out, the only *religious* way in which to regard death is to perceive and feel it as a constituent part of life, as life's holy prerequisite, and *not* to separate it intellectually, to set it up in opposition to life, or, worse, to play it off against life in some disgusting fashion—for that is indeed the antithesis of a healthy, noble, reasonable, and religious view. The ancients decorated their sarcophagi with symbols of life and procreation, some of them even obscene. For the ancients, in fact, the sacred and the obscene were very often one and the same. Those people knew how to honor death. Death is to be honored as the cradle of life, the womb of renewal. Once separated from life, it becomes grotesque, a wraith—or even worse. For as an independent spiritual power, death is a very depraved force, whose wicked attractions are very strong and without doubt can cause the most abominable confusion of the human mind."

Herr Settembrini said no more. He had come to a halt at a generality, but had done so most definitively. He was very serious—he had not spoken in a conversational tone, had refused to allow Hans Castorp any opportunity to pick up the thread or contradict him, and had lowered his voice decisively to mark the end of his statement. He sat there with his mouth closed, his hands folded in his lap, one check-trousered leg crossed over the other, and he gazed sternly at his foot swinging gently in the air.

Hans Castorp was silent, too. Sitting up against his pillows, he turned his face toward the wall and drummed his fingertips lightly on his comforter. He felt he had been lectured to, corrected, even scolded, and there was a great deal of childish sullenness in his silence. This pause continued for some time.

At last Herr Settembrini raised his head again, and said with a smile, "Do you remember, my good engineer, how we once had a similar dispute, one could well say, the same dispute? Our conversation that day— I believe we were out walking—was about sickness and stupidity; and out of a respect for illness, you declared the combination of the two a paradox. I called that respect a gloomy notion that dishonored the very idea of humanity, and to my delight you appeared not all that reluctant to take my objections into consideration. We spoke about the neutrality and intellectual hesitancy of youth, of its freedom to choose, its tendency to experiment with all sorts of standpoints, and of how one need not regard such experiments as final, life-determining options. Would you allow me"—and here Herr Settembrini bent forward on his chair, and with a smile he placed both feet on the floor, tucked his folded hands between his knees, and thrust his head forward at a slight tilt—"would you allow me," he repeated with some emotion in his voice, "to lend you a helping hand in your exercises and experiments and to play a corrective role whenever I see danger looming in the form of some pernicious fixation?"

"But of course, Herr Settembrini!" Hans Castorp was quick to abandon his uneasy, half-defiant attitude; he stopped drumming on his comforter and turned back to his guest with confused affability. "That's extraordinarily kind of you. But I really have to ask myself . . . I mean, in my case it would be . . ."

"Quite *sine pecunia*," Herr Settembrini quoted as he stood up. "A man can't allow himself to be outclassed." They laughed. They heard the first double door open, and in the next moment they heard the latch of the inner one.

It was Joachim, back from the evening social. He blushed when he caught sight of the Italian, exactly as Hans Castorp had done; his tanned face turned one visible shade darker. "Oh, you have a visitor," he said. "How nice. I was delayed. They made me play a game of bridge—at least they tell people it's bridge," he said, shaking his head, "but it turned out to be something quite different. I won five marks."

"Just so its appeal doesn't become a vice," Hans Castorp said. "Yes, yes—Herr Settembrini has done a splendid job of helping me pass the time—though that's a poor way of putting it. I suppose that could apply as well to your sham game of bridge. Whereas Herr Settembrini really did help me employ my time meaningfully. A respectable man should be trying with might and main to get out of here—particularly when he sees sham bridge games breaking out in his midst. But given the chance to listen often to Herr Settembrini and to have him lend a helping conversational hand, I think I almost might want to stay feverish indefinitely and just sit tight here with you all. It wouldn't be long before they would have to give me a silent sister to keep me from cheating."

"I repeat, my good engineer, you are a wag," the Italian said. He took leave of them very courteously.

Left alone with his cousin, Hans Castorp heaved a great sigh. "What a pedagogue," he said. "A humanist pedagogue, admittedly. He just never stops correcting you, sometimes in the form of stories and sometimes more abstractly. And you end up talking with him about things—that you never would have thought you would talk about or even understand. And if I had run into him down in the flatlands, I'm sure I would *not* have understood them," he added.

Joachim usually stayed awhile with him now, sacrificing two or three quarter hours of his evening rest cure. Sometimes they played chess on Hans Castorp's bed table—Joachim had brought a set with him from down below. Later he would leave—lock, stock, and thermometer—for his balcony, and Hans Castorp would have to take his temperature one last time while soft music drifted up, now near, now far, from the night-enshrouded valley. At ten o'clock the rest cure would be over; he would hear Joachim stir; he would hear the couple from the Bad Russian table—and then Hans Castorp would turn over on his side, waiting for sleep to come.

The night was the more difficult half of the day, because Hans Castorp would wake frequently and often even lie awake for hours on end—perhaps because his overheated blood kept him alert or because his fully horizontal mode of life meant the loss of both the desire and the need for sleep. The hours of slumber were, however, animated with varied and lively dreams, and he could go on indulging in them even while lying there awake. Divided as it was into little segments, the day provided him with diversion, but the hours of night, as they marched past in their blurred uniformity, had much the same effect. And when morning drew near, he found it amusing to watch the objects in his room gradually grow visible, emerging from under a veil of gray, to see daylight kindle outside, sometimes only smoldering murkily, sometimes catching bright fire. And before one even thought about it, the moment had come for the robust knock of the bath attendant, announcing that the daily schedule was in force once again.

Hans Castorp had not brought a calendar along for his little excursion, and so he was never quite sure of the current date. Now and then he would ask his cousin to tell him, but he, too, was not always certain about the matter. All the same, Sundays, and in particular every second Sunday with its concert, gave Hans Castorp something to hang on to in his present situation. But this much was certain: September was fairly far advanced now, somewhere toward the middle. The gloomy and cold weather that had reigned in the valley outside when Hans Castorp had first taken to his bed had given way to splendid bright summer days, a whole series of such days, which seemed to have no end. Each morning Joachim would appear in his cousin's room dressed in white flannels, only to find he could not suppress his honest regrets, which sat deep in his soul and young muscles, that Hans Castorp had to forgo such splendid weather. Once he even spoke softly about what a "disgrace" it was that he had to spend it this way—but then, to mollify him, added that he didn't know himself how to take better advantage of it, since experience had taught him to avoid extensive exercise here. And, after all, the wide-open balcony door allowed his cousin to enjoy something of the warm shimmering light out there.

But toward the end of Hans Castorp's prescribed retreat, the weather changed again. It turned foggy and cold overnight, the valley wrapped itself in wet, blowing snow, and the gentle, dry warmth of the radiator filled the room. And it was on that same day, when the doctors came by on their rounds, that Hans Castorp reminded the director that he had been lying there for three weeks now and asked permission to get up.

"What the—is your time up already?" Behrens said. "Let me think. I do declare, it's true. Good God, how quickly we do get old. Not that your condition has changed all that much in the meantime. What? It was normal yesterday? Yes, except for the measurement at six in the evening. Well, Castorp, I don't want to be like that, and so I'll return you to human society. Arise, go thy way, my good man. Within the prescribed borders and limits, of course. We shall do a portrait of your interior here shortly. Make a note of that," he said to Dr. Krokowski as they departed, pointing over his shoulder with a giant thumb at Hans Castorp and training his watery, bloodshot, blue eyes on his pallid assistant. And so Hans Castorp left the "stall."

In rubber boots and with a turned-up coat collar, he accompanied his cousin again for the first time up to the bench beside the water trough and back. As they walked he could not help remarking that he wondered how long the director would have let him lie there if he had not himself mentioned the time was up. And Joachim, his eyes shifting about and his mouth opening as if to utter a hopeless "oh," let his hand trail off in a gesture of immeasurability.

"My God, I See It!"

A WEEK PASSED before Hans Castorp received orders from Head Nurse Mylendonk to report to the X-ray laboratory. He had not wanted to press the matter. It was apparent that this was a busy time for the Berghof, that the doctors and staff had their hands full. New guests had arrived in the last few days: two Russian students, both with heads of thick hair and high-buttoned black blouses without a trace of collar or cuff; a Dutch married couple, who were assigned places at Settembrini's table; a hunchbacked Mexican, who terrified his tablemates with horrible asthma attacks, when he suddenly could not get his breath and would then grab his neighbor, man or woman, in the iron grip of one of his long hands, hold on tight as a vise, and drag his struggling, panicky victim, now shouting for help, down into the pool of dread with him. In short, the dining hall was already as good as full, although the winter season did not begin until October. And Hans Castorp's case was hardly severe enough, high enough on the scale of illness, for him to have any right to claim special treatment. For all her stupidity and ignorance, Frau Stöhr, for instance, was without doubt much more ill than he, not to mention Dr. Blumenkohl. One would have to lack all sense of decorum or hierarchy not to have exercised restraint in Hans Castorp's case—particularly since such sensibilities were essential to the spirit of the house. People who were only slightly ill did not count for much—he had often overheard conversations to that effect. They were spoken of disparagingly and considered inferior by local standards, not only by those of higher or highest rank, but also by those who themselves were only "mildly ill"—which allowed them to shrug off their own cases; while at the same time, by subjecting themselves to such standards, they were able to preserve and enhance their own self-esteem. Which is only human. "Oh, him," they might say about one another, "there's really not much wrong with him, hardly has the right to be here. Doesn't even have a cavity." Such was the spirit of the place—aristocratic in its own special way; and Hans Castorp greeted it out of an inborn respect for law and order of every sort. When in Rome, as the saying goes. Travelers prove their lack of education if they make fun of the customs and values of their hosts, and the qualities that do a person honor are many and varied. Hans Castorp even showed a certain regard and consideration for Joachim—not so much because he was an old-timer here and had served as his guide and cicerone in this world, but more particularly because there was no doubt that he was "seriously ill." But since this was how things were, it was only understandable if someone made as much of his case as possible, even exaggerated a little to be part of the aristocracy or at least get closer to it. Whenever his tablemates asked about his temperature, Hans Castorp, too, would add a few tenths, and he found it impossible not to feel flattered when they shook their fingers at him as if he were a particularly sly rascal. But even if he laid it on a little thick, he was still low on the ladder, as it were, and so patience and reticence were certainly appropriate behavior.

He had resumed the mode of life adapted in his first three weeks—the familiar, regular, and perfectly ordered life at Joachim's side; everything went like clockwork from the first day, as if there had never been an interruption. And indeed it had meant nothing; he became aware of that fact when he first returned to his table. Joachim, who attached definite importance to such tokens, had of course seen to it that a few flowers adorned the returnee's place setting; but Hans Castorp's tablemates greeted him with little ceremony, with essentially no more interest than usual, as if he had been gone for three hours and not three weeks—not so much out of indifference to this ordinary, sympathetic fellow or out of self-absorption and preoccupation with their own interesting bodies, but because they were oblivious to the intervening time. And Hans Castorp had no trouble following suit, because when he took his seat again at the end of the table, between the teacher and Miss Robinson, it seemed as if he had been gone for a day at most.

And if the people at his own table did not make much fuss about the end of his isolation, how could anyone else in the dining hall have done so? Literally no one there had noticed his return—with the sole exception of Settembrini, who came over at the end of the meal to extend a friendly, witty greeting. Hans Castorp, of course, added one further exception of his own, though with what justification we shall have to leave undecided. He told himself that Clavdia Chauchat had noticed his reappearance— the moment she entered, late as always and having first let the glass door slam, her narrow eyes had rested on him, or so it seemed, and had met his own; no sooner had she sat down than she had looked back over her shoulder at him and smiled the same smile he had seen three weeks before, on the day of his examination. And she was so open, even brazen, about it—brazen in regard both to him and to the rest of the guests—that he had not known whether to be overjoyed or, in case it was a mark of disdain, upset. At any rate, his heart had shrunk beneath those looks— which in his eyes had contradicted and denied, in a most flagrant and intoxicating fashion, the reality that he and the sick woman were not so much as social acquaintances—had, in fact, shrunk almost painfully at the first rattle of the glass door, and his breath had come short and shallow as he sat waiting for that moment.

It should also be noted that Hans Castorp's innermost relationship to this patient from the Good Russian table, the interest his modest intellect and his senses now took in this Kirghiz-eyed, softly slinking woman of average stature—in brief, his infatuation (and the word is apt, even though it is a word from "down below," a word of the plains, and might imply that the little song about "how oft it thrills me" was somehow applicable here)—his infatuation, then, had made considerable progress during his isolation. A vision of her had floated before his eyes as he had watched early dawn slowly unveil his room and dusk thicken again come evening. (It had also been floating there very clearly the evening Settembrini had suddenly entered and set the room ablaze with light—which was why he had blushed at the sight of the humanist.) During each hour of his segmented day, he had thought of her mouth, her cheekbones, her eyes—whose color, shape, and placement cut deep into his soul—of her limp back, the way she carried her head, the neck bones above the collar line of her blouse, her arms a radiant illusion under flimsiest gossamer. And if we did not previously mention that this was how the long hours had passed so effortlessly for him, it was because we sympathize with the qualms of conscience that accompanied the terrifying bliss of these visions and images. Yes, terror and fear were bound up with them; hope, joy, and nameless dread could spill over into boundless uncertainty and total extravagance, but at times they could also suddenly press in on his young heart—that is, his heart in the genuine, physical sense—so that he would put one hand to that organ and the other to his brow, as if to shade his eyes, and whisper, "My God!"

For behind his brow were the thoughts or half-thoughts that first conferred true cloying sweetness to his visions and images, thoughts that centered on Madame Chauchat's carelessness and brazenness, on the illness that accentuated and enhanced her body, the illness that embodied her very being and that he now shared with her according to medical dictum. The realization formed behind his brow that Madame Chauchat was taking utter license with those looks and smiles, totally disregarding their not being social acquaintances—as if they were not social creatures at all, as if there were no need for them even to *speak* to one another. And that was what terrified him, in the same way he had been terrified that day down in the examination room, when he had rapidly shifted his searching glance from Joachim's naked upper torso to his eyes—the difference being that it was pity and worry that had been the source of his terror then, whereas other factors were involved here.

And so now life at the Berghof—this blessed and well-regulated life

on a narrow stage—resumed its steady pace. And while Hans Castorp
waited to have a picture taken of his interior, he continued to share that
life with dear old Joachim, doing exactly what he did, hour for hour; and
close proximity with his cousin was probably good for the young man.
It was a proximity based solely on illness; all the same, Joachim had a
great deal of military integrity about him—though, granted, without his
even being aware of it, that integrity was being increasingly satisfied by
rest cures, to the point where they had become, as it were, a substitute
for duties fulfilled in the flatlands, a kind of spurious occupation. Hans
Castorp was not so dull that he had not noticed that much quite accurately,
but he also sensed an inhibiting, restraining effect on his own civilian
sentiments—indeed it may have been this proximity, the example he took
from it and its supervisory aspect, that kept him from overt actions and
blind adventures. For he could observe only too well how Joachim had
to endure the daily, constant assaults of orange-scented handkerchiefs,
round brown eyes, a little ruby, a great many unwarranted giggles, and
an externally well-formed chest; and the common sense and love of honor,
which enabled Joachim to avoid those assaults and flee from them, touched
Hans Castorp, kept him under some control and prevented him from
"borrowing a pencil," as it were, from a certain narrow-eyed person—
which experience taught him he would have been only too ready to do
without Joachim's disciplining proximity.

Joachim never spoke of tittering Marusya, which therefore precluded
Hans Castorp from mentioning Clavdia Chauchat. He restricted himself
to harmless, furtive exchanges at meals with the teacher on his right,
teasing the old maid about her weakness for their supple fellow patient
until she would blush, and all the while trying to maintain his dignity
by imitating old Grandfather Castorp's chin-propping method. He also
pressed her in order to learn new and interesting details about Madame
Chauchat's private life—her origins, her husband, her age, the exact nature
of her illness. Did she have any children? he wanted to know. Oh,
certainly not, no children. What would a woman like her do with children?
Presumably she had been strictly forbidden to have any—and then, too,
what sort of children would they have turned out to be? Hans Castorp
had to concur. It was probably also too late now, he suggested with
rugged objectivity. There were times, he remarked, when Madame Chauchat's face, in profile at least, looked rather severe. Was it possible she
was already past thirty? Fräulein Engelhart violently contested the very
idea. Clavdia, thirty? At the worst, twenty-eight. And as for her profile,
his tablemate forbade him ever to say such a thing again. Clavdia's profile
was one of softest, sweetest youth—though it was, of course, a most

interesting profile as well, not that of some healthy little goose. And by way of punishment and without even pausing, Fräulein Engelhart added that she knew for a fact that Frau Chauchat often entertained a gentleman caller, a fellow countryman who lived in Platz. She received him in her room every afternoon.

The shot was well aimed. Despite everything he could do, Hans Castorp's face looked strained, and even phrases like "you don't say" and "well, I never," with which he tried to parry her opening move, sounded strained. Incapable of simply shrugging off the existence of this fellow countryman as he pretended to do at first, he kept returning to the topic. With twitching lips he asked: A younger man? Young and attractive, from everything she had heard, the teacher replied, although she hadn't actually seen him to judge for herself. Ill? At most, a very mild case. Well, he did hope, Hans Castorp said, that collars and cuffs were more in evidence with him than with her fellow countrymen at the Bad Russian table. And still intent on punishing him, Fräulein Engelhart claimed she was sure they were. Then he admitted that it was a matter that one should look into and earnestly commissioned her to find out what could be found out about the comings and goings of this fellow countryman. But several days later, instead of providing him with more information, she had other, completely different news for him.

She had learned that Clavdia Chauchat was having her portrait painted—and asked Hans Castorp whether he knew about that, too. If not, he could nevertheless be certain that she had it from the very best sources. For some time now, Clavdia had been sitting for her portrait, posing for someone right here in the house. And who was that? Why, the director. *Hofrat* Behrens, who saw her for that express purpose twice daily in his private residence.

This announcement affected Hans Castorp even more than her previous news. He now tried making several forced jokes about it. Well, of course, it was well known that the director did oils—what did the teacher want, it wasn't forbidden, everyone was free to do so. And in the director's own widower's apartments, had she said? Well, he hoped that at least Fräulein von Mylendonk was present for the sittings.

"But she doesn't have the time."

"Surely Behrens doesn't have more time than our head nurse," Hans Castorp replied sternly.

But although that seemed to be his final remark at first, he was not at all prepared to let the subject drop and almost exhausted himself asking questions about every conceivable detail: about the picture itself—its size and whether it was just a head or a seated portrait—about the hours when the sittings were held. Fräulein Engelhart, however, could not satisfy him about these matters, either, and had to put him off with assurances that she would make further inquiries.

Immediately after hearing this news, Hans Castorp took his temperature—it was 99.9 degrees. He was far more worried and pained by the visits that Frau Chauchat paid than by those she received. Her private life—as a topic in and of itself and apart from what happened in it—had already begun to cause him pain and worry, and those same feelings could only intensify once rumors reached him of what was actually happening in her life. Granted, it was perfectly likely that the relationship between the Russian visitor and his countrywoman was quite sober and harmless; but for some time now, Hans Castorp had found himself regarding sobriety and harmlessness as twiddle-twaddle—just as he could not convince himself that oil painting was anything but an excuse for a relationship between an overenergetic, garrulous widower and a narrow-eyed, pussy-footing young woman. The taste the director displayed in his choice of models corresponded all too closely to his own for him to believe there was anything sober about it—and to reinforce his opinion, he needed only to picture the director's purple cheeks and bloodshot pop-eyes.

An observation he made quite by chance on his own during this same period had a different effect on him, though it also served to confirm his own good taste. At the table set crosswise on the cousins' left, the one near the side door, where Frau Salomon and the gluttonous student with glasses sat, there was another patient—from Mannheim, Hans Castorp had heard—a man about thirty years old, with thinning hair, bad teeth, and a timid way of speaking—the same fellow who occasionally played the piano at their evening social gatherings, usually the "Wedding March" from *A Midsummer Night's Dream*. He was said to be very religious, which, as might be expected, was not uncommon among the people up here, or so Hans Castorp had been told. It was said he attended services down in Platz every Sunday and read devotional books during rest cure—books with a chalice or palm fronds on the cover. And, as Hans Castorp happened to notice one day, this fellow's eyes were staring in the same direction as his own; like his own, they were fixed fondly—and shyly and insistently, if not to say fawningly—on Madame Chauchat's supple body. Once Hans Castorp had noticed this fact, he could not help confirming it again and again. He would spot him standing among the other guests in the game room of an evening, gazing gloomily and forlornly at the charming, though flawed woman who was sitting on the sofa in the small salon and chatting with frizzy-haired Tamara (that was the droll-looking girl's name), Dr. Blumenkohl, the man with the concave chest, and the hunch-shouldered youths from her table. He saw him turn away and, as misery played across the upper lip, slowly sneak an over-the-shoulder look out of the corner of one eye. He noticed how he blushed and did not look up, and then *did* look up when the glass door slammed and Frau Chauchat glided to her seat. And several times he watched as the poor fellow took up a position between the door and the Good Russian table so that Frau Chauchat would have to pass by him at the end of the meal. She paid him no regard, but he devoured her at close range with eyes full of profound sadness.

This discovery also caused young Hans Castorp no little worry, although the Mannheimer's sad, greedy looks did not trouble him as much as the private relations between Clavdia Chauchat and Director Behrens—a man very much his superior in age, character, and position. Clavdia paid no attention to the man from Mannheim—if she had, it certainly would not have escaped Hans Castorp's sharpened instincts. And so it was not the nasty thorn of jealousy that pricked his soul in this case. But he did explore all the feelings that intoxication and passion can explore once they catch a glimpse of themselves in the world outside, feelings that are the strangest mixture of disgust and shared emotions. If we are to get on with our story, however, it will be impossible to fathom and analyze all of that. In any case, the added emotional experience of observing the patient from Mannheim was almost too much for a man like poor Hans Castorp to have to deal with all at once.

And so eight days passed until Hans Castorp's X-ray examination. He had not known how many days would have to pass, but one morning at early breakfast he received his orders from the head nurse, who had another sty now—it could not be the same one; apparently she was naturally susceptible to this harmless but disfiguring ailment. He had to report to the laboratory that afternoon—which made it eight days. Hans Castorp was to appear a half hour before tea, along with his cousin, since Joachim was also supposed to have a picture taken of his interior at the same time—his previous one being too old to be considered valid.

And so they both had cut short the main afternoon rest cure by a half hour, had "descended" the stairs to the pseudo-basement at three-thirty on the dot, and now sat in the little waiting room that separated the consulting and X-ray rooms. Joachim, for whom this was nothing new, was quite calm; Hans Castorp was a little feverish with expectation, since until now no one had ever taken a look into his organic interior. They were not alone. Several guests were already seated in the room, tattered illustrated magazines spread over their knees. They all waited together: a young, big bruiser of a Swede, who sat at Settembrini's table in the dining hall and who people said had been so ill when he arrived the previous April that he had been admitted only with great reluctance, but who now had put on eighty pounds and was about to be released as fully cured; a woman from the Bad Russian table, a mother, a wretched soul; and her even more wretched, long-nosed, ugly son named Sasha. The three had been waiting before the cousins' arrival and presumably had precedence on the appointment list. Evidently they were well behind schedule in the adjoining X-ray room, and a long wait appeared likely.

They were very busy in there—you could hear the director's voice giving orders. It was a little past three-thirty when a technical assistant who worked down here opened the door to admit the lucky Swedish bruiser—evidently his predecessor had been let out by way of another exit. Things proceeded more quickly now. Ten minutes later they heard footsteps in the corridor—the stalwart stride of the fully cured Scandinavian, a walking advertisement for the climate and the sanatorium. The Russian mother and Sasha were admitted. As he had noticed previously when the Swede had gone in, Hans Castorp saw that semidarkness, a kind of artificial twilight, reigned in the X-ray room—just as it did in Dr. Krokowski's analytical chamber. The windows had been blacked out, daylight banned, and only a couple of electric bulbs were turned on. Hans Castorp watched as Sasha and his mother were ushered in, and at the same moment the door to the corridor opened and the next scheduled patient arrived—a little early, since the lab was running late. It was Madame Chauchat.

It was Clavdia Chauchat who had appeared suddenly in the little room. Hans Castorp's eyes stared wide when he realized who it was, and he could feel the blood drain from his face and his jaw go slack—his mouth was close to dropping open. Clavdia's entrance had been so random, so totally unexpected—one moment she was not there, and the next she was sharing the little waiting room with the two cousins. Joachim gave Hans Castorp a quick glance and then not only lowered his eyes, but also picked up a magazine he had only just put back on the table, and hid his face behind it. Hans Castorp could not make up his mind to do the same. After first turning pale, his face was now very red, and his heart was pounding.

Frau Chauchat took a seat on a little round chair with rather rudimentary, stubby arms that stood beside the door to the laboratory; she leaned back, crossed one leg lightly over the other, and stared into space, although the nervous distraction of being watched gave a certain sly squint to her Pribislav eyes. She was wearing a white sweater and a blue skirt and held a book, a library book it appeared, on her lap; she lightly tapped out a rhythm with the sole of the shoe resting on the floor.

Barely ninety seconds had passed before she shifted her position, looked around, stood up with a face that seemed to say she did not know what she was doing here or whom to ask—and began to speak. She asked something, directing her question to Joachim, even though he was still engrossed in his magazine and Hans Castorp was sitting there doing nothing at all. She formed the words with her mouth and there was a voice, too, coming from that white throat. It was the voice Hans Castorp already knew—not too low, pleasantly husky, and with a slight edge to it—knew both from a great distance and, once, from up close, when it had spoken words meant for him: "Glad to. But be sure to give it back to me after class." Those words had been spoken in fluent German, however, and in a more definite tone; these now were halting and in broken German, a language to which she had no natural right, but was merely borrowing—just as Hans Castorp had heard her do a few times before, listening each time with a sense of superiority that was simultaneously cradled in humble delight.

One hand in the jacket of her wool sweater, the other at the back of her head, Frau Chauchat asked, "Please, for what time is your appointment?"

And Joachim, glancing quickly again at his cousin and clicking his heels in his seated position, replied, "Three-thirty."

She now continued, "Mine is for three forty-five. What time is it? It is almost four. Someone just went in, am I correct?"

"Yes, two people," Joachim responded. "They were ahead of us. The lab is behind schedule. It looks as if everything has been moved back a half hour."

"That is unpleasant," she said and nervously patted her hair.

"Rather!" Joachim replied. "We've been waiting almost a half hour now."

The two of them conversed, and Hans Castorp listened as if in a dream. For Joachim to speak with Frau Chauchat was almost the same as if he himself were speaking with her—though, of course, totally different, too. Hans Castorp had been offended by Joachim's "Rather!"—it had sounded so impertinent, or at least oddly indifferent under the circumstances. But the main thing was that Joachim spoke, that he was able to speak to her *at all* and perhaps was even showing off a little for his cousin with his impertinent "Rather!"—just as Hans Castorp had himself showed off for Joachim and Settembrini when he had been asked how long he intended to stay and had said, "Three weeks." She had turned to address Joachim, despite the magazine he was holding up in front of his face—because he was a long-term resident, of course, and so she had known him longer, at least by sight. Although there was that other reason, too: a polite social conversation, an articulated exchange was quite appropriate for them, because no savage, profound, terrible secret existed between them. Had someone brown-eyed, with a ruby ring and orange-blossom perfume, been waiting here with them, it would have been up to him, Hans Castorp, to speak up and say, "Rather!"—to stand across from her so sovereign and correct. Although he would have said, "Certainly, mademoiselle, rather unpleasant," and perhaps have pulled his handkerchief from his breast pocket with a little flourish and blown his nose. "Please, be patient. We're in the same situation ourselves." And Joachim would have been amazed at his easygoing manner—presumably, however, without seriously wanting to have changed places with him. No, given the situation, Hans Castorp was not jealous of Joachim, either, even though it was he who had spoken with Frau Chauchat. It did not bother him that she had turned to Joachim; she had taken the circumstances into account in doing so, thereby making it clear that she was aware of those circumstances. His heart was pounding.

After having been treated by Joachim so coolly—indeed, Hans Castorp sensed something of a gentle hostility in good Joachim's attitude toward their fellow patient, a hostility that made him smile despite his own inner turmoil—"Clavdia" tried pacing the room; but there was not enough space for that, and so she, too, picked up a magazine from the table and returned to her round chair with its rudimentary arms. Hans Castorp sat there and stared at her, so long that he had to assume his grandfather's chin-propping pose—which made him look absurdly like the old man. Frau Chauchat had again lightly crossed one leg over the other, and now the slender outline of the whole leg was visible under the blue fabric of her skirt. She was of only average height, which Hans Castorp found very agreeable, just the right size. But she had relatively long legs and was not at all broad in the hips. She was not leaning back now, but was bent forward, her forearms folded and resting on the thigh of the crossed leg, her back rounded and her shoulders hunched so that the bones of her neck stuck out—you could almost see her spinal column under the close-fitting sweater. Her breasts, which were not voluptuous and high-set like Marusya's, but the small breasts of a young girl, were pressed together from both sides. Suddenly Hans Castorp recalled that she was also here waiting to be X-rayed. The director was painting her, interpreting her external appearance with color and oils on canvas. But there in the twilight, he would turn rays on her that would expose the inside of her body. And at the thought, Hans Castorp turned his head to one side, and his face darkened with the shadow of respectability and assumed a look of discretion and propriety that seemed appropriate to such a vision.

The three of them did not have to wait long together. The staff inside was apparently in a hurry to catch up and had made short work of Sasha and his mother. Once again the technician in his white smock opened the door. Joachim stood up and tossed his magazine on the table; Hans Castorp followed him, although not without some apprehension, toward the door. Chivalrous scruples stirred within him, tempting him to address Frau Chauchat politely after all and offer to let her go first—perhaps even in French, if he could manage it. And he hastily searched his memory for vocabulary and syntax. But he did not know if such courtesies were usual here, if the schedule of appointments was not considered far more important than acts of chivalry. But Joachim would surely know, and it did not appear as if he were about to defer to the lady present, despite the troubled, earnest look Hans Castorp threw him. And so he followed his cousin past Frau Chauchat, who glanced up fleetingly from her hunched-over position, and they moved through the door to the laboratory.

He was so numbed by what he had just left behind, by the adventures of the last ten minutes, that he was unable immediately to realign his inner world as he crossed the threshold into the X-ray room. He saw nothing, or only general outlines, in the artificial twilight. He could still hear Frau Chauchat's pleasant, opaque voice saying, "What time is it. . . . Someone just went in. . . . That is unpleasant . . . ," and the timbre of her voice caused a shudder of sweet excitement to pass up and down his back. He could see her knee outlined under her skirt, the back of her neck bent forward under the short, reddish-blond hairs that hung loose from the tucked-up braid, saw the neck bones sticking out—and the shudder passed over him once again.

He now saw Director Behrens standing in front of a cupboard or built-in cabinet, his back to them as they entered; he was inspecting a blackish plate that he held out at arm's length against the dull light of the ceiling lamp. They passed him as they moved deeper into the room, and were themselves passed by the assistant, who was busy getting things ready for the procedure. There was a peculiar odor here—a kind of stale ozone smell in the air. The built-in unit jutted out between the two black-curtained windows, dividing the laboratory into unequal parts. You could make out clinical apparatus of various sorts: glassware, switch boxes, and tall vertical gauges, but also a camera-like box on a rolling stand and rows of glass photographic plates set along the walls. You couldn't tell if you were in a photographer's studio, a darkroom, or an inventor's workshop and sorcerer's laboratory.

Joachim began without further ado to strip to the waist. The assistant, a younger, squat, red-cheeked local in a white smock, instructed Hans

Castorp to do the same—it would go fast, it would soon be his turn. While Hans Castorp was removing his vest, Behrens stepped out of the smaller recess and joined them in the larger part of the room.

"Hello there," he said. "Why, it's our Dioscuri boys—Castor and Pollux. Please, keep all screams of pain to a minimum. Be careful now, we're going to look right through you both. I believe you're afraid to reveal your insides to us, aren't you, Castorp? You may set your mind at ease—our procedures are quite aesthetic. Look here—have you seen my private gallery?" And grabbing Hans Castorp by the arm, he pulled him over to the rows of dark glass plates; he flipped a switch. Illuminated now, the plates revealed pictures. Hans Castorp saw body parts: hands, feet, knees, thighs, calves, arms, pelvises. But the rounded living contours of these fragments of the human body were phantomlike and hazy; like a fog or a pale, uncertain aura, they enclosed a clear, detailed, and carefully defined core: the skeleton.

"Very interesting," Hans Castorp said.

"Very interesting, indeed," the director replied. "Useful visual aids for the instruction of the young. Illuminated anatomy, the triumph of the age. This is a female arm, you can tell by its dainty form, you see—the kind they hug you with on intimate occasions." And he laughed, which set his upper lip and short-cropped moustache a little more askew. The pictures went dark. Hans Castorp turned away to watch the preparations for taking Joachim's interior portrait.

These were under way in front of the built-in unit where the director had been standing as they came in. Joachim had sat down on a kind of cobbler's bench, facing a panel, against which he now pressed his chest, hugging it at the same time with both arms. The assistant helped Joachim improve his position, pushing his shoulders farther foward and massaging his back in a series of kneading motions. He now moved behind the camera, and like a photographer, legs spread wide, bent forward to check the angle; he expressed his satisfaction, and stepping to one side he told Joachim to take a deep breath and hold it until everything was over. Joachim's back expanded and stayed that way. At the same moment, the assistant flipped the appropriate switches. For two seconds the dreadful forces necessary to penetrate matter were let loose—a current of thousands of volts, one hundred thousand, Hans Castorp thought he had heard somewhere. Barely tamed for their purpose, these forces sought other outlets for their energy. Discharges exploded like gunshots. The gauges sizzled with blue light. Long sparks crackled along the wall. Somewhere a red light blinked, like a silent, threatening eye, and a vial behind Joachim's back was filled with a green glow. Then everything calmed down;

the spectacle of lights vanished, and Joachim expelled his breath with a sigh. It was over.

"Next culprit," Behrens said, and poked Hans Castorp with his elbow. "Now don't pretend you're too tired. You'll get a free copy, Castorp. Just think, you'll be able to project the secrets of your bosom on the wall for your children and grandchildren."

Joachim had stepped away; the technician was changing plates. Director Behrens personally showed the novice how he was to sit and hold his body. "Hug it," he said. "Hug the panel. Imagine it's something else if you like. And press your chest up tight, as if it meant sweet bliss. That's it. Breathe deep! Hold it!" he commanded. "Now smile, please!"

Hans Castorp waited, his eyes blinking, his lungs full of air. The thunderstorm burst behind him, hissing, crackling, popping—and fell quiet again. The lens had peered inside him.

He dismounted, confused and dazed by what had happened to him, although he had not felt anything at all during the penetration.

"Well done," the director said. "Now, let's have a look for ourselves."

Joachim, being an old hand at this, had moved back toward the exit door to take up a position at an adjustable frame. Behind him stood the broad structure of the apparatus, a glass retort extruding tubes and half filled with liquid visible on its top rear shelf. In front of him, at chest-level, a framed screen dangled from a series of pulleys. To his left, a red-globed lamp sat amid a panel with a switch box. Seating himself astride a footstool placed in front of the dangling screen, the director turned on the lamp. The ceiling lamp went out, and only ruby light illuminated the scene. With one quick motion, the master extinguished that as well, and the laboratory was wrapped in darkest night.

"Our eyes have to adapt first," the director's voice said in the darkness. "We have to wait for our pupils to get nice and big, like a cat's, in order for us to see what we want to see. I'm sure you can understand that we can't see properly, just like that, with our normal daylight eyes. For our purposes here, we first have to ban any rousing daylight scenes from our minds."

"Oh, but of course," Hans Castorp said, standing now behind the director. He had closed his eyes, because in the pitch-black night it made no difference if they were open or shut. "We first have to let darkness wash over our eyes to see anything—that's obvious. I even find it quite appropriate for us to gather together beforehand, in silent prayer, as it were. I'm standing here with my eyes closed and feeling pleasantly drowsy. But what's that odor?"

"Oxygen," the director said. "That's oxygen that you scent in the air.

A gaseous product of our little parlor thunderstorm, if you will. Eyes open!" he said. "Let the exorcism begin." Hans Castorp obeyed at once.

They heard a switch thrown. A motor started, its angry hum mounting higher and higher, but suddenly reduced again to a drone at the flip of another switch. The floor vibrated steadily. The little red light, a long vertical slit, stared at them, silent and threatening. A spark crackled somewhere. The milky glow of a slowly brightening window, the pale rectangle of the fluorescent screen, emerged out of the darkness. And before it sat Director Behrens astride his footstool—thighs spread wide, fists propped against them, snub nose close to the screen that gave him a view into the organic interior of another human being.

"Can you see it, my lad?" he asked.

Hans Castorp bent down over his shoulder, but first looked up once more into the darkness, to where he assumed Joachim's eyes were staring out, gentle and sad, just as on that day at his checkup. "Do you mind?" he asked.

"Oh, please, go ahead and look," came Joachim's generous reply out of the blackness. And with the floor vibrating under him and great forces crackling and blustering at play around him, Hans Castorp peered through the pale window, peered into the void of Joachim Ziemssen's skeleton. His breastbone merged with his spine into one dark, gristly column. The ribs at the front of his rib cage overlapped those at the back, which looked paler. The collarbone curved upward on both sides, and the bones of the shoulder, the joint where Joachim's arm began, looked lean and angular against the soft halo of flesh. The chest cavity was bright, but one could make out a web of darker spots and blackish ruffles.

"Sharp picture," the director said. "That's the respectable leanness of military youth. I've had potbellies here—impenetrable, could recognize next to nothing. They still haven't invented rays that can get through layers of fat like those. But this is clean work. Do you see the diaphragm?" he asked, and pointed a finger at a dark curve rising and sinking inside the window. "You see this knob here, this little raised spot? That's from when he had pleurisy at the age of fifteen. Take a deep breath!" he commanded. "Deeper! I said *deep!*" And Joachim's diaphragm quivered and rose as high as it would go. The upper parts of the lungs were brighter now, but the director was still not content. "Unsatisfactory," he said. "Do you see the hilum there? Do you see those adhesions? Do you see these cavities here? That's where the toxins come from that make him so tipsy."

But Hans Castorp was preoccupied with something that looked like a sack, or maybe a deformed animal, visible behind the middle column, or mostly to the right of it from the viewer's perspective. It expanded and contracted regularly, like some sort of flapping jellyfish.

"Do you see his heart?" the director asked, lifting his giant right hand from his thigh again and pointing an index finger at the pulsating pendant.

Good God, it was his heart, Joachim's honor-loving heart, that Hans Castorp saw. "I can see your heart," he said in a choked voice.

"Please, go ahead and look," Joachim replied again, and he was probably even smiling meekly up there in the dark. But the director ordered him to be silent and not to exchange sentimentalities. He studied the spots and lines, the blackish ruffles in the chest cavity, while his fellow viewer gazed tirelessly at Joachim's sepulchral form, his dry bones, his bare scaffolding, his gaunt *memento mori*. He was filled with both reverence and terror.

"Yes, yes, I see it," he said several times. "My God, I see it!" He had once heard about a woman, a long-dead forebear on the Tienappel side of the family, who was said to have been endowed or cursed with a troublesome talent that she had borne in all humility and that had caused her to see anyone who would soon die as just a skeleton. Which was exactly how good Joachim now looked to Hans Castorp, although with the aid and under the auspices of physical optics—so that it did not really mean anything and was perfectly normal, particularly since he had expressly obtained Joachim's permission. And yet he felt some sympathy for the melancholy fate of his clairvoyant great-aunt. He was deeply moved by what he saw, or more accurately, by being able to see it, but he was also stung by secret doubts whether it might not be somehow abnormal after all, doubts about whether it was permissible to stare like this amid the quivering, crackling darkness. A deep desire to enjoy the indiscretion blended with feelings of compassion and piety.

A few minutes later he himself was standing in the stocks while the little thunderstorm raged, and Joachim, his body closed from view again, began to dress. Once again the director peered through the milky pane, but this time into Hans Castorp's interior, and from his mutterings—ragtag curses and phrases—it appeared his findings corresponded to his expectations. In response to much begging, he was kind enough to allow his patient to view his own hand through the fluoroscope. And Hans Castorp saw exactly what he should have expected to see, but which no man was ever intended to see and which he himself had never presumed he would be able to see: he saw his own grave. Under that light, he saw the process of corruption anticipated, saw the flesh in which he moved decomposed, expunged, dissolved into airy nothingness—and inside was the delicately turned skeleton of his right hand and around the last joint of the ring finger, dangling black and loose, the signet ring his grandfather had bequeathed him: a hard thing, this ore with which man adorns a body predestined to melt away beneath it, so that it can be free again and move on to yet other flesh that may bear it for a while. With the eyes of his Tienappel forebear—penetrating, clairvoyant eyes—he beheld a familiar part of his body, and for the first time in his life he understood that he would die. And he made the same face he usually made when listening to music—a rather dull, sleepy, and devout face, his head tilted toward one shoulder, his mouth half-open.

The director said, "Spooky, isn't it? Yes, there's no mistaking that whiff of spookiness."

And then he put a stop to those great forces. The floor grew quiet, the spectacle of lights faded, the magic window wrapped itself in darkness. The ceiling lamp went on. And while Hans Castorp threw on his clothes, Behrens gave the young people some information about what he had observed, though with proper regard to their abilities as laymen to comprehend it. As for Hans Castorp's case, the optical and acoustical results corresponded as precisely as one could ever demand of science. Both the old spots and the fresh one had been visible, and there were "strands" that ran from the bronchi well down into the lung itself—"strands with nodules." Hans Castorp would be able to verify that for himself on the X-ray plate, a copy of which he would soon be given as promised. And so: rest, patience, manly discipline, food, thermometers, sleep—just grin and bear it. He turned his back to them. They departed. First Joachim, then Hans Castorp, who glanced back over his shoulder as they left. Ushered in by the technician, Frau Chauchat was now entering the laboratory.

Freedom

H OW DID YOUNG Hans Castorp actually feel about all this? For instance, did the seven weeks he had demonstrably, indubitably spent with these people here feel like a mere seven days? Or did it seem to him just the opposite, that he had lived here now much, much longer than he really had? He asked himself those same questions, both privately of himself and formally of Joachim—but could not come to any decision. Probably both were true: looking back, the time he had spent here thus far seemed unnaturally brief and at the same time unnaturally long. It seemed everything to him, in fact, except how it really was—always presuming, of course, that time is part of nature and that it is therefore permissible to see it in conjunction with reality.

In any case, October was close at hand, might arrive any day now. Hans Castorp had no trouble figuring out that much; and besides, he heard mention made of the fact in the conversations of his fellow patients. "Do you realize that it's only five days till the first of the month?" he heard Hermine Kleefeld say to two young men of her acquaintance, Rasmussen the student and the thick-lipped lad, whose name was Gänser. Dinner was just over, its odors still heavy in the air, and people were lingering among the tables, chatting and putting off their rest cure. "The first of October—I noticed it on the calendar in the management office. This will be the second one I've spent at this cozy resort. Well fine, summer, or what there was of it, is over—we've been cheated out of it, just as we're cheated out of everything else in life." And she sighed with her half a lung, shaking her head and directing her doltish, sleepy eyes at the ceiling. "Cheer up, Rasmussen," she then said, slapping her comrade on one drooping shoulder, "and tell us some jokes!"

"I know only a few," Rasmussen replied, his hands dangling chest-high like fins. "But I don't tell them very well—I'm always too tired."

"Not even a dog," Gänser said between his teeth, "would want to go on living like this much longer." And they laughed and shrugged.

Settembrini had been standing close by, too, a toothpick between his lips, and as they were leaving he said to Hans Castorp, "Don't believe them, my good engineer, never believe them when they squawk—and there's not a one who doesn't, although they all feel very much at home here. Lead a free and easy life—and then demand you pity them. Think they have a right to bitterness, irony, cynicism. 'At this cozy resort!' Well, isn't it cozy? I would certainly say it is, and in the most dubious sense of the word. 'Cheated,' the little minx says—'cheated out of everything in life at this cozy resort.' But send her back to the plains and her life down there would leave you in no doubt that her sole object was to get back up here as soon as possible. Ah yes, irony! Beware of the irony that flourishes here, my good engineer. Beware of it in general as an intellectual stance. When it is not employed as an honest device of classical rhetoric, the purpose of which no healthy mind can doubt for a moment, it becomes a source of depravity, a barrier to civilization, a squalid flirtation with inertia, nihilism, and vice. And since the atmosphere in which we live provides very favorable conditions for this swamp plant to flourish, I may hope—or perhaps I must fear—that you do understand me."

The Italian's remarks were truly the sort that, if Hans Castorp had heard them down in the plains seven weeks before, would have been mere

noise; but his stay up here had made his mind receptive for them—
receptive in terms of intellectual understanding, though not necessarily in
terms of sympathy, which perhaps is the more telling factor. For although
in the depths of his soul he was glad that, despite everything that had
happened, Settembrini continued to speak with him as he did, continued
to teach, to warn, to try to influence him, his own perceptive powers had
advanced to the point where he would criticize the remarks and withhold
his agreement, at least to some extent. "How about that," he thought,
"he talks about irony in almost the same way he talks about music. The
only thing missing is for him to call it 'politically suspect' the moment it
stops being an 'honest and classical means of instruction.' But if 'no
healthy mind can for a moment doubt its purpose,' what sort of irony
is that for heaven's sake, if I may ask?—assuming I am to have a say in
any of this. That would just be dry pedantry!" (Such is the ingratitude
of immature youth. It accepts the gift of learning, only to find fault
with it.)

Nevertheless, he would have found it all too risky to put his insubordination into words. He limited himself to objecting to Herr Settembrini's
critique of Hermine Kleefeld, which seemed unjust to him—or which,
for other reasons, he wanted to see as unjust.

"But the girl is ill," he said. "She is truly, positively very ill and has
every reason to be in despair. What do you want from her, really?"

"Illness and despair," Settembrini said, "are often only forms of depravity."

"And what about Leopardi," Hans Castorp thought, "who explicitly
despaired of science and progress? Or what about our good schoolmaster
himself? He's ill and keeps coming back up here. Carducci wouldn't have
been all that happy with him, either." But aloud he said, "Fine fellow
you are. The young lady may breathe her last any day now, and you call
her depraved. You'll have to explain that for me. If you had said that
illness is sometimes a result of depravity, that would at least have been
plausible, or—"

"Very plausible," Settembrini broke in. "My word! So you would have
agreed had I left it at that?"

"Or if you had said that illness sometimes is made to serve as a pretext
for depravity—I would have accepted that, too."

"*Grazie tanto!*"

"But illness as a *form* of depravity? Which means, not that it arises
from depravity, but is itself depravity? Now that's a paradox."

"Oh, I beg you, my good engineer, do not lay that at my door. I
despise paradoxes. I loathe them. You may assume that everything I said

about irony also applies to paradoxes, and more besides. Paradox is the poison flower of quietism, the iridescent sheen of a putrefied mind, the greatest depravity of all. By the way, I also notice you are coming to the defense of illness yet again."

"No, what you say interests me. It reminds me of some of the things that Dr. Krokowski lectures about on Mondays. He, too, declares illness to be a secondary phenomenon."

"No pure idealist, he."

"What do you have against him?"

"Precisely that."

"Don't you approve of analysis?"

"Not every day. It's very bad and very good, by turns, my good engineer."

"How am I supposed to take that?"

"Analysis is good as a tool of enlightenment and civilization—to the extent that it shakes stupid preconceptions, quashes natural biases, and undermines authority. Good, in other words, to the extent that it liberates, refines, and humanizes—it makes slaves ripe for freedom. It is bad, very bad, to the extent that it prevents action, damages life at its roots, and is incapable of shaping it. Analysis can be very unappetizing, as unappetizing as death, to which it may very well be linked—a relative of the grave and its foul anatomy."

"Well roared, lion," Hans Castorp could not help thinking, as he usually did when Herr Settembrini uttered something pedagogic. But now he said, "We recently participated in some illuminated anatomy downstairs on the ground floor. That's what Behrens called it when he X-rayed us."

"Ah, so you've now scaled to that level, too. Well?"

"I saw the skeleton of my own hand," Hans Castorp said, trying to recall the emotions that had stirred in him at the sight of it. "Have you ever had him show you yours?"

"No, I'm not the least bit interested in my own skeleton. And what was the medical finding?"

"He saw strands, strands with nodules."

"The imp of Satan!"

"You called Director Behrens that once before. What do you mean by it?"

"You may be sure that I choose the term deliberately."

"No, you're not being fair, Herr Settembrini. I'll admit that the man has his weaknesses. After being here awhile, even I don't find the way he talks that congenial; there's something so fierce about it, especially when you think of the grief that he felt at losing his wife up here. But what an admirable, respectable man he is all in all, a benefactor to suffering humankind. I recently met him as he was coming from an operation, a rib resection, a matter of life or death. And to see him like that, coming from such a difficult, practical task, made a big impression on me. He was still flushed and had just lit a cigar to reward himself. I was envious of him."

"How very generous of you. And your sentence is?"

"He did not mention any definite length of time."

"Not bad, either. So let us go and lie down, my good engineer. Assume our positions."

They said good-bye outside room 34.

"Well, go on up to your roof, Herr Settembrini. It must be more amusing to lie there in the company of others than alone. Do you find it entertaining? Are they interesting people, the ones you take your rest cure with?"

"Oh, nothing but Parthians and Scythians."

"You mean Russians?"

"Russians, male and female," Herr Settembrini said, and a tightening was visible at the corner of his mouth. "Adieu, my good engineer."

No doubt about it, he had meant something by that. Hans Castorp entered his room in confusion. Did Settembrini know what was going on with him? Presumably he had been spying on him for educational reasons, taking careful note of where his eyes were directed. Hans Castorp was angry at the Italian, and at himself, too, because it was his own lack of self-control that had provoked the gibe. He gathered up some writing materials to take out with him for his rest cure—because there could be no more delays, a letter home, his third, would have to be written—and went on being angry, muttering things about this windbag and quibbler, who was sticking his nose into things that were none of his business, but who hummed little songs at girls in public. By now, he no longer felt like taking up the task of writing. This organ-grinder and his insinuations had definitely spoiled the mood for it. But one way or the other, he had to have winter clothes, money, underwear, shoes—everything, in fact, that he would have brought with him had he known he would be here not for just three weeks at the height of summer, but . . . but for a still-undetermined period, which, no matter what, was sure to last into some of winter, indeed, given assumptions and circumstances up here, would very probably include the whole season. And that, or at least the possibility of it, would have to be shared with his family. It would require real work this time—making a clean breast of things and no longer pretending otherwise to himself or them.

And it was in this spirit that he wrote, making use of a technique he had frequently seen Joachim employ—sitting in his lounge chair, with his fountain pen in hand and a writing case against his raised knees. He wrote on sanatorium stationery, taken from an ample supply in his table drawer, to James Tienappel, the uncle to whom he felt closest of the three, and asked him to inform the consul. He spoke of an unforeseen vexation, of misgivings that had proved justified, of the necessity, on good medical advice, of spending a part of the winter, and perhaps all of it, up here, since cases such as his own were often more stubborn than those that began more spectacularly and since the important thing, really, was to intervene decisively and so arrest his case's progress for good and all. Seen from this angle, he suggested, it was a stroke of fortune, a happy turn of fate, that he had chanced to come up here and had occasion to be examined; because otherwise he would probably have remained unaware of his condition much longer and perhaps have learned of it in a much more distressing fashion. As for the estimated time of his cure, one should not be surprised if he might have to make a winter of it and would be able to return to the plains hardly any earlier than Joachim. Notions of time here were different from those applicable to trips to the shore or stays at a spa. The month was, so to speak, the shortest unit of time, and a single month played no role at all.

It was cool; he was wearing his overcoat, had wrapped himself in a blanket, and his hands turned red as he wrote. At times he would look up from his paper, covered with reasonable and convincing phrases, and gaze out into the familiar landscape, which he hardly noticed anymore: the long valley, its exit blocked today by pale, glassy peaks; the bright pattern of settlement along its floor, glistening now and then in the sun; and the slopes, covered partly by rugged forests, partly by meadows, from which the sound of cowbells drifted. Writing came more easily as he went along, and he no longer understood how he could possibly have been afraid of this letter. As he wrote, he came to see that nothing could be more plausible than his explanations and that of course his family at home would be in perfect agreement with them. A young man of his social class and circumstances took care of himself when that proved advisable, he made use of facilities set aside expressly for him and people like him. That was only proper. Had he returned home, they would have sent him right back up here upon hearing his report. He now asked them to send the things he needed. And in conclusion he asked that necessary funds be sent regularly. Eight hundred marks a month would take care of everything.

He signed it. That was done. This third letter home was comprehensive, it did the job—not in terms of conceptions of time valid down below,

but in terms of those prevailing up here. It established Hans Castorp's
freedom. This was the word he used, not explicitly, not by forming the
syllables in his mind, but as something he felt in its most comprehensive
sense, in the sense in which he had learned to understand it during his
stay here—though that was a sense that had little to do with the meaning
Settembrini attached to the word. And as he heaved a sigh, his chest
quivered as the wave of terror and excitement that he knew quite well by
now swept over him.

Blood had rushed to his head as he wrote, his cheeks burned. He picked
up Mercury from the nightstand and took his temperature, as if he could
not let this opportunity pass. Mercury climbed to one hundred degrees.

"You see?" Hans Castorp thought. And he added a postscript: "This
letter has been quite an effort. My temperature stands at a hundred degrees.
I see that for the time being I shall have to keep very quiet. You will have
to excuse me if I do not write often." Then he lay back and lifted a hand
to the sky, palm out, just as he had held it behind the fluorescent screen.
But daylight had no effect on its living form, the stuff of it grew even
darker and more opaque against the brightness and just its outer edge
shone reddish. It was the living hand he was accustomed to seeing, wash-
ing, using—not the alien scaffold he had seen in the screen. The analytical
pit he had seen open up before him that day had closed again.

Mercury's Moods

OCTOBER BEGAN as new months are wont to do—their beginnings
are perfectly modest and hushed, with no outward signs, no birth-
marks. Indeed, they steal in silently and quite unnoticed, unless you are
paying very strict attention. Real time knows no turning points, there are
no thunderstorms or trumpet fanfares at the start of a new month or year,
and even when a new century commences only we human beings fire
cannon and ring bells.

In Hans Castorp's case the first day of October was exactly like the
last day of September. The one was just as cold and inclement as the
other, and those that followed were the same. He needed his winter
overcoat and both camel-hair blankets for his rest cure, and not just of
an evening, but during the day, too. If he tried to hold a book, his fingers
turned clammy and stiff, even though his cheeks were flushed with dry
heat. And Joachim was very tempted to put his fur-lined sleeping bag
to use, but then thought better of it, not wanting to pamper himself
too soon.

But several days later, somewhere between the beginning and the middle of the month, things turned around again, and a belated summer burst upon them with absolutely astonishing splendor. Not without good reason, then, had Hans Castorp heard people praise October in these regions. For a good two and a half weeks a splendid sky reigned above mountains and valley, each new day outdoing the last for sheer blue purity; and the sun burned with such intensity that everyone found good reason to dig out his or her lightest summer clothes, the cast-aside muslin dresses and linen trousers; and even the large white canvas sunshade, which had no handle but was ingeniously fixed with a peg and several holes to the arm of the lounge chair, offered only inadequate protection from the midday glare.

"I'm glad I'm still here to enjoy this," Hans Castorp said to his cousin. "It's been so wretched at times—and now it seems as if we already had winter behind us and the nice weather lay ahead." And he was right. There were few signs to indicate the true state of affairs, and even those were inconspicuous. Some maples that had been planted down in Platz, but were barely surviving, had long since despondently shed their leaves; otherwise there were no hardwoods here to give the landscape the characteristic look of the season—only the hybrid Alpine alders, which drop their soft needles like leaves, were bare and autumnal. The rest of the trees adorning the region, whether tall or stunted, were evergreens steeled against winter, the boundaries of which were so vague that it could scatter snowstorms across the whole year; and only several subtle shades of rusty red that lay over the forest told of a dying year, despite the blazing sun. To be sure, if you looked more closely, there were wildflowers that gently made the same point. Gone now were the purple orchis and bushy columbine, even the wild pink, all of which had adorned the slopes at the visitor's arrival. Only the gentian and stubby meadow crocus were still in bloom, and they attested to a freshness hidden within the superficially heated air, a chill that could suddenly go straight to the bone as you lay there singed by the sun, like an icy shiver in the midst of fever.

Inwardly, then, Hans Castorp ignored the structure by which those who husband time measure its passing and divide it into units, counting and naming each. He had paid no attention to the silent onset of the tenth month; he felt only what his senses felt—blazing heat with icy frost hidden within and beneath it, a sensation that was new to him in this intensity and that suggested a culinary comparison: it reminded him, he remarked to Joachim, of an *omelette en surprise*, where ice cream lay wrapped in hot meringue. He often made such comments, letting them fall quickly and offhandedly, though with emotion in his voice, like a man who is chilled and feverish at the same time. To be sure, in between such moments, he could be silent, too, if not to say turned in upon himself; for although his attention was directed outward, it was focused on just one point. All the rest, whether people or objects, lay in a blur of fog—a fog that was engendered in Hans Castorp's own brain and that Director Behrens and Dr. Krokowski would doubtless have declared to be the product of soluble toxins. He even told himself this was the case—not that the insight aroused in him the capacity or even the slightest wish to be rid of his intoxication.

For it is an intoxication that cares only for itself—nothing could be less desirable or more abhorrent than becoming sober again. It holds its own against all impressions that might suppress it, does not tolerate them out of self-preservation. Hans Castorp knew that Frau Chauchat's profile did not flatter her, but made her look rather severe and not all that young—he had even mentioned it himself on occasion. And the result? He avoided looking at her in profile, literally closed his eyes if by chance, whether at a distance or up close, this was the view offered him—it pained him. And why? His reason should have jumped at the chance to assert itself. But we are asking too much of him. At second breakfast on each of these sparkling mornings, he would turn pale at the thrill of seeing Clavdia appear in the lace peignoir that she wore on warm days and that only added to her special fascination—late as always, slamming the door, smiling, both arms lifted slightly at different angles, standing there at attention to present herself to the dining hall. But he was thrilled not so much because she looked so charming, but because her looking that way only enhanced the sweet fog in his head, increased the intoxication that desired itself, that wanted only nourishment and self-justification.

An observer with a mind like Lodovico Settembrini's would surely have seen such a lack of good intentions as depravity, as "a form of depravity." Hans Castorp occasionally thought about the literary views that the man had offered on "illness and despair"—which he had found incomprehensible, or so at least he had pretended. He gazed at Clavdia Chauchat, at the limpness of her back and the way she thrust her head forward; he watched her arrive for meals, always very late, without reason or apology, but simply because she lacked the discipline and energy of good manners; watched how, because of that basic flaw, whether coming or going, she let every door slam behind her, rolled her bread into little pills, and occasionally gnawed at her cuticles. And the unspoken suspicion rose up in him that if she was ill—which she surely was, almost hopelessly ill, since she had been forced to come up here so often and for such long periods—her illness was, if not entirely, then at least in large part, of a moral nature, and was therefore, just as Settembrini had said, not the cause or result of her "carelessness" but in fact identical with it. He also recalled the dismissive gesture with which the humanist had spoken of the "Parthians and Scythians" with whom he had to share his rest cure, a gesture of natural, immediate disdain and disapproval that needed no explanation and that Hans Castorp had understood quite well at one time—back when he, a man who sat up very straight at the dinner table, had detested slamming doors from the bottom of his heart, had never felt tempted to chew his fingernails (if for no other reason than because he had his Maria Mancinis), had been deeply offended by Frau Chauchat's lack of manners, and had been unable to throw off a feeling of superiority whenever he heard this narrow-eyed foreigner attempt his mother tongue.

As matters now stood, Hans Castorp had almost totally renounced such feelings, and instead it was the Italian who annoyed him with that conceited talk about "Parthians and Scythians"—without even specifying the Bad Russian table, where those students sat with heads of thick hair and not a trace of collar or cuff, arguing in their alien tongue, apparently unable to express themselves in any other, a boneless language that reminded Hans Castorp of a thorax without ribs, like the one Director Behrens had described recently. It was true—these people's manners might very well arouse lively distaste in a humanist. They ate with their knives and made an unspeakable mess of their clothes. Settembrini claimed that one of these fellows, a medical student well advanced in his studies, had turned out to be totally ignorant of Latin and did not know, for example, what a *vacuum* was; and from daily first-hand knowledge, Hans Castorp was fairly sure that Frau Stöhr was not lying when she told her tablemates that the couple in room 32 were always still in bed together when the bath attendant came to give them their morning massage.

All of which might be true—yet it was not for nothing that a clear distinction was made between "good" and "bad" tables, and Hans Castorp assured himself that he could shrug off a propagandist for the world republic and beautiful style, who so snootily and coolly—especially coolly, even though he was feverish and tipsy himself—applied the designation "Parthians and Scythians" to both the good and bad tables. Hans Castorp understood only too well how it was intended; after all, he had himself begun to understand the connection between Frau Chauchat's illness and her "carelessness." But the thing was, as he told Joachim one day, you began with annoyance and distaste, and suddenly "something quite different comes up" that "has nothing whatever to do with forming opinions" and then it was all over with such rigor—and suddenly you were no longer receptive to pedagogic influences of the republican and eloquent sort. But what sort of dubious experience, we now ask—much in the spirit of a Lodovico Settembrini—can so paralyze and suspend a man's ability to form opinions, even rob him of the right to form them, or better, induce him to waive that right in a kind of insane rapture? We are not asking the precise name of that experience—since everyone knows it. We are inquiring, rather, about that experience's moral character—and, to be frank, do not expect a very cheering answer. In Hans Castorp's case, its character was apparent not only in the extent to which he stopped forming judgments, but also in the way he began to experiment on his own with the style of life that so bewitched him. He tried out what it was like to let his back go limp and sit slumped in his chair at meals, and found it greatly relaxed the abdominal muscles. Moreover, he tried out going through a door without troubling to latch it behind him, but merely letting it close by itself; and that proved both convenient and easy—as an expression of feeling, it corresponded to the shrug with which Joachim had greeted him that day at the train station and which since then he had often noticed people use here.

To put it simply, our traveler had fallen head over heels in love with Clavdia Chauchat—we use the term "love," whereas we have thus far spoken of infatuation, because we believe we have taken sufficient precautions to prevent any misunderstandings its use might cause. The constituent element of his love, therefore, was not the amiable, tender melancholy found in our little song. It was, instead, a rather reckless and unpolished variation of this folly, a fusion of frost and heat, like a man in a fever or an October day in these lofty regions. What he lacked was the emotion that might have united the two extremes. On the one hand, his love was caught up—and with such an immediacy that it could make the young man blanch and grimace—in Frau Chauchat's knee, the contour of her leg, her back, the nape of her neck, her upper arms and the way they pressed her small breasts together, in brief, caught up in her body, her careless body, so accentuated and vastly enhanced by her illness that it was a second embodiment of her body. And on the other hand, his love was something utterly elusive and amorphous, a thought—no, a dream, the terrifying and infinitely seductive dream of a young man whose answer to certain, though subconsciously posed questions would have been only hollow silence. We have as much right as anyone to private thoughts about the story unfolding here, and we would like to suggest that Hans Castorp would not have stayed with the people up here even this long beyond his originally planned date of departure, if only some sort of satisfactory answer about the meaning and purpose of life had been supplied to his prosaic soul from out of the depths of time.

In any case, being in love inflicted on him all the pain and all the joys that the condition brings with it the whole world over. It is a piercing pain that has something degrading about it, as does all pain, and is such a shock to the nervous system that it takes one's breath away and can make a grown man weep bitter tears. But to do justice to the joys, they were countless, and although they arose out of trivial events, they were no less compelling than the sufferings. Almost any moment in a Berghof day might serve as their source. For example: as he is about to enter the dining hall, Hans Castorp realizes that the object of his dreams is behind him. He clearly anticipates what will happen—an exceedingly simple outcome, but one that nevertheless sends him into raptures and can even cause tears to well up. Eyes meet at close range, his own and her gray-green ones, whose slightly Asiatic shape and placement enchant his very core. He is barely conscious, but even in that state he steps to one side to allow her to precede him through the door. With half a smile and a low *"merci"* she avails herself of this perfectly conventional courtesy and walks past him into the dining hall. He stands there in the gentle breeze as she brushes past him, wild with the happiness of having encountered her and of knowing that the word her mouth has spoken, that little *"merci,"* was intended personally and solely for him. He follows her, staggers off to the right to his own table, sinks down into his chair, and realizes that as "Clavdia," too, takes her seat, she turns around to look at him—with an expression, or so it seems to him, that says she is thinking about their encounter at the door. What an incredible adventure! What joy, what triumph, what boundless rapture! No, Hans Castorp would never have felt this intoxication of fantastic bliss if he had tried to catch the eye of some healthy little goose or other down below in the flatlands, to whom he might have "given his heart" in the legitimate, promising, calm fashion of that old song. With feverish high spirits he greets the teacher, a blush on her downy cheeks after watching it all—and now bombards Miss Robinson with English conversation of such inanity that the old maid, being inept at ecstasy, recoils and measures him with apprehensive glances.

On another occasion they are sitting at supper and the rays of a brilliant sunset fall directly on the Good Russian table. The curtains have been drawn across the windows and the doors to the veranda, but there is a gap somewhere. Cool, but dazzling red light has found a way through it and now lands precisely on Frau Chauchat's head, so that while engaging her concave fellow countryman in conversation she has to raise her right hand to shield herself against it. It is a nuisance, nothing more; no one pays much attention, and the lady herself is probably not even aware of her discomfort. But Hans Castorp notices from across the dining hall—

and he gazes at her for a while. He examines the situation and, following the ray, discovers its source at the arched window in the far corner on the right, between a veranda door and the Bad Russian table, some distance from Frau Chauchat's seat and an almost equal distance from Hans Castorp's own chair. And he comes to a decision. Without saying a word, he stands up. Still holding his napkin and working his way between tables, he walks across the room to the cream-colored curtains, folds one nicely over the other, satisfies himself with a glance over his shoulder that the sunset has been shut out and Frau Chauchat set free—and with a display of great composure, he starts back to his place.

An attentive young man, who did what needed to be done, since no one else noticed to do it. Only a very few people had paid attention to his meddling, but Frau Chauchat had felt the benefit at once and turned around—and held that pose until Hans Castorp had reached his chair again. Turning to look at her as he sat down, he saw her thank him with a smile of friendly surprise and a nod, or better, a thrust of her head. He responded with a little bow. His heart was inert, seemed not to be beating at all. Only after it was all over did his heart begin to pound again, and only then, too, did he notice that Joachim was keeping his eyes directed at his plate—and only afterward did it strike him that Frau Stöhr had nudged Dr. Blumenkohl and suppressed a giggle, while her eyes roamed over her own table and others in search of knowing glances and smiles.

We are describing everyday events; but even everyday events look peculiar if they grow in peculiar soil. There were moments of tension and of gratifying release of tension between the two of them—or if not between them (because to what extent Madame Chauchat was affected remains to be seen), then at least in Hans Castorp's own fantasies and emotions. The beautiful weather held, and the majority of the hotel residents had got into the habit of moving from the dining hall out onto the veranda after their midday meal, to spend a quarter hour together there in the sun; and what went on was very like the scene at the band concerts held every other Sunday. The young people—totally languid, stuffed with roasts and desserts, all slightly feverish—chatted, joked, and flirted with their eyes. Frau Salomon from Amsterdam might sit on the balustrade—hard-pressed on one side by the knees of thick-lipped Gänser and on the other by the Swedish bruiser, who, although completely well now, had extended his stay for a little extra therapy. Frau Iltis had apparently become a widow—in any case, she had of late been enjoying the company of a "fiancé," who had a melancholy, subservient look about him, and whose presence did not prevent her from simultaneously receiving the attentions of Captain Miklosich, a man with a hooknose, waxed moustaches, swelling chest, and menacing eyes. There were other ladies of various nationalities who took their rest cure in the common lounging areas—among them some new faces that had appeared since the first of October and that Hans Castorp would have had difficulty putting a name to. Mingling with them were cavaliers of Herr Albin's sort: seventeen-year-olds with monocles; a young Dutchman with lots of diamonds, a pink face, and a mania for philately; various Greeks, with slicked-down hair and almond eyes, who tended to reach for things at meals; two almost inseparable dandies, nicknamed "Max and Moritz," who were reputed to be great breakers of house rules. The hunchbacked Mexican, who, because he knew none of the languages represented here, wore the expression of a deaf-mute, was forever taking photographs—a comical figure nimbly dragging his tripod from one point on the terrace to another. Even the director might make an appearance in order to do his bootlace trick. The religious fanatic from Mannheim would be slinking about alone in the crowd somewhere, his profoundly sad eyes cast furtively in a certain direction—much to Hans Castorp's disgust.

But to return to some examples of "tension and release of tension," it could happen on such occasions that Hans Castorp might be sitting on an enameled garden chair, his back to the wall, conversing with Joachim, who had been forced to come along against his will, and there would be Frau Chauchat standing at the railing directly opposite, smoking a cigarette with a tablemate. He would speak loudly enough for her to hear him. She would turn her back on him. As is obvious, we have a particular occasion in mind. . . . Conversation with his cousin had not satisfied his chatty affectation, and so he had intentionally struck up a new acquaintance. And with whom? With Hermine Kleefeld. As if quite by chance, he directed a remark to the young lady, and introducing both himself and Joachim to her by name, he pulled over a third enameled chair for her— the better for him to put on his show. Did she know, he asked, what a devilish fright she had given him that day when he had first encountered her while out taking a morning stroll? Yes, *he* was the one at whom she had whistled her heartwarming welcome. And she had achieved her purpose—he was perfectly willing to admit that he had felt as if he had been clubbed from behind, she needed only to ask his cousin. Ha, ha, whistling with her pneumothorax to frighten a harmless wanderer. A wicked game, that was what he called it—downright sinful abuse, if he did say so. He had every reason to be outraged.

Joachim sat there with his eyes cast down, well aware of his utilitarian role in all this, and Mademoiselle Kleefeld for her part took increasing offense as she realized from Hans Castorp's roving, blank glaze that she was only a means to some other end—and all the while Hans Castorp sulked and played coy and turned fancy phrases and made his voice as melodious as possible, until he finally achieved his goal, and Frau Chauchat turned to look directly at the conversational exhibitionist, but only for a moment. And what a look it was: her Pribislav eyes glided quickly over him as he sat there with his legs crossed and came to rest briefly on his yellow boots with an expression of deliberate indifference that looked very much like disdain, precisely like disdain—and then those same eyes turned indolently away, with perhaps a trace of a smile in their depths.

A dreadful, dreadful calamity! Hans Castorp went on speaking feverishly for a while; but when he finally grasped the meaning of that glance at his boots, he broke off, almost in the middle of a word, and fell into silent grief. Bored and offended, Hermine Kleefeld went her way. Not without a certain petulance in his voice, Joachim remarked that they could probably go take their rest cure now. And a broken man with pale lips responded: Yes, they could.

The incident threw Hans Castorp into cruel agony for two long days, during which nothing happened that might serve as a balm for his smarting wound. Why that look? In God's good name, why had she shown him such disdain? Did she see him as some healthy nitwit from down below, whose susceptibilities were of the most harmless sort? As some innocent from the country, an average fellow who strolled about laughing, stuffing his belly, and earning money—a model pupil in the school of life, who could conceive of nothing except the boring advantages of respectability? Was he just a shallow three-week visitor, a nonparticipant in her world? But had he not taken vows as a result of a moist spot? Was he not in their ranks now, one of them, one of "us up here," with a good two months to his credit, and had not Mercury climbed to one hundred degrees again yesterday evening? But that, in fact, was what made his agony perfectly dreadful—Mercury was no longer climbing! Two terrible days of depression had a chilling, sobering, slackening effect on Hans Castorp's nature, which, to his bitter humiliation, manifested itself in a very low temperature, barely above normal, and he came to the cruel realization that his worry and grief had accomplished nothing except to place even greater distance between himself and Clavdia's being and nature.

The third day, the morning of the third day, brought with it gentle release. It was a splendid autumn morning, sunny and fresh, with silver-gray webs spun over the meadows. The sun and the waning moon both stood rather high in the pure blue. The cousins had arisen earlier than usual in order to honor the morning by extending their constitutional a little beyond its normal limits and continuing along the forest path beyond the bench beside the water trough. Joachim, whose temperature had like-wise shown a welcome decline, had seconded this invigorating change of schedule and had not disagreed with Hans Castorp's suggestion. "We're recovered patients," he had said, "rid of fever and toxins, practically ripe for the flatlands. Why shouldn't we buck like colts?" And so, planting their walking sticks firmly, they strolled off bareheaded—because since taking vows, Hans Castorp had, for God's sake, complied with the local custom of not wearing a hat, despite his strong feelings at the beginning about how the practice contradicted his own civilized style of life. They had not yet covered the initial steep rise of the reddish path and were only at about the point where the novice had first encountered the pneu-mothoracic crew, when they caught sight of Frau Chauchat climbing very slowly some distance ahead—Frau Chauchat in white, in a white sweater, white flannel skirt, and even white shoes, her reddish hair glistening in the morning sunlight. More precisely, Hans Castorp had recognized her. Joachim was not aware of the situation until he felt the unpleasant sensa-tion of being tugged or pulled along, the result of his companion's having suddenly picked up the pace and moving ahead swiftly, after first having checked his step abruptly, almost coming to a halt. Joachim did not like being hurried, found it annoying and intolerable; he was soon short of breath, and he coughed. But Hans Castorp, with his eye on his goal and his lungs apparently working superbly, did not let that bother him much. And once Joachim became aware of the actual situation, he merely scowled, said not a word, and kept pace with his cousin—he certainly could not allow him to march ahead alone.

Young Hans Castorp felt invigorated by the beautiful morning. In his depressed mood, his inner energies had quietly recovered some strength, too, and his mind was illumined with the clear certainty that the moment had come to break the spell that had been cast over him. And so he stepped on ahead, pulling a gasping and generally reluctant Joachim with him, and by the time they reached the point where the path leveled out and turned off to the right, they had almost pulled even with Frau Chau-chat. Hans Castorp now slowed the pace again so that he would not look too outlandish from his exertions when carrying out his plan. And just beyond the dogleg in the path, between slope above and drop-off below, among rusty-hued pines with sunlight filtering through the branches, it happened—everything worked out marvelously. Hans Castorp, walking on Joachim's left, caught up with his adorable patient and began to pass her on the right with manly strides. At the moment when he was just even with her, he made a hatless bow and whispered, "Good morning," in a low voice of reverent greeting (but why "reverent," really?)—and heard her respond in kind, wishing him good morning in his own language; her eyes smiling, she acknowledged him with a friendly, not particularly surprised nod. And it was all so different, so totally and blissfully different from that glance at his boots—it was a stroke of good fortune, a turn for the better, indeed for the best, an unparalleled event almost beyond comprehension. It was the longed-for release.

On winged heels, blinded by irrational joy, the proud owner of a greeting, a word, a smile, Hans Castorp hurried forward at the side of maltreated Joachim, who went on staring in silence down the steep hill. It had been a prank, a rather brash one, and in Joachim's eyes there was probably a trace of treachery and malice about it—Hans Castorp was well aware of that. It was not exactly the same as asking a total stranger for a pencil—indeed, it would have been almost rude to pass stiffly by a lady with whom one had been living for months under the same roof and not salute her. And had not Clavdia recently engaged them in a conversation in the waiting room? And so Joachim had to keep his peace. But Hans Castorp understood quite well the other reason why Joachim, with his love of honor, had turned his head away and was walking along in silence, whereas he himself was utterly, trace-kicking happy at his successful prank. No man in the flatlands could have been happier if he had "given his heart" legitimately, cheerfully, and with a promising view to the future to some healthy little goose, and had found success. No, such a man could not be *nearly* as happy as he over the bit of success he had pilfered and secured in one lucky stroke.

After a while, then, he pounded his cousin on the shoulder and said, "Say there, what's wrong? The weather's so beautiful. We'll have to go down to the Kurhaus in Platz later, there'll probably be a concert. Just think. Maybe they'll play that aria from *Carmen*: 'Through every long and lonely hour, in prison there I kept your flower.' What's gnawing at your craw?"

"Nothing," Joachim said. "But you look so flushed that I'm afraid we've seen the end of your lowered temperature."

And it was the end. Hans Castorp's humiliating depression had been vanquished by the greetings he had exchanged with Clavdia Chauchat, and strictly speaking, the real basis of his present satisfaction was his awareness that it had been overcome. Yes, it turned out Joachim was right: Mercury was climbing again! Home from his walk, Hans Castorp consulted him—and he promptly climbed to 100.4 degrees.

Encyclopedia

ALTHOUGH SOME of Herr Settembrini's innuendoes had annoyed Hans Castorp, there was no reason he should have been amazed by them—nor did he have any right to accuse the humanist of pedagogic spying. A blind man would have noticed how things stood with him; he had done nothing to keep it secret. Out of a certain generosity and noble simplicity of spirit, he was a man who tended to wear his heart on his sleeve, which at least distinguished him—to his advantage, if you like— from the love-sick Mannheimer with thinning hair and furtive ways. We would remind our readers that, as a rule, inherent in the condition in which Hans Castorp found himself is an urge, a compulsion, to reveal oneself, a need to be open and to confess, a blind prejudice in one's own favor, and a rage to fill the world with oneself—and the less common sense, reason, and hope apparently involved, the more dismaying it is for those of us of a more sober temperament. It is hard to say how such people actually first come to betray themselves; they cannot, it seems, do or refrain from doing anything that does not betray them—particularly (as a certain gentleman who had no trouble forming opinions remarked) in the company of people who have only two things in their heads: the first being their temperature, the second their temperature. By the latter he meant, for instance, the question of who Frau Wurmbrandt from Vienna, the general consul's wife, had decided would have to pay damages for her loss of fickle Captain Miklosich: the fully mended Swedish bruiser, or Prosecutor Paravant from Dortmund, or—a third possibility—both at once. Because it was certain and general knowledge that the bond linking the prosecutor and Frau Salomon from Amsterdam had, after several months, been broken by mutual agreement and that Frau Salomon, obeying the impulse of her years, had turned to a lad of a more tender age, thick-lipped Gänser from Hermine Kleefeld's table, and had now taken him under her wing—or, as Frau Stöhr put it in her own rather picturesque legalese, had "procured." And so the prosecutor now had a free hand either to do battle over Frau Wurmbrandt, or to come to an understanding with the Swede.

These were the kinds of suits pending among the residents of the Berghof, especially among its feverish youth; and apparently one major factor in all of them was the passageway along the balconies—where one slipped past glass partitions and kept to the railing. These proceedings, then, occupied people's minds, they were an essential component of the local ambiance—and even in saying that, we have not really expressed what was going on. Hans Castorp, in particular, had the funny feeling that in this locale a basic fact of life—which is granted sufficient importance everywhere in the world, whether spoken of in earnest or jest—acquired an accent, a value, a pattern of meaning so serious, and by its very seriousness so new, that this basic fact was cast in an entirely new light, which, if not absolutely appalling, was at least appalling in its newness. Simply mentioning such things causes our own expression to change, and we notice that, although thus far we may have spoken of such questionable liaisons in a light and jocular tone, we did it for the same mysterious reasons people usually speak of them in that fashion—not that it in any way proves the subject to be a matter of levity and jest. And in the environs where we now find ourselves, such would be the case even less than elsewhere. Hans Castorp had believed his was a typical understanding of this fact of life, which normally serves as a favorite topic of jokes, and he may have been right in his belief. But he now realized that he had understood it very inadequately down in the flatlands, had actually been in a state of innocent ignorance. His personal experiences here—the nature of which we have attempted to indicate on several occasions—had forced him at certain moments to cry, "My God!" But they also enabled him to perceive, understand, and internalize the ever-intensifying accent on shock and indescribable adventure that people up here, both generally and individually, attributed to the matter. Not that people did not joke about it here as well. But to a far greater extent than down below, there was something inappropriate about the jokes, something to do with chattering teeth and shortness of breath, something that marked such jokes all too clearly as transparent disguises for the anguish hidden beneath them, or rather for the anguish impossible to hide. Hans Castorp recalled how Joachim's face had turned blotchy and pale the one and only time he had tried to tease him in an innocent, flatland sort of way, by bringing the conversation around to Marusya's physical attributes. He recalled the cool pallor on his own face the evening he had freed Frau Chauchat from the setting sun; and how, on various occasions before and since, he had seen that same pallor on many another face, usually on two at once—for instance on Frau Salomon's and young Gänser's of late, ever since what Frau Stöhr had described in her colorful way had indeed come to pass. We repeat, he recalled all this and realized not only that it would have been difficult not to "betray" oneself under such circumstances, but also that the attempt would hardly have been worthwhile. In other words, if Hans Castorp saw no compelling reason to restrain his feelings and make a secret of his condition, that was probably due not merely to generosity of spirit and guilelessness, but also to a certain encouragement he breathed from the atmosphere all around him.

Had it not been for the difficulty of making acquaintances here, a difficulty to which Joachim had immediately called his attention but the primary cause of which could be traced to the fact that the cousins were, so to speak, a couple or miniature clique within the sanatorium's society and that soldierly Joachim, who was interested solely in regaining his health quickly, was fundamentally opposed to any closer contact or association with his fellow patients—had it not been for that difficulty, then, Hans Castorp would have had, and taken advantage of, many more opportunities to make his feelings known in his generous and guileless way. All the same, Joachim discovered him one evening at the usual social gathering in the company of Hermine Kleefeld, her tablemates Gänser and Rasmussen, and, as a fifth, the lad with the monocle and saltcellar fingernail; with his eyes glittering undeniably brighter than usual and with emotion in his voice, Hans Castorp had delivered an extemporaneous oration on Frau Chauchat's peculiar and exotic facial features, while his audience exchanged glances, nudged one another, and tittered.

It was all very painful for Joachim; but the person who was the source of their amusement seemed insensitive to this revelation of his inner state. Perhaps he thought that if he had left it hidden and ignored, it would never have come into its own. He could be sure of meeting with general sympathy and was willing to accept the schadenfreude that might come with it. Not just people at his own table, but by now those at neighboring tables as well, took delight in watching him blanch and blush when the glass door banged shut at the start of each meal; and indeed he even found some gratification in attracting their attention, since it brought with it a certain external acknowledgment and confirmation of his intoxicated state, which somehow tended both to advance his cause and to encourage his own vague, irrational hopes—and it all made him very happy. It came to the point where people literally gathered to watch the infatuated young man—on the terrace after dinner or on Sunday afternoon when all the guests thronged the concierge's desk to pick up their mail, which on that one day was not delivered to their rooms. It was generally known that he was tipsy as hell, a man in a highly lambent state, who did not care who noticed. And so Frau Stöhr, Fräulein Engelhart, young Kleefeld, her girlfriend with the face of a tapir, the incurable Herr Albin, the young man with the saltcellar fingernail, and various other sanatorium residents would stand there with mouths pulled down at the corners and snort through their noses as they watched him gaze in one particular direction—

a forlorn and passionate smile on his lips, the same flush on his cheeks that had appeared his first evening here, the same glint in his eyes that had been enkindled by the Austrian horseman's cough.

Given this state of affairs, it was actually a good thing that Herr Settembrini would sometimes approach Hans Castorp and start up a conversation, asking him how he was feeling; but it is doubtful whether the younger man knew what thanks he owed him for this humane broad-mindedness. It might happen, for instance, in the lobby on a Sunday afternoon. . . . The guests were pressing around the concierge's desk, hands stretched out for their mail. Joachim was up front with them. His cousin held back, busy watching it all in the state described above, trying to catch Clavdia Chauchat's eye. She was standing nearby with her tablemates, waiting for the crowd at the desk to thin out. It was an hour when all the patients mingled, an hour of opportunities, and for precisely that reason an hour that young Hans Castorp loved and longed for. The week before, he had been so close to Madame Chauchat at the desk that she had bumped against him just the least bit and with a cursory turn of her head had said, "Pardon."

And thank God, he had shown sufficient feverish presence of mind to reply, "Pas de quoi, madame!"

What a godsend, he thought, that you could be certain mail would be distributed in the lobby every Sunday afternoon. One can say that he consumed one whole week waiting for the return of that single hour every seven days—and waiting means racing ahead, means seeing time and the present not as a gift, but as a barrier, denying and negating their value, vaulting over them in your mind. Waiting, people say, is boring. But in actuality, it can just as easily be diverting, because it devours quantities of time without our ever experiencing or using them for their own sake. One could say that someone who does nothing but wait is like a glutton whose digestive system processes great masses of food without extracting any useful nourishment. One could go further and say that just as undigested food does not strengthen a man, time spent in waiting does not age him. Granted, such pure and unalloyed waiting practically never happens.

And so the week had been devoured, it was Sunday afternoon and the distribution of the mail was proceeding as if this were still the Sunday of seven days before. The procedure continued to provide the most exciting opportunities; each minute concealed and offered possibilities of coming into social contact with Frau Chauchat—and Hans Castorp let those possibilities squeeze his heart and make it flutter, but never actually let them become reality. Certain inhibitions stood in the way, some military, some civilian—which is to say, some that were due to Joachim's honorable presence and Hans Castorp's own sense of honor and duty; some, however, were based in the feeling that social contact with Clavdia Chauchat—a *civilized* relationship, with formal pronouns and bows and conversation in French perhaps—was not necessary, not desirable, not the right thing at all. He stood there and watched her smile and talk, just as Pribislav Hippe had smiled and talked in the schoolyard years before, her mouth open rather wide and her slanting gray-green eyes above her strong cheekbones narrowing to little slits. The effect was not "beautiful" at all; but it was what it was, and when a man is in love his aesthetic opinions are no more valid than his moral judgments.

"You are also waiting for dispatches, are you, my good engineer?"

Only one person talked like that, one bothersome person. Hans Castorp winced and turned toward Herr Settembrini, who stood smiling before him. It was his delicate, humanist smile, the one with which he had first greeted the newcomer on the bench beside the water trough—and just as on that day, Hans Castorp now felt ashamed of himself. But despite the many times he had tried to push the "organ-grinder" away for bothering him in his dreams, the waking man proved a better person than the dreaming. The sight of that smile not only shamed and sobered Hans Castorp, but also awakened a sense of gratitude for needs met.

"Dispatches?" he said. "Good God, Herr Settembrini, I'm not an ambassador. There may be a postcard there for one of us. My cousin is checking right now."

"That little limping devil up front already handed me my paltry correspondence," Settembrini said, shoving a hand down into the side pocket of his ineluctable petersham coat. "Interesting matters. Matters of literary and social consequence, I cannot deny it. It is about an encyclopedia—to which a philanthropic institution has done me the honor of asking me to contribute. In short, a fine offer of work." Herr Settembrini paused. "But what about your affairs?" he asked. "How are things in that regard? How are you getting along with your acclimatization, for example? You have not been residing here among us for so long now that, taken all in all, the question can be removed just yet from the agenda."

"Thank you for asking, Herr Settembrini. As before, I am having my difficulties. I think it possible I may very well continue to have them until my last day here. Some people never get used to the air here, my cousin told me the day I arrived. But one gets used to not getting used to it."

"A convoluted process," the Italian said with a laugh. "A strange sort of naturalization. But of course, youth is capable of most anything. It may not get used to things, but it does take root."

"And after all, this isn't a Siberian salt mine."

"No. . . . Ah, you prefer Oriental metaphors. Quite understandable. Asia is devouring us. Tartar faces in every direction you look." And Herr Settembrini discreetly turned his head to glance over his shoulder. "Genghis Khan," he said, "lone wolves on dusky steppes, snow and schnapps, whips and knouts, Schlüsselburg prison and Holy Orthodoxy. They ought to erect a statue of Pallas Athena here in the lobby—as a kind of self-defense. Look there—one of your Ivan Ivanovitches, without cuff or collar, has got into a fight with Prosecutor Paravant. Each claims he should be ahead of the other in the mail line. I don't know who is right, but to my mind, the goddess fights on the prosecutor's side. He's an ass, of course, but at least he knows his Latin."

Hans Castorp laughed—something Herr Settembrini never did. One could not even imagine his ever laughing heartily; he managed little more than a dry, delicate tightness at one corner of his mouth. He watched the young man laugh and then asked, "And the copy of your X-ray—have you received it?"

"I did indeed receive it," Hans Castorp confirmed with importance. "Just recently. Here it is." And he reached for his inside breast pocket.

"Ah, you carry it in your wallet. As a kind of identification, like a passport or membership card. Very good. Let me see." And Herr Settembrini raised the little glass plate framed with black paper up to the light, holding it between the thumb and forefinger of his left hand—a gesture one saw quite frequently up here. As he examined the funereal photograph, a little scowl passed over his face with its black almond-shaped eyes—though it was not clear if his scowl was an attempt to see better or if there were other reasons for it.

"Yes, yes," he said at last. "Here you have your legitimation—thank you so much." And he handed the piece of glass back to its owner, but in sidelong fashion, passing it across his other arm and turning his face away.

"Did you see the strands?" Hans Castorp asked. "And the nodules?"

"You are aware," Herr Settembrini replied languidly, "what store I set by these artifacts. You know, too, that the spots and shadows inside you are for the most part matters of physiology. I have seen hundreds of pictures that looked about the same as yours, and the decision whether they are truly a 'passport' or not lies more or less in the eyes of the beholder. I speak as a layman, but as a layman of many years' experience."

"Does your passport look worse?"

"Yes, somewhat worse. I also know, by the way, that our lords and masters never base a diagnosis solely on such playthings. And so you propose to spend the winter with us, do you?"

"Yes, dear God, I'm beginning to get used to the idea that until my cousin leaves, I won't be leaving, either."

"Which means you're getting used to not getting . . . You did put that very wittily. I hope you've been sent your winter things—warm clothes, sturdy footwear?"

"Everything. Everything nicely taken care of, Herr Settembrini. I informed my relatives, and our housekeeper sent it all express. I can manage here now."

"That eases my mind. But wait—you'll need a sleeping bag, one with fur lining. Where are our minds? This late-summer weather is deceptive. It can be deepest winter within an hour. You'll be spending the coldest months here."

"Yes, the sleeping bag," Hans Castorp said, "that's probably a necessary piece of gear. It has crossed my mind that we—my cousin and I— should go down into town sometime soon and buy one. It's something I'll never use again later, but it's worth it, after all, for four to six months."

"Yes, it is worth it, it is worth it, my good engineer," Herr Settembrini said softly, stepping closer to the young man. "It is truly hideous, you know, the way you are throwing the months around. Hideous, I say, because it is so unnatural, so foreign to your nature, purely a matter of a receptive young mind. Ah, the immoderate receptivity of youth—it can drive an educator to despair, because it is always ready to apply itself to bad ends. Do not ape the words you hear floating in the air around you, young man, but speak a language appropriate to your civilized European life. A great deal of Asia hangs in the air here. It is not for nothing that the place teems with Mongolian Muscovites—people like these." And Herr Settembrini pointed back over his shoulder with his chin. "Do not model yourself on them, do not let them infect you with their ideas, but instead compare you own nature, your *higher* nature to theirs, and as a son of the West, of the divine West, hold sacred those things that by both nature and heritage are sacred to you. Time, for instance. This liberality, this barbaric extravagance in the use of time is the Asian style—that may be the reason why the children of the East feel so at home here. Have you never noticed that when a Russian says 'four hours' it means no more to him than 'one hour' does to us? The idea comes easily to mind that the nonchalance with which these people treat time has something to do with the savage expanse of their land. Too much room—too much time. It has been said that they are a nation with time on their hands—they can afford to wait. We Europeans can't wait. We have just as little time as our noble, tidily segmented continent has space; we must carefully husband the resources of the former just as we do those of the latter—

put them to use, good use, engineer! Our great cities are the perfect symbol—these centers and focal points of civilization, these crucibles of thought. Just as land values rise in cities and wasted space becomes an impossibility, in the same measure, please note, time becomes more precious there, too. *Carpe diem!* An urbanite sang that song. Time is a gift of the gods to humankind, that we may use it—use it, my good engineer, in the service of human progress."

Whatever difficulties certain phrases presented to Herr Settembrini's Mediterranean tongue, he had expressed himself in the most delightful fashion—clearly, euphoniously, and, one may well say, graphically. Hans Castorp could only respond with the brief, stiff, and uneasy bow of a schoolboy on the receiving end of a critical lecture. What could he possibly have replied? This private homily, which Herr Settembrini had delivered surreptitiously, almost in a whisper, behind the backs of the other guests, had been too businesslike, too unsocial, too little like conversation, for him to have expressed approval in any tactful way. One does not respond to a teacher with: "You said that beautifully." Hans Castorp had indeed done that on several previous occasions, if only to preserve some kind of social equality—but the humanist had never before spoken with such pedagogic urgency. There was nothing for him to do but swallow this scolding—like a schoolboy dazed by too much moralizing.

One could tell from Herr Settembrini's expression that he was still busy pursuing his train of thought even after he fell silent. He was still standing so close to Hans Castorp that the latter was forced to bend back just a little. His black eyes were focused in a fixed, thoughtful stare at the young man's face.

"You are suffering, my good engineer," he continued. "And you are suffering in great confusion—who would not notice it just by looking at you? But your attitude to suffering should be a European attitude—not that of the East, which precisely because it *is* weak and prone to illness, is so amply represented here. The East treats suffering with pity and infinite patience. We dare not, we cannot, do the same. We were speaking of my mail. Look here . . . or even better, come with me now. This is impossible. Let us get away from this spot, we'll step in there. I have something to disclose to you that . . . Come along."

And turning on his heels, he pulled Hans Castorp out of the lobby and into the social room nearest the main entrance, which was set up for reading and writing, but was empty at the moment. It had a bright, vaulted ceiling and was paneled in oak; its furnishings included bookcases, a central table covered with newspapers in holders and surrounded by chairs, and desks in nooks beneath window arches. Herr Settembrini strode across the room to a window. Hans Castorp followed him. The door remained open.

"These papers," the Italian said, swiftly extracting a package from the pouchlike side pocket of his petersham coat—an oversize opened envelope, which contained several flyers and a letter that he ran through his fingers for Hans Castorp to see—"these papers bear a letterhead in the French language: 'International League for the Organization of Progress.' They have been sent to me from Lugano, where the league has a branch office. You ask me: What are its principles, its goals? I can tell you in two words. Working from Darwin's theory of evolution, the League for the Organization of Progress advances the philosophical viewpoint that humankind's innermost natural purpose is its own self-perfection. It concludes further that it is the duty of every person who desires to satisfy that natural purpose to cooperate in the cause of human progress. Many have followed that call; there are significant numbers of them in France, Italy, Spain, Turkey, even in Germany. I, too, have the honor to be on the league's membership rolls. A large-scale scientific program of reform has been drawn up, embracing all presently known possibilities for perfecting the human organism. The problem of the health of our race is being studied, including the examination of methods for combating its degeneration, which doubtless is one lamentable side effect of increasing industrialization. Moreover, the league is engaged in founding popular universities, in working to overcome class struggle by every means of social improvement that commends itself for the purpose, and, finally, in eliminating conflict between nations, war itself, by fostering international law. As you can see, the efforts of the league are high-minded and all-embracing. Several international periodicals bear witness to its activities—monthly reviews, which appear in three or four important languages and report in very exciting articles about the progressive development of civilized humankind. Countless local chapters have been established in various countries, their purpose being to inform and educate by means of public lectures and Sunday festivities. Above all the league endeavors to supply materials to progressive political parties everywhere. Do you follow me, my good engineer?"

"Absolutely," Hans Castorp hastened to reply with some vehemence. As he said it, he felt like a man who has lost his footing but luckily catches himself just in time.

Herr Settembrini seemed satisfied. "I assume these are new and surprising vistas for you, are they not?"

"Yes, I must admit this is the first time I've heard about these . . . these efforts."

"If only," Settembrini exclaimed softly, "if only you had heard of them before! But perhaps it is not yet too late for you to hear. Now, as to these flyers—you would like to know what they are about. I shall explain. This past spring the league was called together in solemn convention in Barcelona. You know, I'm sure, that city boasts of a special affinity for ideas of political progress. The convention lasted one whole week and included banquets and ceremonies. Good God, how I wanted to go, how I yearned to take part in its deliberations. But that scoundrel of a director forbade me, threatened me with death. What was I to do? Fearing death, I did not go. I was, as you can well imagine, in despair over the trick my imperfect health had played on me. Nothing is more painful than when our organic, animal component prevents us from serving the cause of reason. All the more intense, then, was my satisfaction upon receiving this letter from the office in Lugano. You are curious about its content, are you? I can well believe it. But first, some quick background information. Heedful of the truth that its task is to further human happiness, or in other words, finally to eradicate human suffering by combating it with practical social work; heedful, further, of the truth that this noble mission can be completed only with the help of social science, whose ultimate goal is the perfect state—the League for the Organization of Progress resolved in Barcelona to publish a multivolumed work, which is to bear the title *The Sociology of Suffering* and in which human sufferings of all classes and species will be treated in detailed, exhaustive, systematic fashion. You will object: What good are classes, species, and systems? And I reply: Order and classification are the beginning of mastery, whereas the truly dreadful enemy is the unknown. The human race must be led out of the primitive stage of fear and long-suffering vacuity and into a phase of purposeful activity. Humankind must be informed that certain effects can be diminished only when one first recognizes their causes and negates them, and that almost all sufferings of the individual are illnesses of the social organism. Fine! This is the purpose of our *Sociological Pathology,* an encyclopedia of some twenty or so volumes that will list and discuss all conceivable instances of human suffering, from the most personal and intimate to the large-scale conflicts of groups that arise out of class hostility and international strife. In short, it will list the chemical elements that serve as the basis for all the many mixtures and compounds of human suffering. Taking as its plumb line the dignity and happiness of humankind, it will supply for each and every instance of suffering the means and measures that seem most appropriate for eliminating its causes. Renowned scholars and experts from all over Europe—medical doctors, economists, psychologists—will participate in drafting this encyclopedia, and the general editorial offices in Lugano will act as the reservoir into which all articles will flow. I can read the question in your eyes: What will be my role in all of this? Let me finish first. This immense work does not wish to see belles-lettres neglected, either, at least to the extent that they speak of human suffering. Literature is therefore to have its own volume, which is to contain, as solace and advice for those who suffer, a synopsis and short analysis of all masterpieces of world literature dealing with every such conflict. And—that is the task with which the letter you see here entrusts your humble servant."

"You don't say, Herr Settembrini! Well, allow me then to offer my most heartfelt congratulations. What a spectacular assignment—simply made for you, I'd say. I'm not the least bit surprised that the league thought of you. And how happy it must make you that you can be helpful in eradicating human suffering."

"It is a very complex task," Herr Settembrini said, musing, "demanding much prudence and vast reading. Especially," he added now, his gaze seemingly lost in the immensity of his mission, "especially because literature has regularly chosen suffering as its topic. Even masterpieces of only second or third rank have been concerned with it in one way or another. But no matter—all the better! However complex the task, it is the sort of work that I can manage even in this cursed place, if need be, although I would hope that I shall not be forced to complete it here. One cannot say," he went on, stepping closer to Hans Castorp again and dampening his voice almost to a whisper, "one cannot say the same of the duties nature has imposed upon *you*, my good engineer. And that is my point, that is what I wanted to warn you about. You know how very much I admire your chosen profession, but because it is practical, and not intellectual, you cannot, unlike myself, pursue that profession anywhere but in the world below. You can be a European only in the flatlands—actively combating suffering in your own fashion, advancing progress, using time well. I have told you of the task that has come my way only to remind you of this, to bring you to yourself, to set your thoughts straight, which are evidently beginning to become confused under these atmospheric conditions. I urge you: Consider your self-respect, your pride. Do not lose yourself in an alien world. Avoid that swamp, that isle of Circe—for you are not Odysseus enough to dwell there unharmed. You will walk on all fours, you are tipping down onto your front limbs already, and will soon begin to grunt—beware!"

While he whispered his warnings, the humanist shook his head urgently back and forth. He fell silent now, scowling, with eyes lowered. It was impossible to reply with a quip or some other evasion, as was Hans

Castorp's usual method—though he did weigh the possibility for just a moment. His eyes were directed at the floor, too. Lifting his shoulders, he asked just as softly, "What should I do?"

"What I told you before."

"You mean leave?"

Herr Settembrini did not reply.

"You mean that I should go back home, is that it?"

"I told you that the very first evening, my good engineer."

"Yes, and at the time I was free to do so, although I thought it unreasonable to throw in the towel just because the local air was a little hard on me. Since then, however, the situation has changed. Since then I've gone for an examination, as a result of which Director Behrens told me flat out that it would not pay for me to return home, that I would have to come back in very short order, and that if I were to continue my life just as before down below, the whole pulmonary lobe would go, willy-nilly, to the devil."

"I know, and now you have your membership card in your pocket."

"Yes, and you say it so ironically—with the right kind of irony, of course, whose purpose cannot be doubted for a moment and which is meant to serve as an honest, classical device of rhetoric—you see, I do pay attention to your words. But after the results of the X-ray, after this photograph here, after the director's diagnosis, will you take the responsibility for sending me back home?"

Herr Settembrini hesitated for a moment. Then he stood up tall, opened his black eyes wide, fixing them firmly on Hans Castorp, and responded with an emphasis that did not lack a certain dramatic, theatrical tone, "Yes, my good engineer. I will take the responsibility."

But Hans Castorp's posture had stiffened as well now. He had put his heels together and was looking just as directly at Herr Settembrini. The battle had been engaged. Hans Castorp stood his ground. He was "strengthened" by forces close-by. Here was a pedagogue—but just outside was a narrow-eyed woman. He did not apologize for what he now said, did not even bother to preface it with, "No offense." He replied, "Then you are more cautious about yourself than you are about other people. *You* did not go to Barcelona against your doctor's orders. Fearing death, you stayed here."

There was no doubt that to some extent this had a disruptive effect on Herr Settembrini's pose. He smiled, but not without difficulty, and said, "I can appreciate a quick answer when I hear one, even when its logic borders on sophistry. I loathe the idea of engaging in that disgusting contest so typical here, otherwise I would reply that my illness is significantly more serious than yours—indeed, I am unfortunately so ill that only by a little artistic self-deception can I eke out the hope of ever being able to leave this place again and return to the world below. Come the day it should be proved totally improper of me to maintain that deception, I shall turn my back on this institution and spend the rest of my days in private lodgings somewhere in the valley. That will be sad, but since the sphere of my work is of the freest, most purely intellectual sort, it will not prevent me from serving the cause of humankind, from defying the spirit of disease to my last dying breath. I have already called to your attention the difference between us in that regard. My good engineer, you are not a man to sustain your better self here—I saw that the first time we met. You reproach me for not having gone to Barcelona. I submitted to that injunction so that I might not destroy myself prematurely. But I did it with gravest reservations, under the proudest, most excruciating protest of my spirit against the dictates of my wretched body. Whether that protest still lives within you as well, seeing that you are following the bidding of the local powers—or whether it is not, rather, the *body* and its evil proclivities that you all too willingly obey . . ."

"What do you have against the body?" Hans Castorp interrupted quickly, staring at him with large blue eyes, the whites broken with bloodshot veins. He was giddy with his own foolhardiness, as was only too obvious. ("What am I saying?" he thought. "This is ghastly. But I've declared war on him, and if at all possible I'm not going to let him have the last word. He'll have it, of course, but that doesn't matter. I'll use it to my advantage all the same. I'll provoke him.") And now he completed his objection by asking, "But you are a humanist, are you not? And if you are, how can you say such bad things about the body?"

Settembrini's smile was not forced this time; he was sure of himself. " 'What do you have against analysis?' " he quoted, his head tilted to one shoulder. " 'Don't you approve of analysis?'—You will always find me ready to provide you with an answer, my good engineer," he said with a bow and a deferential downward sweep of his hand, "particularly when your objections show some wit. You parry my thrusts not without elegance. Humanist—certainly I am that. You will never find me guilty of ascetic tendencies. I affirm, I respect, I love the body, just as I affirm, respect, and love form, beauty, freedom, mirth, and pleasure—just as I champion the 'world,' the interests of life against sentimental flight from the world, *classicismo* against *romanticismo*. I believe my position is perfectly clear. But there is one force, one principle that is the object of my highest affirmation, my highest and ultimate respect and love, and that force, that principle, is the mind. However much I detest seeing that dubious construct of moonshine and cobwebs that goes by the name of 'soul' played off against the body, within the antithesis of body *and* mind, it is the body that is the evil, devilish principle, because the body is nature, and nature—as an opposing force, I repeat, to mind, to reason—is evil, mystical and evil. 'But you are a humanist!' Most certainly I am that, because I am a friend of humankind, just as Prometheus was a lover of humankind and its nobility. That nobility, however, is contained within the mind, within reason, and therefore you will level the charge of Christian obscurantism against me quite in vain."

Hans Castorp waved this off.

"You will," Settembrini insisted, "level that charge quite in vain, simply because in due time, noble humanistic pride comes to see the tie that binds the mind to the physical body, to nature, as a debasement and a curse. Did you know that the great Plotinus is recorded to have said that he was ashamed to have a body?" Settembrini asked, and with such earnest expectation of an answer that Hans Castorp found himself forced to admit that this was the first he had heard of it.

"Porphyrius has recorded it for us. An absurd statement, if you like. But absurdity is an intellectually honorable position, and nothing could be more fundamentally pitiful than to raise the objection of absurdity when the mind attempts to maintain its dignity against nature and refuses to submit to her. Do you know about the Lisbon earthquake?"

"No . . . an earthquake? I've not been reading newspapers here . . ."

"You misunderstand me. Nevertheless, I would note that it is regrettable—though characteristic of the institution—that you have neglected to read what the press has to say. But you have misunderstood me, the natural phenomenon of which I speak is not a current event; it took place, incidentally, some one hundred and fifty years ago."

"Oh, yes! Wait a moment—right! I read somewhere that Goethe said something in his bedroom one night to his valet—"

"Oh—I don't wish to talk about that," Settembrini broke in, closing his eyes and waving one little brown hand in the air. "Besides, you're getting your catastrophes mixed up. You're thinking of the earthquake in Messina. I'm talking about the one that ravaged Lisbon in the year 1755."

"Beg your pardon."

"Well, it was Voltaire who rose up against it."

"What do you mean 'rose up'? What did he do?"

"He rebelled, that's what. He would not accept this stroke of fate, the brutal fact of it. He refused to submit to it. He protested in the name of the mind and reason against this scandalous offense of nature, which destroyed three-quarters of a flourishing city and took thousands of human lives. That astounds you, does it? Amuses you? You may be as astounded as you like, but I shall make so bold as to rebuke you for the smile. Voltaire's position was that of a true descendent of those ancient Gauls who shot their arrows against heaven. You see, my good engineer, there you behold the mind's enmity toward nature, its proud mistrust of her, its greathearted insistence on the right to criticize her and her evil, irrational power. Because she is a power, and it is servile to accept her, to reconcile oneself to her—that is, to reconcile oneself to her *inwardly*. There you see the kind of humanism that absolutely does not become ensnared in contradictions, that is in no way guilty of a retreat into Christian toadying, even though it resolves to see in the body the evil force, the antagonist. The contradiction that you believe you see is always one and the same. 'What do you have against analysis?' Nothing, when it serves the cause of education, liberation, and progress. Everything, when it comes wrapped in the ghastly, gamy odor of the grave. It is no different with the body. One must respect and defend it, when it serves the cause of emancipation and beauty, of freedom of the senses, of happiness and desire. One must despise it insofar as it is the principle of gravity and inertia opposing the flow toward the light, insofar as it represents the principle of disease and death, insofar as its quintessence is a matter of perversity, of corruption, of lust and disgrace."

Settembrini had been standing very close to Hans Castorp as he spoke these final words in an almost flat tone of voice, hurrying to finish before reinforcements for Hans Castorp's side arrived—Joachim had just entered the reading room, two postcards in hand. The man of letters said no more, and the ease with which he changed now to a light conversational tone did not fail to make an impression on his student—if one can call Hans Castorp that.

"There you are, lieutenant. You've probably been looking for your cousin—forgive me. We were deep in conversation—if I'm not mistaken, in something of a little dispute. He is not a bad quibbler himself, your cousin, certainly no harmless foe in a battle of words—when he wants to be."

Humaniora

DRESSED IN WHITE FLANNELS and blue blazers, Hans Castorp and Joachim Ziemssen were sitting in the garden after dinner. It was yet another of those celebrated October days, a day that was both hot and gentle, festal and austere, with a dark blue southern sky above the valley, whose meadows, crossed with paths and dotted with settlements, were still a cheerful green and from whose rugged, wooded slopes came the sound of cowbells—a metallic, serene, simple tone that drifted clear and untroubled through the quiet, thin, empty air and enhanced the gala mood reigning in those high regions.

The cousins were sitting on a bench in front of a circle of young firs at the far end of the garden. The spot lay at the northwest edge of the level, fenced-in area on which the Berghof was set, about 150 feet above the valley floor. They said nothing. Hans Castorp was smoking. In his mind he was quarreling with Joachim for not having wanted to join the others on the veranda and for having insisted instead, against his express wish, that they come out and sit here in the hushed garden before retiring for their rest cure. Joachim was acting like a tyrant. As far as that went, they weren't Siamese twins. They could go their separate ways if they were of different minds. Hans Castorp was not here to keep Joachim company, but was a patient himself. He went on sulking like this—had no trouble sulking, really, since he had his Maria Mancini. His hands in the side pockets of his blazer, his feet shod in brown shoes stretched out before him, he had set the long, dull gray cigar in the center of his mouth, letting it dangle slightly, the first ashes still clinging to the blunt tip in this initial phase; having just eaten a heavy meal, he was enjoying its aroma, which had come back in full force at last. It might well be that getting used to things up here was simply a matter of getting used to not getting used to them—but as for his digestive chemistry and his sensitive, dry mucous membranes that tended to nosebleeds, the adjustment seemed complete at last. He had not even noticed progress in the making, but over the course of these sixty-five or seventy days, the comfort his whole organism found in well-rolled tobacco, whether as stimulant or narcotic, had returned. And he was delighted that he had regained the capacity. Moral satisfaction reinforced physical pleasure. During his period of bed rest, he had made sparing use of the stock of two hundred he had brought with him and so still had some of those left. But in his letter to Schalleen requesting underwear and winter clothes, he had also asked her to order five hundred more from his supplier in Bremen to make sure he wouldn't be caught short. They came in beautiful enameled boxes with gilt depictions of a globe, lots of medallions, and an exposition hall with banners flying.

And as they sat, here came Director Behrens walking through the garden. He had joined the others for the main meal in the dining hall today, had sat at Frau Salomon's table, his gigantic hands folded before his plate. After that, it would appear, he had spent some time on the terrace, adding a personal touch, perhaps showing off his bootlace trick for someone who had never seen it before. Now he came strolling down the gravel path, dressed not in his medical smock, but in a small-checked swallowtail coat, his bowler pushed back on his head, a cigar in his mouth, too—a very black one, from which he drew great, whitish clouds of smoke. His head, or better, his face, with its purplish, flushed cheeks, snub nose, blue watery eyes, and short-cropped moustache, looked small in comparison to his tall, slightly stooped, and skewed figure, with its oversize hands and feet. In a nervous state, he was visibly startled by the sight of the cousins, and even stood there in some embarrassment that his path had led him directly toward them. Employing his usual cheerful lingo, he greeted them with, "Behold, behold, Timotheus!" and expressed his best wishes for their metabolisms. They were about to stand out of respect, but he told them to remain seated.

"No need, no need. Let's have no further fuss about a simple fellow like myself. Don't deserve it at all, inasmuch as you are my patients—both of you now. You needn't do that. No objection to the status quo." And there he stood before them, his cigar held between the first and second fingers of his gigantic right hand. "How's your cabbage-roll doing, Castorp? Let me have a look. I'm a connoisseur. Good ash—what brand of lovely brunette is she?"

"Maria Mancini, *Poste de Banquette*, from Bremen, Director Behrens. Costs little or nothing, a mere nineteen pfennigs, natural color, but an aroma that you don't normally find at the price. Best Sumatra-Havana wrapper, as you can see. I have got very used to them. It's a medium mixture, quite spicy but light on the tongue. She likes you to leave her ash long—I knock it off twice at most. Of course she has her little moods, but the quality control must be especially exacting, because Maria is very dependable and has an absolutely even draw. Might I offer you one?"

"Thank you, let's exchange brands." And they pulled out their cases.

"She has good breeding," the director said, holding out his brand. "Vivacious, you know, vim and vigor. Saint Felix–Brazil, I've always stuck to that sort. Soothes one's cares away, catches fire like brandy, but, all the same, she packs something of a wallop toward the end. A little caution is in order—you can't light one from the other. Would take more of a man than I. But I'd rather have a hearty snack than a whole day of tasteless air."

Each rolled his gift between his fingers, examining the slender body with expert eye—there was an organic, living quality about the even rows of raised and slanted ribs, the tiny pores along the edges here and there, the veins that seemed almost to throb, the little irregularities of skin, the play of light on surfaces and edges.

Hans Castorp put it into words. "There's life in a cigar. It actually breathes. At home I came up with the idea of keeping my Maria stored in airtight metal containers, to keep out the damp. Would you believe it, she died! Within a few weeks she grew sickly and died—nothing left but leathery corpses."

They exchanged what they knew about the best way to store cigars, especially imports. The director loved imported cigars and would have most preferred to smoke heavy Havanas. Unfortunately they did not agree with him, and he told about two little Henry Clays he had taken a liking to one evening at a party and how they had come close to putting him six feet under. "I smoke them both with my coffee," he said, "one after the other, thinking nothing of it. But no sooner am I finished than I have to ask myself what's up. Whatever it is, I'm feeling very rum, stranger than I've ever felt in my life. I arrive home, no little problem in itself, and no sooner am I home than I think I'm about to pop my cork—you know, feet like ice, a cold sweat, you name it, face white as a sheet, heart doing crazy tricks, my pulse going from a thread you can barely feel to a helter-skelter, cross-country spurt, you know, and my brain in a tizzy. I was convinced that I was about to kick the bucket. I say 'kick the bucket,' since that's the phrase that came to me then as the best description of my condition. Because actually I was feeling as euphoric as if this were some sort of shindig, although I was scared stiff, or better, I was out of my mind with fear. But fear and euphoria aren't mutually exclusive, everybody knows that. Some scalawag who's about to have a girl for the first time is afraid, too. So is she. But they simply melt together for euphoria. Well, I was close to melting myself, about to kick the bucket, my chest heaving away. But then Mylendonk's ministrations broke the mood. Ice compresses, a rubdown with a brush, an injection of camphor—and so here I am still among the living."

Hans Castorp had sat there listening in his role as patient, but now he looked up at Behrens, whose blue pop-eyes had filled with tears as he told his tale. His own face mirrored a mind full of thoughts. "You paint sometimes, don't you, Director Behrens?" he suddenly asked.

The director pretended to recoil in astonishment. "What's this? Now where did you get that notion, my lad?"

"Excuse me. I've heard people mention it here and there. I just happened to think of it."

"Well, then I'll not go to the trouble of telling fibs. We're all human and have our weaknesses now and then. Yes, it's been known to happen. *Anch'io sono pittore*, as that Spaniard liked to say."

"Landscapes?" Hans Castorp asked. Circumstances contributed to his laconic, condescending tone.

"As many as you like," the director replied with embarrassed bravado. "Landscapes, still lifes, animals—a fellow like me shrinks from absolutely nothing."

"But no portraits?"

"A portrait or two has probably slipped in now and then. Do you want to commission me for one?"

"Ha, ha, no. But it would be very kind of you to show us your paintings if the opportunity should ever arise."

Joachim, too, after first gazing at his cousin in astonishment, hastened to assure the director that it would indeed be very kind of him.

Behrens was so pleased and flattered that he was almost ebullient. He even turned red with delight, and by now his eyes seemed close to shedding actual tears. "Gladly, gladly!" he cried. "With greatest pleasure! Right here on the spot, if you'd like. Come along, come with me, I'll brew us some Turkish coffee at my diggings." And he took each young man by the arm and pulled them from the bench; linking arms with both, he now led them down the gravel path toward his residence, which, as they knew, was located in the nearby northwest wing of the Berghof.

"I've tried something along that line myself on occasion in the past," Hans Castorp declared.

"You don't say. The real thing in oils?"

"No, no, I never managed anything more than a watercolor or two. An occasional ship, a seascape, childish stuff. But I like to look at paintings, which is why I've taken this liberty."

Joachim, in particular, felt somewhat relieved and enlightened by his cousin's explanation for his startling curiosity—and it was more for his sake than the director's that Hans Castorp had called attention to his own attempts as an artist. They arrived—but here was no splendid portal flanked by lanterns like the one at the end of the driveway on the other side of the building. A few semicircular steps led up to an oaken door, which the director opened with a latchkey, one of many on his key ring. His hand trembled as he did it; he was definitely nervous. They entered a vestibule where you could hang your things, and Behrens placed his bowler on its hook. Once they were inside the short corridor, which opened on both sides to the rooms of his small private residence and was separated from the rest of the building by a glass-paned door, he called for the maid and placed his order. Then with several jovial phrases of encouragement, he admitted his guests through one of the doors on the right.

Two rooms furnished in banal bourgeois style, one opening into the other and separated only by portieres, looked toward the valley: a dining room done in "antique German"; a combination living room and office, with sofa and chairs, bookcases and heavy wool carpets, a fraternity cap and crossed swords hung above a desk, plus a small smoking alcove, done in "Turkish" style. There were paintings everywhere, the director's paintings—the visitors' eyes at once began courteously to wander over them, ready to admire. The director's departed spouse was conspicuously present, in several oils and also in a photograph on the desk. She was a thin, somewhat enigmatic blond in diaphanous garments, who always held her hands folded against her left shoulder—not firmly clasped, but with just the fingertips lying loosely interlaced—her eyes either directed heavenward or cast down, hidden under long lashes that stood out at an angle from the lids. But the late wife never looked straight ahead at her beholder. Otherwise, the paintings were mostly Alpine landscapes— mountains draped in snow and evergreen, mountains with peaks veiled in mist, and mountains whose crisp, sharp outlines stood out against a deep blue sky and betrayed the influence of Segantini. There were also other themes: Alpine dairy sheds, dewlapped cows standing or lying in sun-drenched pastures, a plucked hen among vegetables with its twisted neck dangling over one side of a table, floral arrangements, local mountain folk, and so on—all of them painted in a kind of brisk, dilettante style, with brash clumps of color that often looked as if they had been squeezed onto the canvas directly from the tube and must have taken a long time to dry. The technique occasionally proved effective at covering bad mistakes.

They moved along the walls as if at an exhibition, accompanied by the master of the house, who would now and then provide a title, but usually said nothing, displaying the proud apprehension of the artist, enjoying it all, letting his eyes rest on each work along with those of the strangers. The portrait of Clavdia Chauchat was hung in the living room, next to the window—Hans Castorp had spied it with one quick glance as he entered the room, although it bore only a very distant resemblance to her. He intentionally avoided the spot, keeping his companions pinned down in the dining room by pretending to admire a verdant view of the Sergi Valley with bluish glaciers in the background; well aware that he was in command, he first steered them into the Turkish smoking alcove, which he likewise gave a thorough examination amid much praise, and then surveyed the wall on the entrance side of the living room, sometimes urging Joachim to join him in his complimentary remarks. Finally he turned around and said with measured puzzlement, "Why, I know that face, don't I?"

"Do you recognize her?" Behrens wanted to know.

"Certainly, I'm surely not mistaken. That's the lady from the Good Russian table, the one with the French name . . ."

"Correct. Chauchat. I'm pleased you see the likeness."

"The lady as she lives and breathes," Hans Castorp lied, less out of cunning than out of an awareness that if everything had been as it should be, he ought not to have recognized the lady at all, any more than Joachim had recognized her on his own—dear old outfoxed Joachim, for whom a light now went on, the real light and not the false one Hans Castorp had lit for him.

"Ah, yes," Joachim said softly and set about helping Hans Castorp study the painting. His cousin had certainly known how to recover damages for having been kept away from the gathering on the veranda.

It was a bust in half-profile—somewhat smaller than life-size, with the neck bared, a veil draped across the shoulders and breasts—set in a wide, black, beveled frame edged in gold nearest the canvas. Frau Chauchat looked ten years older than she was—as usually happens when amateurs try to capture character. There was too much red in the face, the nose was very badly drawn, the hair color was wrong, almost that of straw, the mouth was askew; the special fascination of her features had not been brought out, was not even apparent, but only coarsened by exaggeration. The whole thing was a rather botched job, the portrait only vaguely corresponding to the model. But Hans Castorp was not all that scrupulous about the issue of resemblance. The relationship between Frau Chauchat as a person and this piece of canvas was enough for him. The painting was intended to be a depiction of Frau Chauchat, she had sat as the model for it here in this apartment—that sufficed for him.

"As she lives and breathes," he repeated.

"Don't say that," the director objected. "I did a clumsy job. I don't flatter myself that I handled it all that well, although I suppose we had twenty sessions at least. How can one handle an outlandish face like that? At first you think it will be easy to capture it, what with the swing of those hyperborean cheekbones and those eyes that look like cracks in a muffin. Yes, there is something special about her. You get the details right, and bungle the larger effect. A regular puzzle box. Do you know her? It might be better not to have her sit, but to paint her from memory. You know her, then, do you?"

"Yes—no—only superficially, the way one knows people here."

"Well, I know her more internally, subcutaneously, if you get my drift. From her blood pressure, tissue firmness, and lymph circulation, I pretty much know what's what with her—and for good reason. The surface offers greater difficulties. Have you ever noticed the way she walks? Her face is just like her walk. She's a slinker. Take her eyes, for example—I'm not talking about the color, although that's tricky, too. I mean their placement, their shape. There's a slit in the lid, or so you think, and it's on a slant. But that only seems to be the case. The deceptive thing is the epicanthic fold, or a variation on it, that you find among certain races, an extra piece of skin that begins at the flat-bridged nose common among such people and falls like a pleat across the lid down to the inner corner of the eye. But if you pull the skin back taut toward the bridge, their eye is just like ours. A titillating little mystery, but not all that worthy; by light of day, the epicanthic fold turns out to be an atavistic abnormality."

"So that's how it works," Hans Castorp said. "I didn't know that, but it's always interested me what makes their eyes look like that."

"A mirage, a deception," the director confirmed. "If you simply draw it slanted and slit, all is lost. You have to handle it the same way that nature does, create an illusion within the illusion, so to speak, and for that, of course, you need to know all about the epicanthic fold. Knowledge never hurts. Do you see the skin, the epidermis here? Is it lifelike, or not especially so, in your opinion?"

"Terribly," Hans Castorp said, "terribly lifelike skin. I don't think I've ever seen skin so well painted. It's as if you can see the pores." And he brushed the edge of his hand across the skin left exposed by her décolletage, which stood out very white against the exaggerated redness of the face, like a part of the body never exposed to light, evoking, whether intentionally or not, an even stronger sensation of nakedness—a rather crude effect in any case.

All the same, Hans Castorp's praise was justified. Where her tender, though hardly meager bosom lost itself under the bluish drape, its subdued shimmer of white seemed taken from nature. The bare skin had obviously been painted with feeling, and despite a certain aura of sweetness, the artist had been able to endow it with scientific reality and lifelike accuracy. He had used the grainy surface of the canvas under the oils to suggest its uneven texture, particularly where the collarbone delicately protruded. He had not failed to include a mole just where the breasts began, and between their soft swellings there was a hint of pale bluish veins. Under the beholder's gaze, a barely perceptible shiver of sensitivity seemed to pass over this naked flesh—or to put it more boldly, you could imagine that you saw perspiration, the invisible vapors of life, rising from the flesh, that if you were to press your lips against the surface, you would smell a human body, not paint and varnish. We are simply describing Hans Castorp's impressions—but although he was especially receptive to such impressions, it should be noted that in fact Frau Chauchat's bared skin was by far the most remarkable piece of painting in the apartment.

His hands in his trouser pockets, Director Behrens rolled back and forth between the balls of his feet and his heels, regarding his work along with his visitors. "That pleases me, coming from a fellow artist," he said. "It pleases me that you see it. It's a good thing—certainly doesn't hurt—if a man knows something about what's what under the epidermis and can paint what cannot be seen. Or in other words, when a man's relationship with nature is something different from the, let us say, purely lyrical. When, for example, he's a part-time physician, physiologist, and anatomist with some intimate knowledge of life's undergarments. It can work to his advantage. Say what you like, it is a certain plus. That human hide there is a matter of science. You can examine it under a microscope for organic accuracy. And you'll see not just the horny and mucous layers of the outer skin, but along with them, the imagined reticular layer with its sebaceous glands, sweat glands, blood vessels, papillae. And beneath that is the layer of fat, the upholstery, you know—the foundation of fat cells that creates the gorgeous female form. And what a man thinks and imagines, that gets expressed, too. Those things flow into his hand and have their effect. It isn't there and yet it is—and that makes for lifelikeness."

The conversation stirred Hans Castorp's blood—his brow was flushed, his eyes had an eager glint; he had so much to say that he did not know how he should begin to reply. First, he wanted to move the painting from the shadowy wall where it was hanging to some more favorable spot; second, he definitely wanted to develop what the director had said about the nature of skin, a topic in which he had an immense interest; but third, he wanted to try to express more general and philosophical ideas, which were also matters of high priority.

Laying both hands on the portrait to lift it off its hook, he began hastily by saying, "Yes indeed, yes indeed. Very good, that is important. What I want to say is . . . that is, you yourself said, Director Behrens, 'when a man's relationship with nature is something different.' You said it's good if there is something else besides the lyrical—I believe that was your word—or artistic relationship. In short, it helps to regard nature from another viewpoint, the medical viewpoint, for instance. That is terribly relevant—pardon me, sir—I mean, you are so colossally right about that, because we are not dealing with two totally different viewpoints and relationships, but, more precisely, with the same one in both instances, with mere variations on a theme. With shades of meaning, I mean, with modifications of the same general concern, of which artistic activity is merely one part, one form of expression, if I may put it that way. Yes, pardon me, I'm just taking the painting down, there's absolutely no light here. I'll move it over to the sofa there, you'll see whether it doesn't look quite different. I mean to say: what is medical science concerned with? I understand nothing about it, of course, but its main concern is with human beings. And jurisprudence, the making and executing of laws? With human beings as well. And philology, which is usually tied up with some pedagogic profession? And theology, the care of souls, the pastoral office? All of them with human beings. They are all merely shades of one and the same important, primary interest: that is, the interest in human beings. In a word, they are all humanistic professions. And if you want to study them, you first learn classical languages as the basis, do you not? As part of your formal training, as they say. You are wondering, perhaps, why I am speaking about all this, since I am merely a realist, a technician. But not long ago I was lying in my rest cure, and I thought: it's really marvelous, a marvelous arrangement, the way every humanistic profession has the same formal basis, is grounded in the idea of form, of beautiful form, you know—which adds an extra nobility to it all, and emotion, too, in a way and . . . courtesy—so that interest in a given topic becomes something almost chivalrous. I mean—I'm most likely expressing myself very poorly, but one can see that matters of the intellect and beauty, or in other words, science and art, blend together because they have actually always been just one thing; so that artistic activity definitely belongs among the sciences, as a kind of fifth faculty if you like—is no less a humanistic profession, insofar as, to repeat myself, its main theme or concern is human beings. You must admit I'm right. Back when I was making youthful attempts at it, I painted only ships and water, but to my eye, portraiture will always be the most fascinating part of painting, because it has the human being as its subject. Which was why I asked right off whether you, sir, had done anything in that line. Wouldn't it hang much, much better here?"

Both Behrens and Joachim looked at him to see if he was not ashamed of himself for these impromptu babblings. But Hans Castorp was much too involved in his topic to feel any embarrassment. He held the painting against the wall behind the sofa and demanded they tell him if it was not considerably better lit there. At this moment, the maid entered with a tray of hot water, a spirit lamp, and coffee cups.

Pointing her in the direction of the smoking alcove, the director said, "Then your primary interest really ought to be more in sculpture. Yes, right, it does have more light there, of course—if you think it can tolerate that much . . . In sculpture, that is, because it deals in the purest, most exclusive form with human beings in general. But we mustn't let our water boil away."

"That's very true, about sculpture," Hans Castorp said as they moved away; and forgetting to rehang the painting or even to set it aside, he carried it with him, trailing it behind him into the adjoining area. "Certainly the humanist element is revealed most clearly in a Greek Venus or some athlete. When you stop and consider, it is, after all, the true, genuine humanist form of art."

"Well, as far as little Chauchat goes," the director remarked, "she's probably more an object for painting. I'm afraid Phidias or that other fellow whose name ends in that Hebrew-sounding way would have wrinkled up their noses at her sort of physiognomy. What are you doing there? Dragging my daubings around with you?"

"Yes, thanks, I'll just put it here against the leg of my chair—it's fine there for the moment. The Greek sculptors were not very interested in the head, it was more a matter of the body; perhaps that was the real humanistic element in fact. And the female form, that's actually fat, did you say?"

"It's fat," the director said with finality as he closed a cupboard from which he had extracted the utensils for brewing coffee: a cylindrical Turkish mill, a long-handled pot, a divided bowl for sugar and ground coffee—all of brass. "Palmitin, stearin, olein," he said, shaking coffee beans from a tin box into the mill as he began to turn the crank. "As you gentlemen can see, I make it all myself, from scratch. It tastes twice as good. . . . What did you think it was? Ambrosia, perhaps?"

"No, I already knew it on my own. It's just strange to hear it," Hans Castorp said.

They were seated in one corner, between the door and window, in front of a low bamboo table that held a brass tray with Oriental designs, on which the coffee apparatus had been set in the midst of various smoking utensils—Joachim beside Behrens on an ottoman furnished with an abundance of silk pillows, Hans Castorp in a club chair on rollers, against which he had leaned Frau Chauchat's portrait. A bright carpet lay at their feet. The director spooned coffee and sugar into the long-handled pot, poured water over them, and let the liquid come to a boil over the spirit lamp. It foamed up brown in the little onion-pattern cups. When they took a sip, it proved as strong as it was sweet.

"Your form is, too," Behrens said. "Your sculptural outline, if one can speak of it that way, is fat, too, of course, if not to the same extent as a woman's. For our sort, fat normally is only a twentieth of total body weight; a sixteenth for women. Without our subcutaneous cell structure we'd all end up looking like some sort of wrinkly fungus. The fat disappears with age, of course, resulting in the unaesthetic sags we all know so well. The fat is thickest around the female breast and abdomen, the upper thighs—in short, everywhere you find a little something of interest for your hand and heart. And the soles of the feet, they're both fat and ticklish."

Hans Castorp rolled the cylindrical coffee mill between his palms. Like all the furnishings in the room, its origin was probably more Indian or Persian than Turkish—certainly the style of its brass engraving, the surface pattern shiny against the dull background, suggested as much. Hans Castorp studied the design, without making much of it at first. When he suddenly did make something of it, he blushed.

"Yes, that's a tool for single gentlemen," Behrens said. "That's why I keep it locked up, you know. It might ruin my little kitchen fay's eyes. You'll suffer no further harm, I'm sure. It was presented to me as a gift by a patient, an Egyptian princess, who honored us with her presence for one brief year. You see, the pattern is repeated on each of the items. Droll, eh?"

"It's quite remarkable," Hans Castorp replied. "No, no, it doesn't bother me, of course. One can even view it in dead earnest if one likes— although, after all, it's not exactly appropriate on a coffee service. The ancients are said to have decorated their coffins with things like this on occasion. The obscene and the sacred were more or less one and the same for them."

"Well, as far as the princess goes," Behrens said, "she was, I think, given more to the former. I also have some very lovely cigarettes she gave me, extra-fine quality, the sort you bring out on tip-top occasions." And he fetched a bright green box from the cupboard to offer them one. Joachim declined with a click of his heels. Hans Castorp helped himself and smoked the unusually large, wide cigarette, imprinted with a golden sphinx—and it was indeed wonderful.

"If you would be so kind, Director Behrens," he requested, "do tell us something more about skin." He had picked up Frau Chauchat's portrait again, balancing it on one knee. Leaning back in his chair, the cigarette between his lips, he regarded it now. "Not specifically about the fatty layer—we've learned what that's about. But about human skin in general, since you're so good at painting it."

"About skin? Are you interested in physiology?"

"Very much. Yes, I've always taken a great deal of interest in it. The human body—I've always had a singular fondness for it. Sometimes I've asked myself if I shouldn't have become a doctor. In a certain sense, I think, I would not have done badly at it. Because if a man is interested in the body, he is also interested in illness—particularly in that—isn't he? Not that it means all that much, by the way. I could have become any number of things. I could have become a clergyman, too."

"Really?"

"Yes, sometimes I've had the fleeting impression that I would actually have been in my element there."

"But then why did you become an engineer?"

"Purely by chance. External circumstances tipped the scale more or less."

"Well, then—skin, you say? What should I tell you about your sensory envelope? It is your external brain, you see. Ontogenetically speaking, it has the same origin as the apparatus for the so-called higher sensory organs up there in your skull. You should know that the central nervous system is simply a slight modification of the external skin. Among lower animals there is no differentiation whatever between central and peripheral—they smell and taste with their skin. Just imagine it—the skin is their only sensory organ. Must be quite a cozy sensation, when one thinks about it. Whereas with highly differentiated beings like you and me, the skin's sole aspiration is to be tickled. It is an organ that merely wards off danger, sends up signals, though it does keep a damned good eye out for anything that gets too near the body. It even sticks its tactile apparatus out beyond itself—as hair, body hair, which is nothing but keratinized skin that can sense something approaching before the skin itself is touched. Just among us, it's even possible that the skin's task of protecting and defending us may go beyond the merely physical. Do you know how you blush or turn pale?"

"Not precisely."

"Yes, well, frankly, we don't know all that precisely ourselves, at least not when it comes to blushing for shame. The process has not been totally explained, since so far we have been unable to locate dilating muscles along the blood vessels that are activated by the vasomotor nerves. Why the cock's comb actually swells—or whatever other bombastic examples one might mention—remains a mystery, so to speak, particularly since psychological influences are involved. We assume that there are connections between the cerebral cortex and the vascular center in the medulla. And in response to certain stimuli—if you are terribly embarrassed, for instance—both these connections and the vascular nerves to the face come into play, which causes the blood vessels to dilate and fill up, so that you get a head as red as a turkey-cock's—and there you are all swollen with blood till you can hardly see a thing. Whereas in other cases—God knows what awaits you, something perilously beautiful perhaps—the blood vessels of the skin contract, and the skin turns cold and pale and shrinks, and your emotions make you look like a corpse, with leaden eye sockets and a white, pinched nose. But all the while the sympathetic nerves keep the heart thumping right along."

"So that's what happens," Hans Castorp said.

"More or less. Those are all reactions, you see. But since all reactions and reflexes, by their very nature, serve some purpose, we physiologists are almost forced to conclude that such secondary phenomena due to psychological factors are actually meant to protect the body, are defense mechanisms, much like goose bumps. Do you know how you get goose bumps?"

"Can't say I know that exactly, either."

"That's a display put on by the skin's sebaceous glands, which give off the skin's oils, a kind of protein-rich, fatty secretion, you know—not exactly appetizing, but it keeps the skin supple, so that it doesn't dry out and crack or break and remains pleasant to the touch. It's hard to imagine what it would be like to touch human skin without greasy cholesterol. The sebaceous glands have little muscles that can make the glands stand up erect, and when they do that, your skin feels like a rasp—just like the lad in the tale when the princess dumped a pail of minnows over him. And if the stimulus is very strong, the hair follicles become erect, too— and your hair stands on end, on your head and all over your body, like a porcupine defending itself. So now you can say you've learned what it means to have your flesh creep."

"Oh my," Hans Castorp said, "I've already learned that numerous times. I get the shivers rather easily in fact, on all sorts of occasions. What amazes me is that these glands go erect under such a variety of circumstances. When someone runs a stylus over glass, you'll get goose bumps, but it can also suddenly appear at the sound of especially beautiful music. And when I first took communion at my confirmation, it came in waves—the tingling and prickling just wouldn't stop. It's really strange what all puts those little muscles into motion."

"Yes," Behrens said, "a stimulus is a stimulus. The body doesn't give a damn about the meaning of the stimulus. Whether minnows or communion, the sebaceous glands stand up erect."

"Director Behrens," Hans Castorp said, studying the portrait across his knees, "I wanted to come back to what you were saying about the inner processes, the circulation of lymph and such. What is that about? I would love to hear more about it. Lymph circulation, for example, interests me a great deal—if you would be so kind."

"I can well believe it," Behrens replied. "Lymph is the most refined, intimate, and delicate mechanism in the human body. I presume that's what you had in mind in asking. People always talk about the blood and its mysteries, that special juice, as it's called. But the lymph, now that's the juice of juices, the essence, you see, the blood's own milk, a very rarefied liquid—a fatty diet will make it look just like milk, in fact." And in high spirits, employing his special jargon, he began to describe how blood—turned crimson as an opera cape from respiration and digestion, saturated with gases, laden with the slag of waste, brewed out of fat, protein, iron, salt, and sugar, forced through arteries at a temperature of 98.6 degrees by the pumping heart, and keeping both metabolism and animal warmth, in a word, sweet life itself, running in our bodies—began to describe, then, how blood does not enter cells directly, but under pressure sweats an extract, a milky fluid, through the arterial walls and into the tissues, so that it oozes in everywhere, a histological fluid that fills every little crack, stretching and expanding elastic cell tissue. That was what was called cellular tension, or turgor, and in turn turgor was what caused the lymph, after it had exchanged materials with the cells and tenderly rinsed them clean, to be forced back into the lymphatic vessels, the *vasa lymphatica*, and from there into the blood—a liter and a half of it per day. He described the lymphatic vessels, the system of arteries and absorbent tubes; spoke about how breast milk was formed from lymph collected from the legs, abdomen, chest, one arm, and one side of the head; then went on to talk about how at various points in the lymph vessels there were delicate filters called lymph glands, located along the neck, in the armpits, at the crooks of the elbows, the backs of the knees, and similar intimate, sensitive spots on the body. "Swelling can occur at such points," Behrens explained. "That's what got us started on all this—thickening of the lymph glands, here and there, at the back of the knee or the crook of the elbow for instance, rather like the tumors associated with dropsy. And there is always a reason for them, though hardly a welcome one. Under certain circumstances, it may arouse more than a suspicion of tubercular congestion in the lymphatic vessels."

Hans Castorp said nothing. "Yes," he remarked softly after a pause, "it's true. I could easily have become a doctor. The formation of breast milk . . . the lymph of the legs—it all interests me very much. The body!" he suddenly cried in a rapturous outburst. "The flesh! The human body! What is it? What is it made of? Tell us now, this very afternoon, Director Behrens. Tell us, for once and for all, in precise terms, so that we may know."

"It's made of water," Behrens replied. "So you're interested in organic chemistry, too, are you? The human body consists of water for the most part. Nothing better, nothing worse than water—nothing to get excited about. The dry stuff is a mere twenty-five percent of the whole, twenty percent being ordinary egg white, or protein, if you want a little more noble word for it, to which just a little fat and salt is then added. That's about all."

"But what about protein? What is it?"

"Various elements—carbon, hydrogen, nitrogen, oxygen, sulfur. Sometimes phosphorus, too. Your curiosity is becoming quite excessive, I must say. Some proteins are bonded with carbohydrates, mainly glucose and starch. As we age, muscles grow tough, because of increased collagen in the connective tissue—that's the glue, you see, the chief component of bones and cartilage. What else should I tell you? There's a protein in muscle plasma called myosin that coagulates in the muscle fiber and causes rigor mortis."

"Oh, right, when the body goes stiff after death," Hans Castorp said cheerfully. "Very good, very good. And then comes the autopsy, the anatomy of the grave."

"But of course. And you've put it very nicely. Then everything gets a lot more diffuse. We evaporate, so to speak. Just think of all that water. All those other ingredients are not very stable without life. Decomposition takes over, and they resolve into simpler chemical compounds, into inorganic matter."

"Decomposition, corruption," Hans Castorp said, "but that's really just a kind of burning off, isn't it? It all binds with oxygen, if I recall."

"Absolutely correct, oxidation."

"And life?"

"That, too. That, too, my lad. That's oxidation, too. Life is primarily the oxidation of cell protein, that's where our pretty animal warmth comes from, of which some people have a bit too much. Ah yes, life *is* dying— there's no sense in trying to sugarcoat it—*une destruction organique,* as some Frenchman once called it in that flippant way the Frenchies have. And it smells of dying, too, life does. And if we sometimes think otherwise, it's because we have a natural bias in the matter."

"And so if someone is interested in life," Hans Castorp said, "it's death he's particularly interested in. Isn't that so?"

"Well, there's a certain difference all the same. Life means that the form is retained even though matter is being transformed."

"But why retain the form?" Hans Castorp asked.

"Why? Now listen here—there's nothing the least bit humanist about a comment like that."

"Form is namby-pamby nonsense."

"You're in very bold and daring form today, yourself. Literally kicking over the traces. But I'm fading quickly here," the director said. "I'm beginning to feel melancholy," he added, rubbing his eyes with his gigantic hands. "It just comes over me, you see. I've joined you in a cup of coffee, and certainly it tasted good—but suddenly it just comes over me and I get melancholy. You gentlemen will have to excuse me. It was quite a special occasion. I found it great sport."

The cousins had sprung to their feet. They apologized, blaming themselves for keeping the director so long. But he reassured them the contrary was the case. Hans Castorp hastened to return Frau Chauchat's portrait to the adjoining room and hung it in its place again. They did not go back to their quarters by way of the garden. Behrens showed them the way through the building, letting them out through the glass-paned door. In the melancholy mood that had suddenly come over him, his neck vertebrae seemed to protrude even more than usual. He kept blinking his pop-eyes, and the skew of his moustache, caused by that hitch of his upper lip, gave him a mournful look.

As they walked along the corridor and started up the stairs, Hans Castorp said, "Now admit it—that was a good idea of mine."

"It was a change of pace at any rate," Joachim replied. "And you two certainly did use the occasion to discuss a lot of things, I must say. It was all a little haphazard for me. But it's high time we went off to our rest cure—twenty minutes at most until tea. You'll find it a little namby-pamby of me to insist on it, I suppose—now that you've taken to kicking over the traces. But then you don't need your rest cure as badly as I need mine."

Research

AND SO what had to happen happened, and Hans Castorp experienced what he would never have dreamed possible only a short while before. Winter was upon them, the local winter, with which Joachim was already familiar, because it had been raging at full force when he had arrived the previous year. Hans Castorp, however, had been somewhat afraid of its onslaught, although he knew he was definitely well equipped for it. His cousin tried to calm him.

"You mustn't imagine it as all that grim," he said. "It's not exactly the Arctic. You don't feel the cold that much, because the air is so dry and the wind is still. If you wrap yourself up well, you can stay out on the balcony until deep into the night without freezing. It's all about temperature inversions above the fog line—it gets warmer at higher altitudes. People didn't really know about that before. It feels colder, in fact, when it rains. But you have your sleeping bag now, and they'll even turn on the heat a bit if worse comes to worst."

And one certainly couldn't have called it a sneak attack or a violent assault; winter arrived gently, so that at first it did not look all that different from many days that summer had brought with it. For two days the wind was from the south, the sun bore down, the valley seemed shorter and narrower somehow, the background of the Alps at its entrance looked near and stark. Then clouds pushed in from the northeast across Piz Michel and Tinzenhorn, and the valley turned dark. Heavy rains followed. Then it wasn't just rain, but a whitish-gray mixture of snow and rain, and finally just snow that came in squalls that filled the whole valley. The snow continued for several days, and in time the temperature had fallen to the point where the snow could no longer melt. It was wet snow, but it stuck, and the valley now lay under a thin, damp, tattered garment of white that made the rugged evergreen slopes stand out black in contrast. The dining hall radiators were lukewarm by now. That was at the beginning of November, around All Souls', and it was nothing new. It had been much like this in August, and Hans Castorp had long since disabused himself of the idea that snow was the prerogative of winter. No matter what the weather, winter was always in view, if only at a distance—remnants and traces of snow lay glistening in crevices and fissures of the craggy Rhätikon chain that seemed to block the entrance to the valley, and a constant snowy salute came from mountain majesties far to the south. But now both snow and temperature kept falling. The sky, low and pale-gray above the valley, dissolved into relentless flakes that fell without sound and in immoderate, almost disquieting abundance. It grew colder by the hour. Then came a morning when Hans Castorp found it was forty-eight degrees in his room, and the next morning it was only forty-three degrees. Winter's icy chill had set in—in moderation, but it held. The temperature at night had been below freezing, but now it stayed there all day, from morning till evening; and with only brief interruptions, the snow continued a fourth, a fifth, a seventh day. Snow began to accumulate in earnest and present difficulties. Both the path to the bench beside the water trough and the driveway to the valley were kept shoveled clear, but were so narrow that there was no room for someone to move aside. When people met, one party had to step into the snowbank, sinking in up to the knee. All day a horse led by a man at its halter pulled a heavy stone snow-roller through the streets of the resort below; and what looked like an old-fashioned postal carriage on runners, with a plow mounted up front to push great masses of white to each side, commuted between the resort and Davos-Dorf, as the settlement to the north was known. The world—the high, remote, narrow world of the people up here— appeared padded and wrapped under heavy furs, not a post or pillar without its white bonnet. The stairs to the Berghof's main door had vanished and were replaced by a ramp; everywhere massive, comically shaped pillows weighed down the boughs of pine, sliding off now and then in one great mass and bursting in a cloud of white mist that drifted off among the tree trunks. The mountains all around were snow-covered—a rugged blanket on the lower slopes, a softer layer across peaks jutting in various shapes above the tree line. The days were dim, the sun visible only as a wan glow behind the veil of gray. But the snow provided indirect, gentle light—a milky luster that suited this world and its people, even if noses were red under white or brightly colored woolen caps.

At all seven tables in the dining hall, the onset of winter, the "season" in these regions, was the major topic of conversation. A great many tourists and athletes, it was said, had already arrived, filling the hotels in Dorf and Platz. The snow accumulation was estimated at two feet, its consistency perfect for skiing. Across the way people were hard at work on the bobsled run—from the top of the northwest slope of Schatzalp to the valley below—and it was expected to be open within a few days; that was, if a warm foehn wind did not spoil everything. People were looking forward to the activities that healthy guests would soon be pursuing again in the valley below—organized races and contests, which they all planned to attend, even if it meant breaking the rules and playing hooky from rest cure. There was a new sport, Hans Castorp learned, an invention from the north called *skijoring*, a race in which contestants on skis were pulled by horses. That was worth playing hooky for. People talked about Christmas, too.

Christmas! No, Hans Castorp had not even given it a thought until now. He had found it easy to talk or write letters about his doctor's discovery and having to spend the winter here with Joachim. But that also meant, as was now evident, that he would spend Christmas here, and without a doubt there was something unsettling about the idea, for he had never once spent the holidays anywhere but at home, in the bosom of his family. Good God—so that was part of the bargain, too. But he was no longer a child. Joachim seemed to have no trouble with the notion, had resigned himself to it without whining—and after all, Christmas had surely been celebrated around the world under a great variety of circumstances.

All the same, it seemed to him they were hurrying things, talking about Christmas even before the first day of Advent—it was still a good six weeks away. But people leaped right over those six weeks, devoured them there in the dining hall—a mental procedure that Hans Castorp had learned something about all on his own, although he was not yet used to whelmed by the blow that he had temporarily fallen into a strange melancholy and had been seen walking the streets giggling, gesticulating, and talking to himself. He had not returned to his former life, then, but had stayed on here—in part, to be sure, because he did not want to leave her grave behind; but the deciding, and less sentimental, factor had probably been that he had become slightly infected himself and, in his own professional opinion, actually *belonged* here. So he had taken up residence as one of those physicians who not only supervised people's stay here, but also shared their sufferings, who did not battle disease from a position of personal wholeness and independence, but who bore its marks themselves. It was a curious, but certainly not unique situation, with presumably both its beneficial and dubious sides. A warm relationship between doctor and patient is certainly to be welcomed, and there is something to the proposition that only he who suffers can be the guide and healer of the suffering. But can someone truly be the intellectual master of a power to which he is himself enslaved? Can he liberate if he himself is not free? To the average person, the idea of a sick physician remains a paradox, a problematical phenomenon. Instead of being intellectually enriched and morally strengthened by his experience, may he not perhaps find that his knowledge of the disease becomes clouded and confused? He no longer stares down the illness with a hostile eye; he is a biased and hardly unequivocal foe. With all due respect, one must ask whether someone who is part of the world of illness can indeed be interested in curing or even nursing others in the same way a healthy person can.

In his own way, Hans Castorp expressed some of these same doubts and considerations as he chatted with Joachim about the Berghof and its supervising physician; but Joachim countered that one had no way of knowing if Director Behrens was still a patient himself nowadays—presumably he had recovered long ago. It was ages now since he first began to practice here—on his own at first, quickly making a name for himself as both a specialist with a fine ear for auscultation and a sure-handed lung surgeon. And then the Berghof had secured his services, and in the course of what would soon be a decade now, his life had become intimately interwoven with that of the sanatorium. His residence was back there, at the far end of the northwest wing—Dr. Krokowski lived close by. That lady of noble lineage, the head nurse of whom Settembrini had spoken so scornfully and whom Hans Castorp had seen only fleetingly a few times, was in charge of the widower's household. The director lived alone, by the way—his son was studying at a university in imperial Germany and his daughter was already married, to a lawyer in the French part of Switzerland. Young Behrens came home on vacation now and practicing it with the cool grace of some of the old-timers among his fellow patients. Such junctures in the course of the year seemed to give them a hook to hang on to, functioned like a piece of gymnastic equipment for vaulting nimbly over the empty intervals in between. They were all feverish, with accelerated metabolisms, the whole physical organism working at a faster, augmented pace—which may well have had something to do with the way they drove time like a herd before them. He would not have been surprised if they had regarded Christmas as already over and started talking about New Year and Mardi Gras. But the people in the Berghof dining hall were certainly not so flippant and unsteady as all that. They pulled up short at Christmas—it was cause for worry, for racking one's brains. They discussed the communal gift that, following an old institutional custom, would be presented to Director Behrens on Christmas Eve and for which a collection was being started. The previous year he had been given a traveling bag, according to the report of those who had spent more than one year here. There were advocates now of a new operating table, an easel, a fur-lined overcoat, a rocking chair, an ivory stethoscope with some sort of "inlay." And when asked his opinion, Settembrini recommended a lexicographic work currently in preparation, entitled *Sociology of Suffering;* but the only person to second this suggestion was a bookdealer who had recently joined Fräulein Kleefeld's table. There was as yet no consensus. There were difficulties in coming to an agreement with the Russian guests. The collection was now split in two— the Muscovites declaring they wanted to present Behrens a gift of their own. Frau Stöhr was in a state of terrible upset for several days because of a sum of money—ten francs—that she had been foolish enough to lend Frau Iltis to contribute, but which that lady had "forgotten" to repay. She had "forgotten" it—Frau Stöhr used a wide range of calibrated emphases when speaking the word, all of them displaying her profoundest disbelief in such forgetfulness, which apparently was weathering the storm of the many little innuendoes and delicate proddings that Frau Stöhr assured everyone she had employed. On several occasions, Frau Stöhr waived all claims, stating she would forgive Frau Iltis the debt. "I'll pay for both myself and her," she said. "Fine, the disgrace won't be mine." But at last she hit upon a way out, which she then shared with her tablemates, much to their general amusement. She had "management" refund her the ten francs and add the sum to Frau Iltis's bill. And with that, the reluctant debtor had been outfoxed and at least that particular matter was settled.

It had stopped snowing. The overcast broke here and there; leaden-gray clouds parted to reveal glimpses of the sun, whose rays lent a bluish hue to the landscape. Then the sky turned clear. A bright, pure frost reigned, winter's splendor settled over mid-November, and the panorama beyond the arches of the balcony was magnificent—snow-powdered forests, ravines filled with soft white, a glistening sunlit valley under a radiant blue sky. And of an evening, when the almost circular moon appeared, the world turned magical and wondrous—flickering crystals and glittering diamonds flung far and wide. The forests stood out black against white. The regions of the sky beyond the reach of moonlight were dark and embroidered with stars. The sharp, precise, intense shadows of houses, trees, and telegraph poles cast on the sparkling surface looked more real and significant than the objects themselves. Within a few hours after sunset, the temperature sank to twenty degrees, then seventeen degrees. Its natural squalor hidden, the world seemed to be under a spell of icy purity, trapped inside a fantastic dream of fatal enchantment.

Hans Castorp stayed out on his balcony, looking down on the bewitched valley until late into the night, even though Joachim went back in around ten, or a little after. His splendid lounge chair with its three cushions and neck roll had been pulled up close to the wooden railing, topped along its full length by a little pillow of snow; on the white table at his side stood a lighted electric lamp, a pile of books, and a glass of creamy milk, the "evening milk" that was served to all the residents of the Berghof in their rooms at nine each night and into which Hans Castorp would pour a shot of cognac to make it more palatable. By now he was availing himself of every possible means of protection against the cold, the whole paraphernalia. The fur-lined sleeping bag he had purchased in an appropriate shop down in town was buttoned all the way up his chest, and he had ritually wrapped himself in his two camel-hair blankets. He wore a short fur jacket over his winter suit, had a woolen cap on his head, felt boots on his feet, and thickly lined gloves on his hands, although those did not prevent his fingers from turning numb.

What kept him out there so long, until midnight and even later (long after the Bad Russian couple had left the adjacent balcony), was in part the magic of the winter night, particularly since until eleven it was interwoven with music drifting up, now near, now far, from the valley—but primarily it was languor and excitement, both at once and in combination: the languor and weary inertia of his body and the busy excitement of a mind that could find no rest in its preoccupation with the new and fascinating studies the young man had recently taken up. The weather was hard on him, the frost exacted a toll on his physical organism. He ate a great deal, attacking the sumptuous Berghof meals—a roast beef course followed by a roast goose course—with an immense appetite not all that uncommon here, particularly in winter it seemed. At the same time he was subject to fits of drowsiness, so that whether by broad daylight or on moonlit evenings he would often drop off as he thumbed through his books (of which more later), and after a few minutes of unconsciousness, resume his research where he had left off. And when he and Joachim would take their constitutionals in the snow, their lively conversations exhausted him—and he tended here, more than ever had been the case down in the flatlands, to get caught up in his own hasty, unrestrained, even loose chatter. Shivering and dizzy, he would be overcome with a kind of numb intoxication that left his head flushed and hot. Since the onset of winter, his fever chart had been curving upward, and Director Behrens had mentioned something about injections that he liked to give for chronic high temperature and which two-thirds of the guests, including Joachim, regularly received. But Hans Castorp was certain his body was generating increased warmth because of the mental excitement and turmoil that kept him sitting in his lounge chair until very late every sparkling, frosty night. Indeed, the books he was reading with such fascination suggested much the same explanation.

Quite a bit of reading went on at the International Sanatorium Berghof, both in the common lounging areas and on private balconies—this was particularly true of newcomers and short-termers, since residents of many months or even years had long since learned how to ravage time without diverting or employing their minds, had become virtuosi at putting time behind them, and declared openly that only clumsy bunglers in the art needed a book to hang on to. At most they might leave a book lying on their lap or within reach on a table—that sufficed for them to feel their reading needs were taken care of. The sanatorium library was a polyglot affair with many illustrated works—an expanded version of the sort of thing that serves to entertain patients in a dentist's waiting room—and offered its services free of charge. People exchanged novels from the lending library down in Platz. Now and then a book or publication would appear that everyone fought over, and even those who had given up reading would grab for it, with only pretended disinterest. At the period we are describing here, *The Art of Seduction*, a badly printed booklet that Herr Albin had introduced, was making the rounds. It was translated almost word for word from the French, with even the original syntax perfectly preserved, lending a certain demeanor and titillating elegance to its exposition of a philosophy of physical love and debauchery, all in a spirit of worldly, life-affirming paganism. Frau Stöhr had soon read it and found it "stunning." Frau Magnus—the woman who was losing protein—supported her unconditionally. Her husband, the brewer, claimed personally to have profited from reading it, but regretted that his wife had imbibed, since that sort of thing only "spoiled" women and gave them immodest ideas. His remarks significantly increased demand for the publication. Two ladies from the lower common lounging area, Frau Redisch, the wife of a Polish industrialist, and a certain widow Hessenfeld from Berlin, both of them recent October arrivals, became involved in a rather unedifying scene after supper; indeed they came to blows and one of them began screaming hysterically (it might have been Redisch, but could just as easily have been Hessenfeld), and finally, simply sick with rage, had to be taken to her room—all because each claimed she was first in line for the book. Hans Castorp observed the incident from his balcony. Young people were quicker to get hold of the tract than patients of more advanced years. They would study it, sometimes in groups, up in their rooms after supper. Hans Castorp watched the lad with the saltcellar fingernail pass it on to a young lady with blond hair parted neatly in the middle—Fränzchen Oberdank, a lady's companion and housemaid, who was not all that ill and had only recently been brought up here by her mother.

Perhaps there were exceptions, people who spent the hours of their rest cure with some sort of serious intellectual pursuit, some rewarding study of one topic or another, even if they did so only to maintain contact with life on the plains or to give a little weight to time, a deeper draft to its keel, and prevent it from becoming pure time and nothing else. Perhaps besides Herr Settembrini struggling to eradicate suffering and honor-loving Joachim poring over his Russian textbooks, there were here and there people who did likewise, if not among the denizens of the common lounging areas—which was indeed very unlikely—then among the bedridden and moribund. Hans Castorp, at least, was inclined to believe it was so. As for himself, once he found that *Ocean Steamships* no longer had anything to say to him, he had requested that, along with his winter gear, his family send him a few books pertinent to his profession, works on engineering science and the technology of shipbuilding. These volumes, however, now lay neglected, replaced by others from quite a different department, textbooks from a field of study in which young Hans Castorp had developed a sudden interest. These were books on anatomy, physiology, and biology, written in various languages—German, French, and English—and sent him one day by the local bookdealer; evidently he had ordered them, on his own and without a word to anyone, while taking a walk down in Platz alone. (Joachim had had an appointment for an injection or was getting weighed that day.) His cousin was surprised to see them in Hans Castorp's hands. They were expensive books, as scientific works always are. The prices were written both inside the cover and on the jackets. He asked Hans Castorp why, if he really wanted to read such books, he had not borrowed them from the director, who surely had a fine selection of that sort of literature. But Hans Castorp replied that he wanted to own them himself—it was different reading a book that you owned. And besides, he loved to take his pencil and underline at will. Joachim listened for hours to the sound coming from his cousin's balcony: a paper knife slipping through uncut pages.

The volumes were heavy, cumbersome. When reclining, Hans Castorp propped the lower edge on his chest or stomach, which hurt a little but was simply part of the bargain. His mouth hanging half-open, he would let his eyes glide down each learned page illuminated by the reddish light from his shaded lamp, though, if it had come to that, he could just as easily have read by the bright moonlight. His head would lower until his chin lay on his chest, and he would hold that pose awhile—lost in thought perhaps or musing in a doze—half-asleep, before lifting his head for the next page. While the moon followed its prescribed path across the high mountain valley glistening like crystal below, he would read, pursue his study of organized matter, of the characteristics of protoplasm, that self-sustaining, delicate substance that hovers intriguingly between synthesis and dissolution and whose basic forms have remained the same as when it first assumed rudimentary shape. He read with burning interest about life and its sacred, yet impure mystery.

What was life? No one knew. It was aware of itself the moment it became life, that much was certain—and yet did not know what it was. Consciousness, as sensitivity to stimuli, was undoubtedly aroused to some extent at even the lowest, most undeveloped stages of its occurrence; it was impossible to tie the emergence of consciousness to any particular point in life's general or individual history—to link it, for instance, to the presence of a nervous system. The lowest animals had no nervous systems, let alone a cerebral cortex, and yet no one dared deny that they were capable of responding to stimuli. And you could anesthetize life, life itself, not just the special organs capable of the response that informs life, not just the nerves. You could temporarily suspend the responses of every speck of living matter, in both the plant and animal kingdoms, narcotize eggs and sperm with chloroform, chloral hydrate, or morphine. Consciousness of self was an inherent function of matter once it was organized as life, and if that function was enhanced it turned against the organism that bore it, strove to fathom and explain the very phenomenon that produced it, a hope-filled and hopeless striving of life to comprehend itself, as if nature were rummaging to find itself in itself—ultimately to no avail, since nature cannot be reduced to comprehension, nor in the end can life listen to itself.

What was life? No one knew. No one could pinpoint when it had emerged from nature and struck fire. Nothing in the realm of life was self-actuated or even poorly actuated from that point on. And yet life seemed to have actuated itself. If anything could be said about it, then, it was this: life's structure had to be so highly developed that nothing like it could occur in the inanimate world. The distance between an amoeba— a pseudopod—and a vertebrate was minor, insignificant in comparison to that between the simplest form of life and inorganic nature, which did not even deserve to be called dead—because death was merely the logical negation of life. Between life and inanimate nature, however, was a yawning abyss, which research sought in vain to bridge. People endeavored to close that abyss with theories—it swallowed them whole, and was still not an inch less broad or deep. In the search for some link, scientists had stooped to the absurdity of hypothesizing living material with no structure, unorganized organisms, which if placed in a solution of protein would grow like crystals in a nutrient solution—whereas, in fact, organic differentiation was simultaneously the prerequisite and expression of all life, and no life-form could be proved that did not owe its existence to propagation by a parent. What jubilation had greeted the first primal slime fished from the sea's deepest deeps—and what humiliation had followed. It turned out that they had mistaken a precipitate of gypsum for protoplasm. But to avoid one miracle (because it would be a miracle for life spontaneously to arise out of and return to the same stuff as inorganic matter), scientists had found it necessary to believe in another: archebiosis, that is, the slow formation of organic life from inorganic matter. And so they went about inventing transitional and intermediate stages, assuming the existence of organisms lower than any known form, but which themselves were the result of even more primal attempts by nature to create life—attempts that no one would ever see, that were submicroscopic in size, and whose hypothesized formation presupposed a previous synthesis of protein.

What was life, really? It was warmth, the warmth produced by instability attempting to preserve form, a fever of matter that accompanies the ceaseless dissolution and renewal of protein molecules, themselves transient in their complex and intricate construction. It was the existence of what, in actuality, has no inherent ability to exist, but only balances with sweet, painful precariousness on one point of existence in the midst of this feverish, interwoven process of decay and repair. It was not matter, it was not spirit. It was something in between the two, a phenomenon borne by matter, like the rainbow above a waterfall, like a flame. But although it was not material, it was sensual to the point of lust and revulsion, it was matter shamelessly sensitive to stimuli within and without—existence in its lewd form. It was a secret, sensate stirring in the chaste chill of space. It was furtive, lascivious, sordid—nourishment sucked in and excreted, an exhalation of carbon dioxide and other foul impurities of a mysterious origin and nature. Out of overcompensation for its own instability, yet governed by its own inherent laws of formation, a bloated concoction of water, protein, salt, and fats—what we call flesh— ran riot, unfolded, and took shape, achieving form, ideality, beauty, and yet all the while was the quintessence of sensuality and desire. This form and this beauty were not derived from the spirit, as in works of poetry and music, nor derived from some neutral material both consumed by spirit and innocently embodying it, as is the case with the form and beauty of the visual arts. Rather, they were derived from and perfected by substances awakened to lust via means unknown, by decomposing and composing organic matter itself, by reeking flesh.

This was the image of life revealed to young Hans Castorp as he lay there preserving his body warmth in furs and woolens, looking down on the valley glistening in the frosty night, bright beneath the luster of a dead star. The image hovered out there in space, remote and yet as near as his senses—it was a body: dull, whitish flesh, steaming, redolent, sticky; its skin blemished with natural defects, blotches, pimples, discolorations, cracks, and hard, scaly spots, and covered with the delicate currents and whorls of rudimentary, downy lanugo. The body was leaning back, wrapped in the aura of its own vapors, detached from the coldness of the inanimate world, its head crowned with a cool, keratinous, pigmented substance that was a product of its own skin, its hands clasped behind the neck. Gazing out from under lowered lids, the eyes had a slanted look because of a racial variation in the formation of the lid; its mouth was half-open, its lips pouted slightly. Its weight was on one leg, so that flesh protruded where the bone of the supporting hip stuck out, while the relaxed leg was raised so that the knee bent a little to nestle against the inside of the supporting leg and the foot rested on just the toes. There the body stood, leaning charmingly, turning to smile at him, its radiant elbows spread wide in the dual symmetry of its limbs, of its corporeality. The night of its pubic region built a mystic triangle with the steaming pungent darkness of the armpits, just as the red epithelial mouth did with the eyes, or the red buds of the breast with the vertically elongated navel. Under the impetus of brain and of motor nerves extending from the spine, belly and rib cage stirred, the pleuroperitoneal cavity swelled and contracted; the breath, warmed and moistened by mucous membranes along the trachea and laden with secreted material, streamed out between the lips, now that oxygen had bonded with the hemoglobin in the blood deep in the air sacs of the lungs. For Hans Castorp understood that this living body—with its mysterious symmetry of limbs, nourished by blood through a network of nerves, veins, arteries, capillaries, all oozing lymph; with its scaffold of bones, some of them tubes filled with marrow, some like blades, some like bulbs, some torqued vertebrae, but all originating in a gelatinous base that with the help of calcium salts and lime had grown firm enough to support the rest; with its joints made of tendons, cartilage, and slippery, well-oiled balls and sockets; with its more than two hundred muscles; with its central system of organs for nutrition and respiration, for registering and transmitting stimuli; with its protective membranes, serous cavities, and glands pumping secretions; with its complicated interior, a network of pipes and crevices, including openings onto the world outside—understood that this self was a living entity of a higher order, far removed from those simple organisms that breathed, fed, even thought, with just the surface of their bodies, that it was constructed, rather, out of a myriad of small organized units, which all shared a common origin, but had multiplied by constantly dividing, had adapted and combined for various functions, and had then separated to develop on their own and germinated new forms that were both the prerequisite and the effect of its growth.

The body hovering before him, this individual, living self was therefore a huge multiplicity of breathing and self-nourishing entities, which in the course of organic integration and specialization had forfeited their existence as selves to become anatomical elements, but with such a total loss of freedom and direct connection to life that some functioned only in response to stimuli like light, sound, touch, or warmth, whereas others could only cluster in new shapes or secrete digestive juices, and still others had been trained to function solely for defense, support, transport of fluids, or procreation. Relaxation of the rules unifying this organic multiplicity into a single higher self was permitted in some cases, and then a multitude of subordinate individuals would be collected in a loose, muddled way to form a higher living unit. The student brooded over the phenomenon of cell colonies; he learned about transitional organisms, algae, whose individual cells, wrapped in a coating of gelatin, were often widely dispersed, but nevertheless built multicelled formations, which, had they been asked, would not have known if they should be regarded as a settlement of single-celled individuals or as a single living entity, and in providing their answer would have vacillated strangely between the use of "I" and "we." Nature here exhibited an intermediate state between the free individual existence of simple units and the highly social organization of countless elemental individuals such as tissues and organs within a dominant self—the multicelled organism being only one possible form life might take as it passed through the cyclical process leading from procreation to procreation. The act of fertilization, the sexual union of two cells, marked the beginning of the formation of each pluralistic individual, just as it marked the beginning of each successive generation of more elemental forms, and so always led back to itself. The effects of this act lasted through many generations, which could then multiply all on their own in constant repetition, until the moment came when these asexually produced offspring once again found they required renewal by means of copulation, and the circle was closed. A complex living entity, born from the merged nuclei of two parental cells, was in fact a cooperative venture of many generations of individual cells produced asexually; it grew as they multiplied, and the circle of procreation was closed only when sexual cells, individual units specialized for procreation, had been produced within it and now found their way to a new fusion that would propel life onward.

With a volume on embryology propped at the bottom of his sternum, our young adventurer followed the development of the organism from the moment when the sperm, out in front of many just like itself and driven onward by the whipping motion of its tail, crashed headfirst into the gelatin coating of the egg and bored its way through to what is called the mount of conception, a conical protrusion in the outer rim of the egg's protoplasm formed in reaction to the approach of the sperm. In its serious pursuit of variations on this standard procedure, nature had employed every conceivable farce and grotesquerie. In some animal species the male was a parasite in the intestine of the female. There were others where the male placed his arm down the gullet of the female to lay his sperm inside her; the arm, bitten off and vomited back up, now ran away on its fingers, long fooling scientists into believing it to be an independent life-form deserving a Greek and Latin name of its own. Hans Castorp listened to the learned argument between the ovists and animalculists, the former asserting that the egg contains a perfect little frog, dog, or human being and the sperm merely stimulates it to grow, the latter seeing the sperm as a living creature with preformed head, arms, and legs, which then found in the egg a medium on which to feed—until everyone finally agreed to grant equal merit in the process to egg and sperm, both of which had arisen out of what were originally undifferentiated reproductive cells. He watched the single cell of the fertilized egg transform itself into a multicelled organism that grew by cleavage and division, saw the cellular ball nestle up against the lamellae of the mucous membrane, saw the blastula fold in on itself to form a basin or cavity, which then assumed the task of receiving and digesting nourishment. This was the gastrula, the protozoon, the primal form of all animal life, the primal form of flesh-borne beauty. Its two epithelia, the outer and inner, ectoderm and endoderm, turned out to be primitive organs, from whose folds and protrusions were formed glands, tissues, sense organs, the body's appendages. One layer of the ectoderm thickened, folded to form a groove, then closed to build a nerve canal, became the spinal column, the brain. When gelatinous cells began to produce glutens in place of mucin, the fetal fluid solidified into fibrous connective tissue, to cartilage; and he watched as calcium salts and fats were extracted from the surrounding liquid to form bone. The human embryo lay there crouched and cowering, it had a tail— and with its monstrous abdomen, stubby shapeless extremities, and larval face bent down over a bloated belly, it was indistinguishable from an embryonic pig. And according to one branch of science, whose notions of reality were equally unflattering and lurid, the embryo's development seemed to be a hasty recapitulation of zoological genealogy. It even temporarily had gill flaps, like a skate's.

It seemed permissible, or necessary, to view these developmental stages as finding their logical conclusion in the less-than-humanistic picture presented by the finished product: primitive man. His skin was covered with thick hair and equipped with twitching muscles to ward off insects. The olfactory membranes covered an extensive surface; his ears stuck out and were movable, so that they not only played a role in facial expression but also were more adept at catching sound than at present. In those days, the eyes, protected by a third, blinking lid, were at the sides of the head— except for a third eye, of which the pineal gland was a vestige, that was able to patrol the upper air. Primitive man also had a very long intestine, several sets of milk teeth, and air sacs next to the larynx to enhance his roar; the male sexual glands were carried inside the abdomen.

Anatomy presented our researcher with human limbs skinned and prepared for study; it showed him both the surface and the deeper structure of muscles, tendons, and ligaments, those of the thigh, the foot, and especially the arm, the upper and lower arm; it taught him the Latin names that medicine—that adumbration of the humanist spirit—had nobly and chivalrously supplied to distinguish them; and it allowed him to penetrate to the skeleton, an illustration of which offered him new perspectives, revealing the unity of all things human, the interconnection of all disciplines. For here, in a most remarkable fashion, he found himself reminded of his own—or should one say, his former—profession and of the fact that on his arrival he had presented himself to whomever he met, from Dr. Krokowski to Herr Settembrini, as a member of the scientific caste.

In order to study something—just what had been quite unimportant—he had learned in technical college about statics, flexible supports, and loads, about how good construction was the functional use of mechanical materials. It would surely have been childish to think that the engineering sciences and the laws of mechanics had been applied to organic nature, any more than one could say that they had been derived from it. They were simply repeated and corroborated in it. The principle of the hollow cylinder dominated the structure of tubular bones to such an extent that static requirements were satisfied with the precise minimum of solid material. A structure, Hans Castorp had learned, conformable to the demands of tension and pressure put upon it and constructed of nothing more than rods and braces of a mechanically suitable material, will withstand the same weight as a solid made of the same materials. So, too, one could observe that as tubular bones developed, with each increase in solid surface material, the inner portion, which had become mechanically superfluous, was transformed step by step into fatty tissue, the marrow. The bone of the upper thigh was a crane, and in constructing its bony beam, organic nature had given it precisely the same shape and direction that Hans Castorp would have had to draw as lines of tension and pressure in the blueprint of a mechanism subject to similar stresses. He was delighted to see it, for he now realized that his relationship to the femur, and to organic nature in general, was threefold: lyric, medical, and technical. It came as a great inspiration. And these three relationships, he believed, were a unity within the human mind, were schools of humanist thought, variations of one and the same pressing concern.

And yet, for all that, the accomplishments of protoplasm remained quite inexplicable—it seemed that life was prohibited from understanding itself. Not only were most biochemical processes unknown, but it was also their very nature to avoid examination. Almost nothing was understood about the construction and makeup of the unit of life known as the "cell." What good did it do to uncover the components of dead muscle? The living tissue did not permit chemical analysis; the very changes that brought about rigor mortis were enough to make all such experimentation futile. No one understood metabolism, no one knew how the nervous system functioned. What made it possible for taste buds to taste? What made it possible for certain olfactory nerves to be stimulated by various odors? What, indeed, made something smell at all? The specific odor of animals or people resulted from the vaporization of substances that no one could identify. The composition of the secretion called sweat was poorly understood. The glands that excreted it also produced aromas that doubtless played an important role among mammals, but whose significance among humans no one was prepared to claim to know much about. The physiological significance of obviously important parts of the body remained shrouded in darkness. One could, of course, simply disregard the appendix, call it a mystery—except that the appendices of rabbits were regularly found filled with a pulpy substance, and no one could explain either how it ever got back out or was replenished. But what about the white and gray matter in the medulla, what about the optic thalamus and its connection to the eye, or the gray matter in the pons? Brain and spinal tissue deteriorated so quickly that there was no hope of determining its structure. What caused the cerebral cortex to shut down as one fell asleep? What prevented the stomach from digesting itself—which occasionally did happen with corpses? The answer people gave was: Life, a special immunity of living protoplasm—and acted as if they did not notice what a mystical explanation that was. The theory behind such a commonplace phenomenon as fever was self-contradictory. An increase in metabolism caused an increase in the production of body heat. But, then, why did the body not compensate, as usual, by releasing that heat? Instead, sweat production was retarded—was that because of a contraction of the skin? But that could be demonstrated only if a chill was also present—otherwise the skin remained hot. "Hot flashes" would indicate that the central nervous system was the seat both of whatever caused catabolism and of a skin condition we are content to call abnormal, simply because we do not know any better way to define it.

But even so, what was such ignorance in comparison with our confusion when confronted by phenomena like memory—or the even more astounding extended memory that allowed acquired characteristics to be inherited? Anything like a mechanical explanation for these achievements of protoplasm was completely out of the question. Sperm, which transferred the countless, complicated individual and racial characteristics of the father to the egg, was visible only under a microscope; and even the most powerful magnification did not suffice to determine its genesis or allow it to be seen as anything but a homogeneous body—for the sperm of one animal looked like that of every other. Such structural factors forced one to assume that a single cell was no different from the higher life-form of which it was a building block, that it, too, was a higher organism, yet another composite made up of discrete units of life, individual living entities. One progressed from the ostensibly smallest unit to something smaller still, one was compelled to split something elemental into yet more basic elements. No doubt just as the animal kingdom consisted of various species of animals, just as the organism of the human animal consisted of a whole animal kingdom of cell species, so, too, the cell consisted of a new and diverse animal kingdom of elemental, submicroscopic living entities that grew independently, multiplied independently according to the law that each can only produce its own kind, and cooperated by division of labor to serve the next higher level of life.

Those were the genes, the bioblasts, the biophores—Hans Castorp rejoiced in the frosty night to make their acquaintance by name. But even in his excitement, he asked himself just how elemental they might appear under better light. Since they were bearers of life, they had to be organized, because life was based on organization; but if they were organized, they could not be elemental, because an organism is not elemental, but multiple. They were living entities below the level of the cell that they built and organized. But if that was so, despite their incomprehensible smallness, they, too, as living entities had to be built out of something, had to be organized, structured organically. Because to be a living entity was by definition to be built out of smaller, subordinate entities, or better, out of entities organized to serve the higher form of life. There could be no limit to such division as long as it yielded organic entities—that is, those possessing the characteristics of life, in particular the ability to ingest, grow, and multiply. As long as one spoke of living entities, any discussion of elemental units was dishonest, because the concept of an entity carried with it, *ad infinitum*, the concept of the subordinate, organizing unit. There was no such thing as elemental life—that is, something that was both already life and yet elemental.

But although it could not logically exist, ultimately there had to be something of that sort, because the notion of archebiosis—that is, the slow development of life from inorganic matter—could not be dismissed out of hand; and the gap in external nature between living and nonliving matter, which we vainly attempted to close, had to be filled or bridged somewhere deep within organic nature. At some point the division had to lead to "entities," which, although composites, were not yet organized and mediated between living and nonliving matter, groups of molecules that formed a transition between mere chemistry and organized life. But when one looked at chemical molecules, one found oneself at the edge of a yawning abyss far more mysterious than the one between organic and inorganic nature—at the edge of the abyss between the material and non-material. Because the molecule was made up of atoms, and the atom was not even close to being large enough to be called extraordinarily small. It was so small, in fact, such a tiny, initial, ephemeral concentration of something immaterial—of something not yet matter, but related to matter—of energy, that one could not yet, or perhaps no longer, think of it as matter, but rather as both the medium and boundary between the material and immaterial. But that posed the question of another kind of spontaneous generation, far more baffling and fantastic than that of organic life: the generation of matter from nonmatter. And indeed, the gap between matter and nonmatter demanded—at least as urgently as the one between organic and inorganic nature—that there be something to fill it. There must of necessity be a chemistry of nonmatter, of unsubstantial compounds, from which matter then arose, just as organisms had come from inorganic compounds, and atoms would then be the microbes and protozoa of matter—substantial by nature, and yet not really. But confronted with the statement that atoms were "so small they were no longer small," one lost all sense of proportion, because "no longer small" was tantamount to "immense"; and that last step to the atom ultimately proved, without exaggeration, to be a fateful one. For at the moment of the final division, the final miniaturization of matter, suddenly the whole cosmos opened up.

The atom was an energy-laden cosmic system, in which planets rotated frantically around a sunlike center, while comets raced through its ether at the speed of light, held in their eccentric orbits by the gravity of the core. That was not merely a metaphor—any more than it would be a metaphor to call the body of a multicelled creature a "city of cells." A city, a state, a social community organized around the division of labor was not merely comparable to organic life, it repeated it. And in the same way, the innermost recesses of nature were repeated, mirrored on a vast scale, in the macrocosmic world of stars, whose swarms, clusters, groupings, and constellations, pale against the moon, hovered above the valley glistening with frost and above the head of this master of muffled masquerade. Was it illicit to think that certain planets of the atomic solar system—among all those hosts of solar systems in all those milky ways that constituted matter—that the state of some planet or other in that inner world might not correspond to the conditions that made the earth an abode of *life*? For a slightly tipsy young master of the muffling art with an "abnormal" skin condition, who was no longer totally lacking in experience when it came to illicit matters, this was a speculation that bore the stamp of logic and truth and, far from being absurd, seemed as perfectly obvious as it was illuminating. Once the cosmic character of the "smallest" bits of matter became apparent, any objection about the "smallness" of these stars in the inner world would have been quite irrelevant—and concepts like inner and outer had now lost their foundation as well. The world of the atom was an outer world, just as it was highly probable that the earthly star on which we lived was a profoundly inner world when regarded organically. Had not one researcher in his visionary boldness spoken of the "beasts of the milky way"—cosmic monsters whose flesh, bones, and brains were formed from solar systems? But if that was so, as Hans Castorp believed it to be, then at the very moment when one thought one had reached the outermost edge, everything began all over again. But that meant, did it not, that perhaps in inner world after inner world within his own nature he was present over and over again—a hundred young Hans Castorps, all wrapped up warmly, but with numbed fingers and flushed face, gazing out from a balcony onto a frosty, moonlit night high in the Alps and studying, out of humanistic and medical interest, the life of the human body?

He learned pathological anatomy from a volume he was now holding to one side to catch the reddish glow of his table lamp; the text, with a series of illustrations, discussed parasitic cell fusion and infectious tumors. These were tissue formations—and very luxuriant formations they were—caused by foreign cells invading an organism that proved receptive to them and for some reason offered favorable conditions (although, one had to admit, rather dissolute conditions at that) for them to flourish. It was not so much that the parasite deprived the surrounding tissue of its nourishment, but rather, in exchanging materials with its host cell, it formed organic compounds that proved amazingly toxic, indeed ultimately destructive, to the cells of the host organism. Researchers had been able to isolate and concentrate the toxins from several such microorganisms and were amazed to find that, if injected into an animal's bloodstream, even tiny doses of such materials, which could be classified as simple proteins, produced the most acute toxic effects, leading to rapid demise. The external form of this contamination was a rapid growth of tissue, a tumor, pathologically speaking, which was the cells' reaction to the stimulus of bacilli having taken up residence among them. The cells of the mucuslike tissue between which or in which the bacilli resided formed millet-seed-size nodules, some of which were very large indeed and extraordinarily rich in protoplasm containing numerous nuclei. This riotous living, however, soon led to ruin, because the nuclei of these monster cells began to shrink and break down, their protoplasm began to congeal and decompose; other tissues in the vicinity were affected by the same foreign stimuli. Inflammation spread to adjacent blood vessels; lured to the scene of the accident, white corpuscles now arrived; death by congealing proceeded apace. Meanwhile the soluble toxins from the bacteria had long since intoxicated the nerve centers; the organism was already feverish, and with heaving bosom, so to speak, it reeled toward its disintegration.

So much for pathology, the study of disease, with an emphasis on bodily pain, which at the same time was an emphasis on the body, an emphasis on its pleasures—disease was life's lascivious form. And for its part, what was life? Was it perhaps only an infectious disease of matter— just as the so-called spontaneous generation of matter was perhaps only an illness, a cancerous stimulation of the immaterial? The first step toward evil, toward lust and death, was doubtless taken when, as the result of a tickle by some unknown incursion, spirit increased in density for the first time, creating a pathologically rank growth of tissue that formed, half in pleasure, half in defense, as the prelude to matter, the transition from the immaterial to the material. This was creation's true Fall, its Original Sin. The second spontaneous generation, the birth of the organic from the inorganic, was only the sad progression of corporeality into consciousness, just as disease in an organism was the intoxicating enhancement and crude accentuation of its own corporeality. Life was only the next step along the reckless path of spirit turned disreputable, matter blushing in reflex, both sensitive and receptive to whatever had awakened it.

The books lay piled high on the table with the lamp, but one was on the floor mat next to his lounge chair and another, the one Hans Castorp had last been reading, lay across his stomach, its weight making it very difficult for him to breathe, although his cerebral cortex had sent no order to the appropriate muscles to remove it. He had read to the bottom of the page, until his chin rested on his chest and his eyelids fell over his ordinary blue eyes. He beheld the image of life, its voluptuous limbs, its flesh-borne beauty. She had loosened her hands from the back of her neck, and her arms—she spread them wide now, revealing the inner surface, especially the tender skin at the elbow with its blood vessels, two large bluish branching veins—her arms were of inexpressible sweetness. She bent toward him, bent down to him, over him, he sensed her organic aroma, sensed the lacelike pounding of her heart. He felt an embrace, hot and tender, around his neck. Melting with lust and dismay, he laid his hands on her upper arms, there where her grainy skin stretched taut over the triceps and was blissfully cool to the touch. He felt the moist suckle of her kiss on his lips.

Danse Macabre

SHORTLY AFTER THE HOLIDAYS, the Austrian horseman died. Prior to that event, however, was Christmas, two days of festivities—or three, if you counted Christmas Eve—that Hans Castorp had awaited with some anxiety, shaking his head now and then, wondering what they would be like here, only to discover that they came and went like normal days with a morning, afternoon, and evening, with the usual whims of the weather (a slight thaw set in), and were indistinguishable from others of their sort, apart from a little external decoration and the mood that held sway in people's hearts and minds for the time allotted to them, until the days moved on, becoming a recent, then distant past silted with a few novel impressions.

Director Behrens's son, Knut by name, came for a holiday visit and lived with his father in the residential wing—a pretty young man, whose neck vertebrae already stuck out a bit too far as well. You could feel young Behrens's presence in the air. Dressing with special care, the ladies were subject to little fits of laughter and temper, and their conversations were about encounters with Knut in the garden, in the woods, or down in the resort. He had visitors himself, several friends from his university found their way to the valley—six or seven students, who stayed in town, but took their meals at the director's residence and roamed the region with their comrade in a closed troop. Hans Castorp avoided them. If necessary, both he and Joachim reluctantly made detours to avoid meeting these young people. A whole world separated those who belonged to the society of "people up here" from these warbling, walking-stick-swinging wanderers, and he did not want to hear or know anything about them. Besides, most of them seemed to be from the North, some even from his hometown perhaps—and Hans Castorp felt very shy about meeting any-one from Hamburg. He often wondered if someone from home might not suddenly show up at the Berghof, especially since Behrens had re-marked that the city always provided the sanatorium with a handsome contingent. Perhaps there were some here already among the serious cases and the moribund, whom you never saw. Quite visible, however, was a hollow-cheeked merchant, said to be from Cuxhaven, who had been sitting at Frau Iltis's table for a few weeks now. Whenever he spotted him, Hans Castorp was glad both that it was so difficult to come into contact with people who were not tablemates and that his hometown was a large one with many different social spheres. The merchant's insignificant presence greatly reduced the worries he had about the possible appearance of natives of Hamburg.

And so Christmas Eve came ever nearer, until one day it was only just around the corner, and the next day it had arrived. It had been a good six weeks away when Hans Castorp had first been surprised to hear talk about the holidays—as long, if you stopped to count, as his originally scheduled stay plus the period he had spent in bed, which, as Hans Castorp looked back on it now, had seemed a very long time back then, particularly those first three weeks, whereas the same number of days now appeared to add up to very little, almost nothing. The people in the dining hall had been right, he now discovered, to have taken the interval so lightly. Six weeks—why, that was not as many as a single week had days. And what was a week, when you stopped to consider? Just a little circuit from Monday to Sunday—and then it was Monday again. You had only to keep asking about the value and meaning of the next smaller unit to realize that taken together they would not add up to a sum, but rather that such calculations led to diminishment, obliteration, shrinkage, and annihilation. What was a day, measured for instance from the moment you sat down to your midday meal to the return of that same moment twenty-four hours later? Nothing—although it was twenty-four hours. And what was an hour, spent for instance lying in rest cure or taking a walk after a meal—which more or less exhausted the possibilities for using up such a unit of time? Once again, nothing. By their very nature, the sum of these nothings was not all that serious. Things did become serious, however, when you descended to the smallest unit—those sixty seconds times seven you spent with the thermometer between your lips so that you could extend the line on your chart. Those were extremely tenacious, important seconds—they stretched out into a little eternity, leaving extraordinarily dense deposits in the scurrying shadow of grand time.

The holidays proved incapable of disturbing the daily schedule of the residents of the Berghof. A tall, handsome fir had been set up a few days beforehand at the far right end of the dining hall, next to the Bad Russian table; and its piny scent, finding its way among all the aromas of rich food, occasionally reached the noses of the diners and awakened a kind of wistful look in the eyes of some who sat at the seven tables. By suppertime on the twenty-fourth, the tree had been gaily decorated with tinsel, glass balls, gilt cones, little apples in nets, and all sorts of candies; its colorful wax candles burned during the whole meal and for a while afterward. It was said that little trees with candles had been provided for the bedridden, too—one tree per room. A great many parcels had arrived over the last few days. Even Joachim Ziemssen and Hans Castorp had received packages from their distant, low-lying homeland, carefully wrapped gifts that they had then spread out in their rooms: cleverly chosen articles of clothing, neckties, luxury items in leather and nickel, as well as an abundance of holiday pastries, nuts, apples, and marzipan, in such quantities that the cousins gazed at them dubiously, wondering when they would ever find a chance here to eat it all. Hans Castorp was well aware that Schalleen had prepared his package, had even purchased the gifts after dignified consultation with his uncles. A letter from James Tienappel was included, typewritten, but on his heavy private stationery: his uncle sent his own and his father's holiday greetings and best wishes for a speedy recovery. He also made practical use of the occasion to add felicitations for the New Year fast approaching—a procedure that Hans Castorp had himself adopted when from his lounge chair he had penned his own Christmas letter, along with a clinical report, to Consul Tienappel.

The candles on the tree in the dining hall burned, singeing needles that crackled and gave off a scent that reminded all hearts and minds of just what day it was. People had dressed for dinner, the gentlemen in evening clothes, the ladies in jewels, some of them probably sent up from the plains below by loving husbands. Even Clavdia Chauchat had exchanged her customary sweater for a gown with a hint of whimsy, or rather patriotism. A brightly embroidered, belted peasant outfit, in a Russian, or rather Balkan, perhaps even Bulgarian style, it was trimmed with gold spangles, and its many pleats lent her figure an unusual soft fullness. It suited what Settembrini liked to call her "Tartar physiognomy" very nicely, in particular it went well with her "lone-wolf eyes." The mood was very lively at the Good Russian table, where the first pop of a cork was heard from the champagne being served at almost all the tables. At the cousins' table, it was the great-aunt who ordered it for her niece and Marusya, but she treated them all to some. The menu was well chosen, ending with cheese pastry and bonbons, and they finished off with coffee and liqueurs. Now and then a little spray of pine would catch fire, inspiring a moment of shrill, inordinate panic before the flames were put out. At the end of the meal, Settembrini, dressed as always and with a toothpick in his mouth, joined the cousins at their table for a while, teasing Frau Stöhr and offering a few remarks about a carpenter's son, a rabbi to all humankind, whose make-believe birthday it was today. It was uncertain if he had ever even lived. But an idea had been born back then, which had continued to triumph down to the present, and that idea was the dignity of every individual soul, and the equality of all—in a word, individualistic democracy—and in honor of it, he would now empty the glass someone had passed to him. Frau Stöhr found his remarks "amphibious and unfeeling." She stood up in protest, and since people were already moving to join the evening social, her tablemates followed her example.

This evening their gathering was given added dignity and vitality by the presentation of the gift to the director, who stopped by for half an hour with Knut and Head Nurse Mylendonk. The ceremony took place in the social room with the optical toys. The Russians' special present consisted of a very large, round silver plate with the recipient's monogram engraved in the middle—an object whose utter uselessness was immediately obvious. One could at least lie down on the chaise longue the other guests had given him, although it was covered with just a cloth, since it still lacked both cushions and upholstery. But the headrest was adjustable, and Behrens tried it for comfort, stretching out on it with his useless plate still under one arm; pretending to be Fafnir guarding his treasure, he began to snore like a sawmill. Cheers on all sides. Even Frau Chauchat laughed very hard at this performance, so that her mouth stood open and her eyes drew close together, exactly like Pribislav Hippe's whenever he laughed—or so it seemed to Hans Castorp.

No sooner had the director departed than people sat down at the card tables. The Russian group withdrew, as usual, to their little salon. A few guests stood around the dining hall Christmas tree, nibbling at the ornaments and watching the stubs of candles flicker out in their little metal jackets. Widely scattered among the tables already set for breakfast, a few solitary souls sat, each frozen in a distinctive pose and private silence.

Christmas Day was damp and foggy. They were sitting in clouds, Behrens said—there was no such thing as fog up here. But whether clouds or fog, the damp was penetrating. The surface of the snowpack began to thaw, turn porous and slushy. During rest cure, the numbness in face and hands was much more painful than on sunny cold days.

The evening of Christmas Day was marked by a musical presentation, a real concert with rows of chairs and printed programs, just for "people up here" at the Berghof. It was an evening of lieder, presented by a local professional soprano who also gave lessons. Two medallions were pinned at either side of the décolletage of her ball gown; she had arms like sticks and a voice whose unique toneless quality sadly revealed the reason why she resided up here. She sang:

> I bear my song of love
> Within my heart.

The accompanist was likewise local. Frau Chauchat sat in the first row, but disappeared at intermission, so that from that point on Hans Castorp could listen to the music (and it was music, despite the circumstances) with a peaceful heart, reading the text printed in the program as each song was sung. Settembrini sat off to one side for a while, but he also vanished, after first making a few graphic, taut comments about the local's tedious bel canto and adding a satirical remark about how delightful it was that they were all so cozy and snug here together this evening. Truth to tell, Hans Castorp was relieved that the two of them—the narrow-eyed woman and the pedagogue—were gone, and he was free to devote his full attention to the songs. He thought what a fine thing it was that people made music all over the world, even in the strangest settings—probably even on polar expeditions.

The second day of Christmas differed not at all from a Sunday or even a normal weekday, except for the faint awareness of its presence; but once it was over, the Christmas holidays were part of the past—or, just as correctly, lay in the distant future, a year away. It would take twelve months until they would return anew, the circle complete—and after all, that was only seven months more than Hans Castorp had already spent here.

But, as noted, shortly after Christmas, even before New Year, the Austrian horseman died. The cousins learned about it from Alfreda Schildknecht, or Sister Berta as she was known, who tended poor Fritz Rotbein and stopped them in the corridor to inform them of the discreet event. Hans Castorp took profound interest in it all, partly because the signs of life he had heard from the horseman were among his first impressions up here—the first of several, or so it seemed to him, to contribute to the hot flush in his face, which had never left it since—but partly, too, for moral, or one might say, spiritual reasons. He kept Joachim there for a long while as he talked with the nurse, who hung with happy gratitude on his every remark and question. It was a miracle, she said, that the horseman had lived to see the holidays. He had long since proved what a tough cavalier he was—it was hard to know what he had used to breathe with toward the end. True, for days he had kept himself going only with the help of massive amounts of oxygen; had used forty demijohns yesterday alone, at six francs a bottle. That must have run into some money, as the gentlemen could well imagine, especially since his wife, in whose arms he had passed away, had been left quite penniless. Joachim expressed disapproval of such expense. What was the point of these tortures, of clinging to life in such an expensive, artificial way, when the case was hopeless? One could not blame the man for blindly consuming expensive gas keeping him alive, when they had forced it on him. But those treating him ought to have acted more reasonably and have let him walk the inevitable path, for God's sake—regardless of the question of resources, or better, with considerable regard to them. The living had their rights, too, and so on. Hans Castorp disputed this emphatically—his cousin was talking almost like Settembrini, with no respect or reverence for suffering. The horseman had died in the end, and there was nothing funny about that; you could only show your concern, and a dying man deserved every kindness, every honor that could be bestowed on him, Hans Castorp insisted on that. He could only hope Behrens had not screamed at the

man at the end and scolded him irreverently—he hadn't, had he? No need
to worry, Nurse Schildknecht declared. The horseman had made only
one small, imprudent attempt to escape at the very end, by trying to jump
out of bed; but a gentle reminder of the pointlessness of his intention had
sufficed to keep him from attempting anything of the sort again.

Hans Castorp made a personal inspection of the deceased. He did so
in open defiance of the institutional practice of concealment; he despised
the egotism of all the others, who did not want to know, hear, or see
anything, and hoped to reproach them with this act. He had tried to bring
up the subject of this latest death with his tablemates, but had been met
by a unanimous rebuff so sullen that he felt both chagrined and outraged.
Frau Stöhr came close to being rude. How could he even mention such
a thing? she had asked. What sort of upbringing had he had? House rules
carefully screened them, the patients, from coming into contact with such
matters, and now here came a greenhorn sounding off about it—and while
they were trying to eat their roast and with Dr. Blumenkohl present at
that, who could be taken any day. (This last was whispered behind her
hand.) If it happened again she would lodge a complaint. Then and there,
as a result of that rebuke, Hans Castorp had reached his decision, which
he made known to the others, to pay his personal respects to their departed
housemate and say a silent prayer beside his remains. He also prevailed
upon Joachim to join him.

Through the good offices of Sister Berta they were admitted to the dead
man's room, which was on the second floor, directly under their own.
His widow received them—a small, disheveled blond, frazzled from long
nights of watching, pressing a handkerchief to her lips and red nose and
wearing a plaid winter coat with the collar turned up, because it was very
cold in the room. The heat had been turned off, the door to the balcony
was open. The young men said what had to be said in muffled tones, and
then, waved forward by an agonized gesture, they stepped across the
room with a reverential, forward rocking motion, the heels of their boots
never touching the ground, and stood there regarding the dead man on
his bed, each in his own way—Joachim at attention, half bowing in an
official, reserved pose; Hans Castorp relaxed and preoccupied, his hands
clasped before him, his head tilted to one shoulder, with an expression
much like the one he usually wore when listening to music. The horseman's
head was still propped up so that his body—its long frame once the site
of life's ceaseless breeding—looked all the flatter, almost like a plank,
with a slight rise in the blanket from the feet at the other end. A wreath
lay in the vicinity of the knees, with a palm frond projecting from it and
grazing the large, yellow, bony hands folded across the sunken chest. The

face, too, was yellow and bony, with a hooked nose, sharp cheekbones, and a bushy, reddish-blond moustache, so thick that it made the cheeks look even hollower. The eyes were closed unnaturally tight—pressed closed, Hans Castorp could not help thinking, not just closed. They called that the last token of love, although it was done more for the sake of the survivors than of the dead man. And it had to be done very soon, because once too much myosin had formed in the muscles, it was no longer possible, and then he would lie there staring—and that was the end of the sedate notion of "slumber."

A skilled expert at all this, in his element in more than one sense, Hans Castorp stood piously beside the bed. "He looks as if he's sleeping," he said to be kind, although the considerable differences were obvious. And then in a masterfully subdued voice, he began a conversation with the horseman's widow, making inquiries—which demonstrated both medical expertise and moral, religious sympathy—about her husband's long years of suffering, his last days and moments, and the transfer of the body to Kärnten, which was yet to be arranged. The widow, speaking in a nasal, Austrian drawl interrupted occasionally by sobs, found it remarkable for young people to feel and show such concern for other people's troubles. To which Hans Castorp responded that his cousin and he were themselves ill, after all, and that very early in life he himself had stood beside the deathbeds of close relatives, was an orphan twice over, and so death was an old acquaintance, so to speak. What profession had he chosen? she asked. He replied that he "had been" an engineer. —Had been? —Had been, insofar as his illness and a stay up here of still quite indeterminate length had interfered with his plans; this was a critical time in his life, perhaps even a turning point, one could not know for sure. (Joachim stared, scrutinizing him in horror.) And what about his good cousin? —He wanted to be a soldier down in the flatlands, was an officer's candidate. —Oh, she said, military service was certainly one of the more serious professions, a soldier had to reckon with coming into close contact with death and certainly did well to grow accustomed to the sight of it early on. She dismissed the young men with her thanks, and her mood was now imposingly serene, given her anguished situation—in particular the stiff bill for oxygen her spouse had left her. The cousins returned to their own floor. Hans Castorp seemed satisfied with their visit and spiritually moved by the impressions it had left on him.

"Requiescat in pace," he said. "Sit tibi terra levis. Requiem aeternam dona ei, Domine. You see, when it comes to death, when one speaks to the dead or about them, Latin comes into its own. It's the official language in such cases, which only points up how special death is. But it is not out of humanistic courtesy that people speak Latin in their honor. The language of the dead is not the Latin you learn in school, you see, but comes from a totally different sphere, from just the opposite direction one might say. It is sacred Latin, the dialect of monks, a chant from the Middle Ages, so to speak, a kind of muted, subterranean monotone. Settembrini would not be pleased with it, it's nothing for humanists and republicans and pedagogues of that ilk. It comes from a different intellectual direction—from the other one. It seems to me you have to be clear about these two intellectual directions, or dispositions, as they might more accurately be called—the religious and the freethinking. They both have their good points, but what I particularly have against the freethinking one—the Settembrinian one, I mean—is that it assumes that only it truly represents human dignity. That is an exaggeration. In its own way, the other contains a great deal of human dignity, too, and contributes to moral conduct and decorum and noble formality, certainly more than 'freethinking' does—and always with an eye to human weakness and frailty. The concepts of death and corruption play an important role, too. Have you ever seen a production of *Don Carlos*—the way things were done at the Spanish court? When King Philip enters, all in black, decorated with his orders of the Garter and the Golden Fleece, and slowly doffs his hat—which looks very much like one of our modern bowlers—in a kind of wide, upward sweep, and says, 'Ye may cover now, my lords,' or something like that. Well, that's up to the highest standards, let me tell you, not a hint of slipshod manners and simply letting things take their course—just the contrary. And then the queen says, " 'Twas otherwise in my own France"—naturally, it's all too correct and formal for her, she wants life to be more amusing, more human. But what does that mean, human? Everything is human. The Spaniard's fear of God, his humility, his solemnity, his scrupulous austerity is a very worthy form of humanity, I would say. Whereas you can also use the word 'human' to cover up all sorts of weak-willed slovenliness. You do agree I'm right, don't you?"

"Yes, you're right," Joachim said, "of course I can't stand either slovenliness or weak-willed people. There has to be discipline."

"Yes, you say that as a military man, and I must admit, the military understands these things. The widow was quite right to say your profession has something serious about it, because the military always has to reckon with the worst case, which can mean dealing with death. You have your uniforms that sit tight and proper and have stiff collars—that gives you your *bienséance*. Plus you have your idea of rank, your obedience to authority, and take pains to deal honorably with one another, and that's part of the Spanish spirit, too—all out of a kind of piety, and deep down I respect that. It's a spirit that ought to be more prevalent among us civilians, in our customs and conduct—I'd like that better, it would suit me. I think the world and life are such that people ought to dress mostly in black, with a starched ruff instead of your military collar, and deal with one another in a serious, muted, formal way, always keeping death in mind—that's how I'd like it, that would be moral. You see, that's another one of Settembrini's conceited misconceptions—it would be good to bring it up with him sometime. He claims he's the one true representative not only of human dignity, but of morality as well—what with his 'practical, lifelong labor' and his Sunday festivities in honor of progress, as if people didn't have other things besides progress to think about on Sunday. His systematic eradication of suffering. You haven't heard about that yet, by the way, but he gave me a nice lecture on the topic—wants to eradicate it systematically with an encyclopedia. And if the project seems downright immoral to me, what then? I won't say anything to him, of course—he would talk circles around me with his graphic patter and say, 'I am warning you, my good engineer!' But a man can think what he likes—'Sire, give thoughts their freedom.' Let me tell you something," he said in conclusion—they had arrived in Joachim's room, and his cousin was getting ready for rest cure. "Let me tell you something I've decided to do. We live here right next door to dying people, next to awful tribulation and misery, and it's not just that we all act as if it were no concern of ours, but we're even protected, spared any possibility of coming into contact with it, or seeing it. And now they'll sneak the horseman out while we're eating supper or breakfast. I find that immoral. That Stöhr woman got huffy merely because I mentioned someone had died—how silly. And even if she is so ignorant that she believes 'Softly, softly, holy air' comes from *Tannhäuser*—she let that one slip just recently—she could at least show some moral emotions. They all could. I've decided that from now on, I shall show more concern about serious and moribund cases. It will do me good. Just this visit of ours did me some good. Poor Reuter, the fellow in room twenty-seven— I caught a glimpse of him through his door one of my first days here— he surely joined his ancestors long ago, after which they sneaked him out. His eyes were simply huge even back then. But there are plenty of others, the place is full of them, what with new arrivals every day. And Sister Alfreda or the head nurse or even Behrens would certainly help us strike up an acquaintance or two—it can easily be done, I'm sure. Let's assume someone who's moribund has a birthday and we learn about it—it's not hard to come by that sort of information. Fine, we send the fellow, or the lady, whichever, a potted plant for his or her room, a little thoughtful remembrance from two anonymous colleagues, along with best wishes for recovery—which is, one would hope, always a courteous thing to do. And then our names get mentioned, of course, and as weak as he or she may be, we are permitted to say a friendly hello, just through the door, or are even invited into the room for a moment, perhaps, and we exchange a few humane words before he or she slips away. That's how I imagine it. Are you agreed? For my part at least, I plan to do it."

And Joachim did not have any great objection to these plans. "It's against the house rules," he said. "It would mean breaking them, more or less. But Behrens would probably make an exception and give you permission if you made it a point to ask. You can always claim it's out of medical interest."

"Yes, that would be another reason," Hans Castorp said, because, in fact, there were complicated motives behind this wish. His protest against the egotism prevalent here was only one of them. Likewise playing a role was his own spiritual need to take suffering and death seriously, to pay attention to them, a need he hoped would be nourished and satisfied by his getting closer to the seriously ill and dying, as a way of counteracting the numerous rebuffs such a need received daily, even hourly, wherever he turned—including some of Settembrini's insulting pronouncements, which only reinforced his own craving. Examples of such rebuffs were far too numerous to count. If someone had asked Hans Castorp to name a few, he would probably have first mentioned those people at the Berghof who readily admitted that they were not seriously ill, but came up here voluntarily under the official pretext of not feeling well, whereas in reality it was because the style of life, the amusements, here appealed to them, as was the case, for instance, with Widow Hessenfeld, previously mentioned in passing, a lively lady, whose passion in life was betting on things: she would bet with the gentlemen about anything and everything, about the next day's weather, about what the next course would be, about the results of people's monthly checkups and how many months would be added to their sentences; she would bet on certain bobsledders, ice-skaters, or skiers at various athletic contests or championships, on the results of some nascent love affair among the guests, and on a hundred other, often totally trivial and insignificant things, wagering for chocolate or champagne or the caviar enjoyed on festive occasions in the restaurant, for money, for movie tickets, even for kisses, both those given and received—in short, her passion for gambling brought a great deal of lively excitement into the dining hall. Of course, young Hans Castorp could not see his way clear to take such carryings-on very seriously, indeed her mere presence seemed prejudicial to the dignity of this place of suffering.

For it was his sincere desire faithfully to defend and uphold that dignity in his own eyes, however difficult that might be after an almost six-month stay among "people up here." The insights he had gained over time into their lives and doings, their customs and opinions, were not very conducive to such good intentions. There were, for example, the two skinny dandies, "Max and Moritz," the one seventeen, the other eighteen years old, who offered the ladies much stuff for conversation by slipping out each evening to play poker and carouse. Not long before, about a week after New Year—and it must be kept in mind that while we tell our story, the silent, restless current of time sweeps on—news spread at breakfast that the bath attendant had found them that morning lying on their beds still in wrinkled evening clothes. Even Hans Castorp had laughed. But although that incident confounded his good intentions, it was nothing in comparison to the stories told about Herr Einhuf, a lawyer from Jüterbog, a forty-year-old with a goatee and hands furry with black hair, who had been sitting at Settembrini's table for some time now, having replaced the cured Swede. He not only came home drunk every night, but indeed had also not even bothered to do that recently—and had been found outside in the snow. He was considered a dangerous rake, and Frau Stöhr could point to the young lady—engaged to be married down in the lowlands, by the way—who had been seen leaving Einhuf's room at a very late hour, clad in a fur coat, under which she wore nothing more than bloomers. That was scandalous—not just in the general moral sense, but also personally scandalous to Hans Castorp, an offense to his own spiritual strivings. He could not think of the lawyer, moreover, without being reminded of Fränzchen Oberdank, the smoothly coiffed lady's companion and housemaid who had recently been brought up here by her mother, a very dignified provincial lady. Upon admission and after her first checkup, she had been considered only a mild case; but whether she had not been conscientious in her rest cure, whether this was a case in which the air at first was not just good for fighting off illness, but *for* illness, or whether the young lady had become involved in intrigues or excitements that had not done her any good—in any case, four weeks after her arrival, she entered the dining hall upon returning from a new checkup, tossed her purse in the air, and cried in a clear voice, "Hurrah, I have to stay a whole year!" And the entire dining hall had burst into Homeric laughter. But fourteen days later the rumor spread that Herr Einhuf had behaved like a cad to Fränzchen Oberdank. That epithet, by the way, is ours (or better, Hans Castorp's), because for those who spread such news it was hardly a novelty that required such strong language. They shrugged, as if to say that it took two for such affairs, and that presumably nothing had occurred against the wish or will of either participant. At least, to judge from her demeanor, that was Frau Stöhr's moral reaction to the matter.

Karoline Stöhr was a dreadful person. If there was any one thing that interfered with Hans Castorp's well-intentioned spiritual striving, it was this woman—her personality, her very existence. Her endless malapropisms alone would have sufficed. She called death the "grim ripper," called people "impediment" if she wanted to accuse them of being too cheeky, and could talk the most ghastly nonsense about the astronomical causes for a solar eclipse. She called the deep snow-cover a "massive agglomeration"; and one day she caused Herr Settembrini no end of amazement by declaring that she had been reading a book from the sanatorium library that would interest him, entitled *Benedetto Cenelli*, in Schiller's translation. She loved turns of phrases that grated on Hans Castorp's nerves simply because they were clichés or the latest shabby slang—"Isn't that the limit!" or "Bowl me over!" And since the adjective "stunning" had been used for "splendid" or "excellent" for quite some time now—was totally washed out, enervated, prostituted, and therefore obsolete—she had of late seized upon the word "devastating," and now found everything "devastating," whether in earnest or in jest: the bobsled run, their dessert dumplings, and her own body warmth, which sounded equally repulsive coming from her. And then there was her love of gossip—which was excessive. Nevertheless, if she reported that Frau Salomon was wearing her most expensive lace undergarments that day—because she had an appointment for a checkup and always donned fine lingerie for the doctors—there was probably something to it. Hans Castorp himself had the impression that checkups, quite apart from the results, were a source of entertainment for the ladies, for which they attired themselves in their flirtatious best. But what should one say to Frau Stöhr's assertion that Frau Redisch from Posen, who was said to have tuberculosis of the spinal cord, was forced once a week to march naked back and forth in front of Director Behrens in his office for ten minutes? The claim was almost as scandalous as it was improbable, but Frau Stöhr swore it was so by all that was holy—though it was hard to understand how the poor thing could devote such zeal, vigor, and cantankerousness to gossip, when her own problems were giving her so much trouble. For from time to time she was subject to fits of anxious, whining panic, the result of her allegedly increasing "listlessness" and the upward curve of her fever chart. She would come to the table sobbing, tears streaming down her chapped red cheeks, and blubber into her handkerchief that Behrens wanted to order her to bed, but she wanted to know what he had said behind her back about her condition, about just how ill she was—she wanted to look truth in the eye. One day, to her horror, she found her bed had been turned with the foot toward the door, and the discovery almost sent her into convulsions. Her anger, her dread, did not meet with ready understanding; Hans Castorp in particular was slow to comprehend. Well? But so what? Why shouldn't the bed be placed the way it was?

For God's sake, didn't he see?—*Feet first!* She set up a dreadful ruckus, and the bed had to be changed around at once, even though her pillow then faced the light, which was very disruptive to sleep.

None of that was really serious; it said very little to Hans Castorp's spiritual needs. A horrible incident at a meal one day, however, did make an impression on the young man. A new patient, a teacher named Popóv, a gaunt, silent fellow, who now sat at the Good Russian table next to his equally gaunt, silent young bride, turned out to be an epileptic and right in the middle of a meal had a violent fit, falling to the floor with that demonic, inhuman shriek we have all often heard described, and lay there next to his chair, flailing arms and legs about in the most ghastly writhings. What made matters worse was that the fish course had just been served, and it was feared that Popóv might choke on a bone. The uproar was indescribable. The ladies, with Frau Stöhr in the vanguard—though Mmes. Salomon, Redisch, Hessenfeld, Magnus, Iltis, Levi, et al. hardly took second place to her—fell victim to a whole variety of "conditions," with several of them coming close to imitating Herr Popóv. Shrieks rang out—everywhere, nothing but eyes squeezed tight, mouths agape, and twisted torsos. Only one lady preferred to faint quietly. Since they had all been surprised in the middle of chewing and swallowing, choking attacks were common. Some diners made for available exits, including the doors to the veranda, although it was very damp and cold outside. The whole incident, however, took on its own unique, scandalous character, quite apart from the horror of it, primarily because most people could not help associating it with Dr. Krokowski's most recent lecture. In his address the previous Monday (dealing, as always, with love as a force conducive to illness), the psychoanalyst had made special mention of epilepsy, which in preanalytic days had been seen variously as a holy, indeed prophetic affliction or as a sign of demonic possession, but which he described in half poetic, half ruthlessly scientific terms as the equivalent of love, an orgasm of the brain—in brief, made it sound so suspect that his audience was now forced to see Popóv's performance as an illustration of the lecture, a dissolute revelation, a mysterious scandal. The covert flight of the ladies was therefore also an expression of a certain modesty. The director himself was present at the meal, and it was he who, together with Nurse Mylendonk and a few stalwart young diners, carried the ecstatic teacher just as he was—blue, stiff, contorted, and still foaming at the mouth—from the dining hall to the lobby, where the doctors, the head nurse, and other personnel were observed working over the unconscious man for a while, after which he was carried away on a litter. But within a very short time, Herr Popóv was seen sitting serenely beside his equally serene young wife at the Good Russian table, and he finished his midday meal as if nothing had happened.

Hans Castorp had sat through the incident with every outward sign of concerned horror, but ultimately—God help him!—not even this event seemed all that serious. To be sure, Popóv might have choked to death on his mouthful of fish; but, in fact, he had not choked to death and despite all his unconscious cavorting rage had evidently quietly managed to keep from doing so. And then there he sat cheerfully finishing his meal and pretending as if he had never carried on like a crazy drunkard gone berserk—presumably did not even recall what had happened. Nor was there anything to inspire greater reverence for suffering in his appearance; in its own way, this incident, too, bolstered Hans Castorp's impression that he was being exposed up here, against his will, to frivolous slovenliness, and, counter to all local custom, he hoped to offset this process by paying closer attention to those seriously ill and moribund.

On the same floor as the cousins, not far from their own rooms, a young lady named Leila Gerngross lay dying, or so they were told by Sister Alfreda. She had suffered four severe hemorrhages over the last ten days, and her parents had come here with the idea of taking her back home while she still lived; but that did not appear to be a feasible plan— the director said that poor Fräulein Gerngross ought not to be moved. She was sixteen or seventeen years old. Hans Castorp saw a genuine opportunity to realize his plan to send a potted plant and best wishes for recovery. True, it was not Leila's birthday, nor would she, in all probability, live until her next one, which Hans Castorp learned on inquiry was not until spring—yet that did not seem an obstacle to his mission of mercy. On a noonday walk with his cousin, he stopped in a flower shop near the spa hotel; he eagerly breathed in the moist, earthy, aroma-laden air and purchased a pretty potted hydrangea, which he instructed be delivered to the dying girl's room, enclosing a card, left unsigned, on which he wrote, "From two fellow guests, with best wishes for recovery." Pleasantly giddy from the odor of plants and the sultry warmth of the shop, which made his eyes water after the cold outdoors, he completed the transaction with a happy, pounding heart, construing his modest effort as bold, adventurous, and helpful, and secretly ascribing symbolic importance to it.

Leila Gerngross did not enjoy the luxury of private nursing, but was under the direct care of Fräulein von Mylendonk and her doctors; but Sister Alfreda looked in on her occasionally as well, and she reported to the young men how their act of thoughtfulness had been received. Despite her straitened, hopeless condition, the girl had taken childlike pleasure in the strangers' good wishes. The plant stood beside her bed, she caressed it with her eyes and hands, saw to it that it was kept watered, and even during some of the worst coughing fits to which she was subject, she kept her tormented eyes trained on it. Her parents, retired Major Gerngross and his wife, were likewise touched and pleased, but since they had no friends whatever in the house, they could not even hazard a guess as to the givers. Under such circumstances, Nurse Schildknecht had no longer been able to refrain from lifting the veil of anonymity and disclosing the donors' names. She brought the cousins the thanks of the three Gerngrosses—as well as a request that they might all meet. The next day, with the nurse leading the way, the two cousins tiptoed into Leila's chamber of suffering.

The dying girl was a charming young thing—blond, with eyes the exact color of forget-me-nots—who looked fragile, but not all that pathetic, despite a dreadful loss of blood and only meager remnants of lung tissue still available for labored breaths. She thanked them, chatting in a rather monotone but pleasant voice. A rosy glow came to her cheeks and lingered there. After first offering an explanation for his actions—almost an apology, really, since he felt that was expected—both to her and to her parents, Hans Castorp now paid his tender respects in a hushed, emotional voice. It would not have taken much—the impulse was certainly there at least— for him to have knelt on one knee beside the bed; but he did hold Leila's hand in his for a long time—a hot hand that was not merely damp, but downright wet, for the child was perspiring excessively, her sweat glands producing so much water that her flesh would have shriveled and dried out long before this had she not managed to keep pace with her body's transudation by thirstily downing great quantities of lemonade, a full carafe of which stood on her nightstand. Grief-stricken as they were, her parents held up their end of the brief conversation, as good manners demanded, inquiring about the cousins' own circumstances and making other conventional remarks. The major was a broad-shouldered man with a low brow and bristling moustache—a hulk, who quite obviously was innocent of his daughter's susceptibilities and organic biases. It was apparent, rather, that his wife was the guilty party—a small woman with a decidedly consumptive look about her and a conscience evidently weighed down by the dowry she had brought into the marriage. When after ten minutes Leila showed signs of fatigue, or, to be more precise, of over-excitement—her rosy cheeks turned redder, her forget-me-not eyes took on an alarming gleam—and Sister Alfreda began to signal with admonishing glances, the cousins took their leave; Frau Gerngross accompanied them out into the hall, where she broke into self-recriminations that had an odd effect on Hans Castorp. In her remorse, she assured them that it was her fault, her fault alone; the poor child could only have got it from her, her husband was not involved, had played no part in it whatever. But she swore that she had been infected only temporarily, very slightly and superficially, for just a brief time as a young girl. Then she had got over it, had totally recovered, the doctors said—because she had wanted so much to marry, to live and to marry, and she had succeeded, had been completely cured, was perfectly healthy when she married her dear, robust husband, who had never given a thought to such a thing happening. But as unsullied and strong as he was, his influence had not been able to prevent this misfortune. How awful, then, that what had been buried and forgotten had reappeared in the child, who had not got over it, but was succumbing to it, whereas she, the mother, had escaped and lived on into mature adulthood. The poor little thing was dying, the doctors had given up all hope. And it was all due to her former life—she alone was to blame.

The young men tried to comfort her, said something about the possibility of a happy turn for the better. But the major's wife merely sobbed and thanked them once again for everything, for the hydrangea, for diverting the child by their visit, for providing her a little happiness. There the poor thing lay in her lonely torments, while other young girls were enjoying life and dancing with handsome young men—no illness ever took away that desire. They had brought a ray of sunshine into her life—good God, probably the last. The hydrangea had made her the belle of the ball and a chat with two handsome cavaliers had been a nice little flirt for her—as a mother, Frau Gerngross had not failed to notice that.

Hans Castorp was embarrassed by this last remark, particularly by the word "flirt," which Frau Gerngross pronounced incorrectly, supplying it with a German vowel so that it sounded like "fleert"—that annoyed him no end. Nor was he a handsome cavalier, but had visited little Leila out of medical and spiritual conviction, as a protest against the prevailing egotism of the place. In brief, he was a little disgruntled by the turn things had taken, or at least by what the major's wife had to say, but otherwise very excited and pleased at having carried out his plan. Two things in particular lingered in his mind and heart: the earthy odor of the flower shop and Leila's wet hand. And now that a beginning had been made, he arranged an appointment that very day with Sister Alfreda to visit her patient, Fritz Rotbein, who like his nurse was terribly bored, even though, to judge by all the evidence, he had only a short time left.

There was nothing for it—good Joachim would have to come along. Hans Castorp's impulse for altruistic enterprise was stronger than his cousin's reluctance—manifest primarily in Joachim's silence and lowered gaze—because, barring an admission of a lack of Christian charity, he had no cogent explanation to offer. Hans Castorp saw that clearly, and used it to his advantage. He understood very well the military nature of that reluctance. But what if he himself felt excited and pleased by such plans, what if he found them useful? Why then, he would have to ignore Joachim's silent resistance. He discussed with him whether they ought to send young Fritz Rotbein flowers as well, or perhaps take some with them, even though they were dealing with a moribund male. He wanted very much to do it; flowers, he said, were simply proper; he had been especially pleased by his hydrangea gambit—the purple blossoms, the nice full shape. And so he decided that Rotbein's sex was offset by his terminal condition and that a gift of flowers did not require a birthday, particularly since a dying person surely ought to be treated as if every day were his birthday. And with that in mind and his cousin at his side, he again sought out the warm, earthy-scented air of the flower shop; carrying a dewy bouquet of fragrant roses, carnations, and wallflowers, he entered Herr Rotbein's room, ushered in by Alfreda Schildknecht, who had first announced the two young men's visit.

Barely twenty years old, but already graying and balding, the patient was emaciated, his skin waxen; he had large hands, large ears, a large nose; grateful to the point of tears for this diversion and their encouraging words, he actually wept a little out of weakness as he greeted them and accepted the bouquet. Almost immediately, however, in a voice close to a whisper, he turned the conversation to the European flower business and the current boom it was enjoying, especially the nurseries in Nice and Cannes, which daily exported flowers by mail and by the trainload in all directions, to wholesale markets in Paris and Berlin, even supplied Russia. For he was a businessman, and that was where his interests would remain as long as he lived. His father, who manufactured dolls in Coburg, had sent him to England for commercial training, he whispered, and it was there that he had taken ill. His fever had been diagnosed as typhoid in nature and treated accordingly, which meant a diet of broths that had caused him to lose far too much weight. They had let him eat up here, and he had certainly done so, had sat there in his bed, trying to nourish himself by the sweat of his brow. Except it had been too late; his intestine had also been infected, unfortunately, and all the tongue and smoked eel sent him from home had done no good—he could not digest a thing anymore. Now his father was on his way here from Coburg. Behrens had sent him a telegram—because they wanted to take more decisive action, a rib resection, to try it at least, although the chances for success were diminishing. Rotbein whispered all this in a very businesslike voice, viewing even the operation itself as a matter of business—as long as he lived he would regard things from that point of view. The total cost, he whispered, including the spinal anesthetic, would come to one thousand francs, since almost the entire rib cage was involved, six to eight ribs, and the question now was whether it could be seen as a promising investment. Behrens was trying to persuade him, but the doctor's self-interest was only too clear—whereas his own interests seemed more ambiguous, and one could not be sure if it might not be wiser to die in peace with ribs intact.

It was hard to advise him. The cousins suggested that one must also take into consideration the director's splendid talents as a surgeon. They finally agreed that the elder Rotbein, who was already chugging his way here, should have the last word. As they left, young Fritz wept a little again, and although it was only out of weakness, the tears he shed stood in curious contradiction to the dry, businesslike way he spoke and thought. He begged the gentlemen to visit him again, and they gladly promised they would—but never had the chance. The doll-manufacturer arrived that same evening, and the next morning the operation was performed, after which young Fritz was no longer able to receive visitors. Two days later, as Hans Castorp and Joachim were passing Rotbein's room, they noticed it was being fumigated. Sister Alfreda had already packed her bag and departed from the Berghof, having received an urgent call to report to another moribund patient at a different sanatorium. Tucking the cord of her pince-nez behind her ear with a sigh, she had hurried off to nurse him—it was the only prospect that had opened up for her.

On your way to the dining hall or the outdoors, you sometimes saw an empty room, a "vacated" room, ready for fumigation, with furniture piled high and both doors flung wide open—a sight that spoke volumes, and yet was so normal that it said very little, especially when at some point you yourself had taken possession of just such a fumigated, "vacated" room and now called it home. Sometimes, however, you knew who had lived in a particular room, and that always made you stop and think—as was the case both on that occasion and eight days later, when Hans Castorp saw Leila Gerngross's room in the same state. At first his mind rebelled against the commotion he saw inside the room. He was

still standing there observing, perplexed and lost in thought, when the
director happened by.

"Good day, Director Behrens. I was just standing here watching them
fumigate," Hans Castorp said. "Little Leila . . ."

"Hm yes—" Behrens replied with a shrug. After a period of silence,
during which he let this gesture take effect, he added, "You did a proper
bit of courting there at the end—got in just under the wire, didn't you?
I like that about you—taking on my little lung-whistlers in their cages,
seeing as you're in relatively robust health yourself. A nice trait. No,
no—you cannot deny it, it's a very pretty trait in your character. Would
you like me to introduce you to some patients now and then? I've plenty
of other caged finches here—that's if you're still interested. For instance
I'm just about to look in on 'Lady Overblown.' Do you want to come
along? I'll introduce you as a fellow sufferer."

Hans Castorp replied that the director had taken the words right out
of his mouth, had suggested precisely what he had wanted to ask. He
would gratefully accept the offer. But who was this woman, this "Lady
Overblown," and how was he supposed to take the name?

"Literally," the director said. "No metaphors intended. You can let
her tell you herself." A few steps, and they were at "Lady Overblown's"
room. Ordering his companion to wait, the director thrust his way
through both doors. As Behrens entered, there was a burst of bright,
merry laughter inside the room, but any words were broken off as the
door closed. The visitor was greeted by the same laughter when, a few
minutes later, he was allowed to enter and Behrens introduced him to a
blond woman half sitting up in bed, with pillows stuffed behind her, her
blue eyes gazing at him with curiosity. She seemed fidgety and laughed
incessantly—a very high, silvery-bright, bubbly laugh that left her fighting
for breath, which only made her seem that much more nervous, excited,
and titillated. She also laughed at the director's distinctive turns of phrase
as he presented the visitor and then turned to leave. Waving good-bye,
she called out "adieu" and "many thanks" and "see you soon" several
times. She now sighed a musical sigh and laughed a silvery arpeggio,
pressing her hands to her chest heaving beneath her batiste nightshirt—
she was also apparently having difficulty keeping her legs still. Her name
was Frau Zimmermann.

Hans Castorp knew her vaguely by sight. She had sat at the same table
with Frau Salomon and the gluttonous student for a few weeks, and was
always laughing. Then she had vanished without the young man's paying
much attention. She might have left the Berghof, he thought—that is, if
he gave any thought at all to her disappearance. Now he found her here,

under the name of "Lady Overblown"—and was still waiting for an explanation of that.

"Ha ha, ha ha," she bubbled gleefully, her breast fluttering. "A terribly funny man, our Behrens, a fabulously funny, amusing man—laugh till your sides split. Do have a seat, Herr Kasten, Herr Carsten, or whatever your name was. You do have a funny name, ha ha, hee hee. You must excuse me. Do sit down on that chair at the foot of the bed, but pay no mind if my legs start kicking, I really can't . . . ha ha, aaah"—she sighed with an open mouth and then went on bubbling—"really can't seem to help it."

She was almost pretty, had clear, rather too defined, but agreeable features and a little double chin. But her lips were bluish, and the tip of her nose had taken on the same hue, evidently from a lack of oxygen. Her hands were thin and looked very attractive against the lace cuffs of her nightshirt, but she could keep them still no more than she could her feet. Her neck was girlish, with dimples at the collarbone, and her breasts appeared soft and young under the linen sheets, kept in constant shallow motion by both laughter and the struggle for air. Hans Castorp decided he would send her a potted plant, too, or bring her a dewy, fragrant bouquet, imported from the nurseries of Nice or Cannes. With some misgivings, he joined Frau Zimmermann in her volatile, edgy good cheer.

"So you're visiting high-ranking patients, are you?" she asked. "How amusing and kind of you, ha ha, ha ha. But you should know that I don't rank very high on the fever chart—which is to say, I had almost none, really, until recently. Until this little adventure. Just listen, and tell me if it isn't the funniest thing you've ever heard in your life." And now, struggling for air and laughing with many a trill and grace note, she told him what had happened to her.

She had come up here only slightly ill—but ill, all the same, otherwise she would never have come; perhaps more than just *slightly*, but closer to that than seriously ill. Pneumothorax—the new surgical technique that had quickly gained such widespread popularity—had proved marvelously effective in her case. The operation had been a complete success; Frau Zimmermann's condition had improved most gratifyingly. Her husband—for she was married, though she had no children—was told he could expect her home in three to four months. And so, just for the fun of it, she had made a little trip to Zurich—for no other reason than to amuse herself. And she had done so to her heart's content; meanwhile, however, she became aware that she needed a refill and had entrusted a local doctor with the job. A nice, funny young man—ha ha ha, ha ha ha—and what had happened? He had overblown her! There was no other way to put it, the word itself said it all. He had meant well, too well, but had not really understood his task. The upshot was that she had come back up here in an overblown state, with constriction of the heart and shortness of breath—ha! hee hee hee—and Behrens had sworn like a trooper and sent her straight to bed. Because she was now seriously ill— not a patient of highest rank, but one whose case was botched and bungled. Ha ha ha—look at his face, what a funny face! And pointing a finger at Hans Castorp, she laughed so hard at the face he was making that her forehead began to turn purple. But the funniest thing of all, she said, had been the way Behrens had turned the air blue with his ranting and raving. From the moment she had realized she was overblown, just picturing what he would do had set her laughing. "You are literally hovering between life and death," he had shouted, not bothering to mince words. What a bear he was—ha ha ha, hee hee hee—Herr Carsten really must excuse her.

It was not clear why the director's comments had sent her into gales of laughter. Was it because he had "turned the air blue" and she did not really believe him—or that she did believe him, as she surely must, but found the state of "hovering between life and death" too funny for words? Hans Castorp had the impression that the latter was the case and that these sparkling trills and grace notes of laughter were due solely to childish giddiness and silly ignorance—and he did not approve. He sent her flowers all the same—but never saw gleeful Frau Zimmermann again, either. For after being kept under oxygen for several days, she had died in the arms of her husband, who had been called to her bedside by telegram. "A jumbo-size goose," the director had volunteered in summary when he told Hans Castorp the news.

But even before her death, Hans Castorp—in a spirit of sympathetic enterprise and with the help of the director and the nursing staff—had made the acquaintance of other seriously ill patients in the sanatorium, and Joachim had to come along. He had to come along to visit *Tous-les-deux*'s son, the one still left her—the other's room had long since been turned upside down and fumigated with H_2CO. There was also a boy named Teddy, whose condition had recently turned so serious that he had been transferred here from a boarding-school sanatorium called the "Fridericianum." Then there was a Russo-German insurance agent named Anton Karlovitch Ferge, a good-natured martyr; and the unhappy, but very flirtatious Frau von Mallinckrodt, who like the others received flowers and whom Hans Castorp had even fed porridge on several occasions, with Joachim looking on. By now they had gained the reputation of Good Samaritans and Hospitallers.

The day came when Settembrini broached the topic with Hans Castorp.

"Zounds, my good engineer. I've been hearing the most curious things about your behavior. You have thrown yourself into deeds of mercy? Are you pursuing justification by good works?"

"Nothing worth mentioning, Herr Settembrini. Nothing to it, really, nothing to make a fuss over. My cousin and I . . ."

"Oh, leave your cousin out of this. Though you both may have become the topic of conversation, it is you we are concerned with, that much is certain. The lieutenant is a respectable fellow, but his is a simple temperament, not prone to spiritual dangers—the sort that never perturbs a teacher. You'll not convince me he's in charge here. You are the more important personality—and the one in greater danger. You are, if I may put it that way, one of life's problem children, a fellow whom others must look after. And you did once tell me that I might look after you."

"I most certainly did, Herr Settembrini. Once and for all. It's very kind of you. And 'life's problem children' is prettily put. The things you writers come up with! I don't rightly know if I should consider myself flattered by the term, but it does sound pretty, I must say. Yes, well, I have been concerning myself somewhat with 'death's children'—that's probably what you mean. Now and then, when I have time, just in passing, as it were, and not that I neglect my own rest-cure duties, I look in on the serious and critical cases—you know, the ones who come here not for their own amusement and a loose life, but to die."

"It is written, however: let the dead bury their dead," the Italian said.

Hans Castorp raised his arms and made a face that said that a great many things were written, on both sides of the question, and that it was difficult to decide what was right and abide by it. But of course, the organ-grinder would voice a disruptive point of view—that was to be expected. Yet even though Hans Castorp was prepared, as he had been all along, to lend him an ear, to consider his lectures worth listening to—quite noncommittally—and to let himself be pedagogically influenced, that in no way meant that, on the basis of a strictly educational point of view, he should desist from his enterprise, which still seemed to have an important impact, to be beneficial in some vague way—despite Madame Gerngross and her talk about a "nice little fleert," despite the businesslike personality of poor young Rotbein or the foolish trillings of Lady Overblown.

Tous-les-deux's son was named Lauro. He had also been sent flowers—violets from Nice, heavy with the scent of earth—"from two fellow patients, with best wishes for recovery"; anonymity, however, had now become merely a matter of form, and everyone knew from whom such gifts came. And so when *Tous-les-deux*—the pallid, black-clad mother from Mexico—happened to meet the cousins in the corridor, she expressed her gratitude, chiefly by a series of mournfully becoming gestures, and in her clanking French asked for them to receive in person the thanks of her son—*de son seul et dernier fils qui allait mourir aussi*. They did so at once. Lauro turned out to be an astonishingly pretty young man with glowing eyes, an aquiline nose with flared nostrils, and splendid lips above which sprouted a black moustache; but he carried on in such a dramatic, boastful way that the visitors—Hans Castorp no less than Joachim Ziemssen—were both happy to close the patient's door behind them again. During their visit, *Tous-les-deux*—wrapped in her black cashmere shawl, a black veil knotted under her chin, her narrow brow creased by a frown, enormous bags of skin drooping under her jet-black eyes—had paced the room with knees slightly bent; now and then she would approach the two cousins sitting beside the bed and, with her careworn mouth turned down at one corner, repeat her one tragic, parrotlike sentence: "*Tous les dé, vous comprenez, messiés . . . Premièrement l'un et maintenant l'autre.*" Meanwhile, pretty Lauro had gushed on and on in surging, clanking, and unbearably high-flown French phrases about how he intended to die a hero's death, *comme héros, à l'espagnol*, just like his brother, *de même que son fier jeune frère*, Fernando, who likewise had died a Spanish hero. And he went on like that—speaking with broad gestures, ripping back his shirt to expose his yellow chest to the fatal blow—until a coughing fit stifled his rodomontade, bringing delicate, rusty-colored froth to his lips and giving the cousins an excuse to withdraw on tiptoe.

They said nothing further about their visit with Lauro, and even in the quiet of their own rooms, they refrained from judging his behavior. They both enjoyed, however, their visits with Anton Karlovitch Ferge from Saint Petersburg, a fellow with a huge good-natured moustache and a protruding Adam's apple that somehow seemed equally good-natured; he lay there in his bed, recovering very slowly and with great difficulty from an attempted pneumothorax, which, Herr Ferge said, had come within an inch of costing him his life. It had been a severe shock to his system, a pleural shock, which was known to happen sometimes during the fashionable operation. His had been an exceptionally dangerous pleural shock, a total collapse, an alarming swoon—in a word, so severe that the operation had to be broken off and postponed for now.

Whenever Herr Ferge spoke about these events, his good-natured gray eyes grew wide and his face grew pallid—it must have been horrible. "With no general anesthetic, gentlemen. Fine, it's not permitted in cases like ours, we can't handle that—which is understandable, and so as a reasonable man you reconcile yourself to the fact. But the local does not go deep, gentlemen, it numbs only the outermost layer of muscle, you feel them make the incision, although only as a bruising pressure. I'm lying there with my face covered so I can't see anything, and the assistant is holding me on the right and the head nurse on the left. It's as if someone is pressing me, bruising me—it is the muscle tissue that they open up and hold back with clamps. And then I hear the director say, 'So!' And at that same moment, gentlemen, he begins to explore the pleural lining with a blunt instrument—it has to be blunt so it doesn't puncture too soon; he explores to find the right place to make his puncture and let in the gas, but the way he does it, the way he rubs the instrument around the pleural lining—gentlemen, gentlemen, that's what did me in. It was all over for me—simply indescribable. The pleural lining, gentlemen, should never be touched—it ought not, cannot, be touched. It is taboo. The pleural lining is covered by flesh, isolated, inaccessible—for good and all. And now he had exposed it, was exploring it. Gentlemen, it made me sick to my stomach. It was ghastly, gentlemen. I never in my life thought that such a totally hideous, filthy feeling could even exist, except perhaps in hell. I fainted dead away, fell into three faints at once—a green, a brown, and a purple. And it stank at the bottom—the pleural shock affected my sense of smell, gentlemen. There was the unbearable stench of hydrogen sulfide, just like hell itself must stink. And as I blacked out, I heard myself laughing—not a human laugh, but the most indecent, disgusting laugh I've ever heard in my life. Because when they explore your pleural lining, gentlemen, it's as if you are being tickled in the most infamous, intense, inhuman way—that's just what the damn, disgraceful torment feels like. That's what pleural shock is, and may the good Lord spare you the experience."

Anton Karlovitch Ferge came back again and again—and always with that same pallor of horror—to his "filthy" ordeal, reliving many of its torments every time he told about it. He had explained from the start that, being an ordinary man, "higher things" were utterly foreign to him. They shouldn't make any special intellectual or emotional demands of him, and he wouldn't make any of them. But once that was settled, he could tell some very interesting tales about the life he had led before illness wrenched him out of it—the life of a traveling fire-insurance salesman. With Petersburg as home base, he had traveled the length and breadth of Russia, visiting insured factories and ferreting out those in dubious financial condition—because statistics showed that fires occurred most often in factories where business was going badly. Which was why he was sent to investigate each factory on some pretext or other, and report back to his bank, so that they could have time to prevent serious losses by reinsuring or spreading the risk. He told about trips across the great empire in winter, about traveling all night in the incredible cold, stretched out in a sleigh under sheepskins, and when he awoke he could see the eyes of wolves glowing like stars out there in the snow. He had brought boxes of provisions with him, frozen cabbage soup and white bread, which he would thaw out and enjoy whenever they stopped to change horses, and the bread would be as fresh as on the day it was baked. The worst thing was if a sudden thaw set in—then the chunks of cabbage soup he had brought along would melt and leak.

And so Herr Ferge would tell his tales, occasionally interrupting himself to heave a sigh and remark how everything was quite fine now—if only they didn't try to perform another pneumothorax on him. He never spoke of "higher things," but simply stuck to the facts, and it was a delight to listen to him—particularly for Hans Castorp, who thought it useful to hear about the Russian Empire and the life lived there, about samovars, piroshki, Cossacks, and wooden churches with so many onion-shaped steeples that they looked like mushroom colonies. He also had Herr Ferge tell them about the people who lived there, people from the Far North— and so all the more exotic in Hans Castorp's eyes—with Asia in their blood, prominent cheekbones, and a Finno-Mongolian set to their eyes. He listened to it all with anthropological interest, even asked to hear some Russian spoken as well; and the muddy, barbaric, boneless tongue from the East flowed swiftly out of Herr Ferge's good-natured protruding Adam's apple and from under his good-natured moustache. And youth being what it is, Hans Castorp felt all the more entertained because he was now romping in pedagogically forbidden territory.

They often dropped by to spend fifteen minutes with Anton Karlovitch Ferge. From time to time they also visited Teddy, the boy from the Fridericianum, an elegant, refined, blond fourteen-year-old, who had a private nurse and wore white silk tie-string pajamas. He was an orphan, but rich, as he himself admitted. He was waiting now for a serious operation—they hoped to remove some of his worm-eaten parts—but on days when he was feeling better he would sometimes leave his bed for an hour, put on a handsome, sporty outfit, and join the social whirl downstairs. The ladies liked to tease him, and he enjoyed listening to their conversations— when, for example, the talk turned to Einhuf the lawyer, the young lady in bloomers, and Fränzchen Oberdank. Then he would go lie down again. And so Teddy idled his time away elegantly, making it clear that he expected nothing more of life than this.

In room number 50 lay Frau von Mallinckrodt—Natalie was her first name. She had black eyes and wore golden earrings; a flirt who loved her finery, she was nevertheless a perfect Job, a Lazarus in a female body, whom God had visited with every sort of affliction. Her organism seemed to be so inundated by toxins that she was ravaged by numerous illnesses, sometimes alternately, sometimes all at once. Her skin was a particular problem, great portions of it subject to a tormenting itch that erupted here and there into the open sores of eczema, even around the mouth—which was why she found it difficult to use a spoon. Frau von Mallinckrodt suffered by turns from various internal inflammations—of the pleura, the kidneys, the lungs, the periosteum, even of the brain, which would cause her to lapse into unconsciousness; a weak heart, the result of fever and constant pain, was her greatest worry, for it sometimes resulted in food becoming lodged at the top of the esophagus, making it difficult for her to swallow normally. In short, the woman's life was a horror. She was all alone in the world, too, having left her husband and children—as she freely admitted to the cousins—for another man (still half a boy), only to be left in turn by her lover. She now had no home, although she was not penniless—her former husband saw to that. She did not take herself seriously and therefore did not let false pride prevent her from making full use of his decency—or was it enduring love? Well aware that she was a faithless and sinful woman, she bore all the plagues of Job with amazing patience and poise, with a fiery female's elemental powers of resistance; she triumphed over the misery of her dark-skinned body, even turned a white gauze bandage, which she was forced to wear wrapped around her head for some awful reason, into a becoming piece of attire. She was constantly changing her jewelry—beginning each morning with corals and ending each evening with pearls. She had been delighted by the flowers Hans Castorp had sent, regarding them as a gesture more of gallantry than charity, and she invited the two young men for tea at her bedside—drinking hers from a spouted cup; her fingers, including thumbs, were adorned to the knuckles with opals, amethysts, and emeralds. With golden rings dangling at her ears, she quickly told the cousins what had happened to her: about her respectable, but boring husband, her equally respectable and boring children, who had turned out just like their father and whom she had never especially warmed to, and about the half-grown boy with whom she had run off and whose poetic displays of affection she praised at length. But by ruses and coercion, his family had taken him away from her—and the lad had probably been repulsed by her illness, too, which by then had begun to evidence itself in various violent eruptions. Were the gentlemen repulsed by it, too? she asked coquettishly; and her fiery femininity triumphed over the eczema covering half her face.

Hans Castorp felt only disdain for the lad's allowing himself to be repulsed, and he let his disdain be known with a shrug. The poetic adolescent's delicacy only served to spur him to take the opposite course, to find occasion for paying frequent visits to unhappy Frau von Mallinckrodt and for performing little nursing services that required no special training. He would arrive, for instance, just in time carefully to spoon her midday porridge into her mouth, to help her drink from her spouted cup if a bite got stuck in her throat, or to assist her in shifting position in bed—for, in addition to all her other problems, an incision from an operation made it difficult for her to lie down. He performed these little services when he would drop by on his way to the dining hall or after a walk, telling Joachim to go on ahead, that he was just going to check quickly on the case in room 50; and each time he felt his whole being expand with a joy rooted in a sense of helpfulness and quiet importance, but intermingled with a certain jaunty delight in the spotless Christian impression his good deeds made—an impression so devout, caring, and praiseworthy, in fact, that no serious objections whatever could be raised against it, either from a military or a humanistic-pedagogic standpoint.

We have not yet mentioned Karen Karstedt, although Hans Castorp and Joachim took special interest in her. She was one of Behrens's private outpatients, and the director had commended her to the cousins' charity. She had been up here four years now, was penniless herself and dependent on skinflint relatives, who had already taken her away once—she was going to die anyway—and had sent her back only when the director protested. She lived in an inexpensive boardinghouse in Dorf—nineteen years old, a slip of a thing, with smooth oily hair, eyes that shyly tried to hide a glint that matched the hectic flush of her cheeks, and a distinctively husky but sympathetic voice. She coughed almost incessantly and had bandages on all her fingers, the result of open sores from the toxins in her body.

The director had pled her cause to the two cousins—since they were such good-hearted lads—and they were now devoted to her. Flowers were sent, this was followed by a visit with poor Karen on her little balcony in Dorf, and then the three of them began to undertake special outings together. They attended an ice-skating contest, a bobsled race—for the winter sport season in our Alpine valley was in full swing. There was a festival week with any number of entertainments—sports events and performances to which the cousins had paid only occasional, fleeting attention until now. Joachim had been averse to all amusements up here. He had not come here for that sort of thing, was certainly not here to enjoy his stay by organizing his life around a variety of diversions, but solely for the purpose of detoxifying his body as quickly as possible, so that he could take up his duties in the plains below, real duties, not just the duties of rest cure—which, even though it was only a substitute, he was loath to slight in any way. It was forbidden to take part in winter sports, and he had no desire to play the gaping onlooker. And as for Hans Castorp, he felt himself to be, in a very restricted and intimate sense, so very much a part of "the people up here" that he wasted not a thought or a glance on people who saw the valley as a sports arena.

Their charitable interest in poor Fräulein Karstedt, however, brought with it several changes in this respect—and Joachim could not object without seeming un-Christian. On a splendid, frosty, sun-drenched day, they stopped for the sick girl at her modest apartment in Dorf and strolled with her past the elegant shops lining the main street of the English quarter, named for the Hotel d'Angleterre. To the sound of sleigh bells, the idle, pleasure-loving rich from all over the world, residents of the Kurhaus and the other large hotels, promenaded—bareheaded, clad in the latest sports outfits of the most expensive fabrics, and bronzed by the winter sun reflected off the snow. The trio now walked toward the bottom of the valley to the ice rink, which was not far from the resort and in summer served as a soccer field. There was music in the air, the hotel band was playing a concert from a little gallery on the wooden pavilion at the far end of the rectangular rink, behind which snowcapped mountains rose against a deep blue sky. They paid to enter, pushed their way through the crowd assembling on bleachers set up on three sides of the rink, and took their seats to watch. The skaters, wearing brief tricot costumes, the jackets trimmed with fur and braid, swayed to and fro, traced figures, leapt, and spun. A man and a woman, a pair of highly talented professionals ineligible for competition, executed a feat no one else in the world could do—to great applause and a fanfare. The contestants for the race, six young men of various nationalities, sped six times around the wide rectangle—bodies bent low, hands behind their backs, some with a handkerchief pressed to their mouths. A bell rang out while the music played on. From time to time, waves of encouraging cries and applause surged up from the crowd.

It was a very colorful gathering, and the three patients—the two cousins and their protégée—looked about, taking it all in. Englishmen with very white teeth and Scotch tams conversed in French with ladies drenched in perfume and dressed from head to foot in bright-colored wools, some even in trousers. American men, their hair plastered flat against their small heads, wore their fur coats skin-side out and smoked shag-tobacco pipes. Seated among the Germans and Swiss were bearded, elegant Russians, looking barbarically rich, and Dutchmen with traces of Malayan blood—all intermixed with a sprinkling of indeterminate sorts who spoke French and came from the Balkans or the Levant, a motley set of adventurers for whom Hans Castorp had a certain weakness but whom Joachim spurned as dubious and lacking in character. There were also various crazy contests for children, who hobbled across the rink with a snowshoe on one foot, an ice skate on the other. Little boys had to push little girls ahead of them on snow shovels. There was a race with candles—the winner was the first to arrive at the goal with her flame still burning. There were obstacle courses, and races where the contestants had to carry potatoes on a tin spoon and deposit them in watering cans set at the end of the course. High society cheered. People pointed out the richest, most famous, most charming children: the daughter of a Dutch multimillionaire, the son of a Prussian prince, and a twelve-year-old lad whose name was on the label of a world-famous champagne. Poor Karen cheered as well—and coughed each time. She clapped her hands for joy, despite the open sores on her fingers. She was so grateful.

The cousins also took her to the bobsled races. As it came down off Schatzalp, the run ended among buildings on Dorf's western slope, not far from the Berghof, nor from Karen Karstedt's lodgings. A little hut had been built at the finish line, and inside was a telephone that rang whenever a sled began its run. Steered by men and women in white wool and with sashes in various national colors across their chests, the low, flat frames came shooting down, one by one, at long intervals, taking the curves of the course that glistened like metal between icy mounds of snow. You could see red, tense faces with snow blowing in their eyes. There were accidents, too—sleds crashed and upended, dumping their teams in the snow, while onlookers took lots of pictures. There was music playing here, as well. The spectators sat in a little grandstand or thronged the narrow pathway shoveled free next to the course itself. Farther up, wooden bridges spanned the course, and they, too, were crowded with people, who could watch the competing sleds hurtle by under them from time to time. The bodies from the sanatorium on the far slope whizzed down the same course, taking its curves, heading down to the valley, all in the valley, Hans Castorp thought—and remarked on the fact, too.

They even took Karen Karstedt to the Bioscope Theater in Platz one afternoon, because that was something she truly enjoyed. Being used to only the purest air, they felt ill at ease in the bad air that weighed heavily in their lungs and clouded their minds in a murky fog, while up ahead on the screen life flickered before their smarting eyes—all sorts of life, chopped up in hurried, diverting scraps that leapt into fidgety action, lingered, and twitched out of sight in alarm, to the accompaniment of trivial music, which offered present rhythms to match vanishing phantoms from the past and which despite limited means ran the gamut of solemnity, pomposity, passion, savagery, and cooing sensuality. They watched as a rousing tale of love and murder in the court of an Oriental potentate unrolled silently before them; scene after opulent scene sped past, full of naked bodies, despotic lust, and abject servility blind in its zeal, full of cruelty, prurience, and fatal desire—and then suddenly the film slowed to linger revealingly on the muscular arm of an executioner. In short, it had been produced with a sympathetic understanding of its international audience and catered to that civilization's secret wishes. Settembrini, as a man who formed opinions, would surely have denounced this exhibition as a denigration of humanity, and with honest, classical irony would have castigated the misuse of technology that made such cynical presentations possible—or so Hans Castorp thought, and whispered as much to his cousin. Frau Stöhr, however, who happened to be sitting not all that far from the trio, had apparently abandoned herself to the film; her red, uneducated face was contorted with pleasure.

But, then, it was much the same with all the faces they could see. When the last flickering frame of one reel had twitched out of sight and the lights went up in the hall and the audience's field of dreams stood before them like an empty blackboard, there was not even the possibility of applause. There was no one there to clap for, to thank, no artistic achievement to reward with a curtain call. The actors who had been cast in the play they had just seen had long since been scattered to the winds; they had watched only phantoms, whose deeds had been reduced to a million photographs brought into focus for the briefest of moments so that, as often as one liked, they could then be given back to the element of time as a series of blinking flashes. Once the illusion was over, there was something repulsive about the crowd's nerveless silence. Hands lay impotent before the void. People rubbed their eyes, stared straight ahead, felt embarrassed by the brightness and demanded the return of the dark, so that they could again watch things, whose time had passed, come to pass again, tricked out with music and transplanted into new time.

The despot was dispatched by a knife, his mouth opened for a bellow that no one heard. They now saw pictures from all over the world: the top-hatted president of the French republic reviewing a long cordon, then sitting in his landau to reply to a welcoming speech; the viceroy of India at the wedding of a rajah; the German crown prince on a barracks drill field in Potsdam. They observed the life and customs of an aboriginal village on New Mecklenburg, a cockfight on Borneo, naked savages blowing on nose flutes, the capture of wild elephants, a ceremony at the Siamese royal court, a street of brothels in Japan with geishas sitting caged behind wooden lattices. They watched Samoyeds bundled in furs driving sleds pulled by reindeer across the snowy wastes of northern Asia, Russian pilgrims praying at Hebron, a Persian criminal being bastinadoed. They were present at each event—space was negated, time turned back, "then and there" transformed by music into a skittering, phantasmagoric "here and now." A young Moroccan woman dressed in striped silk and harnessed with chains, bangles, and rings, her swelling breasts half-bared, was suddenly brought nearer until she was life-size. Her nostrils were flared wide, her eyes full of animal life, her features vivacious; she laughed, showing her white teeth, held up one hand—the nails seemed lighter than her skin—to shield her eyes, and waved at the audience with the other. People stared in bewilderment at the face of this charming specter, who seemed to see them and yet did not, who was not at all affected by their gaze, and whose laughter and waves were not meant for the present, but belonged to the then and there of home—it would have been pointless to respond. And so, as noted, their delight was mixed with a sense of helplessness. Then the phantom vanished. A bright void filled the screen, the word *Finis* was projected on it, this cycle of entertainments was over, and the people left the theater in silence as a new audience pushed its way in, eager to enjoy another roll of the reels.

Urged on by Frau Stöhr, who had now joined them, they stopped by the Kurhaus café just to please Karen, who clasped her hands together in gratitude. There was music here, too. A little orchestra in red jackets was playing under the direction of a Czech or Hungarian violinist, who stood apart from the rest among the dancing couples, belaboring his instrument with ardent writhings of his body. This was the sophisticated life—people walked about with strange drinks in their hands. The cousins ordered refreshing orangeade for themselves and their protégée—it was hot and dusty in the room; Frau Stöhr, however, drank a sweet liqueur. Things were not in full gear yet at this time of day, she said. The dancing would get much more lively as the evening progressed; countless patients from the various sanatoriums and patients living brazenly on their own at the Kurhaus or other hotels would join in later in much greater number than now, and many a serious case had danced his way to eternity here, first tossing back the beaker of life and then hemorrhaging one last time *in dulci jubilo*. What Frau Stöhr in her ignorance did to the phrase *dulci jubilo* was quite extraordinary; she pronounced the first word as "*dolce*," borrowing it from the Italian musical vocabulary of her spouse, but the second was more reminiscent of "yippee-ay-oh" or God only knew what—and at the sound of her Latin, the two cousins simultaneously made a grab for the straws in their glasses. This did not trouble Frau Stöhr. Instead, obstinately baring her rabbit's teeth, she attempted by way of allusion and innuendo to get to the bottom of the relationship of these three young people, only one part of which was clear to her: that poor Karen, as she remarked, could not help enjoying the high life chaperoned by two such smart young cavaliers. The situation was much less obvious as regarded the cousins; but despite her stupidity and ignorance, feminine intuition allowed her a certain insight, if only a partial and vulgar one. For she understood, as she insinuated, that the real cavalier here was Hans Castorp and that young Ziemssen was merely his assistant; but since she was also well aware of Hans Castorp's partiality for Frau Chauchat, she assumed he was chaperoning poor little Karstedt as a substitute for a woman he evidently did not know how to approach. It was a very inadequate insight, based on vulgar intuition and lacking real moral profundity, and so perfectly worthy of Frau Stöhr—which was why Hans Castorp replied only with a tired, disdainful glance when she expressed it in her coarse, bantering way. It was true, after all, that for Hans Castorp the relationship with poor Karen was a kind of substitute, a vaguely useful device—but that was true of all his other charitable enterprises as well. Yet these pious works were, at the same time, an end in themselves, and the satisfaction he found in feeding porridge to sickly Frau Mallinckrodt, in letting Herr Ferge describe his infernal pleural shock, or in seeing poor Karen clap her hands with joy and gratitude, despite the bandaged fingertips, was not only of a vicarious and relative kind, but also genuine and immediate. It arose from an intellectual tradition diametrically opposed to the one represented by Herr Settembrini's pedagogy, but all the same one quite worthy of the designation *"placet experiri"*—or so it seemed to Hans Castorp.

The little house where Karen Karstedt lived was on the road leading into Dorf, not far from the brook and the train tracks, and so it was easy for the cousins to stop for her when setting out on their promenade after breakfast. Continuing toward the main street of Dorf, they saw Little Schiahorn directly before them, and on its right were three crags called the Green Towers, although they, too, now lay under snow glistening in the sun, and still farther to the right was the summit of Dorfberg. A cemetery was visible about a quarter of the way up its slope: the town cemetery, surrounded by a wall, presumably commanding a lovely view—of the lake, more than likely—which made it an obvious goal for a walk. And the three of them did hike up there one beautiful morning—all the mornings were beautiful now, calm and sunny, frosty yet warm, glistening white under a deep blue sky. The cousins, the one with a brick-red face, the other tanned bronze, walked along without overcoats, which would only have been burdensome in the glaring sun—young Ziemssen wearing sport clothes and rubber galoshes, Hans Castorp dressed much the same, though in long trousers, since he was not the sort who gave much thought to his physique. It was between the beginning and the middle of February of a new year. Yes, the last number in the date had indeed changed since Hans Castorp's arrival up here; when you wrote the date, you added another year. One hand on the world's great chronometer had ticked ahead one space—not one of the largest hands, not the one for millennia for instance, few people then alive would ever see that happen—not the century hand, either, not even the decade hand, no. But the year hand had recently moved one space (although Hans Castorp had not been up here even a year yet, only a little more than half a one), and like some large clocks with a minute hand that jerks only every five minutes, it now stood still and would not advance again soon. The month hand had to move ahead ten more spaces yet, a few more than it had since Hans Castorp had arrived up here. February, however, no longer counted, because once begun, soon finished—once the bill's broken, the money's soon spent.

And so the trio also walked to the cemetery on Dorfberg one day— this excursion, too, is recorded here for the sake of rendering a full account. The suggestion had been Hans Castorp's, and although Joachim had some doubts at first because of poor Karen, he had yielded, admitting that it would have been pointless to play hide-and-seek with her, shielding her out of anxiety, à la cowardly Frau Stöhr, from anything that might remind her of her mortality. Karen Karstedt did not indulge in self-deception about even the final stages of her illness; she knew only too well how things stood and what the necrosis in her fingertips meant. She knew, moreover, that her skinflint relatives would hardly want to hear anything about the expense of transporting her home after her demise and that she would be allotted a modest plot up above for a final resting place. And so one might very well conclude that, as a goal for an excursion, it was more morally fitting than many others—the movie theater or the start of the bobsled run, for instance—particularly since paying a visit to those people up there was nothing more than an act of comradely respect, assuming, of course, that one did not regard the cemetery simply as one of the town's sights, a standard goal for a standard walk.

They worked their way slowly up the path in single file, since it had been shoveled wide enough for only one person to pass, left behind the last villas set high on the slope, and, as they climbed, looked back down

on the landscape in its winter splendor, opening again now in a slightly
shifted perspective. The vista broadened to the northeast toward the entrance to the valley and included the lake, as expected—a frozen, snow-
covered circle surrounded by forest. Beyond its farthest shore, several
steep slopes appeared to meet, and above them were unfamiliar, snow-
clad peaks, overtopping one another against the blue sky. Standing there
in the snow beside the little stone gate to the cemetery, they took in the
view and then entered, swinging aside the unlocked wrought-iron grill
hinged to the stone.

Here, too, paths had been shoveled between railed-in, snow-covered
mounds—gravesites, each containing a series of regular, properly made
beds decorated with stone and metal crosses or little monuments adorned
with medallions and inscriptions. But not another soul was to be seen or
heard. The silence, the solitude, the serenity of the place seemed both
deep and secret, in many senses of those words. Among some shrubbery
stood a little stone angel or cupid, its snowy cap cocked to one side, its
finger to its lips; it might have been taken for the genius of the place—
that is to say, the genius of silence, but of a silence that, although it was
certainly the antithesis and counterpart of speech, and so a silence of
hushed voices, was in no way a silence devoid of substance or incident.
This would probably have been an occasion for the two men to remove
their hats, had they been wearing any. But they were both bareheaded,
even Hans Castorp, and so they merely walked on ahead reverently, in
single file behind Karen Karstedt, who led the way, placing their weight
on the balls of their feet and making what looked like a series of little
bows to the right and left.

The cemetery was irregularly shaped, beginning as a narrow rectangle
facing southward and then opening into two more rectangles, one on
either side. It had obviously had to be enlarged several times by the
annexation of adjacent fields. All the same, the enclosure seemed to be as
good as fully occupied at present, whether along the walls or in the middle,
where the less desirable plots were located. It would have been hard to
say where anyone else could be buried. The three strangers wandered
discreetly for a while along the narrow channels and passageways between
the monuments, stopping now and then to decipher a name, the dates of
birth and death. The gravestones and crosses were unpretentious affairs
placed there at no great expense. As for the inscriptions, the names came
from every corner of the earth, were written in English, Russian or other
Slavic languages, in German, Portuguese, and many more tongues. The
dates, however, had their own delicate individuality—on the whole these
life spans had been strikingly short, the difference in years between birth

and demise averaging little more than twenty. The field was populated almost exclusively by youth rather than virtue, by unsettled folk who had found their way here from all over the world and had returned now for good and all to the horizontal form of existence.

Somewhere deep in the press of resting places, toward the midpoint of the meadow, between two mounds whose gravestones were hung with artificial wreaths, was a flat, regular, unoccupied space, the length of a human body—and the three visitors stopped instinctively beside it. There they stood, the young girl a little ahead of her escorts, reading the tender message of the stones—Hans Castorp relaxed, his hands clasped before him, with open mouth and sleepy eyes; young Ziemssen at attention, not merely erect, but even leaning backward a little. The cousins, both at the same moment, cast stolen sidelong glances at Karen Karstedt's face. She noticed, however, and as she stood there, bashful and demure, she thrust her head forward at a slight tilt and smiled affectedly with pursed lips, blinking her eyes rapidly.

Walpurgis Night

A FEW DAYS PASSED, and young Hans Castorp had now spent seven months up here, whereas Joachim, who already had five months to his credit when his cousin first arrived, could now look back on twelve months, one round year—round in the cosmic sense, as well, for in the time since the small, sturdy locomotive had dropped him off up here, the earth had returned to its starting point, having completed one orbit around the sun. It was carnival time. Mardi Gras was upon them, and Hans Castorp inquired of the one-year-old what that was like up here.

"*Magnifique!*" responded Settembrini, who had happened to meet the cousins on their morning constitutional. "Splendid!" he said. "As rollicking as in the Prater. You'll see, my good engineer. And now the dance is taken up, we play gallants most dashing," he quoted, and went on shooting a volley of taut, satirical words, accompanying his satire with deft gestures of arm, head, and shoulder. "What do you want? Even in the *maison de santé* they throw balls and galas now and then for the fools and cretins, or so I've read—why not here? The program includes various *danses macabres*. Unfortunately a certain number of last year's participants won't be able to appear this time, because the party is over at half past nine."

"You mean . . . oh, I see now—how marvelous!" Hans Castorp

laughed. "What a jokester you are! 'At half past nine'—did you hear, cousin? Herr Settembrini is saying that it's too early for some of 'last year's participants' to spend a little time at the ball. Ha, ha, how spooky. He means the people who have finally put aside all 'lusts of the flesh'— if you know what I mean. But I really am looking forward to it," he said. "I'm all for celebrating holidays just as they fall; we should mark the passing of the year in the usual way, its turning points, I mean, so that the monotony gets divided up. Things would be just too strange otherwise. And so we've had Christmas, and we marked the New Year, and now Mardi Gras is coming. Then it will soon be Palm Sunday—do they bake special pastries here?—then Holy Week, Easter, and Pentecost, which is only six weeks later, and then before you know it, it's the longest day, Midsummer Night, you see, and soon you're into autumn."

"Wait! Wait! Wait!" Settembrini cried, lifting his face heavenward and pressing his palms to his temples. "Silence! I forbid you to play so fast and loose with time!"

"Beg your pardon, I really meant just the opposite. By the way, Behrens will probably decide sooner or later to use injections to try to detoxify me, because I'm constantly at ninety-nine point three, point five, point seven, even point nine. It simply never changes. I am and shall remain one of life's problem children—not that I'm a long-termer. Rhadamanthus has never saddled me with any sentence, but he says it would be pointless to interrupt my cure too soon, especially since I've been up here for so long now—have invested so much time, so to speak. And what good would it do if he were to set a date? It wouldn't mean all that much, because if he says six months, for example, that's always a low estimate— you have to be ready for more. You can see that with my cousin here, who was supposed to be finished by the first of the month—finished in the sense of cured—but at his last checkup Behrens said it would take another four months for him to heal completely. Well, and where are we then? Why, Midsummer Night, just as I said—but not because I wanted to offend you. And then we start heading toward winter. But at the moment we're about to celebrate Mardi Gras, of course. And as you heard I'm all in favor of that, of celebrating things as they come, just as the calendar dictates. Frau Stöhr mentioned that we can get little toy trumpets at the concierge's desk, is that right?"

It was indeed. Already at breakfast on Mardi Gras morning—which was there before you had even got a good bead on it—already at breakfast, the dining hall was filled with the rattling and tootling of all sorts of toy instruments. By noon, streamers were already flying at the table where Gänser, Rasmussen, and Kleefeld sat, and several people—round-eyed

Marusya for instance—were wearing paper hats, which were also on sale at the limping concierge's desk in the lobby. And by evening both in the dining hall and the social rooms the festivities continued to grow until at one point . . . At this juncture we alone know to what these carnival festivities eventually led, thanks to Hans Castorp's enterprising spirit. But we are not about to let our knowledge of what happened disrupt the deliberate pace of our narrative; instead, we shall give time the honor it is due and not rush into things—perhaps we shall even draw these events out a bit, for we share with young Hans Castorp the same moral scruples that for so long had kept him from precipitating such events.

More or less everyone made a pilgrimage to Platz that afternoon to see the carnival in the streets. There were people strolling in masks— Punchinellos and Harlequins, flicking whips that rattled—and flurries of confetti burst among the pedestrians and above the heads of masked passengers in the decorated sleighs jingling past. By suppertime, spirits were already very high at all seven tables, with everyone determined to continue the public gaiety in their own closed circle. The concierge had done a good business in paper hats, rattles, and sacks of favors, and Prosecutor Paravant made a start at keeping the buffoonery going by appearing in a kimono and wearing a false pigtail that belonged, or so someone shouted, to Frau Wurmbrandt, the general consul's wife; he had also used a curling iron to turn his moustaches down, making him look every inch Chinese. Nor was the management taking a backseat to anyone. They had placed a paper lantern on each table, a colorful moon with a candle burning inside, so that when Settembrini entered the dining hall, passing close by Hans Castorp's table, he had an appropriate quote at the ready:

> Behold bright flames illuminated!
> A merry club has congregated.

As he said it, he smiled his delicate, dry smile, but kept on strolling toward his seat, where he was received with a barrage of fragile pellets that burst as they struck, dousing their victim in a spray of perfume.

To put it in a word: the festive spirit was very apparent from the start. Laughter reigned, streamers dangling from the chandeliers wafted in the breeze, confetti floated in the gravy, and soon the dwarf appeared with the first ice-bucket and hurried past with the first bottle of champagne. Lawyer Einhuf set the tone by mixing champagne and burgundy, and now they were all doing it. Once the lights were turned off toward the end of the meal and only the lanterns illumined the dining hall with the soft, colorful glow of a night in Italy, the perfect mood was set. There was general approval at Hans Castorp's table of a note that Settembrini passed to him by way of Marusya, who was decked out in a jockey's cap of green tissue paper, on which he had written in pencil:

> But bear in mind, the mountain's mad with spells tonight,
> And should a will-o'-wisp decide your way to light,
> Beware—its lead may prove deceptive.

Dr. Blumenkohl, who had been doing very poorly again of late, muttered something to himself—with a look on his face, or better, about his lips, that was peculiarly his own—that indicated the source of these verses. For his part, Hans Castorp felt that he ought to reciprocate tit for tat, that he had to respond by writing a jocular note of his own, though it could have been only some very lightweight quotation. He searched his pockets for a pencil, but could not find one, and neither Joachim nor the teacher had one to lend him. His bloodshot eyes wandered eastward for help, to the far left-hand corner of the dining hall. And it was at once apparent that what had been a fleeting notion had dissipated into a wider circle of associations—he turned pale and completely forgot his original intention.

There was reason enough for him to turn pale. Frau Chauchat had likewise dressed for the occasion and was wearing a new gown, or at least a gown that Hans Castorp had never seen on her—of thin, dark, almost black silk that sometimes took on a tawny shimmer; the rounded cut of the neck was small, almost girlish, barely deep enough to expose the throat or even a hint of the collarbone—or her protruding neck bones visible beneath a few stray hairs when she thrust her head forward in that special way. But it left Clavdia's arms bare all the way to the shoulder— her arms, so tender and full at the same time, and cool, one could only presume—so that they stood out extraordinarily white against the dark shadows of silk. The effect was so overwhelming that Hans Castorp closed his eyes and whispered to himself, "My God!" He had never seen a dress cut like that. He was familiar with festive, yet formal ball gowns that revealed, as custom allowed, far more of the human body than this one, yet without causing the least bit of sensation. Poor Hans Castorp—what an error his earlier assumption had been upon first making the acquaintance of those arms through thin gossamer: that once bared, bared against all good reason, those arms would affect him less deeply without the seductive "radiant illusion" of fabric, as he had called it that day. An error, a fatal act of self-deception! The full, heightened, dazzling nakedness of the splendid limbs of a sick, infected organism turned out to be an experience far more potent than that day's "illusion"—a phenomenon for which there was only one response: he lowered his head again and silently repeated, "My God!"

A little later, another note arrived, on which was written:

> A party to your heart's desire,
> With maids who long to marry,
> And bachelors with hearts on fire,
> And hopes extraordinary!

"Bravo, bravo!" someone shouted. They were drinking their mocha now, served in little earthen-brown jugs, and some had liqueurs as well—Frau Stöhr for example, who simply loved to sip sweet spirits. People began to get up and circulate about the room. They visited one another's tables. One group of guests had already moved on to the social rooms, while another stayed where they were in order to apply themselves to more burgundy and champagne. Settembrini came over in person now, coffee cup in hand, a toothpick between his lips, and made himself at home between Hans Castorp and the teacher.

"In the Harz Mountains," he said, "are towns with names like Schierke and Elend—Imps and Misery. Did I exaggerate, my good engineer? Now here's a holy mass, I do declare. But just wait, our mirth's not yet about to fade, we've not yet reached our heights—let alone come to an end. To judge from what one hears, still further masquerades await us. Certain persons have already withdrawn—and therefore we are permitted to make all sorts of assumptions. You'll see."

And indeed new costumes arrived now: ladies in men's clothes, their ample curves making them look as implausible as characters in an operetta, an effect accentuated by black beards drawn on their faces with burnt cork; and vice versa, gentlemen attired in women's clothes, tripping over their skirts—including Rasmussen the student, who wore a black, jet-trimmed gown, its décolletage revealing a pimply chest and ditto back, both of which he tried to cool with a paper fan. A knock-kneed beggar appeared, leaning on a crutch. Someone had put together a Punchinello costume out of white underwear and a lady's felt hat—the face powdered so white that the eyes looked quite unnatural, the lips emphasized in bloody-red lipstick. (It was the young fellow with the saltcellar fingernail.) A Greek from the Bad Russian table strutted about as a Spanish grandee or fairy-tale prince with a cape, paper ruff, and sword—and a pair of purple tights to show off his handsome legs. All these costumes had been hastily improvised after the meal. Frau Stöhr could no longer bear it just to sit there. She vanished, and a short time later reappeared as a cleaning lady, with apron and rolled-up sleeves, the ribbons of her paper hat tied under her chin; she was armed with bucket and broom, which she now put to use, thrusting the wet broom under the table and swabbing between people's feet.

"And here alone comes Baubo now," Settembrini quoted, and added the next line, too, in his clear, graphic voice—its rhyme was "sow." Frau Stöhr heard that—called him an Italian turkey, told him to keep his "filthy jokes" to himself, and, availing herself of the license of carnival, used familiar pronouns. But then, that form of address had gained general usage during the meal. Settembrini was about to reply, when he was interrupted by the racket of loud laughter coming from the lobby. Everyone in the dining hall looked up.

Followed by other guests emerging from the social rooms, two curious figures now made their entrance—they had apparently only just finished with their costumes. The one was dressed in a deaconess's black uniform, but with white horizontal stripes sewn onto it from collar to hem—short stripes, set close together, with a few longer ones here and there, like the markings on a thermometer. She kept one forefinger pressed to her pale lips and carried a fever chart in her right hand. The second person was costumed all in blue—eyebrows and lips tinted blue, the whole face and neck in fact painted blue, a blue woolen cap pulled down over one ear, and a case or slipcover of glazed blue linen, all one piece, pulled down over him, then tied with a string at the ankles and stuffed with pillows to round things off at the stomach. They recognized these two as Frau Iltis and Herr Albin. Both had paper signs hung around their necks, on which were written "Silent Sister" and "Blue Henry." Paired together and moving in a kind of waddle, they circled the room.

To great applause—and clamoring cheers! Frau Stöhr, her broom tucked under one arm, put both hands on her knees and broke into unrestrained, vulgar laughter—her role as a charwoman gave her such license. Only Settembrini showed no response. He cast the winning costumes one quick glance, and then his lips grew very thin beneath the lovely upward sweep of his moustache.

Among those who had found their way back from the social rooms in the wake of Mr. Blue and Miss Silent was Clavdia Chauchat. Accompanied by frizzy-haired Tamara and her tablemate with the concave chest, a Bulgarian in evening dress, she crossed the room, moving toward the table where Gänser and Kleefeld were sitting—and brushing past Hans Castorp's table in her new dress. She stopped now to chat, her hands behind her back, her narrow eyes laughing; her escorts, however, joined the allegorical spooks and followed them out of the room. Frau Chauchat had donned a carnival hat as well—not one she had bought, but the kind children make, a simple tricorn of folded white paper set rakishly to one side—and it looked quite marvelous on her. The skirt of her dark golden-brown silk dress reached only to her ankles and was slightly bouffant. We shall say nothing more about her arms—which were bare to the shoulder.

"Look closer now, my lad!" Hans Castorp heard Herr Settembrini say, as if from some great distance—his eyes were following her as she now left the dining hall by way of the glass door. " 'Tis Lilith."

"Who?" Hans Castorp asked.

The question delighted the man of literature. He replied, "The first wife Adam had. You'd best beware . . ."

Besides the two of them, only Dr. Blumenkohl was still in his seat, at the far end of the table. The rest of the diners, including Joachim, had moved on to the social rooms.

"You're full of poetry and verses this evening," Hans Castorp said. "What's all this about Lilli? You mean Adam was married twice? That's the first I've heard of it."

"According to Hebrew tradition he was. Lilith then became a wraith who haunts young men by night—her beautiful hair makes her particularly dangerous."

"Why, how disgusting! A wraith with beautiful hair. You simply can't stomach things like that, can you? And so here you come and turn the lights back on, so to speak, so you can set young men back on the right path—isn't that what you're up to, Lodovico?" Hans Castorp said giddily. He had drunk quite a bit of burgundy and champagne.

"Now listen—that's enough of that, my good engineer!" Settembrini commanded with a scowl. "You will please use forms of address appropriate to the educated West. No first names. Formal pronouns, if you please. What you are trying to do there doesn't suit you at all."

"But why not? It's Mardi Gras! It's common practice on an evening like this."

"Yes, just to add a little uncivil excitement to things. For people to use informal pronouns or first names when they have no real reason to do so is a repulsively barbaric practice, a slovenly game, a way of playing with the givens of civilization and human progress, against both of which it is directed—shamelessly, insolently directed. Please, do not presume that in calling you 'my lad,' I was addressing you in that fashion. I was merely quoting a passage from the masterpiece of your national literature. I was speaking poetically, as it were."

"So was I. And I'll go on speaking more or less poetically, too—because the moment seems to call for it, that's why I am speaking this way. I'm not saying I find it all that natural and easy to use familiar pronouns. On the contrary, I have to overcome my own resistance, give myself a poke just to be able to do it. But now that I've given myself a poke, I'll go on using them quite happily, with all my heart."

"With all your heart?"

"With all my heart, yes, please believe me. We've been up here together for so long now—seven months, if you stop to count—which isn't all that much by our standards up here, but when viewed from down below, now that I think back on it, it's quite a long time. Well, and so we've spent it here with one another, because life has brought us together here, have seen one another almost every day and had interesting conversations, some on subjects I would not have understood anything about down below. But I certainly have up here—they were very important and relevant, so that whenever we discussed something I paid strict attention. What I mean is, whenever you as a *homo humanus* were explaining things to me—because I didn't have all that much to contribute, of course, given my previous inexperience, and could only feel that everything you said was well worth listening to. About Carducci—but that was the least of it. For instance, about how the world republic is bound up with beautiful style or how time and human progress are related—because if there were no time there couldn't be any human progress, and the world would be just an old water hole, a stinking pond. What would I have known about all that without you! And so I'm simply addressing you with personal pronouns, I can't really help it, you'll have to excuse me—I didn't know how to go about it any other way. I'm not good at that. There you sit and here I am speaking to you like this, and that's that. You're not just anybody, a face with a name, you're a representative of something, Herr Settembrini, a representative here and now and at my side—that's what you are," Hans Castorp declared, slamming the palm of his hand on the tablecloth. "And now I want to thank you," he went on, shoving his glass of champagne and burgundy up against Herr Settembrini's coffee cup, as if to toast him there on the table, "to thank you for having been so kind as to look after me for the past seven months—a young donkey with all sorts of new experiences coming at me—for lending a helping hand in my exercises and experiments and trying to play a corrective role in my life, quite *sine pecunia*, sometimes with stories, sometimes more abstractly. I have the clear feeling that the moment has come to thank you for all that, and to ask for your forgiveness for the times I was a poor student, one of 'life's problem children,' as you put it. I was very touched by your saying that, and it still touches me whenever I think of it. A problem child, that's certainly what I've been for you and your pedagogic streak—you spoke about that the very first day. And of course, that's one of the connections you've taught me about—between humanism and pedagogy. And I would come up with even more if you gave me a little time. Forgive me, then, and don't think badly of me. To your health, Lodovico—I wish you long life. I empty my glass in honor of your literary efforts to eradicate human suffering!" he concluded, and throwing his head back, he downed his burgundy and champagne in two great gulps. "And now let's go join the others."

"My good engineer, whatever has got into you?" the Italian asked, his eyes full of amazement, rising to leave the table as well. "Those sound like words of farewell."

"No—why should it be a farewell?" Hans Castorp said, ducking the issue, not just in a metaphorical sense with his words, but also physically, swinging his upper body around in a wide curve and taking the arm of Fräulein Engelhart, who had come to fetch them. The director was personally tapping a bowl of carnival punch that had been donated by the management, she reported. The gentlemen, she said, would have to come with her at once if they hoped to have a glass of it. And so they left together.

And indeed, there in the middle of his guests, all holding out their little punch glasses to him, Director Behrens was standing beside a round table with a white tablecloth, ladling steaming liquid from a large bowl. He, too, had spruced up his appearance a little for Mardi Gras, for in addition to his white clinical smock, which, as a man ever on professional call, he wore today as always, he had donned a genuine Turkish fez, scarlet red with a black tassel dangling over one ear—costume enough to lend his already striking appearance an even more curious and outlandish look. The white smock emphasized the director's height; and if you took into account the arched neck and pictured him instead pulled up to full height, he seemed a man almost larger than life, topped by a small, colorful head with very peculiar features. At least Hans Castorp thought that face had never looked so odd as it did this evening under its foolish headgear: that snub-nosed, flat physiognomy, purplish and hectic, with blue, watery eyes bulging beneath very blond brows, and a pale, skewed, short-cropped moustache above the hitch of his lips. Bending back from the steam eddying up from the punch bowl, he let the brown liquid—a sugary arrack punch—fall in long arcs from the ladle into the glasses held out to receive it, gushing the whole time in his high-spirited jargon, so that the process was greeted by salvos of laughter all around.

"Old Scratch himself atop them all," Settembrini explained softly, gesturing toward the director—and then was dragged away from Hans Castorp's side. Dr. Krokowski was on hand as well. Short, stout, and stolid, his black shiny smock draped over his shoulders so that the sleeves hung empty in domino fashion, he twisted his wrist around and held his glass up at eye-level as he chatted merrily with a group of cross-dressed masqueraders. Music was struck up. The girl with the face of a tapir played Handel's *Largo* on the violin, accompanied on the piano by the man from Mannheim. This was followed by a Grieg sonata—salon music of a Nordic nature, which met with polite applause, even from the costumed and uncostumed patients seated now, bottles in ice-buckets at their sides, at the two bridge tables that had been set up. The doors stood open, and several guests were standing out in the lobby as well. One group next to the round punch table was watching the director, who was introducing them to a parlor game. He stood there bent down over the table, but with his head held to one side so that everyone could see that he had his eyes closed, and drew blindly with a pencil on the back side of a calling card; and without any help from his eyes, his massive hand traced an outline, the profile of a pig—more simplified and slightly idealized than realistic, but it was undoubtedly a rudimentary pig that he managed to assemble under such handicapped circumstances. It was a clever stunt, and he did it well. The little squinty eye had ended up in approximately the correct position, a little too far back from the snout, but more or less in place; and the same could be said of the pointed ear atop the head or the little legs dangling from the rounded belly; and the opposing arch of the spine continued in the charming little spiral ringlet of a tail. When he finished, people cried, "Ah!" and crowded forward to try it, eager to emulate the master. The problem was that few of them could have drawn a pig with their eyes open, let alone closed. And what monsters were born! They lacked all coherence. The eyes landed outside the head, the legs inside the paunch, which did not come close to joining the rest, and the tail spiraled off alone into nowhere—an independent arabesque, with no organic connection to the amorphous body. They laughed so hard they almost burst. Others joined the group. The cardplayers took notice and came over now, curious, still holding their cards in their hands like fans. The onlookers watched the eyelids of each contestant, making sure there was no peeking, which several were tempted to try in their helplessness; they giggled and snorted while each candidate blundered blindly at the task, then crowed with laughter when he finally opened his eyes and gazed down at his absurd botched job. Seduced by overconfidence, everyone had to try his hand. The calling card, although large, was soon so full on both sides that the abortive attempts overlapped. But the director sacrificed a second one from his case, on which Prosecutor Paravant, after thinking the task through, tried to draw his pig in one continuous line—

with the result that his failure exceeded all others. The decorative design he produced did not even vaguely resemble a pig—or anything else in this world, for that matter. Hulloos, laughter, and raucous congratulations! Someone brought a menu from the dining hall, so that several people, both men and women, could try at once, and for each contestant there was an audience keeping a close eye out and someone waiting to grab the pencil being used. There were only three pencils, belonging to various guests, and people snatched them out of one another's hands. Having introduced his parlor game and seeing that it was a hit, the director departed with his aide-de-camp in tow.

Hans Castorp joined the crowd to watch a contestant, stood looking over Joachim's shoulder, propping one elbow against it while holding his chin tight in all five fingers, his other hand braced at his hip. He talked and laughed. He wanted to draw, too, demanded loudly he be allowed to, and was given the pencil, already just a stump of a thing that you could barely hold between your thumb and forefinger. He cursed the pencil, raised his head toward the ceiling and closed his eyes; loudly damning the useless pencil again and cursing just in general, he hastily drew some atrocity on the paper, at one point missing it entirely and ending up on the tablecloth. "That doesn't count!" he shouted amid well-deserved laughter. "How can I possibly draw with a thing like that—to hell with it!" And he tossed the offending stump into the punch bowl. "Who has a decent pencil? Who'll lend me one? I have to try again. A pencil, a real pencil! Does anyone have a pencil?" he called out to all sides, keeping his left forearm propped against the tabletop, but raising his right hand and shaking it in the air. No one had a pencil for him. He turned around and walked back into the room, continuing to shout—headed directly toward Clavdia Chauchat, who, as he well knew, was standing just beyond the portieres in the little salon, smiling and watching the goings-on around the punch bowl.

Behind him he heard someone calling him—in melodious foreign words: "*Eh! Ingegnere! Aspetti! Che cosa fa! Ingegnere! Un po' di ragione, sa! Ma è matto questo ragazzo!*" But he drowned out the voice by shouting even more loudly himself, and Herr Settembrini could now be seen flinging one hand above his head at the end of an extended arm, a common enough gesture in his homeland (but one whose meaning is hard to put into words). And uttering a long drawn-out "*Ehh—!*" he left the Mardi Gras festivities.

Hans Castorp, however, was standing in the brick schoolyard, staring from close up into a pair of blue-gray-green, epicanthic eyes above prominent cheekbones; and he said, "Do *you* have a pencil, perhaps?"

He was pale as death, as pale as on the day when he had returned from his solitary walk, still splattered with blood, to attend the lecture. Nerves controlling the blood vessels to his face were so successful at their task that the skin of his young face was drained of blood, turned pallid and cold, making the nose pinched and the area under his eyes so leaden that he looked almost like a corpse. But Hans Castorp's sympathetic nerves kept his heart thumping so hard that regular respiration was out of the question, and a shudder ran over the young man, the work of his body's sebaceous glands, which stood erect now, along with their hair follicles.

The woman in the paper tricorn looked him up and down—and her smile betrayed neither pity nor concern for his ravaged condition. Her sex knows no pity or concern when staring at the horrors of passion, an elemental emotion with which the female is apparently much more familiar than the male, who is not at all at ease with it—and if she finds him in that state, she never fails to greet him with mockery and schadenfreude. But then, he would certainly not have thanked her for either pity or concern, either.

"Do you mean me?" the bare-armed patient replied, in response to the familiar pronoun in his question. "Yes, I might." At most, her smile and voice suggested the kind of excitement that comes when the first words in a long, silent relationship are spoken at last—a subtle excitement secretly incorporating into this one moment everything that has happened until now. "You are very ambitious . . . You are . . . very . . . eager," she said, likewise using personal pronouns, continuing to mock him in her exotic accent with its strange *r* and stranger open *e*, and stressing the word "ambitious" on the first syllable, so that in her opaque, pleasantly husky voice it sounded like a word from her mother tongue. She rummaged in her leather handbag, peered down into it, first pulled out a handkerchief, from which she then extracted a silver pencil-holder, a slight, fragile trinket, never intended for serious use. That pencil long ago, the first one, had been more straightforward, handier.

"*Voilà*," she said and picked the little pencil up by the tip, holding it between thumb and forefinger and waggling it back and forth.

She both gave it to him and held it back, so that he took it without actually taking hold of it—raising his hand, very close to the pencil, his fingers ready to grasp it, but not actually grasping; and the gaze from his leaden eye sockets shifted between the object and Clavdia's Tartar face. His bloodless lips were open, and they stayed open, unused, as he said, "You see, I knew it—I knew you'd have one."

"*Prenez garde, il est un peu fragile*," she said. "*C'est à visser, tu sais.*"

And as they both bent their heads down over the pencil, she showed him the standard screw mechanism, from which emerged a very thin, hard needle of graphite that could leave no real mark.

They stood there bending toward one another. He had donned a formal, stiff collar for this evening and so could support his chin on that.

"A poor thing, but thine own," he said, brow to brow with her, gazing down at the pencil, his lips never moving, so that the two labials were left unsounded.

"Oh, and you are witty, too," she replied with a brief smile, raising her head now and letting him take the pencil. (Though God only knew how he had managed to be witty—with apparently not a drop of blood left in his head.) "And so go, step lively, draw, draw well, withdraw to draw." She was sending him wittily on his way, too, it seemed.

"No, *you* haven't drawn yet. *You* must draw now," he said, leaving out the *m* in "must" and taking a step back to let her pass.

"Do you mean me?" she said again, and this time her astonishment seemed directed at more than his request. At first she stood there smiling in some confusion, but then, as if pulled by a magnetic force, followed him as he backed away toward the punch table.

But it turned out that the diversion had lost its appeal, was in its last throes. One person was still drawing, but had no audience. The calling cards were covered with nonsense, everyone having given it a helpless try—but the table was as good as deserted, particularly since a current was now flowing in the opposite direction. Once it became clear that the doctors had left, word quickly spread that there would be dancing. The table was shoved to one side. Scouts were posted at the doors to the reading and music rooms and instructed to give the signal if the "boss," Krokowski, or the head nurse was sighted. A Slavic lad passionately attacked the keyboard of the little walnut piano. The first couples began to spin inside a little circle of spectators seated in chairs and on stools.

Hans Castorp waved good-bye to the table as it drifted away—"Farewell!" he said. He pointed with his chin first to some free chairs he had spotted in the little salon, and then to a sheltered corner just to the right of the portieres. He said nothing, perhaps because the music was too loud. He dragged one chair—this was for Frau Chauchat, almost a reclining throne, with a high, wooden-frame back and plush upholstery—over to the spot he had indicated in his pantomime, and for himself he selected a crackling, creaking wicker chair with scrolled armrests, on which he now sat down beside her, bending forward, his arms on the scrolls, her pencil in his hand, his feet well hidden under his chair. She, however, was forced to lie far back into the plush cushions, with her knees pulled up; nevertheless, she managed to cross one leg over the other and wiggled a foot in the air—her ankle, visible above the rim of her black patent leather shoe, was wrapped in a taut black silk stocking. The people seated in front of them would occasionally get up to dance, making room for those who had tired of dancing. There was a constant coming and going.

"You're wearing a new dress," he said, as an excuse for gazing at her. And now he heard her answer.

"New? You are conversant with my wardrobe?"

"I am right, am I not?"

"Yes. I recently had it made here, by Lukaček, the tailor in the village. He does work for many of the ladies up here. Do you like it?"

"Very much," he said, letting his gaze pass over her again before casting his eyes down. "Do you want to dance?" he added.

"Would you like to?" she asked, her brows raised in surprise, but still with a smile.

"I'd do it, if that's what you want."

"You're not quite as well-mannered as I thought you were," she said. When he dismissed this with a laugh, she added, "Your cousin has already gone."

"Yes, he is my cousin," he confirmed quite unnecessarily. "I also noticed a while ago that he had left. I'm sure he's taking his rest cure."

"He is a very rigid, very respectable, very 'German' young man."

"*Rigid? Respectable?*" he repeated. "I understand French better than I speak it. What you mean to say is that he's pedantic. Do you consider us Germans pedantic—*us other Germans?*"

"We are talking about your cousin. But it's true, you are all a little bourgeois. You love order more than liberty, all Europe knows that."

"*Love . . . love. What is it, exactly? The word lacks definition. What one man has, the other loves, as the German proverb puts it,*" Hans Castorp contended. "I have been giving freedom some thought of late," he continued. "That is, I heard the word mentioned so often, that I started thinking about it. *I'll tell you in French* what it is I've been thinking. *What all Europe refers to as liberty is, perhaps, something rather pedantic, rather bourgeois in comparison to our need for order—that's the point!*"

"*You don't say! How amusing. Was it really your cousin who got you thinking such strange things?*"

"No, *he is truly a good soul*, his is a simple temperament, not prone to dangers, *you understand. But he is not a bourgeois, he is a military man.*"

"Not prone to dangers?" she repeated with difficulty. "*By which you mean to say: a thoroughly steadfast nature, secure in itself? But your poor cousin is seriously ill.*"

"Who told you that?"

"We all know about one another here."

"Did Director Behrens tell you that?"

"Possibly, when he let me see his paintings."

"Don't you mean, when he was painting your portrait?"

"Why not? Did you think it successful, my portrait?"

"Oh yes, extremely. Behrens captured your skin perfectly, oh, truly quite lifelike. I would very much have liked to have been a portrait painter myself, if only to have had the chance to study your skin, as he did."

"Please, sir, speak German!"

"Oh, but I am speaking German, even if I am speaking French. *Painting is the kind of study that is both artistic and medical—in a word: it is, you see, a humanist pursuit.* So what do you say, wouldn't you like to dance?"

"Certainly not—how childish. *Behind the doctor's back. The moment Behrens returns, they will all throw themselves on their lounge chairs. How utterly ridiculous it all is."*

"Do you hold him in such high respect, then?"

"Whom?" she asked, pronouncing the word in a strange, clipped way.

"Behrens."

"Enough of your Behrens already! It's much too small a space for dancing. *And on the carpet besides . . .* Let's just watch the others."

"Yes, let's do that," he concurred, and with her beside him, he turned his grandfather's blue, thoughtful eyes, framed in a pallid face, to watch the costumed patients skip about in the salon here and in the reading room beyond. Silent Sister was capering with Blue Henry, and Frau Salomon, who was dressed like a gentleman in evening clothes—swallow-tail coat, white vest, amply filled shirt, monocle, and painted-on moustache—spun about on her little patent leather high-heeled shoes (which looked very out of place with her long, black men's trousers) in the arms of her Punchinello, whose lips shone bloody red in his whitened face and whose eyes looked like an albino rabbit's. The caped Greek moved his legs in their purple tights in perfect harmony with Rasmussen, whose black, low-cut dress sparkled. The prosecutor in his kimono, Frau Wurmbrandt, the general consul's wife, and young Gänser were dancing as a threesome, their arms thrown around one another. As for Frau Stöhr, she danced with her broom, pressing it to her heart and caressing its bristles as if they were the hair on a man's head.

"Let's do that," Hans Castorp said mechanically again. And so they went on speaking softly, their conversation covered by the piano. "Let's sit here and watch, as if in a dream. It is like a dream for me, you know, for me to be sitting here like this—*like an especially deep dream, for a man must sleep very heavily to dream like this. What I'm trying to say is: it is a dream I know well, have dreamed for a long time, yes, eternally, sitting here with you as I am now. Behold—eternity."*

"A poet!" she said. "A bourgeois, a humanist, and a poet—behold, Germany all rolled into one, just as it should be!"

"I'm afraid we are not at all, not in the least, as we should be," he replied. "Not in any way. We are perhaps life's problem children, that's all."

"Nicely put. Tell me . . . surely it would not have been too difficult to dream your dream before now. It is a little late for monsieur to decide to address his words to his humble servant."

"What good are words?" he said. "Why speak? Speech, discourse—those are nice republican things, I admit. But I doubt if they are equally poetic. One of our fellow residents, who has in fact become something of a friend, Monsieur Settembrini . . ."

"Who just let fly with a few words in your direction."

"Be that as it may, he is no doubt an eloquent speaker, indeed loves to recite beautiful verses—but does that make the man a poet?"

"I deeply regret never having had the pleasure of making the gentleman's acquaintance."

"I can well believe it."

"Ah! You believe it."

"What? But that's just a phrase one uses, with no real significance whatever. As you've surely noticed, I barely speak French. All the same, I would rather speak with you in it than in my own language, since for me speaking French is like speaking without saying anything somehow—with no responsibilities, the way we speak in a dream. Do you understand?"

"More or less."

"That will do. Speech—" Hans Castorp continued, "what a poor business it is! In eternity, people won't speak at all. Eternity, you see, will be like drawing that piglet: you'll turn your head away and close your eyes."

"Not bad! You seem quite at home in eternity, know its every detail, no doubt. I must say I find you a very curious little dreamer."

"Besides," Hans Castorp said, "if I had spoken to you before this, I would have had to use the formal pronoun."

"I see. Do you intend to use only the informal with me from now on?"

"But of course. I've used it with you all along, and will for all eternity."

"That's a bit much, I must say. In any case, you won't have the opportunity to use informal pronouns with me for much longer. I'm leaving."

It took a while before what she had said penetrated his consciousness.

But then he started up, looking about in befuddlement, like someone rudely awakened from sleep. Their conversation had proceeded rather slowly, because Hans Castorp's French was clumsy and he spoke haltingly as he tried to express himself. The piano, which had briefly fallen silent, struck up again, now under the hands of the man from Mannheim, who had taken over for the Slavic lad. He had spread his music out before him, and Fräulein Engelhart now sat down next to him to turn pages. The party was thinning out. The majority of the residents appeared to have assumed the horizontal position. There was no one sitting in front of them now. People were again playing cards in the reading room.

"What are you going to do?" Hans Castorp asked, flabbergasted.

"I am leaving," she repeated, smiling in apparent amazement at the frozen look on his face.

"It's not possible," he said. "You're joking."

"Most certainly not. I am perfectly serious. I am leaving."

"When?"

"Why, tomorrow. *After dinner.*"

A whole world was collapsing inside him. He said, "And where are you going?"

"Very far away."

"To Daghestan?"

"*You're not badly informed. Perhaps—for now at least.*"

"Are you cured, then?"

"*As for that . . . no.* But Behrens doesn't think I can achieve much more here, for the present at least. *Which is why I may now risk a little change of air.*"

"So you will be coming back?"

"That's an open question. Or, rather, the real question is when. *As for me, you know, I love freedom above all else—especially the freedom to choose my place of residence. I can hardly expect you to understand what it means to be obsessed with independence. It's in the blood, perhaps.*"

"*And your husband in Daghestan consents to—your liberty?*"

"*It is my illness that allows me liberty. You see, this is now my third time here. I've been here a year now. I may well return. But you will be far from here long before that.*"

"Do you think so, Clavdia?"

"*And my first name, too! You certainly do take the customs of carnival very seriously!*"

"So you do know how sick I am?"

"*Yes—no—the way one knows things here. You have a little moist spot there inside, a bit of fever, isn't that right?*"

"*A hundred, a hundred point two in the afternoon,*" Hans Castorp said. "And you?"

"*Oh, my case is a little more complicated, you see—it's not that simple.*"

"Within the humanist branch of letters called medicine, there is something," Hans Castorp said, "that they call tubercular congestion in the lymphatic vessels."

"*Ah! You have a spy, my dear, that's quite clear.*"

"And you—please, forgive me! I must ask you something, ask you something very urgent, but in German. That day, six months ago, when I left the table for my checkup—you looked up and watched me go, do you remember?"

"*What sort of question is that? Six months ago!*"

"Did you know where I was going?"

"*Certainly, but only quite by accident.*"

"So Behrens had told you, hadn't he?"

"*You and your Behrens!*"

"*Oh, he rendered your skin in absolutely lifelike fashion. Moreover, he is a widower with glowing cheeks who happens to own a really remarkable coffee service. I can well believe that he knows your body not merely as a doctor, but also as an initiate in another humanistic discipline.*"

"*You have every reason to say you speak as if in a dream, my friend.*"

"*That may be. But you must first let me dream anew, now that you've awakened me so cruelly with that alarm bell about your departure. Seven months beneath your gaze—and now, when I've come to know you in reality, you tell me you're leaving!*"

"*And I repeat, we should have chatted long before this.*"

"So you would have liked that?"

"*Me? You won't slip out of it that easily, my boy. This is about your interests, about you. Were you too shy to approach a woman with whom you are now speaking as if in a dream, or was there someone else who prevented your doing so?*"

"*I told you. I didn't want to address you with formal pronouns.*"

"*What a fraud. Answer me—the gentleman who speaks so eloquently, that Italian who just left our soiree—what words did he let fly just now?*"

"*I didn't understand any of it. The gentleman meant not a whit to me the moment I laid eyes on you. But you forget—it would not have been at all easy to have made your acquaintance in society. Besides, there is my cousin with whom I am involved and who has little or no inclination to amuse himself here; he thinks about nothing except returning to the plains to be a soldier.*"

"*Poor devil. He is, in fact, more ill than he knows. Your friend the Italian, by the way, is not doing very much better.*"

"He says so himself. But my cousin—is that true? You frighten me."

"It is quite possible that he will die if he tries to be a soldier on the plains."

"That he will die. Death. A terrible word, isn't it? But it's strange, the word doesn't impress me so much today. It was more just a conventional phrase when I said, 'You frighten me.' The idea of death doesn't frighten me. It leaves me calm. It arouses no pity—either for dear old Joachim or for myself—to hear that he may die. If that's true, then his condition is very much like my own, and I don't find mine particularly grand. He is dying, and me, I'm in love—fine! You spoke with my cousin once, in the waiting room outside where they take intimate photographs, if you recall."

"I vaguely recall."

"It was the same day that Behrens took your transparent portrait!"

"But of course."

"My God! And do you have it with you?"

"No, I keep it in my room."

"Ah, in your room. As for mine, I always keep it in my wallet. Would you like me to show it to you?"

"A thousand thanks, but I'm not overwhelmed with curiosity. It is sure to look quite innocent."

"Well, I have seen your exterior portrait. But I would much prefer to see the interior portrait you have locked up in your room. Let me ask you something else. From time to time a Russian gentleman who lives in town comes to visit you. Who is he? What is his purpose in coming?"

"You're enormously skilled at espionage, I must say. All right—I'll give you an answer. Yes, he is an ailing compatriot, a friend. I made his acquaintance at another resort, some years ago. Our relationship? We have tea together, we smoke two or three papyrosy, we gossip, we philosophize, we talk about man, God, life, morality, a thousand things. And with that my tale is ended. Are you satisfied?"

"About morality as well! And what discoveries have you in fact made about morality, for example?"

"Morality? It interests you, does it? All right—it seems to us that one ought not to search for morality in virtue, which is to say in reason, in discipline, in good behavior, in respectability—but in just the opposite, I would say: in sin, in abandoning oneself to danger, to whatever can harm us, destroy us. It seems to us that it is more moral to lose oneself and let oneself be ruined than to save oneself. The great moralists have never been especially virtuous, but rather adventurers in evil, in vice, great sinners who teach us as Christians how to stoop to misery. You must find that all very repugnant."

He fell silent. He was still sitting just as at the start—bending toward the woman reclining there in her paper tricorn, his intertwined feet far back under his creaking chair, her pencil between his fingers—and from lowered eyes, Hans Lorenz Castorp's blue eyes, he looked out into the room, which was empty now. The guests had scattered. The piano in the far corner across from them tinkled softly, disjointedly; the patient from Mannheim was playing with just one hand, while the teacher at his side paged through the music, which she now held on her knees. As the conversation between Hans Castorp and Clavdia Chauchat died away, the pianist stopped playing altogether, laying the hand with which he had been doodling back in his lap. Fräulein Engelhart went on thumbing through the music. Only these four were left now from the Mardi Gras party—they sat there motionless. The stillness lasted several minutes. Slowly it weighed down on the couple at the piano until their heads sank deeper and deeper, the Mannheimer's toward the keyboard, Fräulein Engelhart's toward her music. Finally, almost simultaneously, as if by some silent agreement, they stood up circumspectly; ingeniously avoiding any glances toward the other occupied corner of the room, with heads tucked low and arms stiff to their sides, the man from Mannheim and the teacher softly vanished together on tiptoe by way of the reading room.

"*They're all retiring to their rooms,*" Frau Chauchat said. "*Those were the last; it's getting late. Ah yes, our carnival festivities are over.*" And she raised both arms to remove her paper hat from her reddish hair, wound in a braid around her head. "*You know the consequences, monsieur.*"

But Hans Castorp rejected this, keeping his eyes closed and not changing his position in the least. He replied, "*Never, Clavdia. Never will I address you formally, never in life or in death,* if I may put it that way, and surely I may. *That form of address, as cultivated in the West and in civilized society, seems terribly bourgeois and pedantic to me. Why, indeed, use such forms? Formality is the same thing as pedantry! All those things you have established in regard to morality, you and your ailing compatriot—do you seriously suppose they surprise me? What sort of dolt do you take me for? So then tell me, what do you think of me?*"

"*That is a subject requiring little thought. You are a decent, simple fellow from a good family, with handsome manners, a docile pupil to his teachers, who will soon return to the flatlands in order to forget completely that he ever spoke in a dream here and to help repay his great and powerful fatherland with honest labor on the wharves. And there you have your own intimate photograph, taken with no apparatus at all. You do find it a good likeness, I hope?*"

"*It lacks some of the details that Behrens found there.*"

"*Ah, the doctors are always finding something, it's what they're good at.*"

"*You sound like Monsieur Settembrini. And my fever? Where does it come from?*"

"*Oh, go on, it's an episode of no consequence that will pass quickly.*"

"*No, Clavdia, you know perfectly well that what you say is not true and is spoken without conviction, of that I am certain. The fever in my body and the pounding of my exhausted heart and the trembling in my hands, it is anything but an episode, for it is nothing but*"—and he bent his pale face deeper toward hers, his lips twitching—"*nothing but my love for you, yes, the love that overwhelmed me the instant I laid eyes on you, or better, the love that I acknowledged once I recognized you—and it is that love, obviously, that has led me to this place.*"

"*What foolishness!*"

"*Oh, love is nothing if not foolish, something mad and forbidden, an adventure in evil. Otherwise it is merely a pleasant banality, good for singing calm little songs down on the plains. But when I recognized you, recognized my love for you—it's true, I knew you before, from days long past, you and your marvelously slanting eyes and your mouth and the voice with which you speak—there was a time long ago, when I was still just a schoolboy, that I asked you for a pencil, just so I could meet you at last, because I loved you with an irrational love, and no doubt what Behrens found in my body are the lingering traces of my age-old love for you, proof that I was sick even back then.*"

His teeth banged together. While he fantasized, he had pulled one foot out from under his creaking chair, and shoving it out in front of him and letting his other knee touch the floor, he was now kneeling beside her, his head bent low, his whole body quivering. "*I love you,*" he babbled, "*I have always loved you, for you are the 'intimate you' of my life, my dream, my destiny, my need, my eternal desire.*"

"*Come, come!*" she said. "*If your teachers could only see you—*"

But in his despair he merely shook his head, his face still directed toward the carpet, and replied, "*I don't care, I don't care about Carducci and the republic of eloquence and human progress over time, because I love you!*"

She softly stroked the short-cropped hair at the back of his head with one hand. "*My little bourgeois!*" she said. "*My handsome bourgeois with the little moist spot. Is it true that you love me so much?*"

Thrilled by her touch—on both knees now, head thrown back, eyes closed—he went on, "*Ah, love, you know. The body, love, death, are simply one and the same. Because the body is sickness and depravity, it is*

*what produces death, yes, both of them, love and death, are carnal, and
that is the source of their terror and great magic! But death, you see, is on
the one hand something so disreputable, so impudent that it makes us blush
with shame; and on the other it is a most solemn and majestic force—
something much more lofty than a life spent laughing, earning money, and
stuffing one's belly—much more venerable than progress chattering away
the ages—because it is history and nobility and piety, the eternal and the
sacred, something that makes you remove your hat and walk on tiptoe.
In the same way, the body, and love of the body, too, are indecent and
disagreeable; the body's surface blushes and turns pale because it is afraid
and ashamed of itself. But at the same time it is a great and divine glory,
a miraculous image of organic life, a holy miracle of form and beauty, and
love of it, of the human body, is likewise an extremely humanistic affair
and an educating force greater than all the pedagogy in the world! Ah,
ravishing organic beauty, not done in oils or stone, but made of living and
corruptible matter, full of the feverish secret of life and decay! Consider
the marvelous symmetry of the human frame, the shoulders and the hips
and the breasts as they blossom at each side of the chest, and the ribs
arranged in pairs, and the navel set amid the supple belly, and the dark
sexual organs between the thighs! Consider the shoulder blades shifting
beneath the silky skin of the back, and the spine descending into the fresh
doubled luxuriance of the buttocks, and the great network of veins and
nerves that branch out from the trunk through the armpits, and the way
the structure of the arms corresponds to that of the legs. Oh, the sweet inner
surfaces of the elbow and the hollow of the knee, with their abundance of
organic delicacies beneath the padding of flesh! What an immense festival
of caresses lies in those delicious zones of the human body! A festival of
death with no weeping afterward! Yes, good God, let me smell the odor
of the skin on your knee, beneath which the ingeniously segmented capsule
secretes its slippery oil! Let me touch in devotion your pulsing femoral
artery where it emerges at the top of your thigh and then divides farther
down into the two arteries of the tibia! Let me take in the exhalation of
your pores and brush the down—oh, my human image made of water and
protein, destined for the contours of the grave, let me perish, my lips against
yours!"*

When he finished speaking, he did not open his eyes; he remained just
as he was—his head thrown back, his hands stretched out before him,
still holding the little silver pencil—quivering and swaying there on his
knees.

She said, *"You are indeed a gallant suitor, one who knows how to woo
in a very profound, German fashion."*

And she set her paper hat on his head.

"*Adieu, my Carnival Prince! I can predict that you'll see a nasty rise in your fever chart this evening.*"

Then she glided out of her chair, glided across the carpet to the door, where she stopped and turned halfway back to him, one bare arm raised, a hand on the hinge. Over her shoulder she said softly, "*Don't forget to return my pencil.*"

And she left.

6

Changes

WHAT IS TIME? A secret—insubstantial and omnipotent. A prerequisite of the external world, a motion intermingled and fused with bodies existing and moving in space. But would there be no time, if there were no motion? No motion, if there were no time? What a question! Is time a function of space? Or vice versa? Or are the two identical? An even bigger question! Time is active, by nature it is much like a verb, it both "ripens" and "brings forth." And what does it bring forth? Change! Now is not then, here is not there—for in both cases motion lies in between. But since we measure time by a circular motion closed in on itself, we could just as easily say that its motion and change are rest and stagnation—for the then is constantly repeated in the now, the there in the here. Moreover, since, despite our best desperate attempts, we cannot imagine an end to time or a finite border around space, we have decided to "think" of them as eternal and infinite—in the apparent belief that even if we are not totally successful, this marks some improvement. But does not the very positing of eternity and infinity imply the logical, mathematical negation of things limited and finite, their relative reduction to zero? Is a sequence of events possible in eternity, a juxtaposition of objects in infinity? How does our makeshift assumption of eternity and infinity square with concepts like distance, motion, change, or even the very existence of a finite body in space? Now there's a real question for you!

Hans Castorp turned these sorts of questions over and over in his own mind—a mind that, since his arrival up here, had tended to quibble and think indiscreet thoughts of this sort and had perhaps been especially honed and emboldened for grumbling by a naughty, but overwhelming desire, for which he had now paid dearly. He asked himself these questions, asked good Joachim, even asked the valley buried under snow now since time out of mind, although he certainly never heard anything resembling an answer from any party—hard to say which was least helpful. In fact, he asked himself such questions only because he could not find any answers. It was almost impossible to engage Joachim's interest in these matters, since he thought of nothing—as Hans Castorp had himself noted one evening in French—except being a soldier down in the plains, and lived in increasingly bitter conflict with his hopes, which teased him by now drawing nearer, now vanishing into the distance. Indeed, of late he seemed inclined to end the struggle with one decisive blow. Yes, good, patient, honest Joachim, a man given totally to service and discipline, was subject to attacks of insubordination, rising up against the "Gaffky scale," an analytical method by which people down in the laboratory (or, as it was usually called, the "lab") ascertained and specified the degree to which a patient was infected. And, depending on whether only a few isolated bacilli were to be found in the sample analyzed, or whether they were present in untold quantities, the patient was assigned a Gaffky number— on which everything else depended. Every patient had to reckon with it as the infallible indication of his chances of being cured; the number of months or years someone would have to stay here could easily be determined from it—beginning with just dropping by for six months all the way up to a "life sentence," which all too often meant very little in terms of actual time spent. And so it was against the Gaffky scale that Joachim rebelled, openly refusing to believe in its authority—well, not *quite* openly, not to the higher-ups, but to his cousin and even his tablemates. "I've had it up to here; they're not going to make a fool of me any longer," he said loudly, the blood rising in his darkly tanned face. "Two weeks ago, I was two on the Gaffky, a trifle, the best prospects. And today it's nine, a teeming population, and the plains are simply out of the question. How in the devil is a man supposed to know how he stands, it's intolerable. There's a fellow over at Schatzalp, a Greek farmer, sent up here from Arcadia by an agent of the sanatorium—a hopeless case of galloping consumption, they expect his demise any day, but not one bacillus has ever been counted in his sputum. Whereas the fat Belgian captain, who left here healthy just as I was arriving, was ten on the Gaffky, simply swarming with it, and all he had was a tiny little cavity. To hell with Gaffky! I've had it—I'm going home, even if it kills me!" This was how Joachim put it—and it pained everyone to see this gentle, sedate young man in open rebellion. Whenever he heard Joachim threaten to chuck it all, Hans Castorp could not help thinking of certain things he had heard a third party say in French. But he kept his peace—was he supposed to reproach his cousin with the example of his own patience, the way Frau Stöhr did? She actually admonished Joachim not to be so obstinate, but to show some humility and to see in her, Karoline Stöhr, an example of faithful perseverance, of pure willpower: the way she denied herself the pleasure of running the show at home as a housewife in Cannstatt, in order that someday she might be restored whole to her husband, a completely cured wife. No, Hans Castorp really wanted none of that, especially because ever since Mardi Gras his conscience had bothered him; that is to say, his conscience told him that Joachim had to regard a certain incident, about which they never spoke but of which Joachim was undoubtedly aware, as an instance of betrayal, desertion, and faithlessness, particularly when one thought of a pair of round, brown eyes, unwarranted giggles, and orange perfume, to the effects of which he was exposed five times a day—and each time sternly, properly lowered his eyes to his plate. Yes, even in the quiet reluctance with which Joachim responded to his speculations and opinions about "time," Hans Castorp thought he sensed something of a military propriety that included a reproach to his conscience. As for the valley, this winter valley under a deep blanket of snow, to which Hans Castorp likewise directed his metaphysical questions from his splendid lounge chair, its peaks, summits, ridges, and brown-green-reddish forests stood there silent in time, were draped in the web of silently flowing earthly days, now sparkling against the deep blue of the sky, now wrapped in mists, now aglow with the red of the setting sun, now glittering hard as diamonds in a world turned magical by moonlight—but always in the snow, while six unbelievably long months had scampered by. And all the guests declared they could not stand to see any more snow, it disgusted them, summer alone had more than satisfied them in that regard, nothing but masses of snow, day in, day out, mounds of snow, pillows of snow, whole slopes of snow—it was more than any human being could stand, deadly to both mind and spirit. And they put on sunglasses, tinted green, yellow, or red—to protect their eyes, to be sure, but more to protect their hearts.

So, valley and mountains under snow for six months now? Seven! Time sweeps onward while we tell our tale—not only *our* time, the time we devote to the telling, but also the profoundly past time of Hans Castorp and those who share his fate up there in the snow—and it brings forth changes. Everything that Hans Castorp had anticipated—and all too hastily put into words for Herr Settembrini as they returned from Platz that afternoon before Mardi Gras—was well on its way to being fulfilled. Not that Midsummer Night was imminent, but Easter had already passed through the white valley, April was advancing, Pentecost loomed ahead in open view, and spring would soon begin and with it the snow would melt—though not all of it, there was always some on the peaks to the south and in the ravines of the Rhätikon chain to the north, not to mention what would fall all through summer without sticking. But the trundling year definitely promised decisive changes very soon, for it had now been six weeks since the night of Mardi Gras, when Hans Castorp had borrowed a pencil from Frau Chauchat—and given it back to her, though only after first asking for some little memento, which he now carried in his pocket— a time twice as long as Hans Castorp had originally intended to stay up here.

Six weeks had indeed passed since that evening when Hans Castorp had made Clavdia Chauchat's acquaintance and returned to his room considerably later than conscientious Joachim to his; six weeks since the morning after, the day of Frau Chauchat's departure—her departure for now, her temporary departure for Daghestan, far to the east, beyond the Caucasus. That her departure was intended as merely temporary, was a departure only for now, that Frau Chauchat planned to return, although it was not certain just when—hoped to return, indeed would surely return—as to all that, Hans Castorp had received direct, spoken assurances, though not during the conversation in a foreign language we have already shared with our readers, but during an interval we have chosen to pass over in silence by breaking the time-bound flow of our narrative and so allowing only pure time to take its course. At any rate, the young man had received those assurances and comforting promises before returning to room 34 that night. He did not, however, exchange a single word with Frau Chauchat the next day, hardly saw her—only twice, and then from some distance: at dinner, when she had appeared in her blue skirt and white wool sweater, slamming the glass door and gracefully slinking to her table one last time, which set his heart pounding in his throat and almost caused him to hide his face in his hands—only Fräulein Engelhart's sharp gaze had prevented that; and then again, at three that afternoon, as she was leaving, although he had not actually been present, but had merely watched from a hall window with a view to the driveway.

Her departure had taken place in much the same fashion as others Hans Castorp had seen during his stay: the sleigh or carriage stopped at the ramp, driver and porter strapped down trunks, and around the main entrance were gathered sanatorium guests—both friends of the person who, whether cured or not, whether to live or to die, was returning now to the flatlands, and mere onlookers playing hooky from their rest cure to take in the ambiance. A gentleman in a frock coat from the management, perhaps even the doctors, would appear, and then the departing guest came out—usually with a beaming smile, graciously greeting both by-standers and friends left behind, and generally quite animated by the excitement of the moment. And this time it had been Frau Chauchat who emerged, smiling, arms full of flowers, wearing a large hat and a long, coarse traveling coat trimmed with fur; she was accompanied by Herr Buligin, her concave countryman, who was to travel partway with her. Like every other departing guest, she, too, seemed happy and excited, if only because life would surely change—whether a person departed with medical approval or out of weary desperation broke off his stay at his own risk and with a bad conscience. Her cheeks were flushed, she kept up a constant flow of chatter—in Russian, presumably—while someone tucked a fur blanket around her legs. Not just Frau Chauchat's coun-trymen and tablemates were present, but countless other guests were on hand as well. Dr. Krokowski showed up, smiling pithily and showing his yellow teeth under his beard. More flowers were presented. The great-aunt gave her some candies, *"konfekti"* as she called them in Russian; the teacher, Fräulein Engelhart, appeared, as did the man from Mannheim— although he stood off at some distance, watching gloomily; but then his mournful eyes glided up to the window, where he had spotted Hans Castorp, and lingered gloomily there for a while. Director Behrens had not come, having presumably said his good-byes to her on some other private occasion. The onlookers waved and called out, the horses pulled; as the sleigh moved forward, Frau Chauchat's upper body sank back against the cushions and her smiling, slanted eyes quickly surveyed the façade of the Berghof and rested for the fraction of a second on Hans Castorp's face. He was pale as he hurried back to his room and out onto the balcony, from where he could catch another glimpse of the sleigh as it made its jingling way down the approach road toward Dorf; then he threw himself in his chair, and from his breast pocket he pulled his memento—not reddish-brown pencil shavings this time, but a little plate of glass in a narrow frame, which had to be held up to the light for him to see what was there: the portrait of Clavdia's interior, without a face, but revealing the organs of her chest cavity and the tender framework of her upper body, delicately surrounded by the soft, ghostlike forms of her flesh.

How often had he looked at it and pressed it to his lips during the time that had passed since then, bringing forth its changes—changes, for instance, like getting used to life up here without Clavdia Chauchat present in a shared space. And it had happened more quickly than one would have thought: time here was especially conducive to it, was purposely organized so that you got used to things—if only used to not getting used to them. The rattling slam at the start of each of the five sumptuous meals could no longer be reckoned with, it happened no more; and now, somewhere terribly far away, Frau Chauchat was slamming doors—it was an expression of her character, intermingled and bound up with her existence and her illness, much as time was bound up with bodies in space. Perhaps that, that alone, *was* her illness. But although she was invisibly absent, at the same time she was also invisibly present in Hans Castorp's mind—as the genius and guardian angel of the place, whom he had known and possessed for one wicked, riotously sweet hour, an hour quite incongruous with some delicate little song from the flatlands, and whose interior silhouette he now bore next to a heart that had been sorely overtaxed for the last nine months.

During that hour his twitching lips had stammered, in a half-stifled, half-unconscious way, a great many riotous things, some in a foreign tongue, some in his own: suggestions, proposals, mad plans, and ambitions, which had quite rightfully been totally rejected—for instance, that he might hope to accompany this guardian angel, travel with it beyond the Caucasus, to the place its free spirit had chosen as its next abode, never to be separated from it again, along with a good many other similar irresponsible ideas. The only thing this prosaic young man had retrieved from his hour of adventure, however, had been the shadowy token of a pledge—the possibility, bordering on a probability, that Frau Chauchat would return here, sooner or later, for a fourth stay, just as the illness, which indeed gave her such freedom, might dispose. But whether sooner or later, Hans Castorp would in any case "be gone long before that," as she told him again as they parted; and the note of sarcasm in her prophecy would have been even harder to bear had he not understood that some prophecies are made not so that something may come true, but as a kind of spell to *prevent* it from coming true. By predicting what form the future will take, prophets of this sort mock the future by shaming it into not taking that form. And if in the course of both conversations, recorded and unrecorded, the genius of the place had called him, Hans Castorp, a *"joli bourgeois au petit endroit humide"*—in its way, a translation of Settembrini's phrase "problem child of life"—the question then was: which part of this mixed character would prove the stronger, the bourgeois or the other? And the genius had likewise failed to take into consideration that, just as it had departed and returned on several occasions, so, too, Hans Castorp might also return at just the right moment—though, to be sure, the only reason he was still sitting here now was so that he would *never* have to return again, that being, after all, as for so many people up here, the point of his sojourn.

One mocking prophecy from Mardi Gras had been fulfilled: Hans Castorp's fever chart had taken a turn for the worse; he had solemnly traced the initial steep, jagged upward curve, the few halting steps back down, and the steady high plateau that undulated gently above its previous standard level. It was a fever which, in its stubbornness and seriousness, was out of all proportion to any medical finding, or so the director said. "More toxic than we gave you credit for, my friend," he declared. "Well, let's give injections a try! Those will do the trick. In three or four months you'll be fit as a fiddle, if the undersigned has anything to do with it." And so from then on, twice a week, right after his morning constitutional on Wednesday and Saturday, Hans Castorp had to report to the lab for his shot.

Both doctors administered the drug, sometimes the one, sometimes the other, although the director was a virtuoso at it, inserting the needle and squeezing the syringe in one flourish. He paid no attention, however, to where he was sticking the needle, so that it could hurt like hell, leaving a little hardened spot that stung for a long time. The injections were also very hard on the entire system, as much a shock to the nerves as a major athletic feat would have been, which was a token of their inherent potency, likewise evidenced by an immediate, though momentary, rise in temperature. The director had predicted it all, and it all happened as per regulation, with no deviations from the norm worth mentioning. When it finally came your turn, the procedure was quickly taken care of; quick as a flash the antitoxin was under your skin, either in the thigh or arm. Now and then, when the director was in the mood and not melancholy from tobacco, he might actually use the occasion of an injection for a little conversation, which Hans Castorp knew how to steer along the following lines:

"I still enjoy thinking back to that pleasant little chat we had quite by happenstance over coffee in your rooms that day last autumn, Director Behrens. Why, only yesterday, or maybe it was the day before, I was reminding my cousin of it."

"Seven on the Gaffky," the director said. "Latest results. The lad simply will not detoxify. And all the same, pesters and badgers me worse than before to let him go dangle a sword at his side, the nincompoop. Carries on about his fifteen months as if they were eons he had to kill. He is determined to leave, one way or the other—has he told you that, too? You should give him a talking-to, speak your mind, straight out. It will be the ruin of the lad if he starts filling that spot on the upper right with your lugubrious fog too soon. A swashbuckler like that doesn't need a great deal of gray matter, but as the steadier of the two, the civilian, the man with a solid education, you should set his head square on his shoulders before he does anything stupid."

"But I do that, Director Behrens," Hans Castorp replied, keeping the reins in his hands. "I do it whenever he kicks up a row, and I do think he'll listen to reason. But the examples we have here before our eyes are not always the best ones, and that's what does the damage. People are constantly leaving—leaving for the flatlands, all on their own and without permission, and there's even a little celebration, as if it were a genuine departure, which can be tempting for someone of weaker character. Just recently, for example . . . who was it that left just recently? A lady, from the Good Russian table, Madame Chauchat. Took off for Daghestan, I heard. Well, I don't know about the climate in Daghestan, although I'm sure it's less detrimental than up on the coast. But by our definition up here it is the flatlands, even if it may have mountains, in the strict geographic sense—I'm not all that well informed. But how is anyone who's not really cured supposed to live there, where the basic concepts are lacking and no one understands the rules we have up here—and what about rest cures and measuring your temperature? Although she does plan to return, or so she happened to mention to me—now how did we get started talking about her? Ah yes, we ran into you in the garden that day, if you recall, Director Behrens, or better, you ran into us, because we were sitting on a bench, I still know which one, I could even point it out to you, and there we sat smoking. Which is to say, I was smoking, because my cousin for some inexplicable reason doesn't smoke. And you happened to be smoking, too, and we exchanged brands with one another, it just occurs to me again. And I thought your Brazil was excellent, but it has to be handled like a young, spirited colt, otherwise the same thing might happen that happened to you with those two little imported cigars, when your chest started heaving and you almost kicked the bucket—but it turned out all right, so we can laugh about it now. I recently ordered another two hundred Maria Mancinis from Bremen, by the by, I'm really very attached to that bit of merchandise, find it congenial in every way. Although the customs duties and postage do hit rather hard, and if you start adding any more to my bill, I am perfectly capable of converting to some local weed—there are some lovely items in the shop windows. And then we were permitted a look at your paintings—it seems like only yesterday, and what a pleasure it was. I was absolutely dumbfounded by the risks you take with oils, I would never have the courage. We also saw Frau Chauchat's portrait and the first-class way you handled the skin— it was simply inspiring, I must say. But at the time I didn't know your model, or just by sight and name. Since then, shortly before her recent departure, in fact, I've had the chance to become personally acquainted with her."

"You don't say!" the director replied, much as he had—if we may remind the reader—when Hans Castorp had declared before his first examination that he had a little fever. And that was all he said.

"Yes, indeed, I did," Hans Castorp confirmed. "It's been my experience that it isn't all that easy to make acquaintances up here, but it just worked out that way for Frau Chauchat and me at the very last minute and we sort of fell into conversation and . . ." Hans Castorp pulled air in between his teeth. The needle struck home. "Fff!" he sucked in. "That's a critical nerve you happened to hit there, Director Behrens. Oh, yes, yes, hurts like hell. Thanks, a little massage does help. And so got to know one another, conversationally, I mean."

"So! And—?" the director said, nodding as he asked, with the expression on his face of someone expecting a favorable reaction, the tone of the question implying he was awaiting praise that corroborated his own experience.

"I suppose my French was a little weak," Hans Castorp said evasively. "But how could it be all that good, really? Somehow a few things do come to you at just the right moment, and so we managed to communicate fairly well."

"I can well believe it. And—?" the director said, pressing him again. And now he volunteered something of his own: "Rather nice, eh?"

Buttoning his collar now, Hans Castorp stood there with legs and elbows spread, his face turned up to the ceiling. "It's the old story," he said. "Two people, or two families, spend weeks together under the same roof at a resort somewhere, always keeping their distance. And one day they become acquainted, find they like one another, but at the same time it turns out one party is about to leave. Regrettable things like that happen often, I suppose. But nevertheless, one would like to keep in touch, hear something of one another, by mail I mean. But Frau Chauchat . . ."

"Ah, but she doesn't want to, does she?" the director said with a genial laugh.

"No, she wouldn't hear of it. Doesn't she even write you now and then, from her other places of residence?"

"Heaven forbid!" Behrens replied. "She'd never think of it. First because she's too lazy to write, and then, how could she? I can't read Russian—I manage to jabber it a little if need be, but I can't read a word. And you can't either, I'm sure. Well, and the little pussycat can meow some very pretty French and a little stilted High German—but write?

She'd be in completely over her head. Spelling, my dear friend! No, we'll just have to console ourselves, my lad. She's sure to come back, sooner or later, always has. It's a matter of skill, or of temperament, as I've often said. Some people leave now and then and have to come back, and others remain for as long as it takes until they don't need to come back. If your cousin leaves now, and you can tell him this for me, it may very well happen that you'll still be here to witness his solemn return."

"But, Director Behrens, how long do you think that I—"

"That you? I'm talking about *him!*—that he'll not last down there as long as he's been up here already. That is my humble personal opinion, and I'm commissioning you to give him the message, if you'd be so kind."

And that was more or less how their conversations went—cleverly steered by Hans Castorp, but with results that were either nonexistent or ambiguous—ambiguous in terms of how long he would have to stay until someone who left too soon returned again, and as good as nil when it came to the vanished lady. Hans Castorp would hear nothing more from her as long as time and space separated them; she would not write, or give him the chance to do so, either. And when he stopped to consider the matter, how could it have turned out any differently? Had his notion that they ought to write one another not been very bourgeois, very pedantic—particularly when all along he had felt it was unnecessary, even undesirable for them to *speak* to one another? And as he sat beside her that Mardi Gras evening, had he actually "spoken" with her in the manner appropriate to the educated West? Or had he not, instead, prattled on in a foreign tongue, in the less civilized fashion of a dream? And so why write a letter, or even a postcard, like the ones he sometimes sent home to the flatlands to report about the ups and downs in the results of his checkups? Wasn't Clavdia right to feel excused from writing, simply because her illness gave her that freedom? To speak, to write—indeed that was a splendid humanistic and republican achievement, like that of Signore Brunetto Latini, who had written a book about virtue and vice, had given the Florentines their polish and taught them both how to speak and the fine art of guiding their republic by the rules of politics.

Which brought Hans Castorp's thoughts around to Lodovico Settembrini—and he blushed, just as he had blushed the day that the writer had unexpectedly entered his sickroom and suddenly illumined it. Hans Castorp could just as easily have directed his questions about transcendental riddles to Herr Settembrini, if only as a way of challenging him and quibbling, but certainly not in the expectation of receiving an answer from a humanist whose sole concern was this earthly life. But ever since the Mardi Gras party and Settembrini's heated departure from the music room, a coolness had reigned between Hans Castorp and the Italian, the result both of the former's bad conscience and the latter's deep pedagogic indignation, so that they avoided one another and had not exchanged a single word for weeks now. Was Hans Castorp still one of "life's problem children" in Herr Settembrini's eyes? No, he had probably been given up for lost in the eyes of a man who sought morality in reason and virtue. And Hans Castorp's heart hardened against Herr Settembrini; he scowled and pursed his lips whenever their paths crossed—and Herr Settembrini's flashing black eyes would rest on him in silent reproach. And yet that hardened heart softened at once the first time the literary man spoke to him again—after weeks, as noted—though it was only in passing and in the form of a mythological allusion, which to be understood required an education in the traditions of the West. It occurred after dinner; they ran into one another at the door that no longer slammed. Catching up with the young man, but with the intent of moving right on past him, Settembrini said, "Well, my good engineer, how did you like the pomegranate?"

Hans Castorp smiled in confused delight. "I'm sorry—what did you say, Herr Settembrini? Pomegranate? We haven't had any pomegranates, have we? I don't think I've ever . . . no, wait, I did once drink some pomegranate juice and soda. It was too sweet for me."

Already past him now, the Italian looked back over his shoulder and carefully stated: "The gods and mortals have on occasion visited the realm of shades and found their way back. But those who reside in the nether world know that he who eats of the fruits of their realm is forever theirs."

And he walked on, wearing those everlasting pastel checked trousers, leaving Hans Castorp behind, presumably "cut to the quick" by so much trenchant significance—and to some extent he was, although he was also vexed and amused by the notion that he was supposed to be. He muttered to himself, "Latini, Carducci, bibbi-boobi-trappi, just leave me in peace!"

All the same, he was touched and glad that the ice had been broken; for despite his trophy, the macabre gift that he wore next to his heart, he was very fond of Herr Settembrini, set great store by his presence, and the thought of being totally rejected and abandoned would have weighed down on him more heavily than had the feeling of being a schoolboy no longer in the running and enjoying the advantages of disgrace, just like Herr Albin. And yet he did not have the courage to speak to his mentor, and several more weeks passed before Herr Settembrini once again approached his problem child.

The waves of the ocean of time, in their eternal monotone rhythm, washed Easter ashore, and the Berghof celebrated it, just as it took note of all time's stages and turning points in order to avoid undifferentiated tedium. At early breakfast, each guest found a nosegay of violets beside his place setting; at second breakfast, a dyed egg; and at the festive dinner, a little chocolate rabbit decorated with sugar.

"Have you ever taken an ocean voyage, *tenente*—or you, my good engineer?" Herr Settembrini asked, stepping up to the cousins' table after the meal, his toothpick in his mouth. Like most of the guests, they were shaving fifteen minutes from the main rest cure by lingering over coffee and cognac. "These rabbits and dyed eggs remind me of life on a great steamer, when for weeks on end you stare at an empty horizon and a briny desert, under conditions of deluxe comfort that only superficially help you forget the enormity of the situation, an awareness of which lives on as a secret horror gnawing in the deeper regions of your mind. I recognize today's mood; it is the same mood that reigns when the holidays of terra firma are religiously observed on those great arks—as reminders of a world outside, nostalgia as per calendar. Today would be Easter on terra firma, right? Today's the king's birthday on terra firma—and so we celebrate it, too, as best we can, we're only human. Isn't that right?"

The cousins agreed. It really was true. Touched by having been spoken to and spurred on by his own bad conscience, Hans Castorp had high praise for these sentiments, found them witty, choice, and literary, and made every effort to say what he thought Herr Settembrini wanted to hear. To be sure, just as Herr Settembrini had put it so graphically, the comforts on an ocean liner allowed one only superficially to forget the real situation and its dangers, and there was, if he might be permitted to add a comment of his own, even a kind of frivolous provocation about that perfect comfort, somewhat like what the ancients called hubris (in his desire to please, he was even citing the classics)—"I am the king of Babylon," and that sort of thing—in a word, sacrilege. On the other hand, however, the luxury on board manifested ("manifested"!) a great triumph of the human spirit and human dignity—for in bearing luxury and comfort out onto the briny, foamy deep and boldly maintaining it there, man was, so to speak, setting his boot on the neck of the elements, of savage forces, and that manifested the triumph of human civilization over chaos, if he might be permitted the phrase.

Herr Settembrini listened attentively, his ankles crossed, his arms ditto, all the while daintily stroking the sweep of his moustache with his toothpick. "It is remarkable," he said, "how a man cannot summarize his thoughts in even the most general sort of way without betraying himself completely, without putting his whole self into it, quite unawares, presenting as if in an allegory the basic themes and problems of his life. The same thing has just happened with you, my good engineer. What you just said came from the very depths of your personality, and even the present state of your personality found poetic expression. And as before, it is the experimental state."

"*Placet experiri!*" Hans Castorp said nodding and laughing—and with a soft Italian *c*.

"*Sicuro*—when it is a matter of a respectable passion to explore the world and not a matter of depravity. You spoke of 'hubris,' used that very word. But the hubris of reason set against the dark powers is the highest form of humanity, and as such it evokes the rage of the envious gods; *per esempio,* when such a luxury ark founders and plummets to the depths, that is a downfall with honor. Prometheus's deed was one of hubris as well, and his torments on the Scythian cliffs are for us a sacred martyrdom. But what about the other kind of hubris, when a man perishes in wanton experiments with the powers of unreason, with forces hostile to the human race? Is there honor in that? Can that ever be honorable? *Si o no!*"

Hans Castorp stirred his spoon in his cup, although there was nothing in it.

"My good engineer, my good engineer," the Italian said, bending his head forward thoughtfully and letting his black eyes "set." "Are you not afraid of the second circle of hell and the cyclone that tosses and whirls the sinners of the flesh about, those unhappy souls who sacrificed reason for lust? *Gran Dio,* when I picture you being blown and blasted about, tumbling head over heels, it worries me until I could simply topple over myself, like a tumbling corpse."

They laughed, happy to hear him joking and speaking poetically. But then Settembrini added, "Over a glass of wine, on the evening of Mardi Gras, my good engineer, you will recall that you more or less took your leave of me—yes, it was very like a good-bye. And so today it is now *my* turn. You see me standing here before you, gentlemen, about to say my farewells. I am leaving the sanatorium."

They were both totally taken aback.

"It's not possible! You're joking!" Hans Castorp cried, just as he had on another, similar occasion. He was almost as shocked as he had been then.

But Settembrini replied, "Most certainly not. It is just as I've said. Nor should you be all that surprised by my news. I've already explained to you that the moment my hopes of being able to return to the world of work in the foreseeable future should prove untenable, I was determined to fold my tents here and set myself up for the duration somewhere else in the valley. Well, what would you have me do? The moment has come.

I cannot get well, that is settled. I can eke out an existence here—but only here. My sentence, my final sentence has been spoken—and it is life. It has been pronounced by Director Behrens, in that special cheerful way of his. Fine, then I shall accept the consequences. I have rented lodgings, and my few worldly goods and the tools of my literary trade are about to be transported there. It's in Dorf, not very far from here at all. We're sure to meet, I'll not lose sight of you. But as your fellow resident, I now take my leave of you."

This was Settembrini's Easter disclosure. The cousins were plainly extraordinarily moved by it all. They spoke repeatedly and at length with the literary man about his decision: whether he would be able to follow the rules of rest cure on his own; how he would continue the complex, encyclopedic task he had taken upon himself—that survey of literary masterpieces from the perspective of human sufferings and their eradication; and finally, about his future quarters in a building belonging to a "retailer of foodstuffs," as Herr Settembrini put it. The retailer, he reported, had rented the upper floors of his property to a Bohemian ladies' tailor, who was now subletting some of the space.

But these conversations now lay in the past. Time had swept onward, bringing forth more than one change. No longer a resident of the International Sanatorium Berghof, Settembrini had been living with Lukaček, the ladies' tailor, for several weeks. His departure had not been by sleigh, but on foot. Wearing his short yellow overcoat, with a bit of fur trim at the collar and sleeves, and accompanied by a man who transported the writer's earthly and literary baggage in a wheelbarrow, he had been seen walking off, swinging his cane—but only after first stopping at the front door to give a dining attendant's cheek a little pinch with the backs of two fingers. As noted, a good part of April, three-quarters of it, already lay in the shadows of the past, but it was still deepest winter, with room temperatures of barely forty-two degrees each morning, and of twelve degrees outside; and if you left an inkwell out on the balcony overnight, it would be a clump of ice the next morning, a piece of hard coal. But spring was coming, they knew that; on days when the sun shone, there was an occasional, gentle hint of it in the air. Longer periods of thaw could be expected soon, and with them would come inevitable changes at the Berghof—changes that not even the authority of the director's word could hold back, although every day, in the dining hall, in patients' rooms, at every checkup, at every meal, he vigorously combated the prejudice that prevailed against the season of thaw.

Was he dealing with winter athletes, he asked, or patients, people who were ill? Why in the world did they have to have snow, frozen snow?

The coming period of thaw, an unhealthy season? It was the healthiest of all. It could be proven that during thaw there were relatively fewer bedridden patients throughout the valley than during any other time. At this point in the year, the weather everywhere else in the world was worse for patients with lung disease. Anyone with a scintilla of common sense would remain here and make good use of the bracing effects of local conditions. After that, a person would be immune to the effects of any climate anywhere, could stand firm against every onslaught—provided, of course, he waited for healing to take hold completely, and so forth. But that was easy for the director to say—the prejudice against the thaw was firmly entrenched in their minds, and the resort was emptying out. It may well have been that approaching spring was stirring in their bones and making even sedentary folk restless and eager for change—in any case the number of "wild" and "fraudulent" departures from the Berghof was increasing to acute levels. Frau Salomon from Amsterdam, for example— despite the pleasure she took in checkups that allowed her to show off her best laçe undergarments—departed on a totally wild and fraudulent basis, without permission of any kind, and not because she was getting better but because she was doing worse and worse. Her stay up here went back to long before Hans Castorp's arrival; it was more than a year since she had first come here—with a slight infection for which she had been sentenced to three months. After four months she was then told she would "be cured inside of four weeks," but six weeks later, any talk of being cured was simply out of the question—she would have to stay at least another four months. And so it went—after all, this was no prison ship, no Siberian salt mine; and Frau Salomon stayed on and used the time to show off her finest lingerie. But when, with thaw looming up ahead, she had been sentenced to an additional five months—as a result of her latest checkup, revealing a whistle in her left upper lobe and unmistakably harsh tones under her left shoulder—she lost all patience, raised loud protests, and, cursing Dorf and Platz, the famous air, the International Sanatorium Berghof, and its doctors, departed for home, for windy, wet Amsterdam.

Was that a wise thing to do? Director Behrens threw his arms above his shoulders and let them fall; noisily slapping his thighs. By autumn at the latest, he said, Frau Salomon would be back again—but then for good. Would he be proved right? We shall see—for we are bound to this cozy resort for many earthly days yet. But Frau Salomon's case was certainly not the only one of its kind. Time brought forth changes—just as it always had, but those changes had been more gradual, not so striking. There were gaps now in the dining hall, at all seven tables, at both the Good and Bad Russian tables, at those set both lengthwise and crosswise. One could not, however, have gained from this fact a complete picture of the hotel's occupancy rate; there had been arrivals as well, just as at any time of the year; rooms might very well be occupied, but by guests whose freedom of movement was limited by the final stages of their condition. But in the dining hall, as we have said, some persons were missing because they still had such freedom of movement. And others left a gap, a void, much more profound—like Dr. Blumenkohl, who was dead. That look on his face, as if he had something foul-tasting in his mouth, had become more and more pronounced; then he had been confined to his bed, and then he died—no one knew exactly when; the matter was handled with customary tact and discretion. A gap. Frau Stöhr sat next to the gap, and it made her shudder. And so she moved to the other side of young Ziemssen, to the place previously belonging to Miss Robinson, who had been released as cured; across from her now was the teacher, who still sat on Hans Castorp's left, having held faithfully to her post. She was all alone on her side of the table, where three more places were now free. Rasmussen the student, who had daily grown thinner and more listless, was now bedridden and considered moribund; and the great-aunt had gone on a trip with her niece and Marusya of the prominent breasts. We say "on a trip," because that is what everyone said, since it was understood that they would be returning soon enough. They would be back by autumn at the latest—how could one call that a departure? And how very near Midsummer Night already was, especially with Pentecost just around the corner; and once the longest day had come and gone, the year raced downhill from there, toward winter—so that in a way the great-aunt and Marusya were as good as back again. And that was a fine thing, because laughter-loving Marusya was not cured and detoxified by any means; Fräulein Engelhart knew all about some tubercular tumors brown-eyed Marusya had on her full bosom, which had been operated on several times already. And when the teacher shared this information, Hans Castorp glanced furtively at Joachim, whose face had turned blotchy and was bent down over his plate.

The chipper great-aunt had invited her tablemates—that is, the cousins, the teacher, and Frau Stöhr—to a farewell dinner in the restaurant, a lavish feast with caviar, champagne, and liqueurs, during which Joachim had been very quiet, speaking only a few words in almost a whisper, so that the great-aunt, being the benevolent soul she was, told him to cheer up and, suspending the rules of civilized discourse, even addressed him with informal pronouns. "Never mind, old fellow, don't worry. Eat, drink, talk—we'll be coming back soon," she said. "Let us all eat, drink, and chat, and let sorrow take care of itself. God will bring autumn before we even know what's happened. So you be the judge—is there any reason to be sad?" The next morning she gave almost everyone in the dining hall a colorful box of *konfekti* as a memento and then left on her little trip with the two girls.

And Joachim, how was he doing? Did he feel liberated, was his mind easier—or did his spirit suffer great privation when he saw one whole side of the table empty? And his uncharacteristic, rebellious impatience, including his threat to carry out a wild departure of his own if they kept on leading him around by the nose—did that have anything to do with Marusya's being gone? Or was the fact that he did not leave, at least for now, and instead lent an ear to the director's testimonials on the thaw, traceable to full-bosomed Marusya's not having departed for good, to her certain return after only five of the smallest units of local time? Ah, it was probably all true at once, and in equal measure. Hans Castorp could well imagine that was the case, without ever speaking to Joachim. For he refrained from mentioning anything about the matter, just as Joachim avoided the name of someone else who had departed for a while.

But meanwhile at Settembrini's table, who had recently taken the Italian's place?—amid Dutch guests whose appetites were so immense that they all ordered three extra fried eggs before starting on their soup at each five-course midday meal? It was Anton Karlovitch Ferge, the man who had gone through the hell of pleural shock. Yes, Herr Ferge was up and out of bed, his condition so improved, even without pneumothorax, that he spent most of the day dressed and walking about and appeared for meals with his bushy, good-natured moustache and his prominent Adam's apple that somehow seemed equally good-natured. The cousins chatted sometimes with him in the dining hall and lobby, and, as chance dictated, took constitutionals with him now and again, for they had a soft spot in their hearts for this simple martyr, who claimed to know nothing about higher things, but once that was settled, could chat easily about the manufacture of galoshes and the far reaches of the Russian Empire—Samara, Georgia, and such—while they trudged on through fog and slush.

The paths were really barely passable now, were simply melting away, and fogs brewed all around. To be sure, the director claimed it wasn't fog, only clouds; but that was merely verbal chicanery in Hans Castorp's opinion. Spring had to fight a difficult battle for months, all the way to June, with a hundred setbacks into bitterest winter. On sunny days in March, it got so hot out on the balcony that it was almost impossible to lie in a lounge chair, even with light clothes and a sunshade; and there were ladies who pretended it was already summer and appeared at first breakfast in muslin dresses. They could be excused to some extent, given

the peculiar nature of the climate up here, which encouraged confusion
by throwing the seasons into a meteorological jumble; but there was
also a great deal of shortsightedness and lack of imagination in their
impertinence—theirs was the foolishness of creatures of the moment,
incapable of thinking that things may change again, craving constant variety, and devouring time in their impatience. The date was March, it was
spring, that was practically summer, and you got out your muslin dresses
so that you could show them off before autumn came. Which it did, so
to speak. In April, a series of gloomy, chilly, damp days set in, with
steady showers that then turned to snow, flurries of new, wet snow.
Fingers grew numb as you lay on the balcony—both camel-hair blankets
had to be put back into service, and fur-lined sleeping bags were almost
required again; management decided to turn on the heat, and people
complained they had been cheated out of spring. By the end of the month,
everything lay under a heavy blanket of snow; but then foehn winds set
in—just as predicted by experienced, impressionable guests, who had
scented it in the air: Frau Stöhr, Fräulein Levi of the ivory complexion,
even the widow Hessenfeld—they were unanimous in claiming they felt
it before even the smallest cloud appeared above the granite peaks to the
south. Frau Hessenfeld tended to crying jags, Fräulein Levi took to her
bed, and Frau Stöhr, obstinately baring her rabbitlike teeth, announced
almost hourly her superstitious fear of a sudden hemorrhage, for it was
said foehn winds hastened and caused such things. It was now unbelievably
warm, the heat was turned off, people left balcony doors open at night
and it would still be fifty-seven degrees in their rooms the next morning;
the snow was melting fast—turned ice-gray, became porous and honey-
combed; great drifts of it sagged now, seemed to creep back into the earth.
Water seeped, trickled, dribbled everywhere—it dripped, then gushed in
the forests. The shoveled piles of snow along the streets and the pallid
carpets on the meadows disappeared, although the masses of white had
been far too thick to vanish quickly. And the strangest things could
happen—vernal surprises on a walk to the valley, things you had never
seen before, straight out of a fairy tale. Before you lay a wide meadow—
the snow-clad cone of Schwarzhorn towered in the background, the snow-
bound Scaletta Glacier just to its right, and even the wider terrain, with
its hayshed hidden somewhere, still lay under a cover of snow, though it
was thin and sparse now, interrupted here and there by rough, dark
mounds of earth, with tufts of dry grasses sticking up everywhere. But
that meadow there, the cousins noticed—what a peculiar sort of snow-
cover it had: thicker farther back up near the wooded slope, but nearer
in the foreground, where the grass was discolored and ravaged by winter,

there was only a sprinkling of snow, like polka dots, like little flowers. They took a closer look, bent down in astonishment—that wasn't snow, those were flowers, snowdrops, blossoming snow, no doubt of it, little chalices on short stems, white or whitish-blue, a kind of crocus, millions of them, growing so thick you could easily have taken them for snow, into which they blended indiscernibly.

They laughed at their mistake, laughed for joy at the miracle before their eyes, this charming mimicry of snow by organic life hesitantly finding its way back into the world. They picked a few, examined them, studied their delicate chalices, made boutonnieres of them, wore them home, put them in water glasses in their rooms—for the valley's inorganic paralysis had lasted a long, long time, despite its diversions.

But the snow flowers were soon covered again by real snow, and the same thing happened to the blue soldanella and the red cowslips that had next appeared. Yes, what a very difficult time spring had making any headway in its conquest of winter. It was thrown back ten times before it finally gained a toehold up here—until the next burst of winter, with white flurries, icy winds, and warm radiators. At the beginning of May (for May arrived while we were talking about snowdrops), it was absolute torment to sit out on the balcony and try to write a postcard to the plains, your fingers aching from the raw November damp; and the half-dozen hardwoods in the valley were as bare as flatland trees in January. The rain went on for days, it poured one whole week, and without the compensations of the lounge chair it would have been very hard to spend so many hours reclining out there, your face numbed and wet from the damp murk of clouds. But ultimately, it proved to be a clandestine spring rain, and more and more, the longer it lasted, disclosed itself as such. Almost all the snow melted away beneath it; there was no white left, only patches of dirty ice-gray here and there, and now the meadows truly began to turn green.

What a comforting sight those green meadows were after an infinity of white. And another green appeared as well, its delicate, tender softness far exceeding the green of new grass—young clusters of needles on the larches. When taking his constitutionals, Hans Castorp could not help caressing them and brushing them against his cheek—their softness and freshness were so irresistibly enchanting. "It's enough to make a botanist of you," the young man said to his companion. "A man could really and truly decide to become a scientist from the pure joy of watching nature reawaken after one of our winters up here. That's gentian you see there on that slope, my man, and right there is a kind of little yellow violet I don't recognize. But here we have buttercups, no different from the ones down below, from the family Ranunculaceae, a compound flower, as I recall, an especially charming plant, bisexual, you can see the great number of stamens and several pistils, the androecium and gynoecium, if I remember correctly. I really think I shall add some botanical tomes to my collection, just to become somewhat better informed about this part of life, this realm of knowledge. Yes, just look at the world's colorful variety."

"It gets even better in June," Joachim said. "The valley's famous for its wildflowers. But I don't think I'll wait for them. Your wanting to study botany—picked that up from Krokowski, did you?"

Krokowski? What did he mean? Oh, that's where he got it—because Dr. Krokowski had recently been carrying on botanically in his lectures. (It would be quite a mistake, in fact, to assume that just because time had brought forth so many changes, Dr. Krokowski was no longer giving his lectures.) Dressed in his frock coat—though no longer in sandals, which he wore only in summer and so would soon be wearing again—he delivered them, as before, every two weeks, every second Monday in the dining hall, just as on that day when Hans Castorp, early in his stay, had arrived late, splattered with blood. The psychoanalyst had spoken for nine months about love and illness—never too much at once, always in small portions, little talks of half or three-quarters of an hour, in which he displayed the treasures of his knowledge and thought; and everyone was under the impression that he would never have to stop, that it would go on like this forever. It was kind of a biweekly *Thousand and One Nights* spun out at random, and, like Scheherazade's stories for a curious prince, each lecture was calculated to please its audience and prevent acts of violence. In its very boundlessness, Dr. Krokowski's theme recalled an enterprise to which Settembrini was devoting his labor, the encyclopedia of suffering; and like that project, it proved equally rich in its applications—as witnessed by the lecturer's recent digression into botany, or more precisely, fungi. He had, by the way, changed his topic somewhat perhaps—it was now more a discussion of love and *death*, which led to numerous reflections of a half poetic, half ruthlessly scientific nature. And it was in this context that the scholar had come around to speak—in his drawling East European accent with its *r* produced by a single tap of the tongue—of botany, or better, of mushrooms: those rank, fantastic creatures from life's twilight world, fleshly by nature, so similar to animal life that products of animal metabolism, proteins and glycogen, an animal carbohydrate, were found in their chemical makeup. And Dr. Krokowski had spoken about one fungus, famous since classical antiquity for its form and the powers ascribed to it—a morel, its Latin name ending in the adjective *impudicus*, its form reminiscent of love, and its odor, of death. For the stench given off by the *impudicus* was strikingly like that of a decaying corpse, the odor coming from a greenish, viscous slime that carried its spores and dripped from the bell-shaped cap. And even today, among the uneducated, this morel was thought to be an aphrodisiac.

Well, that had been a little much for the ladies, declared Prosecutor Paravant—who was managing to survive the thaw with the moral assistance of the director's propaganda. And even Frau Stöhr, who as a woman of principle had likewise held her ground and met head-on every temptation to make her own wild departure, had remarked to her tablemates that Krokowski had really been rather "obscure" today with his classical mushroom. The unfortunate woman actually said "obscure"—disgracing her illness with her unspeakable malapropisms.

What Hans Castorp found amazing, however, was that Joachim would refer at all to Dr. Krokowski's botany, for they spoke as little of the psychoanalyst as they did of Clavdia Chauchat or Marusya—they never alluded to him, passing over his ways and works in silence. But now suddenly Joachim had mentioned the assistant by name—in an ill-tempered tone of voice, just as his remark that he would not be waiting for the wildflowers to bloom had sounded quite ill-tempered, too. Dear old Joachim—of late he appeared to be close to losing his equilibrium. There was an edgy quaver to his voice whenever he spoke, and he was not at all his old gentle, prudent self. Was it orange-blossom perfume that he lacked? Was their teasing him with Gaffky numbers driving him to despair? Could he not resolve in his own mind whether to stay here until autumn or to depart on a fraudulent basis?

In reality, it was something entirely different that brought the edginess to Joachim's voice and made him mention the recent lecture on botany in such a sarcastic tone. Hans Castorp knew nothing at all about it—or rather, he did not know that Joachim knew; for as a man who had kicked over the traces, as a pedagogic problem child of life, he himself knew what that something was only too well. In a word, Joachim was onto his cousin's tricks, he had accidentally eavesdropped on an act of betrayal, much like the one Hans Castorp had committed on the evening of Mardi Gras—a new treachery, exacerbated by the indisputable fact that it had become a habit with him.

One part of the eternal monotony of time's rhythm, of the diverting, standard segmentation of the normal day, which was always the same, to the point where each day was so confusingly like, so identical with, the next that it could be taken for it, a fixed eternity that made it hard to understand how time could ever bring forth changes—one part of the undeviating schedule (as our readers will recall) was that Dr. Krokowski made his rounds every day between half past three and four o'clock, moving from room to room, or rather balcony to balcony, lounge chair to lounge chair. And the Berghof day had itself come round many times now since that day when Hans Castorp, lying there in his horizontal position, had felt hurt because the assistant had made a detour around his room, leaving him to his own devices. The visitor in August had long ago become a comrade—Dr. Krokowski frequently called him that when he stopped to check on him, and although, as Hans Castorp remarked to Joachim, that military word, with its exotic *r*, a single palatalized tap of the tongue, sounded dreadful coming from the assistant, it did not fit all that badly with his rugged, virile, jovial manner, which both demanded your cheerful trust and yet at the same time had its dubious side, since it was always contradicted somehow by his black pallor.

"Well, comrade, how's it going, how's it coming?" Dr. Krokowski said, arriving from the Russian barbarians' balcony and stepping up to the head of Hans Castorp's lounge chair; and as on every other day, the patient lying there with his hands folded across his chest smiled up in amiable vexation at the ghastly word "comrade" and gazed at the doctor's yellow teeth revealed beneath his black beard. "Had a fine rest, did we?" Dr. Krokowski continued. "Fever chart on the decline or on the rise today? Well, doesn't mean much—it'll be fine by your wedding day. My regards." And with that farewell, which likewise sounded ghastly, since he pronounced it like "d'gods," he would move on, heading for Joachim's balcony. These were merely his rounds, no more than a quick check on things.

Sometimes, to be sure, Dr. Krokowski might stay a little longer, standing there broad-shouldered, smiling his manly smile, chatting with his "comrade" about this and that—the weather, departures and arrivals, the patient's general mood, good or bad, and about his personal affairs, too, his home, his prospects—until he would finally say, "My d'gods," and move on. Hans Castorp, hands clasped behind his head for a change, would respond with a smile of his own to all the questions—with a pervasive sense of revulsion, to be sure, but with a ready answer to everything. They would lower their voices to chat, and although the glass partition did not completely separate the balconies, Joachim next door could not make out what they were saying—did not even try for that matter. He would hear his cousin get up from his lounge chair and walk back into the room with Dr. Krokowski, presumably to show him his fever chart; and then the conversation might continue a while longer, to judge from the delay before the assistant appeared at Joachim's door by way of the hall.

And what were these comrades chatting about? Joachim did not ask; but if one of us chose not to follow his example and posed the question, then, by way of general observation, it might very well be noted that considerable material was available for an intellectual exchange between such men and comrades, both of whose basic perspectives bore an idealistic stamp—one of them having educated himself to believe that matter is the spirit's Original Sin, a nasty rank growth in response to a stimulus, whereas the other, as a doctor, was accustomed to teaching that organic illness was a secondary phenomenon. Yes, we might note that there was much to discuss and share: about matter as a disreputable degeneration of the immaterial, about life as an impudency of matter, about illness as life's lascivious form. With the ongoing series of lectures as a basis, the conversation could then have moved from love as a force conducive to illness, to the nonphysical nature of its indications, to "old" and "new" areas, to soluble toxins and love potions, to light piercing the dark subconscious, to the blessings of psychoanalysis and the transference of symptoms—but then what do *we* know, since for us this is all merely guesswork, a hypothetical answer to the question about the subject of the chats between Dr. Krokowski and young Hans Castorp.

Moreover, they no longer chatted—that was all over, it had lasted only a brief while, a few weeks. More recently, Dr. Krokowski treated this patient no differently from the way he treated all others. On his rounds, he generally confined himself to "Well, comrade?" and "My d'gods." But Joachim had made a discovery—of the aforementioned act he considered a betrayal on Hans Castorp's part. Although it should be said that, as a military innocent, he made it quite accidentally, without resorting to any sort of spying. He had simply been summoned one Wednesday morning, in the middle of his first rest cure, to be weighed by the bath attendant in the basement—and that was when it happened. He was coming down the stairs, with their tidy linoleum steps and a view to the door of the general consulting room, which stood between the two X-ray rooms— the organic one on the left, and around the corner on the right, two steps lower, the psychoanalytical one, with Dr. Krokowski's visiting card on the door. Halfway down the stairs, Joachim stopped in his tracks when he saw Hans Castorp suddenly emerge from the consulting room where he had just been given his injection. Quickly closing the door with both hands and without looking around, Hans Castorp turned now to the right, toward the door with the thumbtacked calling card; with a kind of forward rocking motion, he reached it in a few soundless strides. He knocked, bending forward and holding his ear next to his rapping fingers. And then Joachim heard the word "Enter!" in the resounding baritone of the occupant, with that exotic, tapped *r* sound and a diphthongized distortion of the vowel—and saw his cousin vanish into the twilight of Dr. Krokowski's analytical pit.

Someone Else

Long days, the longest, in terms of hours of sunlight—objectively speaking, that is, since their astronomical length has nothing whatever to do with whether they seem to pass swiftly or can divert us. The vernal equinox now lay three months in the past, the summer solstice had arrived. But the natural year followed the calendar only very reticently up here; only now, within the last few days, had spring definitely arrived, a spring without any hint of summer's oppressiveness—with spicy, light, thin air, with a radiant, silvery-blue sky and blossoming meadows as colorful as a child's paint box.

Hans Castorp found the slopes full of flowers, the same ones that had just been ending their bloom when Joachim had gathered a few to put in his room as a friendly greeting—yarrow and bluebells. It was a sign that the year was coming full circle. But along with new emerald-green grass, what a wealth of organic life had now emerged from the soil on the slopes and wide meadows—stars, chalices, bells, and whimsies that filled the sun-drenched air with subtle fragrances: great masses of Alpine campion and wild pansies, daisies, marguerites, cowslips in red and yellow—much larger and more beautiful than any Hans Castorp remembered seeing in the flatlands, that is, to the extent that he had ever paid attention to them—plus nodding soldanella, little ciliated bells of blue, purple, and pink, a specialty of the region.

He gathered up these delights, brought bouquets home, but for serious purposes—less to decorate his room than to follow through on his plan and study them with a strictly scientific eye. He had bought some paraphernalia for his project: a book on general botany, a handy trowel for digging up plants, a herbarium, a powerful magnifying glass; and the young man went to work on his balcony, dressed for summer again now, in one of the suits he had brought with him at the very start—this, too, another token that the year had come full circle.

Fresh flowers stood in several water glasses on various surfaces provided by the furniture in his room, even on the little lamp table next to his splendid lounge chair. Half-faded flowers, wilting but not yet dry, were strewn across the balcony floor and scattered along the railing; others had already been carefully spread out between sheets of blotting paper that absorbed their moisture and were weighted down with stones, so that once the specimens were dry, Hans Castorp could paste them in his album with strips of gummed paper. There he lay, his knees pulled up, one leg crossed over the other, his field guide facedown on his chest, the spine forming a little gable; he held the thick beveled circle of his magnifying glass up to his ordinary blue eyes and examined a blossom, whose corolla he had partly removed with his pocketknife so that he could study its receptacle, which now swelled to a bizarre fleshy structure under the powerful lens. The anthers on the tips of filaments spilled their yellow pollen, the pitted pistil stood up rigid from the ovary, and if you cut through it, you could see the delicate channel down which a sugary excretion flushed grains and bags of pollen into the receptacle itself. Hans Castorp counted, probed, and compared; he investigated the structure and placement of sepals and petals, of male and female sex organs, compared them to diagrams and illustrations, determined to his satisfaction that the structures of plants he knew were scientifically correct, and then proceeded to those whose names he did not know, identifying them with his Linnaeus according to class, cohort, order, family, genus, and species. With so much time on his hands, he put comparative morphology to work and made considerable progress in botanical taxonomy. Under each of the dried plants in his herbarium, he wrote in a fine calligraphic hand the Latin names humanistic science had gallantly bestowed upon them, plus a list of their distinguishing characteristics. He showed this to good Joachim, who was quite amazed.

In the evening he would study the stars. He became fascinated by the passing year—although he had watched some twenty summers pass on earth without ever having been concerned about it before. We automatically used a term like "vernal equinox," because we knew that when we came to this topic, such terminology would reflect Hans Castorp's own thinking. For of late he had developed a fondness for tossing around such nomenclature, and his cousin was amazed by his knowledge of this subject as well.

"The sun will very soon enter Cancer," he might remark while they were out on a walk. "Do you understand what that means? It's the first summer sign of the zodiac, you see. And then the sun moves on through Leo and Virgo to the point where autumn begins, at the equinox toward the end of September, when the sun passes across the celestial equator, just as it did recently in March, when it entered Aries."

"I must have missed that," Joachim said peevishly. "What are you rattling on about? Entered Aries—and that's part of the zodiac?"

"Quite right, the zodiac. The ancient heavenly signs—Scorpio, Sagitta-rius, Capricorn, Aquarius, and all the rest—how can someone not be interested in it? There are twelve of them, you should at least know that much, three for each season, ascending and descending, a circle of constellations through which the sun moves—it's all so splendid! Imagine, they found it painted on the ceiling of an Egyptian temple—a temple of Aphrodite, by the way—not far from Thebes. The Chaldeans already knew about it, too—the Chaldeans, if you please, that ancient tribe of Semitic or Arabic magicians, highly trained astrologists and diviners. They had already studied the celestial zone in which the planets move, dividing it into twelve constellations or signs, the *dodecatemoria*, which have come down to us. Now that's splendid! That's humanity!"

"And now you're starting in on 'humanity,' just like Settembrini."

"Yes, like him—or not quite like him, either. You have to take human-ity as it is, but it's still splendid. I like to think back to the Chaldeans when I'm lying there watching the planets, the ones they already knew about, because they didn't know them all, clever as they were. But I can't see the ones they didn't know, either. Uranus was only recently discovered through a telescope, about a hundred and twenty years ago."

"Recently?"

"I'd call it 'recently' in comparison to the previous three thousand years, if you please. But when I'm lying there and watching the planets, then those last three thousand years seem fairly 'recent' themselves, and somehow I feel very intimate with those Chaldeans, who watched them, too, and wrote poetry about them—and that's what humanity means."

"Well, that's nice. You certainly have some grand ideas in your head."

"You call them 'grand' and I call them 'intimate'—what they're called doesn't make any difference. But when the sun enters Libra, about three months from now, then the length of the days will have decreased until day and night are equal, and will continue to decrease until around Christ-mas—you know all that. But, please consider this: that while the sun moves through the winter signs—Capricorn, Aquarius, and Pisces—the length of the days is increasing again. And then we come back to the point where spring begins, for the three thousandth time since the Chal-deans, and the days go on lengthening until the year comes round again and summer begins."

"That's obvious enough."

"No, it's all smoke and mirrors! The days get longer during winter, and when we get to the longest one, the twenty-first of June, the beginning of summer, they start getting shorter again and it all heads right back downhill toward winter. You call it obvious, but once you disregard the obvious part, it can momentarily set you into a panic, make you want to grab something to hold on to. It's really like some great practical joke, so that the beginning of winter is actually spring, and the beginning of summer is actually autumn. It's as if we're being led around by the nose, in a circle, always lured on by the promise of something that is just another turning point—a turning point in a circle. For a circle consists of nothing but elastic turning points, and so its curvature is immeasurable, with no steady, definite direction, and so eternity is not 'straight ahead, straight ahead,' but rather 'merry-go-round.' "

"Stop!"

"Midsummer Night!" Hans Castorp said. "Midsummer Night celebrations, with fires and dances around the leaping flames, everyone joining hands. I've never seen it, but I've heard that's how primitive tribes do it, celebrating the first night of summer, which is actually the beginning of autumn—the year's high noon, its zenith, and it's all downhill from there. They dance and whirl and cheer. And what are these primitives cheering about—can you explain that to me? Why are they so boisterous and merry? Because they are now headed back down into the dark, maybe? Or is it because things have gone uphill until now, and the turning point has come, the slippery turning point, Midsummer Night? Is it melancholy mirth at the high-point? I'm just describing it as I see it, in the words that come to mind. Melancholy mirth and mirthful melancholy—that's the reason why those primitives are cheering and dancing around the flames. They do it out of constructive despair, if you want to put it that way, in honor of the practical joke of the circle, of eternity that has no permanent direction, but in which everything keeps coming back."

"I don't want to put it that way," Joachim muttered, "please don't lay the blame on me. Those are awfully grand notions you're playing with when you're lying there of an evening."

"Yes, I won't deny it—you keep yourself busy with more practical matters, with your Russian grammar. You should soon be fluent, my man, and that can only be to your great advantage—if there should be a war, which God forbid."

"Forbid? You're talking like a civilian. War is necessary. Without war the world would soon go to rot, as Moltke said."

"Yes, it has that tendency. I'll grant you that much," Hans Castorp added, intending to return to the Chaldeans, who had also waged war and conquered Babylon, although they were Semites, and so practically Jews—when both of them at the same time noticed two gentlemen just ahead, who had heard them talking and interrupted their conversation now to turn and look back.

They were on the main street between the Kurhaus and the Hotel Belvedere, on the way back to Davos-Dorf. The valley was dressed in its Sunday best, in delicate, soft, and cheerful colors. The air was delightful—pure, dry, clear, sun-drenched, filled with a symphony of blithe wildflower fragrances.

They realized that it was Lodovico Settembrini at the side of a stranger, but it appeared that he did not recognize them or at least did not want to encounter them, because he quickly turned his head away and dived back into the conversation with his companion, gesticulating and at the same time trying to move quickly on ahead of them. But when the cousins caught up with him on the right and greeted him with friendly bows, he pretended to be pleasantly surprised, exclaimed, "*Sapristi!*" and "Damned if it isn't!" but then held back as if to let the two of them pass and move on ahead; they, however, did not understand what he wanted—or better, simply paid no attention since they did not see the point. Genuinely pleased to see him after what had been a rather long separation, they stopped and shook his hand, asked how he was doing and glanced at his companion, expecting to be introduced. And so they forced him to do something he evidently preferred not to do, whereas to them it seemed the most natural and logical thing in the world: to make formal introductions—which Settembrini now did, with obligatory gestures and good-natured phrases, but so that they all had to shake hands across his chest as they half stood there, half kept moving.

It turned out that the stranger, who was about Settembrini's age, lived in the same house with him. He was the other person to whom Lukaček, the ladies' tailor, had sublet rooms. His name, as nearly as the young men could make out, was Naphta. He was a small, skinny, clean-shaven man, and so ugly—caustically, one could almost say corrosively, ugly—that the cousins were astonished. Somehow everything about him was caustic: the aquiline nose dominating the face; the small, pursed mouth; the pale gray eyes behind thick lenses in the light frames of his glasses; even his studied silence, from which it was clear that his words would be caustic and logical. As was the custom here, he wore neither hat nor overcoat, but he was very well dressed: his suit was dark blue flannel with white pinstripes, its cut elegant, understated, stylish—which did not escape the scrutiny of the cousins' sophisticated eyes, though their gaze was immediately countered by an even sharper, more caustic inspection of their persons. If Lodovico Settembrini had not known how to wear his threadbare petersham and checked trousers with such grace and dignity, the figure he cut in this fine company would not have been to his advantage. But such was not the case, particularly since his checked trousers had been freshly pressed, so that at first glance you might have thought them new—doubtless the work of his landlord, the young men thought in passing. But although in terms of expensive, sophisticated clothes, ugly Herr Naphta had one thing in common with the cousins, it was more than just his advanced years that allied him with his neighbor in contrast to the younger men; there was definitely something else, too, which might best be attributed to the matter of complexion—that is, one pair was either tanned or sunburnt, whereas the other two were pale. Over the course of the winter, Joachim's face had turned an even deeper bronze, and Hans Castorp's face glowed pink under his blond hair. Herr Settembrini's exotic pallor, however, which looked quite refined against his black moustache, had been left totally unaffected by the sun's rays; and his companion, although a blond—with metallic, colorless, ash-blond hair that he combed straight back from his receding forehead—likewise had the dull white skin characteristic of some darker races. Two of the four were carrying walking sticks—Hans Castorp and Settembrini; as a military man, Joachim never bothered with a cane, and after the introductory handshakes, Naphta immediately crossed his hands behind his back. They were small, dainty hands, just as his feet were dainty, too—but all in proper proportion to the rest of his body. He had a cold, but no one paid any attention to his feeble and not very wholesome coughs.

Settembrini had at once elegantly overcome any trace of the embarrassment or annoyance he had shown upon first seeing the young men. He seemed in the best of moods and wittily helped all three get better acquainted—calling Naphta a *"princeps scholasticorum,"* for example. Mirth, he claimed, quoting Aretino, "held brilliant court in the hall of his breast" today—and that was the work of spring, a spring that he could only praise. As the gentlemen knew, he harbored considerable ill will against the world up here, had surely disparaged it often enough. Yet one must give the Alpine spring its due—for the moment, spring was atoning for all the horrors of the region. There was none of the confusion and provocation of spring down on the plains—no seething in the depths, no damp odors, no sultry vapors. And instead—clarity, serenity, a dry, austere charm. It was all to his taste, it was superb!

They walked four abreast in a ragged row, as much as possible, but when they passed people coming from the opposite direction, Settembrini, on the right flank, was forced to step out into the road; or the line would be broken up when someone else temporarily dropped back and yielded the right-of-way—Naphta, for instance, on the left, or Hans Castorp, who had been walking between the humanist and Joachim. Naphta laughed in short bursts muted by his cold, and his voice sounded like a piece of cracked porcelain when you rap it with a knuckle.

Tilting his head to point at the Italian, he said with a drawl, "Just listen to our rationalist here, our Voltairian. He's praising nature because even in her fertile phase she does not confuse us with mystic damps, but provides classical austerity. And yet, what is the Latin word for moisture?"

"*Humor*," Settembrini cried back over his left shoulder, "and the humor in our professor's observations about nature can be found in the fact that, like Saint Catherine of Siena, he sees the wounds of Christ in the markings of a red cowslip."

Naphta countered, "That would be more witty than humorous. But 'tis said we must bring our spirits to bear upon nature. And she sorely needs it."

"Nature," Settembrini said, lowering his voice and no longer speaking over his shoulder but merely looking down at it, "certainly has no need of your spirit. It is itself spirit."

"Doesn't your monism bore you?"

"Ah, so you admit that it is solely for the sake of your own amusement that you divide the world into two hostile camps, sundering God and nature."

"I find it interesting you would use the term 'amusement' for what I have in mind when I speak of Spirit and the Passion."

"To think that someone like you, who uses such grand words for such shameless purposes, can accuse me of demagoguery."

"And so you still believe that Spirit is shameless, do you? But it cannot help being what it is: dualistic. Antithesis, dualism—that is the motivating, passionate, dialectical, spiritual principle. To see the world divided into hostile camps, that is Spirit. All monism is boring. *Solet Aristoteles quaerere pugnam.*"

"Aristotle? Aristotle shifted the reality of universal ideas to the individual. And that is pantheism."

"False. If you posit substantial character in the individual, that is, if you transfer the essence of things from the universal to the particular, as Thomas and Bonaventura did, being true Aristotelians, you have then removed the world from its unity with the highest idea, it becomes something outside God, and so God becomes transcendent. That is classic medievalism, my dear sir."

" 'Classic medievalism,' now isn't that a delicious phrase."

"I beg your pardon, but I grant the term 'classic' its place where it is applicable, that is, whenever an idea has achieved its apogee. Antiquity was not always classic. I have observed an aversion on your part to . . . to the absolute, to the broader application of categories. You do not want Spirit to be an absolute. You want Spirit to be democratic progress."

"I hope we are agreed in our conviction that Spirit, however absolute it may be, can never become the advocate of reactionary forces."

"Nevertheless, it is always the advocate of freedom."

"Nevertheless? Freedom is the law of brotherly love, not of nihilism and malice."

"Both of which you apparently fear."

Settembrini flung an arm in the air. The skirmish broke off. Joachim looked in bewilderment from one to the other, and Hans Castorp raised his eyebrows and gazed down at his path. Naphta's words had been caustic, apodictic—even though it was he who had defended a larger definition of freedom. Particularly unpleasant was the way he contradicted you with his "False!"—thrusting his lips forward at the final *s* and then closing them to a pucker. Settembrini had countered him in jaunty fashion for the most part, but had also added considerable warmth to his remarks, whenever he exhorted his opponent to agreement on certain fundamental points, for instance. But now that Naphta had fallen silent, the Italian began to provide the cousins with explanations of who this stranger was— explanations he assumed they might very well need in the wake of his debate with Naphta. And the latter let him proceed and paid little attention. He was professor of classical languages for advanced students at the Fridericianum, Settembrini declared, emphasizing the title of the introductee with great pomposity, the way Italians do. Naphta's fate was much the same as his, Settembrini's, own. His health had brought him up here five years before, and having discovered that his stay would be a long one, he had left the sanatorium and taken private lodgings with Lukaček, the ladies' tailor. A brilliant Latinist—having been educated in a school run by a religious order, as he put it rather vaguely—he had very wisely secured himself a position as an instructor at the local secondary school, and did great credit to that institution. In brief, Settembrini did not stint in his praise of ugly Herr Naphta, despite the rather abstract argument they had just had—a dispute that would very soon be taken up again.

Settembrini now went on to offer Herr Naphta some information about the cousins, from which it became apparent that he had previously told him about these young men. This, then, was the young engineer who had come to visit for three weeks, only to have Director Behrens discover a moist spot; and this young hope of the Prussian military was Lieutenant Ziemssen. And he spoke of Joachim's general disgust and plans to depart—and made sure to add that one would doubtless be doing the engineer a disservice if one did not ascribe to him the same impatience to return to his work.

Naphta made a wry face and said, "The gentlemen have an eloquent advocate. Far be it from me to doubt that he has aptly interpreted your thoughts and wishes. Work, work—beg your pardon, but he is about to chide me as an enemy of mankind, an *inimicus humanae naturae*, for daring to recall a time when his fanfare to labor would not have achieved its accustomed effect—a time, that is, when the opposite of his ideal was held in incomparably higher esteem. Bernard of Clairvaux, for instance, taught about a ladder of perfection unlike anything Herr Lodovico has ever conceived in his wildest dreams. Would you like to hear about it? His lowest rung was found at the 'treadmill,' the second in the 'plowed field,' the third and most praiseworthy, however—now don't listen to this part, Settembrini—was 'a bed of rest.' The treadmill is the symbol of life in the world—not badly chosen, I must say. The plowed field represents the soul of worldly man, where preachers and spiritual teachers labor—already a more honorable level. The bed, however—"

"Enough! We know!" Settembrini cried. "Gentlemen, he will now describe for you the purpose and use of the libertine's couch."

"I did not know you were such a prude, Lodovico. After all, I've seen you wink at the girls. Where's your pagan open-mindedness? The bed, then, is the place where lover and beloved cohabit, a symbol of contemplative retreat from the world and its creatures for the purpose of cohabitation with God."

"Phooey! *Andate, andate!*" the Italian demurred, almost in a whimper. Everyone laughed. But then Settembrini continued with dignity, "Ah, no, I am a European, an Occidental. Your ladder is pure Orient. The East despises action. Lao-tzu teaches that doing nothing is more beneficial than anything between heaven and earth, that if humankind were to stop all activity, perfect peace and happiness would reign on earth. There's cohabitation for you."

"You don't say. And Western mysticism? And quietism? Among whose adherents one may include Fénelon, who taught that every act is flawed, since the will to act is an affront to God, who alone can will to act. I need only mention Molinos's propositions. It seems to me that the spiritual possibility of finding salvation in repose is widespread throughout all mankind."

At this point Hans Castorp spoke up, breaking into their conversation with the courage of simple souls. He stared into space and declared, "Contemplation, retreat—there's something to it, sounds quite plausible. One could say that we live at a rather high level of retreat from the world up here. At five thousand feet, we recline in our lounge chairs—and remarkably comfortable they are—and look down on the world and its creatures and think things over. To tell the truth, now that I stop and think about it, my bed—and by that I mean my lounge chair, you understand—has proved very beneficial over the last ten months, made me think more about things than I ever did in all my years down in the flatlands, I can't deny that."

Settembrini gazed at him with mournful, flashing black eyes. "My good engineer," he said in a choked voice, "my good engineer." And he grabbed Hans Castorp by the arm and pulled him back a little from the others, as if he had some private advice to give him behind their backs. "How often have I told you that a man must know who he is and think thoughts befitting him. A man of the West, despite all other propositions, has only one concern: reason, analysis, deeds, progress—not the idle couch of a monk!"

Naphta had been listening. He looked back and said, "Monks! We have monks to thank for what culture there is on European soil. We have them to thank that Germany, France, and Italy aren't covered with primeval forests and swamps, but provide us with grain, fruit, and wine. Monks, my dear sir, certainly performed hard work."

"*Ebbè*—so you see!"

"Please hear me out. The work of the religious orders was not an end in itself, that is, a narcotic. Nor was its purpose to improve the world or achieve commercial advantage. It was a purely ascetic exercise, a part of the discipline of penitence, a means of salvation. It afforded protection against the flesh, served to mortify the senses. Such work—permit me to point out—was of a totally asocial nature. It was pure, unadulterated religious egoism."

"I'm much obliged to you for the explanation and am happy to see that the blessings of labor can stand the test, even against the will of man."

"Against his intention, yes indeed. What we observe here is nothing less than the difference between what is utilitarian and what is humane."

"What I observe, with some annoyance, is that you are once again dividing the world in two."

"I regret having aroused your displeasure, but one must differentiate and systematize things in order that the idea of the *homo Dei* may be kept free of all impurities. You Italians invented money changing and banking—may God forgive you. But the English invented economic social theory, and humanity's guardian angel will never forgive them that."

"Ah, but that same guardian angel was alive and working among the great economists of that island. You wanted to say something, my good engineer?"

Hans Castorp denied that he did, but then said something after all— and both Naphta and Settembrini listened in some suspense. "You must look favorably, then, on my cousin's profession, Herr Naphta, and sympathize with his impatience to take it up. I am a thorough civilian myself, my cousin often reproaches me for it. I've never even done military service, am an out-and-out child of peace, and sometimes I've even thought that I might very easily have become a clergyman—as I've mentioned on various occasions, just ask my cousin. But disregarding my own personal preferences—though perhaps, strictly speaking, I needn't disregard them so entirely—I have a great deal of sympathy and affinity for the military life. There is something devilishly earnest about it all, something 'ascetic,' if you will—that was, I believe, the term you were kind enough to use just now—and one must always reckon that one will have to deal with death, just as, ultimately, the clergy must deal with it as well—with what else, really? That is where soldiers get their *bienséance*, and their idea of rank and obedience to authority and Spanish sense of honor, if I may put it that way. And it really doesn't matter much whether one is wearing a stiff uniform collar or a starched ruff, the end result is the same, an 'ascetic' result, as you put it so splendidly just now. I don't know whether I've succeeded in making my train of thought . . ."

"Oh, yes indeed," Naphta said, with a glance at Settembrini, who was twirling his cane and gazing at the sky.

"And that's why, I presume," Hans Castorp went on, "you must feel some sympathy for my cousin Ziemssen's inclinations, given what you just said yourself. I'm not thinking here of 'church and king' or whatever other phrases people—perfectly well-meaning people, who simply like their world kept in good order—may sometimes come up with to justify the association between the two. No, what I mean is that the work of the professional soldier, that is, his military service—and it *is* called service—is done for no commercial advantage whatever and has no relation to any 'economic social theory,' as you call it, which is why the English have so few soldiers, a couple for India and a couple for parades at home—"

"There is no point in your going on, my good engineer," Settembrini interrupted. "From an intellectual standpoint, the soldier's life is simply not worth discussing—and I say this without wanting to do the lieutenant any disservice—because it is a life of pure form, without any content whatever. Your standard soldier is the mercenary who can be hired for one cause or another. In brief, soldiers fought for the Spanish Counter-Reformation, for Napoleon, for Garibaldi—and now we have Prussian soldiers. I shall be quite willing to talk about soldiers when I find out what it is they're fighting *for*."

"The simple fact that they *do* fight," Naphta retorted, "remains an obvious characteristic of the profession, on that much we can agree. Possibly that does not suffice to make it 'worth discussing from an intellectual standpoint,' but it does remove them to a sphere beyond the ken of any bourgeois affirmation of life."

"What you like to call the 'bourgeois affirmation of life,' " Herr Settembrini replied—setting the corners of his mouth in a taut line under the sweep of his moustache, so that only the front of his lips moved, and screwing his neck up out of his collar at an odd backward slant— "will always be found ready to advocate ideals of reason and morality and to impress them on young, wavering minds by whatever means available."

Silence ensued. The young men stared straight ahead in embarrassment. After they had walked a few more steps, Settembrini returned his neck to a more natural position and said, "You should not be amazed that this gentleman and I argue frequently—it is done in a spirit of friendship and on the basis of previous understandings."

That helped—it was chivalrous and humane of Herr Settembrini. But Joachim, likewise harboring the best of intentions and hoping to move their conversation harmlessly along, spoke up now—yet it sounded almost as if he did so under some pressure or duress, against his will, as it were. "It so happens my cousin and I were talking about war just now as we came up behind you."

"I heard," Naphta said. "I caught a bit of it and looked around. Were you talking politics? Discussing the situation in the world?"

"Oh, no," Hans Castorp said with a laugh. "That's hardly a topic for us. My cousin's profession makes it quite inappropriate for him to concern himself with politics, and I voluntarily forgo the pleasure—don't understand a thing about it. I've never once glanced at a newspaper since I've been here."

As on a previous occasion, Settembrini found this reprehensible; he at once proved to be very well informed about major current events—and approved of what was happening, since things were taking a course favorable to civilization. The general European atmosphere was imbued with ideas of peace and plans for disarmament. Democratic ideals were on the march. He claimed to have confidential information that the Young Turks had just completed preparations for their revolutionary uprising. Turkey as a constitutional nation-state—what a triumph for humanity!

"The liberalization of Islam," Naphta scoffed. "Excellent. Enlightened fanaticism—how fine. The matter is of some concern to you, by the way," he said, turning to Joachim. "If Abdul Hamid falls, that's the end of your influence in Turkey, and England will set itself up as protector. You should take our Settembrini's contacts and information very seriously," he said to both cousins; and this, too, sounded impertinent, as if he thought them uninclined to do so. "He knows what's what when it comes to national revolutions. His friends at home have good ties to the English Balkan Committee. But what becomes of the 'Reval program,' Lodovico, if your progressives meet with success? Edward the Seventh will no longer be able to allow the Russians an exit through the Dardanelles; and if Austria manages somehow to pull herself together for a more active policy in the Balkans, then . . ."

"You and your visions of catastrophe!" Settembrini parried. "Nicholas loves peace. We have him to thank for the Hague Conventions, superior moral realities that will abide."

"Correct—Russia needed to catch her breath after that little mishap in the Far East."

"Shame, shame, my dear sir. You should not mock humankind's longing for social perfection. Any nation that thwarts such endeavors will undoubtedly find itself the object of moral ostracism."

"What good would politics be, if it didn't give everyone the opportunity to make moral compromises."

"You are an advocate of Pan-Germanism, then, are you?"

Naphta shrugged shoulders that stood unevenly. He was not only ugly, he was also slightly hunchbacked. He disdained to answer.

Settembrini rendered his opinion: "What you've said is, in any case, cynical. You are determined to interpret democracy's noble endeavors to assert itself internationally as mere political cunning."

"You want me to see such efforts as idealism or even some sort of religiosity, is that it? They are nothing but the last, feeble twitches of what little instinct for self-preservation a doomed international system still has. The catastrophe will, indeed must, follow—is coming toward us from all directions, in all guises. Take British policy. England's need to secure buffer states around India is legitimate. But with what results? Edward knows as well as you or I that the potentates in Saint Petersburg have to make good their losses in Manchuria and desperately need to distract their own revolutionaries. But all the same, he can't help steering Russian expansionism toward Europe, reawakening sleeping rivalries between Saint Petersburg and Vienna."

"Oh, Vienna! You are worried about that universal impediment because you recognize the rotten imperium of which it is the capital, as a mummified version of the Holy Roman Empire."

"And I find you are a Russophile, presumably out of humanistic sympathies for caesaropapism."

"Democracy, my dear sir, has more to hope for from the Kremlin than from the Hofburg, and it is a disgrace that the land of Luther and Gutenberg—"

"Not only a disgrace, but probably also an act of stupidity. But such stupidity is the instrument of fate."

"Oh, I'll have none of your fate! Human reason needs only to *will* more strongly than fate, and it *is* fate."

"Man can only will what already is his fate. And capitalist Europe wills its own, as well."

"One believes war is inevitable, if one does not loathe it sufficiently."

"Such loathing is a leap in logic if it does not begin with the nation-state."

"The nation-state is the principle that guides this world's affairs—though you wish to ascribe that to the Devil. But once you make nations free and equal, defend the small and weak from oppression, establish justice, fix national borders—"

"The Brenner Pass as the border, I know. The liquidation of Austria. If only I knew how you intend to accomplish all that without war."

"And I would be only too glad to know when you ever heard me condemn a war of national liberation."

"But didn't I just hear—"

"No, I must confirm what Herr Settembrini says," Hans Castorp remarked, breaking into the argument, which he had followed as they walked along, tilting his head to one side or the other, depending on the speaker. "My cousin and I have often had the privilege of conversing with him about these and similar matters—what I mean is, of course, that we listened to him develop and spell out his opinions. And I can confirm, as I'm sure my cousin also recalls, that Herr Settembrini has more than once waxed enthusiastic for the principle of motion and rebellion, of improvement in the world—hardly a principle of peace, I don't suppose—and has noted that great efforts still lie ahead before such a principle will have triumphed everywhere and the universal, happy Republic of the World is established. I am more or less quoting him, although his words, of course, were much more graphic and literary than mine, but that's obvious. One thing that has remained exactly in my memory, and I can quote it verbatim—because as a seasoned civilian I was somewhat appalled by it—was his saying that such a day would come, if not on the feet of doves, then on the pinions of eagles (it was the eagle pinions that appalled me, as I recall) and that the fatal blow must be struck against Vienna, if we wish to bring about universal happiness. So that one cannot say that Herr Settembrini has repudiated war. Am I not correct, Herr Settembrini?"

"More or less," the Italian said curtly, turning his head away and swinging his cane.

"Worse luck," Naphta said with an ugly smile. "Now you've been convicted by your own pupil of harboring warlike tendencies. *Assument pennas ut aquilae . . .*"

"Voltaire himself affirmed wars that spread civilization, even advised Frederick the Second to go to war against the Turks."

"And instead, he allied himself with them—hee hee. And then there's the Republic of the World. I shall refrain from inquiring what becomes of the principle of motion and rebellion once happiness and confederation have been established. For in that moment, rebellion becomes a crime."

"You know very well, as do these young gentlemen, that the human progress of which I speak is conceived as infinite."

"All motion, however, is circular," Hans Castorp said. "In both space and time, as we learn from the laws of periodicity and the conservation of mass. My cousin and I were speaking about that earlier. Can one speak of progress when motion is a closed system without any direction? When I am lying there of an evening and observing the zodiac—the half of it that we see, that is—and think back to those ancient wise peoples—"

"You should not brood and dream, my good engineer," Settembrini interrupted, "but steadfastly trust those instincts of your years and race that compel you to action. You also need to pair your scientific learning with the idea of progress. In the immeasurable expanses of time, you see how life moves onward and upward from infusoria to man, and you cannot deny that infinite possibilities for further perfection still await humankind. But if you are determined to stick with mathematics, it, too, will lead you in a spiral from perfection to perfection; and you can take solace in the precepts of our eighteenth century, which taught that man was originally good, happy, and perfect, that it is only through social errors that he has been perverted and ruined, and that by working critically to rebuild society he shall become good, happy, and perfect again."

"What Herr Settembrini neglects to add," Naphta broke in, "is that the Rousseauian idyll is merely a rationalist's bastardization of the Church's doctrine of man's original sinless, stateless condition, of his primal direct relationship to God as a child of God, to which condition he shall return. Once earthly forms have dissolved, the reestablishment of the City of God will take place where earth and heaven, the natural and the supernatural, meet—salvation is transcendent. As for your capitalist world republic, dear doctor, it is quite curious to hear you speak of 'instinct' in that context. Instinct is certainly on the side of the nation-state, for God has implanted in man natural instincts that have caused the world's peoples to separate into various nations. War—"

"War," Settembrini exclaimed, "even war, my dear sir, has on occasion been forced to serve progress—as you yourself must grant me, if you will recall certain events from your own favorite epoch, by which I mean the Crusades. Those wars on behalf of civilization served mightily to enhance economic and commercial relations between peoples and united Western man under the banner of a single idea."

"You are suddenly very tolerant of that idea. And so, might I courteously remind you that, although the Crusades did stimulate international commerce, they did anything but bring about international reconciliation. On the contrary, they taught peoples to differentiate themselves one from the other and fostered the growth of the concept of the nation-state."

"Quite true, at least in regard to a given people's relation to their clergy. Yes, it was during that period when a sense of national honor began to solidify against hierarchical pretension."

"And yet, what you call hierarchical pretension is actually nothing less than the idea of unifying mankind under the banner of the Spirit."

"We know that spirit—thanks, but no thanks."

"It is clear that your nationalist mania loathes the world-conquering cosmopolitanism of the Church. If only I knew how you reconcile that with your loathing of war. Your repristination of antiquity's cult of the state surely makes you a champion of a positive interpretation of law, and as such—"

"Have we moved on to law? The idea, my dear sir, of both natural law and universal reason is alive in international law and—"

"Pooh, your international law is once again merely a Rousseauian bastardization of the *ius divinum*, which has nothing to do with either nature or reason, but is based upon revelation."

"Let us not quarrel over terms, professor. What I honor as natural and international law, you may go right ahead and call *ius divinum*. The main thing is that above the positive law of nation-states there arises a universal law with a higher jurisdiction, which allows disputed questions between parties to be settled by courts of arbitration."

"Courts of arbitration—the very idea! A bourgeois court of arbitration that decides questions of life and death, ascertains God's will, and ordains the course of history. Fine, that takes care of the dove's feet. But what about the pinions of eagles?"

"Bourgeois civilization—"

"Nonsense, the bourgeoisie doesn't know what it wants. They scream about doing something to halt the decline in the birthrate, demand that the costs of raising and educating children be reduced—and all the while we're suffocating in the throngs, and every profession is so overcrowded that the brawl over a few scraps of bread will soon eclipse all previous wars. Open spaces and green cities! Toughen the nation's youth! But why toughen them if civilization and progress demand there be no more war? War would take care of all those problems, and provide the solutions. Toughen our youth and at the same time combat the decline in the birthrate."

"You're joking—not even trying to be serious. Our conversation is at an end, and just in time. We're home," Settembrini said and for the cousins' sake pointed with his cane to a little house before whose gate they had now halted. It was a modest structure just this side of Davos-Dorf, separated from the road only by a small yard. Rising from bared roots, wild grape twined around the front door and, clinging to the wall, stretched an arched arm toward the ground-floor window on the right, the display window of a small grocery. The ground floor belonged to the grocer, Settembrini explained. Naphta's lodgings and the tailor's shop were the next floor up, his own residence was in the attic—a quiet studio.

In a surprising burst of cordiality, Naphta expressed the hope that further meetings would come from this first one. "Do come visit us," he said. "I would say, 'Come visit me,' if Dr. Settembrini here did not have prior claims on your friendship. Come by anytime you like, whenever you feel the need for a little colloquy. I enjoy exchanging views with young people, am perhaps not totally lacking in my own pedagogic tradition. Our Master of the Lodge"—he pointed at Settembrini—"may wish to claim that all pedagogic proclivities, even the very calling itself, belong to bourgeois humanism—but one must take issue with him there. We shall see you soon again, I'm sure."

Settembrini demurred. There were problems, he said—the lieutenant's days up here were numbered and the engineer would now be doubling his efforts at rest cure in order to follow his cousin back down to the plains soon.

The young people agreed with them both, first the one and then the other. They accepted Naphta's invitation with bows, and in the next moment they were nodding and shrugging to indicate that Settembrini's objections were justified. And so the matter was left open.

"What did he call him?" Joachim asked as they climbed the looping road to the Berghof.

"I understood him to say 'Master of the Lodge,' " Hans Castorp said, "and have been wondering about it myself. It's probably a joke of some kind—they both have such odd names for each other. Settembrini called Naphta '*Princeps Scholasticorum*'—which isn't bad. The scholastics were sort of the scribes of the Middle Ages, the dogmatic philosophers, if you like—hmm. The Middle Ages came up several times—and it reminded me how that very first day Settembrini said there was a medieval ring about a lot of things up here. The topic came up because of Adriatica von Mylendonk, because of her name. So how did you like *him*?"

"The little fellow? Not very well. I liked some things he said. Courts of arbitration are goody-goody nonsense, of course. But I didn't think that much of him. A fellow can say all sorts of fine things—but what good is that, if he's a dubious character? And there is something dubious about him, you can't deny it. His story about the 'place of cohabitation' was definitely suspect. And that nose is Jewish, too—take a good look at him. And only Semites are such puny physical specimens. Do you seriously intend to visit the man?"

"But of course we'll visit him," Hans Castorp declared. "And as for being puny—that's just the soldier talking. The Chaldeans had noses like that, too, and they were damn sharp people, and not just when it came to occult sciences. There is something of the occult about Naphta, too— I find him more than a little intriguing. I can't say I've got him figured out after only today, but if we get together with him often enough, maybe we'll both be able to. And I don't think it's out of the question that we'll learn a thing or two out of this."

"Oh, you and your learning! You're always learning up here—about biology and botany and slippery turning points. And you started in on 'time' your first day here. When what we're here to do is to get healthier, not more clever—healthier, until we're truly healthy, so they can finally let us go free and send us back to the flatlands cured."

" 'Freedom dwells within the mountains!' " Hans Castorp intoned giddily. "First tell me what freedom is," he went on in normal tones. "Naphta and Settembrini were arguing about just that and couldn't agree. 'Freedom is the law of brotherly love,' Settembrini says, and that sounds like it comes from his ancestor, the Carbonaro. But however brave that Carbonaro was, and our Settembrini himself may be—"

"Right—he got uneasy when the conversation turned to personal courage."

"I do believe he's afraid of some things Naphta is *not* afraid of, you see, and that his freedom and courage are somewhat namby-pamby concepts. Do you think he has enough courage '*to lose himself or to let himself be ruined*'?"

"What are you speaking French for?"

"Oh, just because. The atmosphere is so international. I don't know who ought to like that more—Settembrini with his bourgeois world republic, or Naphta with his hierarchical cosmopolitanism. I was paying attention, you see, but none of it was clear. Instead, the more they talked the more confused I got."

"That's how it always is. When people talk and spout opinions, the result is always confusion. I'm telling you, it doesn't matter what sort of opinions a man has, but whether he's a decent fellow. The best thing is to have no opinions at all and just do your duty."

"Yes, you can say that—as a mercenary, someone whose life is pure form. It's different for me. I'm a civilian, more or less responsible for myself. But it upsets me to see such confusion—what with the one preaching about an international world republic and loathing war on principle, but at the same time so patriotic that the Brenner Pass is the only possible border and he's willing to fight a civilizing war over it; and the other claiming the nation-state is the Devil's own work and gushing about the unification of all mankind, only to turn around and defend the law of natural instincts and make fun of peace conferences. We definitely have to go find out what we can learn from all this. You say our job is to get healthier, not more clever. But the two must be compatible, damn it. And if you don't believe that, then you're dividing the world in two—which is always a great mistake, let me tell you."

The City of God and Evil Deliverance

RECLINING ON HIS BALCONY, Hans Castorp identified a plant that had started to flourish in a great many places now that the astronomical summer had begun and the days were growing shorter again: columbine, or aquilegia, from the family Ranunculaceae, a long-stemmed herbaceous perennial, with blue and violet, sometimes almost reddish-brown flowers and flat, spreading, weedlike foliage. The plant could be found most everywhere, but it grew in particular abundance on the remote meadow where he had first noticed it almost a year before—the same secluded woodland valley with footbridge and bench where his premature, freewheeling walk had come to such a disconcerting end. He had been revisiting the spot now and then of late.

It was not all that far, really, when you went about it a little less impetuously than he had done that day. If you started at the bobsled finish line in Dorf and worked your way up the slope along a forest path with several wooden bridges that crossed the run as it descended from Schatzalp, you could—omitting detours, arias, and exhausted pauses— be there in twenty minutes. And if the weather was good and Joachim was tied up at the Berghof by a checkup, X-ray, blood sample, injection, or weigh-in, Hans Castorp might hike up there after second breakfast, occasionally after first; sometimes he even used the hour between tea and supper for a visit to his favorite spot; and then he would sit down on the same bench where he had had that nasty nosebleed, tilt his head to catch the sound of the rushing brook, and enjoy the closed landscape with its banks of blue columbine blossoming once again in the meadow.

Had he come only for that? No, he sat there so that he could be alone to remember, to think back over the past months with all their many and varied impressions and adventures, which were not easy to sort out, because they often seemed interlaced, blending into one another until palpable reality was often no longer distinguishable from what had merely been thought, dreamed, or imagined. But adventures they had been—so much so that whenever he recalled them, his heart, skittish since his very first day up here, would stop still and then begin to pound. Or was his skittish heart startled simply by the intellectual realization that the blue columbine—here in the same spot where Pribislav Hippe had appeared to him as he lay in a state of reduced vitality—was not still blooming, but blooming once again, that "three weeks" would soon be one whole adventurous year come full circle?

He no longer got nosebleeds, however, when he sat down on the bench beside the torrent—that was a thing of the past. The process of acclimatization, which from the very start Joachim had described as difficult and which had indeed proved to be so, had advanced to a point where, after eleven months, it had to be regarded as complete—further progress in that area was hardly noticeable now. His digestive chemistry had stabilized and adjusted. His Maria Mancinis tasted good again; the nerves of his dry mucous membranes had long since become receptive to the delicate aroma of the brand (a bargain at the price), so that for sentimental reasons he continued to order them from Bremen whenever his supply ran low, although the shop windows of an international resort displayed very inviting wares. Did not Maria act as a kind of connection between him, a man withdrawn from the world, and his former home in the flatlands? Did it not maintain and preserve those connections more effectively than, for instance, the postcards he now and then sent to his uncles, particularly since the intervals between them had been growing steadily longer the more he appropriated local conceptions of how to handle time on a grand scale? As a favor to the recipients, he usually sent picture postcards, with pretty views of the valley in either its snow-covered or summery state and just enough space for him to inform his kinsmen about the doctor's latest statement after a monthly checkup or complete physical—for instance, that from what the doctor could both hear and see, some improvement was undeniable, but that he was not yet detoxified and that his chronically slightly raised temperature came from the continued presence of some small areas, which, if he were only patient, would definitely vanish completely so that he would never have to return here again. He could be certain that any literary efforts beyond these were not demanded or expected of him. The world he was addressing was not one with a tradition of humanistic rhetoric; the answers he received were no more effusive than his postcards and usually accompanied the monies needed for his maintenance here—interest on his paternal inheritance, the conversion of which into Swiss currency worked so much to his advantage that he never used up one installment before the next arrived from home. The letters consisted of a few typewritten lines signed by James Tienappel, with greetings and best wishes for recovery from his great-uncle and sometimes from seafaring Peter as well.

The director, Hans Castorp reported home, had recently discontinued his series of injections. For such a young patient, he was not reacting well; they had resulted in headaches, fatigue, loss of appetite and weight, had at first raised his "fever" slightly, but then had not got rid of it. It continued to glow as a dry, subjective flush in his pink face, a reminder that for this child of the lowlands with their intoxicatingly damp meteorology, acclimatization consisted primarily of getting used to not getting used to things—which, by the way, Rhadamanthus himself, with his purple cheeks, had never done. "Some people never get used to it," Joachim had responded right off, and this did appear to be the case with Hans Castorp. Even the tremor of his head, which had begun to bother him soon after his arrival up here, gave every indication of not wanting to clear up, but would invariably start again when he was walking or talking, or even sitting there in the blue-blossoming meadow, thinking back over the complexity of his adventures; in fact, Hans Lorenz Castorp's dignified chin-propping method had almost become a habit for his grandson as well—and he never used it without being reminded of the old man's stiff collar, that interim form of his ceremonial ruff, of the soft golden hollow of the baptismal bowl, the religious sound of "great-great-great," and similar secret, private associations, all leading to yet another round of reflection on the complexity of his life.

Pribislav Hippe no longer appeared living before him, as he had eleven months before. His acclimatization was complete, he had no more visions, his body no longer lay inert on the bench while his innermost self wandered in some distant present—nothing of that sort happened. And when the memory of it came back to him, its vivid clarity stayed within normal, healthy bounds; and then Hans Castorp would pull from his breast pocket the glass memento that he kept in a heavy envelope he carried in his wallet—a little rectangle, which when held parallel to the ground was a black, opaque, reflective surface, but when held up to the sky, grew light and revealed very humanistic things: the transparent picture of a human body, with rib cage, the outline of the heart, the curve of the diaphragm, the bellows of the lungs, plus scapulae and humeri, all surrounded by a pale, hazy halo, the flesh—of which, against all reason, Hans Castorp had tasted on Mardi Gras. Was it any wonder, then, that his skittish heart stopped and did a somersault whenever he looked at this memento? And then to the sounds of the rushing brook and amid blue-blossoming columbine, he would lean back against the crude wooden bench, cross his arms, tilt his head to one shoulder, and begin to reminisce about it "all."

That sublime image of organic life, the human body, hovered before him just as it had on that frosty, starlit night when he had pursued his learned studies; and in contemplating its inner aspect now, young Hans Castorp was caught up in a great many questions and distinctions—the sort that dear old Joachim did not think it was his duty to be concerned about, but for which, as a civilian, Hans Castorp had begun to feel a responsibility, even though down in the flatlands he had never noticed such questions, probably never would have noticed them, but certainly did here, where one looked down on the world and its creatures from the contemplative retreat of five thousand feet and thought one's thoughts, even if they were probably the result of enhanced activity of the body, which was caused by soluble toxins and made your face burn with a dry flush. And in considering that inner aspect, he also thought of Settembrini, the pedagogic organ-grinder, whose father had come into the world in Greece and who explained love for that sublime image to be a matter of politics, rebellion, and eloquence, whereby the citizen's pike was consecrated on the altar of humanity; he thought, too, of Comrade Krokowski and what the two of them had been doing in his darkened suite for some time now, thought of the two sides of analysis and how it was not only beneficial to action and progress, but also a relative of the grave and its foul anatomy. He called up images of the two grandfathers, placing them side by side, the rebel and the faithful servant, who both wore black but for different reasons, and he considered their merits. He went on to deliberate such vast complexities as form and freedom, mind and body, honor and disgrace, time and eternity—and was overcome by a brief, but frantic dizzy spell at the thought that the columbine was blooming again and the year had come full circle.

He had a special term for this responsible preoccupation with his thoughts as he sat at his picturesque, secluded spot: he called it "playing king"—a childish term taken from the games of his boyhood, and by it he meant that this was a kind of entertainment that he loved, although with it came fear, dizziness, and all sorts of heart palpitations that made his face flush even hotter. And he found it not unfitting that the strain of all this required him to prop his chin—and the old method seemed perfectly appropriate to the dignity he felt when "playing king" and gazing at that hovering sublime image.

"*Homo Dei*"—that had been ugly Naphta's term for the sublime image when he was defending it against English social theory. Was it any wonder, then, that Hans Castorp, given his civilian sense of responsibility and interest in "playing king," felt that he and Joachim were obliged to pay him a little visit? Settembrini did not like the idea—Hans Castorp was shrewd and sensitive enough to see that quite clearly. The humanist had been displeased by their first meeting, had obviously tried to thwart it and pedagogically prevent the young people—himself in particular, the cunning problem child noted—from making Naphta's acquaintance, even though he personally associated and argued with him. That is how teachers are. They allow themselves to enjoy the interesting stuff, claiming they are "adults," but forbid it to young people, even demand that they acknowledge just how "unadult" they are. It was a good thing that the organ-grinder had no real right to forbid young Hans Castorp from doing anything—did not even make the attempt. The problem pupil needed only to ignore his sensitivities and pretend innocence, and there was nothing to prevent him from cordially accepting little Naphta's invitation—which he did after the main rest cure one Sunday afternoon, only a few days following that first meeting. Joachim had to come along for better or worse.

It was only a few minutes' walk from the Berghof down to the little house with the grapevine twined about its door. They entered, passed the door to the grocery on the right, and climbed a set of narrow brown stairs that brought them to another door. There was only one name on the plate beside the bell: Lukaček, Ladies' Tailor. The door was answered by a half-grown lad with close-trimmed hair and red cheeks; he was dressed in a kind of uniform—a striped footman's jacket and gaiters. They asked for Professor Naphta and, since they had no calling cards, made sure he could repeat their own names. He left them there, saying he would inform Herr Naphta—he used no title. A door stood open immediately opposite, and they could see into the tailor's shop, where Lukaček, despite its being Sunday, was sitting cross-legged atop a table, sewing. He was a pale, bald man; from beneath an oversize, drooping nose, a black moustache hung down morosely on both sides of his mouth.

"Good afternoon," Hans Castorp said.

"How do," the tailor said in Swiss dialect, although that seemed to match neither his name nor appearance and sounded rather false and odd.

"Working so hard, even on a Sunday?" Hans Castorp added with a nod.

"It's urgent," Lukaček replied curtly and took a stitch.

"Something elegant, I suppose," Hans Castorp guessed. "It's needed right away for a ball or party, is that it?"

The tailor left the question unanswered, bit off his thread, and threaded again. After a while he nodded in agreement.

"Will it be pretty?" Hans Castorp asked anew. "Will it have sleeves?"

"Yep, sleeves, it's for an ol' lady," Lukaček replied with a heavy Bohemian accent. The page returned to interrupt their conversation, which had been carried on through the open door. Herr Naphta would be pleased to receive the gentlemen, he reported, and asked them to follow; he opened another door, two or three steps farther on the right, behind which was a heavy portiere that he also lifted aside for the young men to enter. Standing there in slippers on a moss-green carpet, Naphta greeted his guests.

Both cousins were surprised by the luxury of the two-windowed study into which they had stepped—indeed, they were dazzled, for they had not expected anything of the sort given the shabby little house with its dingy corridor and stairway, in contrast to which Naphta's furnishings seemed almost fabulously elegant, when in point of fact they weren't, nor would Hans Castorp or Joachim Ziemssen normally have regarded them as such. But the decor was first-rate, and so ornate that despite the desk and bookcases the room did not have much of a masculine look. There was too much silk, burgundy and purple silk: silk curtains to conceal the shoddy doors, silk valances above the windows, and silk upholstery on a sofa and armchairs grouped at the far end of the room, opposite a second door and directly below a tapestry covering almost the entire wall. The baroque chairs, with little upholstered cushions on the arms, were placed around a circular, brass-trimmed table; behind this stood the sofa, likewise baroque and strewn with silk plush pillows. The bookcases, fitted with glass doors and green silk curtains, filled the walls at the sides of both doors; they were mahogany, as was the desk, or rather the rolltop secretary, which had been placed between the two windows. In the corner, to the left of the sofa and chairs, was a work of art: a painted wooden sculpture set atop a large pedestal draped in red, a profoundly terrifying work, a naive pietà—very effective, almost grotesque. The Mother of God, her hood drawn up, her brows furrowed in agony, her mouth skewed and gaping in lamentation; the Man of Sorrows on her lap, a primitive figure, badly out of scale, the crudely fashioned body revealing an ignorance of anatomy, the drooping head studded with thorns, the face and limbs splattered and dripping with blood, thick globs of congealed blood at the wound in the side, nail marks on the hands and feet—this showpiece definitely lent the silk room a special accent. The wallpaper visible above the bookcases and at the sides of the windows was also apparently the work of the tenant, with vertical stripes in the same green as the soft carpet spread over the simple red floor-covering. Only the low ceiling was more or less beyond help; it was cracked and bare—although a small Venetian chandelier had been hung. The windows were hidden by floor-length cream-colored curtains.

"We've come by for our little colloquy," Hans Castorp said, his eyes directed more at the pious horror in the corner than at the occupant of this surprising room, who was commending the cousins for having kept their word. Gesturing hospitably with his little right hand, he was trying to lead them to the silk-upholstered chairs, but Hans Castorp, as if spellbound, headed straight for the wooden sculpture and stopped in front of it, his hands on his hips and his head tilted to one side.

"What is this you have here?" he said softly. "It's frightfully good. I've never seen such suffering. Very old, of course, is it not?"

"Fourteenth century," Naphta replied. "Presumably from the Rhineland. You're impressed, aren't you?"

"Enormously," Hans Castorp said. "It couldn't help making an impression on one. I would never have thought that anything could be simultaneously so ugly—beg your pardon—and so beautiful."

"Works of art from a world in which the soul expresses itself," Naphta responded, "are always beautiful to the point of ugliness and ugly to the point of beauty. It is indeed a law. We are dealing with beauty of the Spirit, not of the flesh, which is basically stupid. And abstract, as well," he added. "The beauty of the body is abstract. Only inner beauty, the beauty of religious expression, possesses true reality."

"How kind of you to define and differentiate the matter so clearly," Hans Castorp said. "Fourteenth?" he inquired, just to be sure. "Thirteen hundred and something? Yes, perfect textbook Middle Ages—I see in it, as it were, some notions about the Middle Ages that I've been working on of late myself. Actually, I never knew anything about the period. I'm a man of technology and progress, to the extent my opinions count in this world. But up here the whole issue of the Middle Ages has been brought home to me in various ways. Certainly there was no economic social theory in those days, that much is clear. Do you know the artist's name?"

Naphta shrugged. "What does it matter?" he said. "We should not even ask, because at the time it was created no one asked, either. There is no miracle-worker, no Mr. Individual Creator behind it—it is an anonymous, communal work of art. It comes, of course, from the very advanced Middle Ages, the Gothic—*signum mortificationis*. You'll not find the crucifixion glossed over and prettified here, the way the Romanesque period thought it best to deal with things—no kingly crown, no majestic triumph over the world and martyrdom. The entire work is a radical proclamation of suffering and the weakness of the flesh. It is not until the Gothic that tastes turn to true pessimistic asceticism. You're probably unfamiliar with *De miseria humanae conditionis* by Innocent the Third— a very witty literary work, from the end of the twelfth century. But only later did this sort of art provide the illustrations for it."

"Herr Naphta," Hans Castorp said, heaving a sigh, "every word of everything you've said interests me. '*Signum mortificationis*,' was that it? I shall make a note of it. And just before that you mentioned 'anonymous and communal,' which also appears worth some serious thought. Sad to say, you guessed correctly about my not knowing the writings of that pope—I assume Innocent the Third was a pope. Did I understand you to say that the work is ascetic and witty? I must admit I've never thought those two things could go hand in hand, but now that I consider it, it seems quite plausible—any discussion of human misery would offer a chance for witty remarks at the expense of the flesh. Is the work to be had somewhere? If I brush up on my Latin perhaps I can read it."

"I have the book," Naphta replied, pointing his head toward one of the bookcases. "It is at your disposal. But won't you please sit down? You can regard the pietà from the sofa. And here's our afternoon snack—"

The little page had brought tea, plus a pretty silver-trimmed basket containing slices of layer cake. And who should come through the open door behind him—gliding swiftly, smiling delicately, exclaiming, "Zounds!" and "*Accidenti!*" It was Herr Settembrini, who lived one floor up and just happened to drop by to keep these gentlemen company. He had seen the cousins coming, he said, from his little window and had quickly finished off the encyclopedic page he had been working on, so that he, too, could join the party. His arrival seemed the most natural thing in the world—justified both by his old acquaintance with the Berghof residents and his relationship with Naphta, which despite profound differences of opinion was evidently characterized by regular and very lively visiting back and forth. And, indeed, the host showed no surprise as he casually greeted him as one of their number. All this, however, did not prevent Hans Castorp from gaining two distinct impressions from his arrival. First, he had the feeling that Herr Settembrini had dropped by in order to keep him and Joachim—or, actually, just him—from being left alone with ugly little Naphta and to provide a pedagogic counterweight by his presence; second, it was quite evident that he had no objection to using the occasion to leave his lodgings in the attic for a while, exchanging them for Naphta's silk-adorned room and a properly served tea. He first rubbed his yellow hands—and a line of black hair grew down the side of each, to just below the little finger—and then helped himself. With obvious relish, indeed with open praise, he dined on layer cake, each narrow, curving slice of which was richly veined with chocolate.

The topic of conversation continued to be the pietà, for Hans Castorp kept both one eye and his remarks fixed on it as he turned now to Herr Settembrini, trying to bring him into critical contact, as it were, with the work of art, even though the humanist's aversion to this bit of decor could very easily be read from the expression on his face when he twisted around to look at it—he had taken a seat with his back to that particular corner. Too polite to say what he thought, he confined himself to remarks concerning errors in proportion and anatomical defects in the figures; such offenses against the truth of nature did not come close to moving him, he said, since they were based not on any primitive lack of skill but arose out of willful malice, out of an antagonistic principle. And Naphta maliciously agreed, saying that it certainly was not a question of any lack of technical skill. It was, rather, a matter of the emancipation of the Spirit from the bonds of nature, indeed, the work proclaimed a religious contempt for nature by refusing to submit to it. But when Settembrini declared that such a neglect of nature and a refusal to study her led humankind down a false path and then began in taut words to contrast an absurd formlessness—to which the Middle Ages and epochs that imitated it were addicted—with classicism, with the Greco-Roman heritage of form, beauty, reason, and serenity born of natural piety, for classicism alone was destined to further the human enterprise, Hans Castorp interrupted him and asked how all that fitted in with Plotinus, who, as was well known, was ashamed of his own body, and with Voltaire, who in the name of reason had rebelled against the scandalous earthquake in Lisbon? Absurd? Yes, this work, too, was absurd, but when one stopped and considered the matter, one could, in his opinion, call absurdity an intellectually honorable position, and so the absurd enmity toward nature in Gothic art was ultimately as honorable as the gesture of a Plotinus or a Voltaire, for it expressed the same emancipation from facts and givens, the same proud unwillingness to be enslaved, the same refusal to submit to dumb powers, that is, to nature.

Naphta broke into that laugh of his that sounded like a porcelain plate and ended in a cough.

Settembrini said loftily, "You wrong our host with your display of wit, for it is equally a display of ingratitude for this delicious cake. But I wonder if gratitude is one of your concerns—that is, presuming one shows gratitude by making good use of gifts received."

But when Hans Castorp blushed at this, he went on charmingly, "You are known to be a wag, my good engineer. Despite your amiable scoffing at the Good, I do not doubt in the least that you also love it. You know yourself, of course, that the only intellectual protest against nature that can be called honorable is one that keeps in mind the dignity and beauty of man and never one that, even if it does not aim at man's degradation and debasement, nevertheless accomplishes just that. You are also aware what inhuman abominations, what bloodthirsty intolerance—without which the artifact behind me would not exist—that epoch brought forth. I need only remind you of those who persecuted heretics, dreadful inquisitors like the bloody Konrad of Marburg with his foul priestly rage against everything that resisted his heavenly rule. You, I am sure, would never approve of the sword or the stake as an instrument of brotherly love."

"All the same, it was in love's service," Naphta declared, "that machinery was set in motion by which the cloister cleansed the world of its wicked citizens. All ecclesiastical punishments, even death at the stake, even excommunication, were imposed to save souls from eternal damnation, which cannot be said of the mad exterminations of the Jacobins. Allow me to remark, that every sort of torture, every bit of bloody justice, that does not arise from a belief in the next world is bestial nonsense. And as for the degradation of man, its history coincides exactly with the rise of the bourgeois spirit. The Renaissance, the Enlightenment, and the teachings of nineteenth-century science and economics have omitted nothing, absolutely nothing, that seemed even vaguely useful for furthering such degradation, beginning with modern astronomy—which turned the focal point of the universe, that sublime arena where God and Satan struggled to possess the creature whom they both ardently coveted, into an unimportant little planet, and, for now at least, has put an end to man's grand position in the cosmos, upon which astrology was likewise based."

"For now?" And as Herr Settembrini asked his sly question, his expression was much like that of an inquisitor who is waiting for his victim to stumble and confess incontestable crimes.

"Why, of course—for a couple of centuries," Naphta affirmed coldly. "The honor of the scholastics will be vindicated in this regard as well, if I am not mistaken. Indeed the process is well under way. Copernicus will be routed by Ptolemy. The theory of heliocentrism is now being opposed by intellectual forces whose efforts will presumably attain their desired goal. Science will find itself philosophically constrained once again to grant earth all the honors that Church dogma wished to preserve for it."

"What? What? Intellectual opposition? Philosophically constrained? Attain their desired goal? What sort of voluntarism are you spouting now? And what about unbiased research? What about pure knowledge? What about the truth, my dear sir, which is so intimately bound up with freedom, and its martyrs—whom you claim have slandered the earth, but who are instead the planet's most beautiful and everlasting ornaments?"

Herr Settembrini had a forceful way of posing questions. He sat up straight and pelted little Herr Naphta with righteous words, his voice swelling so powerfully toward the end that you could hear just how certain he was that his opponent's answer could take only one form—embarrassed silence. He had been holding a piece of cake between his fingers as he spoke, but now he laid it back on his plate, unwilling to take a bite after such questions.

"My good friend," Naphta replied with sour composure, "there is no such thing as pure knowledge. The validity of ecclesiastical science— which can be summarized in Saint Augustine's statement: 'I believe, that I may understand'—is absolutely incontrovertible. Faith is the vehicle of understanding, the intellect is secondary. Your unbiased science is a myth. Faith, a world view, an idea—in short, the will—is always present, and it is then reason's task to examine and prove it. In the end we always come down to '*quod erat demonstrandum.*' The very notion of proof contains, psychologically speaking, a strong voluntaristic element. The great scholastics of the twelfth and thirteenth centuries were unanimous in their conviction that nothing could be true in philosophy that was theologically false. Let us set theology aside, if you like. A human race, however, that refuses to accept the proposition that nothing can be true in science that is false in philosophy, is not human. The argumentation of the Holy Office against Galileo stated that his theses were philosophically absurd. There can be no more cogent argument than that."

"*Eh, eh!* Our poor, great Galileo's arguments proved to be the more valid ones. No, let's be serious, *professore.* Here in the presence of these two attentive young people, answer one question for me, please: Do you believe in truth, in objective, scientific truth? That to strive for it is the highest law of morality? That its triumphs over authority are the most glorious page in the history of the human spirit?"

Heads turned from Settembrini to Naphta—Hans Castorp's more quickly than Joachim's. "Such a triumph is an impossibility," Naphta replied, "because the authority is man himself—his interests, his dignity, his salvation—and there can be no contradiction between man and truth. They coincide."

"Which means that truth is—"

"Whatever profits man is true. Nature herself is summarized in him; in all of nature, only he is created, and nature is solely for him. He is the measure of all things and his salvation is the criterion of truth. Theoretical knowledge with no practical application in the realm of man's salvation is so totally uninteresting that we must deny it any value as truth and exclude it entirely. The Christian centuries were united in their view that the natural sciences were of no significance to man. Lactantius, whom Constantine the Great chose to be his son's tutor, put the question quite directly: how would it help him gain his salvation if he knew the sources of the Nile or the ravings of physicists about the heavens? Try to answer that one sometime! And if Platonic philosophy was preferred above all others, it was because it did not concern itself with the study of nature, but with the study of God. I can assure you that mankind is about to find its way back to this point of view, to recognize that the task of true science is not the pursuit of worthless information, but rather the elimination on principle of what is pernicious, even of what is merely without significance as an idea, and, in a word, to proclaim instinct, moderation, choice. It is childish to believe that the Church defended darkness against the light. Rather, she did what was right, right three times over, in declaring criminal any 'unbiased' striving for a knowledge of things, that is to say, any striving that casts aside those spiritual concerns aimed solely at winning salvation. What has led man into darkness, and will continue to lead him ever deeper is 'unbiased'—that is, aphilosophical—natural science."

"What you are preaching is pragmatism," Settembrini responded, "and you need only transfer it to the political realm to perceive how totally destructive it is. Whatever profits the state is good, true, and just. Its salvation, its dignity, its power is the criterion of morality. Fine—and with that you have opened the door wide for every sort of crime. And as for human truth, justice for the individual, democracy—well, you'll see what becomes of them."

"I move we apply a little logic here," Naphta retorted. "Either Ptolemy and the scholastics are right, and the world is finite in time and space, which means that God is transcendent and the polarity of God and world is maintained, so that man, too, leads a dualistic existence, and the problem of his soul rests in the conflict between what his senses register and what transcends his senses, making all social issues entirely secondary—this is indeed the only form of individualism that I recognize as logically consistent. Or, conversely, your Renaissance astronomers discovered the truth, and the cosmos is infinite, which means there is no world that transcends the senses, no dualism; the world beyond is absorbed into this world, the polarity of God and nature is annulled, and since the human personality is no longer the battlefield of two hostile principles, but rather harmonious and unified, all human conflict stems from the clash between the interests of the individual and of society as a whole, and so the purposes of the state become the law of morality, just as in good old heathen days. It's either one or the other."

"I protest," Settembrini cried, holding his teacup out at arm's length toward his host. "I protest your insinuation that the modern state dooms the individual to the hell of slavery. And I protest yet a third time, against the harrowing alternative you have presented us with: Prussianism or Gothic reaction. The sole purpose of democracy is to provide an individualistic corrective to the absolutism of the state. Truth and justice are the crown jewels of individual morality; and should a conflict arise with the interests of the state, they may very well appear to be hostile to it, but in fact are directed toward the state's higher—one may even say, transcendent—good. The Renaissance as the origin of the deification of the state? What sham logic! The achievements that the Renaissance and the Enlightenment wrested from the past—and may I emphasize, my dear sir, the struggles contained in that verb—were individual human personality, human rights, and human freedom."

His listeners, who had held their breath during Herr Settembrini's grand rejoinder, breathed out again now. Hans Castorp could not help slamming his hand, though with restraint, on the edge of the table. "Brilliant!" he said with clenched teeth. And even Joachim seemed deeply satisfied, despite what had been said about Prussianism. But then they both turned back to the other disputant, who had just been rebuffed—Hans Castorp, in fact, with such eagerness that he placed both elbows on the table and propped his chin in one hand, much as he had when drawing his pig, so that he was staring from close up directly into Herr Naphta's face.

He sat silent, his skinny hands in his lap, a caustic look on his face. "I was attempting to introduce logic into our conversation," he said, "and you have replied with high-mindedness. I am more or less aware that the Renaissance gave birth to what is known as liberalism, individualism, humanistic citizenship, and all that. But your emphasis on that verb leaves me cold, inasmuch as the heroic age that 'wrested' your ideals came to an end long ago—those ideals are dead, or at best lie twitching in their death throes, and those whom they had hoped to finish off have got their foot in the door again. You call yourself, if I am not mistaken, a revolutionary. But you are badly mistaken if you think that future revolutions will end in freedom. After five hundred years, the principle of freedom has outlived its usefulness. A pedagogic method that regards itself as a daughter of the Enlightenment and employs educational methods based on criticism, on the liberation and nursing of the ego, on the breaking down of ordained living patterns—such a pedagogy may still achieve moments of rhetorical success, but for those who know and understand, it is, beyond all doubt, sublimely backward. All institutions dedicated to genuine education have always known that there can be only one central truth in any pedagogy, and that is: absolute authority and an ironclad bond—discipline and sacrifice, renunciation of the ego and coercion of the personality. It is ultimately a cruel misunderstanding of youth to believe it will find its heart's desire in freedom. Its deepest desire is to obey."

Joachim sat up straight. Hans Castorp blushed. Herr Settembrini twirled his handsome moustache excitedly.

"No!" Naphta continued. "The mystery and precept of our age is not liberation and development of the ego. What our age needs, what it demands, what it will create for itself, is—terror."

He had uttered this last word more softly than any he had spoken thus far—and without gestures, at most, a quick flash of his glasses. All three of his listeners had flinched, even Settembrini, who quickly recovered, however, and smiled.

"And might one inquire," he asked, "who or what—you see, I'm all ears, I don't even know how to put my question—who or what, do you believe, will be the agents of this—I do not gladly repeat the word—this terror?"

Naphta sat silent, his eyes sparkling, a caustic look on his face. He said, "I am at your service. I don't believe I am mistaken in assuming we are agreed in our presupposition of an ideal primal condition of man, a stateless condition that knew no compulsion, where the relationship to God was direct and childlike, where there was neither sovereignty nor service, no law, no punishment, no injustice, no union of the flesh, no class differences, no labor, no property, but only equality, fraternity, and moral perfection."

"Very good. I agree," Settembrini declared. "I agree except for the point about union of the flesh, which obviously must always have been the case, since man is a highly developed vertebrate, no different from other animals."

"As you wish. I am merely establishing fundamental agreement as to man's original, paradisial condition, without law and with a direct childlike relation to God, all of which was lost in the Fall. I believe we can walk side by side a little farther down this path by tracing the state to a social contract, which takes sin into account and protects against injustice and which we both therefore regard as the origin of sovereign authority."

"*Benissimo!*" Settembrini exclaimed. "Social contract—that's the Enlightenment, that's Rousseau. I would never have thought—"

"Beg your pardon, but we now come to a parting of the ways. Given the fact that all sovereignty and authority were originally vested in the people, who then transferred all legislative and other powers to their prince, your school of thought deduces, first and foremost, the people's right to revolt against the crown. Whereas we—"

"We?" Hans Castorp thought, listening intently. "Who is 'we'? I definitely must ask Settembrini later who it is he means by 'we.' "

"—we, for our part," Naphta continued, "are perhaps no less revolutionary than you, but we have always deduced, first and foremost, the supremacy of the Church over the secular state. For even if the state's ungodliness were not branded on its brow, one need only note a simple historical fact—that its origins can be traced to the will of the people and not, like those of the Church, to divine decree—and thereby prove that the state is, if not exactly a manifestation of evil, then at least a manifestation of dire necessity and sinful shortcomings."

"The state, my dear sir—"

"I know what you think of the nation-state. 'Above all else, love of the fatherland and a boundless hunger for glory.' That is Virgil. You amend him with a little liberal individualism, and call it democracy; but your fundamental relationship to the state remains completely untouched. You are apparently not disturbed by the fact that money is its soul. Or would you contest that? Antiquity was capitalist because it idolized the state. The Christian Middle Ages clearly saw that the secular state was inherently capitalist. 'Money will become our emperor'—that is a prophecy from the eleventh century. Do you deny that it has literally come true, making life itself a veritable hell?"

"My dear friend, you have the floor. I am impatient to make the acquaintance of the great unknown that is the agent of terror."

"Brash curiosity for a spokesman of a social class that is itself the agent of the freedom that has ruined the world. If need be, I can do without your counterarguments—I am quite familiar with the political ideology of the bourgeoisie. Your goal is a democratic empire, the world-state, the apotheosis of the principle of the nation-state on a universal plane. And the emperor of your empire? We know him. Yours is a gruesome utopia, and yet—on this very point we find ourselves more or less in agreement. For there is something transcendent about your capitalist world republic— indeed, the world republic is the transcendent secular state, and we are one in our faith that on some distant horizon a final perfect condition awaits mankind that will correspond to his original perfect condition. Since the days of Gregory the Great, the founder of the City of God on earth, the Church has seen it as her task to bring mankind back under divine rule. His papal claim to temporal authority was not made for its own sake; proxy dictatorship was, rather, a means, a path to a redemptive goal, a transitional phase from the heathen state to the kingdom of heaven. You have spoken to our pupils here about the Church's bloody deeds and her chastening impatience—but that was very foolish of you, for the zeal of the godly cannot, by definition, be pacifistic. And Gregory himself said: 'Cursed be the man who holds back his sword from shedding blood.' We know power is evil. But if the kingdom is to come, the dualism between good and evil, between this world and the next, between power and the Spirit, must be temporarily abrogated and transformed in a principle that unites asceticism and dominion. That is what I call the necessity of terror."

"But its agent! Its agent!"

"You even ask? Can it be your Manchester eyes have failed to notice the existence of a social theory that promises the victory of man over economics, a social theory whose principles and goals coincide exactly with those of the Christian City of God? The Church fathers called 'mine' and 'yours' pernicious words, described private property as usurpation and thievery. They repudiated private ownership, since, according to the divine law of nature, the earth is the common property of all mankind and therefore its fruits are likewise intended for the common use of all. They taught that only greed, itself a consequence of the Fall, defends the rights of property, since it also invented exclusive ownership. They were humane enough, anticommercial enough, to call economic activity per se a danger to the salvation of the soul, that is, to humanity. They hated money and finance and called capitalist wealth fuel for the fires of hell. With all their hearts they despised the economic principle that declares price is the result of the workings of supply and demand, and they damned those who lived by the fluctuations of the market as exploiters of their neighbors. Even more blasphemous in their eyes was another form of exploitation, that of time—the monstrosity of receiving a bonus, that is, interest paid on money, from the simple passage of time and thereby perverting a universal divine institution, time itself, to one's own advantage and the detriment of others."

"*Benissimo!*" Hans Castorp cried, availing himself in his eagerness of Herr Settembrini's favorite expression of approval. "Time . . . as a universal divine institution—now that is extremely important!"

"Indeed it is," Naphta remarked. "These humane minds were disgusted by the idea of wealth increasing automatically and placed all speculation and transactions involving interest under the rubric of usury, making every rich man either a thief or the heir of a thief. They went even further. Like Thomas Aquinas, they regarded trade in general—the basic commercial act of buying and selling for a profit without having altered or improved the product—as a despicable occupation. They were not inclined to assign a high value to labor in and of itself, because it is an ethical, not a religious act, performed in the service of life, not of God. And since labor was concerned exclusively with life and its maintenance, they demanded that both personal profit and public esteem be measured by the productive effort involved. They considered the peasant and the craftsman honorable people, but not the merchant or the industrialist. They wanted goods to be produced on the basis of need and loathed the idea of mass production. Well, then—after having been buried for centuries, all these economic principles and standards have been resurrected in the modern movement of communism. The correspondence is perfect, down to the meaning of international labor's claim of dominion over international marketeering and speculation. In the modern confrontation with bourgeois-capitalist rot, the world's proletariat embodies the humanity and criteria of the City of God. The point of the dictatorship of the proletariat, the political-economic demand for salvation in our time, is not dominion for its own sake and for all eternity, but only a temporary abrogation of the polarities of mind and Spirit under the sign of the cross. It is a way of overcoming the world by ruling the world, a transition; its point is transcendence, the kingdom itself. The proletariat has taken up Gregory the Great's task, his godly zeal burns within it, and its hands can no more refrain from shedding blood than could his. Its work is terror, that the world may be saved and the ultimate goal of redemption be achieved: the children of God living in a world without classes or laws."

So ended Naphta's caustic oration. The little gathering was silent. The young men looked to Herr Settembrini—they would take their cue from him.

"Amazing," he said. "I certainly must admit my shock—I had not expected this. *Roma locuta*. And what a speech! With our very own eyes, we have witnessed a hieratic death-defying leap—and if that is a contradiction in terms, then Herr Naphta has 'temporarily abrogated' it. Ah, yes. I repeat, it is amazing. Can you even conceive that there might be any objections, professor—even objections based purely on consistency? You attempted a while ago to help us understand a Christian individualism founded in the dualism between God and the world, and tried to prove its preeminence over all politically determined morality. A few minutes later you are advocating a socialism that ends in dictatorship and terror. How do you reconcile the two?"

"Opposites," Naphta said, "may very well be reconciled. But what is mediocre and makeshift will never be. Your individualism, as I made bold to remark before, is a makeshift thing, a series of concessions. It corrects your heathen state morality with a little Christianity, a little 'individual rights,' a little so-called freedom, that is all. Whereas an individualism that proceeds from the cosmic, astrological importance of the individual soul, an individualism that is not social, but religious, that experiences its humanity not as a contradiction between self and society, but between self and God, between flesh and Spirit—such a genuine individualism can be reconciled very nicely with a community rich in ties of commitment and obligation."

"So it's both anonymous and communal," Hans Castorp said.

Settembrini looked at him wide-eyed. "Silence, my good engineer!" he commanded with a severity attributable to his own nervous tension. "You may learn, but please do not perform." And now turning back to Naphta he said, "That is one possible answer, but only one. It comforts me a little. But let us confront it in all its consequences. Along with industry, your Christian communism rejects technology, the machine, progress itself. In denying what you call marketeering, the world of money and finance, which antiquity valued much more than farming and handicrafts, it also denies freedom. For it is as clear as clear can be that, just as in the Middle Ages, all private and public relationships will be bound to the soil, even—and I do not find it easy to say this—even the individual personality. If only the soil can provide a living, then it alone can provide freedom. Craftsmen and peasants, no matter in what honor they may be held, own no land, they are vassals of those who do own it. Indeed, until well into the late Middle Ages, the majority of people, even those in the cities, were vassals. Here and there in the course of our discussion, you have made mention of human dignity. But now you are advocating an economic system whose morality deprives the individual of freedom and dignity."

"There is much that we might say about dignity or the lack thereof," Naphta replied. "For now, I would be most gratified if in this context you might find reason to see freedom less as a lovely gesture and more as a problem. You maintain that the morality of Christian economics, with all its beauty and humanity, creates men who are not free. I, on the other hand, declare that the issue of freedom—or, to put it more concretely, the issue of cities—as highly moral an issue as it may be, is historically associated with a most inhuman degeneration of economic morality, with the many horrors of modern marketeering and speculation, with the satanic rule of money, with commerce."

"I must insist that you not hide behind reservations and paradoxes, that you confess clearly and unambiguously that you are the blackest reactionary."

"The first step toward true freedom and humanity would be to cast off your quaking fears of the term 'reactionary.' "

"Well, then, enough," Herr Settembrini declared with a slight quiver in his voice, pushing his plate and cup away—both empty now—and getting up from the silk sofa. "That is enough for today, enough for any one day, it seems to me. Professor, we thank you both for the tasty hospitality and the very scintillating conversation. The rest cure calls my friends back to the Berghof, but before they go, I would like to show them my monk's cell upstairs. Come, gentlemen. *Addio, padre!*"

And now he had even called Naphta *"padre"*—Hans Castorp took note of it with raised brows. No one objected to Settembrini's breaking up the party, taking charge of the cousins, or failing to suggest the possibility that Naphta might join them. The young people said their good-byes, likewise expressing their thanks, and were in turn encouraged to come again. They left with the Italian, but not before Hans Castorp was sent on his way with the loan of a crumbling paperback edition of *De miseria humanae conditionis.* To reach the almost ladderlike stairway to the top floor, they had to pass Lukaček's door again and noticed the peevish tailor was still sitting on his table, working on the sleeved dress for the old lady. The top floor, by the way, was not a floor at all, it was simply a garret—with naked beams that supported the shingled roof, with the feel of a granary in summer and the odor of warm wood. The garret, however, had two small rooms that were both occupied by the republican capitalist—one serving as the bedroom, the other as the study of the literary contributor to the *Sociology of Suffering.* He cheerfully showed his lodgings to his young friends, called them private and cozy, thereby supplying them with the right words by which they could then praise his quarters— which they did in unison. They both found it quite charming—private and cozy, just as he had said. They stepped into the little bedroom—it had a small rag rug and a narrow, short bed set back in a dormer—then returned to the study, furnished no less sparely, but all the same with a certain chilly order about it, if not to say stateliness. Clumsy, old-fashioned rush-bottom chairs—four in all—were symmetrically arranged beside the doors, and the divan was also pushed against the wall, so that the middle of the room was taken up exclusively by the round table with its green cloth and a rather commonplace water carafe—either for decoration or refreshment—an upended glass over its neck. Books, some bound, some simply sewn, leaned tipsily against one another on a small bookshelf, and next to the open window stood a rickety, long-legged folding lectern with a little thick felt rug below, just large enough for one person to stand on. Hans Castorp struck a pose there for a moment, trying it out—it was Herr Settembrini's working place, where great literature was being transformed into encyclopedic material from the viewpoint of human suffering. He propped his elbows on the slanting surface and offered his opinion that it was a private and cozy place to stand and work. He suggested that it must have been much the same when Lodovico's father, with his long, finely chiseled nose, had once stood at his lectern in Padua—and learned that he was standing at the actual lectern of that deceased scholar, and indeed, that the rush-bottom chairs, the table, even the water carafe, had come down from him; not only that, but the rush-bottom chairs had also belonged to the Carbonaro grandfather and had once adorned the walls of his law office in Milan. That was impressive. The contours of the chairs suddenly took on a look of political agitation in the young men's eyes, and Joachim got up from the one where he had been sitting cross-legged and unsuspecting, glanced at it mistrustfully—and did not sit back down. Hans Castorp, however, still standing at the lectern of Settembrini the elder, was pondering how the son now worked here to combine the politics of his grandfather and the humanism of his father into literature. Then all three of them left. The writer had offered to accompany the cousins home.

They said nothing for part of the way, but their silence was all about Naphta, and Hans Castorp could wait—he was certain that Herr Settembrini would come around to speaking of his housemate, that in fact he had come with them for that very purpose.

After a sigh that sounded like a preface to his remarks, the Italian began to speak. "Gentlemen—I would like to warn you."

When he paused briefly at this point, Hans Castorp of course asked in feigned amazement, "Warn us about what?" He might just as easily have asked "about whom?" but he kept things impersonal as a way of demonstrating his total innocence, although even Joachim knew what was going on.

"About the person whose guests we just were," Settembrini replied, "and to whom I introduced you, very much against my will and intentions. As you know, chance wished it otherwise. I could not help it, but I bear the responsibility and it weighs heavily on me. It is at the very least my duty to point out to you as young people certain intellectual risks you run in associating with that man and to beg you, moreover, to keep your relations with him within certain prudent limits. His form is logic, but his nature is confusion."

Well, yes, that was true, Hans Castorp suggested, there was something a little uncanny about Naphta, he did say some rather strange things at times; it had almost sounded as if he really believed the sun revolved around the earth. But all in all, how could they, the cousins, ever have concluded it might be unadvisable to associate with one of his, Herr Settembrini's, friends? He had said himself it was through him that they had made Naphta's acquaintance; they had met him in his, Settembrini's, company—and he took walks with him, came down to tea all on his own. All of which proved—

"To be sure, my good engineer, to be sure." Herr Settembrini's voice sounded gentle, resigned, but it had a slight quiver in it as well. "Such things can be said in reply, and you have so replied. Fine, I am ready to accept responsibility. I live under the same roof with the gentleman, it was inevitable that we would meet, that one thing would lead to another, that we would become acquainted. Herr Naphta is a man of intellect— and that is rare. He is loquacious by nature—and so am I. Let those who would judge me do so—I took advantage of the opportunity to cross intellectual swords with an opponent who is, after all, my equal. There is no one else, far and wide. In brief, it is true that I visit him, that he visits me, that we take our strolls together. We argue. We argue almost every day, to the point of drawing blood. And I must admit the very contrariness of his thoughts, their antipathy to my own, add a special allure to our meetings. I need the friction. Opinions cannot live unless they have the chance to do battle—and I am firm in mine. But could you claim the same for yourselves—you, lieutenant, or you, my good engi- neer? You enter the fray unarmed against such intellectual chicanery. If exposed to the influences of this half-fanatic, half-malicious humbug, both your minds and souls are in danger."

Yes, yes, Hans Castorp said, that was probably true, his cousin and he, they were more or less prone to such spiritual dangers. It was the old story of life's problem children—he understood. But on the other hand, one could just as easily quote that old motto of Petrarch's, Herr Settem- brini knew the one he meant. But in any case, the ideas Naphta advanced were well worth listening to: one had to be just. That part about commu- nistic time, and how no one should be paid a bonus simply because it passed—that had been excellent. And then it had been very interesting to hear certain ideas on pedagogy, about which he probably would never have known a thing without Naphta.

Herr Settembrini pressed his lips together, and so Hans Castorp hurried to add that he himself, of course, would refrain from taking sides or endorsing any viewpoint, but he had found it worth listening to what Naphta said about the desires of youth. "But you must explain one thing for me," he went on. "Well, your Herr Naphta—I call him 'your Herr Naphta' to indicate that I do not necessarily find myself in sympathy with him, but that on the contrary, my attitude is one of considerable reservation—"

"Very wise of you!" Settembrini exclaimed gratefully.

"Well, he said a great many things about money, the soul of the state, as he put it, and spoke out against property, because it's thievery, and against capitalist wealth in general, which he said, I believe, was fuel for the fires of hell—at least if I'm not mistaken that's how he put it—and sang the praises of the medieval injunction against interest. And yet, he himself—excuse me, but he himself must be . . . It really is quite a surprise to enter that room—all that silk."

"Ah, yes," Settembrini said with a smile, "that sort of taste is very characteristic."

"All the beautiful old furniture," Hans Castorp went on, remembering. "The pietà from the fourteenth century, the Venetian chandelier, the little footman in livery, and as much chocolate layer cake as you could eat. Which means he must himself be—"

"Herr Naphta," Settembrini replied, "is no more a capitalist than I."

"But?" Hans Castorp asked. "I am waiting for the 'but' in your response, Herr Settembrini."

"Well, those people never let any of their own starve."

"Who are 'those people'?"

"The fathers."

"Fathers? Fathers?"

"I am speaking, my good engineer, of the Jesuits."

There was a pause. The cousins were obviously taken aback.

"What? Good God in heaven!" Hans Castorp exclaimed. "I'll be damned—so the man's a Jesuit?"

"You have guessed it," Herr Settembrini said delicately.

"No, I never—but, then, who would ever have thought it? So that's why you called him *padre*?"

"That was just a little exaggerated courtesy," Settembrini replied. "Herr Naphta is not a priest. His illness is to blame for his not having gone further by now. But he did complete his novitiate and take his first vows. Illness forced him to break off his theological studies. He then spent a few years serving at one of the Society's schools as a prefect—a headmaster, a principal in charge of their young pupils. That suited his pedagogic interests. And he can continue to pursue them here, too, teaching Latin at the Fridericianum. He's been here five years now. It's not clear when or if he will be allowed to leave here. But he is a member of the Society, and even if the ties were looser, he still would lack for nothing. I told you that he is a poor man, by which I mean one without possessions. Regulations, of course. But the Society has unlimited wealth at its disposal and takes care of its own, as you saw."

"I'll be damned," Hans Castorp muttered. "And I didn't even know, never even thought that there still actually was such a thing. A Jesuit— so that's it! But tell me one thing: if he's so well taken care of by those people, why in the world would he live . . . I certainly don't want to disparage your lodgings, Herr Settembrini, you have a very charming place there with Lukaček, it's so nice and private, and especially cozy, too. But what I mean is—if Naphta is so flush, to use the vulgar term, why doesn't he rent a different apartment, something grander, with a normal entrance and big rooms, in a large, fine home? There's something almost furtive, even bizarre about the way he lives there in his little hole with all that silk."

Settembrini shrugged. "He must have his reasons," he said. "Perhaps it's a matter of tact, or taste. I assume it eases his anticapitalist conscience to dwell in poor man's quarters, and that he compensates for it by the style in which he lives. Discretion probably plays a role as well. It's best not to flaunt the fact that the Devil is paying all your bills. You put on a nice unpretentious façade, and then behind it indulge your priestly penchant for silk."

"How extraordinary," Hans Castorp said. "I must admit, this is all absolutely new and exciting for me. No, we really are very grateful, Herr Settembrini, for your having introduced us. Believe you me, we shall be paying him many a nice visit. That's absolutely certain. A relationship like that broadens one's horizons in quite unexpected ways, gives one some insight into the world, into a kind of life about which one had not the vaguest. A proper Jesuit! And by saying 'proper,' it's my way of reminding myself of what all is running through my mind right now, the things I'll have to keep an eye on. What I am saying is: is he a proper one? I know well enough that you don't think there can be anything proper about having the Devil pay all one's bills. But what I mean goes beyond that to the next question: is he a proper *Jesuit*? That's what is running through my mind. He said things—you know the things I mean— about modern communism and the godly zeal of the proletariat that cannot refrain from shedding blood. In short, things I won't amplify on—but your grandfather with his citizen's pike was a perfect little lamb in comparison, if you'll pardon the expression. How does that work? Do his superiors agree with him? Does that square with Roman doctrine, for which the Society weaves its web of intrigue all around the world—or so I'm told? Isn't it—what's the word—heretical, unorthodox, incorrect? That's what I'm wondering about in regard to Naphta, and I'd be glad to hear what you think."

Settembrini smiled and said, "It's very simple. Herr Naphta is first of all a Jesuit, a good and proper Jesuit. But second, he is a man of intellect—otherwise I would not seek out his company—and as such he is always looking for new combinations, adaptations, connections, modern permutations. You saw that even I was surprised by his theories. He had never before revealed so much of himself to me. I used the stimulus that your presence obviously provided to provoke him to speak his last word on certain matters. And it certainly turned out droll enough—ghastly in fact."

"Yes, yes. But why didn't he become a *padre*? He's surely old enough."

"I told you, it was his illness that temporarily prevented it."

"Fine, but don't you think that if he's a Jesuit first and a man of intellect, with permutations, second—that the second part has something to do with his illness?"

"What are you trying to say?"

"No, wait, Herr Settembrini, all I mean is that he has a moist spot, and that prevents him from becoming a priest. But his permutations would probably have prevented it as well, and to that extent his permutations and his moist spot go together, so to speak. In his own way he's one of life's problem children, too, a *handsome Jesuit with a little moist spot*."

They had reached the sanatorium. Before separating, they stood for a while in the fenced-in area out front, forming their own little group, while a few patients loitering at the main entrance watched them as they talked.

Herr Settembrini said, "To repeat myself, my young friends, I am warning you. I cannot prevent your cultivating this acquaintance now that it has been made, if curiosity impels you to do so. But arm your hearts and minds with mistrust, never let your critical resistance down. I will characterize the man for you in a single word. He is a voluptuary."

The cousins grimaced. Then Hans Castorp asked, "A what? I beg your pardon, but he's part of the Society. They have to take certain vows, as far as I know, and besides he's so sickly and puny."

"You are speaking foolishness, my good engineer," Herr Settembrini responded. "His physical frailty has nothing to do with it. And as for his vows, there is such a thing as mental reservation. I spoke, however, in a broader, more intellectual sense, a perspective I assumed you would understand by now. You may still recall when I visited you in your room one day—long ago now, terribly long ago. You were just completing your period of bed rest after having been accepted as a patient."

"But of course. You entered my room, it was dusk, and you turned on the light. I remember as if it were yesterday."

"Good. And we started to chat—as happens frequently, thank God—about higher things. I believe, in fact, we spoke about life and death, about the dignity of death, to the extent that it is a constituent and prerequisite of life, and about how it can degenerate into something grotesque if we commit the abominable error of isolating it as an intellectual principle. Gentlemen," Herr Settembrini continued now, stepping very near to the young men, spreading the thumb and middle finger of his left hand into a wide fork, as if to concentrate their attention, and raising the forefinger of his right hand in warning, "imprint this on your minds: the intellect is sovereign, its will is free, it defines the moral world. If it isolates death in a dualistic fashion, then by that act of intellectual will, death becomes real in actual fact—*actu,* do you understand? It becomes a force of its own opposed to life, an antagonistic principle, the great seduction—and its kingdom is lust. And why lust, you ask? And I reply: Because it loosens and delivers, because it is a deliverance, and not deliverance from evil, but evil deliverance. It loosens morals and morality, it delivers from discipline and self-control, liberates for lust. In warning you about this man, with whom I have unwillingly made you acquainted, in demanding that you gird yourselves three times round with a critical spirit when you are dealing with him and discussing things, I do so because all his thoughts are of lust; they stand under the aegis of death, a most depraved force—just as I told you that day, my good engineer, I very clearly recall using that phrase, for I always keep in mind useful and apt words I have used on occasion—a most depraved force directed against morals, progress, labor, and life. And it is the sublime duty of the pedagogue to defend young souls against its mephitic breath."

One could not speak in finer, clearer, more rounded phrases than Herr Settembrini. Hans Castorp and Joachim Ziemssen expressed their warmest thanks for what he had told them, took their leave, and climbed the stairs to the main entrance of the Berghof; and Herr Settembrini returned to his humanist's lectern, one floor above Naphta's silken cell.

The visit we have described here was the cousins' first with Naphta. It was followed by two or three more, one in fact in the absence of Herr Settembrini; and each of them provided young Hans Castorp with a great many things to consider whenever the sublime image, now called *homo Dei,* hovered before his mind's eye as he sat at his secluded spot in the blue-blossoming meadow and "played king."

An Outburst of Temper/
Something Very Embarrassing

AND SO AUGUST BEGAN, and among its first days, slipping past
without incident, was the anniversary of our hero's arrival up here.
It was over now, and that was good—for Hans Castorp had watched its
coming with some uneasiness. That was normal—no one was fond of
anniversaries of arrival. Those who had been here a year or more did not
mention them. True, people never failed to take advantage of any excuse
for festivities or toasts and augmented the high-points in the year's rhyth-
mic pulse with as many private, irregular beats as possible by gathering
in the restaurant to feast and pop corks in celebration of birthdays, physical
exams, imminent wild or authorized departures, and similar events—but
patients greeted these memorial days with pure silence, let them glide by,
and truly forgot to observe them in the certainty that others would not
recall them very clearly either. They made sure that time was properly
segmented, kept an eye on the calendar and its recurring cycle of external
events. But the measuring and counting of the time that bound each person
to space up here, of personal, individual time—that was for newcomers
and short-termers; established residents reserved their praise for unmeasured time and unheeded eternity, for the day that was always the same,
and each person delicately presumed everyone else harbored the same
sentiment. It would have been considered totally uncouth and cruel to
mention to someone that he or she had been here for three years to the
day—it was not done. Frau Stöhr herself, however lacking in other respects, showed perfect tact and refinement in this regard and had never
been guilty of such an offense. Her illness and the fever in her body were,
to be sure, bound up with her great ignorance. Only recently she had
told her tablemates about the "affectation" in the tips of her lungs and
then, when conversation turned to historical matters, declared that remembering dates had always been her "ring of Polycrates"—which was likewise greeted by rather frozen expressions on the faces of those around her.
But it was unthinkable that she would have reminded young Ziemssen, for
instance, of his anniversary in February, though the thought probably
occurred to her, since her unhappy head was filled with useless dates
and facts and she loved keeping track of other people's affairs. Custom,
however, held her in check.

It was the same on Hans Castorp's anniversary. She had indeed tried to give him a meaningful wink at breakfast, but when his only response was a vacant stare, she quickly pulled back. Even Joachim had said nothing to his cousin, although he was well aware of the date on which he had met his "three-week guest" at the station in Dorf. Joachim was not very talkative by nature—definitely not as talkative as Hans Castorp had become up here, not to mention certain humanists and humbugs of their acquaintance—but the silence he had adopted of late was peculiar and impressive. Only monosyllables passed his lips—while the muscles in his face worked hard. It was clear that for him the station at Dorf was associated with more than arrivals or meeting guests. He was corresponding regularly with the flatlands now. Decisions were ripening within him. The preparations he was making were almost concluded.

July had been warm and sunny. But at the start of the new month, bad weather set in—damp, gloomy days, with a mixture of snow and rain, then snow, clear and simple; and except for an occasional splendid burst of summer, the bad weather continued for the rest of the month and on into September. At first the rooms held the warmth of the preceding summer days—fifty-five degrees, which was considered comfortable—but they quickly grew colder and colder. People were glad to see snow cover the valley, because that sight—and only that sight, since falling temperatures accomplished nothing—moved management to turn on the heat, at first only in the dining hall, but then in the rooms as well, so that when you unwrapped yourself from your blankets at the end of a rest cure and came back into the room from the balcony, your moist, numb hands could feel warmth stirring in the radiator, even if the dry heat only made your cheeks burn all the more.

Was this winter? The senses could not avoid that conclusion, and people complained that they had been "cheated out of summer"—although, abetted by natural and artificial circumstances, people had cheated themselves out of it by squandering both internal and external time. Reason tried to tell them beautiful autumn days would follow, a whole succession of days so warm and splendid that they might very well deserve the honor of being called summer—that is, if one ignored the sun's crossing the sky lower and setting earlier each day. But the effect of the winter landscape on the general mood was stronger than any such consolation. You stood at your closed balcony door and stared with disgust at the squalls and flurries—just as Joachim was standing there now.

"Is winter starting up again already?" he asked in a choked voice.

From behind him in the room, Hans Castorp responded, "It would be a little early for that—it can't be for good yet. Although it does have a look of terrible finality about it. If winter means darkness, snow, cold, warm radiators—then this is winter again, there's no denying. And when you think that it was only just winter, that the thaw is barely over—at least it *seems* that way, doesn't it, as if spring were only yesterday? It can put you in a foul mood momentarily, I admit. It's deleterious to a basic human love of life—let me explain what I mean. I mean the world is normally arranged so that it meets people's needs and is salutary to their love of life, there's no denying that. I wouldn't go so far as to say that the natural order—the size of the earth, for instance, or the time it takes for it to turn on its axis or orbit the sun, the alternation of day and night, the change of seasons, the rhythm of the cosmos, if you like—that all that has been measured out to suit our needs. That would surely be too simple, too brazen—what the philosophers call teleology. But the fact is, thank God, that our needs and the general, fundamental facts of nature are in harmony. I say 'thank God,' because it really is a reason to praise God. And down in the flatlands, when summer comes, or winter, then the time since the previous summer, or winter, is always the same, and the season seems new and welcome—that's the foundation of our love of life. But up here with us, that order, that harmony is disturbed—first of all, because there are no real seasons, as you yourself once noted, but merely summer days and winter days all mixed up higgledy-piggledy. And besides, there really is no time that you can notice passing, so that the new winter, when it does come, isn't new, but just the old one again; and that explains the discontent you feel when peering out through the windowpane."

"Many thanks," Joachim said. "And now that you have explained the matter, I suppose, you're so content that you're even content with its being like this, even though it's . . . no!" Joachim said. "Enough!" he said. "It's a filthy mess. The whole thing is a monstrous, disgusting, filthy mess, and whatever you may think, I—" And he strode rapidly out of the room, angrily pulling the door to behind him—and there was almost no doubt that those were tears in his beautiful, gentle eyes.

Hans Castorp was left behind, perplexed. He had never taken certain of his cousin's resolves all that seriously—at least not as long as they remained pronouncements. But now that Joachim had fallen silent, with the muscles in his face working so hard, and begun behaving as he just had, Hans Castorp took fright, because he understood that the officer was man enough to act—turned pale with fright, for both of them, for both Joachim and himself. *It is quite possible that he will die*, he thought—but that information was secondhand at best; and so it became mixed with the pain of an old suspicion he had never been able to suppress

entirely and he thought, "Can it be that he'll leave me alone up here—
even though it was I who came up here just to visit him?" And then he
thought, "How horrible, how absurd—so horrible and absurd that I can
feel my face turning cold and my heart pounding irregularly. Because if
I stay behind up here alone—and that is what I'll do if he leaves, it's
totally out of the question for me to go with him—then it will be—my
heart's standing absolutely still now—it will be for good and all, because
I'll never, ever find my way back to the flatlands alone."

This was the frightening course Hans Castorp's thoughts took. And
that same afternoon, he was to gain certainty about the turn things had
taken: Joachim declared the die was cast, the blow struck, his decision
made.

They had descended into the bright basement for their monthly checkups—it was after tea, one day early in September. As they entered the
dry heated air of the consulting room, they found Dr. Krokowski at his
desk and the director leaning against the wall, his arms crossed, his face
very purple—in one hand he held his stethoscope and was tapping it
against his shoulder. He yawned and stared at the ceiling. "Greetings,
boys!" he said in a dull voice that was a further indication of a very
languid mood—melancholy, general resignation. Evidently he had been
smoking. But he was vexed by objective problems as well, about which
the cousins had already heard: the sort of sanatorium affair with which
everyone was only all too familiar. A young lady, Ammy Nölting was
her name, had first been admitted in the fall two years previous and then
discharged as fully cured in August, nine months later—but was back
before September was even out, claiming that she "did not feel well" at
home. Last February her lungs were found clear of any sounds and she
had been returned to the flatlands. Around the middle of July, however,
she had resumed her old place at Frau Iltis's table. This same Ammy had
been discovered at one o'clock in the morning in her room with another
patient named Polypraxios, a young Greek chemist whose father owned
dye-works in Piraeus—the same fellow whose well-turned leg had aroused
justifiable admiration at the Mardi Gras party. The discovery was made
by a jealous friend, who had found her way to Ammy's room by the
same route Polypraxios had taken, that is, by way of the balcony, and in
her rage and pain over what she saw there had begun shrieking so dreadfully that people came running. Word spread like wildfire. Behrens had
no choice but to expel all three—the Athenian, Fräulein Nölting, and her
girlfriend, who in her passionate rage had paid little attention to her own
honor—and had just been discussing the whole unsavory affair with his
assistant, who, by the way, had been treating both girls privately. Even

as he examined the cousins, he went on talking about the matter in a melancholy, resigned tone of voice, for he was such an expert in auscultation that he could simultaneously listen to a patient's interior, talk about something else, and dictate what he had heard to his assistant.

"Yes, yes, gentlemen, the damn libido," he said. "The whole affair is great sport for you, of course—it doesn't matter to you. Vesicular. But the director of a sanatorium gets a noseful, believe you—muffled—believe you me. Can I help it if phthisis is accompanied by increased concupiscence? Slight roughness? I didn't arrange things this way, but before you know what's happened you're running a cathouse. Diminished under the left shoulder. We provide analysis, a chance to talk things out—and a hell of a lot of good it does. The more the rhonchial pack talks things out the more lecherous they become. I advocate mathematics. Better here, the old sound is gone. Keeping oneself occupied with mathematics, I say, is the best medicine for cupidity. Prosecutor Paravant, who was severely afflicted, threw himself into math—he's busy squaring the circle these days, and it has greatly eased his problem. But most of them are too dull-witted or too lazy for that, God help them. Vesicular. You see, I'm quite aware that young folks go to the dogs all too easily here, and I used to attempt to take occasional measures against their debauchery. But then one day some lad or lover looked me straight in the eye and asked what business it was of mine. And since then I've been only a doctor. Weak rattling, top right."

He was finished now with Joachim; he slipped his stethoscope into the pocket of his smock and rubbed both eyes with his gigantic left hand— a habit of his when he "faded" and felt melancholy. Half-mechanically and between moody yawns, he rattled off his sales talk: "Well, Ziemssen, keep your chin up. Things don't always happen the way we find them described in a physiology textbook. There's still a hitch or two, and you haven't entirely cleared up your troubles with Gaffky, either—you even went up a notch or so here recently. It's six this round, but that's no reason to be down in the dumps. You were more ill when you first arrived, I can show you the records to prove it, and with another five, six moneths—did you know that people used to say 'moneth' rather than month? Much more euphonious, I think. I've decided to use only 'moneth' myself."

"Director Behrens," Joachim began—he was standing there naked from the waist up, but still at attention, his chest thrust forward, his heels together, and with a face as blotchy as it was the first time Hans Castorp had noticed that this was how his tanned face looked when it turned pale.

"If you do your duty for another half year or so," Behrens broke in over his halting start, "keeping your boots polished and such, then your career is made. You can take Constantinople, you'll be robust enough to bust a whole Prussian regiment."

Who knows, given the director's melancholy state, how much more balderdash of this sort there would have been, if the sight of Joachim, standing there at undaunted attention, obviously determined to speak—and speak courageously—had not disconcerted him.

"Director Behrens," the young man said, "I wish to report that I have decided to depart."

"What's this? You're going off and leaving us? I thought you wanted to join the military someday, a healthy man."

"No, sir, I have to leave now—one week from today."

"Someone tell me—am I hearing right? You want to toss in the towel, you want to cut and run? Do you know that's desertion of duty?"

"No, that is not how I see it, Director Behrens. I have to return to my regiment."

"Although I'm telling you that I can definitely discharge you in six months, but not one day before?"

Joachim's pose was growing more and more official. He tucked in his stomach and in a choked, bluff voice he said, "I have been here for a year and a half, Director Behrens. I can wait no longer. You originally told me three months, sir. My cure has been regularly extended, until another year and a quarter have now passed, and I am still not well."

"Is that my fault?"

"No, Director Behrens. But I cannot wait any longer. I can't wait for a total cure up here, otherwise I will miss this opportunity. I have to go back down. I need some time to outfit myself and take care of other matters."

"Do you have your family's approval for what you're doing?"

"My mother approves. It's all arranged. I will be joining the seventy-sixth as an ensign on the first of October."

"No matter what the risk?" Behrens asked, staring at him with his bloodshot eyes.

"Yes, sir, Director Behrens, sir," Joachim replied with trembling lips.

"Well, fine, then, Ziemssen." The director's facial expression changed, his body relaxed, everything seemed to go slack. "Fine, then, Ziemssen. At ease. Go ahead, leave—and God be with you. I see you know what you want. Take over. The responsibility is definitely yours and not mine from the moment you do take over. Man is master of his fate. You travel at your own risk. I wash my hands. But never fear, it may turn out all right. Yours is a fresh-air profession. It may very well be that it does you good and you'll make the grade."

"Yes sir, Director Behrens, sir."

"Well, and what about you, my young member of the civilian population? I suppose you want to go along?"

It was Hans Castorp's turn to answer. He stood there as pale as he had at the examination that had ended with his being admitted one year before, was standing on the very same spot, and his heart was once again hammering visibly against his ribs. He said, "I would prefer to make that dependent on your approval, Director Behrens."

"My approval? Fine!" And he grabbed Hans Castorp by one arm and pulled him to him. Listened and tapped. But dictated no results. It all went rather quickly. When he was done, he said, "You may leave."

Hans Castorp stammered, "You mean . . . but how can that be? Am I cured?"

"Yes, you're cured. The spot at the upper left isn't worth talking about. Your temperature has nothing to do with it. I can't tell you what causes that. I assume it's of no further importance. As far as I'm concerned, you may leave."

"But, Director Behrens. You're not really serious, are you?"

"Not serious? What do you mean? What would make you think that? What sort of person do you suppose I am, if I may ask? What do you take me for, the owner of a cathouse?"

It was an outburst of temper. The rush of hot blood to the director's face turned his purple cheeks a deep violet; his skewed lip and little moustache were wrenched until upper teeth could be seen at one side of his mouth. He thrust his head forward like a bull. His bloodshot, watery eyes popped from their sockets.

"I won't stand for it!" he shouted. "I don't own anything here. I'm merely an employee. I'm a doctor. I am *only* a doctor, do you understand? I am not anyone's procurer. I'm no Signor Amoroso working the Toledo in beautiful Naples, do you understand? I serve suffering humanity. And if you have formed a different opinion of me, you can go to hell, to pot, or to the dogs—take your pick. *Bon voyage!*"

And with long, even strides he walked out the door—the door leading to the X-ray waiting room—and slammed it behind him.

The cousins looked helplessly to Dr. Krokowski, but he merely buried his nose deeper in his papers. They scrambled to put on their clothes.

As they climbed the stairs, Hans Castorp said, "That was really dreadful. Have you ever seen him like that before?"

"No, never like that. But superiors throw temper tantrums. The only thing to do is maintain perfect composure and let it pass right over you. He was upset, of course, by the Polypraxios-Nölting affair. But did you see," Joachim went on, and his joy at having fought the good fight rose visibly, making him catch his breath, "did you see how he backed off and capitulated when he realized that I was serious? All you have to do is show your spunk and not let them get the upper hand. And now I've been given permission more or less—he said himself that I'd probably make the grade—to leave a week from today." And correcting himself, he added, "To be with my regiment inside of three weeks." He did not even mention his cousin, but restricted his exuberant comments to his own fate.

Hans Castorp did not reply. He said nothing about Joachim's "permission" to leave, or about his own, although the topic might easily have been addressed. He got himself ready for his rest cure, stuck his thermometer in his mouth, put perfected skills to work and with a few deft, sure motions of the sacred art—about which no one in the flatlands had the vaguest— he wrapped his two camel-hair blankets around him to form a solid, unbroken cylinder, and lay there quietly on his splendid lounge chair, in the cold damp of the early autumn afternoon.

Rain clouds hung low; the fantasy flag had been taken down. There were still remnants of snow on the wet boughs of the silver fir. From the common lounging area below, from where he had first heard Herr Albin's voice a little more than a year ago, the low hum of conversation now rose to him as he lay in his rest cure, his fingers and face quickly turning clammy and stiff in the cold. He was used to it and was grateful for the opportunity that the local style of life—which for him had long since become the only conceivable style—provided him to lie there safe and secure and think things through.

It was definite: Joachim would be leaving. Rhadamanthus had discharged him—not officially, not as a cured man, but with a kind of semiapproval all the same, in recognition of Joachim's perseverance. He would take the narrow-gauge train back down to the lowlands via Landquart and Romanshorn, then pass over the wide, unfathomable lake (whose frozen surface, as legend had it, a man had ridden across on horseback), and travel the length of Germany to arrive home. He would live there in the world of the flatlands, among people who had not the vaguest about how one had to live, about thermometers, about the art of wrapping oneself, about fur-lined sleeping bags, about three promenades a day, about—it was difficult to say, difficult to enumerate all the things people down there did not know about; but the notion that Joachim, after having spent more than a year and a half up here, would now be living among such ignorant people, that notion, which applied only to Joachim—and merely from a great distance and only quite hypothetically to himself—so confused Hans Castorp that he closed his eyes and dismissed it with a gesture of his hand. "Impossible, impossible," he murmured.

But since it was impossible, that meant he would go on living alone up here without Joachim, didn't it? Yes. And for how long? Until Behrens discharged him as cured—in earnest, not like today. But first of all, that was a point in time so indefinite that you could only describe it, as Joachim had done on some occasion or other, with a trailing gesture of immeasurability, and second, did that make the impossible any more possible? It was more like the opposite. And to be fair, he had to admit that a hand had now been offered him, now, when the impossible was perhaps not quite so impossible as it would be later—Joachim's wild departure could be a support, a guiding hand on the road back to the flatlands, which he would never, ever find all on his own. And what if humanistic pedagogy were to learn of this opportunity? Oh, how it would exhort him to grab that hand and accept its guidance. But Herr Settembrini was only a representative—of things and forces worth hearing about, but not without qualification, as if nothing else existed. The same applied to Joachim. He was a soldier, yes indeed. He would be departing at almost the same moment when Marusya of the prominent breasts was supposed to return (it was common knowledge that she would be back on October first); whereas for him, Hans Castorp the civilian, a departure seemed impossible, because—to put it openly and succinctly—he had to wait for Clavdia Chauchat, about whose return he had heard nothing at all. "That is not how I see it," Joachim had said when Rhadamanthus mentioned desertion, and Joachim had doubtless interpreted it as more of the gloomy director's hot air. But things were surely different for him as a civilian. For him—yes, no doubt about it! He had lain down here in the cold and damp today for the sole purpose of wresting this crucial insight from his mixed emotions—for him to grab this chance of a fraudulent or semifraudulent departure to the flatlands would constitute real desertion of duty, desertion from the vast responsibilities that had grown up out of his vision of the sublime image, the *homo Dei,* a betrayal of the hard, exciting duties of "playing king," which though they might overtax his natural energies nevertheless made him wildly happy whenever he fulfilled them on his balcony or in the blue-blossoming meadow.

He pulled the thermometer from his mouth, more violently than he had ever done before, except for that first time, the day the head nurse had sold him this dainty gadget, and he gazed down at it with the same eagerness as he had then. Mercury had climbed very robustly, reaching 100 degrees, almost 100.2.

Hans Castorp threw his blankets aside, jumped up, and quickly walked the length of his room, to the door and back. Then resuming his horizontal position, he called out softly to Joachim and asked about his fever chart.

"I'm no longer measuring," Joachim replied.

"Well, I have a temp," Hans Castorp said, borrowing Frau Stöhr's abridged form of the word. Joachim responded with silence from his side of the glass partition.

And he did not say anything later that day or the next, either, did not inquire about his cousin's plans or decisions, which, given the short time involved, would be revealed all by themselves, either by actions or by the failure to act—and indeed they were, by the latter. Hans Castorp appeared to have joined the quietists, who claimed that to act was an affront to God, who alone can will to act; his activities during this week, at any rate, were limited to a visit with Behrens. Joachim was quite aware of this consultation—the subject and outcome were as plain as the nose on his face. His cousin, he was sure, had declared he would take the liberty of setting greater store by the director's earlier and frequent warnings that his case should be completely cured so he would never have to return again, than by hasty words spoken in a moment of impatience. He had a temperature of one hundred degrees, he could not believe he had been officially discharged, unless the director's recent remarks were to be taken as an order of expulsion, although he, the speaker, was unaware of having given any cause for such a measure; he had therefore decided, after considering the matter calmly and in conscious distinction to Joachim Ziemssen, to remain here and wait until he was completely detoxified. To which the director had surely responded, more or less verbatim, with, "*Bon*, fine!" and "No harm meant!" and then gone on to say that was what he called being reasonable and that he had seen right off Hans Castorp had more talent for being a patient than that trace-kicking swashbuckler. And so on.

Joachim guessed that this was the course their conversation had taken, and his guess was fairly accurate; and so he said nothing and simply observed in silence that, unlike himself, Hans Castorp was not making any preparations for departure. And dear old Joachim had enough to do just looking after himself. He really could not worry about his cousin's whereabouts or fate. As is easy to imagine, a storm was raging in his breast. It was a good thing, perhaps, that he no longer kept track of his temperature, having—so he claimed—dropped his thermometer and broken it. Such measurements might well have brought forth disconcerting results—particularly given Joachim's dreadfully excited state, in which he would by turns flush darkly with joy and grow pale with anticipation. He could no longer lie still; Hans Castorp heard him pacing his room four times a day, during those hours when the rest of the Berghof assumed the horizontal position. A year and a half! And now it was back down to the flatlands, back home, where he would actually join his regiment— even if only with semipermission. It was no small matter, definitely not. Listening to that restless pacing, Hans Castorp could certainly sympathize with his cousin. Joachim had lived up here for eighteen months—a year come full circle, and half again—had profoundly settled in, become accustomed to the routine, to the undeviating path of life here, had walked it seventy times seven times, in all seasons. And now he was to return home, to an alien land, to ignorant people. What difficulties in acclimatization awaited one there? Was it any wonder, then, that Joachim's excitement consisted not just of joy but also of fear, that the anguish of saying farewell to everything familiar kept him pacing his room?—And that is without even mentioning Marusya.

But joy predominated. Dear old Joachim's heart and words were brimming over with it; he spoke about himself, never mentioning his cousin's future. He talked about how new and fresh everything would be—life, himself, time, each day, each hour. He would know solid time again, the slow, momentous years of youth. He spoke about his mother, Hans Castorp's half aunt Ziemssen, who had those same gentle, black eyes and whom he had not seen during all his time in the mountains, because, like her son, she had been put off from month to month, season to season, and so could never actually decide to pay him a visit. He smiled and spoke enthusiastically about the oath he would soon be taking—in a solemn ceremony he would stand beneath the flag and swear his allegiance to it, to the banner. "What's that?" Hans Castorp asked. "Are you serious? To a flagpole? To a scrap of cloth?" Yes, indeed; and in the artillery the oath was sworn, symbolically, to a cannon. Well, the civilian remarked, those were certainly fervent customs, something for emotional fanatics, one might say. To which Joachim simply nodded with happy pride.

He was caught up in preparations; he paid his final bill in full at the office and began packing his bags days ahead of time. He packed summer and winter clothes, gave his fur-lined sleeping bag and camel-hair blankets to the porter to have them sewn into linen sacks—he might have use for them sometime on maneuvers. He began to say his good-byes. He paid a farewell visit to Naphta and Settembrini—alone, his cousin did not join him, did not even ask what Settembrini had said about Joachim's imminent departure or Hans Castorp's imminent non-departure, whether he had said, "I see, I see," or "Yes, yes," or both, or *Poveretto*." It was all of no interest to Hans Castorp, apparently.

Then came the eve of departure, when Joachim did everything for the last time—each meal, each rest cure, each promenade—and took his leave of the doctors and the head nurse. And then came the day itself. Joachim arrived at breakfast with glowing eyes and cold hands, since he had not slept at all, and hardly ate a bite. When the dwarf reported that his baggage was strapped to the carriage, he hastily jumped to his feet to bid farewell to his tablemates. As she said her good-byes, Frau Stöhr wept great tears, the unsalty, free-flowing tears of the uncultured; and in the next moment, behind Joachim's back, she turned to the teacher, shook her head, and wagged one hand, its fingers splayed—her sour expression reflecting a vulgar skepticism about Joachim's permission to depart and how he would manage now. Hans Castorp watched her as he stood there drinking the rest of his tea, ready to follow his cousin out. There was still some tipping to do, and then came the official farewell in the lobby, extended by a representative of the management. As always, patients had gathered to watch the departure: Frau Iltis of the "stirletto," Fräulein Levi of the ivory complexion, drastic Herr Popóv and his wife. They waved their handkerchiefs as the carriage, rear brake set, skidded down the driveway. Joachim had been given roses. He was wearing a hat. Hans Castorp was not.

It was a splendid morning, the first sunny day after a long gloomy period. Outlined against the blue were the unchanged hallmarks of Schiahorn, Green Towers, and Dorfberg—Joachim's eyes rested on them. What a shame he had to depart in such beautiful weather, Hans Castorp remarked; there was something almost spiteful about it, because a last inhospitable impression always made parting easier. To which Joachim replied that things didn't have to be made easier for him, that this was excellent drill weather, which he would certainly·be able to use down below. Otherwise they said little. As things stood for each of them and between them, there was in fact little to say. Besides, the limping concierge was right in front of them, up on the box next to the driver.

Sitting up straight, thrown back against the cabriolet's hard cushions, they crossed the brook and then the narrow tracks, following the street running alongside them and faced by an irregular pattern of buildings, and halted now on the gravel apron in front of the Dorf railroad station, which was not much more than a shed. Hans Castorp was startled to recognize it all again; he had not seen the station since his arrival at dusk thirteen months before. "This is where I arrived," he said superfluously. And Joachim simply replied, "Yes, so you did," and paid the driver.

The bustling, limping concierge took care of everything—the ticket, the baggage. They stood side by side on the platform, next to the miniature train, right in front of the little gray-upholstered compartment where

Joachim had claimed a seat with his coat, plaid blanket, and roses. "Well, make sure you swear that oath fervently," Hans Castorp said; and Joachim responded, "I intend to." And what else? They exchanged final regards to be paid both to people down below and up here. Then Hans Castorp stood there drawing figures on the asphalt with his cane. At the "all aboard" call, he looked up in surprise; he stared at Joachim. Joachim stared at him. They shook hands. Hans Castorp managed a vague smile; his cousin's eyes were serious, sad, urgent. "Hans!" he said—good God! Had the world ever known a more embarrassing moment? He had called Hans Castorp by his first name. Their whole lives long they had used informal pronouns and phrases like "my man," and now, in defiance of all cool, reserved custom, in a moment of the most embarrassing exuberance—a first name. "Hans," he said, and in desperate anguish he squeezed his cousin's hand, and the latter noticed Joachim's head trembling from lack of sleep and the excitement of the trip, just as his own did when he "played king." "Hans," he said imploringly, "come soon!" And then he swung himself up on the footboard. The door closed, there was a whistle, the cars banged against each other, the little locomotive pulled, the train glided away. The traveler waved from the window with his hat; the man left behind waved with his hand. He stood there a long time, alone, his heart in turmoil. Then he slowly walked back up the road that Joachim had led him along little more than a year before.

An Attack Repulsed

T**HE WHEEL TURNED.** The clock hand jerked. Orchis and columbine had ceased blooming, as had the wild pink. The deep blue stars of gentian and the pale, poisonous blossoms of meadow crocus appeared again in the wet grasses, and there was a reddish cast to the woodlands. The autumn equinox had passed, All Souls' was coming into view—and for expert consumers of time, that meant so were the first Sunday in Advent, the shortest day of the year, and Christmas. But for now, there was a succession of beautiful October days—days like the one on which the cousins had viewed the director's oil paintings.

Since Joachim's departure, Hans Castorp no longer sat at Frau Stöhr's table—the same table that had been abandoned by the late Dr. Blumenkohl and where Marusya had sat, stifling her unfounded mirth in her orange-scented handkerchief. New guests, total strangers, were sitting there now. Two and a half months into our friend's second year, management had assigned him a different seat, at a neighboring table set crosswise to his old one, between it and the Good Russian table and farther toward the veranda door on the left—in short, Settembrini's table. Yes, Hans Castorp was now sitting in the same spot the humanist had deserted; like his old place, it was at one end of the table, opposite the "doctor's chair," which was reserved at each of the seven tables for the director and his aide-de-camp.

At the far end on his left, the hunchbacked amateur photographer from Mexico sat perched on several pillows, wearing the facial expression of a deaf man, the result of linguistic isolation; on his right was seated the old maid from Transylvania, a lady who, as Herr Settembrini had complained, demanded that everyone take an interest in her brother-in-law, although no one knew the man, nor wished to know him. At certain times of the day, she could be seen at the railing of her balcony doing hygienic deep-breathing exercises—her chest, flat as a platter, rising and falling and her cane with a niello-silver handle, which she also used on her constitutionals, held straight across the back of her neck. A Czech gentleman sat across from her; people called him Herr Wenzel, since no one could pronounce his real last name. In his day, Herr Settembrini had tried to utter its intricate succession of consonants—not, however, as an honest attempt at its wild jungle of sound, but as an amusing challenge for his own hopelessly elegant Latinity. Although this Bohemian was as stocky as a badger and displayed an appetite quite amazing even for people up here, he had been asserting for four years now that he would soon die. At their evening socials, he would occasionally plunk out the songs of his homeland on a ribboned mandolin or talk about his sugar-beet plantation, where only pretty maids worked. Closer to Hans Castorp, then, one on each side of the table, came Herr and Frau Magnus—the beer-brewer from Halle and his wife. Melancholy hung like a cloud over them, because both were steadily losing vital products of metabolism—Herr Magnus, sugar; Frau Magnus, protein. The mood of pallid Frau Magnus in particular seemed without a glimmer of hope; she exuded bleakness of spirit the way a cellar exudes damp. And perhaps even more explicitly than ignorant Frau Stöhr, she represented the union of sickness and stupidity that Hans Castorp had declared intellectually offensive—for which Settembrini had rebuked him. Herr Magnus was more talkative and lively by nature, although in ways that had once aroused Settembrini's literary impatience. He was also inclined to temper tantrums and had frequently clashed with Herr Wenzel about politics or other matters, for he was incensed by the nationalist aspirations of the Bohemian, who likewise declared himself an advocate of temperance and would sometimes cast moral aspersions on the brewer's profession, whereupon the latter would turn red-faced and defend the incontestable benefits to health found in the beverage with which his interests were so intimately entwined. On such occasions, Herr Settembrini's humor had at one time helped to smooth matters over; but although he sat in the same chair now, Hans Castorp was less adept at this and unable to lay claim to the necessary authority.

With only two of his tablemates was he acquainted more personally. The first, his neighbor on the left, was A. K. Ferge, the good-natured martyr from Saint Petersburg, from under whose bushy reddish-brown moustache came anecdotes about the manufacture of galoshes and tales of distant regions, the Arctic Circle, and the perpetual winter at North Cape. Hans Castorp even took his constitutionals with him now and then. The other person, however, who would join up with them whenever he met them along the way and who sat at the far end of the table across from the hunchbacked Mexican, was the man from Mannheim with the thinning hair and bad teeth—his name was Wehsal, Ferdinand Wehsal, a merchant by trade, the same man whose eyes had constantly clung with such gloomy hunger to the charming Frau Chauchat and who, ever since Mardi Gras, had sought out Hans Castorp's friendship.

He did so with dogged humility, gazing up out of devoted eyes, a look that Hans Castorp found disgusting and horrible, for he understood its complex meaning, but that he nevertheless struggled to return in a humane, calm fashion. Knowing that the slightest frown was sufficient to terrify and cow the pitiful, sensitive fellow, he tolerated Wehsal's servile habit of seizing every opportunity to bow and scrape, sometimes allowed him to carry his overcoat on their promenades—and Wehsal would bear it over one arm with a kind of reverence—and even put up with the Mannheimer's conversation, and very gloomy conversation it was. Wehsal loved to pose questions such as whether there was any point in declaring one's love to someone who did not even know one was alive—a hopeless declaration of love, what did the gentlemen think of that? For his part, he thought very highly of it, was of the opinion that it brought infinite happiness. Such an act of confession might arouse disgust and entailed much self-abasement; all the same, it established, if only for a moment, intimate contact with the desired object, dragging her into one's confidence, into the element of one's passion, and although it meant that everything was over, such eternal loss was not too much to pay for desperate bliss—for confession was a form of violence, all the more enjoyable for the disgust it encountered. At this, Hans Castorp's face darkened and Wehsal shrank back, but more in response to the presence of good-natured Herr Ferge—who had often emphasized that all higher, more complicated things were

utterly foreign to him—than to any judgmental moral rectitude in our
hero's expression. Since our intent all along has been to make him no
better or worse than he was, it should also be noted that when poor
Wehsal approached him privately one evening and begged with ashen
words for God's sake to please tell him in strict confidence about his
experiences that night of the Mardi Gras party, Hans Castorp had complied with calm charity, although, as the reader can well imagine, he did
not permit anything the least bit base or frivolous to sully that hushed
scene. All the same, we have our reasons for excluding him and ourselves
from it, and will merely add that afterward Wehsal bore his friend's
overcoat with twice the reverence.

But enough of Hans's new tablemates. The seat on his right was occupied, though only temporarily, for just a few days, by a visitor, just as
he himself had once been, by a guest, a relative from the flatlands, an
envoy from those regions, one might say—in a word, by Hans's uncle
James Tienappel.

It was strange suddenly to have sitting beside him a representative and
ambassador from home, the scent of an old, vanished, earlier life, of an
"upper world" that lay so far below, still clinging fresh to the weave of
the man's English suit. But it had been inevitable. Hans Castorp had been
quietly expecting such a raid from the flatlands for a long time now, had
even correctly guessed the person who would actually be entrusted with
the task of reconnaissance—but that had not been hard to do. Seafaring
Peter was more or less out of the question, and as for Great-uncle Tienappel, it was understood that wild horses could not drag him to regions
whose barometric pressures he had every reason to fear. No, it would
have to be James who was commissioned to check up on the missing
family member. Hans Castorp had expected him before this. But once
Joachim had returned home alone and spread the news among their relatives of how things stood up here, an attack was due, indeed overdue;
and so Hans Castorp had not been the least bit surprised when, barely
two weeks after Joachim's departure, the concierge handed him a telegram,
whose content he surmised even as he opened it: an announcement of the
imminent arrival of James Tienappel. He had business in Switzerland and
had decided to use the occasion to visit Hans on his mountaintop. He
would be there the day after next.

"Fine," Hans Castorp thought. "Lovely," he thought. And even silently added something like, "Just as he pleases." And addressing the
approaching visitor, he thought, "If you only knew!" In short, he received
the news with great calm, passed word along to both Director Behrens
and management, had them ready a room—Joachim's old one was still

available. Two days later, at around eight in the evening, the same time of day that he himself had arrived—although it was dark now—he hired the same hard-riding vehicle in which he had seen Joachim off, to take him to the station in Dorf and fetch the envoy from the flatlands who had come to check up on him.

Crimson-faced and wearing neither hat nor overcoat, he stood at the edge of the platform as the little train rolled in, stood under the window of his relative's compartment, and directed him to get off now—he was here. Consul Tienappel—he was a vice-consul, having generously relieved the old man of his honorary duties as well—emerged from his compartment half-frozen and wrapped in his winter coat (because there really was a biting chill to the October evening, its air very close to what one would call clear and frosty, indeed it was sure to freeze by morning), stepped forward expressing his amused surprise in the somewhat spare, but very civilized phrases of a northwestern German gentleman, greeted his nephew, or quasi cousin, emphasizing his satisfaction at how splendid he looked, discovered that the limping attendant had taken care of all his baggage problems, and climbed up with Hans Castorp onto the high, hard seats of the carriage. They drove off under a starry sky; leaning his head back and pointing a forefinger into the air, Hans Castorp elucidated the fields of heaven for his uncle, or quasi cousin, tracing with words and gestures one twinkling constellation here, another there, and calling planets by name; his relative, meanwhile, paid more attention to his companion than to the cosmos, remarking to himself that, although it was certainly possible and hardly crazy to speak here and now about the stars, there were surely several other more obvious topics. Since when was he so well informed about what was up there, he asked Hans Castorp; to which the latter replied that it was knowledge acquired from his rest cure, from lying on his balcony every evening—spring, summer, fall, and winter. What? He spent his nights lying on a balcony? Oh, yes. And the consul would be doing the same—he would not have much choice in the matter.

"But of course, to be sure," James Tienappel concurred, somewhat intimidated by his foster brother, who spoke so calmly and in a monotone; the crisp autumn evening was close to freezing, yet there beside him sat Hans Castorp without hat or overcoat. "The cold doesn't affect you, does it?" asked James, who was shivering despite the inch-thick fabric of his coat; and if there was something both hurried and halting about the way he put his question, it was because his teeth were very close to chattering.

"We're never cold," Hans Castorp replied calmly and curtly.

The consul could not get his fill of staring at that profile. Hans Castorp did not ask about relatives and acquaintances at home, but James conveyed their regards, including those of Joachim, who had joined his regiment and was glowing with pride and happiness; Hans Castorp calmly accepted these greetings without inquiring further about conditions at home. James felt uneasy about something, though he was not sure whether that something had its origin in his nephew or in his own weariness from travel; looking about him without being able to see much of the Alpine valley's landscape, he took a deep breath of air and let it out again, declaring it excellent. Certainly, his companion replied, it was not world-famous for nothing. This air had special properties. Although it accelerated the metabolism, the body was still able to store protein. Of course it could heal sickness, but its first effect was greatly to enhance illnesses that everyone carried latent within them, because the impetus and stimulus this air gave the whole organism brought illness to exuberant eruption, so to speak. Beg pardon, exuberant? But of course. Had he never noticed that there is something exuberant about the eruption of illness, as if the body were celebrating? "But of course, to be sure," his uncle hastened to reply, losing control of his lower jaw; he now explained that he could stay only eight days, or rather, just a week, seven days actually, perhaps even only six. And since, as he had noted, Hans Castorp was looking robust and really quite splendid thanks to his stay at the sanatorium, which had gone on much longer than expected, he assumed that his nephew would be returning home with him now.

"Well, let's not be reckless about this," Hans Castorp said. Uncle James was talking like someone from down below. Once he had been here awhile and looked around a bit and settled in, he would soon see things differently. The point was a total cure, totality was the decisive factor, and Behrens had recently saddled him with another six months. At this point his uncle addressed him as "my boy," and asked if he was crazy. "Have you gone completely crazy?" he asked. A vacation was what it was, a good year and a quarter long, and now six months more! In God's good name, a man didn't have all that much time! At which point, Hans Castorp laughed calmly and gazed briefly at the stars. Yes, time—as for human time, well, James would have to revise any ideas about time he had brought up here with him before they could discuss that topic. Tienappel promised he would have a serious discussion with the director about Hans's case the next morning. "Do that," Hans Castorp said. "You'll like him. An interesting fellow, brash and melancholy at the same time." And then he pointed to the lights up on Schatzalp and casually mentioned how they used the bobsled run to bring bodies down.

The gentlemen dined together in the Berghof's restaurant, after Hans Castorp had shown his guest to Joachim's room and given him a chance to tidy himself up a bit. The room had been fumigated with H_2CO, Hans Castorp said—just as thoroughly as if it had not been a case of a fraudulent departure, but a departure of a very different sort, not an exodus, but an exitus. And when his uncle asked him what he meant, the nephew replied, "Jargon. Our way of putting things. Joachim deserted—deserted to the colors. That's possible, too. But hurry now, otherwise you won't get a hot meal." And so now there they sat across from one another at the raised table in the cozy warmth of the restaurant. The dwarf promptly arrived to serve them, and James ordered a bottle of burgundy, which was placed on the table cradled in a basket. They toasted glasses and let the gentle glow course through them. The younger man spoke about life up here and the change of seasons, about certain people they would see in the dining hall, about pneumothorax, explained about the operation, mentioning good-natured Ferge's case in particular and expounding on the ghastly nature of pleural shock—the green, brown, and purple faints Herr Ferge claimed to have experienced, the hallucinated odor that was part of the shock, the burst of laughter as he blacked out. He paid for their meal. As was his custom, James ate and drank heartily, his appetite having been whetted even more by the trip and the change of air. But from time to time he broke off taking nourishment; and he would sit there, his mouth full of food he had forgotten to chew, his knife and fork dangling idly at a low angle over his plate, and fix his eyes on Hans Castorp, apparently without even being aware of it—not that his nephew seemed to mind. The veins at Consul Tienappel's temples, just below his thinning blond hair, were swollen.

They did not talk about home, said nothing about personal or family affairs, business or civic matters, did not mention the firm of Tunder and Wilms (dockyards, machine works, and boilers), where they were still waiting for their young trainee to join the firm, though they surely had so many other things to do that one might well ask if they were still waiting at all. James Tienappel had mentioned all these matters during their carriage ride, of course, but the topics had fallen away, as good as dead, as if they had bounced off Hans Castorp's calm, resolute, and genuine indifference, which acted as a kind of immunity that kept anything from touching him, just as he was insensitive to the chill of the autumn evening and could reply, "We're never cold." Maybe that was also why his uncle sometimes gazed at him with that fixed stare. Their conversation also included the head nurse, the doctors, Dr. Krokowski's lectures—it turned out that James would be able to attend one if he stayed eight days. Who had told him, the nephew, that he, the uncle, wanted to attend the lecture? No one. He had simply assumed it, taken it for granted, so calmly, so resolutely, that the mere idea of not participating suddenly appeared in such a strange light to James himself that he hastily added, "But of course, to be sure," in an attempt to forestall any suspicion that he had, even for a moment, planned something so outrageous. Such was indeed the vague, yet compelling power that caused Herr Tienappel to stare, quite unconsciously, at his cousin—with his mouth open now, by the way, because he could no longer breathe through his stuffy nasal passages, although the consul did not have a cold as far as he knew. He listened to his relative talk about the disease that formed the common professional bond for everyone here, and of people's susceptibility to it; about Hans Castorp's own modest, but chronic case, about how the bacillus irritated the cells of the tissue in the bronchi and air sacs of the lungs, about the formation of tubercles and the production of soluble intoxicating toxins, the deterioration of the cells and the process of caseation, which if it continued to petrify into chalky scar tissue meant a beneficial arrest of the disease, but if it went on to build ever-larger soft foci, created cavities that ate away at everything around them and finally destroyed the entire organ. He heard about the accelerated or galloping form of this process, which could lead to one's exitus within a few months, even weeks, heard about pneumectomy, the director's skillfully executed craft, about lung resections, like the one that would be performed the next day, or at least very soon, on a recently arrived serious case, a once very attractive Scottish woman, who was now suffering from *gangraena pulmonum*, gangrene of the lungs, so that a blackish-green infection was raging inside her, forcing her to breathe a vaporized solution of powdered carbolic acid all day just to keep from losing her mind in revulsion at her own body—and suddenly, much to his own surprise and great embarrassment, the consul burst out laughing. The laughter came in loud snorts, until in his dismay he thought better of it and suddenly recovered, coughed, and tried to gloss over his inane conduct by any means possible; but he was relieved to see—a relief that contained the seeds of renewed disquiet—that Hans Castorp had paid no attention at all to what had happened, although he could hardly not have noticed, but simply passed over it with a disregard that did not look like tact, consideration, or politeness, but instead like pure indifference or callousness—a tolerance so vast it was almost eerie, as if he had taught himself long ago not to be surprised by such incidents. But now—and it was unclear whether he hoped to cloak this outburst of levity with common sense and reason, or whether he had something else in mind—quite out of the blue, the consul picked up on a topic one might hear at a men's club, and with the swollen veins pulsing at his temples, began to talk about a so-called *chansonette* whom he had heard singing in a café, a quite incredible young thing, who was currently appearing in Sankt Pauli and whose fiery charms, which he described in detail for his cousin, had simply knocked the breath out of all the gentlemen in the city-state they called home. His tongue grew a little thick as he talked, although he need not have let it disturb him, since his companion's eerie tolerance apparently extended to that phenomenon as well. In any case, the overpowering fatigue of travel, to which he now fell victim, gradually became so obvious that it was not even half past ten when he suggested they end their tête-à-tête; and he was not exactly pleased when, as they crossed the lobby, they ran into the frequently mentioned Dr. Krokowski, who had been sitting with his newspaper right by the door of the reading room and whom the nephew now introduced to his uncle. The consul hardly knew what else to reply to the doctor's jovial, rugged greeting except, "But of course, to be sure," and was glad when his nephew announced he would fetch him for breakfast the next morning at eight and he could then proceed by way of the balcony to Joachim's disinfected room, light his usual bedtime cigarette, and stretch out at last on the deserter's bed. Dozing off twice with the glowing cigarette between his lips, he only by a hair missed starting a general conflagration.

James Tienappel, whom Hans Castorp addressed by turns as "Uncle James" or simply "James," was a long-legged gentleman nearing forty, who wore English suits and linens white as cherry blossoms; he had thinning, canary-yellow hair, very close-set blue eyes, a straw-colored moustache trimmed so close that it was almost not there, and perfectly manicured hands. A husband and father now for several years, he had not, however, been required to leave the old consul's roomy villa on Harvestehuder Weg. He was married to a woman who had come from his own social circle, a lady as civilized and refined as he, who spoke in the same soft, rapid, pointedly polite fashion. At home he gave the impression of a very energetic, prudent, and—despite his elegance—cold, practical man of business; but when traveling in regions whose customs were strange to him, in the south of Germany, for instance, he was all too quick to be polite and self-effacing and assumed a certain impetuous amiability, which was in no way the result of insecurity about his own culture, but on the contrary reflected both an awareness of its solid integrity and a desire to improve on his own aristocratic tendencies—even amid customs he found simply incredible, he would show no surprise whatever. "Naturally, but of course, to be sure," he was always prompt to say, so that no one would think that, although he might be quite refined, he *was* rather narrow-minded. Having come here on a definite practical mission—that is, for the express purpose of having an energetic look around, of checking up on his "lackadaisical" young relative, as he put it, of "prying him loose" and taking him home—he was quite aware that he was operating on foreign soil; and from the first moment, he had been acutely sensitive to a suspicion that he was now the guest of a world, a social community, with a self-assurance as intact as that of the world from which he came, indeed surpassing it in that regard, so that his business energies were at once in conflict with his good breeding—in very serious conflict, because the self-assurance of the world of his hosts turned out to be truly overwhelming.

This was precisely what Hans Castorp had foreseen when he responded to the consul's telegram with, "Just as he pleases." But one should not suppose he consciously took advantage of the inner strengths of the world around him and used them against his uncle. He had been part of this world too long for that; and it was not he who made use of it against this aggressor, but vice versa; so that everything happened now with a kind of matter-of-fact simplicity—from the first moment when the consul felt a vague suspicion drift over him, emanating from his nephew and telling him that his project was hopeless, until the very end, the final conclusion, to which, admittedly, Hans Castorp could not help appending a melancholy smile.

The next morning, right after breakfast, during which the permanent resident introduced his guest to the circle of tablemates, Tienappel learned from tall, colorful Director Behrens—who came rowing through the dining hall, gliding about, his black and pale assistant in his wake, and strewing his rhetorical morning question, "Sleep well?"—learned, as we said, from the director that not only had it been a tip-top notion to provide his lonely nephew a little company up here, but that he had also acted very much in his own interest, since he was apparently totally anemic. Anemic—he, Tienappel, was anemic? Was he ever, Behrens said, and pulled one of James's eyelids down with a forefinger. First-class case, he said. It would be a very clever move if Hans Castorp's good uncle would spend a few weeks here reclining comfortably on his balcony and in general emulate the fine example set by his nephew. In his condition one could do nothing wiser than to live for a while as if one had a light case of *tuberculosis pulmonum*, which was always present at any rate. "But of course, to be sure," the consul promptly replied and his mouth hung politely, eagerly open for quite a while as he watched the long-necked man row away, while his nephew stood there callous and casual beside him. Then, as prescribed, they promenaded to the bench beside the wooden trough, and afterward James Tienappel enjoyed his first hour of rest cure, to which practice he was introduced by his nephew, who supplemented the plaid roll James had brought along with a camel-hair blanket of his own—one being more than enough for Hans Castorp, given the lovely autumn weather—and instructed his uncle, step by step, in the traditional art of wrapping oneself; in fact, once the consul had been transformed into a smooth, cylindrical mummy, Hans Castorp undid it all, in order to have his uncle repeat the whole established procedure on his own, intervening only occasionally to improve his technique. He also taught his uncle how to attach the canvas sunshade to the arm of his chair.

The consul made little jokes. The flatland spirit was still strong within him, and he made fun of the things he had been taught, just as he had made fun of the prescribed promenade after breakfast. But when he saw the calm, uncomprehending smile with which his nephew responded to his jokes, the way it perfectly mirrored this whole community's intact self-assurance, he took alarm; and fearing the loss of his business energies, he quickly concluded that he would have that decisive conversation with the director about his nephew at once—that very afternoon if at all possible—while he still had a spirit of his own and energies from the world below with which to attack, for he could feel those energies vanishing and the spirit of the place joining forces with his own good breeding in a dangerous alliance against them.

He felt, moreover, that it had been quite unnecessary for the director to suggest he adopt the customs of the patients here because of his anemia—he would have done so all on his own. No other course of action was conceivable, or so it seemed. To what extent Hans Castorp's calm, callous self-assurance made things seem that way, and to what extent they actually were that way, making any other course of action indeed inconceivable and impossible—that was, from the very start, something no well-bred gentleman could have decided. Nothing, then, could be more obvious than that the first rest cure would be followed by a lavish second breakfast, leading inevitably to a promenade down to Platz, whereupon Hans Castorp tied his uncle up again—tied him up, there was no other word for it—and left him lying there under an autumn sun in a lounge chair whose comfort was quite indisputable, indeed laudable, just as he himself lay there until the vibrating gong called them back into the society of patients for their midday meal, which turned out to be first-class, tip-top, and so lavish that the ensuing rest cure was more than mere custom, but a true necessity performed out of personal conviction. And so the day proceeded until the substantial supper, which was followed by a gathering in the social rooms, with optical gadgets for everyone's amusement. How could there be any objection to the pressures of a daily schedule so gentle and so self-evident; indeed, there could have been no reason whatever to object, even if the consul's critical abilities had not been diminished by a condition that he could not actually call sickness, but that consisted of both fatigue and agitation, accompanied by a sense of being simultaneously feverish and chilled.

Official channels were used to bring about the impatiently awaited discussion with Director Behrens; Hans Castorp commissioned the bath attendant to pass the request on to the head nurse; this resulted in Consul Tienappel's being given an opportunity to make that eccentric lady's acquaintance. She suddenly appeared before him as he lay on his balcony, and her exotic manners made considerable demands on the good breeding of that helpless, cylindrically wrapped gentleman. He was told to please be patient for a few days—since, man alive, the director was busy; Christian principles demanded that operations, checkups, and suffering humankind take precedence. Since he was himself ostensibly healthy, he would have to get used to the idea that he was not the number one person around here, that he had to step back and wait his turn. It would be a different matter if he wished a general examination—which would certainly not surprise her, Adriatica. And she told him to focus his eyes directly at her—yes, they definitely had a dull flicker. Just look at him lying there. It did not, on the whole, appear to her as if everything were quite as it should be, he did not seem all that "spotless" to her, if he caught her meaning—and so was he asking for an examination or for a private discussion? Why, for the latter, of course, for a private discussion, the consul assured her from his recumbent position. Well, then, he would have to wait until further notice. The director seldom had time for private discussions.

In short, everything went quite differently from how James had assumed it would, and the conversation with the head nurse was like a shove that kept him off-balance. He was too civilized to tell his nephew—whose calm indifference made it quite clear that he was in agreement with the way things were done up here—how terrifying he had found the woman, and so he simply rapped on his nephew's door and circumspectly inquired if he did not also think the head nurse just a little odd. After first casting a fleeting, speculative glance in the air, Hans Castorp halfway assented to the idea by asking in return whether Head Nurse Mylendonk had sold him a thermometer. "No. Me? Is she in the business?" his uncle replied. But the worst part was how clearly his nephew's face said that he would not have been surprised if what he had asked had in fact occurred. "We're never cold" was written in that expression. The consul, however, was cold, was constantly freezing although his head was hot; and he stopped to consider that if the head nurse had offered him a thermometer, he would have refused it, and yet it would not have been the right thing to do somehow, since it would be impolite to use someone else's, his nephew's for example.

Several days passed, four or five. The envoy's life proceeded along the tracks laid down for him, and it seemed inconceivable it could have proceeded any other way. The consul experienced life here, gathered impressions—and we do not wish to spy on him any further. One day he happened to notice a little plate of dark glass that Hans Castorp had placed atop his chest of drawers along with several other personal items by way of decoration for his tidy room; he picked it up from the little carved wooden stand in which it rested and, holding it up against the light, discovered it was the negative of a photograph. "What's this?" Uncle James asked, still staring at it—and an honest question it was. The portrait had no head, it was the skeleton of a human torso inside a foggy halo of flesh—the torso of a woman, he realized. "That? A souvenir," Hans Castorp replied. And then his uncle said, "Pardon me!" put the portrait back on its stand, and quickly left the room. We mention this merely as one example of his experiences and impressions during those four or five days. He also attended one of Dr. Krokowski's lectures, since it was unthinkable that he could excuse himself from it. And as for the private discussion he hoped to have with Director Behrens, he was granted his wish on the sixth day. He was sent for, and after breakfast he descended to the basement, determined to have a serious word with the man about his nephew and the way he was spending his time.

But when he came back upstairs, he asked in a much smaller voice, "Have you ever heard the like?"

It was clear, however, that Hans Castorp had indeed heard the like before, that this would not make him feel cold, either; and so the consul broke off and simply responded to his nephew's rather indifferent general query by saying, "Oh, nothing, nothing." And then he did something that was to become a habit with him: he scowled, pursed his lips, stared up and away to one side, and then violently tossed his head around and stared in exactly the opposite direction. Had the consul's discussion with Behrens taken a different direction from what he had intended? Had it included not just the topic of Hans Castorp but of James Tienappel himself, so that as it went on it lost the character of a private discussion? To judge from the consul's conduct, it had. He seemed to be in high spirits—he would chatter away, laugh for no reason, poke his nephew in the stomach with his fist and exclaim, "Why hello there, old boy!" But every now and then that look would come over him, and he would stare first in one direction, then in another. But his eyes were also following a more definite path, too—at the table, on their walks, at the evening socials.

The consul had at first paid no particular attention to a certain Frau Redisch, the Polish industrialist's wife, who sat at the same table as the gluttonous student with the circular glasses and the temporarily absent Frau Salomon; and indeed she was only one of many ladies who took their rest cure in the common lounging area—a rather plump and buxom brunette, no longer all that young, graying already, but with a dainty double chin and lively brown eyes. Most assuredly, in matters of civilized behavior she could not have held a candle to Madame Tienappel down in the flatlands. But one Sunday evening in the salon after supper, the consul made a discovery, thanks to a black, very low-cut sequined gown: Frau Redisch had very feminine, soft, white, close-set breasts and a cleavage visible from a considerable distance. And this discovery had stirred the mature, refined man to the depths of his soul, thrilling him as if this were a totally new, unexpected, unheard-of phenomenon. He sought out and made Frau Redisch's acquaintance, carried on a long conversation with her, first standing, then seated—and went to bed humming. The next day Frau Redisch was no longer wearing a black sequined gown, but a dress that covered almost all of her; the consul, however, knew what he knew and remained faithful to that first impression. He made a point of catching up with the lady on their walks, so that he could stroll beside her and chat with her, turning and bending toward her in a special, insistent, but charming way; he toasted his glass to her at dinner, and she responded with a smile, revealing several sparkling gold-capped teeth; and in a conversation with his nephew he declared her to be an absolutely "divine creature"—and at once began to hum again. Hans Castorp calmly, patiently endured it all, with a face that said this was as things were meant to be. It, however, did not exactly increase the older man's authority and was hardly consistent with his mission.

The meal at which he toasted Frau Redisch with his glass—twice in fact, once over fish ragout and then later over sorbet—was a meal at which Director Behrens was seated at the same table as Hans Castorp and his guest, for he regularly worked his way around all seven and there was always a place set for him at the upper end of each. He was seated between Herr Wehsal and the hunchbacked Mexican, with whom he spoke Spanish—because he was a master of many languages, including Turkish and Hungarian—and folding his gigantic hands before his plate and hitching his moustache more askew, he watched with protruding, bloodshot, blue eyes as Consul Tienappel raised his glass of bordeaux to Frau Redisch at her table. Later in the course of the meal, the director gave a little lecture, having been prodded to do so when, from the other end of the table, James had asked him out of the blue what happened, exactly, when, a body decayed—the director had studied anatomy, and the human body was most decidedly his business, he was, so to speak, a prince of the body, if one could put it that way, and so would he now please explain the process by which the body decomposed.

"First of all, your guts burst," the director replied, propping his elbows on the table and leaning forward over his folded hands. "There you are lying on your wood shavings and sawdust, and the gases, you see, swell you up, blow you up until you're immense, the way frogs look when naughty boys blow air into them, until you're a regular balloon, and then your abdomen can no longer take the pressure and bursts. Bang! You relieve yourself noticeably—the same thing happens to you that happened to Judas Iscariot when he fell headlong from the bough—your bowels gush out. Yes, and after that you're actually socially acceptable again. If granted a holiday, you could visit your heirs without causing much offense. You stink yourself out, so to speak. And if you were to go for a stroll, you'd be quite the fine fellow, much like the citizens of Palermo who are hung up in the Capuchin catacombs near the Porta Nuova. There they hang dry and elegant, enjoying universal respect. All you have to do first is stink yourself out."

"To be sure," the consul said. "Much obliged." And the next morning he had vanished.

He was gone, had left with the earliest narrow-gauge train for the plains below—not without first having settled his affairs, of course. The very idea! He had paid his bill in full, including the fee for a complete physical examination; then, without so much as a word to his nephew, he had quietly packed his two bags—probably that very evening or early the next morning while everyone was still asleep. And when Hans Castorp entered his uncle's room to fetch him for first breakfast, he found it empty.

He stood there arms akimbo and said, "I see, I see." It was at this point that the melancholy smile spread over his face. "Ah, yes," he said and nodded. So he had turned tail and run, head over heels, in silent haste, as if he had seized the resolve of the moment, dared not for the life of him let that moment pass, had thrown his things into his bags and off he had gone. Alone, not with his nephew, not in fulfillment of his honorable mission, but overjoyed at having escaped, even if it was all alone—the upright citizen and deserter to the flag of the flatlands, Uncle James. Well, *bon voyage*.

Hans Castorp did not let on to anyone that he had not known about his relative's imminent departure, particularly not to the limping porter, who had accompanied the consul to the station. A postcard arrived from Lake Constance, in which James Tienappel wrote that he had received a telegram requiring his immediate return to the plains on business. He had not wanted to disturb his nephew—a white lie. "Best wishes for a continued pleasant stay." Was that meant to mock him? If so, Hans Castorp thought it was very forced mockery, because his uncle had definitely not been in a mood for jests or mockery when he rushed off like that, but rather had come to the profound realization—and had turned pale with fright picturing it to himself—that upon his return to the flatlands, after a stay of only eight days, everything down there would seem totally false, unnatural, and wrong for a good while, that instead of heading off to his office after breakfast, he ought to take a short constitutional, then ritually wrap himself in blankets, and assume a horizontal position in the open air. It was this terrifying realization that had been the direct cause of his flight.

And that was the end of the attempt by the flatlands to reclaim Hans Castorp. The young man admitted quite openly to himself that such total failure, which he had seen coming, was of decisive importance for his relationship to the people down there. For the flatlands it meant a final shrug, the abandonment of any claim; for him, however, it meant freedom finally won, and by now his heart no longer fluttered at the thought.

Operationes Spirituales

LEO NAPHTA came from a small town on the border between Galicia and Volhynia. His father, about whom he spoke with respect (apparently out of the sense that he had outgrown his origins sufficiently to be able to judge them kindly) had been the village *shohet*—a profession very different from that of a Christian butcher, who was a tradesman, a man of business. Not so Leo's father. He held an office, a spiritual office. Having been examined in his godly skills by the rabbi, who then authorized him to slaughter acceptable animals according to the Law of Moses and the regulations of the Talmud, Elia Naphta was himself filled with a quiet religiosity; there had been something priestly about him and his blue eyes, which, as his son described them, had glittered like stars and radiated a solemnity recalling ancient times when the slaughtering of animals had indeed been the duty of priests. When Leo, or Leib as he was known in his childhood, had been allowed into a farmyard to watch his father fulfill his ritual office—with the help of his assistant, a powerful, athletic Jewish lad, next to whom slender Elia with his round, blond beard seemed all the more delicate and frail—and had seen him flourish the large butcher knife and cut deep into the neck vertebrae of the bound and hobbled, but fully conscious animal, had seen the assistant catch the spurting, steaming blood in basins that filled rapidly, the boy had watched the spectacle with the eyes of a child, which see through externals to essentials; indeed, the son of star-eyed Elia may have been particularly gifted in that regard. He knew that Christian butchers were obliged first to stun beasts with the blow of a club or an axe before they killed them, that this requirement was intended to prevent animals from being cruelly tortured; whereas his father, although much wiser and more delicate than those louts—and with eyes like stars, which not one of them had—proceeded according to the Law and administered the lethal cut while the creature was still fully conscious and then let it bleed until it buckled and fell dead. Leib was a mere boy, but he saw that the methods of those clumsy goyim, though excusably charitable, were also profane, that they did not honor sacred things in the same way his father's solemn pitilessness did; and so for him the idea of piety became bound up with cruelty, just as the sight and smell of spurting blood was bound up in his mind with the idea of what is holy and spiritual. For he saw quite clearly that his father had not chosen his bloody profession out of the same brutal enjoyment that those Christian louts, or even his own Jewish assistant, took in their strength, but had done so, despite his delicate physique, for star-eyed, spiritual reasons.

Elia Naphta had in fact been a brooding introvert; he was not just a scholar of the Torah, but a critic of Scripture who discussed its contents with the rabbi and frequently argued with him. Throughout the district, he was thought of as someone special, and not just by those of his own creed, as someone who knew more than others—about religious matters in part, but also about other things that made him seem a little uncanny, or at the least, out of the ordinary. There was something unorthodox and sectarian about him, as if he were conversant with God, a *baalshem* or *zaddik*, a miracle man, particularly since, using only blood and spoken charms, he had once healed a woman with a loathsome skin condition and on another occasion had cured a boy of seizures. But this same aura of a somewhat perilous piety, in which the bloody odor of his profession played its role, had also been his undoing. During a pogrom, a panic of rage unleashed by the unexplained deaths of two Christian children, Elia had met a terrible end: he had been found hanging on the door of his own burning house, crucified to it with nails; and his wife, although bedridden with consumption, had fled the region with her children, little

Leib and four others—all of them with arms raised, crying in loud lamentation.

Thanks to Elia's foresight, the family was not entirely penniless when they at last came to rest in a little town in Vorarlberg, where Frau Naphta found a job in a cotton mill, at which she worked as long as her strength allowed. The older children attended the local grammar school; although the intellectual offerings of this institution were sufficient for Leo's brothers and sisters, that was anything but the case for him, the oldest. From his mother he had acquired incipient lung disease; from his father, however, in addition to a frail physique, he had inherited an exceptional mind— intellectual gifts that very early on were joined with haughtiness, vaunting ambition, and an aching desire for more elegant surroundings, a passionate need to move beyond the world of his origins. As a lad of fourteen or fifteen, he had obtained books and impatiently and unsystematically gone about educating himself outside of school and providing his mind with nourishment. He thought and said things that caused his sickly mother to tilt her head, raise her shoulders, and fling her emaciated hands in the air. By both his manner and answers in religion class, he attracted the attention of the district rabbi, a pious and learned man, who took him on as a private pupil, satisfying the boy's love of formal knowledge with Hebrew and the classics and his passion for logic with mathematics—for all of which the man received very scant thanks. Over time it became clear that he had nursed a viper at his bosom. Just as things had once gone between Elia Naphta and his rabbi, so they went now—teacher and student did not get along, religious and philosophical friction increased, grew worse and worse. The honest old scholar suffered every abuse imaginable as a result of young Leo's intellectual obstinacy, captiousness, skepticism, contrariness, and cutting dialectical logic. Moreover, Leo's restive mind and sophistry soon showed a rebellious streak; he made the acquaintance of the son of a social-democratic member of the Reichsrat, and following the lead of this hero of the masses, had directed his mind along political paths, turning his passion for logic to the field of social criticism. The old Talmudic scholar was a loyal citizen, and Leo's speeches made his hair stand on end—they marked the end of what little understanding existed between teacher and student. In short, there came a day— at just the same time that Leo's mother, Rachel, lay dying—when the master threw Naphta out, and forbade the boy ever to enter his study again.

It was at that same period, immediately after his mother's demise, that sixteen-year-old Leo made the acquaintance of Father Unterpertinger. He was sitting alone on a bench in the park atop a little hill known as Marga-

ret's Head, just west of town and with a view to the Ill River and the
wide, serene Rhine valley—was sitting there lost in gloomy, bitter thought
about his fate and his future, when a strolling member of the faculty of
the Morning Star, the local boarding school run by the Society of Jesus,
sat down next to him, laid his hat on the bench, crossed one leg over the
other under his order's cassock, and after reading awhile in his breviary
struck up a conversation, which soon turned very lively and proved decisive for Leo's further destiny. The Jesuit, a well-traveled man with cultured manners, a pedagogue by passion, a judge of men, a fisher of men,
sat up and took notice at the first sardonic, clearly articulated answers
the wretched young Jewish lad gave to his questions. A caustic, tormented
spirituality drifted toward him in those words; probing deeper, he discovered both knowledge and a maliciously elegant mode of thought—all the
more surprising, given the young man's tattered exterior. They spoke
about Marx, whose *Kapital* Leo Naphta had studied in a popular edition,
and then moved on to Hegel, of whom, or about whom, he had also read
enough to be able to offer a few striking comments. Whether due to his
general bent for paradox or out of courtesy, he called Hegel a "Catholic"
thinker; and in response to the priest's smiling question about the basis
for this comment, inasmuch as Hegel was actually the state philosopher
of Prussia and generally considered a Protestant, Leo had replied: the
very term "state philosopher" confirmed he was correct in pointing to
Hegel's Catholicity in the religious sense, if not, of course, in regard
to Church dogmatics. *For* (and Naphta was particularly fond of that
conjunction—in his mouth it gained something triumphantly inexorable,
and his eyes would flash behind his glasses whenever he could insert it),
for politics and Catholicism, as concepts, were psychologically related;
they formed a single category embracing all objective, actual, active, actu-
alizing reality, and as such stood in contradiction to pietist Protestantism,
which had emerged out of mysticism. The political-pedagogic nature of
Catholicism, he added, was apparent in the Jesuit order, which had always
regarded education and statecraft as its domains. And he also mentioned
Goethe, who, though rooted in pietism and most assuredly a Protestant,
had also had a strong Catholic side, evident in his objectivism, his doctrine
of the active life, and his defense of private confession—as a teacher he
had been virtually a Jesuit.

Naphta may have made these remarks because he believed them, or
because he found them witty, or simply because as a poor man he wanted
to flatter his hearer and was well aware of how to help and how to harm
himself—but the priest was less interested in the truth of his statements
than in the general cleverness they revealed. As the conversation unfolded,

Leo's personal situation became clear, and the meeting ended with Unter-pertinger's request that Leo visit him at his school.

And so Naphta was permitted to enter within the walls of the Stella Matutina, whose challenging academic and social atmosphere had long been an object of his own intellectual longings and appetites; what was more, this turn of events had given him a new teacher and patron far more capable than his previous one of appreciating and fostering his character, a master whose value lay in his cool cosmopolitanism, and it was the lad's greatest desire to enter such circles. Like many gifted Jews, Naphta was by instinct both a revolutionary and an aristocrat—a socialist, yet obsessed with the dream of participating in a proud, elegant, exclusive, closely circumscribed world. The first statement that the presence of a Catholic theologian had elicited from him, even though a purely analytical compari-son, had been a declaration of love for the Roman church, which he saw as an elegant and yet spiritual power—that is, anti-worldly, anti-material, and thus revolutionary. And his homage was genuine, rooted deep within his nature; for, as he himself explained, Judaism—thanks to its earthy, practical character, its socialism, its political spirituality—was far nearer to the Catholic sphere, was incomparably more closely related to it, than to the self-absorption and mystical subjectivity of Protestantism; this meant that it was decidedly less intellectually disruptive for a Jew to convert to the Roman church than for a Protestant to do so.

Having quarreled with the shepherd of his original religious community, orphaned and abandoned, yet filled with a longing for life's purer air, for a form of existence to which his talents entitled him, and having long since reached the age of legal consent, Naphta was so impatient to convert that his "discoverer" was spared any effort to win this soul—or better, this unconventional mind—for the world of his own religious confession. The priest saw to it that, even before his baptism, the lad was given temporary shelter and spiritual nourishment at the Stella. Leo moved in— but only after first abandoning, with the cool callousness of an intellectual aristocrat, his younger brothers and sisters to charity and a fate suited to their lesser talents.

The grounds of the institution were as extensive as the buildings them-selves, which provided space for four hundred pupils. The complex in-cluded forests and meadows, a half-dozen athletic fields, agricultural buildings, including stalls for hundreds of cows. The institution was a boarding school, a model farm, an academy of higher learning, and a temple for the muses—for there were constant theatrical and musical performances. Life was both stylish and monastic. The discipline and elegance, the hushed serenity and intellectual challenge, the well-ordered

and well-tended life, the precise yet richly varied schedule—it all spoke
to Leo's profoundest instincts. He was beyond happy. He took his excellent meals in a huge refectory, where the rule of silence reigned—which
was also the case in the corridors—and where a young prefect sat at his
lectern in the middle of the room, high above the diners, and read to
them. Leo showed a burning zeal for his studies and, despite a weakness
of the chest, mustered all his strength to hold his own at games and sports.
The devotion with which he listened to daily morning mass and worshiped
at the solemn Sunday service could only delight his priestly pedagogues.
His social deportment was no less satisfactory. On holiday afternoons,
after partaking of cake and wine, he and his fellow students—in gray-
and-green uniforms with stiff collars, striped trousers, and caps—went
for a walk in closed formation.

He was grateful beyond bounds for the respect shown his origins, his
infant Christian faith, his personal status in general. No one seemed to
realize that he lived and studied free of charge. The rules of the institution
diverted the attention of his classmates from the fact that he had no family,
no home. The receipt of all packages of food and sweets was expressly
forbidden, and if something did arrive, it was distributed evenly among
them all. The cosmopolitanism of the Stella prevented his racial traits from
being noticed. There were other young foreigners—Portuguese South
Americans, who looked more "Jewish" than he, and so the very term
lost meaning. The Ethiopian prince who had been admitted at the same
time as Naphta was a very elegant-looking Moor with woolly hair.

In his rhetoric year, Leo let it be known that he wished to study
theology and, if he should be found worthy, to join the order. The result
was that his scholarship was transferred from the "second tier," with its
more modest board and room, to the "first tier," where meals were served
by waiters, and the neighbors on each side of his cubicle were a Silesian
count von Harbuval and Chamaré and a marquis di Rangoni-Santacroce
from Modena. He graduated with honors and, true to his resolve, exchanged the life of a boarding-school pupil for that of a novice in nearby
Tisis—a life of service and humility, of silent subordination and religious
training, from which he wrested intellectual pleasures congruent with his
earlier wild fantasies.

His health, meanwhile, grew worse—less as a direct result of external
severities of the novitiate life, which provided sufficient recreation, than
of internal ones. The educational system, in its clever subtlety, both met
and encouraged his own natural tendencies. His days and part of his nights
were filled with *operationes spirituales*, with examinations of conscience,
with introspection, deliberation, and meditation, and he went about it

with such malicious, peevish passion that he found himself ensnared in a thousand difficulties, contradictions, and disputes. He was the despair—and the great hope—of his father confessor, whose life he daily made a hell with raging dialectics and a total lack of simplicity. *"Ad haec quid tu?"* Leo would ask, his eyes flashing behind his glasses. And driven into a corner, there was nothing the priest could do except admonish him to pray for his soul to find peace—*"ut in aliquem gradum quietis in anima perveniat."* Except that, once achieved, such "peace" resulted in a total dulling and deadening of the personality, until a man was a mere tool and his peace that of the graveyard, the eerie external tokens of which Brother Naphta could study in the hollow eyes of faces all around him—and which he would never succeed in achieving, except by way of physical ruin.

It spoke well of the spiritual quality of his superiors that his protests and doubts in no way prejudiced their regard for him. The father provincial himself summoned Naphta at the end of his two-year novitiate, spoke with him, and approved his admission to the order. The young scholastic, having received the four minor orders—doorkeeper, acolyte, lector, and exorcist—and having sworn his "simple" vows, admitting him at last into the Society, now departed for the Jesuit college at Falkenburg in Holland to begin his theological studies.

He was twenty years old at the time, and three years later, thanks to a deleterious climate and intellectual exertion, his inherited illness had advanced to the point where a further stay would have been fatal. A sudden hemorrhage alerted his superiors to the problem; after hovering for weeks between life and death and still in precarious health, he was sent back to where he started. He returned to the institution where he had been a pupil and was given a position as prefect, a supervisor of the students, a teacher of philosophy and humanities. This hiatus was prescribed by regulation in any case—except that one normally returned to college after a few years in order to conclude the seven-year course of instruction. This was now denied to Brother Naphta. His illness continued; his doctor and father superior decided it would be more appropriate for him temporarily to serve pupils where the air was healthy and outdoor farm work available. He received the first of the major orders, which gave him the right to chant the Epistle at solemn mass on Sunday—a right, however, which he never exercised, first because he was completely unmusical and second because illness had left his voice cracked and hardly suitable for singing. He did not advance beyond the subdiaconate—was never ordained deacon or priest. But when both hemorrhages and fever persisted, he had come up here for a long-term cure, which was paid for by his order and was now into its sixth year—hardly a cure by now and more a kind of categorical form of life at rarefied heights, mitigated by his duties as a teacher of Latin at the local school for tubercular boys.

HANS CASTORP learned the general outline and details of all this in conversations with Naphta himself during visits to his silken cell, either alone or accompanied by his tablemates, Ferge and Wehsal, whom he had introduced there; or he might meet him out on a promenade and stroll back with him to Dorf. The story came to him on various occasions, in fragments and as connected narratives, and not only did he himself consider it highly remarkable, but he encouraged Ferge and Wehsal to do so as well, which they did—the former, of course, with a qualifying reminder that all higher things were foreign to him (for only the experience of pleural shock had ever lifted him above life's most unpretentious levels); the latter, however, with obvious pleasure in the happy course an oppressed man's life had taken, even though—since all good things must come to an end—it was now at a standstill and appeared to be foundering in their common malady.

For his part, Hans Castorp regretted this standstill and thought with pride and concern about honor-loving Joachim, who with one heroic, courageous effort had ripped to shreds the tough fabric of Rhadamanthine rhetoric, sought out his flag, and now, in Hans Castorp's imagination, stood clutching it, three fingers of his right hand raised to swear his oath of loyalty. Naphta, too, had sworn an oath to a flag; he, too, had been received beneath a banner, as he himself put it when explaining the nature of his order to Hans Castorp. But apparently, given his adaptations and permutations, he was not as loyal as Joachim was to his—although, to be sure, whenever Hans Castorp, both as a civilian and child of peace, listened to this has-been or would-be Jesuit he felt reinforced in his view that each of these two men would take pleasure in the occupation and status of the other, as something closely related to his own. For each was as much a military calling as the other, in every sense: in asceticism and hierarchy, in obedience and Spanish sense of honor. The latter, in particular, prevailed in Naphta's order, which had originated in Spain and whose rules of spiritual exercise—in some sense the equivalent of those that Frederick the Great later promulgated for his Prussian infantry— were first drawn up in Spanish, so that Naphta frequently used Spanish phrases in his stories and lessons. He would speak of *dos banderas*, of the two flags to which armies rallied for the great struggle—the flags of heaven and hell, the former in the region of Jerusalem, with Christ as the *capitán general* commanding the armies of the good, and the latter on the plains of Babylon, with Lucifer as *caudillo* or chieftain.

Had not the Morning Star been a regular military academy, whose pupils, divided into "divisions," were honorably exhorted to spiritual-military *bienséance*—a combination "stiff collar" and "Spanish ruff," if one could put it that way? Ideas of honor and excellence played a significant role in Joachim's profession—and were equally conspicuous, Hans Castorp thought, in the order in which Naphta had unfortunately been unable to advance very far due to illness. Listening to him, one might believe that the order consisted of nothing but very ambitious officers inspired by a single thought: to make their mark—*insignes esse,* as the Latin had it. According to the teaching and rules of its founder and first general, the Spaniard Loyola, they accomplished more and served more splendidly than those who acted purely out of common sense. Rather, they accomplished their work above and beyond the call of duty (*ex supererogatione*), not only by resisting the insurrections of the flesh (*rebellioni carnis*), which was, after all, the task of every man of average common sense, but also by doing battle against every inclination of the senses, against both love of self and love of the world, against things that are normally permitted. Because in battling the enemy, to attack (*agere contra*) was better and more honorable than simply to defend oneself (*resistere*). Weaken the enemy and break him—those were the instructions in their field handbook; and here again its author, the Spaniard Loyola, was of one mind with Joachim's own *capitán general*, the Prussian Frederick, whose rule of war was: "Attack! Attack!" "Jump into your enemy's pants!" "*Attaquez donc toujours!*"

But Naphta's and Joachim's worlds had something else special in common: their relationship to blood and the axiom that one should not refrain from shedding it. On that they were in fierce agreement—as worlds, as orders, as professions; and a child of peace found it worth his while to listen to Naphta talk about the martial monks of the Middle Ages, who, although ascetics to the point of exhaustion, were likewise filled with a spiritual lust for power and did not refrain from bloodshed in order to bring about the City of God and its transcendent world dominion; or about belligerent Knights Templar, who considered death in battle against unbelievers more meritorious than death in one's bed and for whom slaying and being slain for the sake of Christ was no crime, but the highest glory. It helped if Settembrini was not present for such lectures. Otherwise, he played the role, as always, of the bothersome organ-grinder and trumpeted peace, even though he remained hardly averse to his holy, civilizing, patriotic war against Vienna—and Naphta, of course, was sure to repay such passion and weakness with sarcasm and disdain. In any case, whenever the Italian warmed to that cause, Naphta would champion a Christian world citizenship, claim every land and no land as his fatherland, and caustically recall the phrase of Nickel, a former general of the order, who declared patriotism "a plague and the surest death of Christian charity."

And, of course, what prompted Naphta to call patriotism a plague was asceticism—what all did he not subsume under that concept, what all, in his opinion, did not oppose asceticism and the kingdom of God! Not only our ties to family and homeland did so, but also those to health and life. Asceticism was even his basis for reproaching the humanist whenever he trumpeted peace and happiness; Naphta would belligerently accuse him to his face of love of the flesh (*amor carnalis*) and love of physical comfort (*commodorum corporis*), call it utter bourgeois irreligion to ascribe the least value to life and health.

Then there was the great colloquy on health and sickness, which arose out of differences that became apparent one day, very close to Christmas, as they walked through the snow to Platz and back. They all took part: Settembrini, Naphta, Hans Castorp, Ferge, and Wehsal—all of them slightly feverish, frequently shivering in the Alpine chill, numbed and excited by the walk and the discussion; and, whether, like Naphta and Settembrini, they participated more actively or merely followed the conversation and broke in with only brief remarks, they were all so avidly involved that they often forgot where they were and stopped to form a deeply engrossed, gesticulating group, all speaking at once and blocking the walkway, unconcerned about strangers who had to detour around them or stopped to lend an ear, listening in astonishment to such extravagant talk.

Actually the dispute had started over Karen Karstedt—poor Karen with the open sores on her fingers, who had died recently. Hans Castorp had been unaware of her sudden turn for the worse and exitus; otherwise he would gladly have taken part in her burial, both out of friendship and his admitted love of funerals in general. But the local custom of discretion had meant that he learned of Karen's demise too late and that she had already been placed in a permanent horizontal position, in the garden of the cupid whose snowy cap was cocked to one side. *Requiem aeternam.* He offered a few friendly words in her memory, which inspired Herr Settembrini to make sarcastic remarks about Hans's charitable activities—his visits to Leila Gerngross, business-minded Rotbein, overblown Frau Zimmermann, the braggart son of *Tous-les-deux*, and the tormented Natalie von Mallinckrodt—and then went on to sneer at the expensive flowers with which the engineer had shown his devotion to such a totally wretched and ridiculous crew. Hans Castorp had then pointed out that those who had received his attentions, with the exception, for now, of Frau von Mallinckrodt and the lad named Teddy, were all quite dead; in response, Settembrini asked whether that made them any more respectable. There was such a thing, Hans Castorp replied, that one might call Christian reverence for human misery. And before Settembrini could rebuke him, Naphta began to speak of pious excesses of charity witnessed in the Middle Ages, amazing examples of fanaticism and ecstasy in the care of the sick—the daughters of kings had kissed the stinking wounds of lepers, with the express purpose of becoming infected, had called the ulcerated sores to which they exposed themselves "roses," had drunk the water with which they had bathed those festering bodies, and had declared they had never drunk anything so tasty.

Settembrini pretended he was going to vomit. It was less the sheer physical repulsiveness of such scenes and ideas that turned his stomach, he said, than the monstrous insanity evident in such a conception of active charity. And pulling himself up straight and regaining his serene dignity, he spoke about modern, progressive forms of humanitarian nursing, the slow, steady victory over epidemic disease, and went on to contrast such horrors with the achievements of medical science, hygiene, and social reforms.

During the centuries he was talking about, Naphta responded, such decent bourgeois measures would have served neither side—would have been of no more use to the ill and suffering than to the healthy and happy, who had wanted to demonstrate their charity not so much out of compassion as out of the desire to save their own souls. Efficacious social reforms would have deprived the latter of the most important means of justification, and the former of their sanctified state. And so it had been in the interest of both parties to perpetuate poverty and illness, and that attitude had held as long as it had been possible to maintain a purely religious view of things.

A squalid view of things, Settembrini asserted, and he felt himself almost above combating such an attitude. For the notion of a "sanctified state" or what the engineer had called "Christian reverence for misery"—though the phrase was surely not his own—was a fraud based on deception, on misplaced feelings, on a psychological blunder. The sympathy that the healthy person felt for someone who was ill, which could intensify to the point of awe, since he was unable to imagine how he could ever bear such suffering himself—such sympathy was utterly exaggerated. The sick person had no right to it. It was based on a misperception, a failure of

imagination, because the healthy person was attributing his own mode of
experience to the sick person, making of him, so to speak, a healthy
person who had to bear the torments of sickness—a totally erroneous
idea. The sick person was just that, sick, both by nature and in his mode
of experience. Illness battered its victim until they got along with one
another: the senses were diminished, there were lapses in consciousness,
a merciful self-narcosis set in—all means by which nature allowed the
organism to find relief, to adapt mentally and morally to its condition,
and which the healthy person naively forgot to take into account. A
perfect example was this tubercular pack up here, with their frivolity,
stupidity, depravity, their aversion to becoming healthy again. In short,
if the sympathetic or awestruck healthy person were to become sick himself, to lose his health, he would soon see that illness is a state in and of
itself, though certainly not an honorable one, and that he had been taking
it all too seriously.

At this, Anton Karlovitch Ferge flared up to defend his pleural shock
against such sneers and slanders. What—taken his pleural shock too seriously? Well, thanks very much, but beg your pardon! His large Adam's
apple and his good-natured moustache bobbed up and down, and he
demanded some respect be shown for what he had gone through. He was
just an ordinary man, a traveling insurance agent, and higher things were
utterly foreign to him—this conversation, in fact, was far beyond him.
But if Herr Settembrini presumed to include pleural shock, for example,
in what he had said—that ticklish hell with its sulfur stench and faints in
three colors—then all he could say was thanks very, very much, but beg
your pardon. There had not been a trace of diminished senses or merciful
self-narcosis or failures of imagination, but only the biggest, crudest piece
of filth on God's green earth, and anyone who had not undergone that
beastly experience as he had could not even begin to—

"Oh my, oh my yes," Settembrini said. Herr Ferge's collapse was
growing more and more glorious as time went on, until it had become
almost a halo around his head. He, Settembrini, had little respect for sick
people who felt entitled to other people's admiration. He was himself
more than a little ill; but without any affectation, he could say he was
more inclined to be ashamed of the fact. In any case, his remarks had
been impersonal, philosophical, and what he had said about the nature
of the sick and the healthy, about the difference in their experiences, was
a solid argument. The gentlemen had only to think of the mentally ill, of
hallucinations, for example. If one of his companions, the good engineer
or Herr Wehsal, for example, should happen to see his dead father sitting
in the corner of his room at dusk that evening, see him look up and hear

him speak—it would be absolutely horrible for the beholder, a dreadfully shocking, distressing experience, so disconcerting that he would doubt his own senses, his very reason, and feel he had to vacate his room as soon as possible and put himself under psychiatric care. Was that not so? But the joke was that this could not happen to any one of these gentlemen, because their minds were healthy. And if it ever should occur, then they would not be healthy, but sick, and instead of reacting like a healthy person, that is, turning tail and running in horror, they would think it quite normal, join in the conversation, the way people who hallucinate did. The belief that one would be healthy enough to regard one's hallucination as a horror—that was the failure of imagination of which healthy people were guilty.

Herr Settembrini spoke very graphically, very drolly, about the father in the corner. They all had to laugh, even Ferge, although he was still offended by the disparagement of his infernal adventure. The humanist then took advantage of this animated mood to explain further about how one ought to pay no attention to those who suffered from hallucinations, to *pazzi* in general, advancing the proposition that such people let themselves get carried away, quite illegitimately, and often had it within their power to control their madness, as he had himself observed on several visits to madhouses. Because whenever a doctor or a stranger appeared on the threshold, the hallucinating patient would usually cease grimacing, talking, and gesticulating and behave himself, as long as he knew he was being watched, letting himself go again only afterward. Letting oneself go, in fact, was doubtless a definition of madness in many cases, inasmuch as it was a way of fleeing from great affliction and served weak natures as a defense against the overpowering blows of fate, which such people felt they could not withstand in their right mind. But then anyone could use that excuse, so to speak; and he, Settembrini, had brought many a madman back to reality, at least temporarily, by confronting his fiddle-faddle with a pose of unrelenting reason.

Naphta laughed scornfully, whereas Hans Castorp stated he believed every word Herr Settembrini had said. When he pictured him with his moustache, smiling and staring some feebleminded fellow directly in the eye, he could well understand why the poor man would have pulled himself together and given reality its due, however unwelcome a disturbance Herr Settembrini's visit must have been for him. But Naphta had also visited madhouses, and he recalled having entered a "violent ward," the kind of place that offered scenes and images for which, good God, Herr Settembrini's reasonable stare and decorous influence would hardly have been a match. Grotesque images of horror and torment straight out of Dante: naked madmen living their lives squatting in tubs of water, in every pose of mental anguish and terrified stupor, some screaming aloud in lament, others with arms raised and mouths gaping as they burst with laughter—all the ingredients of hell merged in one.

"Aha!" Herr Ferge said, and took the freedom of recalling the laughter that had burst from him as he had blacked out.

And in short, Herr Settembrini's unrelenting pedagogy could have packed its bags when confronted with those faces in the "violent ward," on which a shudder of religious awe would have had a more humanizing effect than the sort of arrogant moralizing about reason with which this Most Worthy Knight of the Sun and Vicar of Solomon here had chosen to combat madness.

Hans Castorp had no time to concern himself with the titles Naphta had bestowed upon Herr Settembrini. He hastily promised himself to probe the issue at the first opportunity. At the moment, however, their current discussion consumed his total attention, because Naphta now went on to discuss in caustic fashion the general biases that induced humanists to honor health on principle and dishonor and belittle sickness whenever possible—a position, however, that revealed a remarkable and almost praiseworthy self-abnegation on Herr Settembrini's part, since he was himself ill. Such an attitude, which was no less faulty for all its dignity, arose from a regard and reverence for the body, which could only be justified if the body still existed in its original God-given state, rather than in a state of humiliation (*in statu degradationis*). For although created immortal, it had become subject to decay and abomination as part of the general impairment of nature brought about by Original Sin, was now mortal and corruptible, and should be regarded merely as a prison, the stocks in which the soul was entrapped, its sole purpose being to awaken within us a feeling of shame and confusion (*pudoris et confusionis sensum*), as Saint Ignatius had put it.

The same feeling, as was well known, that the humanist Plotinus had expressed, Hans Castorp exclaimed. But flinging his arm high above his head, Herr Settembrini demanded he not confuse the two points of view, adding that the engineer would do better to remain receptive to ideas.

Naphta now proceeded to prove that the awe in which the Christian Middle Ages had held the suffering human body was derived from religious affirmation in the face of the afflictions of the flesh. For festering sores were not only conspicuous reminders of the body's sunken state, but also, in reflecting the venomous corruption of the soul, they awakened a desire for edifying spiritual compensation; whereas the bloom of health was a deceptive phenomenon, an offense to the conscience that it was best to disavow by bowing low in profound humility before human frailty. *Quis me liberabit de corpore mortis huius?* Who shall deliver me from the body of this death? That was the voice of the Spirit, and it would be the voice of true humanity for all eternity.

No, that was a benighted voice, in Herr Settembrini's opinion—which he delivered with much emotion. The voice of a world upon which the sun of reason and humanity had never risen. Yes indeed, his own body might be venomous, but he had kept his mind healthy and uninfected enough to defy Naphta's priestly views concerning the body and to ridicule what he called the soul. He went so far as to celebrate the human body as the veritable temple of God, whereupon Naphta declared our stuff to be nothing more than a curtain between us and eternity, which resulted in Settembrini's forbidding him ever to use the word "humanity" again—and so on.

Faces numbed with cold, heads bare, but feet in rubber galoshes, they moved along the sidewalk, its deep layer of snow strewn with ashes and crunching underfoot, or plowed through looser mounds of snow in the road—Settembrini in his winter coat, its beaver collar and lapels worn so smooth and hard that it had a rather mangy look, though he wore it elegantly all the same; Naphta in a black, ankle-length coat that buttoned to the neck, fully lined with fur, but not so that anyone could see it. And as they moved along, they argued their principles with great personal urgency, although frequently they did not speak to one another, but instead each would turn to Hans Castorp to deliver his views, lecturing him, while pointing a head or thumb at the real opponent. Hans Castorp was trapped between them; turning his head back and forth, he would agree first with one, then with the other, or he would come to a stop, bending his body backward and gesticulating with a hand inside its fur-lined goatskin glove, and offer some opinion of his own—some highly unsatisfactory comment, of course; meanwhile Ferge and Wehsal circled the three of them, now walking in front, now behind, now forming a single row, until oncoming traffic broke the group up again.

Inspired by some casual remark, the debate turned to more concrete subjects, moving quickly with the growing interest and participation of all through a series of issues: corporal punishment, cremation, torture, and the death penalty. It was Ferdinand Wehsal who brought up the subject of flogging, and one could read the excitement on his face, or so Hans Castorp thought. It was not surprising that Herr Settembrini, invoking the dignity of man in sterling words, spoke out against the brutal practice, both from a pedagogic and juridical point of view; nor was it any more surprising, though perhaps it was astounding simply because

of the gloomy brazenness of his words, that Naphta spoke out in favor
of the bastinado. According to him, it was absurd to jabber on about the
dignity of man in this instance, for our true dignity was based in the Spirit
and not the flesh, and since the human soul was only too inclined to suck
its entire love of life from the body, the administration of pain to the
body was a highly commendable means by which to spoil the soul's desire
for sensual pleasure and, as it were, drive it back out of the body and
into the spiritual realm, thereby restoring the latter's dominion. How
foolish to object that there was something particularly ignominious about
blows administered as corporal punishment. Saint Elizabeth had been
disciplined by her father confessor, Konrad von Marburg, until he drew
blood, "transporting her soul," as legend put it, "to the third choir of
angels," and she had herself laid the rod to an old woman who was too
sleepy to make her confession. Would anyone venture in all earnestness
to declare as barbaric and inhumane the self-flagellation practiced among
members of certain orders and sects, and in general by people of more
profound capacities, in order that they might strengthen their own spiritual
principles? Nations that considered themselves genteel may have abolished
corporal punishment, but the belief that its abolition was a mark of true
progress was only the more comic for being so unshakable.

Well, in any case, Hans Castorp remarked, it was absolutely certain
that within the polarity of body and mind, the body doubtless embodied—
ha ha—embodied the evil, devilish principle, because the body was part
of nature, naturally—naturally part of nature, that wasn't bad, either—
and nature, in contradistinction to the mind, to reason, was doubtless
evil—mystically evil, one might say, if one dared employ a little of one's
education and knowledge. And having once established that point of view,
it was only logical, then, to treat the body accordingly, to bestow upon
it certain disciplinary methods, which, if one dared take another risk,
might likewise be called mystically evil. Perhaps, if Herr Settembrini had
had a Saint Elizabeth at his side back then, when the infirmities of his
body had prevented him from attending the convention for progress in
Barcelona, why then . . .

They all laughed, and before the humanist could fly off the handle,
Hans Castorp quickly told about a thrashing he had once received—a
punishment still administered sometimes in the lower grades of his high
school, where there had been riding crops in every room; and although
social disparities had prevented teachers from laying a hand on him, he
had once been thrashed by a bigger classmate, a lout of a fellow, who
had applied the supple switch to his thighs and calves, right through his
thin stockings, and it had hurt something awful, he would never forget,

it had been beastly, almost mystical, and to his shame he had heaved great sobs and hot tears of rage and agony had flowed—and here Hans Castorp begged Herr Wehsal's pardon for using the obscure word "*Wehsal*" for "agony." He had also read that even the strongest cutthroats, when they were flogged in prison, blubbered like children.

And while Herr Settembrini hid his face in both hands—revealing very shabby leather gloves—Naphta asked in a chill, statesmanlike voice how else intractable criminals should be handled if not with stocks and cudgels, which were very stylish furnishings for a prison in any case. A humane prison was a half-measure, an aesthetic compromise, and although Herr Settembrini was a master of beautiful rhetoric, he understood nothing about aesthetics. And as for pedagogics, the conception of human dignity that sought to ban corporal punishment had its roots, to hear Naphta tell it, in the liberal individualism of the era of bourgeois humanism, in the Enlightenment's absolutism of the ego, which was about to atrophy and be replaced by a wave of newer, less namby-pamby social concepts, ideas of submission and obedience, of bridles and bonds, and since such things were not to be had without holy cruelty, flogging would thus be regarded with quite a different eye.

"Yes, like watching someone flog a dead horse into obedience," Settembrini scoffed; to which Naphta replied that since for our sin God had visited our bodies with the gruesome ignominy of rot and decay, there was no indignity in the same body's receiving an occasional beating—which immediately brought them to the topic of cremation.

Settembrini applauded it. One could in fact remedy that ignominy, he said gaily. Both out of idealism, and for practical reasons, humankind was about to provide the remedy. And he explained that he was assisting in preparations for an international congress on cremation, which in all probability would be held in Sweden. Working from previous experience in the field, they were planning to construct a model crematorium and hall of urns, and the hope was that it would encourage further far-reaching developments. What a moldy, obsolete practice burial was! Cities were expanding; so-called memorial parks were being forced out to the periphery—wasting space and driving up the price of land. And what a disillusioning effect the necessary use of modern vehicles had on the funeral procession. Herr Settembrini had all sorts of apt, sensible remarks to make on the subject. He joked about the figure cut by a widower bent low with grief and making his daily pilgrimage to the graveside of his dear departed wife to converse with her there. To engage in such idyllic practices, a man had to have an amazing surplus of one of life's most precious commodities: time. Not to mention the way the hustle and bustle in modern large cemeteries would spoil any atavistic sentimentality. The destruction of the body by fire—what a neat, hygienic, dignified, and indeed heroic idea that was in comparison with letting it decompose miserably on its own and be assimilated by lower forms of life. Yes, and even emotional needs—the human desire for immortality—did better by this new method. For what were lost in the flames were the body's more mutable components, which even in life were burned up in the body's metabolism; but those components that participated least in life's steady flow and that accompanied human beings through their adult life almost without change, proved to be the most fireproof; they formed the ashes, and by collecting them, the survivors kept what was immortal about the deceased.

"Very nice," Naphta said—oh, that was very, very pretty. The ashes as the immortal part of man.

Ah, but of course Naphta would like nothing better than for humankind to retain its irrational attitude toward biological fact; of course he would defend the primitive religious level on which death was a terror wrapped in horrors most mysterious and so prevent the phenomenon from being viewed with the clear eye of reason. What barbarism! The fear of death came from epochs of lowest human culture, when violent death was the rule, and the terror rightly associated in man's emotions with a violent death had been wedded to the idea of death itself for ages now. But more and more, thanks to the development of hygienics and the consolidation of personal security, natural death was becoming the norm; and for the modern workingman the thought of eternal rest after having exhausted one's energies in labor was not at all horrible, but rather perfectly normal and desirable. No, death was neither a terror nor a mystery, it was an unambiguous, reasonable, physiologically necessary, and welcome phenomenon, and to dwell on the thought of it longer than was seemly was to rob life itself. Which was why the model crematorium and its hall of urns, the "Hall of Death" as such, had been planned with an adjoining "Hall of Life," where architecture, painting, sculpture, music, and poetry would be united, so that the mind of the survivor might be directed away from the experience of death, from dull mourning and idle laments, toward the good things of life.

"And as quickly as possible," Naphta scoffed. "Mustn't let him overdo the rites of death in an unseemly fashion; mustn't let him get carried away thinking about the simple fact of death—without which, of course, there would be no such thing as architecture, painting, sculpture, music, or poetry."

"He deserts to the colors," Hans Castorp said dreamily.

"Your statement is incoherent, my good engineer," Settembrini said in reply, "yet its reprehensibility still shines through. The experience of death must ultimately be the experience of life, or else it is only a wraith."

"Are they going to decorate their 'Hall of Life' with obscene symbols, like the ones found on many ancient sarcophagi?" Hans Castorp asked in all seriousness.

There was sure to be a fat feast for the senses, Naphta declared. In oils and marble, the body would be celebrated in classicistic taste—the sinful body, which they rescued from decay, although that should come as no surprise, since it was those same tender feelings about the body that prevented even physical chastisement nowadays.

It was at this point that Herr Wehsal introduced the topic of torture— one could read the excitement on his face. Interrogation under torture, what did the gentlemen think of that? When traveling on business in towns that were historic centers of civilization, he, Ferdinand, had always enjoyed visiting those secluded places where that sort of probing of the conscience had once been practiced. He knew the torture chambers in Nuremberg and Regensburg, had examined them closely for educational purposes. For the sake of the soul, people had certainly subjected the body to less than tender treatment, in oh-so-many ingenious ways. There had not even been screams. The pear had been shoved into the open mouth, the famous pear, not a very tasty fruit, to be sure—and then silence had reigned as they went about their business.

"*Porcheria,*" Settembrini muttered.

All due regard for their pear and silent business—but in Ferge's opinion, no one had ever come up with anything more vile than the exploration of the pleura.

That had been done for his own good!

And in a case where an impenitent soul had violated the law, temporary merciless procedures were no less justifiable. Besides, torture had been a rational step forward.

Naphta was truly no longer in his right mind.

Oh, yes he was, very much so. As a belletrist, Herr Settembrini apparently did not have an overview of the history of medieval law at his immediate command. That history had in fact been one of the progressive application of human reason, by which, on the basis of purely rational concerns, God had gradually been removed from the administration of justice. Trial by ordeal had been abandoned, because over time it became apparent that might was victorious even when it was not in the right. People of Herr Settembrini's sort, the doubters and critics, had observed this fact and seen to it that the old naive form of justice was replaced by the Inquisition, which no longer depended on God's intervening on behalf of truth, but was aimed at obtaining the truth through the confession of the accused. No sentence without a confession. One had only to listen to commonfolk even nowadays, the instinct ran deep: no matter how strong the links in the chain of proof, a sentence was considered illegitimate if there was no confession. And how did one obtain it? How did one find the truth beyond all suspicion, beyond all circumstantial evidence? How did one look into the heart and mind of a man who dissembled and denied? If the Spirit was willfully malicious, one had no recourse but to turn to the body, which one could get hold of. Reason dictated the use of torture as the means to obtain that indispensable confession. But the person who had demanded and initiated the process that led to confession—that had been Herr Settembrini. It was he who had originated torture.

The humanist begged the other gentlemen not to believe it. That was a diabolical joke. If it had all happened the way Herr Naphta claimed, if reason had indeed been the inventor of something so ghastly, that would only prove how bitter was reason's need of assistance and enlightenment, how little cause admirers of natural instinct had for fearing the world could get too reasonable. Except, of course, that the previous speaker had been very much mistaken. Such a perversion of justice could not be attributed to reason, because the real cause had been a belief in hell. You needed only to look around in museums and torture chambers: those pincers, racks, screws, and branding irons were obviously the products of a deluded childish fantasy, created out of the pious desire to imitate what went on in the otherworld's chambers of everlasting torment. They had apparently believed, moreover, that they were actually helping the malefactor. They had assumed his poor soul was struggling to confess and that the flesh, as the principle of evil, stood opposed to its better intentions. They had truly thought they were doing him a favor by breaking his body with torture. The madness of ascetics.

And had the ancient Romans suffered from the same madness?

The Romans? *Ma che!*

Why, they had also used torture as part of the judicial process.

Logical stalemate. Hans Castorp attempted to help them over it—as if it were his job—by imperiously taking over the conversation and tossing in the issue of the death penalty. Torture had been abolished, although examining magistrates still had ways of softening up the accused, but the death penalty seemed to be immortal, there was no doing without it. The most civilized nations clung to it. The French system of deportation had been very unsuccessful. One simply did not know what should be done with certain subhuman creatures except behead them.

Those were not "subhuman creatures," Herr Settembrini informed him. They were human beings like the engineer, like himself—although weak-willed victims of an imperfect society. And he told them about a hardened criminal, a mass murderer, the sort of man prosecutors loved to portray in their closing arguments as a "brute" and a "beast in human form." The man had covered the walls of his cell with verses. And they hadn't been bad verses, either—much better than those occasionally penned by prosecutors.

That might cast a rather strange light on art, Naphta reposted, but was in no way remarkable otherwise.

Hans Castorp said he had expected Herr Naphta would know how to react in defense of executions. Naphta, he continued, was certainly just as much a revolutionary as Herr Settembrini, but in a defensive, reactionary sense—he was a revolutionary of reaction.

The world, Herr Settembrini said with a self-assured smile, would glide right past the revolution of inhuman reaction and move on to its real agenda. Herr Naphta would rather impugn art than admit it could make a human being of even the worst reprobate. Youth in search of light would never be won over by that kind of fanaticism. An international league whose goal was the abolition of capital punishment had just been formed in all civilized countries. Herr Settembrini had the honor of being a member. The venue for its first convention had not yet been chosen, but humankind could be certain that the speakers whom it would hear there would come armed with arguments. And he supplied those arguments himself, including both the ever-present possibility of a false verdict, whereby justice itself was executed, and the hope of rehabilitation, which ought never to be abandoned. And quoting the biblical verse "Vengeance is mine," he pointed out that the state, if its purpose was ennoblement and not coercion, should not repay evil with evil, and went on to repudiate the concept of "punishment," after first having refuted that of "guilt," basing his argument on scientific determinism.

Whereupon "youth in search of light" was forced to watch as Naphta took each argument, one after the other, and wrung its neck. He ridiculed the philanthropist's reluctance to shed blood, his reverence for life, claimed that such a reverence for life belonged to only the most banal rubbers-and-umbrellas bourgeois periods, but that the moment history took a more passionate turn, the moment a single idea, something that tran-scended mere "security," was at work, something suprapersonal, some-thing greater than the individual—and since that alone was a state worthy of mankind, it was, on a higher plane, the normal state of affairs—at that moment, then, individual life would always be sacrificed without further ado to that higher idea, and not only that, but individuals would also unhesitatingly and gladly risk their own lives for it. His good adversary's philanthropy, he said, was aimed at robbing life of all its difficult and deadly serious aspects; its goal was the castration of life, and the same went for the determinism of its so-called science. The truth was, however, that determinism could never abolish the concept of guilt—indeed it could only add to its terrible gravity.

Not bad. So he was demanding that society's unlucky victims should feel terribly guilty and enter the bloody arena out of personal conviction, was that it?

Exactly. The criminal was as imbued with guilt as he was with self. For he was what he was, and was neither able nor willing to be anything else—and that was his guilt. Herr Naphta removed guilt and merit from the empirical world to the metaphysical. Our deeds, our actions were predetermined, of course, that was not where our freedom lay—but in being. Man was as he wanted to be, and would never cease to want to be until his extermination. "For the life of him" he had gladly slain others, and so it was not too high a price to exact life from him. Let him die then, for he had satisfied the deepest lust of his heart.

The deepest lust?

The deepest.

Lips were pursed. Hans Castorp gave a little cough. Wehsal had set his jaw askew. Herr Ferge sighed.

Settembrini responded with a subtle remark: "It seems some generalizations reflect on the person making them. You feel a desire to kill, do you?"

"That's no business of yours. If I did, however, I would laugh right in the face of any ignorant humanitarian who tried to keep me on a diet of pap until I died in my bed. It is nonsense, of course, for a murderer to outlive his victim. The two of them, eye to eye, are alone together in a way that two people are alone in only one other similar circumstance, the one receptive, the other active—and they share a secret that will unite them forever. They belong together."

Settembrini confessed coolly that he lacked the requisite organ for this murderous mysticism and that he did not miss it at all. Not that he was denigrating Herr Naphta's religious talents—they doubtless exceeded his own—he was merely admitting a lack of envy. He felt an insurmountable need for tidiness that kept him out of that realm where a reverence for human misery—as experimental youth had put it earlier—reigned, not only in a physical but also in a psychological sense, a realm where, in short, virtue, reason, and health meant nothing, but where vice and illness were held in extraordinary honor.

Naphta agreed that virtue and health were not part of the religious condition. Much would be gained by making it clear that religion had absolutely nothing to do with reason and morality. For, he added, religion had nothing to do with life. Life was based on conditions and principles that belonged in part to epistemology and in part to ethics—the former being time, space, and causality; the latter, morality and reason. All such matters were not only foreign and of no significance to religion as such, but also inimical to it; for they were the constituents of life, or so-called health, which was to say, ultraphilistine, utter bourgeois existence—to which the religious world was ordained to be the absolute opposite, indeed the very genius of opposition. Not that he, Naphta, would want to deny the possibility of a certain genius in the sphere of life. There was a "bour-geoisiosity" of life, whose monumental genius was indisputable, a philis-tine majesty, which one might well consider worthy of respect, as long as one realized that as it stood there in all its dignity, legs astraddle, hands at its back, chest thrust forward, it was the incarnation of irreligiosity.

Hans Castorp raised a schoolboy forefinger. He did not wish to offend either side, he said, but apparently the subject had now turned to progress, to human progress, and so in a certain sense to politics, the republic of eloquence, the civilization of the educated West; and in that regard he would like to say that the difference, or if Herr Naphta preferred, the opposition between life and religion could be traced to that between time and eternity. Because progress occurred only within time; there was no progress in eternity, no politics or eloquence, either. There one laid one's head back onto God, so to speak, and closed one's eyes. And that was the difference between religion and morality—though put in a rather confused fashion.

The naiveté of his words, Settembrini said, was less problematic than his fear of giving offense and his tendency to make concessions to the Devil.

Well, as far as the Devil went, he and Herr Settembrini had discussed him over a year ago. "*O Satana, O ribellione!*" To which Devil was he making concessions, then? The one involved with rebellion, labor, and criticism, or the other one? You were taking your life in your hands—a Devil on the right, a Devil on the left, how in the hell were you supposed to survive?

That was not a proper characterization, Naphta said, of the way Herr Settembrini wished to see things. The decisive factor in the humanist's view of the world was that God and the Devil were two different persons or principles and that "life" was the bone of contention between them—very much after the medieval model, by the way. In reality, however, they were one, were united in their opposition to life, to the bourgeoisiosity of life, to ethics, reason, virtue; they were the single religious principle that they represented together.

"What a revolting hodgepodge—*che guazzabuglio proprio stomache-vole!*" Settembrini cried. God and evil, the holy and the criminal all jumbled together. No judgment, no will, no capacity to reject what was vile. He wondered if Herr Naphta knew just what he was repudiating—and with young people listening—by jumbling up God and the Devil and denying the ethical principle in the name of his depraved Holy Duality. He was repudiating—it made him sick to say it—*values*, every standard of value. Fine—good and evil did not exist, only a morally chaotic void. The individual, in all the dignity of his critical faculties, did not exist, just an all-devouring, all-leveling community, and a mystical submersion in it. The individual—

How charming—Herr Settembrini was back to calling himself an individualist. To be that, however, one needed to know the difference between morality and blessedness, which the gentleman, as a good *illuminatus* and monist, most certainly did not. Wherever life was stupidly regarded as an end in itself, with no questions asked about a meaning or purpose beyond it, what one found were social ethics, species ethics, vertebrate ethics, but not individualism—that resided solely in the realm of the religious and mystical, in that so-called chaotic void. Just what was Herr Settembrini's morality, what was its point? It was bound to life, and so merely utilitarian—unheroic, miserably so. Its sole objective was for a person to grow old, rich, happy, and healthy—period; he considered a philistine gospel of reason and work to be ethics. But as far as he, Naphta, was concerned, he once again took the liberty of calling that a shabby bourgeoisiosity of life.

Settembrini begged for moderation here, although his voice was filled with passion, because he found it intolerable that Herr Naphta kept talking about the "bourgeoisiosity of life" in such a—God only knew why—disdainful, aristocratic tone, as if *the opposite*—and everyone knew what the opposite of life was—was somehow more noble.

More new catchwords. Now the issue was nobility, aristocracy. Hans Castorp, flushed and weary from the frosty air and all these uncertainties, his mind reeling as he wondered whether the way he was putting things was too feverishly daring or even comprehensible, admitted haltingly that he had always imagined death wearing a starched Spanish ruff, or at least in some sort of semi-uniform with a high stiff collar, whereas life always wore a little, normal, modern collar. And then aghast at his own social blunder, at the drunken dreaminess of his words, he assured them that was not what he had meant to say. But was it not true that there were people, certain individuals, whom one found it impossible to picture dead, precisely because they were so vulgar? That was to say: they seemed so fit for life, so good at it, that they would never die, as if they were unworthy of the consecration of death.

Herr Settembrini hoped he was not wrong in assuming that Hans Castorp had made such a remark merely so that it could be contradicted. The young man would always find him ready to assist intellectually in warding off such assaults. "Fit for life," had he said? And had used the term in a pejorative sense? "Worthy of life"—that was the term he should have used instead. And then his thoughts would order themselves in a true and beautiful manner. "Worthy of life"—and at once, by means of the simplest, most legitimate sort of association, one was reminded of the term "worthy of love," which was so intimately related to the former that one could say that whatever was worthy of life was truly worthy of love. And joined together, the two terms—"worthy of love" and "worthy of life"— became what one called noble.

Hans Castorp found that charming, well worth listening to. Herr Settembrini had won him over entirely with his graphic theory. Because say what one might, what one would—and several things might be said, for example that illness was a higher level of life and so possessed a kind of solemnity—this much was certain: illness meant an overemphasis on the physical, sent a person back to his own body, cast him back totally upon it, as it were, detracted from the worthiness and dignity of man to the point of annihilation by reducing man to mere body. Illness, therefore, was inhuman.

Illness was supremely human, Naphta immediately rebutted, because to be human was to be ill. Indeed, man was ill by nature, his illness was what made him human, and whoever sought to make him healthy and attempted to get him to make peace with nature, to "return to nature" (whereas he had never been natural), that whole pack of Rousseauian prophets—regenerators, vegetarians, fresh-air freaks, sunbath apostles, and so forth—wanted nothing more than to dehumanize man and turn him into an animal. Humanity? Nobility? The Spirit was what distinguished man—a creature set very much apart from nature, with feelings very much contrary to nature—from the rest of organic life. Therefore, the dignity and nobility of man was based in the Spirit, in illness. In a word, the more ill a man was the more highly human he was, and the genius of illness was more human than that of health. It was astonishing how someone who played the philanthropist could close his eyes to such basic truths of humanity. Herr Settembrini was forever going on about progress. As if progress, to the extent such a thing existed, was not due solely to illness, or better, to creative genius, which was one and the same thing as illness. As if those who were healthy had not always lived from the achievements of illness. There had always been people who had willingly entered into illness and madness in order to win knowledge for mankind—and knowledge, having been wrested from madness, became health and, once obtained by heroic sacrifice, its possession and use were no longer conditioned by illness and madness. That was the true death on the cross.

"Aha," Hans Castorp said to himself, "you improper Jesuit with your permutations and interpretations of the crucifixion. It's clear enough why you did not became a priest, *a handsome Jesuit with a little moist spot!* Well, lion, roar," he thought, turning toward Herr Settembrini. And "roar" he did, declaring everything Naphta had said to be chicanery, humbug, confusion. "Admit it," he shouted at his adversary, "admit it, by your responsibility as a pedagogue, confess it before the ears of impressionable youth, say it straight out: your Spirit is illness. No doubt of it, that will rouse them for your Spirit, that will win them to the faith. Go ahead and explain how illness and death are noble, but health and life are sordid—that's the surest method for engaging these pupils in the service of humanity. *Davvero, è criminoso!*" And like a knight entering the lists, he championed the nobility of health and life, the nobility that had been granted by nature and did not need to fear Spirit. "Form!" he said. And Naphta grandiloquently responded, "Logos!" But he who would not hear of the logos, said, "Reason!" And the man of the logos defended "Passion!" Confusion reigned. "Objective reality," shouted one; "The self!" cried the other. Finally one side was talking about "Art!" and the other about "Criticism!" And both constantly returned to "Nature!" and "Spirit!" and to which of them was more noble, and to the issue of "true aristocracy." But there was no clarity, no order, not even of a dualistic and militant sort; for it was all not only contradictory, but also topsy-turvy, and the disputants not only contradicted one another, but also themselves. Settembrini had frequently sung the oratorical praises of "criticism," but now it was its opposite—which he called "art"—that he claimed was the more noble principle. And although Naphta had frequently stepped forward as the defender of "natural instinct" against Settembrini's contention that nature was merely a "dumb power," a brutal fact, a stroke of fate, to which reason and human pride dared not submit, he now took up his position on the side of the Spirit and of "illness," for there alone were to be found nobility and humanity. Settembrini, meanwhile, had become the advocate of nature and its nobility of health, ignoring any previous notions of emancipation. And matters were no less confusing when it came to "objective reality" and the "self"—indeed, the confusion here, which was in fact always the same confusion, was so hopeless and literally confused that no one knew any longer who was the devout soul and who the freethinker. In caustic words, Naphta forbade Herr Settembrini to call himself an "individualist," because he denied the polarity of God and nature and defined the question of humanity, the problem of man's interior conflict, as simply the conflict between the individual and larger social units, and so was wedded to a bourgeois morality that was tied to life, understood life as an end in itself, saw its sole purpose in unheroic utility, and viewed all moral law as invested in the state; whereas he, Naphta—well aware that mankind's inner conflict was based instead on the contradiction between what the senses register and what transcends the senses—represented true, mystical individualism and was in actuality the genuine man of freedom and subjectivity. But if that was the case, Hans Castorp thought, how did that square with "anonymous and communal"—just to select *one* of the many contradictions? Or, going one step farther, with those striking remarks to which Naphta had treated Pater Unterpertinger in their colloquy about Hegel and the "Catholicity" of that state philosopher, about how "politics" and "Catholicism" were psychologically related and formed a single objective reality? Had not education and statecraft always been the special domain of Naphta's order? And what an education that was! Herr Settembrini was certainly a zealous pedagogue, zealous to the point of being a tiresome bother; but his principles could not approach Naphta's when it came to ascetic, self-mortifying objectivity. Absolute authority! An ironclad bond! Coercion! Obedience! Terror! There might be something to it, but it showed very little consideration for the dignity of the individual and his critical faculties. It was a drill book written by Frederick the Prussian and Loyola the Spaniard, so devout and strict that it drew blood—leaving only one question: how did Naphta actually achieve such bloody, unconditional certainty, since he admitted he did not believe in pure knowledge as such, in unbiased research, in short, not even in truth, in objective, scientific truth, the search for which formed the highest law of all human morality for Lodovico Settembrini. In that regard, it was Herr Settembrini who was pious and strict, and Naphta who was lax and slovenly, referring truth back to man and declaring that whatever profited man was true. To make truth that dependent on man's own interests—was that not itself philistine utilitarianism, a bourgeoisiosity of life? So that you really could not call it ironclad objectivity; there was more freedom and subjectivity to it than Leo Naphta would have been willing to admit—it was in its own way just as "political" as Herr Settembrini's didactic statement that freedom was the law of brotherly love. And that clearly meant that his freedom, like Naphta's truth, was tied to just one thing: man. But that made it decidedly more devout than free—yet another juxtaposition of terms that tended to slip away when you began defining things. Oh, this Settembrini! It was not for nothing that he was a man of letters—the grandson of a politician and the son of a humanist. He was so noble-minded about the beauties of emancipation and criticism—and hummed little tunes at girls on the street. And then there was caustic little Naphta, who was bound to strict vows—and such a freethinker that he came close to being a libertine himself, making the Italian look like the dupe of virtue, so to speak. Herr Settembrini was afraid of the "absolute Spirit," wanted to restrict "spirit" to democratic progress, and nothing else—was horrified by militant Naphta's religious licentiousness, which made a jumble of God and the Devil, the holy and the criminal, genius and illness, which recognized no values, no judgments of reason, no will. Who, then, was actually free, who was devout? What constituted man's true state and condition: obliteration in all-devouring, all-leveling community, which was a simultaneously voluptuous and ascetic act; or "critical subjectivity," where bombast and strict bourgeois virtue were at loggerheads? Ah, principles and viewpoints were constantly at loggerheads, there was no lack of inner contradictions, making it all extraordinarily difficult for a civilian to exercise responsibility, not merely to decide between opposites, but also to keep them apart as neat, separate specimens—until a civilian was sorely tempted to plunge headlong into Naphta's "morally chaotic void." Everything was intertwined and at cross-purposes, a great general confusion—and Hans Castorp thought he saw that the disputants would have been less embittered, if during their dispute each had not been the harasser of his own soul.

They had walked together all the way to the Berghof; and then the three who lived there accompanied the other two back to their little house, where they all stood outside in the snow for a long time while Naphta and Settembrini continued their argument—for pedagogic purposes, as Hans Castorp well knew, in order to shape the impressionable minds of youth in search of light. All these things were much too high for Herr Ferge, however, and Wehsal proved less interested once the subject was no longer flogging or torture. Hans Castorp probed the snow with his cane, hung his head, and pondered the great confusion.

At last they parted. They could not stand there forever—and their subject was boundless. The three Berghof residents turned homeward, and the two pedagogic rivals were forced to enter their little house, the one climbing to his silken cell, the other to his humanist's garret with its lectern and water carafe. Hans Castorp, however, retired to his balcony—

his ears full of the hubbub and alarums of two armies, one from Jerusalem, the other from Babylon, advancing under the *dos banderas* and joining now in the confused tumult of battle.

Snow

FIVE TIMES A DAY, the diners at all seven tables expressed unanimous dissatisfaction with this year's winter. They were of the opinion that it was very negligent in fulfilling its duties as an Alpine winter and had failed to provide the meteorological medicine for which these regions were famous, in the quantities promised by the brochure, familiar to long-termers, and envisioned by newcomers. A massive deficit in sunlight—a significant factor in the cure—was noted; without those helpful rays, recuperation was doubtless retarded. And whatever Herr Settembrini might think of the sincerity with which these mountain guests went about getting well so that they could leave "home" and return to the flatlands, they did at any rate demand their rights, wanted full value for the money spent by their parents or spouses; and so they grumbled in the dining hall, the elevator, and the lobby. And management proved quite sensible about accommodating its guests and compensating for their losses. Another apparatus for "artificial sunlight" was purchased, since the two in service could not meet the demands of those who expected electricity to help them get a tan—a color that flattered the young girls and women and gave the men a splendidly, irresistibly athletic look despite their horizontal lifestyle. That look reaped its rewards in reality, too; the women, although fully aware of the purely cosmetic and technical origin of such virility, were foolish—or hardened—enough that they gladly chose to be deceived, to be carried away by the illusion, to let it capture their feminine hearts. "My God," a red-haired, red-eyed patient from Berlin remarked one evening in the lobby. It was Frau Schönfeld, and she was speaking about a cavalier with long legs and a sunken chest—he had already undergone pneumothorax—whose calling card read "*Aviateur diplômé et Enseigne de la Marine allemande*" and who always appeared at dinner in formal dress, though never at supper, as per navy regulations, or so he claimed. "My God," she said, voraciously eyeing the ensign, "what a marvelous tan the fellow has from the sunlamp. Looks as if he's been out hunting eagles, the devil does." And in the elevator he gave her goose bumps, bending down to her ear and whispering, "Just wait, you nymph! You'll pay for that devastating glance you shot my way!" And skirting the glass panels of balconies, the devil and eagle-hunter found his way to the nymph.

All the same, it was generally felt that such artificial rays did not really compensate for the year's deficit in genuine sunlight. Two or three days of full sunshine a month—even when they burst so splendidly out of the blur of foggy gray and thick cloud cover, spreading a deep, deep velvet blue behind the white peaks, scattering sparkling diamonds, and delightfully searing your face and the back of your neck—two or three such days over the course of so many weeks were not enough to help the mood of people whose fate justified their making extraordinary demands in the way of consolation and who presumed that in return for having renounced the joys and torments of flatland humanity, they had signed on for an easy and enjoyable, if rather lifeless life—on perfectly favorable terms, until time itself was abrogated. Nor did it help for the director to remind them that even under such circumstances life at the Berghof bore little resemblance to a stay on a prison ship or in a Siberian salt mine, or for him to praise the advantages of the local air, so thin and light, which like the pure ether of the spheres lacked all earthly admixtures, good or bad, and protected them from the fumes and vapors of the plains even without the sun; gloom and protest spread, threats of wild departures were the order of the day, and some were even carried out, despite sad examples like Frau Salomon, recently returned from her willful stay in windy, wet Amsterdam, whose case had once been stubborn but not serious, but now looked very much like a life sentence.

Instead of sun, there was snow, great, colossal masses of snow, more snow than Hans Castorp had ever seen in his life. The previous winter had truly not lacked for snow, but its output had been puny in comparison with this year, which produced it in monstrous, reckless quantities, reminding you of just how bizarre and outlandish these regions were. It snowed day after day, and on through the nights, in light flurries, in heavy squalls—but it snowed. The few paths still passable were like tunnels, with snow piled man-high on both sides, forming walls like slabs of alabaster, grainy with beautiful sparkling crystals, a surface guests found useful for drawing pictures or writing messages—news, jokes, ribaldries. And between the walls, the snow was packed so thick, despite all the shoveling, that here and there you came across holes and soft spots where you could suddenly sink in, sometimes up to the knee. You had to pay close attention to keep from accidentally breaking a leg. The benches had vanished, had sunk beneath the snow—here and there the back of one might stick up out of its white grave. Down in town, street level had shifted oddly until shops had become cellars you entered by descending stairways of snow.

And more snow kept falling on top of the rest, day in, day out, drifting down softly through the moderately cold air (five to fifteen above zero), which did not freeze you to the bone—you barely noticed, it felt more like twenty or twenty-five degrees; the air was still and so dry it took the sting out. The mornings were very dark; they ate breakfast by the light of the artificial moons in the dining hall with its cheerfully stenciled arches. Outside was gloomy nothing, a world packed in grayish-white cotton, in foggy vapors and whirling snow that pushed up against the windowpanes. The mountains were invisible, although over time something of the nearest evergreen forest might come into view, heavily laden with snow, only to be quickly lost in the next flurry; now and then a fir would shake off its burden, dumping dusty white into gray. Around ten o'clock the sun would appear like a wisp of softly illumined vapor above its mountain, a pale spook spreading a faint shimmer of reality over the vague, indiscernible landscape. But it all melted into a ghostly delicate pallor, with no definite lines, nothing the eye could follow with certainty. The contours of the peaks merged, were lost in fog and mist. Expanses of snow suffused with soft light rose in layers, one behind another, leading your gaze into insubstantiality. And what was probably a weakly illumined cloud clung to a cliff, motionless, like an elongated tatter of smoke.

Around noon the sun broke halfway through, struggling to melt the fog into blue, an attempt that fell far short of success. Yet there was a momentary hint of blue sky, and even this bit of light was enough to release a flash of diamonds across the wide landscape, so oddly disfigured by its snowy adventure. Usually the snow stopped at that hour of the day, as if for a quick survey of what had been achieved thus far; the rare days of sunshine seemed to serve much the same purpose—the flurries died down and the sun's direct glare attempted to melt the luscious, pure surface of drifted new snow. It was a fairy-tale world, childlike and funny. Boughs of trees adorned with thick pillows, so fluffy someone must have plumped them up; the ground a series of humps and mounds, beneath which slinking underbrush or outcrops of rock lay hidden; a landscape of crouching, cowering gnomes in droll disguises—it was comic to behold, straight out of a book of fairy tales. But if there was something roguish and fantastic about the immediate vicinity through which you laboriously made your way, the towering statues of snow-clad Alps, gazing down from the distance, awakened in you feelings of the sublime and holy.

Afternoons, between two and four, Hans Castorp would lie on his balcony—wrapped up nice and warm, his head propped neither too high nor too low, but just right, against the adjustable back of his splendid lounge chair—and look out over the pillowed railing to the forests and mountains. Laden with snow, the greenish-black pine forest marched up the slopes, and between the trees every inch of ground was cushioned soft with snow. Above the forest, mountains of rock rose into whitish gray, with vast surfaces of snow broken occasionally by dark, jutting crags and ridges gently dissolving into mist. Snow was falling silently. Everything grew more and more blurred. Gazing into cottony nothing, eyes easily closed and drifted into slumber, and at just that moment a shiver passed over the body. And yet there could be no purer sleep than here in this icy cold, a dreamless sleep untouched by any conscious sense of organic life's burdens; breathing this empty, vaporless air was no more difficult for the body than non-breathing was for the dead. And upon awakening, you found the mountains had vanished entirely in the snowy fog, with only pieces of them, a summit, a crag, emerging for a few moments and disappearing again. This soft, ghostly pantomime was extremely entertaining. You had to pay close attention to catch each stealthy change in the misty phantasmagoria. Freed of clouds, a huge, primitive segment of mountain, lacking top and bottom, would suddenly appear. But if you took your eye off it for only a minute, it had vanished again.

There were blizzards that prevented you from staying out on the balcony, when the wind drove great masses of white before it, covering the floor, furniture, everything, with a thick layer of snow. Yes, it could storm, even in this high, peaceful valley. The empty air would riot, until it was so full of whirling flakes that you could not see one step in front of you. Gusts that could suffocate you drove flurries in wild, driving, sidelong blasts, pulled snow up from the valley floor in great eddies, set it whirling in a mad dance—it was no longer snowfall, it was a chaos of white darkness, a beast. The whole region went on a monumental, unbridled rampage, and only the snow finches, which could suddenly appear in flocks, seemed to feel at home in it.

And yet Hans Castorp loved life in the snow. He found it similar in many ways to life at the shore: a primal monotony was common to both landscapes. The snow, a deep, loose, unblemished powder, played the same role here as yellowish-white sand did down below; both felt clean to the touch; you shook the dry, icy white from your shoes and clothes just as you brushed off the crushed stones and shells from the bottom of the sea—neither was dusty, neither left a trace behind. And wading through snow was just as difficult as wading through sand dunes, except when the sun melted the surface during the day and it froze hard again at night: then you moved across it as lightly as across a parquet floor— it was the same easy, pleasant feeling you got walking over the smooth, firm, springy, salt-rinsed sand at the edge of the sea.

But this year the massive accumulation from so many snowfalls had seriously limited everyone's movement in the open—except for skiers, of course. The snowplows did their work; but they had trouble keeping open even the town's main street and most frequented paths, and the few free passageways, all of them ending in impassable drifts, were crowded with the traffic of the healthy and sick, locals and hotel guests from around the world; pedestrians, however, were constantly in danger of being toppled by sledders, ladies and gentlemen who came sweeping, swerving, and careering down the slopes on their childish vehicles, leaning far back, feet outstretched, yelling warnings in tones that revealed just how importantly they took the enterprise; and no sooner had they reached the bottom than they turned around, grabbed the rope, and pulled their fashionable toys back uphill.

Hans Castorp was fed up with such promenades. He had only two great wishes: the first, and stronger, was to be alone with his thoughts to "play king," and his balcony permitted him to do that, at least perfunctorily. His other wish, however, bound up with the first, was to enjoy a freer, more active, more intense experience of the snowy mountain wilderness, for which he felt a great affinity; but as long as he remained a mere unarmed, unchariceted pedestrian, his wish could never be fulfilled; and had he attempted it, he would have found himself up over his chest in snow the moment he pressed on beyond the shoveled paths, all of which quickly came to an end.

And so one day during his second winter up here, Hans Castorp decided he would buy skis and learn how to use them—well enough at least for his practical purposes. He was no athlete, had never been interested in sports, did not pretend he was, the way many Berghof guests did—the ladies in particular, who decked themselves out in sporty outfits to match the spirit of the place. Hermine Kleefeld, for example—although her lips and the tip of her nose were blue from shallow breathing—loved to appear at lunch in woolen trousers, and after the meal she would loll about, knees spread wide, in one of the wicker chairs in the lobby. If Hans Castorp had asked the director for permission to carry out his eccentric plan, he would have been rebuffed in no uncertain terms. Athletic activities were strictly forbidden to all members of their society up here, both at the Berghof and at similar institutions; for although the air seemed to fill the lungs so easily, it made great demands on the heart; and in Hans Castorp's case, his clever remark about "getting used to not getting used" to things was as valid as ever, and his fever, which Rhadamanthus traced to a moist spot, persisted stubbornly. Why else would he even be here? His wishes and plans were both inconsistent and prohibited. But let there be no misunderstanding here—he had no ambition to emulate fresh-air dandies and rakish athletes, who if fashion had demanded it, would have been just as fanatic about playing cards in a stuffy room. He certainly felt that he was part of a different, more restricted society, was anything but a tourist; and his more recent, broadening perspective had brought with it attenuating duties and a dignity that distanced him from others, so that he was not of a mind to join them in their romps or to roll in the snow like a fool. He was not interested in escapades, he would proceed in moderation. Rhadamanthus might very well have authorized such plans, but house rules would have required him to forbid them. And so Hans Castorp decided to proceed behind his back.

He happened to speak to Herr Settembrini about his intentions. The Italian almost embraced him for joy. "Why, yes, but of course, my good engineer. For God's sake, do it! Don't ask anyone—just do it. Your guardian angel has been whispering in your ear. Do it at once, before the happy notion deserts you. I'll come along, go to the shop with you; let's be off at once to purchase those blessed utensils. I would gladly accompany you into the mountains, moving alongside you with wings on my heels, like Mercury himself—but I dare not. Ah, to dare it—and I would if it were only a matter of 'dare not.' But I cannot, I am a ruined man. But as for you—it most definitely cannot hurt you, not if you're reasonable and don't overdo it. And what if it does hurt you just a tad—it will still have been the work of your guardian angel, which . . . but I shall say no more. What an excellent plan! Here for two years and still capable of such inspiration! Oh, no, you're solid at the core; there's no reason to despair of you. Bravo, bravo! You shall tweak the nose of your Prince of Shades up there. Buy your racing footwear, have it sent to me or Lukaček, or to the retailer of foodstuffs downstairs. You can fetch it from there to go out and practice, and away you'll glide."

And that is how it was done. With Herr Settembrini looking on and playing the critical expert, although he knew absolutely nothing about sports, Hans Castorp purchased a pair of spiffing skis in a specialty shop on the main street—good solid ash, shellacked a light brown, with first-rate leather straps and pointed tips turned up slightly; he also bought poles with iron tips and snow rings, and could not be talked out of carrying it all on his shoulder to Settembrini's quarters, where he quickly came to an agreement with the grocer about storage for his equipment. Having spent a great deal of time watching how skis were used, he began to practice on his own—but well away from the crowds on the beginners' hill; he chose an almost treeless slope not far behind the Berghof, and he would blunder up and down it every day, occasionally with Herr Settembrini watching from a little distance, propped on his cane, his ankles charmingly crossed, greeting each improvement in skill with cries of "Bravo!" One day Hans Castorp was steering his way down the shoveled, looping path, on his way back to Dorf to return his skis to the grocer's, when he ran into the director—but nothing came of it. Behrens did not even recognize him, although it was a bright afternoon and the beginner almost ran him down. Wrapped in a cloud of cigar smoke, the director stomped on past.

Hans Castorp discovered that you quickly learn a skill if you truly need to. He made no pretense of becoming a virtuoso. What he required to know he learned in a few days, without overheating or having to fight for breath. He worked hard at keeping his feet nicely parallel, leaving a set of even tracks, practiced how to push himself off by steering with his poles, learned to negotiate obstacles, leaping over little mounds with arms widespread, rising and falling like a ship on a stormy sea; and after about the twentieth try he no longer upended when he put on the brakes by executing a telemark turn at full speed, sticking one leg out and bending the other at the knee. He gradually increased the range of his activities. One day Herr Settembrini saw him vanish in a burst of white fog; cupping his hands and calling after him to be careful, the contented pedagogue turned homeward.

The wintry mountains were beautiful—not in a gentle, benign way, but beautiful like the wild North Sea under a strong west wind. They awakened the same sense of awe—but there was no thunder, only a deathly silence. Hans Castorp's long, pliant footwear bore him in all directions: along the slope on the left in the direction of Clavadel or to the right on past Frauenkirch and Glaris, the shadowy ghost of the Amselfluh massif looming up out of the fog behind them; he also skied the valley of the Dischma and the hills rising behind the Berghof, in the direction of the wooded Seehorn, only the very tops of its two snow-clad peaks visible above the tree line, and toward the Drusatscha woods, behind which he could see the pale, murky outline of the Rhätikon chain buried under snow. He even took his skis in the cablecar to the top of Schatzalp to glide about happily up there, abducted into a world of shimmering, powdery slopes, sixty-five hundred feet above sea level, from where in good weather he had a glorious panorama of the scene of his adventures.

He reveled in the skill he had acquired, which opened up inaccessible worlds and almost obliterated barriers. It permitted him the solitude he sought, the profoundest solitude imaginable, touching his heart with a precarious savagery beyond human understanding. On one side might be a wooded ravine plunging into snowy mists, and on the other a rocky precipice with monstrous, cyclopean masses of snow that formed vaulted caves and humpbacked domes. When he would stop—not moving a muscle, so that he could not hear even himself—the silence was absolute, perfect, a padded soundlessness, like none ever known or perceived anywhere else in the world. There was not a breath of wind to brush softly against the trees, not a rustle, not the call of a bird. It was primal silence to which Hans Castorp listened as he stood there, leaning on one pole, his head tilted to the side, his mouth open; and silently, unrelentingly the snow went on falling, drifted down in a gentle hush.

No, this world with its fathomless silence did not receive a visitor hospitably. He was an invader who came at his own risk, whose presence was only tolerated in an eerie, foreboding way; and he could sense the menace of mute, elemental forces as they rose up around him—not hostile, but simply indifferent and deadly. Born a stranger to remote, wild nature, the child of civilization is much more open to her grandeur than are her own coarse sons, who have been at her mercy from infancy and whose intimacy with her is more level-headed. They know next to nothing of the religious awe with which the novice approaches her, eyebrows raised, his whole being tuned to its depths to receive her, his soul in a state of constant, thrilled, timid excitement. Dressed in his long-sleeved camel-hair vest and leggings, Hans Castorp actually felt rather impudent standing there on his deluxe skis, listening to the primal silence, to the deadly hush of the winter wilderness; and the sense of relief he felt stir within him on the way home, when the first human dwellings emerged out of the shroud, made him that much more aware of his previous state and told him that for hours now his mood had been one of secret, holy fear. On Sylt, he had stood dressed in white trousers, safe, elegant, and reverent beside the mighty, rolling surf, as if it were a caged lion, yawning and showing its fearful fangs and cavernous gorge. Then he would go for a swim, and a lifeguard would blow on his little horn to warn those brash enough to venture beyond the first breaking wave, or merely to get too close to its onrushing storm—and even the final thrust of the cataract was like the slap of a giant paw against the back of his neck. As a young man, Hans Castorp had learned the exhilarating thrill of brushing up against powers whose full embrace would destroy you. What he had not learned back then, however, was a taste for extending the thrilling contact with deadly nature until it threatened with its full embrace—had not learned to venture out into the enormity as a weak, if well armed and reasonably well equipped child of civilization, or at least to postpone fleeing before the enormity until contact with it verged on a peril that knew no limits, until it was no longer the last thrust of foam and a soft paw, but the wave itself, the gorge, the sea.

In a word: Hans Castorp had found courage up here—if courage before the elements is defined not as a dull, level-headed relationship with them, but a conscious abandonment to them, the mastering of the fear of death out of sympathy with them. Sympathy? Yes, within his narrow, civilized breast Hans Castorp did feel sympathy with the elements; and there was a connection between that sympathy and the newfound sense of dignity that he had felt watching silly people on their sleds and that had made a deeper, wider, less comfortable solitude than that afforded by his hotel balcony seem fitting and desirable. From his lounge chair he had observed fog-shrouded mountains, the dance of snowstorms, and in his soul had been ashamed of gaping at it from across the breastwork of comfort. And that was why he had learned to ski—not because the sport was a fad or he had been born with a love of physical activity. And if there was something uncanny about the enormity of the snowing, deadly silence— and as a child of civilization he most certainly felt there was—both his intellect and senses had long ago tasted of the uncanniness up here. A colloquy with Naphta and Settembrini was not exactly a canny experience, or at the least led into uncharted and dangerous regions; and if we can speak of Hans Castorp's sympathy with the vast winter wilderness, it is because he found it to be, notwithstanding the devout awe it awakened, a suitable arena where he could resolve his tangle of ideas, a convenient spot for someone who, without knowing quite how it had happened, found himself burdened with the duties of "playing king" in regard to the state and condition of the *homo Dei*.

There was no one here, no meddlesome fellow tooting danger on his little horn, unless it might have been Herr Settembrini, who had called out through his cupped hands to Hans Castorp as he vanished. But filled with courage and sympathy, he had paid no more attention to that call at his back than he had to the words that rang out behind him as he took certain steps on the evening of Mardi Gras: "*Eh, ingegnere, un po' di ragione, sa!*"

"Ah, my pedagogic Satana, with your *ragione* and *ribellione*," he thought, "I like you. True, you're a windbag and organ-grinder, but you mean well, mean better than that caustic little Jesuit and terrorist, that Spanish torturer and flogger with his flashing glasses. And I like you better, too, although he's almost always right when you two argue and scuffle pedagogically for my poor soul, like God and the Devil struggling over a man in the Middle Ages."

His legs powdered with snow, he poled his way along, heading for some pale elevation rising higher and higher in a series of broad-sheeted terraces, leading he knew not where—perhaps nowhere. At some point he could no longer make out, their upper regions blended with the sky, which was the same foggy white. No peak, no ridge was visible; it was a misty nothing toward which Hans Castorp pushed his way. And since the real world, the valley populated by human beings, very quickly closed behind him again and was lost from sight, and since no sound could reach him from down there now, he was soon deep in his solitude before he even knew it, more deeply lost than he could ever have wished, so deep that the feeling verged on fear, which is the prerequisite of courage. *"Praeterit figura huius mundi,"* he said to himself in a Latin that was not humanist in spirit, but a phrase he had picked up from Naphta. He stopped and looked about him. There was nothing to be seen everywhere, absolutely nothing except a few very small snowflakes descending from the white above to the white below, and the silence all around took its power from what it did not say. And as his gaze faltered in the white void blinding him, he felt his heart stirring, pounding from the climb—the cardiac muscle, whose animal shape and pulses he had observed, wickedly spied upon perhaps, amid the crackling sparks of the X-ray chamber. And that stirring sent a wave of emotion over him: a simple and reverent sympathy with his heart, his human heart, with its questions and riddles, beating all alone up here in the icy void.

He pushed on, moving ever higher, skyward. Sometimes he would thrust the end of his ski pole into the snow and watch blue light jump from the deep hole as he pulled it out. It was fun—he stood there for a long time, just trying out this little optical phenomenon over and over. It was such a peculiar, delicate greenish-blue light, icy clear and yet dusky, from the heights and from the depths, mysterious and seductive. It reminded him of the light and color of a certain pair of eyes, slanting eyes that spoke of destiny, the ones Herr Settembrini, taking a disparaging humanistic view, had called "Tartar slits" and "lone-wolf eyes"— reminded him of eyes seen long ago and ineluctably rediscovered, of Hippe's and Clavdia Chauchat's eyes. "Glad to," he whispered into the soundlessness. "And don't break it. *Il est à visser, tu sais.*" And in his mind he heard melodious words coming from behind, urging reason.

A foggy wood emerged a little way ahead on his right. He turned toward it to have some earthly goal before his eyes, instead of white transcendence—and suddenly he was racing downward, though he had seen no dip in the terrain. The blinding light prevented his making out any sort of contour; he could see nothing really, everything blurred before his eyes. Obstacles could rise up unexpectedly right in front of him. Unable to make out the angle of decline, he let the slope pull him downward.

The woods that had attracted him lay beyond the trough into which he had unintentionally descended. The slope was covered with loose powder, and after following it a little distance, he realized that it fell away to one side, toward the mountain. He was heading down the trough now, its walls rising on both sides—it seemed to be a fold, a narrow pass leading into the mountain itself. And then the tips of his skis were pointing upward again; the ground rose, there were no more side walls to climb; Hans Castorp's uncharted route led him upward again, across the open face of the mountain.

He saw the evergreen wood below and behind him now; turning around he quickly descended to the snow-laden firs, a last spur of steep, fogged-in forests, that jutted like a wedge out into open ground. He rested beneath the boughs, smoked a cigarette. His soul was still weighed down, oppressed, tense from the profound silence, the dangerous solitude, but he was proud of having conquered it and felt a courage that came from his intrinsic right to such surroundings.

It was three o'clock in the afternoon. He had set out shortly after dinner, intending to cut most of the main rest cure and tea as well and still be back by nightfall. The thought that he would have several hours to roam in vast open spaces filled him with a delightful calm. He had some chocolate in his breeches pocket and had slipped a little bottle of port into his vest.

The sun's position could hardly be made out for the thick fog that encompassed it. Behind him, at the entrance to the valley, at the notch in the mountains that he could not see, clouds were darkening, and the thickening mist seemed to be advancing. It looked like snow, more snow—it was in such short supply, after all—a good, solid squall of it. And in fact, little soundless flakes were falling more heavily now across the slope ahead.

Hans Castorp stepped out from under the tree to let a few fall on his sleeve and to examine them with the connoisseur's expert eye. They looked like shapeless tatters, but more than once he had held his good magnifying glass up to them and knew that they were collections of dainty, precise little jewels: gemstones, star insignia, diamond brooches—no skilled jeweler could have produced more delicate miniatures. Yes, there was something special about this light, loose, powdery white stuff that weighed down the trees, covered the breadth of the land, and carried him along on his skis, something that made it different from the sand on the shore at home, of which it had reminded him. It was not made up of tiny grains of rock, but, as everyone knew, consisted of myriads of water droplets, violently gathered up and frozen into manifold, symmetrical crystals—little pieces of an inorganic substance, the wellspring of protoplasm, of plants and human beings; and among all those myriads of magical stars in their secret, minuscule splendor never intended for the human eye, no two were alike. It was all the result of an endless delight in invention, in the subtlest variation and embellishment of one basic design: the equilateral, equiangular hexagon. And yet absolute symmetry and icy regularity characterized each item of cold inventory. Yes, that was what was so eerie—it was anti-organic, hostile to life itself. Snowflakes were too regular; when put into the service of life, the same substance was never so regular as that. Life shuddered at such perfect precision, regarded it as something deadly, as the secret of death itself; and Hans Castorp thought he understood why the architects of ancient temples had intentionally and covertly built little deviations from symmetry into their rows of columns.

He pushed off, skidding forward on his wooden runners, and headed first along the edge of the woods and then down across the deep snow of the slope into the fog below; rising and falling, skiing effortlessly with no particular goal, he moved through the dead terrain, which with its bare, billowy expanses, dry vegetation of dark, solitary, jutting scrub pines, and horizon bounded by soft swells, bore a striking resemblance to a landscape of dunes. Hans Castorp nodded his head in satisfaction when he stopped to feast his eyes on the similarity; his face stung, his limbs tended to tremble, and a peculiar, intoxicating blend of excitement and weariness came over him, but he found it all quite tolerable because it was so familiar, reminding him of the stimulating, yet sleep-inducing effects of air drenched with the sea. He was delighted by this freedom to roam, by his own winged independence. No path ahead demanded he follow it, and none lay behind him either, to lead him back the way he had come. At first he had left tracks in the snow with his poles, planting them deep, but very soon he quite intentionally freed himself of their tutelage, because it reminded him of the man blowing his little horn and seemed inconsistent with his own innermost feelings for this vast winter wilderness.

Turning now to the right, now to the left, he pushed his way along between snow-clad hillocks, behind which lay another slope, then an open plain, then a great mountain, whose softly cushioned ravines and passes seemed inviting and accessible. Yes, the lure of distance and height, of one solitude opening onto the next, had a very strong effect on Hans Castorp, and though it meant risking getting back late, he pressed ahead ever deeper into the wild silence, into this uncanny world that boded no good—ignoring a tense uneasiness that was growing into real fear as the sky continued to darken much too early, falling like a gray veil over the whole region. Fear made him realize he had secretly, and more or less purposely, been trying to lose his bearings all this time, to forget in what direction the valley and town lay—and that he had been totally successful at it. And yet he could tell himself that if he turned around now and held a course downhill, he would quickly reach the valley, though possibly at some distance from the Berghof—all too quickly; he would be back too early, would not have used his time to the full. Although if he waited until the snowstorm overtook him, he might very well not be able to find his way home all that soon. But he refused to flee ahead of time because of that—let fear, genuine fear of the elements, oppress him as much as it liked. His actions were hardly those of a sportsman, because a sportsman is a man of caution, who gets involved with the elements only as long as he knows he is their lord and master and prudently yields when he must. But there is only one word for what was happening in Hans Castorp's soul: defiance. And although the word certainly can be used pejoratively, even when—or particularly when—a sense of wicked adventure is bound up with genuine fear, if we give it a little thought this much at least becomes clear: that a great many things gather (or, as Hans Castorp the engineer would have said, "accumulate") in the soul of a young person, of a young man who has lived for years as this young man had; and then comes a day when something elemental erupts in a fierce, impatient cry of "Oh, so what!" or "I'll chance it!"—when, in short, prudence is defied, even repudiated. And so he plunged ahead in his long, wooden slippers, gliding down the slope and pushing his way up the next hill, atop which, a little farther off, stood a wooden hut—a hayshed or little barn, with its roof weighted down with stones. It faced the next mountain, whose ridges bristled with firs and above which more foggy peaks towered. The rock wall directly behind the hut was steep and dotted with scattered groups of trees, but it could be circumvented by following what looked like a moderate climb on the right, from where you would then be able to see what lay beyond; and Hans Castorp set out to research the matter, leaving the open field with the hut behind him and skiing down into a rather deep ravine that dropped off from right to left.

He had just begun to climb again when—admittedly, just as expected—it began to snow and blow with a vengeance. In a word, the snowstorm that had been threatening for so long had now arrived—that is, if the term "threat" can apply to blind, unknowing elements that have no intention of destroying us, which might be reassuring in some sense, but are monstrously indifferent, and even that only secondarily. "Hello there!" Hans Castorp thought and came to a stop as the first gust drove a thick flurry against him. "That's quite a little breeze. Goes right to the bone." And, indeed, it was a very ugly wind. One did not notice the general dreadful

cold—it was approaching zero, in fact—when the dry air was still and
inert, as was usually the case; it felt almost balmy. But the moment the
wind picked up, the cold cut through flesh like a knife, and when it really
started blowing, as now—because that first sweeping gust had been only
a harbinger—seven fur coats could not suffice to protect your bones from
the horrendous icy blast. Hans Castorp, however, was not wearing seven
fur coats but only a woolen vest, which would normally have been quite
enough for him—he even found it annoying at the first hint of sunshine.
The wind, by the way, was at his back, and somewhat to one side,
so there was little reason to turn around and take it head-on; and this
consideration, added to his obstinacy and his basic "Oh, so what!" attitude, only made the crazy fellow push on, dodging the few isolated firs
and bearing down on the mountain in the hope of getting beyond it.

There was certainly no pleasure in this, however. All he could see were
dancing flakes, which seemed not to fall but simply to fill the air in a
throng of dense eddies; the icy blasts singed his ears with sharp pain, took
the strength from his legs, and numbed his hands, until he no longer knew
if he was holding his poles or not. The snow blew into his collar and
melted down his back, it flung itself across his shoulders and pelted his
right side; he felt as if he were turning into a snowman, a pole held stiff
in each hand. But as unbearable as these conditions were, they were mild
by comparison, for when he turned around things only got worse. And
yet the return home had now become a task he could probably put off
no longer.

And so he stopped, gave an angry shrug, and turned his skis around.
The head wind promptly took his breath away, so that he had to go
through the awkward procedure of turning around once more just to get
some air and regain enough composure to confront his indifferent foe.
By lowering his head and carefully regulating his intake of breath, he then
managed to set off in the opposite direction—only to be surprised, despite
his own forebodings, at how difficult it was to make any progress, primarily because he could see nothing and was so short of breath. He was
forced to halt every other moment, either to turn for a gulp of air or with
head still bent low to blink up ahead—and see nothing but white darkness,
although he needed to avoid running into trees or being toppled by some
other obstruction. Masses of flakes flew directly into his face, then melted,
freezing his features. They flew into his mouth and vanished with a faint
watery taste, plastered his eyelashes, making him squint and blink, inundated his eyes until there was no hope of even trying to see—which would
have been useless in any case, because the veil of blinding white obstructed
his view and made the act of seeing almost totally impossible. And when

he forced himself to look, he was staring into nothing, into white, whirling nothing. Only at odd intervals did ghostly shadows of the external world loom up before him: a scrub pine, a stand of firs, the pale silhouette of the barn he had just passed.

He skied past the shed, trying to find his way back across the open slope where it stood. But there was no way; to keep to one direction, the approximate direction of home and the valley, was more a matter of luck than sense, because although he could sometimes just make out his hand in front of his face, he never once saw the tips of his skis; and had he been able to see better, there were still plenty of other impediments to frustrate his progress: snow full in the face, a storm as an adversary that robbed you of air and constantly forced you to turn and snatch for a breath—how could any man, be he Hans Castorp or someone much stronger, have made any progress here? He stopped, gasped, blinked to squeeze the water out of his eyelashes, knocked away the coat of snowy armor that encased the front of his body—and realized that under these circumstances, it was unreasonable even to hope for progress.

Hans Castorp was making progress nonetheless—or rather, he was moving. But whether it was purposeful movement, movement in the right direction, or whether it might not have been better to stay where he was (which, however, did not seem feasible), that remained to be seen. Even theoretically, chances were against it; and from a practical point of view, Hans Castorp soon came to believe that there was something not right about the ground under his feet, that it was somehow not what it should be, by which he meant the gentle slope that he had regained only after an exhausting climb back up the ravine and that needed to be retraversed. The level stretch had been too short, the ground was rising again. Apparently the rage of the storm, coming from the southwest, from the entrance to the valley, had pushed him back. He had been making false progress for a good while now; wrapped in a vortex of white night, he had worn himself out blindly working his way ever deeper into the indifferent menace.

"Wouldn't you know!" he said between his teeth and pulled up short. He did not choose words full of pathos, although it seemed to him at that moment as if an icy hand had gripped his heart, making it twitch and then hammer rapidly against his ribs, just as it had the day Rhadamanthus first discovered the moist spot on his lung. For he realized he had no right to grand words and gestures—he had chosen defiance and all the hazards of his present situation could be chalked up against himself alone. "Not bad," he said and felt how his facial features, the muscles governing the expression on his face, no longer obeyed his will and were incapable of revealing anything, whether fear, rage, or disdain—they were frozen. "What now? Down across here and then straight ahead, following my nose right into the wind? Easier said than done," he added with a choked gasp, but all the same went on speaking in a whisper as he forced himself into motion again. "But I have to do something, I can't just sit down and wait here until I'm covered beneath hexagonal symmetry. And then when Settembrini comes to check up on me with his little horn, he'll find me squatting here with eyes turned to glass, a snowy cap cocked to one side." He realized he was talking to himself—and saying rather strange things at that. He reprimanded himself for it, but went right on, sotto voce, but emphatically, even though his lips were so numb that he did not bother to use them and spoke without the consonants that they helped form, which then reminded him of a previous occasion on which the same thing had happened. "Shut up and try to make some progress here," he said. And then he added, "It seems to me you're talking drivel, that you're a little muddleheaded. And in certain respects, that is not good."

And this realization—that in terms of his getting out of there this was not good—was a pure ascertainment of reason, a conclusion reached by an alien, impartial (though, granted, concerned) person. But the more physical part of him was inclined to abandon itself to the muddled state threatening to engulf him as exhaustion grew; he did take note of this tendency, however, and let his thoughts linger on it. "This is the typical mode of experience of someone lost in a mountain snowstorm, who never finds his way home," he thought as he struggled along, the phrases emerging in tattered, breathless fragments—discretion forbade his putting it more explicitly. "Someone hearing about it later imagines how ghastly it must have been, but forgets that illness—and my present situation is more or less an illness—batters its victim until they get along with one another. The senses are diminished, a merciful self-narcosis sets in—those are the means by which nature allows the organism to find relief. And yet you have to fight against such things, because there are two sides to them, they're really highly ambiguous. And your evaluation all depends on which side you view them from. They mean well, are a blessing really, as long as you don't make it home; but they also mean you great harm and must be fought off, as long as there is any chance of getting home—which is my case, since I do not intend, my stormily pounding heart does not intend, to lie down and be covered by stupid, precise crystallometry."

In reality he was already badly battered, and was struggling against his incipient sensory muddle—but in a muddled and feverish way. And when he discovered that once again he had left the level stretch much too soon, this time on the other side, it seemed, where the slope fell away, he was not as frightened as he would have been in a healthy state. For with the wind coming at him on a slant, he had set off downhill again, which he ought not to have done now—but that seemed easiest at the moment. "It's all right," he thought, "I'll get my bearings again once I'm down there." Which is what he did, or so he thought, or perhaps he was not really sure—or, what was more ominous, began not to care whether he did or not. All this came from those ambiguous attacks, which he fought off only feebly now. The familiar blend of languor and excitement— which was the constant condition of a Berghof guest whose acclimatization consisted of his getting used to not getting used to things—had grown so strong in both component parts that it was no longer even a question of his taking prudent action against such attacks. Dazed and giddy, he quivered with exhilaration, just as he often did after a colloquy with Naphta and Settembrini, except this time the feeling was incomparably stronger— which may have been how he came to excuse his own inertia in fighting off such attacks of self-narcosis by reminiscing drunkenly about their discussions. And so despite his disdain and outrage at the idea of being covered up by hexagonal symmetry, he began to babble away to himself, be it sense or nonsense: this feeling of duty that kept telling him to fight off any suspicious diminishing of his senses—it was mere ethics, just a shabby bourgeoisiosity of life, philistine irreligiosity. The desire, the temptation, to lie down and rest crept into his mind disguised as the notion that in desert sandstorms an Arab threw himself on his face and covered his head with his burnous. The only objection he could find to following that example was that he had no burnous and could not very easily pull his woolen vest up over his head—although he was certainly no child and knew from several sources pretty much how people froze to death.

After a fairly rapid descent and another level stretch, the path now led back uphill—a steep hill. But that was not necessarily wrong, for now and again the route to the valley would have to go uphill, too; and as for the wind, it had peevishly changed direction, since Hans Castorp now had it at his back and was glad for that, in any case. Was the wind bending him forward or was that soft white incline before him, veiled by dusky flurries, drawing him onward, pulling him down toward it? All he had to do was submit to it, lean just a little farther, and the temptation was very great—as great as he had seen it described in books, where it was termed typical and dangerous. But that in no way lessened the present, dynamic temptation, which claimed the prerogative of individuality, refusing to be relegated to the familiar and general or to be mirrored in such descriptions, and which declared itself unique and incomparably urgent—

without, of course, being able to deny that it was a temptation whispered from one particular corner, the promptings of a creature in Spanish black with a snow-white, pleated ruff; and bound up with the idea and image were all sorts of gloomy, caustically Jesuitical, and misanthropic notions, the torture and corporal punishment that were such abominations to Herr Settembrini, who with his barrel organ and *ragione* could only appear ridiculous in his opposition to them.

But Hans Castorp proved to be an upright fellow, and he withstood the temptation to lean forward. He could see nothing, but he struggled and moved on—perhaps to some purpose, perhaps not, but he did his part and kept at it, despite the increasingly heavy weights the icy storm tied around his legs. And when the climb proved too steep, he turned to one side, without giving much thought to the consequences, and glided on the slant for a while. Opening his tightly clenched eyelids to peer ahead was an exertion that had proved so useless that he felt little incentive to attempt it. And yet he could see some things now and then: a gathering of firs, a brook or ditch, whose blackness, caught between overhanging layers of snow, stood out against the terrain; and when just for variety's sake his route led him downhill again—against the wind now—he spied at some distance, as if hovering there in the storm-swept tangle of veils, the outline of a man-made edifice.

What a welcome, comforting sight! His stout heart had pulled him through, despite all adversity, and now the first human dwellings had appeared as a sign that the populated valley was near. Perhaps there were people there; maybe they would take him in, let him wait under their roof for the bad weather to end, and provide him with directions or a guide if real darkness had fallen by then. Although it took all his energy to climb against the wind, he made for that chimerical something, which often vanished entirely in the gloom, and when he finally arrived he realized—in dizzy outrage, amazement, and terror—that it was the familiar hut, the hayshed with its roof weighted down by stones, which he had now reconquered after many a detour and so much upright exertion.

What a hell of a state of affairs! From Hans Castorp's frozen lips came formidable curses, though with the labial sounds omitted. In order to get his bearings, he stomped his way around the hut and determined that he had arrived at the back end of it after a good hour—or so he estimated—of pure, futile folly. But that's what the books said would happen. You ran around in a circle, toiling onward, with the feeling in your heart of doing something useful, when in fact you were tracing a wide, foolish arc that led back on itself, just as the teasing year came full circle. And so you wandered around and never found your way home. Hans Castorp

took a certain satisfaction in recognizing the standard phenomenon,
though it frightened him, too, and he slapped his thighs in rage and
astonishment that something so universal had arrived right on schedule
even in his own unique, individual situation.

The isolated shed was barred, the door locked, there was no way in.
But all the same, Hans Castorp decided to stay here for now, since the
overhanging roof provided the illusion of some hospitality, and the side
of the hut facing the mountains, which Hans Castorp now sought out,
actually did offer a little protection against the storm, if you leaned back
so that one shoulder touched its rough-hewn logs—since long skis made
it inconvenient to press your back to it. Thrusting his poles into the snow
beside him, he now propped himself at an angle, and stood there with
his hands in his pockets, the collar of his woolen sweater turned up;
counterbracing himself with his outside leg, he let his reeling head rest
against the plank wall, closed his eyes, and squinted over his shoulder
only now and then, across the ravine to the mountain wall opposite, dimly
visible at times through the curtain of snow.

His position was relatively cozy. "I can stand here all night if need
be," he thought. "That is, if I change legs now and then, turn over on
my other side, so to speak, and of course move around a little every once
in a while—that's indispensable. Even if I'm clammy on the outside, I've
garnered some inner warmth by all the moving around I've done, and so
my excursion wasn't totally useless, even if I did pass on, round and
round, from hut to hut. 'Pass on'—what sort of an expression is that?
It's never used, or at least hardly ever, for what's been happening to me.
I used it quite arbitrarily, simply because my head is a little muddled.
And yet, in its way it's an apt expression, seems to me. It's a good thing
I'm able to hold out, because all this bustling about in the bustling snow
is a bustling nuisance that can easily last till morning, and even if it lasts
only until nightfall, that's bad enough, because there's just as great a
danger of passing on, or passing round and round in circles, in the dark
as there is in a snowstorm. It must be evening by now, close to six—to
think of all the time I've wasted passing on. Just how late is it, really?"
And so he looked at his watch—although it wasn't easy to fish it out of
his clothes with fingers so numb that they couldn't feel anything—at his
gold watch with the monogrammed spring case, which was still doing
lively, faithful duty here in this lonely wasteland, just as was his
heart, his touching human heart tucked inside the organic warmth of his
rib cage.

It was half past four. What the devil—it had been almost that late
when the storm first broke. Was he supposed to believe that his confused

wanderings had lasted barely one quarter of an hour? "Time has slowed down for me," he thought. "Passing on is boring, it seems. But it will be fully dark by five or five-thirty, that much is certain. Will it stop before then, stop in time to keep me from passing on even more? I could drink a sip of port to that—just to fortify myself a little."

The only reason he had pocketed a bottle of this amateurish drink was that it was available for purchase in little flasks at the Berghof, intended for guests going on excursions, but certainly never for anyone illicitly wandering off and getting lost in the snow and frost of the mountains and then waiting for night to fall. Had his mind been less muddled, he would have had to admit that in terms of getting back home this was perhaps the worst thing he could have done; and indeed he told himself as much after he had taken a few sips, which produced an immediate effect, much the same effect as that caused by Kulmbach beer his first evening up here, when with a lot of loose, disreputable talk about fish sauces and the like he had offended Settembrini—Herr Lodovico, the pedagogue, who could keep madmen from letting themselves go, return them to reason with just a glance, and whose melodious little horn Hans Castorp now heard in the air around him, the signal that his oratorical teacher was now approaching at a forced march to free his troublesome pupil, life's problem child, from his mad situation and lead him home. Which was pure nonsense of course, it was the Kulmbach beer he had drunk by mistake that made him think that. Because firstly, Herr Settembrini did not have a little horn, but only his barrel organ, which had a folding leg so he could set it up on the cobblestones and cast a humanistic eye up at the houses as it played its familiar songs; and secondly, he knew nothing about what was going on, since he no longer lived at Berghof Sanatorium, but at Lukaček's, in his little garret with a water carafe, just above Naphta's silken cell—and had no right, and no opportunity, either, to interfere, just as he had had no such right to do so on Mardi Gras night, when Hans Castorp had found himself in a position equally as mad and difficult, when he had given *son crayon*, his pencil, Pribislav Hippe's pencil, back to the ailing Clavdia Chauchat. But what was that about "position"? Was that a horizontal position? But that meant you had to be lying down, that was the only way the word achieved its true and special meaning, rather than remaining merely metaphorical. Horizontal, that was the position appropriate to long-term members of "society up here." Was he not accustomed to lying down in the open air, in the snow and frost, by night as well as by day? And he was about to sink down to rest, when the realization suddenly came to him, grabbed him by the collar, so to speak, that these babbling thoughts about his "position" could likewise be due only to the effects of Kulmbach beer, had arisen solely from an impersonal desire to lie down and sleep, the same typical and dangerous desire you found discussed in books, a desire that was trying to delude him with its sophistries and puns.

"That was a major blunder," he admitted. "The port was not the right thing—just a few sips and my head feels much too heavy, it's all I can do to hold it up. And my thoughts are all muddled, and I end up making insipid plays on words that I dare not trust—and not just the basic idea that first occurs to me, but the second one, too, which is a critique of the first, that's where I get into trouble. 'Son crayon'! In this case that means 'her' pencil, not 'his,' and you only say 'son' because 'crayon' is masculine—all the rest is just a vapid joke. Why am I even bothering with this, when there are much more urgent matters at hand—for example, the leg I'm using to brace myself bears a striking resemblance to the wooden folding leg on Settembrini's barrel organ, which he nudges with his knee so that he can move across the cobblestones and get closer to the window and hold out his velvet hat, so that the lass upstairs can throw something down to him. And all the while there's this impersonal force tugging at my hands to get me to lie down in the snow. Movement is the only thing that can help. I have to move, to make up for that Kulmbach beer and limber up my wooden leg."

He pushed off with his shoulder. But he had no sooner moved away from the shed and taken a step forward than the wind swung its scythe at him and drove him back to the protection of the wall. This was doubtless the spot assigned to him, and he would have to get used to it for now, although he was free to vary his position by leaning against his left shoulder and bracing himself with his right leg, while shaking his left to bring it back to life. "Never leave the house in weather like this," he thought. "Moderate variety is allowed, but no wild innovation or picking quarrels with the bride of the wind. Keep still and just let your head hang low if it's so heavy. It's a good wall, good logs that seem to give off a certain warmth, to the extent you can speak of warmth in this case—the discreet, peculiar warmth of wood, though it may be more a matter of mood, more subjective. Ah, all those trees! Ah, the living climate of the living! And the fragrance!"

It was a park that lay before him, just below the balcony where he was evidently standing—a wide, luxuriantly green park of hardwoods, of elms, planes, beeches, maples, birches, with subtle gradations in the colors of the full, fresh, glossy foliage. Their tops rustled gently in the breeze, and the air was perfumed with their delicate, moist balm. A warm shower passed over, but the rain was translucent. You could see high up into the sky, and the air was filled with a glistening rush of ripples. How beautiful! Oh, the breath of home, the scent and richness of the lowlands—he had gone so long without it. The air was full of birdcalls, of dainty, ardent, sweet piping, twittering, cooing, warbling, and sobbing, though not a single creature was to be seen. Hans Castorp smiled, took a deep, grateful breath. And meanwhile it all turned more beautiful still. A rainbow stretched across a flank of the landscape, a strong, perfectly formed arch, all its moist colors shimmering in pure splendor and flowing like rich oils down into the dense, lustrous green. It was like music, like the sound of harps, joined by flutes and violins. The surging of blue and violet was especially marvelous. And then it all merged and sank in a magical blur, was transformed, unfolded anew, grew more and more beautiful. It was just like a day many years before, when Hans Castorp had been privileged to hear a world-famous singer, an Italian tenor, from whose throat the power of grace-filled art had poured out over the hearts of men. He had held a high note—beautiful from the very first. And then gradually, from moment to moment, the passionate tone had opened up, swelled, unfolded, grown ever brighter and more radiant. It was as if veils, visible to no one before, were falling away one by one—and now the last, or so they thought, revealing the purest, most intense light, and then one more, the ultimate, and then, incredibly, the absolute last, releasing a glory shimmering with tears and a brilliance so lavish that a hollow sound of rapture had gone up from the audience, almost in protest and contradiction, it seemed, and even he, young Hans Castorp, had felt a sob well up within him. And it was the same with this landscape now, transforming itself, opening onto an ever-growing radiance. Blue floated. The glistening curtain of rain fell away—and there lay the sea, a sea, the Mediterranean, deep deep blue, sparkling with silver, a marvelously beautiful bay, opening to haze on one side and embraced on the other by mountain ranges receding to paler and paler blues, dotted with islands where towering palm trees grew or you saw the glint of little white houses set among groves of cypress. Oh, oh, enough, all so undeserved—what a bliss of light, of deep pure sky, of sun-drenched water. Hans Castorp had never seen it before, not even anything like it. He had never vacationed in the south, taken so much as a sip of it, knew only his own rough, pallid sea and clung to it with clumsy, childish emotion, but he had never reached the Mediterranean—Naples, Sicily, Greece. And yet he *remembered* it. Yes, it was that peculiar sense of recognition he celebrated now. "Ah, yes, that's how it is!"—a cry went up within, as if he had always carried this blue sunshine now spreading before him secretly in his heart, hiding it even from himself. And this "always" was wide, infinitely wide, as wide as the sea there on his left, where the sky settled down upon it in soft violet hues.

The line of the horizon lay high, its vastness seemed to climb—this was because Hans was gazing down on the bay from a considerable height. The mountains reached out on all sides, beginning with wooded foothills that ran down into the sea, then rising in a semicircle from a midpoint in the distance to where he was, and extending on behind him. It was a mountainous coast, and here he sat, crouching on sun-warmed stony steps; the ground fell away from him in tiers of moss-covered boulders and undergrowth, down to the level shoreline, where little harbors and ponds could be seen among reeds and shingled blue bays. And this whole sunny region—these easily scaled coastal heights, these laughing rock-bound pools, and the sea itself, as far as the islands where boats sailed past now and then—was populated in all directions: people, children of the sea and sun, were stirring and resting everywhere, intelligent, cheerful, beautiful, young humanity, so fair to gaze upon. And at the sight, Hans Castorp's whole heart opened wide—painfully, lovingly wide.

Lads exercised trotting, whinnying, head-tossing horses, ran beside them, one hand on the halter, tugged at their long bridles when they reared, or rode them bareback, naked heels drumming at the animals' flanks, out into the sea—and then the muscles of the boys' golden-tan backs played in the sunlight and the cries they exchanged or shouted to the horses sounded inexplicably enchanting. Maidens were dancing beside a bay that extended far inland and mirrored its shores like a mountain lake. One girl, her hair wound in a knot, but with a few, especially charming stray strands at the back of her neck, sat with her feet dangling in a little dell and played a shepherd's pipe, her eyes gazing out over her capering fingers to her playmates dressed in long, loose robes, some of whom stood alone, smiling, arms spread wide, while others danced in couples, leaning against one another, temples sweetly touching; and at the piper's back—bent to one side in a long, graceful, white curve because of the way she held her arms—still more of her sisters sat or stood together, embracing, watching, and talking quietly. Another group of young men were engaged in archery. What a happy, friendly sight it was—the way the older lads worked with the unskilled, curly-haired boys, helping them string their bows, showing them how to draw and take aim, supporting them when they reeled back laughing from the recoiling bow as the arrow left it with a whir. Still others were fishing. They lay on their stomachs across flat rocks along the shore; wiggling a leg in the air and holding a line down into the sea, one fellow would turn his head for a leisurely chat with his neighbor, who from the same odd angle stretched his body and threw his bait far out to sea. There was also a group busy dragging, pulling, and shoving a deep-drafted boat with mast and boom into the water. Children played and hooted among the breaking waves. A young woman lay stretched out on her back, gazing up and behind her; with one hand she clutched her flowered garment tight above her breasts and with the other reached into the air, demanding a twig with fruit, which a narrow-hipped lad standing at her head held out at arm's length, teasing her. Some young people reclined in niches in the rocks, others hesitated at the edge of the pool, arms crossed, hands clutching their shoulders, testing the cool water with their toes. Couples strolled along the shore, and each lad's lips were pressed to the ear of the girl he escorted. Long-haired goats leapt from ledge to ledge, watched over by a young shepherd, who stood farther up and wore a little hat cocked over his brown curls, the brim rolled up at the back; he leaned against his long staff, grasping it tightly in one hand, setting the other to his hip.

"It's all so very charming," Hans Castorp thought, touched to the quick. "They're all so pleasant, so winning. How pretty, healthy, clever, and happy they are. It's not just their well-formed bodies—a cleverness and warmth comes from within them, too. That is what moves me, makes me love them so—the spirit and purpose, if I can put it that way, that lies at the basis of their being and allows them to live together like this." What he meant was the vast friendliness, the courteous honesty common to all these sunny people in their dealings with one another; he meant the gentle reverence, which, though hidden beneath smiles, they showed one another at every turn, almost imperceptible and yet so evident in both the physical connections and the deep-seated ideals that bound them all; he meant the dignity, bordering on gravity, though totally fused with good cheer, which alone defined their every deed, an ineffable spiritual influence, earnest yet never gloomy, devout yet always reasonable— though not lacking a certain ceremonial quality. For there on a round, mossy stone, a young mother, dressed in a brown garment that fell away from one shoulder, sat nursing her child. And each person who passed offered her a special greeting that fully expressed what was so eloquently tacit in their general conduct—the young men turned to the mother and quickly, formally, lightly crossed their arms against their chests and bowed their heads with a smile; the maidens approached with just a hint of a curtsy, much like the fleeting genuflection with which visitors honor the high altar in a church, but then made sure to add several energetic, cheerful, cordial nods. Their formal homage mixed with genial friendship, plus the deliberate mildness with which the mother looked up from her baby, while still helping him drink with gentle pressure from her forefinger, to acknowledge with a smile the reverence shown her—it all suffused Hans Castorp with rapture. He could not get his fill of gazing, and yet he asked himself anxiously if he was in fact allowed to gaze upon them, if it was not a punishable crime for an outsider—who felt so ugly and clumsy and base—to spy upon such sunny, civilized happiness.

There seemed to be no objection. Just below where he was sitting, a pretty lad, with a full head of hair brushed to one side and falling down across his brow and temples, stood with his arms crossed on his chest a little distance away from his friends—not in sorrow or defiance, but merely casually off to one side. And the boy looked directly at him, turned his eyes up toward him, and, watching the watcher, his gaze passed back and forth between Hans Castorp and the scenes on the shore. Suddenly, however, he looked beyond and behind him, into the distance, and in a flash that smile of courteous, brotherly deference common to them all vanished from his beautiful, finely chiseled, almost childlike face, and, without so much as a frown, it took on a grave expression, an inscrutable blank look of deathlike reserve, as if it were made of stone— which hardly reassured Hans Castorp and sent a shiver of fear over him, tinged with a vague premonition as to what it might mean.

He looked in the same direction. Towering behind him were huge columns, piled cylindrical blocks with no bases and with moss growing in the joints—the columns of a temple gate, and he was sitting on the open stairway that led to it. With a heavy heart he stood up and descended along one side of the stairs; entering the deep portal, he emerged onto a street paved with flagstones, which soon led him to other propylaea. He passed through them as well, and now the temple stood before him—its massive foundation was weathered a grayish green; a steep flight of stairs led up to the broad façade, its pediment resting on the capitals of powerful, squat, tapering columns; here and there a fluted, round block had slipped out of position and protruded slightly. Hans Castorp labored to climb the steep stairs, helping himself with his hands at times; sighing heavily to relieve the growing pressure around his heart, he now reached the forest of columns. It was very deep, and he walked among its rows as if in a grove of beech trees beside a pallid sea. He kept his distance from the middle of the temple, tried to avoid it. And yet he kept coming back to it, and now found himself at an opening in the rows of columns, before him a group of statuary: two stony female figures on a pedestal, a mother and daughter, it appeared. The one was seated—an older, dignified matron clad in a heavily pleated tunic and drape, a veil drawn over her wavy hair, her vacant, starless eyes truly mild and godlike, yet with a plaintive set to the brows; held in her maternal embrace, the other figure, a young woman with a round face, stood with arms and hands buried in the folds of her cloak.

Hans Castorp stood gazing at the statues, and for some dark reason his heart grew even heavier with fear and foreboding. Hardly daring to risk it, he felt himself compelled to circle behind the figures and move on through the next double row of columns. The metal doors to the sanctuary stood open, and the poor man's knees almost buckled under him at what he now saw. Two half-naked old women were busy at a ghastly chore among flickering braziers—their hair was gray and matted, their drooping witches' breasts had tits long as fingers. They were dismembering a child held above a basin, tearing it apart with their bare hands in savage silence— Hans Castorp could see pale blond hair smeared with blood. They devoured it piece by piece, the brittle little bones cracking in their mouths, blood dripping from their vile lips. Hans Castorp was caught frozen in the gruesome, icy spell. He wanted to cover his eyes with his hands and could not. He wanted to flee and could not. They went on about their grisly work, but they had seen him now and shook bloody fists and damned him soundlessly with the filthiest, lewdest curses of his hometown dialect. He felt sick, sicker than he had ever felt in his life. Trying desperately to pull himself away, he slipped and fell against the column at his back. Still in the grip of cold horror, foul scolding whispers still in his ears, he found himself lying in the snow, his head resting on one arm, his legs stretched out before him, his skis still on.

It was not a genuine awakening; he simply lay there blinking, relieved to be rid of those repulsive women, although it was less than clear to him, and not all that important, if it was a temple column or a hayshed at his back, and he went on dreaming, as it were—no longer in visions, but in thoughts hardly less perilous and tangled.

"I thought so—it was only a dream," he babbled to himself. "A very enchanting, very dreadful dream. At some level, I knew all along that I was making it up myself—the park, the trees, the sweet moist air, and all the rest, lovely or hideous—knew it ahead of time almost. But how can a person know something like that, make it up, to exhilarate and terrify himself? Where did I get that beautiful bay with those islands, and the temple precincts, to which the eyes of that lovely lad who stood off by himself directed me? We don't form our dreams out of just our own souls. We dream anonymously and communally, though each in his own way. The great soul, of which we are just a little piece, dreams through us so to speak, dreams in our many different ways its own eternal, secret dream—about its youth, its hope, its joy, its peace, and its bloody feast. Here I lie against my column, with real remnants of my dream still inside my body—both the icy horror of the bloody feast and the previous boundless joy, my joy in the happiness and gentle manners of that fair humanity. It all comes to me, I say. I have a legal right to lie here and dream such things. I have experienced so much among the people up here, about kicking over the traces, about reason. I have passed on with Naphta and Settembrini into these dangerous mountains. I know everything about humankind. I have known flesh and blood, I gave Pribislav Hippe's pencil back to ailing Clavdia. But he who knows the body, who knows life, also knows death. Except that's not the whole thing—but merely a beginning, pedagogically speaking. You have to hold it up to the other half, to its opposite. Because our interest in death and illness is nothing but a way of expressing an interest in life—just look at how the humanistic faculty of medicine always addresses life and its illness so courteously in Latin. But that is only an adumbration of one great, urgent concern, which in fullest sympathy I shall now call by its name: life's problem child, man himself, his true state and condition. I know quite a bit about him, have learned a great deal among the people up here, after having been driven up here from the flatlands—almost took my breath away. I really do have a fair overview from here at the base of my column. I dreamed about the nature of man, and about a courteous, reasonable, and respectful community of men—while the ghastly bloody feast went on in the temple behind them. Were they courteous and charming to one another, those sunny folk, out of silent regard for that horror? What a fine and gallant conclusion for them to draw! I shall hold to their side, here in my soul, and not with Naphta, or for that matter with Settembrini—they're both windbags. The one is voluptuous and malicious, and the other is forever tooting his little horn of reason and even imagines he can stare madmen back to sanity—how preposterous, how philistine! It's mere ethics, irreligious, that much is certain. And yet I'm not going to take little Naphta's side, either, with his religion that's nothing more than a *guazzabuglio* of God and the Devil, good and evil, just made for someone to tumble headlong into its void and perish mystically there. My two pedagogues! Their arguments and contradictions are nothing but a *guazzabuglio*, the hubbub and alarum of battle, and no one whose head is a little clear and heart a little devout will let himself be dazed by that. With their question of 'true aristocracy'! With their nobility! Death or life—illness or health—spirit or nature. Are those really contradictions? I ask you: Are those problems? No, they are not problems, and the question of their nobility is not a problem, either. Death kicks over its traces in the midst of life, and this would not be life if it did not, and in the middle is where the *homo Dei*'s state is found—in the middle between kicking over the traces

and reason—just as his condition is somewhere between mystical community and windy individualism. I can see all that from my column here.
And in that state let him commune with himself, fine, gallant, genial, and
respectful—for he alone is noble, and not that set of contradictions. Man
is the master of contradictions, they occur through him, and so he is more
noble than they. More noble than death, too noble for it—that is the
freedom of his mind. More noble than life, too noble for it—that is the
devotion of his heart. There, I have rhymed it all together, dreamed a
poem of humankind. I will remember it. I will be good. I will grant
death no dominion over my thoughts. For in that is found goodness and
brotherly love, and in that alone. Death is a great power. You take off
your hat and tiptoe past his presence, rocking your way forward. He
wears the ceremonial ruff of what has been, and you put on austere black
in his honor. Reason stands foolish before him, for reason is only virtue,
but death is freedom and kicking over the traces, chaos and lust. Lust,
my dream says, not love. Death and love—there is no rhyming them,
that is a preposterous rhyme, a false rhyme. Love stands opposed to
death—it alone, and not reason, is stronger than death. Only love, and
not reason, yields kind thoughts. And form, too, comes only from love
and goodness: form and the cultivated manners of man's fair state, of a
reasonable, genial community—out of silent regard for the bloody banquet. Oh, what a clear dream I've dreamed, how well I've 'played king'!
I will remember it. I will keep faith with death in my heart, but I will
clearly remember that if faithfulness to death and to what is past rules
our thoughts and deeds, that leads only to wickedness, dark lust, and
hatred of humankind. *For the sake of goodness and love, man shall grant
death no dominion over his thoughts.* And with that I shall awaken. For
with that I have dreamed my dream to its end, to its goal. I've long been
searching for that truth: in the meadow where Hippe appeared to me, on
my balcony, everywhere. The search for it drove me into these snowy
mountains. And now I have it. My dream has granted it to me so clearly
that I will always remember. Yes, I am overjoyed and filled with its
warmth. My heart is beating strong and knows why. It beats not for
purely physical reasons, the way fingernails grow on a corpse. It beats
for human reasons and because my spirit is truly happy. The truth of my
dream has refreshed me—better than port or ale, it courses through my
veins like love and life, so that I may tear myself out of my dreaming
sleep, which I know only too well can be fatal to my young life. Awake,
awake! Open your eyes. Those are your limbs, your legs there in the
snow. Pull yourself together and stand up! Look—good weather!"

It turned out to be very difficult to liberate himself from the bonds that had woven around him and still tried to hold him down; but the impulse to counter them proved stronger. Hans Castorp propped himself on his elbows, valiantly pulled his knees up, tugged, shoved, wriggled himself to his feet. He stamped the snow with his skis, hugged himself, beat his ribs, shook his shoulders, while his eyes searched excitedly and eagerly here, there, everywhere in the sky, as soft blue peered through the gray-blue gauze of the clouds, now drifting aside to reveal the narrow sickle of the moon. Gentle dusk was falling. No wind, no snow. The whole mountain face opposite, including its ridge of rough firs, was visible now, lay peaceful before him. Shadows now reached halfway up it; but the upper portion was bathed in softest pink. What was happening, what was the world up to? Was it morning? Had he lain there in the snow all night without freezing to death, despite what the books said? No body parts were frostbitten, nothing broke off with a tinkle as he stamped and shook and hugged—and not feebly, either—trying at the same time to fathom his situation. Ears, fingertips, and toes were numb, but nothing more, no worse than they often were after a stay on his balcony on a winter night. He managed to pull out his watch. It was ticking. It had not stopped the way it did if he forgot to wind it of an evening. It wasn't five yet—not by a long shot. Not for another twelve, thirteen minutes. Amazing! Could it be that he had lain there in the snow for only ten minutes or a little longer, had fantasized all those daredevil thoughts, those images of happiness and horror, while the hexagonal monster moved on as quickly as it had come? Well, then, he had been remarkably lucky in terms of getting home. Because his dreams and fantasies had twice taken a turn to bring him back to life: once in horror, the second time out of joy. It seemed that life meant well by its highly confused problem child.

Whatever the case might be, whether it was morning or afternoon (but without doubt it was still late afternoon or early evening), there was nothing about the external circumstances or his own personal condition to prevent him from skiing back home, and that is what Hans Castorp did—boldly making a beeline, so to speak, speeding toward the valley, where lights were already burning when he arrived, although a trace of daylight reflecting off the snow had been quite enough to light his way. He came down Brämenbühl, following along the edge of the forest, and was in Dorf by half past five; he stored his equipment at the grocer's, rested a bit in Herr Settembrini's garret, and gave him a full report of how he had been overtaken by the snowstorm. The humanist was duly horrified. He flung one hand high above his head, scolded him roundly for such dangerous folly, and promptly lit the spluttering fire of his little alcohol stove and brewed some strong coffee for the exhausted engineer—which did not prevent Hans Castorp from falling asleep in his chair.

An hour later he was cradled in the highly civilized atmosphere of the Berghof. He did justice to his supper. His dream was already beginning to fade. And by bedtime he was no longer exactly sure what his thoughts had been.

A Good Soldier

HANS CASTORP had been receiving word from his cousin right along, at first high-spirited good news, then less favorable reports, until finally they were only feeble attempts at concealing a truly sad state of affairs. The series of postcards had begun with the cheerful announcement that Joachim had assumed his duties with all due fervent ceremony, during which, as Hans Castorp replied in his card, he presumably had sworn poverty, chastity, and obedience. The joyous mood continued: each new stage of his smoothly advancing career—made all the easier by his passionate love for what he was doing and the sympathy of his superiors—was hailed with a new postcard. Since Joachim had spent a few semesters at the university, he was excused both from officer's school and service as an ensign. He was promoted to the rank of noncommissioned officer at New Year and sent a photograph of himself with his stripes. Every one of his brief dispatches glowed with his delight in the hierarchy of which he was now a part—rigidly honorable, ironclad, and, in its own doggedly humorous way, flexibly humane. He provided anecdotes about his sergeant, a surly, fanatical soldier, who was caught in the awkward position of dealing with a younger, fallible subordinate, who nevertheless already visited the officer's casino and was destined to be his superior one day. It was a crazy, droll situation. He also mentioned that he had been put on the list of candidates for the officer's exam. By the beginning of April, Joachim was a lieutenant.

There was obviously no happier man, no one who could have been more at home in this style of life or have found in it a greater fulfillment of his wishes. He took a kind of embarrassed delight in telling about the first time he had approached the town hall in dress uniform and had waited until he was well past before saluting to release the sentry from stiff attention. He wrote about the little annoyances and satisfactions of duty, about the rattlingly splendid esprit de corps and the sly loyalty of his orderly, about comic incidents during drills or classes, about inspections and regimental love feasts. He occasionally mentioned social events as well—visits, banquets, balls. But not a word about his health.

Until late spring. And then he wrote that he had taken to his bed—had, sad to say, been put on sick list: a cold, a fever, a matter of a few days. He was back on duty at the beginning of June, but by the middle of the month he had to "rest on his oars" again, and he complained bitterly about his bad luck; he could not hide his fears that he might miss taking part in major maneuvers in early August, to which he had so been looking forward. Nonsense, by July he was hale and hearty again, for several weeks, until a major physical suddenly loomed up ahead—ordered because of the cursed fluctuations in his temperature. A great deal would depend on its outcome. Hans Castorp heard nothing about the results of this exam for a good while, and when he finally did, it was not in a letter from Joachim—perhaps because he was not in any condition to write or was simply too ashamed—but in a telegram from his cousin's mother, Frau Ziemssen. She announced: "Doctors compelled to put Joachim on medical furlough of several weeks. Alps suggested, immediate departure advised, reserve two rooms. Reply prepaid. Aunt Luise."

It was the end of July when Hans Castorp stepped out on his balcony and hastily skimmed this dispatch, then read and reread it. And as he did, he nodded lightly, not just with his head, but with his whole upper body, and said between clenched teeth: "Yes, yes, yes. I see, I see, I see." Suddenly he was overcome with joy: "Joachim is coming back!" But then he fell silent again and thought: "Hmm, hmm, serious news. You could even call it a nice mess. Damn, it all went quickly—already ripe for home! His mother's coming along"—he called her "his mother," not "Aunt Luise," any sense of kinship, of family relationships, having dwindled imperceptibly until such people were almost strangers—"that does give one pause. And just before those maneuvers that the good man was so hot for. Hmm, hmm, isn't that a pretty twist, a nasty twist, a hard fact to contradict all ideals. The body triumphs, has other plans than the soul, and gets its way—quite a comedown for high-minded types who teach that the body must obey the soul. It seems they don't know what they're talking about, because if they were right, a case like this would cast a dubious light on the soul. *Sapienti sat,* I know what I'm saying. For the question *I* am raising here is whether it is not wide of the mark to see them as opposites, and whether they aren't in cahoots instead, haven't rigged the game—which never occurs to the high-minded types, luckily for them. Not that I would want for the world to insult you, my good Joachim, or your zealot's love of duty. What you do, you do in all honesty—but I ask you, what is honesty, if the body and soul are in cahoots? Could it be you have not forgotten certain refreshing fragrances, prominent breasts, and pointless giggles that await you at Frau Stöhr's table? Joachim is coming back!" he thought yet again and experienced a shiver of joy. "He'll be arriving in bad shape, apparently, but we two shall be together again. I won't have to live quite so much to myself now. That's good. Although everything can't be just like before. His room is occupied, after all—Mrs. Macdonald coughs away in that hollow cough of hers and keeps her little son's photograph next to her on the table, or clutches it in her hand. But she's in the last stages, and if the room hasn't been reserved for anyone else, why then . . . but for now, it will have to be another one. Twenty-eight is vacant, as far as I know. I'll go see management right away, and Behrens, too, for sure. This is news—sad in one sense, but spiffing in another. Big news, in any case. I'll just wait for my 'd'gods' comrade, he'll be here any moment, since it's already half past three, I notice. I want to ask him if in light of this case he's still of the opinion that the body is secondary."

He visited the management office before tea. The room he had in mind, down the corridor from his own, was available. Frau Ziemssen could likewise be accommodated. He hurried to see Behrens. He met him in the lab, a cigar in one hand, a test tube with a foul-colored liquid in the other.

"Director Behrens, what do you think has happened?" Hans Castorp began.

"More trouble as always," the pneumotomist replied. "This is Rosenheim from Utrecht," he said, pointing to the test tube with his cigar. "Ten on the Gaffky. And who comes storming in here but Schmitz, the manufacturer, complaining that Rosenheim has been spitting on the walkways—with ten on the Gaffky. And I'm supposed to scold him. And if I scold him, he'll blow up, because he's testy beyond belief—and has rented three rooms for his family. I can't send him packing, because then I'll have the administration down on me. So you see the fracases a fellow is constantly getting involved in, even when he would much rather keep quiet and go his pure and spotless way."

"What a stupid affair," Hans Castorp said, with the insight of a chummy old-timer. "I know both gentlemen. Schmitz is always so proper and pushy, and Rosenheim is sloppy to excess. But hygiene is probably not the only reason for friction, I would say. Schmitz and Rosenheim are both friends of Doña Perez from Barcelona, who sits at Kleefeld's table— that's more than likely at the root of the matter. I suggest a general reminder about the prohibition against spitting, and then wink at the rest."

"Of course I wink at the rest. I'm getting blepharospasmosis from all the winking I do. But what brings you down here?"

And Hans Castorp divulged his sad, but for all that, spiffing news.

Not that the director was in the least surprised. He would not have been in any case; Hans Castorp had kept him informed right along about Joachim's condition—whether he had inquired or not—and the bed rest in May had been signal enough.

"Aha," Behrens replied. "Well, now. And what did I tell you? What were my very words to both you and him—not ten but a hundred times? So there you are. He had his way, his heaven on earth for nine months. But not a totally detoxified heaven on earth, and there's scant blessing in that—but the escape artist wouldn't believe old man Behrens. And you should always believe old man Behrens, otherwise you end up the worse for wear and don't realize it until it's too late. And so he made lieutenant—no objections there. But what good did it do him? The Lord God searches the heart and sees not rank or station, we all stand naked before Him, from general down to lowly private." He rambled on like this for a while, rubbing his eyes with the same gigantic hand in which he held his cigar, but finally said that Hans Castorp had bothered him enough for now. There were diggings to be had for Ziemssen, he presumed, and the moment the engineer's cousin arrived he should take to his bed forthwith. As far as he, Behrens, was concerned, he bore no grudges, but held his paternal arms wide, was ready to kill a fatted calf for the prodigal.

Hans Castorp telegraphed back. He also told anyone who would listen that his cousin was returning, and all those who knew Joachim were both sad and happy to hear the news, and were sincere in both emotions, because Joachim's orderly, chivalrous demeanor had won him general goodwill; and a common response, though left unspoken, was that Joachim was the best of the lot up here. We looked no one square in the eye, but we assume there were many who felt a certain satisfaction in Joachim's having to leave his soldierly profession and resume an orderly, horizontal life with the rest of us up here. Frau Stöhr, as we know, had felt that way from the first; she found her own vulgar skepticism, with which she had sent Joachim on his way down to the flatlands, confirmed, and did not mind praising herself for it. "Rotten, rotten," she said. She had known there was something rotten about the whole affair from the first and could only hope that Ziemssen's obstinacy had not turned it putrid—"putrid," she said, in her infinite vulgarity. It was really much wiser to stick to one's guns, the way she did—she, too, had a life down in the flatlands, in Cannstatt, to be precise, a husband and two children, but she knew how to contain herself.

There was no further reply, either from Joachim or Frau Ziemssen. Hans Castorp was left uncertain of the day and hour of their arrival—which is why he was not at the station to meet them, when, three days after he had sent off his telegram, they were suddenly simply there. Laughing excitedly, Lieutenant Joachim burst in on his cousin, who was in the midst of his evening rest-cure duties.

They had arrived on the same train that had brought Hans Castorp two years before—years neither short, nor long, simply without time, rich with experience and yet null and void. It was even the same time of year, exactly the same: one of August's first days. As noted, Joachim's mood was cheerful, ebullient in fact, as he entered Hans Castorp's room, or rather exited it, having stridden double-time across it to step out onto the balcony and greet his cousin with a smile. His breath came quick, muffled, ragged. His long journey was behind him—the road that led through many a landscape and across the lake that was like a sea, and then squeezed its way, up, up, to this place again. And there he stood now as if he had never left, and was received by his relative, who rose halfway out of the horizontal to shout his hellos and well-well's. His color was ruddy—perhaps from life in the open air, perhaps from the flush of travel. Not even bothering to look at his own room, he had hurried directly to room 34 to greet his companion from the old days, which were now present days again. His mother had gone to see to her toilette. They were going to have dinner in ten minutes—in the restaurant, of course. Hans Castorp would have to eat a bite with them, or at least have a sip of wine. And Joachim dragged him along to room 28, where everything was just the same as on the evening of Hans's arrival, except the other way around: Joachim chatted away feverishly, washed his hands in the sparkling basin, and Hans Castorp watched—amazed, by the way, and to some extent disappointed, to see his cousin in civvies. There was no visible trace of Joachim's new career, he remarked. He had been picturing him as an officer, in his uniform, and here he stood in dull gray, like everyone else. Joachim laughed, told him he was naive. No, he had left his uniform at home. Uniforms had their problems. You couldn't pop in just anywhere wearing a uniform. "I see, thanks for letting me know," Hans Castorp said. But Joachim was obviously unaware of any possible insult in his explanation, and now inquired about the residents of the Berghof and the latest news—not only without any arrogance, but indeed with the insistent animation of the traveler come home. Then Frau Ziemssen appeared through the door connecting the rooms, greeted her nephew in the manner people often choose on such occasions, that is, she pretended to be pleasantly surprised to find him here, although her surprise betrayed a certain melancholy, was muffled by strain and silent worry—about Joachim evidently. They then took the elevator down.

Luise Ziemssen had the same beautiful, black, gentle eyes as Joachim. Her hair was black, too, though mixed with gray now, the coiffure held firmly in place by an almost invisible hairnet, befitting, somehow, her whole personality—which was composed, gently restrained, and friendly in a formal sort of way—and lending a certain dignity to her obviously simple nature. It was clear, as Hans Castorp was not surprised to discover, that she did not understand, was in fact slightly offended by Joachim's good cheer, his rapid breathing, his impulsive words—behavior that presumably contradicted his disposition at home or during the trip. Their arrival here was a sad one for her, and she believed she should act accordingly. She could not reconcile herself to Joachim's turbulent emotions, to his sense of having returned home, which for the moment outweighed everything else and inspired him to breathe drunkenly of the old air again—our incomparably light, empty, incendiary air up here. This was all obscure to her. "My poor boy," she thought, and watched while her poor boy abandoned himself to exuberant exchanges with his cousin, reliving a hundred memories, asking a hundred questions, and throwing himself back in his chair with a laugh at every answer. Several times she said, "Now, children!" And then finally she said something meant to sound happy, but it emerged as a dismayed, gentle rebuke: "I've truly not seen you like this for ages, Joachim. It seems we had to travel all the way here to get you back to how you were on the day of your promotion." Which, of course, put an end to Joachim's exuberance. His mood turned sour, he came back to earth, fell silent, ate none of his dessert, even though a very tasty chocolate soufflé with whipped cream was served (but Hans Castorp ate it for him, though only an hour had passed since his more than ample supper), and finally did not even dare look up—quite probably because of the tears in his eyes.

That had certainly not been Frau Ziemssen's intent. She had hoped merely to introduce a more serious note, for decorum's sake—quite unaware that moderation and the golden mean were out of place here, that there was only the choice between extremes. And seeing her son so downcast, she appeared close to tears herself and was grateful to her nephew for his attempts to revive his despondent cousin's spirits. Yes, in terms of guests, Joachim would find many changes and novelties, though in his absence there had also been instances of a restoration to a former state of affairs. The great-aunt, for example, had returned—with companions. The ladies were seated, as always, at Frau Stöhr's table. Marusya laughed a lot, and heartily.

Joachim said nothing. Hans Castorp's comments had reminded Frau Ziemssen, however, that she had met someone quite by chance, and before she forgot she wanted to extend greetings she had been asked to pass on. A woman, a rather pleasant lady in fact, though she did live alone and her eyebrows were a bit too regular, who had approached their table in a restaurant in Munich, where they had spent a day between trains, came over to say hello to Joachim. A former fellow patient—Joachim would remember the name . . .

"Frau Chauchat," Joachim said quietly. She was at a sanatorium in the Allgäu at present, and wanted to go on to Spain come autumn. But apparently she intended to return here for the winter. She sent her warmest regards.

Hans Castorp was no child, he could control the nerves to the veins that make your face turn pale or blush. He said, "Oh, her? What do you know, she's emerged from beyond the Caucasus again. And she's off to Spain?"

The lady had mentioned some town in the Pyrenees. "A pretty woman, quite a charming lady. Pleasant voice, pretty gestures. But very free in her manners, careless," Frau Ziemssen remarked. "Spoke to us as if we were old friends, asked a great many questions, went on and on, although Joachim tells me he never actually made her acquaintance. Curious."

"That comes from the Asiatic East and her illness," Hans Castorp replied. One ought not to attempt to measure things by humanistic standards there, it didn't work. But that was something to think about—Frau Chauchat's plan to go to Spain. Hmm. Spain—it lay equally as far from the humanistic middle, not toward the soft side, but the hard. Spain was not a lack of form, but an excess of form, death as form, so to speak—not death as dissolution, but death as something austere, black, elegant, and bloody, the Inquisition, starched ruffs, Loyola, the Escorial. He would be interested to know how Frau Chauchat liked Spain. She would probably have to get over slamming doors there, and perhaps those two extrahumanistic camps would compensate for one another, have a humane effect on her. But then, too, something very nasty and terroristic might come of the East's going off to Spain.

No, he did not turn red or pale, but the impression this unexpected news of Frau Chauchat had on him was obvious from his words, to which, of course, the only possible reply was awkward silence. Joachim was less shocked; he knew from previous experience how subtle his cousin's mind had become up here. But Frau Ziemssen's eyes registered great consternation. She reacted exactly as if Hans Castorp's remarks had been crude and indecent, and after an embarrassed silence she ended their meal with a few tactful words to gloss things over. Before they parted, Hans Castorp passed on the director's order that Joachim should remain in bed the next day in any case, at least until the director examined him. As for everything else—well, they would see. And the three relatives were soon lying in their rooms, doors open to the fresh air of the Alpine summer night, each lost in her or his thoughts—Hans Castorp engrossed chiefly in the news that Frau Chauchat was expected to return before another six months had passed.

And so, as advised, poor Joachim had marched back home again for a little extra therapy. "A little extra therapy" had evidently been the term employed down in the flatlands, and they let him use it up here as well. Even Director Behrens took up the phrase, although his very first move was to saddle Joachim with four weeks of bed rest: it was necessary just to repair the worst damage, to reacclimatize him, and to stabilize his body temperature for now. He knew how to avoid being nailed down as to how long such extra therapy would last. Frau Ziemssen—a sensible, reasonable, though in no way sanguine lady—took the director aside and suggested the fall, October perhaps, as a date for Joachim's discharge, and Behrens agreed with her to the extent that by then one would at least be further along than one was at present. She was quite taken by him, by the way. He was chivalrous, he addressed her as "gracious lady," his bloodshot, protruding eyes gazed at her with manly sincerity, and despite her grief she could not help laughing at all his fraternity phrases. "I know he's in the best of hands," she said, and departed for Hamburg only eight days after she had arrived, since there was no serious need for her to offer special care, and besides, Joachim had a relative for company.

"Well, cheer up," Hans Castorp said, as he sat down on his cousin's bed in room 28. "It will be this fall—the boss has more or less committed himself. You can depend on it, count on it. October—that's when it will be. Some people go to Spain then, but you'll be returning to your *bandera*, to perform distinguished service above and beyond the call of duty."

It was his daily chore to console Joachim, especially for his having to be here and miss the grand war games that had begun in early August—because he could not get over that, expressed out-and-out self-contempt for being so damned weak-willed, for having succumbed at the last moment.

"*Rebellio carnis*," Hans Castorp said. "What can you do? The bravest officer can't help that—even Saint Anthony could hum you a tune about it. For God's sake, there are maneuvers every year, and you know what time is like up here. It doesn't exist. You haven't been gone long enough to have trouble getting back into the swing of things. Your little extra therapy will be over quick as a flash."

All the same, Joachim had experienced too great a revitalization of his sense of time while down in the flatlands for him to have no fear of the next four weeks. But on all sides there were people willing to help him get through them; the general regard in which his orderly demeanor was held manifested itself in visits from near and far. Settembrini came, was sympathetic and charming—and having always called Joachim "lieutenant," he now addressed him as "*capitano*." Naphta dropped by as well, and from the sanatorium itself old acquaintances appeared one by one, making use of a spare fifteen minutes to sit down on his bed, adopt his phrase about "extra therapy" as their own, and have him tell them about what all had happened to him—the ladies Stöhr, Levi, Iltis, and Kleefeld; the Messrs. Ferge, Wehsal, et al. Several even brought him flowers. When his four weeks were over, he got up, and his fever had been dampened to where he could walk about and take a seat in the dining hall between his cousin and Frau Magnus, the brewer's wife, at the same corner spot where Uncle James had sat, and, for a few days, Frau Ziemssen as well.

And so the young men lived side by side again just as before; yes, and to restore the scene even more precisely, Joachim inherited his old room beside Hans Castorp's, once Mrs. Macdonald, her son's photo in her hands, had sighed her last—though to be sure, only after it had been thoroughly sterilized with H_2CO. Actually, when viewed from an emotional perspective, it was more that Joachim lived at Hans Castorp's side, and no longer the other way around—for the latter was now the old-timer, whose existence his cousin simply shared for a brief time as a visitor. For Joachim tried hard to keep his eye squarely on October, although certain nodes in his central nervous system refused to obey humanistic norms and hindered a compensatory distribution of body warmth through the skin.

And they resumed their visits to Settembrini and Naphta, as well as walks with those two antagonistic allies; when they were joined by A. K. Ferge and Ferdinand Wehsal, which frequently happened, that made a party of four before which the two intellectual adversaries could engage in constant duels—and we could not hope to present them in their entirety without fear of likewise losing ourselves in the same desperate infinitude into which they daily threw themselves for their large audience, although Hans Castorp chose to see his own poor soul as the chief object of their dialectic rivalry. He had learned from Naphta that Settembrini was a Freemason—which made no less an impression on him than had the Italian's revelation of Naphta's Jesuit origins and patronage. He had been flabbergasted to hear that there really and truly was such a thing; and he had diligently sounded the terrorist out on the beginnings and character of this curious institution, which in a few years would celebrate its two-hundredth anniversary. And whereas Settembrini had spoken behind Naphta's back in tones of pathos-laden admonition about the Jesuit, as if he were somehow diabolic, Naphta made unperturbed fun of the other man and the sphere he came from, suggesting that the whole thing was terribly old-fashioned and backward, an attempt at bourgeois enlightenment perpetrated by yesterday's freethinkers, when in fact it was nothing more than a wretched intellectual mirage, which its self-deluded adherents ludicrously believed was full of revolutionary life.

"What do you expect?" Naphta said. "His grandfather was a Carbonaro, which means charcoal-burner, by the way. From him he got his charcoal-burner's faith in reason, freedom, human progress, and the whole moth-eaten classicistic-bourgeois ideology of virtue. You see, what confuses the world is the incongruity between the swift flight of the mind and matter's vast clumsy slowness, its dogged persistence and inertia. One must admit such an incongruity would suffice to excuse the mind's lack of interest in reality, because as a rule the mind is disgusted by reality's ferment long before it erupts in revolution. Indeed, to a lively mind, a dead intellect is more abhorrent than basalt, which at least does not make any claims to life and thought. Rocks like basalt, remnants of former realities, which the Spirit has left so far behind that it refuses even to associate the notion of reality with them, persist in their dogged way; their very lumpish, dead continuance unfortunately prevents them in their inanity from realizing how inane they are. I am speaking in generalities, but you will know how to apply my words to those humanitarian freethinkers, who believe themselves to be heroes still standing up against authority and domination. Ah, and the catastrophes by which free thought hopes to prove its own vitality—ah, those latter-day, spectacular triumphs for which it prepares itself and which it dreams of someday celebrating! The mere idea would be enough to bore the living Spirit to death, if it did not know that it shall emerge from such catastrophes as the true victor and beneficiary—fusing, as it does, elements of the old with the new to create an authentic revolution. . . . And how is your cousin doing, Hans Castorp? You know I've always had a great liking for him."

"Thanks, Herr Naphta. It seems everyone takes an honest liking to him—he's obviously such a fine lad. Even Herr Settembrini has a genuine soft spot for him, although he must disapprove, of course, of a certain fanatical terrorism that goes with Joachim's profession. And now I hear he's a Freemason—what do you know! Makes a man stop and think, I must say. It puts his personality in a whole new light, makes a lot of things clearer. I wonder if he sometimes places his feet at just the right angle and adds a special grip to his handshake? Not that I've ever noticed anything . . ."

"Our good Third-Degree Master," Naphta replied, "has probably moved beyond such childishness. I assume that the rituals of the lodges have gone through a rather pathetic adjustment to the more prosaic spirit of the modern bourgeoisie. They are probably ashamed of the old ceremonies, see them as uncivilized hocus-pocus—and for good reason, since it really would be rather preposterous to dress atheistic republicanism up as a mystery. I don't know what horrors they used to test Herr Settembrini's stamina—whether they led him blindfolded down various corridors and then let him wait in some dark vaulted chamber before the doors were thrown wide to reveal the mirrors and bright lights of the lodge hall. Or if they solemnly catechized him, holding up a skull and three candles, threatening his bared breast with swords. You'll have to ask him that yourself, but I fear you won't find him very talkative, because even if it was all done in a more bourgeois fashion, he was nevertheless sworn to silence."

"Sworn? To silence? They really do that?"

"Certainly. Silence and obedience."

"Obedience, too. But listen here, professor—it seems to me he would have no reason, then, for criticizing any fanaticism or terrorism in my cousin's vocation. Silence and obedience! I never would have thought that a freethinker like Settembrini could submit to such blatantly Spanish requirements and vows. I detect something downright military, Jesuitical, about this Freemasonry."

"You detect correctly," Naphta responded. "Your divining rod is twitching and tapping away. At its root, the very idea of the lodge is inseparably tied to the notion of the absolute. It is, therefore, terroristic—that is, anti-liberal. It relieves the individual of the burden of conscience, and in the name of an absolute goal, it sanctifies every means—even bloody, criminal means. There are indications that at one time the brotherhood of the lodge was symbolically sealed with blood. A brotherhood is never something visible, but always an organization that, by its very nature, is absolutist in spirit. You didn't know, did you, that the founder of the Illuminati, a society that for a while almost fused with Freemasonry, was a former member of the Society of Jesus?"

"No, that's new to me, of course."

"Adam Weishaupt modeled his humanitarian secret society strictly on the Jesuit order. He was himself a Mason, and the most distinguished Masons of the period were Illuminati. I am speaking of the second half of the eighteenth century, which Settembrini would not hesitate to describe to you as a period of decline in his guild. In reality, however, it was in fullest bloom, as were secret societies in general. It was an age when Freemasonry achieved a higher life—a life of which it was later purged by people of the same sort as our philanthropist, who would most definitely have joined those who at the time accused it of Jesuitical obscurantism."

"And they would have had good reason?"

"Yes—if you like. Banal freethinkers would have had reason to think so. It was a time when our own priests wanted to breathe the spirit of Catholic hierarchy into Freemasonry, and there was even a flourishing Jesuit lodge at Clermont, in France. It was, moreover, the period when Rosicrucianism infiltrated the lodges—a very strange brotherhood, which, you should note, united the purely rational, sociopolitical goals of improving the world and making people happy with a curious affinity for the occult sciences of the East, for Indian and Arabic wisdom and magical knowledge of nature. At the time, many lodges went through a period of rectification and reform, in the spirit of the 'strict charges'—an explicitly irrational, mysterious, magical, alchemistic spirit, to which the higher degrees of the Scottish Rite owe their existence. Building on the old military ranks of apprentice, fellow, and master, new degrees called grand masters were added, leading to hieratic realms filled with Rosicrucian occultism. It was a matter of reaching back to certain religious orders of knights in the Middle Ages, to the Knights Templar in particular—you know, the ones who swore vows of poverty, chastity, and obedience before the patriarch of Jerusalem. Even today, one high degree of Masonry bears the title of 'Grand Duke of Jerusalem.' "

"New to me, all new to me, Herr Naphta. I'm starting to see through our Settembrini's tricks. Not bad—'Grand Duke of Jerusalem.' You should call him that sometime, too, just as a joke. He recently gave you the nickname of '*Doctor Angelicus*.' That cries out for revenge."

"Oh, there are a whole lot of similar imposing titles for the higher degrees in the Grand and Templar lodges of the strict charges. There is a Perfect Master, a King of the East, a Grand High Priest, and the thirty-first degree is called Exalted Prince of the Royal Mysteries. You will note that all these names bear some connection to Oriental mysticism. The reemergence of the Templars had meant nothing less than the establishment of such connections; it had introduced the ferment of irrationality into an intellectual world concerned with rational, practical social improvement. All of which gave Freemasonry a new fascination and luster, which explains the increased popularity it enjoyed at the time. It attracted various elements who were weary of their century's sophistries, of its humane, dispassionate enlightenment, and were thirsty for stronger elixirs. The order's success was such that the philistines complained that it was alienating men from domestic bliss and a reverence for women."

"Well, then, professor, it's quite understandable why Herr Settembrini doesn't like to recall the blossoming of his order."

"No, he does not like to recall that there was a time when his society was the object of all the antipathies that freethinkers, atheists, and rationalistic encyclopedists usually reserve for the Church, Catholicism, monks, and the Middle Ages. You heard me say Masons were accused of obscurantism . . ."

"But why? I'd like to understand that more clearly."

"I shall be glad to tell you. The strict charges meant a deepening and broadening of the order's traditions, a transference of its historical origins back to an occult world, to the so-called Dark Ages. Those who held the higher degrees of the lodges were initiates in the *physica mystica*, bearers of a magical knowledge of nature—which means, in fact, great alchemists."

"And now I have to summon all my faculties and try to remember what alchemy was more or less about. Alchemy—making gold, the philosopher's stone, *aurum potabile* . . ."

"Yes, that's the popular understanding. Put more academically, it is the purification, mutation, and refinement of matter, its transubstantiation to something higher, its enhancement, as it were. The *lapis philosophorum*, which is the male-female product of sulfur and mercury—the *res bina*, the bisexual *prima materia*—was nothing more and nothing less than the principle of that enhancement, the application of external influences to force matter upward: magical pedagogy if you will."

Hans Castorp said nothing. But he blinked, and glanced upward out of the corner of his eye.

"The primary symbol of alchemistic transmutation," Naphta went on, "was the crypt."

"The grave?"

"Yes, the scene of corruption. It is the epitome of all hermetism— nothing less than the vessel, the carefully safeguarded crystal retort, in which matter is forced toward its final mutation and purification."

" 'Hermetism'—that's well put, Herr Naphta. 'Hermetic'—I've always liked that word. It's a magic word with vague, vast associations. Forgive me, but I can't help thinking about our old canning jars, the ones our housekeeper in Hamburg—her name's Schalleen, with no Frau or Fräulein, just Schalleen—has standing in rows on shelves in her pantry: hermetically sealed jars, with fruit and meat and all sorts of other things inside. There they stand, for months, for years, but when you need one and open it up, what's inside is fresh and intact, neither years nor months have had any effect, you can eat it just as it is. Now, it's not alchemy or purification, of course, it's simple preservation, which is why they're called preserves. But the magical thing about it is that what gets preserved in them has been withdrawn from time, has been hermetically blocked off from time, which passes right by. Preserves don't have time, so to speak, but stand there on the shelf outside of time. But enough about canning jars. That didn't get us very far. Beg your pardon, you were going to teach me more."

"Only if you'd like me to. The apprentice must be fearless and hungry for knowledge—to speak in the style of our topic. The crypt, the grave, has always been the primary symbol in their initiation ceremony. The apprentice, the novice hungry to be admitted to such knowledge, must remain undaunted by the grave's horrors; the rules of the lodge demand that he be tested by being led down into the crypt and that he remain there until he is brought forth by the hand of an unknown brother. Which is the reason for the maze of corridors and dark vaulted chambers through which the neophyte must wander, for the black cloth with which the halls of lodges of the strict charges are draped, for the cult of the coffin, which plays such an important role in their meetings and initiation ceremonies. The path of the mysteries and purification is beset with dangers, it leads through the fear of death, through the realm of corruption, and the apprentice, the neophyte, is the young man who is hungry for the wounds of life, demands that his demonic capacity for experience be awakened, and is led by shrouded forms, who are merely shades of the great mystery itself."

"Thank you so much, Professor Naphta. Excellent. So that is what is called hermetic pedagogy. It certainly can't hurt for me to have heard something about that, too."

"All the less so, since it is a guide to final things, to an absolute confession of those things that transcend the senses, and so to our goal. The alchemistic rites of such lodges have led many a noble, inquisitive mind to that goal in the decades since. But surely I need not spell it out, since it cannot have escaped you that the degrees in the Scottish Rite are but a surrogate for another hierarchy, that the alchemistic knowledge of the Master Mason is fulfilled in the mystery of transubstantiation, and that the mystic tour with which the lodge favors its novices clearly corresponds to the means of grace, just as the metaphoric games of its ceremonies are reflections of the liturgical and architectural symbols of our Holy Catholic Church."

"Oh, I see!"

"Beg your pardon, but that is not all. I already took the liberty of suggesting that the development of Freemasonry from guilds of respectable manual laborers is historically extraneous. The strict charges, at least, provided lodges with human foundations that went far deeper. Like certain mysteries in our Church, the lodges' secrets have a clear connection to the solemn cults and holy excesses of primitive man. As regards the Church, I am thinking of the supper that is a feast of love, the sacramental partaking of body and blood. As regards the lodges, however—"

"Just a moment. One moment for a marginal comment. There are also so-called regimental love feasts in the disciplined community to which my cousin belongs. He often wrote me about them. Of course, except for people getting a bit drunk, it's all quite respectable, not nearly as rough as things get in cadet taverns or—"

"—as regards the lodges, however, I was referring to the cult of the crypt and coffin, to which I previously called your attention. In both cases, we are dealing with a symbolism of last and ultimate things, with elements of orgiastic primal religion, with unbridled nocturnal sacrifices in honor of dying and ripening, of death, transformation, and resurrection. You will recall that both the cult of Isis and the Eleusinian mysteries were carried out in dark caves at night. Well, there were and are a great many mementos of Egypt in Freemasonry, and among its secret societies were some that used the name Eleusinian. Those lodges held feasts, feasts of the Eleusinian mysteries and the secrets of Aphrodite, which at last got the female involved—and the Feast of Roses, an allusion to the three blue roses on the Masonic apron, which, it seems, frequently ended in bacchanalian excess."

"Now, now, what's this I hear, Professor Naphta? And it's all part of Freemasonry? And I'm supposed to picture our clearheaded Herr Settembrini mixed up with all that?"

"You'd be doing him a great injustice. No, Settembrini knows absolutely nothing about any of it. I told you, after all, that later on people like him purged the lodges of all elements of a higher life. The lodges were modernized, humanitarianized—good God. They were led back from their aberrations to reason, usefulness, and progress, to the battle against prince and priest—in short, to social happiness. The conversations inside them are once again about nature, virtue, moderation, and the fatherland. And, I assume, about business as well. In a word, it is bourgeois misery organized as a club."

"What a pity. A pity about the Feast of Roses, too. I'll have to ask Settembrini if he's ever even heard of it."

"The doughty Knight of the T-square!" Naphta scoffed. "You must realize that it was not all that easy for him to be admitted to the site where the temple of humanity is being built, because he's as poor as a church mouse, and they not only demand higher education, humanistic education, but, beg your pardon, one must also be well-to-do just to afford the hefty initiation fees and annual dues. Education and property—behold the bourgeoisie! There you have the foundations of the liberal world republic!"

"Yes indeed," Hans Castorp said, laughing, "there you have it right in front of your nose."

"And yet," Naphta added after a pause, "I would advise you not to take the man and his cause all too lightly, would even go so far, now that we are on the subject, as to beg you to be on your guard. Inanity is not synonymous with innocence. Nor is obtuseness necessarily harmless. These people may have poured a great deal of water into wine that was once quite heady, but the concept of brotherhood is itself strong enough to tolerate a lot of water. It retains traces of its fecund secret; nor can there be any doubt that Freemasonry has its hand in world politics, just as there is more to our charming Herr Settembrini than the man himself—standing behind him are powers, whose kin and emissary he is."

"Emissary?"

"Well, yes—proselytizer, fisher of souls."

"And what sort of emissary are you?" Hans Castorp thought. But aloud he said, "My thanks, Professor Naphta. I'm much obliged to you for your reminder and warning. Do you know what? I'm going to go up one floor now, if you can call it a floor, and check the pulse of our lodge-brother in disguise. An apprentice must be fearless and hungry for knowledge. And cautious, too, of course. Caution is definitely required when one is dealing with emissaries."

There was no reason to be shy about turning to Herr Settembrini for further information; inasmuch as the Italian had never been particularly careful about making a secret of his membership in that harmonious society, he could not reproach Herr Naphta for a lack of discretion in the matter. The *Rivista della Massoneria Italiana* lay open on his table; Hans Castorp had simply never noticed it before. And so when he brought the conversation around to the "royal craft," as if he had never been in any doubt about Settembrini's association with it, he met with little reticence. There were topics, of course, that the literary man would not discuss, and at their mention he simply set his lips tight with some ostentation, presumably bound by the terroristic oath that Naphta had said drew a veil of secrecy over the curious organization's ceremonial usages and his own rank within it. But otherwise he was downright boastful and provided his inquisitive visitor a full picture of the fellowship's worldwide operation, with approximately 20,000 lodges and 150 grand lodges, even reaching the cultures of Negro republics like Haiti and Liberia. He was also quite liberal about naming names of those great men who had been or were now Masons: Voltaire, Lafayette, and Napoleon, Franklin and Washington, Mazzini and Garibaldi; and among the living, the king of England and a great many other men, members of governments and parliaments, in whose hands lay the affairs of Europe.

Hans Castorp expressed respect, but no surprise. It was much the same with university fraternities, he suggested. Their members stuck together their whole lives and knew how to take care of their own, so that it was difficult for anyone to get very far in the hierarchy of civil service without having been a member of a fraternity. It was, therefore, perhaps counterproductive for Herr Settembrini to present the membership of such prominent men as an argument in favor of the lodges, since one might turn it around and assume that if so many of his brothers occupied important posts, that only proved the power of the society, which surely was much more deeply involved in the affairs of the world than Herr Settembrini was willing to admit.

Settembrini smiled. He even fanned himself with the issue of *Massoneria* he was holding in his hand. Was that intended as a trap? Was he now supposed to make imprudent statements about the lodge's political nature, its fundamentally political character? "Cunning, but pointless, my good engineer! We admit we are political, admit it frankly, openly. We discount the odium that a few fools—most of them residing in your native land, my good engineer, hardly any elsewhere—attach to that word. For the man who loves his fellow man, there can be no distinction between what is political and what is not. The apolitical does not exist—everything is politics."

"Without exception?"

"I am well aware that there are those who enjoy pointing to the apolitical origins of Masonic thought. But those people are merely playing with words, drawing distinctions that it is high time we recognize to be imaginary and absurd. Firstly, the Spanish lodges, at least, took on a political tone from the very beginning."

"I can well conceive of that."

"You can conceive of very little, my good engineer. Do not presume that you can conceive of much of anything on your own, but rather attempt to receive and ponder. And therefore I beg you—in your own best interest, as well as in the interest of your own country and of Europe itself—to imprint on your mind the 'secondly' that I am about to offer. Secondly, you see, Masonic thought was never apolitical, not at any time—it could not be, and if it ever believed itself to be, then it was denying its true nature. What are we? Masons and hodmen who build, all with but one purpose. The good of all is the fundamental principle of our brotherhood. And what is this good, this building we build? The well-crafted social edifice, the perfection of humanity, the new Jerusalem. And what in the world does that have to do with politics or the lack thereof? The social problem, the problem of human coexistence is politics, is politics through and through, nothing but politics. And the man who consecrates himself to it—and he who withdraws from that sacred task does not deserve the name of man—belongs to politics, foreign and domestic. He understands that the craft of the Freemason is the art of governance."

"Governance?"

"He knows that among those Illuminati who were Masons there was a regent degree."

"Very nice, Herr Settembrini. The art of governance—and I like your regent degree, too. But I need to know one thing: are you Christians, all you fellows there in your lodge?"

"*Perchè?*"

"Forgive me, I shall put it another way, more generally, more simply. Do you believe in God?"

"And I shall give you an answer—but why do you ask?"

"I wasn't trying to trap you just now. But there is a biblical story, where someone tries to trap the Lord with a Roman coin, and the answer he receives is that one should render unto Caesar the things that are Caesar's, and unto God the things that are God's. It seems to me this method of differentiating establishes the difference between what is political and what is not. If there is a God, then the difference exists. Do Freemasons believe in God?"

"I pledged I would give you an answer. You are speaking of a unity that we are working to achieve, but which, to the great sorrow of all good men, does not yet exist. An international union of Freemasons does not exist. It shall be established—and I repeat, we are very quietly, very diligently working to achieve it. And then, without a doubt, we shall likewise be united in our religious confession—and it will be: '*Écrasez l'infâme.*' "

"Will it be compulsory? That would hardly be tolerant."

"You are hardly up to dealing with the problem of tolerance, my good engineer. But imprint this on your mind: tolerance becomes a crime when applied to evil."

"So, then, God would be evil?"

"Metaphysics is evil. For it serves no purpose except to lull us to sleep, to sap us of the energy we should bring to building the temple of society.

Only a generation ago, the Grand Orient of France provided us a fine model by erasing the name of God from all his works. We Italians followed his example."

"How Catholic of you!"

"By which you mean?"

"I find it terribly Catholic—erasing God."

"What you are trying to say is—"

"Nothing worth hearing, Herr Settembrini. You should not pay any real attention to my babblings. It just seemed to me at the moment as if atheism were something dreadfully Catholic, as if one erased the name of God so that one could be that much better a Catholic."

And if Herr Settembrini followed this with a pause, it was clear that he did so solely out of pedagogic circumspection. After a proper period of silence, he replied, "My good engineer, I have not the remotest desire to disconcert or offend you in your Protestantism. We were speaking of tolerance. It is superfluous for me to emphasize that I feel more than tolerance for Protestantism, that I have the deepest admiration for it as the historical opponent of forces that enslave the conscience. The invention of the printing press and the Reformation are and shall remain Central Europe's two most sublime contributions to humanity. Without question. But, considering what you have just said, I do not doubt you will understand me implicitly when I point out that this is only one side of the matter, that there is a second. Protestantism harbors within it certain elements—just as the Great Reformer himself harbored such elements within his personality. I am thinking here of a sentimentality, a trancelike self-hypnosis that is not European, that is foreign and hostile to our active hemisphere's law of life. Just look at him, this Luther. Look at the portraits, both as a young man and later. What a skull, what cheekbones, what a strange set to the eyes. My friend, that is Asia. I would be surprised, would be astonished, if Wendish-Slavic-Sarmatian blood was not at work there, and if it was not this massive phenomenon of a man—and who would deny him that—who proved to be a fatal weight placed on one of the two precariously balanced scales of your nation, on the Eastern scale, which caused—and still causes—the Western scale to fly heavenward."

Herr Settembrini had moved now from his humanist's folding lectern to the round table with its water carafe, closer to his pupil, who was sitting on the backless divan pushed up against one wall, his elbows on his knees and his chin propped in one hand.

"*Caro!*" Herr Settembrini said, "*Caro amico!* Decisions must be made—decisions of incalculable significance for the future happiness of Europe, and your country will have to make them, they must come to fruition within its soul. Positioned between East and West, it will have to choose, will have consciously to decide, once and for all, between the two spheres vying for its heart. You are young, you will take part in this decision, you have been called to exercise an influence upon it. And so let us bless the fates that have thrown you upon these dreadful shores, giving me the opportunity to influence your educable youth with my not unskilled, not yet totally enfeebled words, and to make you aware of the responsibility that you and your country bear, while the civilized world looks on."

Hans Castorp sat there, chin in hand. He stared out the dormer window; a certain obstinacy could be read in his ordinary, blue eyes. He said nothing.

"You are silent," Herr Settembrini said, deeply moved. "You and your country allow unconditional silence to reign, a silence so opaque that no one can judge its depths. You do not love the Word, or do not possess it, or sanctify it only in a sullen way—the articulate world does not and cannot learn where it stands with you. My friend, that is dangerous. Language is civilization itself. The Word, even the most contradictory word, binds us together. Wordlessness isolates. One presumes that you will seek to break out of your isolation with deeds. You will ask your cousin Giacomo"—Herr Settembrini had fallen into the habit of calling Joachim "Giacomo"—"you will ask your cousin Giacomo to step out in front of your silence. 'And two he has slain all unaided, the others his sword have evaded.' "

And because Hans Castorp had begun to laugh, Herr Settembrini smiled, too, likewise pleased for the moment with the effect of his graphic words.

"Fine, let us have a laugh," he said. "You'll always find me ready for mirth. 'Laughter is the sparkle of the soul,' as an ancient once said. And we have strayed to other matters that, I admit, are laden with difficulties, to problems we have encountered in our preparations for an international union of Masons, questions posed in particular by Protestant Europe. . . ." And warming to his topic, Herr Settembrini continued speaking of this international union, which had been born in Hungary and whose longed-for realization would surely confer upon Freemasonry the power to change the world. He casually showed Hans Castorp correspondence he had received from foreign Masonic dignitaries concerning this matter, a handwritten letter from the Swiss Grand Master, Brother Quartier la Tente of the Thirty-third Degree; and he discussed the plan to declare Esperanto the official world language of Freemasonry. His zeal lifted him to the world of high politics; his eye sweeping here and there, he appraised the chances revolutionary republican ideas might have in his own land, in Spain, in Portugal—and claimed to be in contact with persons who stood at the top of the Grand Lodge in that last-named monarchy. Affairs were most assuredly ripening toward decision. Hans Castorp should think of him when, in the very near future, events unfolded rapidly there. Hans Castorp promised he would.

It should be noted that these Masonic colloquies—held separately between the apprentice and each of his mentors—had taken place during the period before Joachim's return home to the people up here. The discussion to which we now turn, however, occurred during his second stay and in his presence, at the beginning of October, nine weeks after his return; and Hans Castorp always remembered this particular gathering under an autumn sun on the terrace of the Kurhaus in Platz, where they sipped refreshing drinks, because his secret worries about Joachim had begun that day, worries aroused by statements and symptoms that would normally not arouse concern, a sore throat and hoarseness in particular, harmless irritations, which nevertheless Hans Castorp saw in a peculiar light somehow, the light, one might say, that he believed he saw shining deep in Joachim's eyes, those eyes that had always been so gentle and large, but which that day, for the very first time, had grown indescribably larger and deeper, and along with their usual calm, inner light had taken on a meditative and—one has no choice but to use the word—*ominous* expression, which it would be quite wrong to say Hans Castorp had not liked, he had in fact liked it, except that it had also given rise to his worries. In short, one cannot help speaking about it in confusion commensurate with his confused impressions.

As for the conversation, the controversy—a controversy between Settembrini and Naphta, of course—it was about something entirely different, only loosely connected with their special discussions about Freemasonry. Besides the cousins, Ferge and Wehsal were also present, and everyone joined in eagerly, although not everyone was up to the subject. Herr Ferge, for example, expressly said he was not. But an argument carried on as if it were a matter of life and death, and with such wit and polish as if it were *not,* but merely an elegant competition—and that was how all disputes were carried on between Settembrini and Naphta—such an argument is, in and of itself, quite naturally entertaining to listen to, even for someone who understands little of it and only vaguely comprehends its significance. Raising their eyebrows, total strangers sitting nearby eavesdropped on the altercation, captivated by the passion and finesse of the interchange.

This took place, as we said, in front of the Kurhaus, one afternoon after tea. The four guests from the Berghof had run into Settembrini there, and then quite by chance Naphta had joined them. They were sitting around a little metal table, drinking various alcoholic beverages diluted with soda—anisette, vermouth. Naphta, who had taken his tea here, had ordered wine and cake, apparently a reminiscence of his student days; Joachim frequently moistened his sore throat with real lemonade, which he drank very strong and sour, for its astringent, soothing effect; and Settembrini was enjoying simple sugared water, but drank it through a straw in a very charming, appetizing way, as if sipping the most costly of beverages.

"What is this I hear, my good engineer? What rumor has come to my ears? Your Beatrice is returning? Your guide through all nine rotating spheres of paradise? Well, I can only hope that you will not totally disdain the friendly guiding hand of your Virgil as well. Our ecclesiastic here can confirm for you that the world of the *medio evo* is not complete if Franciscan mysticism lacks the opposing pole of Thomistic insight."

Everyone laughed at all this facetious erudition and looked now at Hans Castorp, who was also laughing and lifted his glass of vermouth to toast his "Virgil." And it may be hard to believe, but the next hour was consumed by the inexhaustible intellectual fracas that grew out of Herr Settembrini's harmless, though flamboyant remarks. For Naphta, in response to what had admittedly been something of a challenge, immediately went on the attack, impugning the Latin poet whom Settembrini, as they all knew, idolized, indeed ranked above Homer; whereas on more than one occasion Naphta had shown a caustic disregard of Virgil and of the Latin poets in general—and promptly and maliciously used this opportunity to do so again. It was solely because he shared the all too charitable biases of his age, he said, that the great Dante had taken that mediocre scribbler seriously and had assigned him such an important role in his own epic, a role to which Herr Lodovico probably assigned far too much Masonic significance. When, in fact, there was nothing to that fawning poet laureate and flunky of the Julians, that oh-so-urbane inkslinger and rhetorical show-off without a spark of creativity, whose soul, if he had one, was secondhand at best, who was not a poet at all, but a Frenchman togged out in a full Augustan wig of flowing curls.

Herr Settembrini did not doubt that the honorable gentleman had means and methods by which to reconcile his office as a teacher of Latin with his disdain for the glories of Roman civilization. Though it did seem necessary to remind him that such opinions also put him at variance with the judgment of his favorite era, which not only had not disdained Virgil, but had also, in its naive fashion, rightly honored his greatness by making him a mighty seer and sorcerer.

It was all in vain, Naphta responded, that Herr Settembrini appealed to the naiveté of those victorious morning years of Christianity—which had only proved its creative force by making demons of those it conquered. Moreover, the teachers of the early Church had never wearied of warning people against the lies of the philosophers and poets of antiquity, and in particular against sullying themselves with the lush eloquence of a Virgil. Indeed, the present day, when once again one age was heading for the grave even as a proletarian age was dawning, was a particularly appropriate time for respecting such sentiments. And as for the rest of his charge, Herr Lodovico could be sure that he, Naphta, pursued his modicum of bourgeois activity, to which the former had been kind enough to allude, with all due *reservatio mentalis* and that he recognized a certain irony in having found a niche in an educational institution devoted to classical rhetoric, a pedagogy whose life span even the most sanguine would estimate only in decades.

"You Christians studied them," Settembrini exclaimed, "studied the classical poets and philosophers until you broke out in a sweat, attempted to make their precious heritage your own, just as you used the stones of their ancient edifices for your meeting houses. Because you were well aware that no new art could come from your own proletarian souls and hoped to defeat antiquity with its own weapons. And so it will be again, so it will always be. And you with your crude visions of a new morning will likewise have to be taught by those whom—so at least you would like to persuade yourselves, and others—you despise. For without education you cannot prevail before humanity, and there is only *one* kind of education—you call it bourgeois, but in fact it is human." A question of decades—until the end of humanistic education? Only good manners prevented Herr Settembrini from breaking into mocking, carefree laughter. A Europe that knew how to preserve its eternal treasures would coolly, calmly proceed with the agenda of classical reason and ignore any proletarian apocalypses that might be envisioned here or there.

As to the world's agenda, Naphta sarcastically replied, Herr Settembrini did not appear very well informed about that. A matter that the Italian evidently preferred to take for granted would be the next item on that agenda: whether the classical tradition of the Mediterranean was intended for all humanity, and therefore eternal in human terms, or whether it had not merely been the intellectual fashion and trimmings of one particular epoch, the bourgeois liberal age, which could then die with it. It would be a matter for history to decide, and he recommended Herr Settembrini not let himself be lulled into any sort of certainty that the decision would be rendered in favor of his Latin conservatism.

It was a particular bit of impudence on little Naphta's part to call Herr

Settembrini, the declared servant of progress, a conservative. They all felt it—most bitterly, of course, the gentleman in question, who twirled his sweeping moustaches while he searched for a counterblow, giving his foe time to engage in further attacks against classical models, against the rhetorical literary tradition of European education and schooling, with its mania for grammatical form, which only served the interests of bourgeois class domination and had long since become an object of ridicule among the masses. Yes, these gentlemen had no idea what a huge joke all our doctor degrees, our whole mandarin educational system, was to the masses, how they ridiculed our public grammar schools, that instrument of the dictatorship of the bourgeoisie, maintained under the delusion that by watering down scholarship one educated the commonfolk. The masses had long since learned that for the education and discipline needed in the battle against the decaying bourgeoisie they should look elsewhere than to coercive schools imposed by the authorities; and by now every idiot knew that the school system developed from the cloisters of the Middle Ages was as anachronistic and absurd as a periwig, that no one owed his real education to schools anymore, and that free, open instruction by public lectures, exhibitions, films, and so forth was far superior to that found in any schoolroom.

In the mixture of revolution and conspiracy that Naphta had served up to his hearers, Herr Settembrini responded, the obscurantist element had predominated in a most unsavory fashion. Although one found pleasure in Naphta's concern for the enlightenment of the common people, that pleasure was diminished somewhat by the fear that what prevailed here was an instinctual tendency to shroud the commonfolk and the world in illiterate darkness.

Naphta smiled. Illiteracy! And now Settembrini had spoken the word he evidently believed would instill true terror, had held up the Gorgon's head at the sight of which everyone would dutifully turn ashen. He, Naphta, regretted having to disappoint his vis-à-vis, for he found the humanist fear of the very word "illiteracy" merely amusing. One would have to be a Renaissance man of letters, a verbal dandy, a Gongorist, a Marinist, a fop of the *estilo culto*, to endow the disciplines of reading and writing with such exaggerated educational importance and imagine that intellectual night reigned where such skills were lacking. Did Herr Settembrini not recall that the greatest poet of the Middle Ages, Wolfram von Eschenbach, had been illiterate? In those days it was thought disgraceful to send to school any lad who did not wish to become a cleric, and this scorn for the literary arts, on the part of the aristocracy and commonfolk alike, had remained the hallmark of genuine nobility; whereas the literary man, that true son of humanism and the bourgeoisie, who could read and write—which nobles, warriors, and common people could do only poorly or not at all—could do nothing else, understood absolutely nothing about the world, and remained a Latin windbag, a master of speech, who left real life to honest folk, which was why he had also turned politics into a bag of wind, full of rhetoric and beautiful literature, called radicalism and democracy in party jargon, and so on and so forth.

And here came Herr Settembrini! His opponent's contempt for the love of literary form, he cried, only too plainly revealed a taste for the frenzied barbarism of certain epochs, but without such a love no true humanity was possible, or even conceivable, not now, not ever. Nobility? Only a misanthrope could christen the lack of the Word—raw, mute reality itself—with such a name. Nobility was, rather, a certain lofty abundance, *generosità*, which revealed itself by ascribing to form a human value quite independent of content; the cultivation of public speaking as an art for art's sake, this legacy of Greco-Roman civilization, which humanists, the *uomini letterati*, had restored for those who spoke Romance languages, for them at least, was the source of every further meaningful idealism, including political idealism. "Yes, my good sir. What you would like to revile as the disjuncture of speech and life is nothing more than a higher unity in beauty's crown, and I have no fear which side high-minded youth will always take in a struggle where the choice is between literature and barbarism."

Hans Castorp's attention had been directed only partly to the conversation, for he was preoccupied with the presence of a warrior, of a person who was the representative of genuine nobility, or rather with the new look in that person's eyes, and he flinched at Herr Settembrini's last words, sensing that they had been addressed to him and demanded an answer; but then he merely made the same face he had made the day Settembrini had solemnly tried to force him to decide between "East and West"—a face, that is, full of reservations and obstinacy—and said nothing. They carried everything to extremes, these two, as was probably necessary for the sake of argument, and squabbled fiercely over the most extreme choices, whereas it seemed to him that what one might, in a spirit of conciliation, declare truly human or humane had to lie somewhere in the middle of this intolerant contentiousness, somewhere between rhetorical humanism and illiterate barbarism. But to avoid annoying either man, he did not say this, and watched, wrapped in reservations, as they went at it, spitefully helping one another to get lost in a thousand trivialities, all because Settembrini had made a little joke about Virgil the Latin poet.

The Italian would not yield, but brandished the Word like a sword, triumphed with it. He rose up to defend literary genius, celebrated the history of literature from the first moment when man chiseled symbols into stone as a monument to his knowledge and emotion. He spoke of the Egyptian god Thoth, identical with the Hellenistic god Hermes the Thrice Great, and worshiped as the inventor of writing, the patron of libraries, the inspiration for all intellectual endeavor. He bent a metaphorical knee before Hermes Trismegistos, the humanistic Hermes, the master of the palaestra, whom mankind could thank for the sublime gift of the literary word, of agonistic rhetoric. All of which roused Hans Castorp to remark that this Egyptian must have been a politician as well, playing on a grander scale the same role as Signor Brunetto Latini, who had given the Florentines their polish and taught them how to speak and the fine art of guiding their republic by the rules of politics. To which Naphta responded that Herr Settembrini was cheating a little and had given his Thoth Trismegistos all too sleek an image. For he had been a monkey, moon, and soul god—a baboon with a crescent moon above his head and above all, under the name of Hermes, a god of death and the dead, a grabber and guide of souls, who by late antiquity had become a great sorcerer and served the cabalistic Middle Ages as the father of hermetic alchemy.

What, what? Thoughts and images tumbled topsy-turvy in Hans's mental workshop. There sat death, a humanistic rhetorician clad in a blue coat; and when you focused on this philanthropic and pedagogic god of literature, what you saw crouching there had a monkey face, with the symbols of night and sorcery on its brow. He resisted the image, waved it off with one hand, with which he then covered his eyes. But in the darkness into which he fled to escape confusion, he could hear Settembrini's voice droning on in praise of literature. Not just the great thinkers, he exclaimed, but the great doers in every age as well, had been part of literature; and he named Alexander, Caesar, Napoleon, named Frederick the Prussian and other heroes, even Lassalle and Moltke. It did not trouble him in the least when Naphta tried to send him packing to China, a land afflicted with the most bizarre idolatry of the ABC's ever known to history, where you could become a field marshal if you could sketch all forty thousand characters—which surely had to warm the humanist's heart. *Eh, eh,* Naphta knew quite well that he wasn't talking about sketching, but about literature as the basic impulse of humanity, about the human spirit, which, mock as he might, was spirit per se, the miracle uniting analysis and form. That was what awakened our appreciation for all things human, weakened and dispelled foolish prejudices and beliefs, led to the civilizing ennoblement and improvement of humankind. And it did so by creating highly refined morals and sensitivities, while at the same time, and without any fanaticism, teaching healthy doubt, justice, and tolerance. The purifying, sanctifying effect of literature, the destruction of passions through knowledge and the Word; literature as the path to understanding, to forgiveness, and to love; the redemptive power of language, the literary spirit as the noblest manifestation of the human spirit per se; the man of letters as the perfect man, the saint—such were the radiant tones of Herr Settembrini's hymn of apology. Ah, but his adversary was not tongue-tied, either; he knew how to disrupt this angelic hallelujah with nasty, brilliant protests, declaring himself a partisan of life and its conservation and an opponent of the spirit of sedition lurking beneath such seraphic dissemblance. The miraculous unification that Herr Settembrini had warbled on about, so he declared, was a sham, a sleight-of-hand trick, because form, which the literary spirit was so proud of uniting with principles of inquiry and discrimination, was merely a form of illusion and lies, not a genuine, natural form growing out of life. This so-called benefactor of mankind talked a fine game about purification and sanctification, but in fact he was bent upon the emasculation of life, wanted to let it bleed to death. Yes, his spirit, his zealous theory violated life itself, and whoever wanted to destroy passions wanted nothingness, pure nothingness—pure indeed, since "pure" was the only attribute that could still be attached to nothingness. And it was precisely there that Herr Settembrini revealed himself for what he truly was, the man of progress, of liberalism, of bourgeois revolution. For progress was pure nihilism, and the liberal bourgeois was in truth a man of nothingness and the Devil—yes, he denied God, the conservative, positive Absolute, and instead pledged allegiance to the devilish Anti-Absolute, and in his deadly pacifism marveled at how devout he was. Yet he was anything but devout, was a traitor to life, who deserved to be brought before the Inquisition and the Fehme, to be put to the painful question—et cetera.

And indeed Naphta was clever at making his points, turning a hymn of praise into something diabolic and presenting himself as the incarnation of abiding, disciplined love, so that once again it had become a pure impossibility to decide where God and the Devil, life and death, were to be found. The reader can believe us when we say, however, that his opponent was man enough to respond with a brilliant comeback, which he then received in kind; and so it went for a while and the conversation flowed on into issues previously touched upon. But Hans Castorp was no longer listening, because at one point Joachim had mentioned that he was feeling feverish, almost certainly from his cold, but did not know what he should do, since colds were hardly *reçus* here. The two duelers passed over the remark, but Hans Castorp had, as we noted, been keeping a worried eye on his cousin, and now departed with him in the middle of a rebuttal, leaving it to the remaining audience, consisting of Ferge and Wehsal, to provide sufficient pedagogic impetus for a continuation of the argument.

On the way home, he got Joachim to agree that official channels should be opened to deal with his cold and sore throat—this meant asking the bath attendant to inform the head nurse, which would then result in something being done for his sufferings. And it proved the thing to do. That very evening, right after supper, Adriatica knocked on Joachim's door—Hans Castorp happened to be in the room with him—and asked in her squawky voice what the young officer's problems and wishes were. "Sore throat? Hoarseness?" she repeated. "Man alive, what sort of antics are these?" She attempted to fix him with a piercing stare, and it was not Joachim's fault their eyes did not meet—hers were the ones that wandered off. Experience had taught her that she was not meant to execute the procedure, but she kept trying. With the aid of a sort of metal shoehorn that she pulled from the bag hanging from her belt, she looked down into the patient's throat, asking Hans Castorp to provide light with the nightstand lamp. Standing on her tiptoes and gazing at Joachim's uvula, she said, "Man alive, tell me—have you ever swallowed the wrong way?"

What did you answer to that? For the moment, as long as she was peering down his throat, there was no way to reply; but even when she had let him go, Joachim was still at a loss for an answer. Of course he had swallowed the wrong way now and then, eating or drinking something. That was the common fate of humanity—that couldn't be what she meant by her question. So he asked her why she had asked, said he couldn't remember the last time it happened.

Well, fine; it was just something that occurred to her. He had caught a cold, she said—to the amazement of both cousins, since the word "cold" was taboo here at the Berghof. In such cases the director's laryngoscope was sometimes required for a closer examination of the throat. As she departed, she left some Formamint, plus a bandage and some gutta-percha for moist compresses during the night; and Joachim made use of both and said he noticed definite relief from these remedies; and he continued to use them, especially since his hoarseness would not go away, indeed grew worse over the next few days, although his sore throat was gone, more or less.

He had, by the way, only imagined that his fever came from his cold—the objective findings were as usual. Along with the results of the director's examination, this meant that honor-loving Joachim would have to stay with his little extra therapy before he could rush off to the colors again.

The October deadline passed quietly. No one mentioned it—not the director and not the cousins to one another; they simply ignored it in silence with downcast eyes. To judge from what the X-ray plate showed and what Behrens dictated to his psychoanalytic aide-de-camp during Joachim's monthly checkup, it was only too clear that there could be no question of a departure, unless it was fraudulent, because this time it was a matter of Joachim's remaining on duty up here with iron self-discipline, until he had been made fully weatherproof—only then could he fulfill his oath by service in the flatlands.

This was the watchword, with which everyone pretended to be in silent agreement. The truth was, however, that no one was quite certain whether anyone else believed this watchword in the depths of his soul; and because of their doubts the cousins would turn their downcast eyes away—but only after their eyes had first *met*. This had happened often since the colloquy on literature, the day when Hans Castorp had first noticed a new light and the *ominous* expression deep in Joachim's eyes. It happened once at the dinner table—when Joachim, still hoarse, quite unexpectedly choked on something, so violently he could hardly get his breath. And while Joachim gasped behind his napkin and Frau Magnus, his neighbor, pounded on his back in the time-honored fashion, the cousins' eyes met in a way that frightened Hans Castorp even more than the incident itself, which of course could happen to anyone; and then Joachim lowered his eyes, hid his face in his napkin, and left the table and the dining hall to cough himself out elsewhere.

He returned after ten minutes, a little pale, smiled, apologized for the disturbance he had caused, and then rejoined the others in disposing of the rich, heavy meal. This trivial incident was even forgotten afterward, was not mentioned once. But when the same thing happened again a few days later, not at dinner this time, but at their ample second breakfast, though without their eyes meeting—since Hans Castorp was bent down over his plate and went on eating, seeming to pay no attention—they could not avoid commenting on it after the meal; and Joachim cursed that damn woman, Fräulein Mylendonk, who had put a bug in his ear with that question of hers out of nowhere, had put notions in his head, had cast a spell on him, damn her. Yes, it was apparently the power of suggestion, Hans Castorp said—an amusing, though annoying instance of it. And from then on, once they had called the thing by its name, Joachim defended himself successfully against this sorcery, paid close attention at meals, and did not swallow the wrong way, or at least no more often than unbewitched people. It was nine or ten days later before it happened again, and there was no need to comment on it.

All the same, he was summoned to Rhadamanthus out of turn. The head nurse had informed on him, which was really not all that foolish of her; there was a laryngoscope in the house, after all, and given Joachim's stubborn hoarseness, which sometimes progressed to a total loss of voice for hours, and given his sore throat, which returned whenever he neglected to keep his throat moistened with medications that increased salivary flow, there seemed sufficient reason to take that ingenious instrument from the cupboard—not to mention the fact that although Joachim swallowed the wrong way with normal infrequency, he did so only because of the special care he took when eating, so that he was almost always slow to finish his meal.

And so the director scoped, mirrored, and gazed deep and long down Joachim's throat; immediately afterward, the patient appeared on Hans Castorp's balcony, as explicitly requested, to give a report. It had been a ticklish nuisance, he confided in a half-whisper, since this was the main rest cure and silence was the rule. All Behrens had done was babble on about inflammation of this and that, had said that the throat would have to be painted every day and that he would start the procedure the next morning, since he first had to prepare the cauterant. So, then, inflammation, cauterization. Hans Castorp's head was full of thoughts and associations that extended as far as people like the limping concierge and the woman who had kept one hand pressed to her ear for a whole week and was told nevertheless to set her mind at ease; there were questions on the tip of his tongue, but he could not get them out and decided instead to ask them of the director in private. His comments to Joachim were limited to an expression of satisfaction that the annoyance was under control now that the director had taken a hand in the matter. Behrens was a brick of a fellow and would come up with a cure. To which Joachim nodded without looking at his cousin, turned, and walked across to his own balcony.

And how did things stand with honor-loving Joachim? In the last few days his glance had become very unsteady and reticent. Only recently Head Nurse Mylendonk had failed yet again in an attempt to fix his gentle, dark eyes with a piercing stare; but if she were to try her luck again, it was no longer absolutely certain how things would turn out. At any rate, he avoided such meetings of the eye, and even when they did occur (because Hans Castorp looked at him often), it did not make his cousin feel any better. Hans Castorp stayed behind on his balcony, depressed and sorely tempted to go see the boss then and there. But that was no good, since Joachim would have heard him get up, and so he decided he had best put it off and catch Behrens sometime later in the afternoon.

But with no success. Strange. He found it impossible to get hold of the director, either that evening or for the next two whole days. Of course,

Joachim was part of the problem, since he was not supposed to notice, but that did not begin to explain why he could not manage a conference, why, try as he might, he could not lay his hands on Rhadamanthus. Hans Castorp searched and asked for the director all over the sanatorium and was sent here or there, where he was sure to find him—only to discover he was no longer there. Behrens was present at one meal, but sat a good distance away, at the Bad Russian table, and vanished before dessert. A few times Hans Castorp saw him climbing the stairs or standing in the corridor talking with Krokowski, the head nurse, or another patient; he would watch and wait to buttonhole him. But he had looked away for just a moment, and Behrens was gone.

On the fourth day he succeeded. From his balcony, he spotted his quarry in the garden, giving instructions to the gardener. Slipping hastily out of his blankets, he hurried downstairs. The director, his neck arched, was just rowing off toward home; Hans Castorp broke into a trot, even took the freedom of shouting—but got no response. He caught up at last, out of breath, and brought his man to a halt.

"What are you doing here?" the director snapped, his eyes bulging. "Should I have someone give you a special copy of the house rules? As far as I know, it's main rest cure. Your fever chart and your X-ray give you no particular right to go free-lance. We should erect a statue out here somewhere, a scarecrow divinity who will skewer anyone philandering about between two and four. Just what do you want?"

"Herr Behrens, I simply must speak to you for a moment."

"So I've noticed, you've had your mind set on that for some time now. You've been setting traps for me, as if I were some young miss, or God knows what sort of object of your affections. What do you want from me?"

"Beg your pardon, but it's about my cousin, Herr Behrens. His throat is being painted. I'm sure things are progressing well. It is harmless, isn't it, if I may ask?"

"You want everything to be harmless, Castorp, that's the sort of fellow you are. You're not at all averse to getting involved in things that are not harmless, but then you treat them as if they were, and you think that will ingratiate you with God and man. You're something of a coward, man, a phony, and if your cousin calls you a civilian, that's merely a very euphemistic way of putting it."

"That may well be, Herr Behrens. There can be no question that I have many weaknesses of character. But that's the point—there can be no question of that at the moment, and what I've been trying to get from you for three days now is simply—"

"For me to tell you the sweet, sugary, diluted truth. You want to badger me and bore me, until I reinforce your damn phoniness so that you can enjoy your innocent sleep, while others wake and watch and let the gale winds blow."

"My, but you are being hard on me, Herr Behrens. It's just the opposite, I wanted to—"

"Yes, hard on you—and that's not up your alley. Your cousin is quite a different sort of fellow, a man cut from different cloth. He knows what's what. He knows and says *nothing*, do you understand? He doesn't go around tugging on people's sleeves, asking to be hoodwinked with harmlessness. He knew what he was doing, what he was risking, and that's a man for you, who knows how to keep a stiff upper lip, to keep his mouth shut, which is a manly art, but not the sort nice little bipeds like yourself can understand. But this much I'll tell you, Castorp, if you start making a scene, raise a hue and cry and give your civilian feelings free rein, I'll hand you your walking papers. Because men want the company of men up here, if you understand me."

Hans Castorp was silent. His face, too, was blotchy now when it turned pale, his tan too coppery actually to lose color. Finally, his lips quivering, he said, "Thank you, Herr Behrens. I now know what's what myself, since I assume you would not have spoken so—how shall I put it— impressively if things were not serious with Joachim. I dislike scenes and hues and cries myself—that was unfair of you. And when it comes to discretion, I can hold my own, I think I can assure you of that."

"You're fond of your cousin, aren't you, Hans Castorp?" the director asked, suddenly grasping the young man's hand and gazing down at him from his blue, bloodshot, protruding eyes with their white lashes.

"What can I say, Herr Behrens? Such a close relative and such a good friend and my comrade up here." Hans Castorp gave a little sob and turned one heel up and out, so that the foot rested on just the toes.

The director promptly dropped the hand. "Well, then be good to him for these next six to eight weeks," he said. "Just give your native harmlessness free rein—that will please him best. And I will be here, too, to make things as comfortable as possible for an officer and a gentleman."

"It's his larynx, isn't it?" Hans Castorp asked with a nod to the director.

"Laryngeal tuberculosis," Behrens confirmed. "Rapid deterioration. And the tracheal membranes are already looking nasty, too. It may be that shouting orders at drill could have created a *locus minoris resistentiae*. But we'll have to be ready for all sorts of diversions. Not much hope, my lad—none at all, actually. To be sure, we'll do everything possible and feasible."

"His mother . . ." Hans Castorp said.

"Later, later. No hurry. See to it that she slowly gets the picture, but with tact and taste. And now it's off to rest-cure duty with you. He's sure to notice. And it must be awkward to have people talking about you like this behind your back."

Every day Joachim went to have his throat painted. It was a beautiful autumn; his treatments often meant that he came late to dinner in his white flannels and blue coat, looking proper and military, offering curt, friendly, manly, unruffled greetings, begging to be excused for his tardiness, and then sitting down to his meal, which was now prepared especially for him since he could not eat the regular menu for fear of choking. He was served soups, stews, and porridges. His tablemates were quick to realize the situation. They responded to his greetings with poignant courtesy and warmth, addressing him as "Herr Lieutenant." In his absence they asked Hans Castorp about him, and people even came over from other tables to ask. Frau Stöhr arrived wringing her hands and making uncultured lamentation. But Hans Castorp replied only in monosyllables, admitted the seriousness of the situation, but also lied to a certain extent—though honorably, out of a sense that one ought not to abandon Joachim so soon.

They took their walks together, dutifully promenaded three times a day, but only the limited distance expressly prescribed by the director to avoid all unnecessary expenditure of energy. Hans Castorp walked on his cousin's left—in days past they had taken up positions, right or left, as chance would have it; but Hans Castorp now kept consistently to the left. They did not speak much, only the phrases a normal day at the Berghof brought to their lips, nothing more. There was nothing to say about the topic that stood between them, particularly not for people so reserved by custom, who used first names only on the rarest of occasions. All the same, from time to time something would well up urgently inside Hans Castorp's civilian breast, and he would be close to pouring out his feelings. But that was impossible. And what had welled up so painfully, so stormily, sank back and died away.

Joachim walked beside him, his head bent low. He stared at the ground as if examining the soil. It was so strange. Here he walked, so proper and orderly, greeted passersby in his chivalrous way, paying strict attention, as always, to his appearance and *bienséance*—and he belonged to the earth. Well, we all will belong to it sooner or later. But to belong to it when one is so young and has served the colors for such a short time and with such goodwill and joy, that is bitter—even more bitter and incomprehensible for Hans Castorp walking beside him, knowing everything, than for the man who belongs to the earth—whose proper, silent knowledge is actually more academic and less real to him, is less his concern than his companion's. In fact, our dying is more a concern to those who survive us than to ourselves; for as a wise man once cleverly put it, as long as we are, death is not, and when death is, we are not; and even if we are unfamiliar with that adage, it retains its psychological validity. There is no real relationship between us and death; it is something that does not apply to us at all, but at best to nature and the world at large—which is why all creatures can contemplate it with composure, indifference, irresponsibility, and egoistic innocence. Hans Castorp saw a great deal of this innocence and irresponsibility in Joachim's character during these weeks and understood that although his cousin knew, that did not mean it was difficult for him to observe a decorous silence about his knowledge, for his inner relationship to it was loose and merely theoretical; and in terms of any practical considerations, it was all ordered and governed by a healthy sense of propriety, which no more permitted a discussion of such knowledge than it does of any of the many indelicate functions we are quite aware condition life, but do not prevent us from preserving *bienséance*.

And so they walked and said nothing about the indecencies of nature. And even Joachim's earlier agitated and angry complaints—about missing maneuvers and generally neglecting his military duties in the flatlands— had died away. And yet why, despite such great innocence, did that expression of sad shyness keep creeping back into his gentle eyes—that same unsteadiness that might have ended in victory for the head nurse, had she chanced it one more time? Was it because he knew that his cheeks looked hollow, that his eyes looked crossed? Because over these last weeks such changes were much more visible than when he had first returned from the flatlands, and his tanned face was turning more yellow and leathery from day to day. It was as if the same surroundings that had prompted Herr Albin to think of nothing but enjoying the boundless advantages of disgrace, had caused Joachim only shame and self-reproach. What or whom was he dodging when he hid his once so open gaze? How strange that a creature feels ashamed before life and slinks into its den to perish, convinced that it cannot hope to encounter any respect or reverence for its sufferings and death throes—and rightly so, for joyous birds on the wing show no honor to a sick comrade in their flock, but instead peck him angrily, disdainfully with their beaks. That is base nature's way— but a very human, loving mercy swelled up in Hans Castorp's breast when he saw that dark, instinctive shame in poor Joachim's eyes. He walked on the left, made a point of doing so; and since Joachim had become somewhat unsteady on his feet, Hans Castorp was sure to offer him a hand when they were confronted with a gentle meadow slope; overcoming his customary reserve, he would put an arm around him, might even forget for a while to remove it again from Joachim's shoulders, until his cousin shook him off in slight annoyance and said, "Say there, what's this? We look like two drunks wandering along."

But there came a day when young Hans Castorp saw the sadness in Joachim's eyes in a different light; it was in early November—the snow was already deep—and Joachim had been given orders to stay in bed. By then it was difficult for him to manage even stews and porridges, and every second bite went down the wrong way. The time had come for a strict liquid diet, and Behrens used the occasion to prescribe constant bed rest as a means of preserving the patient's energies. It was on the eve of Joachim's retiring to his bed for good, his last evening on his feet, that Hans Castorp happened upon him—in conversation with Marusya, with Marusya of the unwarranted giggles, the orange-scented handkerchiefs, and the externally well-formed chest. It was after supper, during the evening social, out in the lobby. Hans Castorp had been in the music room and came out to see what had become of Joachim, and he found him standing in front of the tiled stove, next to Marusya's chair—a rocking chair and Joachim was holding onto it with his left hand, tilting it back, so that Marusya was in a reclining position, looking up out of her little, round, brown eyes into Joachim's face, which was bent down over hers, uttering soft, disjointed phrases, to which she would occasionally respond with a smile or a nervous, disparaging shrug.

Hans Castorp beat a hasty retreat, but not before he realized that other guests of the sanatorium, as was common here, were watching the scene with an amused eye—without Joachim's noticing, or perhaps caring. What a sight: Joachim recklessly indulging in conversation with high-breasted Marusya, a person with whom he had never exchanged a single word during the whole time they had sat at the same table and at the mention of whose name he had always lowered his eyes and assumed a stern, reasonable, honor-loving expression, though his face had turned blotchy and pale. And it shocked Hans Castorp more than any other sign of his poor cousin's failing strength that he had noticed over the past weeks. "Yes, he is lost," he thought and sat quietly for a while in the music room to give Joachim time for whatever it was he was allowing himself out there in the lobby on his last evening.

From then on Joachim assumed a permanent horizontal position, and Hans Castorp wrote to Luise Ziemssen about it—wrote to her from his splendid lounge chair that he must now add to his earlier occasional reports the news that Joachim was bedfast and that although his cousin had said nothing, one could see in his eyes that it was his wish to have his mother beside him, and that Director Behrens had expressly seconded this unspoken wish. He gently, clearly made that point as well. It was no wonder, then, that Frau Ziemssen took the earliest, fastest train she could find to join her son. She arrived only three days after this humane alert had been sent off, and Hans Castorp fetched her by sleigh from the station in Dorf—stood there in a snow flurry on the platform before the little train arrived and composed his face, so that Joachim's mother would not be too alarmed at first glance, but would not read any false message of good cheer in it, either.

How often must these scenes of greeting have happened here, how often had two people rushed toward one another, the traveler who had just climbed from the train urgently searching the eyes of the person who had come to greet her. Frau Ziemssen gave the impression that she had run here all the way from Hamburg. Her face was flushed, she clasped Hans Castorp's hand and pulled it to her breast; glancing anxiously all about, she hastily posed her almost furtive questions, which Hans Castorp avoided answering by thanking her for having come so quickly—it was spiffing of her. How happy Joachim would be to see her. Yes, well, he was bedridden for now, primarily because of the liquid diet he was on, which of course could not help affecting his energies. But there were, if need be, all sorts of other expedients, intravenous feeding for example. But then, she would see for herself.

She saw, and at her side, Hans Castorp saw, too. Until that moment the changes that Joachim had undergone in the last weeks had not been so noticeable—young people do not have much of an eye for such things. But now, standing beside the mother who had rushed here from elsewhere, he looked at his cousin with her eyes, as it were, as if he had not seen him for a long time, and saw clearly and distinctly what she doubtless also recognized and Joachim certainly knew better than either of them: that he was a *moribundus*. Joachim grasped Frau Ziemssen's hand with hands that were as yellow and wasted as his emaciated face, from which his ears, the one minor sorrow of his youth, stuck out more than ever; but despite that regrettable disfigurement, suffering had stamped his face with an expression of austere earnestness, even pride, and he still looked very manly—although the lips beneath his dark little moustache seemed too full now against the shadows of his hollow cheeks. Two deep creases were engraved in the yellowish skin between his eyes, which although they had sunk deep into their bony sockets, were larger and more beautiful than ever. Hans Castorp took comfort in that, because all the worry, gloom, and unsteadiness had vanished from them now that his cousin was bedfast, and only the light he had noticed early on was visible in their calm, dark—and, to be sure, *ominous*—depths. Joachim did not smile as he held his mother's hand and whispered his welcome. He had not even smiled when she first entered the room; and that immobility, that immutability in his expression said everything.

Luise Ziemssen was a brave woman. She did not go to pieces at the sight of her fine son. As composed and restrained as the almost invisible hairnet holding her hair in place, as detached and energetic as the people of her native land were known to be, she took charge of Joachim's care, was spurred on to maternal battle by what she saw, and was firm in her faith that if anything could be done, it would be done thanks only to her energy and vigilance. And when a few days later she agreed to bring in a nurse, it was certainly not for the sake of her own comfort, but only because she knew what was fitting and proper. And Sister Berta—Alfreda Schildknecht, to be precise—was hired; carrying her black handbag, she appeared at Joachim's bedside. But whether day or night, Frau Ziemssen's jealous energies left Sister Berta little to do, and she had plenty of time to stand out in the hallway, the cord of her pince-nez tucked behind one ear, and keep a curious eye on things.

She was a prosaic soul, this Protestant nurse. But one day, when left in the room with Hans Castorp and her patient, who definitely was not asleep, but lying on his back with his eyes open, she blithely remarked, "I never would have dreamed it, either—that I would be nursing one of you gentlemen to the bitter end."

Hans Castorp's face registered his horror and fury, and he shook a fist at her. But she hardly seemed to understand what he wanted—since, quite rightly, the idea would never have occurred to her that it might be more tactful to spare Joachim and she was much too businesslike to think that anyone, and certainly not a close relative, could possibly indulge in self-deception as to the nature and outcome of the case. "Here," she said, pouring some cologne on a handkerchief and holding it under Joachim's nose, "do something nice for yourself, Herr Lieutenant." And indeed there was little point now in trying to pull the wool over Joachim's eyes—except for tonic effect, as Frau Ziemssen put it when she spoke to her son about his recovery in a brisk, stirring voice. For there could be no mistaking two obvious facts: first, Joachim was approaching death with his mind clear; and second, he did so contentedly and at peace with himself. Only in his last week, at the end of November, after the weakness in his heart had become noticeable, were there times when his mind would wander and he would suddenly grow confused about his condition and speak hopefully and happily of a speedy return to his regiment and of taking part in the grand maneuvers that he obviously thought were still under way. It was at this same period, however, that Director Behrens stopped holding out any hopes whatever and told the family it was only a question of hours.

Even the most manly men succumb to credulous, oblivious self-deception; the phenomenon is as natural as it is melancholy when the process of deterioration approaches its fatal end—natural and impersonal and beyond all individual conscious effort, much as the temptation to wander in circles overcomes someone who is lost or sleep ensnares someone freezing to death. Hans Castorp's grief and worry did not prevent him from focusing objectively on this phenomenon, and he formulated awkward, but clearheaded observations about it in his conversations with Naphta and Settembrini, when he would report to them about his cousin's condition; he was rebuked by the Italian, however, for observing that there was an underlying error in the conventional notion that philosophical credulity and sanguine trust in the good are expressions of health, whereas pessimism and condemnation of the world are signs of illness; because otherwise the bleak final state could not bring forth an optimism, compared to whose awful rosiness the preceding gloom seemed a coarse, but healthy expression of life. At the same time, he could also report to them, thank God, that Rhadamanthus allowed for some hope amid the hopelessness and prophesied a gentle, painless exitus despite Joachim's youth.

"An idyllic affair of the heart, my gracious lady," he said, holding Luise Ziemssen's hand in his two shovel-size mitts and gazing down at her from his protruding, watery, bloodshot blue eyes. "I'm so glad, so tremendously glad that things are taking this serene course, and that he will not have to suffer edema of the glottis and other such beastly problems—he will be spared a great many vexations. His heart is giving out rapidly, luckily for him, luckily for us. We shall do our duty, do what we can with camphor injections, with little danger of side effects. I think I can promise that he will sleep a lot toward the last and dream pleasant dreams, and if at the very end he is unable to sleep, his passing will nevertheless be swift, imperceptible—it won't even matter much to him, you can be sure of that. It's always that way, really. I know death, I'm one of his old employees. He's overrated, believe me. I can assure you there's almost nothing to him. The drudgeries that do on occasion *precede* death can hardly be credited to him, since they just prove that someone is alive and kicking and may lead back to life and health. But if anyone ever did come back, they could not tell you much about death, since we don't actually meet him. We come out of darkness and return to darkness, with some experiences in between. But we don't experience the beginning and the end, birth and death. We are not subjectively aware of them, they exist only in the world of objective events—and that's that."

This was the director's way of offering consolation. We shall hope it did some good with a woman as reasonable as Frau Ziemssen. And his assurances did turn out, for the most part, as predicted. In his weakened state, Joachim slept for many hours during his final days, and probably dreamed dreams he thought pleasant—of military maneuvers in the flat-lands, we assume. And when he did awaken and was asked how he felt, he would always answer, though somewhat indistinctly, that he felt fine and happy—although he had hardly any pulse left and ultimately did not even notice the prick of the hypodermic. His body felt nothing; they could have burned and pinched him, it would have made no difference to Joachim at that point.

And yet he had undergone great changes since his mother's arrival. Shaving had become difficult for him, and although he had a heavy beard that grew rapidly, nothing had been done about it for eight or ten days, so that his waxen face with its gentle eyes was now framed by a full black beard—a warrior's beard, the kind a soldier might grow out in the field. It looked handsome and manly on him, they all said. Yes, the beard—though not it alone—suddenly changed Joachim from a youth to a mature man. Like a clock whirring too fast, he had been living rapidly, galloping through each stage of life that time would never allow him to reach. Over his last twenty-four hours he became an old man. His weak heart caused his face to swell, giving it a strained look that made Hans Castorp think that at the least dying must be a great labor, although Joachim no longer seemed to notice it much, because his senses were diminished and he had lapses in consciousness. The swelling was worst around the lips, and the inside of his mouth was dry or numbed; together these conditions obvi-ously made it difficult for Joachim to speak, he mumbled like a very old man and was himself quite annoyed by the impediment. If only he could speak, he said thickly, everything would be fine—it was a damn nuisance.

What he meant by "everything would be fine" was not exactly clear—it became quite evident that his condition tended to create ambiguities, and he expressed himself equivocally more than once, seemed both to know and not to know, and at one point, apparently overcome by a wave of approaching devastation, he shook his head almost in remorse and declared that he had never felt this bad, never in all his life.

Then his mood turned intransigent, sternly diffident, even boorish; he would not listen to any more fibs or pretty stories, refused to answer them, and stared strangely straight ahead. Especially after the young pastor—whom Luise Ziemssen had summoned and who, to Hans Castorp's regret, had not worn a starched ruff but only Geneva bands—arrived to pray with him, his attitude grew more officially military and his wishes were only blunt commands.

Around six in the evening he began to do something curious. He repeatedly stretched out his right arm, the one with the gold bracelet around the wrist, until it was at about his hip, then raised his hand slightly and pulled it back again along the blanket with a raking or scraping motion, as if he were collecting or gathering something.

At seven o'clock he died—Alfreda Schildknecht was out in the hall, only his mother and cousin were present. He had slipped down too far in his bed and curtly demanded to be propped back up again. As Frau Ziemssen attempted to follow his instructions and was slipping an arm around his shoulders, he remarked rather hastily that he would have to draft and send a letter requesting his leave be extended, and no sooner had he said it than his "swift passing" took place—which Hans Castorp watched reverently by the light of the red-shaded table lamp. The gaze faltered, the unconscious strain left the features, the painful swelling vanished rapidly from the lips, a more handsome, youthful look spread across our Joachim's silenced countenance, and it was over.

Luise Ziemssen turned away sobbing, and so it was Hans Castorp who reached out with his ring finger to close the eyelids of the motionless form that no longer breathed, then carefully laid the hands together on the blanket. Then he stood there, too, and wept, let the tears flow down his cheeks, like those that had stung the cheeks of the English naval officer—the colorless liquid that flows at every hour everywhere in the world, so richly and bitterly that earth's vale has poetically been named after it: an alkaline, salty liquid that our body secretes from glands when our nerves are subjected to the shock of pain, whether physical or psychological. He knew that it also contains traces of mucin and protein.

The director came after being notified by Sister Berta. He had been there only a half hour before to give an injection of camphor, had just missed the moment of swift passing. "Yes, well, he has it behind him," he said simply, rising back up with his stethoscope from Joachim's quiet breast. And then he extended a hand to each relative and added a little nod. He stood for a while together with them beside the bed, gazing at Joachim's impassive face with its warrior's beard. "Crazy lad, crazy fellow," he said thrusting his head back over one shoulder at the body lying there. "Wanted to force it, you see—because of course all his duties down below were force and violence—did his duty with a fever, come hell or high water. The field of honor, you see—hightailed it for the field of honor, kicked over the traces. But honor was the death of him, or—if you turn it the other way around—death did him the honor. Crazy kid he was, crazy fellow." And he left, taking long strides and bent forward so that his neck vertebrae protruded.

It was agreed that Joachim should be returned home, and the Berghof took care of all arrangements necessary for the transport and whatever else seemed fitting and stately. His mother and cousin barely had to lift a finger. By morning, Joachim lay on his bed dressed in a ruffled shirt and with flowers placed beside him, and in the bright light reflected off the snow he looked even more handsome than he had at his passing. Every trace of strain was gone from his face; it had stiffened as it turned cold and was now pure, silent form. Little dark curls fell down across his immobile, yellowish brow, which looked as if it were made of some noble, yet delicate material halfway between wax and marble, and the arch of his lips was full and proud under his slightly curly moustache. An antique helmet would have looked good on that head, as was noted by several visitors who came by to say farewell.

Frau Stöhr wept with enthusiasm at the sight of what had once been Joachim. "A hero! A hero!" she cried several times and demanded that they play Beethoven's *Erotica* at his graveside.

"Silence!" Settembrini hissed in her direction. Both he and Naphta were in the room with her, and he was sincerely moved. He gestured with both hands for those present to look at Joachim, insisting they mourn with him. "*Un giovanotto tanto simpatico, tanto stimabile!*" he exclaimed over and over.

Naphta did not look up from his own constrained pose, but he could not refrain from whispering a cutting remark in Settembrini's direction: "I'm glad to see you have feelings not just for freedom and progress, but for serious matters as well."

Settembrini swallowed the insult. Perhaps he felt that under the circumstances Naphta was temporarily in a superior position; perhaps it was this momentary supremacy of his foe that he had been attempting to counter with lively expressions of grief and that now silenced him—and kept him silent when Leo Naphta exploited his fleeting advantage by declaring with caustic sententiousness: "The error of literary men is to believe that only the Spirit makes us respectable. The opposite is closer to the truth. Only where there is *no* Spirit are we respectable."

"Well," Hans Castorp thought, "there's a Delphic remark for you. And if you purse your lips tight after delivering it, that will certainly intimidate everyone for a bit."

That afternoon the metal coffin arrived. Joachim's transfer into this stately container trimmed with rings and lion's heads was strictly a one-man job, or so the fellow who brought it claimed, an associate of the undertaking establishment that had been hired, who was dressed in a short, black frock coat and wore a wedding ring on his plebeian hand, the yellow circlet embedded deep in flesh, which had, so to speak, over-grown it. One might have been tempted to think his frock coat gave off a grisly odor, but that would have been pure prejudice. The man made it clear, however, that he fancied himself a specialist whose activities had to take place backstage, with only the results of his endeavors displayed for pious review by the bereaved—all of which aroused Hans Castorp's mistrust. This was not at all what he had in mind. He agreed that Frau Ziemssen should withdraw, but refused to bow out himself and stayed behind to lend a hand; he grabbed the body under the armpits and helped transfer it from bed to coffin, where Joachim's remains then lay solemnly bedded atop linen sheets and a tasseled pillow, with candelabra provided by the Berghof set on either side.

Two days later, however, something occurred to convince Hans Castorp to detach himself emotionally from this shell and leave things to the professional, that offensive guardian of piety. Joachim, whose expression so far had been earnest and honorable, began to smile under his beard. Hans Castorp could not help admitting that this smile bore within it the seeds of degeneration—and it filled his heart with a sense of haste. Thank God, the body would soon be picked up, the coffin closed and screwed shut. Setting aside his native reserve, Hans Castorp touched his lips in a gesture of tender farewell to the stone-cold brow of what had once been Joachim, and despite his misgivings, turned his back on the undertaker and meekly followed Luise Ziemssen out of the room.

We let the curtain fall now, to rise but one more time. But while it rustles to the floor, we wish to join Hans Castorp, left behind on those distant heights, as he gazes in his mind down on a wet garden of crosses in the lowlands, watches a sword flash and then lower, hears barked commands and the three volleys that follow, the three fervent rounds of honor bursting above Joachim Ziemssen's soldier's grave, thick with matted roots.

7

A Stroll by the Shore

CAN ONE NARRATE TIME—time as such, in and of itself? Most certainly not, what a foolish undertaking that would be. The story would go: "Time passed, ran on, flowed in a mighty stream," and on and on in the same vein. No one with any common sense could call that a narrative. It would be the same as if someone took the harebrained notion of holding a single note or chord for hours on end—and called it music. Because a story is like music in that it *fills* time, "fills it up so nice and properly," "divides it up," so that there is "something to it," "something going on"—to quote, with the melancholy reverence one shows to statements made by the dead, a few casual comments of the late Joachim, phrases that faded away long ago, and we are not sure if the reader is quite clear just how long ago that was. Time is the *element* of narration, just as it is the element of life—is inextricably bound up with it, as bodies are in space. It is also the element of music, which itself measures and divides time, making it suddenly diverting and precious; and related to music, as we have noted, is the story, which also can only present itself in successive events, as movement toward an end (and not as something suddenly, brilliantly present, like a work of visual art, which is pure body bound to time), and even if it would try to be totally here in each moment, would still need time for its presentation.

That much is perfectly obvious. But that there is a difference is equally clear. The time element of music is singular: a segment of human earthly existence in which it gushes forth, thereby ineffably enhancing and ennobling life. Narrative, however, has two kinds of time: first, its own real time, which like musical time defines its movement and presentation; and second, the time of its contents, which has a perspective quality that can vary widely, from a story in which the narrative's imaginary time is almost, or indeed totally coincident with its musical time, to one in which it stretches out over light-years. A musical piece entitled "Five Minute Waltz" lasts five minutes—this and only this defines its relationship to time. A story whose contents involved a time span of five minutes, however, could, by means of an extraordinary scrupulosity in filling up those five minutes, last a thousand times as long—and still remain short on boredom, although in relationship to its imaginary time it would be very long in the telling. On the other hand, it is possible for a narrative's content-time to exceed its own duration immeasurably. This is accomplished by diminishment—and we use this term to describe an illusory, or, to be quite explicit, diseased element, that is obviously pertinent here: diminishment occurs to some extent whenever a narrative makes use of hermetic magic and a temporal hyperperspective reminiscent of certain anomalous experiences of reality that imply that the senses have been transcended. The diaries of opium-eaters record how, during the brief period of ecstasy, the drugged person's dreams have a temporal scope of ten, thirty, sometimes sixty years or even surpass all limits of man's ability to experience time—dreams, that is, whose imaginary time span vastly exceeds their actual duration and which are characterized by an incredible diminishment of the experience of time, with images thronging past so swiftly that, as one hashish-smoker puts it, the intoxicated user's brain seems "to have had something removed, like the mainspring from a broken watch."

A narrative, then, can set to work and deal with time in much the same way as those depraved dreams. But since it can "deal" with time, it is clear that time, which is the element of the narrative, can also become its *subject*; and although it would be going too far to say that one can "narrate time," it is apparently not such an absurd notion to want to narrate *about time*—so that a term like "time novel" may well take on an oddly dreamlike double meaning. And indeed we posed the question about whether one could narrate time precisely in order to say that we actually have something like that in mind with this ongoing story. And in touching upon the wider question of whether those gathered around us were quite clear about how long it had actually been since the now-deceased, honor-loving Joachim wove those comments about time and music into a conversation (which in fact revealed a certain alchemistic enhancement of his own character, since such remarks were not part of his upright nature), we would hardly have been irritated to learn that our readers really were no longer quite clear about the matter at the moment—hardly irritated, indeed we would be content, for the simple reason that a general sympathy for our hero and his experiences naturally lies in our own interest. And he, Hans Castorp, was not quite certain about the matter himself, and had not been for a good while. That uncertainty is very much part of his novel, a "time novel"—whether taken in one sense or the other.

How long had Joachim actually lived up here with him, whether measured until his wild departure or taken as a whole? What had been the date on the calendar of his first defiant departure? How long had he been gone, when had he returned, and how long had Hans Castorp himself been here when he did return and then took leave of time? How long, to set Joachim aside for now, had Frau Chauchat not been present? How long, purely in terms of years, was it now since she was *back again* (because she was back again); and how much earthly time had Hans Castorp spent at the Berghof until the day she came back? In response to all such questions—assuming someone had posed them to him, which, however, no one did, not even he to himself, for he was probably afraid of posing them—Hans Castorp would have drummed his fingertips on his brow and most assuredly known no definite answer: a phenomenon no less disquieting than the temporary inability to tell Herr Settembrini his own age on his first evening here; indeed, it represented a worsening of that incapacity, for he now seriously no longer knew at any time just how old he was.

That may sound bizarre, but it is far from improbable or unprecedented, and given certain conditions it can happen to any of us at any time; under such conditions, nothing could prevent us from sinking into profound ignorance about the passage of time and so about our own age. The phenomenon is possible because we lack an internal organ for time, because, that is, if left on our own without external clues, we are totally incapable of even approximate reliability when estimating elapsed time. A group of miners buried by a cave-in, and cut off from observing the sequence of day and night, were rescued at last and guessed the period of time they had spent in the dark, between hope and despair, at three days. And it had been ten. One would think that in such an agonizing situation time would have had to have seemed longer to them. And yet it had shrunk to less than a third of its objective proportions. And judging from that, it appears that under confusing conditions, man in his helplessness tends to experience time in a greatly diminished form rather than to overestimate it.

No one disputes, of course, that it would have been no great burden for Hans Castorp, had he truly wanted, to reckon his way out of ignorance and into clarity, just as any reader can do with no great difficulty if he should feel that this blurred, tangled web offends his common sense. As for Hans Castorp, he did not feel all that at ease with the blurry tangle, perhaps; but he was not about to waste any exertion wrestling himself free in order to determine how old he had now become up here. What held him back were scruples of conscience—although it was patently most unconscionable to pay no attention to time.

We do not know if he should be exonerated because circumstances favored his lack of good intentions—that is, if one chooses not to speak of his bad intentions. Frau Chauchat's return (and her return had been very different from anything Hans Castorp had dreamed—but of that at the appropriate time) had coincided with a return of the season of Advent and the year's shortest days; the beginning of winter, astronomically speaking, had been imminent. In reality, however—that is, apart from any theoretical system—in terms of snow and cold, it had been winter now for God knew how long; winter had been interrupted, as always, only very briefly by scorching summer days with a sky whose blue was so inordinately deep that it verged on black—by summer days, then, that could occur in the midst of winter, too, if you ignored the snow, which, by the by, could also fall at any time during summer. How often Hans Castorp had chatted with the late Joachim about the grand confusion that mixed up the seasons higgledy-piggledy, robbing the year of its divisions and making it diverting in a boring sort of way, or boring in a diverting sort of way, until, as the late Joachim had put it out of pure disgust early on, there was no time as such. What got mixed up so higgledy-piggledy in this grand confusion were those emotional concepts and states of consciousness that define "still" and "again"—which is one of the most bewildering, perplexing, and bewitching experiences there is. And from his very first day up here Hans Castorp had felt an immoral appetite to taste that experience—in particular at the five prodigious meals in the cheerfully stenciled dining hall, where he had had his first slight, and relatively innocent, dizzy spell of this sort.

Since then, this deception of mind and senses had assumed much larger dimensions. Time, although the subjective experience of it may be weakened or even abrogated, is an objective reality to the extent that it is active and "brings forth." Are hermetically sealed preserves on the shelf outside of time? That is a question for the professional philosopher—and it was only out of youthful presumption that Hans Castorp had got himself mixed up in the topic. We do know that time does its work even on a hibernating dormouse. A physician has attested to the case of a twelve-year-old girl who fell asleep one day, and remained asleep for thirteen years—during that time, however, she did not remain a twelve-year-old girl, but grew into an adult female. How could it be otherwise? The dead man is dead and has left our temporal world behind; he has a lot of time, which is to say, he has none at all—personally speaking. That does not prevent his nails and hair from growing, or that all in all—but we shall not repeat the slang idiom that Joachim once used in this same context and that at the time offended Hans Castorp's flatland sensitivities. His hair and nails were growing, too, growing quickly it seemed, because a fringe of hair kept overlapping the edges of the ears; and he frequently sat, a white cape wrapped around him, in the adjustable chair in the barber shop on the main street of Dorf and had his hair cut—he was forever sitting there, it seemed. Or rather, when Hans Castorp sat there and chatted away with the fawning barber deftly doing his work, after time had done its, or when he stood at his balcony door and cut his nails with the shears and file he had taken from a pretty velvet etui, he was suddenly overcome with the old dizziness that was mixed with a scary sense of curious delight, an ambiguous dizziness that made him feel not only unsteady, but also beguiled by his whirling inability to differentiate between "still" and "again," out of whose blurred jumble emerge the timeless "always" and "ever."

We have often declared that we do not wish to make him any better or any worse than he was, and so we do not want to hide the fact that he frequently took countermeasures to try to atone for the reprehensible pleasure he found in mystic disturbances that he quite consciously and intentionally elicited himself. He would sit, his watch open in his hand—his flat, smooth gold pocket watch with his monogram engraved on its spring case—and look down at its round porcelain surface encircled with a double row of black and red Arabic numerals, at the two splendid delicately ornamented golden hands spreading in different directions, and at the slender second hand busily pecking its way around its own special circle. Hans Castorp would gaze steadily at it, trying to slow and expand a few minutes, to hold time by the tail. The little hand tripped along paying no heed to the numerals as it came up on them, touched and passed them, left them behind, far behind, and returned to come up on them again. It had no sense of goals, segments, measurements. It could have stopped at the 60 for a moment or at least given some tiny signal that something had been accomplished. But from the way it quickly moved past it, treating it no differently than any unnumbered mark, it was evident that the whole set of numerals and strokes had only been *laid under* its path, and that it just kept going, and going. And so Hans Castorp would slip this product of the jeweler's art back into his vest pocket and let time take care of itself.

How can we help principled flatlanders understand the changes taking place in our young adventurer's interior economy? The scope of his dizzying equations grew. Where previously, by yielding just slightly, he had not found it easy to separate the "now" of today from that of yesterday, or the day before yesterday, or the day before that, when all were alike as peas in a pod, of late that same "now" was apt, even likely, to muddle its present with a present that had prevailed a month or a year before, and to fuse into an "always." But since his moral states of consciousness kept "still," "again," and "next" separate to some extent, the temptation grew to expand relational terms like "yesterday" and "tomorrow"— words by which "today" holds the past and the future at arm's length— and to apply them to still larger contexts. It is not difficult to imagine creatures, on smaller planets perhaps, who administer a miniaturized time and for whose "short" life the nimble, mincing steps of our second hand possess the dogged spatial frugality of an hour hand. But it is also possible to imagine creatures whose space requires time to move at a pace so monumental that in their experience our terms for describing intervals like "just now" and "in a bit" acquire the vastly expanded meaning of "yesterday" and "tomorrow." That would be, we repeat, not only possible, but when viewed in the spirit of a tolerant relativism à la "when in Rome," it might also be considered legitimate, healthy, and respectable. But what should one think of a son of this earth—at an age, moreover, when a day, a week, a month, a semester should play an important role in life and bring a great many changes and much progress—who one day acquires the disgraceful habit, or at least yields occasionally to the pleasure, of saying "yesterday" for "a year ago" and "tomorrow" for "a year from now"? There is no doubt that it would be appropriate to judge him as "lost and confused" and worthy of our gravest concern.

There are situations in life on earth, or circumstances of landscape (if one can speak of "landscape" in this case), in which a confusion and obliteration of temporal and spatial distances, ending in total dizzying monotony, is more or less natural and legitimate, so that immersion into its magic during a vacation, for instance, might likewise be considered legitimate. We are talking about a stroll by the shore—a state of being for which Hans Castorp always felt a great partiality; and, as we know, he gratefully enjoyed thinking of life in the snow as reminiscent of the rolling dunes of his homeland. We assume that our reader's experiences and memories will join us as we expand on this marvelous state of lostness. You walk and walk, and you never get back home on time, because you are lost to time and it to you. O sea—we sit here telling our story far from you, but our eyes and heart turn toward you now, and we explicitly invoke you, speak your name aloud, making you as present as you constantly have been, are, always will be, in our silent thoughts . . . Blustering wasteland, spanned by pale, bright gray, drenched with a dry, salty tang that clings to our lips. We walk and walk along the light springy beach strewn with seaweed and tiny shells, our ears swathed by the wind, by the great, ample, mild wind that passes freely through space, unencumbered and without malice, filling our heads with a gentle numbness—we wander, wander and watch the roiling sea send tongues of onrushing foam to lick our feet and fall back again. The surf seethes, wave upon silken wave crashes with a bright thud against the level beach—here, there, on sandbars farther out. And the universal turmoil, the tenderly booming din closes our ears against every other voice in the world. Profound contentment, knowing forgetfulness. Sheltered in eternity, let us close our eyes. No, look, there in the foamy gray-green expanse as it loses itself, diminishing vastly against the horizon, there is a sail. There? What sort of there? How far? How near? You do not know. It dizzyingly evades all certainty. To say how far the boat is from the shore you would have to know its size. Small and near, or large and distant? And in your ignorance, your gaze falters, for no organ, no internal sense, can tell you for sure. We walk and walk—how long has it been now? How far? It does not matter. And at every step, nothing changes—"there" is "here," "before" is both "now" and "then." Time drowns in the unmeasured monotony of space. Where uniformity reigns, movement from point to point is no longer movement; and where movement is no longer movement, there is no time.

The scholastics of the Middle Ages claimed to know that time is an illusion, its flow toward objective consequences due solely to our sensory apparatus, and that the true state of things is a permanent now. Was he walking by the sea, that professor who was first struck by this notion, the faint bitter taste of eternity on his lips? In any case, we repeat that we are speaking of vacation scenes, of fantasies in moments of leisure, of which the moral intellect quickly has its fill, like a vigorous man who has rested long enough in the warm sand. For us to criticize the methods and forms by which human beings come to know things, to question their validity per se, would be absurd, dishonorable, antagonistic, if we did so for any other purpose than to point out those limits to reason that reason can never overstep without being guilty of neglecting its own tasks. We can only be grateful to a man like Herr Settembrini for characterizing metaphysics as "evil" as he once did when speaking, with his usual pedagogic decisiveness, to the young man with whose fate we are concerned and whom on one occasion he very aptly called a "problem child of life."

And we can best honor the memory of a young man, who though departed is still dear to us, by saying that the critical principle can and must have only one meaning, purpose, and goal: the idea of duty, the command given by life itself. Yes, when law-giving wisdom critically staked out the limits of reason, it also planted the flag of life at those same boundaries and proclaimed that it is man's soldierly duty to serve beneath that banner. But Hans Castorp's military cousin had been a "zealot"—as a melancholic show-off once said—and that had led to a fatal outcome. Might we perhaps find some excuse for our young hero's behavior in assuming that such an outcome encouraged him in his disgraceful management of time, in his wicked dawdling with eternity?

Mynheer Peeperkorn

MYNHEER PEEPERKORN, an elderly Dutchman, had for some time been a guest of the Sanatorium Berghof, which quite rightly appended the adjective "international" to its name. Peeperkorn's nationality and color—for he was a colonial Dutchman, a man from Java, a coffee-planter—would hardly be an incentive, or better, would not of itself be sufficient cause for us to introduce Pieter Peeperkorn (for that was what he called himself, saying, "Pieter Peeperkorn will now regale himself with a schnapps") at this late juncture in our story; for, good Lord, what shades and hues were not to be found in the society of the successful institution under the medical management of *Hofrat* Doctor Behrens, that polyglot of the idiomatic phrase. An Egyptian princess, for instance, had also recently become a guest, the same woman who had once given the director his remarkable coffee service and those sphinx cigarettes, a sensational lady with heavily ringed, nicotine-stained fingers and bobbed hair, who except for the main meal of the day, for which she dressed in finest Parisian fashion, went about clad in a man's jacket and pleated trousers, but otherwise wanted nothing to do with men and devoted her equally indolent and fierce favors exclusively to a Jewish woman from Romania, with the very plain name of Frau Landauer, even though Prosecutor Paravant was so taken by Her Royal Highness that he neglected his mathematics and practically played the fool for love; and not only was there the lady herself, but included in her small retinue was a castrated Moor, a sickly, frail fellow, who despite his fundamental defect, which Karoline Stöhr loved to deride, clung more tightly to life than anyone else and proved inconsolable when presented with the picture taken of the interior that lay beneath his dusky skin.

Compared to such figures, then, Mynheer Peeperkorn might seem almost colorless. And although this chapter of our story might, like an earlier one, bear the title "Someone Else," no one need worry that yet another instigator of intellectual and pedagogic confusion has now made an appearance. No, Mynheer Peeperkorn was certainly not a man to bestow logical confusion upon the world. He was a totally different sort of fellow, as we shall see. But that he nevertheless spread great confusion over our hero can be understood from what now follows.

Mynheer Peeperkorn arrived at the station in Dorf on the evening train with Madame Chauchat and rode in the same sleigh with her to the Berghof, where he also took his evening meal with her in the restaurant. They had arrived not merely simultaneously, they had arrived *together*; and it was this companionship, which continued, for example, in seating arrangements that placed Mynheer beside the returnee at the Good Russian table, opposite the doctor's chair, the seat from which Popóv the teacher had once put on his wild and dubious performances—it was this companionship that upset our good Hans Castorp, because he had failed to see anything of the sort coming. The director had announced the day and hour of Clavdia's return in his own fashion. "Well, Castorp, old boy," he had said, "it pays to be perseverant. Our little pussycat will come slinking home evening after next. Was all in her telegram." But he had said nothing about Frau Chauchat's not arriving alone; maybe he had not known himself that she and Peeperkorn would be traveling together—at least he pretended surprise when Hans Castorp more or less took him to task the day after their joint arrival.

"Can't tell you where she picked him up," he declared. "Probably met him on the trip back from the Pyrenees, I suppose. Hmm, yes, you'll have to take him into the bargain for now, my languishing Céladon, nothing's going to help you there. A firm friendship, you see. It appears they even share traveling expenses. From what I hear, the man is filthy rich. Retired coffee magnate, you see, Malayan valet, lives in opulence. But he's not here just for the fun of it, by the way, because in addition to a proper mucus obstruction caused by alcohol, it appears to be a case of a malign tropical fever, intermittent, you see, protracted, chronic. You will have to be patient with him."

"To be sure, to be sure," Hans Castorp replied superciliously. ("And what about you?" he thought. "How are you taking this? If I'm not sadly mistaken, you can't be all that blasé, either, given what went on before, you purple-cheeked widower with your lifelike oils. A great deal of schadenfreude in your comments, it seems to me, and yet when it comes to Peeperkorn, we're companions in misery, so to speak.") "Odd duck, definitely an eccentric," he said aloud with a dismissive shrug. "Robust and spare—at least that's the impression I got from him this morning at breakfast. Robust and yet spare at the same time, those are the adjectives one would have to use to describe him, I believe, although the two terms usually don't go together. He's a tall, broad-shouldered man, to be sure, and likes to stand with his legs set wide apart, his hands buried in his trouser pockets—I couldn't help noticing they're sewn in vertically, instead of on the slant the way yours and mine are, the way pockets generally are in the better classes. And when he stands there carrying on in his guttural Dutch way, there is something undeniably robust about him. But his beard is sparse—long, but so sparse you feel as if you could count the hairs, and his eyes are quite small and pale, too, almost colorless—I simply can't help it. And it doesn't do any good when he tries to open them wide, it just gives him those deep creases that first extend up toward the temples and then spread horizontally across his brow. High, red brow, you know, in a circle of white hair—cut long, but sparse all the same. His eyes are small and pale, no matter how big he tries to make them. And that vest of his adds a clerical touch, despite the checkered frock coat. Those are my impressions from this morning."

"I see you've given him the once-over," Behrens replied, "and have a good eye for his peculiarities. Very reasonable of you, because you'll have to come to terms with his being here."

"Yes, I suppose we shall," Hans Castorp said. It has been left to him to provide a general description of this new, unexpected guest, and he did not do a bad job of it—we could not have done all that much better ourselves. To be sure, he had observed Peeperkorn from the best possible position. As we know, during Clavdia's absence he had moved into neighborly proximity to the Good Russian table, which, although parallel to his own, was pushed slightly forward toward the veranda door. Hans Castorp and Peeperkorn were both seated at the narrow end of their respective tables, their backs to the middle of the room, more or less beside one another, with the Dutchman a little ahead of Hans Castorp, making discreet observation easy—and he could also glance across and see Frau Chauchat in three-quarter profile. Supplemental to Hans Castorp's accomplished sketch, we might add that Peeperkorn's upper lip was clean-shaven, his nose large and fleshy, and his mouth equally large, with irregularly shaped lips that looked somehow ragged. His hands, moreover, were rather broad, but ended in long tapering fingernails; and he used them when he spoke (and he spoke in an almost incessant stream, although Hans Castorp could not quite comprehend what was said) in a series of exquisite gestures that riveted his listeners' interest—the subtly nuanced, well-chosen, precise, tidy, cultured gestures of an orchestra conductor—

a forefinger bent to form a circle with a thumb or a palm held out wide, but with tapering nails, to caution, to subdue, to demand attention, only to disappoint his now smiling, attentive listeners with one of his very robustly prepared, but incomprehensible phrases; or rather, he did not so much disappoint people as transform smiles into looks of delighted amazement, because the robustness, subtlety, and significance of the preparation largely compensated, even after the fact, for what he failed to say and produced a satisfying, amusing, and enriching effect all its own. Sometimes it would be followed by no utterance at all. He would gently lay one hand on the forearm of the tablemate to his left, a young Bulgarian teacher, or on Madame Chauchat's to his right, then raise that same hand at an angle to command them all to sit in silent expectation of what he was about to say, would then gaze down at a spot on the tablecloth in the vicinity of his captive—lifting his eyebrows until the creases, which started up from the corners of his eyes and then turned in a right angle across his brow, grew even deeper and more masklike—and open his large, ragged lips as if he were about to utter something of vast import. After a moment, however, he would exhale, forgo it all, wave it aside as if to say, "At ease!" and, having accomplished nothing, turn back to his coffee, which he had them brew extra-strong for him in a machine he had brought with him.

And after he had taken a sip, he would continue as follows: restraining further conversation with one hand, he created silence the way a conductor hushes the cacophony of instruments being tuned and with a commanding, cultured gesture summons his orchestra to begin the concert; for his large head with its encircling flames of white hair, with its pale eyes, deeply creased brow, long beard, and exposed, pained lips looked so unquestionably imposing that everyone obeyed his gesture. They all fell silent, smiled, and looked at him expectantly; here and there someone would add a nod of encouragement to his smile.

In a rather low voice, he said, "Ladies and gentlemen. Fine. How very fine. That *set*-tles it. And yet you must keep in mind and never—not for a moment—lose sight of the fact that—but enough on that topic. What is incumbent upon me to say is not so much *that,* but primarily and above all *this*: that we are duty-bound, that we are charged with an inviolable— I repeat with all due emphasis—*inviolable* obligation—*No!* No, ladies and gentlemen, not that I—oh, how very mistaken it would be to think that I—but that *set*-tles it, ladies and gentlemen. Settles it completely. I know we are all of one mind, and so then, to the point!"

He had said nothing; but his head had looked so incontrovertibly imposing, the play of features and gestures had been so definitive, compelling, and expressive that all of them, including eavesdropping Hans Castorp, believed that they had heard something very important or, to the extent that they were aware of the lack of anything communicated and of any thought completed, they simply did not miss it. We might ask ourselves how a deaf person would have felt. Drawing a false conclusion from the expression he saw as to the content of what was expressed, he might have fretted that because of his handicap he had missed something of intellectual substance. Such people tend to be suspicious and bitter. A young Chinese fellow, however, at the other end of the table, whose knowledge of German was scant, had not understood, but had both heard and seen, and announced his own happy satisfaction by calling out *"Très bien!"*—and even applauded.

And Mynheer Peeperkorn came "to the point." He sat up straight, expanded his broad chest, buttoned his checkered frock coat over his high-buttoned vest—and his white head was regal. He waved a dining attendant over—it was the dwarf—and although she was very busy, she instantly obeyed his forceful gesture and took a position next to his chair, milk jug and coffeepot still in hand. Even she could not help nodding encouragement to him; spellbound by those pale eyes under deep creases, a smile playing across her large, elderly face, she gazed attentively at his forefinger bent to form a circle with his thumb, the other three fingers jutting erect, each topped by a sharp fingernail lance.

"My child," he said, "—fine. Very fine, so far. You are small—but what is that to me? On the contrary! I take it as something positive. I thank God you are the way you are, and that by your smallness, which betrays such character—well, fine. What I desire of you is likewise small, small and full of character. But first, what is your name?"

She smiled and stammered and finally said that her name was Emerentia.

"Splendid!" Peeperkorn cried, throwing himself against the back of his chair and stretching one arm out to the dwarf. The tone of his cry seemed to say, "Well, who could object to that! It's all so wonderful!"—"My child," he continued now in an earnest, almost stern voice, "that exceeds my every expectation. Emerentia—you pronounce it with modesty, but the name—and taken together with your person—in short, it reveals the loveliest possibilities. 'Tis well worth musing upon, giving rein to all the emotions that well up in one's chest, so that one may—but as a nickname, you must understand, my child, as a *nick*name—it might be Rentia, or even Emchen would cheer the heart—but for the moment I shall without hesitation hold fast to Emchen. So then, Emchen my child, listen well: a little bread, my dear. Wait! Stay! Let there be no misunderstanding. I can read from your relatively broad face that there is the danger of—bread,

Renzchen, but not baked bread, of that we have a sufficiency, in all shapes and sizes. Not baked, but distilled, my angel. The bread of God, clear as crystal, my little Nickname, that we may be regaled. I am uncertain whether what I intend by using that term—I might suggest 'a cordial for the heart' as an alternative, if that term did not likewise run the danger of being taken in a more common, thoughtless sense—but that *set*-tles it, Rentia. Settles it, over and done! Or rather, in light of our duty, our holy obligation—for example, the debt of honor incumbent upon me to turn with a most cordial heart to you, so small but full of character—a gin, my love! To gladden my heart, might I say. A gin, a Schiedam gin, my Emerenzchen. Make haste to bring it to me."

"A gin, neat," the dwarf repeated, spun once around completely, looking for somewhere to set down her jug and pot, which she then placed on Hans Castorp's table, right next to his place setting, apparently not wanting to bother Herr Peeperkorn with it. She hurried off, and her patron promptly received what he wanted. The little glass was so full that the "bread" ran down on all sides and formed little puddles in his plate. He clasped it between his thumb and middle finger and raised it to the light. "And so," he declared, "Pieter Peeperkorn will now regale himself with a schnapps." And after first chewing it briefly, he swallowed the distilled grain. "Now," he said, "I view you all with refreshed eyes." And he took Frau Chauchat's hand from where it lay on the tablecloth and lifted it to his lips, then laid it back down and let his own hand rest atop it for a while.

A peculiar man, a man of some personal authority, though rather vague—the society of the Berghof was very taken by him. He had recently retired from his colonial affairs, it was said, and was home free. They spoke of his splendid house in The Hague and his villa in Scheveningen. Frau Stöhr called him a "money magnet" and could point to a pearl necklace that Madame Chauchat had been wearing with her evening gowns since her return and that in Karoline's opinion could hardly be considered evidence of Transcaucasian marital gallantry, but rather was the result of "shared travel expenses." She winked as she said it; unrefined by sickness and suffering, she now pointed with her head in Hans Castorp's direction and pulled down the corners of her mouth to parody his distress, mocking and ruthlessly exploiting his sad state. He kept his composure. He even corrected her malapropism with some wit. She had misspoken herself, he said—the word was magnate. But magnet was not all that bad, either, since Peeperkorn was obviously a very attractive man. And in response to Fräulein Engelhart, who without looking at him asked, with a dull blush and a skewed smile, how he liked their new guest, he said with perfect equanimity that Mynheer Peeperkorn was a "blurred person-ality"—a personality, true, but a blurred one. The precision of this charac-terization showed both his objectivity and his composure; it put the teacher off-balance. But in the case of Ferdinand Wehsal, who offered a twisted remark about the unexpected circumstances under which Frau Chauchat had returned, Hans Castorp proved there are glances that are every whit as unambiguous as the most precisely articulated words. "Poor wretch!" that glance said as it measured the man from Mannheim, and said it in a way that excluded even the remotest possibility of any other interpretation; and Wehsal acknowledged that glance and stomached it, even nodded and displayed his rotten teeth; but from then on, he refrained from carrying Hans Castorp's overcoat when they went for walks with Naphta, Settembrini, and Ferge.

But good God, he could carry it himself, preferred to carry it himself, and had handed it over to the poor wretch now and then just to be friendly. But no one in our circle could fail to note that Hans Castorp had been hit hard by these totally unforeseen circumstances, which ruined all his mental preparations for greeting the partner of his carnival adventure on her return. Or better: the circumstances made preparations superflu-ous—that was the humiliating part.

His intentions had been of the most delicate, prudent sort—nothing even vaguely impetuous or awkward. He had not given a thought to fetching Clavdia from the station, for instance—and a good thing the idea had not occurred to him. He had been quite uncertain whether a woman, one whose illness granted her such freedom, would even want to admit the fantastic events of that dreamy night of masquerade in a foreign lan-guage. Or would she perhaps prefer that he immediately remind her? No, nothing obtrusive, no coarse claims on her. Even if one granted that his relationship to the slant-eyed patient had by its very nature exceeded the bounds of Western reason and behavior, what had to be maintained now was very civilized formality, even, for the present, a feigned forgetfulness. A cavalier's greeting from table to table—nothing more than that at first. On some later occasion, he might politely approach the traveler and casu-ally inquire about how she had been doing of late. The real meeting would then follow at the appropriate time as a reward for his level-headed chivalry.

But, as noted, all this delicacy seemed futile now, since his actions had been robbed of their spontaneity and thus of any value. The presence of Mynheer Peeperkorn completely ruled out the possibility of any tactics *except* those of uttermost reserve. Hans Castorp had been sitting on his balcony on the evening of their arrival, had watched the sleigh move slowly up the looping driveway, and had seen the driver on his box, beside him the Malayan valet, a little yellow-skinned man wearing a bowler and sporting a fur collar on his overcoat—and sitting in back, at Clavdia's side, the stranger, his hat pulled down over his eyes. Hans Castorp had not slept much that night. The next morning he had no difficulty learning the name of this unsettling fellow traveler, including the gratis news that the two of them had taken adjoining rooms on the second floor. Then had come first breakfast, during which he had sat at his place, waiting with a pale face for the glass door to slam. It did not. Clavdia's entrance took place silently, because Mynheer Peeperkorn closed the glass door behind her; tall, broad-shouldered, the high brow of his mighty head encircled by white flames, he followed in the footsteps of his traveling companion, who, head thrust slightly forward, moved toward her table with her familiar catlike gait. Yes, it was she, unchanged. Forgetting himself and his plan, Hans Castorp held her in his sleepy gaze. That was her reddish-blond hair, no more elegantly coiffed than usual, just a simple braid wound around her head; those were her "lone-wolf eyes," her rounded neck, her lips, which seemed fuller than they were because they were accented by cheekbones that gave a charming concavity to her cheeks. "Clavdia!" he thought with a shudder. And he looked her unexpected companion directly in the eye, not without a defiant toss of his head to mock the masklike face and the grandeur of the figure, not without challenging his own heart to make fun of this exalted personage, whose current rights of possession were cast in a very odd light by certain past events: *certain* past events, indeed—not dark, uncertain events from the realms of amateur portraits, which had had the power to disquiet him at one time. Frau Chauchat still had the same way of smiling and standing at attention, as if presenting herself to society before taking her seat; and Peeperkorn devotedly stood behind her and a bit to one side as she performed her little ceremony, and then took his own seat next to her at the end of the table.

Nothing came of the cavalier's greeting from table to table. In "presenting" herself, Clavdia had let her eyes sweep right past Hans Castorp and all the farther regions of the room; nothing happened at their next meeting in the dining hall, either; and the more meals that passed without his eye meeting hers—unless you counted Frau Chauchat's blind, sweeping, impassive gaze if she happened to turn around during a meal—the more unsuitable it would have been to attempt his cavalier's greeting. During the brief evening social gatherings, the two traveling companions kept to the little salon. They sat side by side on the sofa surrounded by their tablemates; and Peeperkorn, whose magnificent countenance stood out bright red against the white of his flaming hair and beard, drank the rest of the bottle of red wine he had ordered for dinner. He drank a bottle at every main meal, sometimes one and a half, even two, not to mention the "bread," with which he started every meal, including first breakfast. Apparently this regal man required unusual amounts of regalement. He likewise found regalement in extra-strong coffee, which he drank several times a day—not just in the morning, but at noon from a large cup, and not just after the meal, but during it, along with his wine. Both wine and coffee, Hans Castorp heard him say, were good for fever—quite apart from their regaling effect, they were very good for his intermittent attacks of tropical fever, one of which kept him bedfast in his room for several hours the second day after his arrival. Quartan fever, the director called it, because it struck the Dutchman down approximately every fourth day—it started with chattering teeth, then came a hot flush, and finally the sweats. It was said that he had a swollen spleen from it as well.

Vingt et un

AND SO TIME PASSED—weeks, three or four probably, that at least is our guess, since we cannot possibly depend on Hans Castorp's judgment and ability to gauge such matters. The weeks slipped past without bringing forth any real change; but as for our hero, they brought forth a permanent disdain for those unforeseen circumstances that demanded unrewarding reticence of him: for the circumstance that called itself Pieter Peeperkorn whenever it downed a schnapps; for the bothersome presence of this regal, imposing, and vague man—bothersome indeed and in a much cruder fashion than Herr Settembrini had "bothered" him in the old days. Deep vertical furrows of contempt and ill humor formed between Hans Castorp's eyebrows, and from under those furrows he gazed at the returned traveler five times a day, happy at least to gaze at her, but filled with scorn for the exalted personage who had not the least notion what an odd light past events cast upon him.

One evening, however, for no particular reason, the evening social in the lobby and public rooms turned more lively than usual. There had been music, Gypsy melodies, jauntily executed on the violin by a Hungarian student; and then Director Behrens, who had likewise appeared for fifteen minutes, accompanied by Dr. Krokowski, got someone to play the melody of the "Pilgrims' Chorus" on the bass register of the piano, while he stood close by and attacked the treble with a brush that he

bounced over the keys in a parody of violin arpeggios. Bursts of laughter.
Shaking his head magnanimously at his own friskiness, the director then
left the social rooms amid loud applause. The convivial mood continued,
more music followed, but nothing that demanded their particular attention; people gathered with their drinks for dominoes and bridge, amused
themselves with the optical gadgets, and stood chatting in little groups
here and there. Even the people from the Good Russian table mingled
with the others in the lobby and the music room. Mynheer Peeperkorn
could be seen moving about—one could not avoid seeing him, for that
majestic head towered above its surroundings, overwhelming everything
with royal vigor and import. And although those who now gathered
around him might at first have been drawn to him merely by his rumored
wealth, very soon it was his personality and it alone to which they clung.
Oblivious to all else, they stood there smiling and nodding encouragement.
Caught in the spell of that pallid gaze from beneath those mighty creases
on his brow, held in suspense by the emphatic cultured gestures of his
long-nailed hands, they were not even vaguely aware of being disappointed
by the incomprehensible, fragmented, muddled, indeed useless statements
that followed.

And if we look around for Hans Castorp in this setting, we will find
him in the reading room, the same room where once (though this "once"
is vague, since neither narrator, reader, nor hero is quite clear anymore
as to the degree of pastness involved) he had been party to important
disclosures concerning the organization of human progress. It was quieter
here; he shared his retreat with only a few others. A man was writing at
one of the double lecterns that stood beneath a dangling electric lamp. A
lady with two pince-nez on her nose was sitting in front of the bookcases
paging through an illustrated magazine. Hans Castorp picked up a newspaper, and moving toward the open door that led to the music room, he
sat down, his back to the portieres, on the chair that happened to be
there—a plush-covered Renaissance chair, with a high, straight back and
no arms, for those who wish to visualize it. The young man held his
paper the way one holds a newspaper to read it, but instead of reading,
he tilted his head to listen to the scraps of music mingled with conversation
coming from the room adjacent; but the gloom on his brow suggested
that he did so with only half an ear and that his thoughts were wandering
down unmusical paths, thorny paths of disappointing circumstances,
which, at the end of a long wait, had made an awful fool of the young
man who had gladly waited—bitter paths of disdain that before long
would end in a decision and its execution: he would lay his newspaper
down on this uncomfortable chair he had happened upon, walk through

the far door that led to the lobby, and exchange this convivial fiasco for
the frosty solitude of his balcony and the company of Maria Mancini.

"And your cousin, monsieur?" a voice asked behind him, above his
head. It was an enchanting voice to his ear—an ear expressly fashioned
to perceive that dry, sweet huskiness as utmost pleasure, as the essence
of pleasure brought to one perfect pinnacle. It was the voice that long
ago had said: "Glad to. And don't break it"—a compelling voice, a voice
of destiny; and if he had heard right, it had asked about Joachim.

He slowly lowered his newspaper and lifted his face a little higher so
that his head was raised, but with only his cowlick touching the straight
chairback. He even closed his eyes a little, but immediately opened them
again, and without changing the position of his head directed his gaze up
and to one side into nowhere. Poor fellow—one might have been tempted
to say he had the look of a clairvoyant or a sleepwalker. He wanted to
hear the question repeated, but that did not happen. And so he was not
even certain whether she was still standing behind him, when after a
considerable pause he belatedly answered in almost a whisper: "He's dead.
He did his duty down on the plains and he died."

He noticed himself that "dead" was the first word of any importance
that had been spoken between them. He also noticed at once that her lack
of fluency in his language meant she had to choose simple phrases to
express her sympathy.

From behind and above him, she said, "How sad. What a pity. Quite
dead and buried? Since when?"

"It's been some time now. His mother took him back down with her.
He even grew a warrior's beard. They fired three salvos above his grave."

"He had earned them. He was a very fine man. A much finer man than
most—than certain people."

"Yes, he was a fine fellow. Rhadamanthus always talked about his being
a zealot. But his body wanted things otherwise. *Rebellio carnis* is what
the Jesuits call it. He was always concerned about his body, in an honorable way, I mean. But his body let something dishonorable invade it,
played a trick on his zealotry. But, then, it is more moral to lose oneself
or let oneself be ruined than to save oneself."

"I see monsieur is still a philosophical ne'er-do-well. Rhadamanthus?
Who is that?"

"Behrens. Settembrini calls him that."

"Ah, Settembrini, I know—that's the Italian fellow. I did not like
him. He was not a humane person." (The voice pronounced the word
"*hu*mane," with the accent on the first syllable and drew it out in an
indolent, fanciful sort of way.) "He was arrogant." (The accent was on

the second syllable.) "He is no longer here? I am stupid. I do not know what that means—Rhadamanthus."

"It's a humanistic thing. Settembrini has moved out. We've done some extensive philosophizing in the meantime. He and Naphta and I."

"Who is Naphta?"

"His adversary."

"If he is his adversary, then I would like to make his acquaintance. But did I not say that your cousin would die if he tried to be a soldier down on the plains?"

"Yes, you did, Clavdia."

"Let us have none of that, monsieur!"

A long period of silence. He did not apologize. He waited, his spine pressed against the high chairback, his gaze clairvoyant at hearing that voice anew; but he was once again uncertain whether she was still behind him, afraid that the scraps of music from the next room might have drowned out her departing footsteps. But there it was again at last.

"And monsieur did not even go to his cousin's funeral?"

"No," he replied, "I said my good-byes to him here before they closed the casket—he was starting to smile. You can't believe how cold his brow was, Clavdia."

"Again! Is that any way to talk to a lady whom you hardly know?"

"Should my words be humanistic rather than humane?" (And automatically he drawled the last word out sleepily, as if he were stretching and yawning.)

"*Quelle blague!*—You've been here the whole time?"

"Yes. I've been waiting."

"For what?"

"For you, Clavdia."

A laugh above his head—and with it a trumpeted word: "Fool!"— "For me? They just wouldn't let you out of here, that's all."

"Oh yes they would. Behrens discharged me once in a fit of temper. But it would only have been a wild departure. Because in addition to the old scars from long ago, from my school days, you know, Behrens has found a fresh spot and that's what causes my fever."

"There's still a fever?"

"Yes, always a little. Almost always. It varies. But it's not an intermittent fever."

"*Des allusions?*"

He did not reply. He scowled and looked clairvoyant. After a while he asked, "And where were you, Clavdia?"

A hand slapped the back of his chair.

"*Mais c'est un sauvage!*—Where was I? Everywhere. In Moscow"— the voice pronounced it "Muoscow," drawing the word out in the same indolent way it did "*hu*mane"—"in Baku, in German spas, in Spain."

"Oh, in Spain. How was it?"

"So-so. Travel is difficult. The people are half Moors. Castile is very dry and hard. The Kremlin is more beautiful than that castle or monastery there at the foot of the mountains . . ."

"The Escorial."

"Yes, Philip's castle. An in*hu*mane castle. I liked a folk dance in Catalonia better, the sardana—to bagpipes. I danced along with them. Everyone joins hands and moves in a circle. The whole town square is full. *C'est charmant.* It is *hu*mane. I bought a little blue cap, the kind that all the local men and boys wear, almost a fez, a *boina.* I wear it for my rest cure and at other times, too. Monsieur will have to judge whether it suits me."

"Which monsieur?"

"The one here in this chair."

"I thought, perhaps, Mynheer Peeperkorn."

"He has already judged. He says I look charming in it."

"Did he say that? All the way to the end? Spoke the whole sentence all the way to the end so that you could understand it?"

"Ah, it appears someone is in a bad mood. Someone wants to be malicious, sarcastic. Monsieur is trying to make fun of other people who are much greater and better and more *hu*mane than he and his . . . *ami bavard de la Méditerranée, son maître grand parleur.* But I will not permit someone to speak of my friend—"

"Do you still have my interior portrait?" he interrupted in a melancholy voice.

She laughed. "I will have to look for it."

"I carry yours here. And then I have a little stand on my chest of drawers where I put it at night and—"

He did not finish. Peeperkorn was standing in front of him. He had been looking for his traveling companion; he had come through the portieres and stood now in front of the chair of the man he had seen chatting with her, stood there like a tower, right at our hero's feet, so close in fact that Hans Castorp had trouble getting out of his chair to take a position between the two of them—once he realized, despite his sleepwalker gaze, that he should stand up to be polite. He had to slide out of it sideways, so that our three principal characters now stood in a triangle, the chair in the middle.

Frau Chauchat complied with the demands of Western civilization and introduced the gentlemen to one another. An acquaintance from before, she said, referring to Hans Castorp—from her previous stay here. Herr Peeperkorn's presence needed no further explanation. She said his name, and the Dutchman attentively turned his gaze to the young man, his eyes pale beneath the almost idol-like arabesques of his creased brow and temples, and extended a hand—the back of it was all freckles, a sea captain's hand, Hans Castorp thought, if you discounted those lancelike nails. He was standing now directly under the influence of Peeperkorn's massive personality ("personality"—one glance at him, and the word would not leave your mind; suddenly you knew what a personality was and the more you saw of him the more you were convinced that this was the only way a personality could look); and malleable youth felt crushed beneath the weight of this broad-shouldered, red-faced sixty-year-old, with white flames that encircled his head, painfully ragged lips, and a long, narrow beard that reached down to his high-buttoned, clerical-style vest. Peeperkorn was courtesy personified, by the way.

"My dear sir," he said, "by all means. No, permit me, sir—by all means. I am making your acquaintance this evening—the acquaintance of a promising young man—and I do so, my dear sir, quite deliberately, fully engaging all my energies. I like you, sir. I—don't mention it. Settled. You appeal to me."

There was nothing one could say in return. His cultured gestures were all too peremptory—he liked Hans Castorp. And Peeperkorn drew appropriate conclusions, which he now made known or suggested by gestures that his traveling companion helpfully supplemented with spoken approximations.

"My child," he said, "fine, very fine. How would it be—I beg you to understand me correctly. Life is short, whereas our ability to meet its challenges is but—those are facts, my child. Laws. In-ex-or-a-bilities. In short, my child, in short and for good and all—" And he held his last expressive gesture, which both yielded to her and waived all responsibility for any substantial misinterpretation she might make despite his broad hints.

Apparently Frau Chauchat had practice in determining the direction of his semiwishes. She said, "Why not? We could stay here awhile together, perhaps a game and a bottle of wine. Why are you standing there?" she asked, turning to Hans Castorp. "Look lively. We cannot leave it at just the three of us, we shall need company. Who is still in the salon? Invite whomever you find. Fetch a few friends from the balconies. We shall ask Dr. Ting-Fu from our table."

"Absolutely," Peeperkorn said. "Agreed. Excellent. Hurry, young friend! Obey! We shall form our own little group. We shall play and eat and drink. We shall feel as if we—absolutely, young man!"

Hans Castorp took the elevator to the third floor. He knocked at the door of A. K. Ferge, who then roused Ferdinand Wehsal and Herr Albin from their chairs in the lower lounging area. Prosecutor Paravant and both Magnuses were still in the lobby. Frau Stöhr and Fräulein Kleefeld were found in the salon, and it was there that a large card table was set up beneath the chandelier, with chairs and little serving tables set all around. Mynheer greeted each guest as he or she arrived, his pale, polite eyes gazing out from under an arabesque of attentively raised brows. They were twelve in all when they sat down, with Hans Castorp seated between their majestic host and Clavdia Chauchat. Cards and chips were set out once they had agreed on a few rounds of *vingt et un,* and Peeperkorn summoned the dwarf and in his imposing manner ordered wine, an '06 Chablis, three bottles to start with, and some sweets—whatever dried fruits and pastries could be found. And when these good things arrived, he greeted them with gusto, rubbing his hands and attempting to share his emotions in a few words that broke off impressively, but nevertheless proved quite effective, at least as a general display of personality. He then laid both hands on his neighbor's forearm, raised one forefinger with its lancelike nail, and, bathing in general approval, demanded they all pay particular attention to the splendid golden hue of the wine in their goblets, to the sugar sweated from the Malaga grapes, to a particular kind of salt and poppy-seed pretzel, which he termed "divine"—and then with one peremptory cultured gesture nipped in the bud any objection to so forceful a word. He took charge of the bank at first, but quickly gave it over to Herr Albin, remarking, if they understood correctly, that its duties prevented him from freely enjoying the occasion.

The gambling was obviously of secondary importance to him. They would be playing for next to nothing, or so he exclaimed when they agreed to his suggestion of fifty centimes as the minimum wager—although that was a great deal for most of the participants. Prosecutor Paravant and Frau Stöhr blanched and flushed by turns, and she in particular would writhe in dreadful struggles trying to decide whether to buy another card at eighteen. She would squeal loudly whenever Herr Albin coldly and routinely dealt her one that was too high, dashing her hopes—and Peeperkorn would laugh heartily.

"Squeal, madame, squeal," he said. "The sound is shrill, yet full of life and emerges from deepest—but drink, regale your heart anew." And he poured for her, poured for his neighbor and himself, ordered three more bottles, and touched glasses with Wehsal and Frau Magnus—still wasting away on the inside—since these two seemed most in need of cheering up.

Faces quickly took on higher and higher color from the truly marvelous wine—with the exception of Dr. Ting-Fu's. It remained as yellow as ever, and the ratlike slits shone jet-black; stifling his giggles, he placed very high wagers—and had shamelessly good luck. And the others did not want to be left behind. His gaze floating vaguely, Prosecutor Paravant defied fate by betting ten francs on a less than promising first card, turned pale each time he paid for another, and won twice his money back, because Herr Albin had foolishly put his trust in the ace he had been dealt and doubled every bet. And the thrill was not limited to the person who instigated it. The whole table felt it; even Herr Albin—who wagered with the cold calculation of a croupier in a Monte Carlo casino, where he claimed to have been a regular patron—only partially mastered his agitation. Hans Castorp played for high stakes as well, as did Hermine Kleefeld and Frau Chauchat. They moved on to other games: *tours; chemin de fer; ma tante, ta tante,* and the ever-risky *différence.* And each time rascal luck tickled their nerves, there would be a moment of exaltation or despair, an eruption of anger or a hysterical fit of laughter, and all their outbursts were in genuine earnest and would have sounded no different had these been the ups and downs in life's fortunes.

And yet it was not only, not even primarily, the gambling and the wine that brought forth these high-tension emotions around the table and made faces flush and shining eyes grow wider, so that the whole party was engaged in what might be called a common strenuous effort, all holding their breath in almost painful concentration on the moment. It was, rather, that all these effects could be traced to the influence of one masterful nature among those present, to the "personality" among them, to Mynheer Peeperkorn, who held the reins in his grandly gesticulating hands and bound them all to the spell of the hour with the drama of his countenance, with pale eyes gazing out from under the monumental creases of his brow, with words and compelling pantomime. What did he say? Nothing very intelligible, and even less so the more he drank. But they hung on his words, smiled and nodded and stared with raised eyebrows at that circle he formed with his forefinger and thumb while the other fingers stood erect like lances and his regal countenance labored to speak; they did not resist, they gladly allowed their emotions to wait upon him and abandoned themselves with a passion that went far beyond anything they would normally have trusted themselves to feel. It was too much for some of them, this abandonment. Frau Magnus, at least, felt indisposed and came close to fainting; she stoutly refused to return to her room, but did acquiesce to lie down on the chaise longue and let them apply a moist napkin to her brow. She soon rose, however, and returned to the group.

Peeperkorn claimed her trouble was the result of insufficient nourishment. Raising one forefinger, he enlarged upon his theme in imposing, broken phrases. One must eat, eat properly, in order to give life's demands their due, he informed them, and then ordered refreshments for everyone: a selection of meats and cold cuts, tongue, goose breast, and roast beef, sausages and ham—plates piled with delicacies and garnished with little balls of butter, radishes, and parsley until they resembled showy flowerbeds. But though they all helped themselves lustily to this repast (despite an ample supper, whose substantiality need not be described further), Mynheer Peeperkorn took only a few bites before declaring it to be "gimcrackery"—with a fury that betrayed the frightening unpredictability of such a masterful nature. And when someone tried to come to the defense of the fare, he exploded: his massive head swelled, he banged his fist on the table and pronounced it all a lot of damn garbage, reducing everyone to embarrassed silence, since he had paid for it and, as their host, could say what he pleased about his largesse.

Anger, incomprehensible though it might be, looked splendid on him, by the way, as Hans Castorp in particular was forced to admit. It did not distort his features or diminish him as a man, and its very incomprehensibility—and no one would have had the impudence to attribute it to the quantities of wine he had enjoyed—lent him something grand and majestic, so that they all deferred to him and did not attempt another bite of food. It was Frau Chauchat who calmed her traveling companion. She patted his broad captain's hand, still resting on the table where it had fallen, and coaxed him with the suggestion that one could always order something else, something warm, if he liked and if the chef could be talked into it. "My child," he said, "fine." And retaining his full dignity, he made an effortless transition from rage to composure and kissed Clavdia's hand. He would like omelets for himself and his friends—a good *omelette aux fines herbes* for everyone, so that they might all give life's demands their due. He sent a hundred francs along with his order to convince the kitchen staff to return to work.

And his general delight in things returned completely when several steaming dishes appeared—canary yellow sprinkled with green—spreading the bland odor of eggs and butter through the room. They helped themselves along with Peeperkorn, who presided over their enjoyment and with fragments of phrases and compelling, cultured gestures exhorted them to appreciate, indeed fervently to savor, these gifts of God. He ordered Dutch gin, a round for everyone, and insisted that they all approach it with eager devotion and partake of its clear dew, from which rose the robust aroma of grain and the faint whiff of juniper.

Hans Castorp smoked. Frau Chauchat likewise indulged in filter-tipped cigarettes that she took from a Russian enameled box decorated with a speeding troika, which she had laid within easy reach on the table; nor did Peeperkorn scold his neighbor for yielding to the pleasure, though he did not smoke himself, never had. If they understood him correctly, the consumption of tobacco was, in his opinion, one of those over-refined pleasures, the cultivation of which meant robbing the simpler gifts of life of their majesty—gifts and claims to which our emotional vigor scarcely did justice as it was. "Young man," he said to Hans Castorp, fixing him with his pale gaze and subduing him with a cultured gesture, "young man—whatever is simple! Whatever is holy! Fine, you understand me. A bottle of wine, a steaming dish of eggs, pure grain spirits—let us first measure up to and enjoy such things before we—absolutely, my dear sir. Settled. I have known people, men and women, cocaine-sniffers, hashish-smokers, morphine addicts. Fine, my dear friend. Agreed. Let them. We should not reprove or judge. And yet for what should come first, for what is simple, grand, direct from the hand of God, for such things these people were all—settled, my friend. Condemned. Cast out. They failed to give such things their due. Whatever your name may be, young man—fine, I knew it, but have since forgotten—depravity lies not in cocaine, not in opium, not in vice as such. The unforgivable sin lies in—"

He halted. Turning his face to his neighbor, he wrapped himself, tall and broad, in a grandly expressive silence that demanded understanding—one forefinger upraised; the mouth irregular and ragged beneath a naked, red upper lip still somewhat raw from shaving; the strained tracery of creases across the bare brow encircled by white flames; the little pale eyes held wide—and in his eyes Hans Castorp saw something like a flicker of terror at that crime, that one great sin, that unpardonable transgression, to which he had alluded and which, in trying to fathom its horror, he had condemned to silence with all the spellbinding energy of a vague but commanding personality . . . Objective, matter-of-fact terror, Hans Castorp thought, but personal terror, too, something to do with his own life, with the regal man himself. What Hans Castorp saw flickering there for just a moment, it seemed, was *fear*, not minor, everyday fear, but panic and dread; and despite all the reasons for his hostile feelings toward Frau Chauchat's majestic traveling companion, Hans Castorp had by nature too much respect for others not to be shaken by what he saw.

He lowered his eyes and nodded to give his majestic neighbor the satisfaction of having been understood. And then he said, "That is probably true. It may be a sin—and a token of our inadequacies—to indulge in refined tastes without having given the simple, natural gifts of life, the great and holy gifts, their due. That is your opinion, if I understand you correctly, Mynheer Peeperkorn. And although I had never thought of it that way before, now that you mention it, I can only concur with you wholeheartedly. It is probably all too seldom that full justice is done to such healthy and simple gifts of life. Certainly most people are too weak-willed and inattentive, too unscrupulous and emotionally drained, to do them justice—it is more than likely the case."

The grand man was highly gratified. "Young man," he said, "agreed. Permit me to say—but not one word more. I beg you to drink with me, to quaff our glasses down to the last drop, arm in arm. That does not mean that I am offering you the brotherhood of informal pronouns—I was about to do so, but have reconsidered. That would be a bit too hasty. I shall more than likely do so, however, within the foreseeable future. Depend on it! But if you wish and insist on it now—"

Hans Castorp's gesture implied that he seconded the delay Peeperkorn had proposed.

"Fine, young man. Fine, comrade. Inadequacies—fine. Fine and horrifying. Unscrupulous—very fine. Gifts—not so fine. Demands! Life's holy, feminine demands upon our manly honor and vigor—"

Hans Castorp was suddenly confronted with the realization that Peeperkorn was very drunk. And yet his drunkenness did not belittle or demean him, caused him no disgrace, but rather, when joined with the majesty of his nature, it only made him grander and more awe-inspiring. Even drunken Bacchus, Hans Castorp thought, had propped himself on his exuberant companions without losing anything of his divinity, and ultimately it depended on *who* was drunk—a personality or a tinker. He steeled himself against any loss of respect for this overwhelming traveling companion, whose cultured gestures had grown flaccid and whose tongue was thick.

"Brotherhood—," Peeperkorn said, throwing his massive body back in free and proud intoxication and stretching one arm out over the table to bang it with a flaccidly clenched fist, "in the offing—in the near offing, though discreetly reconsidered for now, fine. Settled. Life, young man, is a woman, a woman sprawled before us, with close-pressed bulging breasts and a great, soft belly between those broad hips, with slender arms and swelling thighs, with eyes half-closed in mocking defiance, demanding our most urgent response, the proof or collapse of our resilient manly desire—collapse, young man, do you understand what that means? The defeat of feeling in the face of life, that is the inadequacy for which there is no pardon, no pity, no honor, but only merciless shame and scornful laughter—*set*-tled, young man, and spewed out again. Ignominy and disgrace are mild terms for such ruin and bankruptcy, for such ghastly humiliation. It is the end, the despair of hell itself, doomsday . . ."

As he spoke, the Dutchman had thrown his massive body back farther and farther, while at the same time his regal head sank to his chest as if he were about to fall asleep. But at this last word, he raised his flaccid fist for two more heavy blows to the tabletop, and slight Hans Castorp, edgy from the gambling and wine and these very peculiar circumstances, flinched and gazed in frightened awe at this powerful man. "Dooms-day"—the word fit him perfectly. Hans Castorp could not recall ever having heard anyone use the word, except perhaps in religion class; and it was no accident, he thought, for of all the people he knew, who among them was fit to release such a thunderbolt—or better, who had the *stature* for it? Little Naphta might have made use of it, but it would have been a usurpation, mere caustic chatter, whereas in Peeperkorn's mouth the thunderbolt was trumpeted forth with its full crashing, booming, biblical impact. "My God—what a personality!" he thought for the hundredth time. "I have stumbled upon a personality, and he is Clavdia's traveling companion." Feeling rather tipsy himself, he spun his wineglass in place with one hand and thrust the other into his trouser pocket, squinting with one eye from the smoke of the cigarette in the corner of his mouth. Should he not have kept silent after the aforesaid thunderbolt? What could his prim voice accomplish? But discussion was a habit now, thanks to his democratic mentors—both were basically democratic, although the one struggled not to be—and he got caught up in one of his own ingenuous commentaries.

"Your remarks, Mynheer Peeperkorn," he said (what a way to put it—remarks; did one make "remarks" about doomsday?), "lead my thoughts back again to what we previously agreed upon about the nature of vice: that it is an insult to the simple, and as you said, holy, or, as I might put it, classic gifts of life—those gifts of life that have stature, so to speak—an insult to them to show a preference for acquired refinements, in which one 'indulges,' as one of us two expressed it, whereas one 'embraces' or 'devotes oneself to' the great gifts. But therein lies, or so it seems to me, the excuse—forgive me, I am by nature inclined to excuse (though excuses have no real stature, as I am only too aware)—the excuse, then, for vice, to the extent, that is, that vice is based upon 'inadequacy,' as we have called it. You said things of such great stature in regard to the terrors of inadequacy, that I find myself quite confounded. But what I mean is, vice is surely not insensitive to such terrors, but on the contrary, gives them their full and just due, to the extent that what drives a man to vice is the failure of feeling in the face of the classic gifts of life; which therefore does not imply, or does not necessarily imply, an insult to life, since it might equally as well be interpreted as an embracing of life. Indeed, inasmuch as these refinements are meant to intoxicate or excite us—are stimulants, as they say—they support and enhance the intensity of feelings, which means, then, that their purpose and goal are life itself, a love of feeling, are inadequacy's way of striving for feeling . . . what I mean is . . ."

What was he talking about? What sort of excess of democratic impudence had led him to speak of "one of us two," when it was a matter of a personality and himself? Had he found the courage for such impertinence in past events that cast certain current rights of possession in a very odd light? Or was he simply feeling his oats? Was that why he had got himself tangled up in this brazen analysis of "vice"? Well, it was up to him to get himself out now—for he had clearly conjured up dreadful forces.

All during his guest's speech, Mynheer Peeperkorn had remained flung back in his chair with his head sunk to his chest, so that there was some doubt if Hans Castorp's words had impinged on his consciousness. But now as the young man grew more confused, the older man gradually began to rear up out of his chair, taller and taller, to full size—his majestic head swelling and turning red, the arabesques on his brow rising and spreading, his little eyes growing ever larger in pale threat. What was going to happen? A temper tantrum seemed to be brewing that would make his previous outburst look like minor annoyance. Mynheer's lower lip was braced in mighty fury against his upper lip, so that both corners of his mouth were pulled down and his chin was thrust forward, and slowly his right arm lifted above the table to the level of his head, then higher still, the fist clenched, poised to deliver an annihilating blow to this democratic chatterbox, who—both filled with terror and yet savoring the eerie sight of eloquent regal wrath unfolding before him—had difficulty hiding his fear and a panicky desire to flee. He hastily decided to try to head things off.

"Naturally, I have expressed myself poorly. The whole thing is a matter of stature, nothing more. Whatever has stature cannot be called vice. Vice never has stature. Over-refined tastes have no stature. But since time immemorial, the human striving for feeling has in fact had one means ready at hand, one drug, one intoxicant, that belongs to the classic gifts of life and bears the stamp of the simple and holy, and thus is no vice—one means of stature, if I may put it that way. Wine—the gods' gift to man, as the humanistic peoples of antiquity claimed, the philanthropic invention of a god who is in fact associated with civilization, if I may be permitted the allusion. For we learn that it is thanks to the art of planting and pressing the grape that man emerged from his savage state and achieved culture. And even today nations where the grape grows are considered, or consider themselves, more cultured than wineless Cimmerians—a most remarkable fact. For it asserts that culture is not a matter of reason and well-articulated sobriety, but rather is bound up with enthusiasm, with intoxication, and the sense of regalement. Is that not, if I may be so bold as to inquire, your opinion in this matter as well?"

What a rascal our Hans Castorp is. Or, as Herr Settembrini would have expressed it with belletristic delicacy, what a "wag"—reckless, even brazen, when dealing with personalities, but just as clever at extricating himself when he must. In the most ticklish situation he had managed—with good grace and quite impromptu—a vindication of drink; he had, moreover, just in passing, brought the conversation around to "civilization," of which, to be sure, little was evident in Mynheer Peeperkorn's primitive, menacing pose; and finally, by asking his question, had relaxed that grandiose pose—it would have been quite inappropriate to respond with a raised, clenched fist. The Dutchman backed off from his antediluvian gesture of fury; he slowly lowered his arm to the table, his face lost its swollen redness; his expression seemed to say "cheers!" with only a conditional, after-the-fact threat still lingering there. The thunderstorm cleared, and Frau Chauchat intervened as well, calling her traveling companion's attention to the general decline in conviviality.

"Dear friend, you are neglecting your guests," she said in French. "You are devoting yourself too exclusively to this gentleman, with whom you doubtless have important matters to discuss. But meanwhile the game has almost come to a halt, and I fear people are growing bored. Shall we end our party?"

Peeperkorn turned immediately to the rest of the table. It was true: demoralization, lethargy, and stupor were rampant. Guests were horsing around like unsupervised schoolchildren. Several of them were close to dozing off. Peeperkorn immediately grabbed the slack reins. "Ladies and gentlemen!" he cried, raising a forefinger—and the long tapering nail was like a brandished sword or a waving banner, and his words were like those of a captain halting an incipient rout with the cry of "Let him who is no coward follow me!" And the engagement of his personality promptly had a bracing, focusing effect. They roused themselves, replaced slack faces with bright ones, nodded and smiled back into their mighty host's pale eyes beneath the idol-like tracery of his brow. Binding them all under his spell and calling them back to his service, he lowered the tip of his forefinger to the tip of his thumb and let the other long nails stand erect at one side. He spread his captain's hand, cautioning and restraining them, and from his painfully ragged lips came words whose discursive ambiguity had compelling power over their minds thanks to the personality behind them.

"Ladies and gentlemen—fine. The flesh, ladies and gentlemen, is as we know—settled. No, permit me to say it—'weak.' So it is written. 'Weak,' which means it tends to see the demands—but I appeal to your—in short and for good and all, ladies and gentlemen, I ap-*peal* to you. You will say—sleep. Fine, ladies and gentlemen, agreed, excellent. I love and honor sleep. I venerate its deep, sweet, refreshing bliss. Sleep must be counted among the—how did you put it, young man?—among the classic gifts of life, among its first, its primal, I beg you, ladies and gentlemen, its highest gifts. And yet please observe and recall: Gethsemane! 'And he took with him Peter and the two sons of Zebedee. Then he saith unto them, tarry ye here, and watch with me.' Do you recall? 'And he cometh unto the disciples, and findeth them asleep, and saith unto Peter, What, could ye not watch with me one hour?' Fervent, ladies and gentlemen. Incisive. Stirring. 'And he came and found them asleep again: for their eyes were heavy. And saith unto them, Sleep on now, and take your rest. Behold the hour is at hand.' Ladies and gentlemen—excruciating, heartwrenching."

And indeed they were all profoundly moved and embarrassed. He had crossed his hands over his breast and scant beard, his head tilted to one side. His pale eyes had faltered as those words spoken from the throes of lonely death crossed his ragged lips. Frau Stöhr sobbed. Frau Magnus heaved a great sigh. Prosecutor Paravant felt it incumbent upon him, as the party's representative as it were, to speak in their behalf, to offer in a low voice a few words to their honored host. There must be some mistake here. They were fresh and alert, gay and merry, engaged with all their hearts and souls. It was such a lovely, festive, absolutely extraordinary evening—they all understood and felt it, and for now no one would even think of making use of the gift of life called sleep. Mynheer Peeperkorn could depend on his guests, on every single one of them.

"Agreed! Excellent!" Peeperkorn cried and sat up straight. His hands now loosened, parted, were spread and raised, palms outward, as if in heathen prayer. His grand physiognomy, only just now animated with Gothic agony, blossomed with luxurious good cheer; even a sybaritic dimple made a brief appearance on one cheek. "Behold the hour is at hand—" And he told them to deal him a card, set a horn-rimmed pince-nez on his nose, its high bridge jutting up into his brow, and ordered champagne: three bottles of Mumm and Co., *Cordon rouge, très sec;* plus petits fours—luscious cone-shaped little delicacies, tenderest pastries glazed with colored sugar and marbled with chocolate or pistachio creams, each presented on a paper doily with a lacy trim. Frau Stöhr licked her fingers with gusto. Herr Albin released the first cork from its wire prison, a task of indolent routine, aimed the bottle at the ceiling, let the mushroom-shaped cork slip from its decorated neck with the pop of a toy gun, and then, as dictated by elegant tradition, wrapped the bottle in a napkin before pouring. Noble foam had moistened the linen on the little serving table. They all chinked shallow goblets and drank the first glass down, electrifying their stomachs with its ice-cold, fragrant tickle. Eyes glistened. The card game was over, although no one had troubled to gather up the cards and money from the table. The party gave itself over to its own blissful idleness; they exchanged disconnected small talk, scraps of elevated emotions, which in their primal state as ideas had promised ultimate beauty, but on the way to being spoken turned into fragmentary, slack-lipped gibberish, some of it indiscreet, some of it incomprehensible, all of it likely to have aroused angry embarrassment in any sober person who might have happened upon them, but accepted without complaint by the participants, who were all cradled in the same irresponsible mood. Frau Magnus's ears had turned red and she admitted that she felt as if life were coursing through her—which did not seem to please Herr Magnus. Hermine Kleefeld leaned her back against Herr Albin's shoulder and held out her goblet for more champagne. Directing his bacchanalia with long-lanced, cultured gestures, Peeperkorn saw to it that supplies kept coming. He ordered coffee after the champagne, double mochas, which were once again served with "bread," or sweet liqueurs—apricot brandy, chartreuse, crème de vanille, and maraschino—for the ladies. Later there was pickled herring and beer, and finally tea, including a Chinese chamomile, for anyone who had drunk enough champagne or liqueurs and did not wish to return to more serious wine, as had Mynheer, who, well after midnight, rang for a simple, sparkling Swiss red for himself, Frau Chauchat, and Hans Castorp—and poured down glass after glass in honest thirst.

At one o'clock the festivities were still under way, held together partly by the leaden palsy of drink, partly by the unusual pleasure of making a night of it, partly by the effect of Peeperkorn's personality, and partly by the deterrent example offered by Saint Peter and friends, whose weakness of the flesh no one wanted to emulate. Generally speaking, the females seemed less endangered in this regard. The men sat with legs stretched out before them, puffing up their red or pallid cheeks and merely quaffing mechanically from time to time, apparently no longer inspired by the task at hand; the women, however, were more industrious. Propping her bared elbows on the table, Hermine Kleefeld held both cheeks in her hands and laughed, displaying the enamel of her front teeth to a giggling Dr. Ting-Fu; meanwhile, Frau Stöhr sat with one shoulder rolled forward, her chin tucked up against it, and flirted with the prosecutor, attempting to enslave him. Frau Magnus was so far gone that she was sitting on Herr Albin's lap, tugging at both his earlobes—to which Herr Magnus reacted with what appeared to be relief. Someone had asked Anton Karlovitch Ferge to entertain them with his tale of pleural shock, but he could not manage his recalcitrant tongue and frankly admitted his incapacity—which was unanimously greeted as cause for another drink. Wehsal wept bitterly for a while, out of the depths of a misery into which he could give them no insight, since his tongue, too, was no longer in service; but coffee and cognac got him back on his mental feet again. His whimpering tones and his wrinkled trembling chin with tears dripping down it aroused Peeperkorn's eminent interest, and he stood there now with a raised forefinger and a raised brow of arabesques, calling everyone's attention to Wehsal's condition.

"That is—," he said. "That is indeed—no, permit me to say: holy! Dry his chin, my child—here, take my napkin. Or no, better still, refrain. He himself chooses not to do it. Ladies and gentlemen—holy! Holy in every sense of the word, both Christian and heathen. A primal phenomenon. A phenomenon of first—of highest—no, no, that is—"

This "that is—that is indeed—" supplied the keynote for the directive, explanatory comments with which he steered the party along—always accompanied by precise cultured gestures that were close to burlesque by now. He would typically raise the circle he made with bent forefinger and thumb to just above his ear, while coyly tilting and turning his head away—and the emotions this evoked were much like those one might feel watching an elderly priest of some alien cult hitch up his robes and dance with strange grace before the sacrificial altar. Then he would sprawl back again in all his grandeur, lay one arm across the back of a neighboring chair, and bewilder them all by demanding they plunge with him into his vivid, keen imaginings of morning—of a frosty, dark winter morning, when the yellowish glow of a nightstand lamp is mirrored in the window-pane and shines out into bare branches, stiff in the icy fog of a morning harsh with the cries of crows. With a few suggestive phrases, he could turn a prosaic everyday scene into stark reality, so that they all shivered when he now spoke of the ice-cold water in the sponge that you pressed to the back of your neck on such a morning—and called it holy. It was a mere digression, an instructive example to sensitize them to the basics of life, an impromptu fantasy, which he then dropped to turn his official and emphatic emotional engagement back to the immediate demands of the late hour's festive abandon. He was manifestly, indiscriminately in love with each and every female in sight—without respect of person. His advances to the dwarf were such that the crippled woman grinned until her aged, oversize face was a wreath of wrinkles; he paid Frau Stöhr compliments that made the vulgar woman roll her shoulder forward even farther and turned her affectations into almost crazed antics; he asked Fräulein Kleefeld to kiss him on his great, ragged lips and charmed even disconsolate Frau Magnus—and all without any detriment to the tender devotion he showed his traveling companion, whose hand he gallantly and frequently pressed to his lips. "Wine," he said, "women—that is—that is indeed—permit me to say—doomsday—Gethsemane—"

Around two o'clock the rumor sprang up that "the boss"—Director Behrens, that is—was moving toward the social rooms at a forced march. And in that same moment, panic raged among the unnerved guests. Chairs and ice-buckets were upended. People fled via the library. In a fit of royal fury at the sudden disruption of his feast of life, Peeperkorn first banged his fist on the table and then called out after the scattering company—something about "spineless slaves"—but nevertheless reconciled himself somewhat to the idea presented by Hans Castorp and Frau Chauchat that his banquet had lasted for almost six hours now and would have to come to an end at some point in any case, even lent his ear to a reminder about sleep's holy refreshment, and at last consented to let them escort him to bed.

"Assist me, my child. Assist me on the other side, young man," he said to Frau Chauchat and Hans Castorp. And so the two of them helped him heave his ponderous body out of the chair and now offered their arms; linked together with them, he walked, or staggered, down the path toward bed, with legs spread wide and mighty head tilted toward one raised shoulder, lurching now toward one of his escorts and now toward the other. In allowing them to support and pilot him, he was in fact treating himself to a kind of regal luxury. Presumably, had it been necessary, he could have walked on his own—he disdained such an effort, however, which could have served only one small, inferior purpose: to hide his drunkenness out of embarrassment. And he was evidently not in the least embarrassed by it; on the contrary, he luxuriated grandly in it and took royal delight in jostling his escorts to the right or left as he tottered along.

On the way, he commented: "Children—nonsense—one is absolutely not—if at this moment—you would see for yourselves—ridiculous—"

"Ridiculous," Hans Castorp confirmed. "No doubt about it. One gives the classic gifts of life their due by boldly staggering in their honor. But in all seriousness . . . I, too, have had my share, but despite any so-called drunkenness, I am perfectly aware what a special honor it is for me to bring a manifest personality to his bed. Indeed the effects of intoxication are so minor that in terms of stature, where there can truly be no comparison—"

"Come, come, my little chatterbox," Peeperkorn said; he lurched, forcing Hans Castorp against the banister and pulling Frau Chauchat along with him.

It was obvious now that the rumor about the director's approach had been an idle threat. Perhaps the weary dwarf had invented it to break up the party. In light of which, Peeperkorn stopped in his tracks and was about to turn back to continue drinking; but from both sides came better council, and so he let them set him back into motion.

The Malayan valet, a little man in a white necktie and black silk slippers, stood waiting in the corridor outside the door to his master's apartment, and he received him with a bow, laying one hand across his chest.

"Kiss one another!" Peeperkorn commanded. "Place a good-night kiss upon the brow of this charming woman, young man," he said to Hans Castorp. "She will have no objection, and will repay you in kind. Do it for my sake and with my blessing." But Hans Castorp declined.

"No, Your Majesty," he said. "I beg your pardon, but it would not do."

Leaning against his valet now, Peeperkorn raised those arabesques high and demanded to know why it would not do.

"Because I cannot exchange kisses on the brow with your traveling companion," Hans Castorp said. "I wish all a pleasant rest. No, from any point of view, that would be utter nonsense."

And since Frau Chauchat was already moving toward the door to the room, Peeperkorn let this headstrong young man go, although he stared after him for a good while, gazing over both his own shoulder and the Malayan's, his brow deeply creased in amazement at such an act of insubordination, to which his royal nature was quite unaccustomed.

Mynheer Peeperkorn (Continued)

MYNHEER PEEPERKORN remained at the Berghof the entire winter—as much of it as was left—and well into spring, so that toward the end of his stay there was a quite memorable excursion (which included Settembrini and Naphta) to Flüela Valley and its waterfall. —The end of his stay? So he did not stay on longer than that? —No, no longer. —So he departed? —Yes and no. —Yes and no? No mystery-mongering, please. Surely it can be said straight out. Lieutenant Ziemssen died, not to mention a good many less honorable folks who have joined the dance of death. And so our vague Peeperkorn was carried off by his malignant tropical fever, is that it? —No, that's not what happened to him. But why this impatience? Not everything can be known right off. That must still be taken as one of the conditions of life and of storytelling, and surely no one is about to rebel against God-given forms of human understanding. Let us honor time at least to the extent that the nature of our story allows. There is not that much time left in any case, it's rushing by slapdash as it is, or if that's too noisy a way of putting it, it's whisking past hurry-scurry. A little hand measures our time, minces along as if measuring seconds; and yet, whenever it cold-bloodedly moves past a high-point without bothering to stop, that still means something, though God only knows what. We have been up here years now, that much is certain—a dizzying stay, an addict's dream, but without opium or hashish. The censor will soon be after us. And yet to counter all this nasty befuddlement we have intentionally introduced a great deal of clear reason and rigorous logic. It is not by accident, please note, that we have chosen to associate with minds like those of Messrs. Naphta and Settembrini, instead of surrounding ourselves with vague Peeperkorns—which leads us, in fact, to a comparison that in many respects and particularly in regard to *stature* can only be resolved in favor of this late arrival, just as it was resolved in Hans Castorp's own mind as he lay on his balcony and admitted that those two hyperarticulate mentors, tugging at both sides of his soul, simply shrank beside Pieter Peeperkorn, until he was inclined to call them the same name the Dutchman had called him in a fit of drunken royal banter—"little chatterboxes"—and decided it was a piece of good luck that hermetic pedagogy had also brought him into contact with such a manifest personality.

This personality had appeared on the scene as Clavdia Chauchat's traveling companion and therefore as a tremendous disruption—but Hans Castorp did not let that alter his judgment of the man. He did not, we repeat, let it alter his honestly deferential, if at times slightly brash sympathy for a man of stature—simply because that man shared traveling expenses with a lady from whom Hans Castorp had borrowed a pencil on Mardi Gras evening. That would not have been like him—though we are quite aware that many a lady or gentleman in our circle of readers may be offended by such a "lack of temperament" and would prefer that he despise and avoid Peeperkorn, that he refer to him, at least to himself, as nothing but an ass, a babbling old sot, instead of visiting the Dutchman during his intermittent attacks of fever, when he would sit down beside the bed for a chat (a word that applies, of course, only to *his* contribution to the conversation, not to the words of the grand Peeperkorn) and let the power of that personality work upon him the way new sights work upon a tourist thirsty for knowledge. For that is what he did, and we recount the fact, indifferent to the danger of its reminding anyone of Ferdinand Wehsal and of how he carried Hans Castorp's overcoat. There is no resemblance. Our hero was no Wehsal; the depths of misery were not for him. He was simply not a "hero," which is to say, he did not let his relationship with the man be determined by the woman. Holding to our principle of not making him any better or worse than he was, we can state that he simply refused—not consciously, not expressly, but quite naively refused—to let ideas out of novels undermine his sense of justice when dealing with his own sex or limit the experiences he needed for growth in this arena of life. That may not please the ladies—we believe we can say that Frau Chauchat was instinctively annoyed by it, one or two pointed remarks that she let slip, and which we shall insert at some juncture, indicated as much. But perhaps it was this personality trait that made him such a suitable object for pedagogic rivalry.

Pieter Peeperkorn often lay sick in bed—that he did so on the day after that first evening of cards and champagne should come as no surprise. Almost all the guests at that extended and intense party were in a sorry state, not excluding Hans Castorp, who had a bad headache, but did not let that affliction prevent him from paying a sick call on his host of the previous evening; when he ran into the Malayan on the second floor, he asked him to pass on the request and was told he would be welcome.

Entering through a parlor that separated Frau Chauchat's room from the Dutchman's bedroom, which contained two beds, he discovered the latter was conspicuously more spacious and more elegantly furnished than the average Berghof room. There were silk-upholstered easy chairs and tables with legs that had soft, curving lines; a white carpet covered the floor, and the beds were not the customary hygienic deathbeds, but quite splendid affairs: of polished cherry, with brass hardware and a little canopy—without curtains—that joined the two beds as a kind of small, protective baldachin.

Peeperkorn was lying in one of the beds, with books, letters, and newspapers strewn across a red silk quilt, and was reading the *Telegraaf* with the help of his high-bridged, horn-rimmed pince-nez. Next to him on a chair was a tray with coffee things and on his nightstand, amid glasses of medicine, was a half-empty bottle of wine—the simple, sparkling Swiss red of the night before. To Hans Castorp's quiet amazement, the Dutchman was not wearing a white shirt, but a woolen affair with long sleeves that buttoned at the wrists and an open, collarless neck, the smooth fabric clinging to the old man's broad shoulders and massive chest. This outfit set the human grandeur of that head in strong relief against the pillow, in part lending it a less bourgeois, more working-class look, in part suggesting a sculptured, immortalized bust.

"By all means, young man," he said, grabbing his pince-nez by its high bridge and removing it. "I beg you, please—not at all. On the contrary." And Hans Castorp sat down beside him, hiding his sympathetic surprise—if indeed genuine admiration was not the emotion his sense of justice demanded of him—behind amiable, bright chatter, which Peeperkorn seconded with magnificent scraps of conversation and very compelling gestures. He did not look good—looked worse for wear in fact, yellow, downright sick. Toward morning he had had an attack of fever, which always left him exhausted and was accompanied now by the unpleasant consequences of drink.

"We overdid it last night," he said. "No, permit me to say—overdid it badly. You are still—fine, and so it makes no real—but at my age and in my compromised—my child," he said, turning with mild, yet resolute sternness to Frau Chauchat, who had just entered from the parlor, "—fine, fine, but I repeat, better attention should have been paid, I should have been prevented from—" Something like gathering royal wrath came to his face and voice as he spoke these words. But one needed only to imagine what sort of a storm would have erupted had anyone seriously attempted to disturb him in his drinking, to realize just how unfair and unreasonable such an objection was. It was probably just a part of grandeur. His traveling companion ignored it, too, and greeted Hans Castorp, who had risen from his chair—though she did not extend him her hand, but simply smiled and gestured for him "oh, but please" to resume his seat and "oh, but please" not to let her interrupt his tête-à-tête with Mynheer Peeperkorn. She busied herself with this and that in the room, instructed the valet to remove the coffee things, disappeared for a while, then returned again on cat's feet, but did not sit down, just stood there and joined briefly in their conversation, or—to record Hans Castorp's general impression—monitored it a bit. But of course! It had been no problem for her to return to the Berghof in the company of a personality of grand stature; but when the man who had waited for her here so long now displayed the reverence due such a personality, from man to man, she revealed her own uneasiness in pointed phrases like "oh, but please." Hans Castorp could only smile at it—but he bent down over his knees to hide his smile and experienced the inner glow of joy.

Peeperkorn offered him a glass of wine from the bottle on the nightstand. Under such circumstances, the Dutchman remarked, the best thing was to pick up where one had left off the night before, and this sparkling wine had the same good effect as soda water. He touched glasses with Hans Castorp, who as he sipped watched the freckled, lance-nailed captain's hand, the woolen shirt buttoned just above its wrist, lift the glass to the broad, ragged lips that now formed around the rim and toss the wine down the bouncing workingman's, or sculptured bust's, gullet. They then spoke about the medicine on the nightstand, a brown liquid, from which Peeperkorn took the spoonful Frau Chauchat urged upon him. It was an antipyretic, mainly quinine. The Dutchman gave his guest a little sample, just so he could experience its rich, bitter, spicy taste; and he went on to praise quinine at some length, because its beneficial effects were not limited simply to destroying germs and regulating body temperature, but it also deserved to be celebrated as a tonic that retarded the metabolism of protein and enhanced one's appetite. In short, it was a true regaling cordial, a splendid drink that invigorated, stimulated, and quickened the system—an intoxicating drug, as well, by the way; one could very easily get a little tipsy and mellow from it, he said, gesturing with both fingers and head as he had the night before in the grand jocular fashion that made him resemble a dancing heathen priest.

Yes, a splendid substance, this china-bark! European pharmacology had known of it, by the way, for less than three hundred years, and chemistry had discovered quinine less than a hundred years before—that is, the alkaloid that was the basis of its virtue—discovered and to some extent analyzed it, though thus far the chemists could not claim to understand its composition well enough to produce it artificially. In general, our pharmacologists would do well not to be too overweening about their knowledge, for they had the same problem with a great many things: they knew this and that about the dynamics and effects of a substance, but any question as to precise causes all too frequently proved an embarrassment. The young man needed only to look at toxicology. No one would be able to give him any information about the elementary properties that produced the effects of so-called poisons. Snake venoms, for instance, why, no more was known about them than that, as animal products, they were included among the complex proteins, were made up of simpler proteins that in certain—but as yet quite uncertain—combinations packed a wallop. Introduced into the bloodstream, they brought forth results we considered quite astounding, simply because we were not used to equating protein and poison. But the world of substances, Peeperkorn said— holding the ring of perfection and the three finger lances up next to his head, which he had now lifted from the pillow to gaze out with pale eyes from under the arabesques of his brow—the world of substances was such that they all concealed both life and death simultaneously, all were both therapeutic and poisonous. Pharmacology and toxicology were one and the same thing—we were healed by poisons, and a substance considered an agent of life could, under certain circumstances, in a single convulsion kill within seconds.

He spoke very forcefully and with unusual coherence about medicines and poisons, and Hans Castorp tilted his head and nodded as he listened, less concerned with the contents of what was said, which seemed very important to the Dutchman, than with quietly exploring the effects of the man's personality, which ultimately was as inexplicable as the effects of snake venoms. Dynamics, that was everything in the world of substances, Peeperkorn said, all else was relative. Quinine was a therapeutic poison, too, of first-class potency. Four grams of it caused dizziness, deafness, shortness of breath, produced blurred vision like atropine, intoxicated like alcohol; and the workers in quinine factories had bloodshot eyes and swollen lips, suffered from skin rashes. And he began to talk about the cinchona, the china-bark tree, about the primeval forests of the Cordillera, where it grew at altitudes above ten thousand feet, which was why the bark, known as "Jesuits' powder," had been so late in coming to Spain— though the natives of South America had long known its powers. He described the Dutch government's massive cinchona plantations on Java, from which each year many millions of pounds of the bark were exported in the form of reddish, cinnamon-like quills to Amsterdam and London. There was something about bark as such, the tissue between the epidermis and the cambium of ligneous plants, Peeperkorn said—it almost always possessed extraordinary dynamic virtues, both for good and evil. Primitive peoples' understanding of such drugs far exceeded our own. On some islands east of New Guinea young people prepared a love potion from the bark of a particular tree, presumably a poisonous species like the *Antiaris toxicaria* of Java, which like the manzanilla tree exhaled toxic vapors that could fatally stupefy man and beast. They took the bark of this tree, then ground it into a powder, mixed the powder with rasped coconut, rolled the mixture in a leaf, and roasted it. They then sprinkled the tea from this mixture into the face of the desired reluctant lover while she slept, causing her to burn with love for whoever sprinkled it. Sometimes it was the bark of roots that had such qualities, like those of a vine on the Malay peninsula called *Strychnos tieuté*, with which the natives mixed snake venom to make upas-rajah, a drug that when introduced into the bloodstream, with a dart or arrow for instance, led to almost instant death, although there was no one who could have told young Hans Castorp how it actually did so. This much was clear, however: upas stood in close dynamic relationship to strychnine. Peeperkorn was sitting up in bed now and with a lightly trembling captain's hand he would occasionally set the wineglass to his ragged lips and take great, thirsty gulps. He went on to speak about the "crow's-eye tree" of the Coromandel coast, from whose orange-yellow berries, the "crow's eyes," was extracted the most dynamic alkaloid of all, called strychnine. Keeping his voice at a low whisper, while lines creased his raised brow, he described the ash-gray branches, the garishly shiny leaves, and the yellow-green blossoms of this tree, so that as young Hans Castorp pictured it in his mind's eye, the image was both dismal and hysterically garish, leaving him with a rather eerie feeling.

Frau Chauchat broke in now, saying that this was not good for Peeperkorn, that the conversation was fatiguing him, might cause another fever attack, and as much as she disliked interrupting their visit, she really did have to ask Hans Castorp to let that be all for now. Which he did, of course; but over the next few months, he would often sit at the regal man's bedside after one of these quartan attacks—while Frau Chauchat came and went, casually monitoring the conversation or participating with a few words of her own. And even on days when Peeperkorn was free of fever, Hans Castorp would spend several hours with him and his pearl-necklaced traveling companion. For when the Dutchman was not confined to bed, he seldom failed to gather about him a small, constantly changing assortment of Berghof guests for after-dinner games with wine and other regalements, either in the social rooms as on that first occasion, or in the restaurant; and Hans Castorp would take his customary seat between the great man and the careless woman. They kept company even outdoors, took walks together, and were joined at times by Herr Ferge and Herr Wehsal, and soon by Settembrini and Naphta as well, for they could not have failed to run into those intellectual adversaries; Hans Castorp thought himself very lucky to be able to introduce them to Peeperkorn, and, at last, to Clavdia Chauchat as well—and was totally unconcerned whether the disputants welcomed these new acquaintances and connections. He was quietly confident that they required a pedagogic object and would rather put up with unwelcome society than entirely forfeit the chance to thrash out their differences before him.

And he was not mistaken in assuming that the members of his motley circle of friends would at least get used to not getting used to one another. To be sure, there was quite sufficient tension, strain, and even silent hostility among them; and we ourselves are amazed that our inconsequential hero managed to keep the group together. Our only explanation is that there was something shrewdly life-affirming in our hero's nature, which allowed him to find everything "worth listening to" and which one might also call obligingness, in the sense that it not only bound him to very different kinds of people and personalities, but also to some extent linked them to one another.

What a strange interweaving of relationships it was! We are intrigued by the idea of making that tangle of threads visible to all for just a moment, much as Hans Castorp himself was able to observe it with a shrewd and life-affirming eye on their walks together. There was miserable Wehsal, whose desire for Frau Chauchat continued to smolder and who humbly revered Peeperkorn and Hans Castorp, the former for his command of the present, the latter for events in the past. There was Clavdia Chauchat herself, that charming, softly treading patient and traveler, who was Peeperkorn's vassal, by choice and conviction, to be sure—yet the sight of a cavalier from a long-ago Mardi Gras night on such good terms with her lord and master always made her somewhat uneasy, honing her emotions to a point. But was not the annoyance she felt in this regard somehow reminiscent of her relationship to Settembrini, young Hans Castorp's pedagogic friend? To that eloquent orator and humanist, whom she could not stand and called arrogant and inhumane? How she would have loved to have confronted him and demanded to know what those words (spoken in his Mediterranean tongue, of which she understood not a syllable more than he of hers, though with none of his supercilious contempt)—what those words had been that he had called after the agreeable young German, just as the lad was about to approach her that night, this pretty little bourgeois lad who came from a good family and had a moist spot? Hans Castorp—"head over heels in love," as people say, and yet not in the happy sense of the idiom, but as one loves when it is forbidden and unreasonable, when there are no calm little songs from the flatlands to be sung, terribly in love, dependent, subjugated, suffering and serving— was nevertheless a man who remained shrewd enough amid his slavery to know exactly what his devotion was worth, and would continue to be worth, to the slinking patient with the enchanting "Tartar slits"; and she could be constantly reminded of its worth, or so he told himself despite his suffering subjugation, by the behavior of Herr Settembrini, who only too openly confirmed her own suspicions by attitudes as dismissive toward her as humanistic courtesy allowed. The worst part—or, in Hans Castorp's eyes, the best—was that she did not find any real compensation, either, in her relationship to Leo Naphta, in whom she had set some hope. Granted, she did not have to deal here with Herr Lodovico's fundamental repudiation of her character, and the essentials for conversation were somewhat more favorable, so that the two of them, Clavdia and the caustic little man, would sometimes move away from the others to talk: about books, about questions of political philosophy, where they found agreement in radical answers; and Hans Castorp sometimes ingenuously joined in as well. Yet she could not help noticing that the parvenu, being a cautious man like all parvenus, showed a certain aristocratic restraint toward her; his Spanish terrorism ultimately had little in common with her own door-slamming, vagabonding "*hu*maneness." And last and subtlest of all, there was a gentle malice that was hard to define, but which she, with a woman's heightened awareness, surely had to feel drifting toward her from *both* adversaries, Settembrini and Naphta (and indeed her Mardi Gras cavalier felt it as well), and which had its origin in their relationship to Hans Castorp: the pedagogue's inherent ill will toward women as a disruptive and distracting element, a silent and primal hostility that united the two men by abrogating their intense pedagogic rivalry.

And did not this animosity also play a role in the two dialecticians' attitude toward Pieter Peeperkorn? Hans Castorp thought he noticed something of that, perhaps because he had expected it to be much worse and had been more than a little impatient to introduce the royal stammerer to his own two "viziers," as he sometimes jokingly called them, and to study the effect. Mynheer did not seem quite as grand out in the open as in a closed room. The soft felt hat that he wore pulled down deep hid the white flames of hair and massive tracery of his brow and made his features look smaller, shrank them as it were; even his red nose lost some of its majesty. And he was less good at walking than standing. He took small steps and had a habit of letting the full weight of his great body, including the head, tilt toward the foot he had just put forward, which made him look more like a kindly, senile old man than a king. Although he always stood pulled up to full height, he did not usually walk that way, but compressed himself somehow. Even then, however, he towered over Herr Lodovico and was several heads taller than little Naphta; but that was not the only reason why his presence weighed so heavily— so overwhelmingly heavily, just as Hans Castorp had pictured it in his imagination—on the existence of the two political theorists.

So heavy was the weight that in comparison they seemed diminished, impaired—which not only the sly observer noticed, but also, without doubt, those involved, both the two frail hyperarticulate gentlemen and the grand stammerer himself. Peeperkorn certainly treated Naphta and Settembrini with courtesy and attention—with a respect that Hans Castorp would have called ironic, if the insight that irony and great stature are incompatible had not prevented him from doing so. Kings know nothing of irony—not even when employed as an honest device of classical rhetoric, not to mention its more complicated forms. And so the Dutchman's behavior toward Hans's friends was characterized by what might better be called a refined, but grand mockery, sometimes hidden under slightly exaggerated seriousness, sometimes quite open. "Yes-yes-yes-yes!" he might say, waving an admonishing finger at them, while turning his head away with a droll smile playing on his ragged lips. "That is—those are— Gentlemen, let me call your attention to—cerebrum, cerebral, you understand. No—no, agreed, extraordinary, that is, it just goes to show—" They took their revenge by exchanging glances—their eyes would meet and then turn heavenward in despair—and even attempted to draw Hans Castorp into the game; he, however, refused.

There came a day when Herr Settembrini directly confronted his pupil, and so betrayed his own pedagogic uneasiness. "But in God's name, my good engineer, he is just a stupid old man. What do you see in him? Can he do anything for you? It is beyond all reason. It would be clear enough—though not necessarily praiseworthy—if you were simply taking him into the bargain, if in seeking out his company you were seeking out that of his current sweetheart. But it is impossible not to notice that you pay almost more attention to him than to her. I implore you, help me understand this."

Hans Castorp laughed. "By all means," he said. "Agreed! The fact is, as we know—permit me to say—fine!" And he tried to ape Peeperkorn's cultured gestures as well. "Yes, yes," he said, and laughed again. "You find that stupid, Herr Settembrini, and certainly it is vague, which in your eyes is worse than stupid. Ah, stupidity. There are so many different kinds of stupidity, and cleverness is one of the worst. Hello! Why, I think I've just coined a phrase, a *bon mot*. How do you like it?"

"Very much. I cannot wait for your first collection of aphorisms. Perhaps there is still time, however, to ask you to take into account certain observations we have occasionally made concerning the misanthropic nature of paradoxes."

"It shall be done, Herr Settembrini. Absolutely—shall be done. No, in this *bon mot* of mine, you do not see me in hot pursuit of paradoxes. I was merely trying to point out the great difficulty one has in defining 'stupidity' and 'cleverness.' It is so hard to keep them separate, they are so intertwined. I know very well how you hate any sort of mystical *guazzabuglio* and are a man who believes in values and judgments—value judgments—and I quite agree with you. But the issue of 'stupidity' and 'cleverness' is at times a complete mystery, and it must be permissible to concern oneself with mysteries, always presuming it is an honest attempt to get to the bottom of them, if possible. Let me ask you this question: Can you deny that he has us all in his pocket? I'm putting it crudely, and yet, as nearly as I can tell, you cannot deny it. He puts us in his pocket, and somehow or other he has the right to make fun of us all. But why? And how? And where does it come from? It is certainly not a matter of his cleverness. One can hardly speak of cleverness in this case, I admit. He is much more a man of fuzziness and feelings, feelings are his cup of tea, so to speak—if you'll forgive me the colloquial phrase. What I am saying is this: it is not by way of cleverness that he puts us in his pocket, not through intellectual prowess. You wouldn't stand for that. And it really is out of the question. But surely it is not physical prowess, either! It cannot be because of his broad captain's shoulders, or any raw brute force, or because he could lay any one of us flat with his fist—it would never occur to him that he could, and if it did, why, a few civilized words would calm him down. And so it's not physical, either. And yet the physical dimension does play a role, without a doubt—not in the sense of brute strength, but in another, more mystical sense—the moment anything physical plays a role, things always get mystical. And the physical merges into the intellectual, and vice versa, and cannot be differentiated, and stupidity and cleverness cannot be differentiated. But the effect is there, the dynamic effect, and we find ourselves stuck in his pocket. And for that we have only one word at hand, and that word is 'personality.' We use the word in another, perfectly reasonable sense, too: we are all personalities—moral and legal and all those other sorts of personalities. But that is not what I mean. I'm talking about a mystery that extends beyond stupidity and cleverness, and that is what we need to concern ourselves with—partly to get to the bottom of it, if possible, and partly, to the extent that it is not possible, to edify ourselves. And if you are for values, then, in the end, personality is a positive value, too, I should think—a more positive value than stupidity or cleverness, positive in the highest degree, *absolutely* positive, like life itself—in short, a value for life and in that sense suitable for our earnest consideration. And that's how I thought I should respond to what you said about stupidity."

Of late, Hans Castorp no longer got tangled up and confused during such gushings. He did not get stuck, but said his piece to the end, came to a full stop, lowering his voice and going his way like a man—although he always blushed and was actually somewhat afraid of the critical lull that would follow his own silence and give him time to feel embarrassed.

Herr Settembrini let silence reign. Then he said, "You deny that you are in hot pursuit of paradoxes. By now you should know that I have an equal dislike of seeing you in hot pursuit of mysteries. By turning personality into an enigma, you run the danger of idol-worship. You are venerating a mask. You see something mystical where there is only mystification, one of those hollow counterfeits with which the demon of corporeal physiognomy enjoys taunting us on occasion. You have never spent any time in theatrical circles, have you? So you do not know those thespian faces that can embody the features of a Julius Caesar, a Goethe, and a Beethoven all in one, but whose owners, the moment they open their mouths, prove to be the most miserable ninnies under the sun."

"Fine, a freak of nature," Hans Castorp said. "And yet not just a freak, not just something to taunt us. For people to be actors, they must have talent, and talent is something that goes beyond stupidity and cleverness, it is itself a value for life. Mynheer Peeperkorn has talent, too, no matter what you may say, and he uses it to put us in his pocket. Set Herr Naphta in the corner of a room and have him deliver a lecture on Gregory the Great and the City of God, something well worth listening to—and in the other corner have Peeperkorn stand there with his strange mouth and a brow raised in great creases and say nothing except, 'By all means! Permit me to say—settled!' And you will see people gather around Peeperkorn, down to the last man, and Naphta will be left sitting there alone with his cleverness and his City of God, although he can express himself so clearly that it makes your blood and spit run cold, to use one of Behrens's phrases."

"You should be ashamed of yourself, worshiping success like that," Herr Settembrini chided him. "*Mundus vult decipi.* I do not demand that people flock around Herr Naphta. He is a dreadful obstructionist. But I would be inclined to stand at his side in the imaginary scene you have just painted with such reprehensible relish. Go ahead and despise distinctions, precision, logic, the coherence of the human word. Go ahead and despise it in favor of some sort of hocus-pocus of insinuation and emotional charlatanry—and the Devil will definitely have you in his—"

"But I assure you, he can speak coherently when he warms to his topic," Hans Castorp said. "He once told me about dynamic drugs and poisonous Asian trees, and it was so interesting it was almost eerie—interesting things are always a little eerie—and yet it was interesting not in and of itself, but actually only in connection with the effect of his personality. That was what made it both eerie and interesting at the same time."

"Of course, your weakness for things Asian is well known. And indeed I cannot treat you to such wonders," Herr Settembrini replied, and with such bitterness that Hans Castorp quickly explained that the benefits of the Italian's conversation and teaching were to be found in an entirely different arena, of course, and no one would even think of making comparisons that would be unfair to both parties.

Herr Settembrini, however, ignored and scorned this bit of courtesy. "In any case," he continued, "one can only admire your businesslike composure, my good engineer. It borders on the grotesque, you must admit. As things stand—well, your dunderhead has stolen your Beatrice. I call a spade a spade. And what do you do? It is unprecedented."

"A difference in temperament, Herr Settembrini. A difference having to do with the heat of one's blood, one's sense of chivalry. Of course, as a man of the South, you would probably suggest poison or a dagger or at the least shape the matter along social and emotional lines, in short, have me play cock of the walk. That would be very manly of me, to be sure, socially masculine and gallant. But I see it differently. I am not at all manly in the sense that I regard other men as my rivals in courting—perhaps I am not masculine at all, but most certainly not in the sense that I automatically termed 'social,' although I don't really know why. I ask my sluggish heart if there is anything I can reproach him for. Did he knowingly wrong me? Insults must be done with intention, or they are not insults. And as for 'wrong'—why, there I should have to turn to *her*, which I certainly have no right to do, none at all, and most especially not in regard to Peeperkorn. Because first of all, he is a personality, which means something to women in and of itself, and second, he is not a civilian like me, but a kind of military man, like my poor cousin. What I mean is, he has a *point d'honneur*, honor is his cup of tea, and that is a matter of feeling, of life. I'm talking nonsense, I know, but I would rather babble away and at least partially express something difficult than reproduce impeccable clichés. That is perhaps a military trait in my own character, if I may say so."

"Say it in any case," Settembrini replied with a nod. "That would definitely be a trait one might praise. The courage of self-recognition and expression—that is literature, that is humanity."

And so they parted on satisfactory terms on this occasion; Herr Settembrini brought the exchange to a conciliatory conclusion, and had good reason for doing so. His position was certainly not so inviolable that he could afford to push the limits of such rigor; a conversation about jealousy put him on rather slippery ground. At some point he would have had to admit that, given his pedagogic streak, his own masculinity was not of a strictly social, cock-of-the-walk nature, either, which explained why the grand Peeperkorn was as much a disruption to his meditations as were Naphta and Frau Chauchat; and finally, he could not hope to disabuse his pupil of the effects of a personality and superior nature, effects from which neither he nor his partner in cerebral matters was able to exclude himself.

The two of them did best when intellectual breezes blew, when they debated and could capture the attention of the strollers with one of their elegant, passionate, academic arguments (though the tone of voice implied that it was one of the most burning questions of the day, of life itself) the burden of which they more or less carried alone, thereby neutralizing for its duration the presence of the man of "stature," who could offer only a brow creased in astonishment and some vague mocking scraps of commentary. But even under such circumstances, his weight was felt; he cast a shadow over the conversation, until it seemed to lose its brilliance, to forfeit its very substance somehow. His was a counterforce that they all could feel, but of which he was surely not even aware, or aware to God only knew what extent; but its weight was of no use to either argument, so that the issue itself seemed to pale, to lose its critical importance, indeed—though we hesitate to say it—to take on the stamp of frivolity. Or, to put it another way: their life-and-death duel of wits was constantly establishing some sort of subterranean connection to this epitome of stature strolling beside them and was enervated by its magnetism. There is no other way to characterize this mysterious process, so very annoying to the debaters. One can only say that, had there not been a Pieter Peeperkorn, the others would have felt much more constrained to take sides, when, for example, Leo Naphta defended the fundamental, archrevolutionary nature of the Church against the teachings of Herr Settembrini, who asserted that her sole historical purpose had been to serve as the patron of the dark forces of inertia and reaction and then went on to claim that the affirmation of life and a future open to revolution and renewal was bound up with the opposing principles of enlightenment, science, and progress, which had arisen in the glorious epoch that witnessed the rebirth of classical education—and drove home this profession of faith with gestures and a burst of eloquence. Whereupon Naphta felt obliged to offer cold, caustic proof—and his proof was almost blindingly incontrovertible—that the Church was the embodiment of the religious, ascetic ideal, and at her core not even remotely an advocate or supporter of forces whose concern was to maintain themselves: worldly education and civil authority, for instance; rather, from time immemorial the Church had inscribed radical overthrow upon her banner—destruction, root and branch. Everything that presumed itself worth preserving and that the pallid, cowardly, conservative bourgeoisie attempted to preserve—state and family, worldly art and science—had always stood in conscious or unconscious opposition to the religious ideal, to the Church, whose innate tendency and unswerving goal was the dissolution of the existing world order and the remaking of society on the model of an ideal, communistic City of God.

Herr Settembrini then took the floor, and by God, he knew how to make the most of it. How deplorable, he said, to confuse true Luciferian revolutionary thought with a general revolt of every bad instinct. Over the centuries, the Church's love of innovation had consisted of Inquisitions, whose task was to throttle all life-affirming ideas, to suffocate them in the smoke of the stake; but nowadays she was sending out her emissaries to announce that she was all for upending things, that her goal was to replace freedom, education, and democracy with dictatorship of the mob and barbarism. *Eh, eh*—that was indeed a dreadful sort of contradictory consistency, a consistent contradiction.

His adversary, Naphta responded, showed no lack of the same contradictions and consistencies; he thought of himself as a democrat, and yet expressed himself as something less than a friend of the common man and equality, indeed displayed a reprehensible aristocratic arrogance by describing the world's proletariat, who were called to provisional dictatorship, as a mob. But obviously he did behave like a real democrat when it came to the Church, which, as one proudly had to confess, represented the most noble force in human history—noble in the final and highest meaning of the word, nobility of the Spirit. For the ascetic Spirit—if he might be permitted a tautology—the Spirit that denied and destroyed the world, was nobility itself, the aristocratic principle in its purest form; it could never be popular, and indeed the Church had been essentially unpopular throughout the ages. If Herr Settembrini would bother to do a little research on the literature of the Middle Ages he would discover that fact: the people—taken in the widest sense—had always had a crude distaste for the Church and her ways, as evidenced, for example, in their regard for certain legendary monks, creations of popular fantasy, who opposed the ascetic ideal with wine, women, and song in a downright Luther-like fashion. Over time, all the instincts of worldly heroism, the cult of the warrior, even courtly poetry, had become more or less open in their opposition to the religious ideal, and thus to the hierarchy. For all that had been mere "world" and mob rule in comparison to the nobility of the Spirit represented by the Church.

Herr Settembrini thanked him for jogging his memory. The figure of the monk Ilsan in the epic *Rosengarten* contained a great many refreshing traits when compared with the graveyard aristocracy so highly praised here; and if he, Settembrini, was no friend of the German reformer to whom allusion had been made, they would nevertheless find him ready fervently to defend a doctrine based on democratic individualism against any sort of spiritual and feudal yearnings to dominate the personality.

"Oh my!" Naphta suddenly cried. Apparently the point was to suggest that the Church suffered from a lack of democracy and did not value human individuality, was that it? And what about the humane, unbiased character of canon law? Roman law made legal standing dependent upon citizenship; Germanic law, on one's being a free man within the tribe. But canon law demanded only orthodoxy and membership in the ecclesiastical community and, casting aside all national and social considerations, allowed slaves and prisoners of war the right to bequeath and inherit property.

Such rights, Settembrini remarked cuttingly, were probably not maintained without a sidelong glance at the "canonical share," which had to be subtracted from every will. And then he went on to speak of "clerical demagoguery," of the absolute lust for power that condescended to rouse the denizens of the underworld when the gods quite understandably did not wish to hear from them, and suggested that the Church was apparently more concerned with the quantity than the quality of souls saved, which indicated a profound lack of spiritual nobility.

A lack of noble intent—the Church? Herr Settembrini's attention was called to the implacable principle of aristocracy that lay behind the idea that shame can be inherited: the transference of major guilt to—democratically speaking—innocent offspring; the lifelong blemish attached to natural children, for example, including their lack of legal standing.

Naphta was told to be silent on that account—first, because it was an outrage to humane feelings, and second, because he, Settembrini, had heard enough evasions and could see through the tricks of his opponent's apologetics to the thoroughly infamous and devilish cult of nihilism, which desired to be called Spirit and managed to perceive something legitimizing and sanctifying in the acknowledged unpopularity of the ascetic principle.

And at this Naphta begged them to forgive him for laughing out loud. The nihilism of the Church, had he said? The nihilism of the most realistic system for exercising authority in the history of the world? Could it be that Herr Settembrini had never been touched by that breath of humane irony with which the Church continually made concessions to the world, to the flesh, cleverly acquiescing in order to disguise the ultimate consequences of the ascetic principle and letting the influence of the Spirit establish order by not opposing nature all too sternly? And so he had never heard of the refined priestly concept of indulgence, under which even a sacrament was included—marriage, to be precise, which unlike the other sacraments was not a positive good, but a defense against sin, conferred solely to limit sensual desire and to instill moderation, so that the ascetic principle, the ideal of chastity, might be affirmed without defying the flesh with unpolitic severity?

How could Herr Settembrini not help inveighing against such an atrocious misuse of the idea of the "politic," against this gesture of shrewd, conceited forbearance that the spirit—or what passed for spirit in this case—extended to its alleged guilty opposite, in the presumption that such "politic" action was necessary, when in truth no such noxious indulgence was required; he could not help castigating a damnable dualistic interpretation of the world that cursed the universe—in particular life itself *and* its fancied opposite, the spirit: for if the one was evil, then the other, as its pure negation, had to be evil as well. And he championed the innocence of lust—and Hans Castorp was reminded of that humanist's spare garret with its lectern and rush-bottom chairs and water carafe; whereas Naphta, after first claiming that lust could never be without guilt and that nature should, if you please, have a bad conscience in the presence of the Spirit, went on to refute the nihilism of the ascetic principle by defining the Church's policy of spiritual indulgence as "love"—and Hans Castorp found the word "love" sounded very odd coming from caustic, gaunt little Naphta.

And on and on it went, we know the game; Hans Castorp knew it, too. We listened along with him for a moment in order to observe, for instance, how such a peripatetic passage-at-arms might sound under the shadow of the personality strolling beside the combatants and how his presence might secretly enervate their struggle. And, indeed, a clandestine compulsion to take the presence of that personality into consideration killed the spark that normally leaped between the two—it was reminiscent of the dull, lifeless feeling that overcomes you when an electrical outlet turns out to be dead. Fine, that was that. Nothing crackled between the antagonists now, no lightning flashed, no current surged. The presence that intellect thought to neutralize, neutralized intellect instead. Hans Castorp observed it all with astonished curiosity.

Revolution and preservation—they looked to Peeperkorn as he trudged along with his hat pulled down low, hardly cutting a particularly grand figure as he tilted to one side with each step; they watched him jerk his head in jest toward the combatants, and heard those wide, irregular, ragged lips say: "Yes—yes—yes! Cerebrum, cerebral, you understand. That is—it just goes to show that—" And behold, the electrical outlet was dead as a doornail. They tried another one, resorted to stronger appeals, took up the issues of nobility, aristocracy, popularity. No spark. As if pulled by some magnetic force, the conversation turned personal. Hans Castorp pictured Clavdia's traveling companion lying in bed under his red silk quilt, in his collarless woolen shirt, half old proletarian, half royal bust—and with a feeble twitch the nerve of the argument died. Turn up the voltage! Here, negation and the cult of nihilism—there, the eternal yes and the Spirit's loving inclination toward life! But when you looked at Mynheer Peeperkorn—and the secret pull in his direction was irresistible—where was the nerve, the lightning flash, the current? In short, nothing happened, and that was, to use Hans's term, no more and no less than a mystery. It was something for him to jot down for his collection of aphorisms: one either expresses a mystery in the simplest words, or not at all. And to express this one, if we must, the only thing to say, as bluntly as possible, is that Pieter Peeperkorn—with his regal mask, his high, creased brow, his poignantly ragged lips—was both at the same time. Both viewpoints seemed to fit him, to cancel one another out when you looked at him: both this and that, the one as well as the other. Yes, this stupid old man, this masterful zero! He did not paralyze the nerve of antithesis with confusion and obstructionism the way Naphta did; he was not ambiguous like him, or if so, then in an entirely contrary, positive fashion—he was the staggering mystery that went not only beyond mere stupidity and cleverness, but also beyond so many of the other opposites that Settembrini and Naphta conjured up to create high tension for pedagogic purposes. Personality, so it seemed, was not pedagogic—and yet, what an opportunity it presented for a tourist thirsty for knowledge. What a strange feeling to watch this ambiguity coming from a king when the disputants began to speak of marriage and sin, the sacrament of indulgence, the guilt and innocence of lust. He tilted his head toward his shoulder and chest, the pained lips separated and spread, the mouth gaped in slack lamentation, the nostrils flared wide as if in anguish, the creases on the brow rose and spread, lending the eyes a look of pale suffering—a picture of bitterness. And behold, in a flash the martyrdom blossomed into sensuality. The tilt of the head suddenly implied roguishness; the lips, still open, smiled lewdly; the sybaritic dimple, familiar from earlier occasions, appeared in one cheek—and there was the dancing heathen priest, who jerked his head in jest and pointed in a cerebral direction. And they heard him say: "Ah, yes, yes, yes—agreed. That is—those are—it just goes to show—the sacrament of lust, you understand—"

And yet, as we have said, Hans Castorp's diminished friends and mentors were still at their best when arguing. They were in their element then, whereas "stature" was not, and one could at least be of differing minds as to what role it actually did play. But they were undoubtedly at a disadvantage when wit and Word and Spirit were no longer at issue, and the topic turned to facts, to earthy, practical affairs, to those questions and things where masterful natures truly prove themselves. Then it was all over for the antagonists, they stepped back into the shadows, became insignificant, and Peeperkorn grabbed the scepter—directed, decided, ordered, commanded, controlled. Was it any wonder, then, that he strove to achieve this state of affairs and to leave logomachy behind? He suffered as long as it reigned, or if it reigned too long; not out of vanity, however—Hans Castorp felt sure of that. Vanity has no stature, and greatness is never vain. No, Peeperkorn's desire for reality was rooted in something else: in "fear," to put it quite bluntly—in his obsession with honor, in the zeal for duty that Hans Castorp had tried to explain to Herr Settembrini and wanted to declare as a kind of military trait.

"Gentlemen—," the Dutchman said, raising his lance-nailed captain's hand in a gesture that both implored and commanded. "Fine, gentlemen, agreed, excellent! Asceticism—indulgence—sensual lust—let me say that—by all means! Eminently important! Eminently controversial! And yet, permit me to say—I fear that we are about to commit a—ladies and gentlemen, we are avoiding, we are irresponsibly avoiding the holiest of—" He took a deep breath. "This air, ladies and gentlemen, this day's foehn air so rich in character, so tenderly enervating, suggestive and reminiscent of spring's fragrance—we should not breathe it in merely so that in the form of—I implore you: we should not do it. That is an insult. For its own sweet, simple sake, we must totally and fully—oh, and with our highest and most perceptive—settled, ladies and gentlemen! And only as an act in purest praise of its properties should we then release it from our—but I must break off, ladies and gentlemen. I must break off in honor of this—" He had stopped now to lean back and look up, shading his eyes with his hat; they all followed his example. "I call your attention," he said, "to the heights above, far above us, to that black speck circling up there against the singular blue, shading into black— It is a bird of prey, a large bird of prey. It is, if I am not totally—gentlemen, and you my child, it is an eagle. I most emphatically call your attention—you see! That is no buzzard, no vulture—were you all as farsighted as I, what with my advancing—yes, my child, to be sure, advancing. My hair is white, to be sure. You could then tell as clearly as I from the blunt curvature of his pinions—an eagle, ladies and gentlemen. A golden eagle. He circles directly above us in the blue, without beating his wings he hovers there in those magnificent heights above our—and, to be sure, peers out from his keen, farsighted eyes beneath the jutting bone of the brow. The eagle, gentlemen, Jupiter's bird, the king of his race, the lion of the air! He has feathered legs and a beak of iron, an iron hook at the very tip, and talons of horrendous power, claws that turn inward, one long rear claw that forms an iron vise with those at the front. Look, like this!" And he tried to mimic an eagle's claw with his own lance-nailed captain's hand. "Good fellow, why do you peer and circle there!" he cried, turning to look back up. "Plummet! Strike that head, those eyes, with your iron beak, rip open the belly of the creature whom God has— Agreed! Settled! Your talons shall be tangled in its entrails and your beak shall drip with blood—"

He was bursting with enthusiasm, and that was the end of the promenaders' interest in Naphta and Settembrini's antinomies. And the sighting of the eagle had other unspoken effects on decisions and activities that now followed under Mynheer's direction: they made a stop; there was food and drink, quite outside the normal schedule, but with appetites now stimulated by silent thoughts of the eagle, a bout of eating and drinking, like so many that Mynheer initiated outside the Berghof, wherever he happened to be—in Platz or Dorf, at an inn in Glaris or Klosters, to which they would take the little train on excursions. They enjoyed the classic gifts under his majestic direction: coffee with cream and country breads, or rich cheeses and fragrant Alpine butter, which also tasted marvelous with hot, roasted chestnuts, all washed down by as much Veltliner red as the heart desired; and Peeperkorn would accompany these impromptu meals with grand tattered phrases, or he might demand a tale from Anton Karlovitch Ferge, the good-natured martyr to whom all higher things were utterly foreign, but who knew some very down-to-earth details about the manufacture of Russian galoshes—sulfur and other ingredients were added to raw rubber, and the finished boots were then lacquered and "vulcanized" at temperatures over two hundred and fifty degrees. He also told them about the Arctic Circle, to which business had taken him on several occasions, about the midnight sun and the perpetual winter at North Cape. And the descriptions emerged from his gnarled throat and from under his overhanging moustache: the steamer had looked very tiny against those massive cliffs and the steel-gray surface of the sea. And streaks of yellow light had spread across the sky—the northern lights. And it all had seemed very spooky to him—not just the whole scene, Anton Karlovitch had even seemed spooky to himself.

Such were the tales of Herr Ferge, the only person in the little group who stood outside its interwoven relationships. Speaking of which, there are two brief conversations from this same period that should be recorded, two curious, tête-à-tête interchanges our unheroic hero had with Clavdia Chauchat and her traveling companion, with each of them alone, that is—the first in the lobby one evening, when the "bothersome disruption" was lying upstairs with a fever; the second, one afternoon at Mynheer's bedside.

The lobby lay in semidarkness. The regular social gathering had been dull and cursory; the guests had departed early for their balconies and the late rest cure—those, that is, who did not follow unhealthy paths down into town, to dance and gamble. Only one ceiling lamp was lit somewhere in the deserted lobby, and the adjoining social rooms were hardly any brighter. But Hans Castorp knew that Frau Chauchat, who had eaten supper without her lord and master, had not yet returned to

the second floor and was lingering behind in the reading room; and so
he, too, hesitated to go upstairs. He was sitting at the far end of the
lobby, in an area one wide step up from the main space and separated
from it by two white arches with wood-paneled columns—was sitting
next to the tiled stove in a rocking chair like the one that had cradled
Marusya when Joachim engaged her in the only conversation they ever
had. He was smoking a cigarette, which was more or less permitted in
the lobby at that hour.

And here she came, he heard her footsteps, her dress trailing behind;
she was beside him, she was holding a letter by one corner and waving
it back and forth in the air, and she said in her Pribislav voice: "The
concierge is gone. Do give me a *timbre-poste*."

She was dressed in filmy dark silk this evening, a gown with a rounded
neckline and loose sleeves that gathered to buttoned cuffs at the wrists.
It was the sort of dress he was very partial to. There was the added touch
of her strand of pearls, which shimmered softly in the twilight. He looked
up into her Kirghiz eyes. "*Timbre?*" he repeated. "I don't have one."

"What, not a one? *Tant pis pour vous*. Not prepared to do a lady a
favor?" She pouted her lips and shrugged. "I'm disappointed. Gentlemen
should at least be punctual and dependable. I was under the impression
that you had sheets of them folded up and tucked away in a little pocket
of your wallet, all arranged according to denomination."

"No, why should I?" he said. "I never write letters. To whom, really?
At most a postcard now and then, and they're prestamped. To whom
should I be writing letters? I have no feeling whatever for the flatlands
anymore, I've lost that somehow. We had a folk song in school, that
went, 'The world is lost to me now.' That's how it is with me."

"Well, then, at least give me a *papyrosa*, my lost young man," she said,
sitting down opposite him next to the stove, on a bench cushioned with
a linen pillow. She crossed one leg over the other and held out her hand.
"It seems you come equipped with those." And without a word of thanks,
she nonchalantly took a cigarette from the silver case he held out to her,
then accepted a light from the pocket lighter he let flicker before her face
as she leaned forward. There was a voluptuousness in this spoiled woman's
"do give me," in the way she took without a word of thanks; but beyond
that, there was also a sense of mutual human—or better, *hu*mane—
interests, of sharing, of a naturalness, at once both savage and tender, in
the act of giving and taking.

With the critical eye of a lover, he remarked on all this to himself. Then
he said, "Yes, always have those. I always come equipped with those.
One must have them. How would one possibly manage without them?

That's what people call a passion, I believe. I am, to be frank, not a passionate man, but I do have my passions, detached passions."

"I find it terribly reassuring," she said, letting the inhaled smoke pour back out, "to hear that you are not a passionate man. But, then, how could you be? That would be a degeneration of the species. Passion—means to live life for life's sake. But I am well aware you Germans live it for the sake of experience. Passion means to forget oneself. But you do things in order to enrich yourselves. *C'est ça.* You haven't the least notion how repulsively egoistic that is of you and that someday it may well make you the enemy of humankind."

"Now, now! The enemy of humankind, just like that? That's quite a generalization, Clavdia. Do you have anything in particular, anyone special in mind when you say we do not live for life but for enrichment? You women don't usually moralize like that for no good reason. Ah, yes, morality. It's one of the things Naphta and Settembrini argue about. It is part of the great general confusion. A man doesn't really know whether he lives for his own sake or for life's sake, and no one can tell him for sure which it is, either. I think the boundaries are rather fluid. There is both egoistic sacrifice and sacrificial egoism. I suppose that on the whole it's the same with love. Of course, it's probably immoral of me that I'm unable to pay much attention to what you're saying about morality, since mainly I'm just happy that we're sitting here together, just as we did one time before and never again, not once since you came back. And that I can tell you how absolutely perfect those narrow cuffs look at your wrists, and how I love the way light silk billows around your arms—arms I know well . . ."

"I'm leaving."

"No, please, don't go. I shall pay all due respect to circumstances and personalities."

"One should at the least be able to count on that much from a man without passion."

"There, you see—you mock me, Clavdia, you scold me, just because I—you're going to leave, just because I . . ."

"If you wish to be understood, I would ask you to speak in a less fragmentary fashion."

"And so I'm not to benefit, not the least little bit, from all your practice in guessing at fragments? That's unfair—or at least I would say so if I weren't well aware that it is not a matter of fairness."

"Oh, no. Fairness is a detached passion. In contrast to jealousy, with which a detached person would simply make himself ridiculous."

"You see? Ridiculous. So, then, allow me my detachment. I repeat:

how could one possibly manage without it? For example, how could I have stood the waiting without it?"

"Beg your pardon?"

"Waiting for you, Clavdia."

"*Voyons, mon ami.* I will not dwell on the foolish stubbornness of your continuing to use my first name and informal pronouns. You are surely weary of my mentioning that by now—after all, I am not a prude, not some outraged bourgeois housewife."

"No, you aren't. Because you are ill. Illness gives you your freedom. It gives you a certain—wait, a word has just come to mind that I have never used before—it gives you a certain genius."

"We shall speak of genius some other time. That is not what I wanted to say. I demand only one thing. You cannot pretend that I had anything to do with your waiting—if indeed you did wait—that I encouraged you to wait, or even gave you permission to do so. You will please acknowledge here and now that the opposite is the case."

"Gladly, Clavdia, but of course. You did not ask me to wait, I waited quite on my own. I understand completely that it is a matter of importance to you—"

"There is something impertinent even in the way you concede the point. You are, on the whole, an impertinent person, God knows why. Not only in your dealings with me, but in general. Even your admiration, your deference is impertinent somehow. Don't think I don't notice. I should not even be talking to you, given your impudence, particularly not when you dare speak of waiting. It is irresponsible of you still to be here. You should have gone back to your work long before this, *sur le chantier*, or wherever it was."

"And now there is no genius whatever about you. You are speaking quite conventionally, Clavdia. Those are phrases. You can't mean that the way Settembrini does; but if not, how do you mean it? You said it just for something to say, I cannot take it seriously. I shall not undertake a wild departure, like my poor cousin, who died, just as you predicted he would, trying to do his duty in the flatlands, and who probably knew himself that he would die, but preferred that to continuing his rest-cure duties here. Fine, that's why he was a soldier. But I am not, I am a civilian. For me it would be deserting the colors to do what he did, to go down to the flatlands at all costs, despite Rhadamanthus's prohibition, and try to be of use and serve progress. That would be base ingratitude and the worst disloyalty to my illness and to genius and to my love for you, from which I bear both old scars and new wounds, and to those arms of yours, that I know well—though I must admit it was only in our dream, a dream with a touch of genius, that I came to know them, which certainly implies no consequences or duties for you, no limitations on your freedom."

She laughed, the cigarette still in her mouth, and her Tartar eyes narrowed to slits; leaning back against the wainscoting and supporting herself on both sides with her hands, one leg still crossed over the other, she jiggled her foot in its patent leather shoe.

"*Quelle générosité! Oh là, là, vraiment*, it's precisely the way I've always imagined an *homme de génie*, my poor little fellow."

"Enough of that, Clavdia. I am certainly no *homme de génie* by birth, any more than I am a man of stature—good God, no. But purely by chance—let us call it chance—I have been forced upward into these regions where genius flourishes. In a word—though you probably are not aware that there is such a thing as alchemistic, hermetic pedagogy—an enhancement, a transubstantiation to something higher, if you understand what I mean. Naturally, the substance that is forced upward by the application of external influences must have a little something to it to begin with. And I know very well just what there was to me: I have been an intimate of sickness and death for a very long time, and even as a boy I borrowed a pencil from you, in the same irrational way I did again on that Mardi Gras night. But irrational love is a mark of genius, because death, you see, is the principle of genius, the *res bina*, the *lapis philosophorum*, and it is also the pedagogic principle. For the love of death leads to the love of life and humanity. That is how it is. It came to me up on my balcony, and I am delighted to be able to tell it to you. There are two ways to life: the one is the regular, direct, and good way. The other is bad, it leads through death, and that is the way of genius."

"You are a silly philosopher, Hans Castorp," she said. "I can't claim that I understand everything in that complicated German brain of yours, but what you say sounds *hu*mane, and no doubt you are a good young man. And one must admit, you behaved quite *en philosophe*."

"All too *en philosophe* for your taste, Clavdia, is that it?"

"That's enough impertinence—it gets to be a bore. For you to wait like that was stupid and quite impermissible. But you aren't angry with me, are you, because you waited in vain?"

"Well, it was rather hard, Clavdia, even for a man with detached passions—hard on me and hard-hearted of you to come back with him, because of course you knew from Behrens that I was still here, waiting for you. But I've told you that I think of that night simply as a dream, our dream, and that I concede you have your freedom. After all, I did not really wait in vain, because you are here again, we are sitting next to one another just as then, I can hear the wonderful edge to your voice, so familiar to my ear for a very long time; and under that billowing silk are arms that I know well—though, granted, your traveling companion is lying upstairs in a fever, the great Peeperkorn, who gave you those pearls . . ."

"And with whom you are on such friendly terms, for your own enrichment."

"Don't hold it against me, Clavdia. Even Settembrini scolded me about it, but that's simply conventional prejudice. The man is a godsend—good Lord, he's a personality. He's well on in years—but so what. I would still understand completely how as a woman you must feel immense love for him. And you do love him very much, don't you?"

"All due deference to your philosophizing, my little German Hans," she said, passing her hand through his hair, "but I would not consider it *hu*mane to speak to you about my love for him."

"Ah, Clavdia, why not? I think humanity begins where people of no genius think it is already at an end. We can go ahead and talk about him. Do you love him passionately?"

She bent forward to toss the butt of her cigarette into the grate beside her, then sat back and crossed her arms. "He loves me," she said, "and his love makes me proud and grateful and devoted to him. That's something you can understand—or you're unworthy of the friendship he has offered you. His feelings compel me to follow him and help him. How could I not? Judge for yourself. How could it be *hu*manly possible to disregard his feelings?"

"Impossible," Hans Castorp agreed. "No, it would be quite out of the question, of course. How could any woman ever bring herself to disregard his feelings, disregard his fear of the feeling of being left behind in Gethsemane, so to speak."

"That's not a stupid way to put it, Hans," she said, and her slanted eyes grew fixed, lost in thought. "You understand. Fear of the feeling . . ."

"It doesn't take much to understand that you have to follow him, even though—or perhaps precisely because—there must be something rather fearful about his love."

"*C'est exact* . . . fearful. There are a lot of worries—you know, difficulties." She had taken his hand now and was playing with his fingers without even noticing. Suddenly, however, she looked up with a frown and said, "Stop. Isn't it rather shabby of us to speak about him this way?"

"Certainly not, Clavdia. No, not in the least. It's really quite human, quite humane of us. You love that word, you draw it out and accent it with such enthusiasm. I've always enjoyed listening to you say it. My cousin Joachim did not like it, as a soldier, that is. He thought it implied a general weak-willed slovenliness, and in that sense, then, a boundless *guazzabuglio* of tolerance. And I have my own reservations about it, too, I grant you. But if it implies freedom and genius and kindness, then there really is something fine about it, and we can go right ahead and use it in our conversation about Peeperkorn and the difficulties and worries he causes you. They all stem from his penchant for honor, of course, from his fear that his feelings will fail him, the same fear that makes him love the classic gifts, the regalements, the way he does. We can speak of it with all due reverence, because everything about him has stature, the magnificent stature of a king, and we demean neither him nor ourselves when we speak about it humanely."

"It has nothing to do with us," she said. She had crossed her arms again. "One would not be a woman if one were unwilling to risk being demeaned for the sake of a man, a man of stature, as you put it, who regards one as the object of his feelings and his fears about feelings."

"Most definitely, Clavdia. Very well put. Because, then, even being demeaned brings with it a certain stature, and a woman can look down from the heights of her demeaned position to those who have no royal stature, and speak in that disparaging tone you used just now when you asked about *timbres-poste* and said: 'Gentlemen should at least be punctual and dependable.' "

"Are you so sensitive, Hans? Don't be. To hell with sensitivities—agreed? I used to be sensitive at one time. I admit it, since we're sitting here together this evening. I was annoyed by your detachment, and that you were on such good terms with him for the sake of your own egoistic experience. And yet I was delighted, too, even grateful to you, that you showed him such respect. There was a great deal of loyalty in your conduct. And even if it was mingled with some impertinence, I still had to give you credit for it in the end."

"That was very kind of you."

She looked at him. "It appears you are incorrigible. I will tell you straight out: you are a subtle young man. I don't know whether you have any depth, but you definitely have subtlety. Which is a good thing, by the way—one can live with that. It can provide the basis for friendship. Shall we build a friendship, establish an alliance for someone, instead of against someone as is usual? Will you give me your hand on it? I am afraid . . . afraid sometimes of being alone with him, emotionally alone, *tu sais*. He can be frightening. I'm afraid sometimes that something may happen to him. It makes me shudder. I would love to have some good person on my side. *Enfin*, if you would like to hear it, perhaps that is why I came back here with him."

They were sitting knee to knee, he tilted forward in his rocking chair, she on the bench. She had squeezed his hands as she spoke these last words directly into his face.

"To me? Oh, that is lovely," he said. "Oh, Clavdia, that is quite extraordinary. You brought him to me? And you still want to claim my waiting was stupid and impermissible and quite in vain? It would be terribly gauche of me if I did not know how to value your offer of friendship, a friendship with you for his sake."

And then she kissed him on the mouth. It was one of those Russian kisses, the sort that are exchanged in that vast, soulful land at high Christian feasts, as a token and seal of love. But even as we record this kiss exchanged between a notoriously "subtle" young man and a charming, slinking, and still equally young woman, we cannot help finding in it a reminder of Dr. Krokowski's elaborate, if not always unobjectionable way of speaking about love in a gently irresolute sense, so that one was never quite sure whether he meant its sanctified or more passionate and fleshly forms. Are we doing the same thing here, or were Hans Castorp and Clavdia Chauchat doing the same thing with their Russian kiss? But what would be our readers' reaction if we simply refused to get to the bottom of that question? In our opinion, it is analytically correct, although—to use Hans Castorp's phrase—"terribly gauche" and downright life-denying, to make a "tidy" distinction between sanctity and passion in matters of love. What's this about "tidy"? What's this about gentle irresolution and ambiguity? Isn't it grand, isn't it good, that language has only *one* word for everything we associate with love—from utter sanctity to the most fleshly lust? The result is perfect clarity in ambiguity, for love cannot be disembodied even in its most sanctified forms, nor is it without sanctity even at its most fleshly. Love is always simply itself, both as a subtle affirmation of life and as the highest passion; love is our sympathy with organic life, the touchingly lustful embrace of what is destined to decay—*caritas* is assuredly found in the most admirable and most depraved passions. Irresolute? But in God's good name, leave the meaning of love unresolved! Unresolved—that is life and humanity, and it would betray a dreary lack of subtlety to worry about it.

And so while Hans Castorp's and Frau Chauchat's lips meet in a Russian kiss, let us lower the lights in our little theater for a change of scene. For our concern now is the second of the two conversations we promised to disclose, and after relighting the scene—it is the soft illumination of a late spring afternoon, the thaw has begun—we discover our hero in his customary place beside the great Peeperkorn's bed, deep in respectful, friendly conversation. After four o'clock tea in the dining hall—at which

Frau Chauchat had appeared alone, as she had at all three previous meals that day, and then set off at once for a shopping trip down in Platz— Hans Castorp had asked to be admitted for his usual sick call on the Dutchman, partly to show the old man some attention and entertain him a little, partly to be edified by his personality: in short, for reasons both life-affirming and irresolute. Peeperkorn laid his *Telegraaf* aside, tossed his horn-rimmed pince-nez atop it after slipping it by the bridge of his nose, and extended a captain's hand to his visitor, while his broad, ragged lips stirred with a vague, but pained expression. Red wine and coffee were within reach as usual; the coffee things, splattered brown from recent use, stood on the chair beside the bed—Mynheer had taken his usual afternoon cup, strong and hot, with sugar and cream, and he was still in a sweat from it. His regal face, encircled by white flames, was flushed, and little beads of moisture stood out on his brow and upper lip.

"I'm sweating a little," he said. "Welcome, young man. On the contrary. Have a seat. It is a sign of weakness when one no sooner enjoys a hot drink than— Would you please? Quite, right, the handkerchief. Thanks so much." The flush soon left his face, however, making way for the yellow pallor that usually came to the man's face after a malign attack. The quartan fever had been fierce that morning, in all three of its stages—the chill, the hot flush, and the sweats—and Peeperkorn's little pale eyes gazed out dully from under the idol-like tracery of his brow.

"It is—by all means, young man," he said. "I might even say, by all means 'appreciated'—absolutely. Very kind of you to pay a sick old man—"

"A visit?" Hans Castorp asked. "Not really, Mynheer Peeperkorn. I am the one who should be very grateful just to be allowed to sit here awhile. I get incomparably more out of it than you, my reasons are purely egoistic. And what a misleading description that is—'a sick old man.' No one would guess that is supposed to mean *you*. What a totally false picture that is."

"Fine, fine," Mynheer replied and closed his eyes for several seconds. Now he threw his majestic head back against the pillow, raising the chin high; he folded his long-nailed fingers over the broad regal chest outlined under his woolen shirt. "Fine, young man, or rather, you mean well, of that I am certain. It was pleasant yesterday afternoon—yes, yes, only yesterday afternoon—at that hospitable inn—I have forgotten the name— where we enjoyed those excellent scrambled eggs and salami and that wholesome country wine."

"It was splendid!" Hans Castorp confirmed. "We all partook of down-right illegal portions—the chef at the Berghof would be justly offended if he had seen us. In short, we all, without exception, did some intensive work there. The salami was the genuine Italian article. Herr Settembrini was quite touched, ate it with tears in his eyes, so to speak. He is a true patriot, as you know, a democratic patriot. He has consecrated his citizen's pike on the altar of humanity just so that salami will have to pass through customs at the Brenner Pass someday."

"That is immaterial," Peeperkorn declared. "He is a chivalrous man and can carry on a high-spirited conversation, a cavalier, although apparently he does not enjoy the privilege of changing his attire often."

"Never, in fact," Hans Castorp said. "Never has the privilege. I have known him for a long time now and am on the friendliest of terms with him, which is to say, he very kindly took me on because he thought I was 'a problem child of life'—that's just a phrase we two use and would require lengthy explanation—and works very hard to influence me and set me on the right course. But I have never seen him, be it summer or winter, in anything except those checked trousers and that threadbare double-breasted coat. He wears those old things, however, with remarkable decorum, quite the cavalier, I can only concur with you there. The way he wears them is a triumph over poverty, and I certainly prefer his poverty to Naphta's elegance, which always seems uncanny somehow, the Devil's own elegance, so to speak, and he gets the funds from dubious sources—I've caught a glimpse or two of his circumstances."

"A chivalrous and high-spirited man," Peeperkorn repeated without picking up on the remark about Naphta, "although—permit me a qualification—although not without his prejudices. Madame, my traveling companion, is not especially fond of him, as you perhaps may have noticed; she expresses little sympathy for him, doubtless because in his behavior toward her those very prejudices are in fact—not a word, young man. Far be it from me, as to Herr Settembrini and your friendly sentiments toward him—settled. I would not think of asserting that, in terms of the courtesy a cavalier owes a lady, he would ever—agreed, dear friend, absolutely unobjectionable. And yet there is a certain boundary, a reserve, a certain stand-off-ish-ness, which, humanly speaking, makes Madame's feelings toward him eminently—"

"Understandable. Logical. Eminently justified. Forgive me, Mynheer Peeperkorn, for having arbitrarily completed your sentence. I risk it only because I am convinced of your complete acquiescence. There is nothing particularly remarkable in her reaction, not when one takes into account how very much the behavior of women—and you may well smile that at my tender age I generalize about women in this way—is dependent on the behavior of a man toward them. Women, if one may put it this way, are reactive creatures, with little original initiative, careless to the point of being passive. Allow me, please, to attempt to develop my thought somewhat, though in labored fashion. In matters of love, a woman, as nearly as I can determine, primarily regards herself as simply an object, she lets things come at her, she does not choose freely, she makes her own subjective choice in love only on the basis of the man's choice, so that, if you will permit me to add this final point, her freedom of choice— presuming, of course, that the man in question is not too sorry a specimen, and even that cannot be regarded as all too strict a requirement—her freedom of choice, then, is prejudiced and corrupted by the fact that *she* has been chosen. Good God, I'm speaking in banalities, but when one is young, everything is, of course, new—new and astounding. You ask a woman: 'Do you love him, then?' And she opens her eyes wide, or even bats them, and replies, 'He loves me so much.' And now try to imagine that sort of answer from a man—forgive me for correlating the two. Perhaps there are men who would have to answer that way, but they are simply and utterly ridiculous, tied to love's apron strings, to put it epigrammatically. I would like to know what sense of self-worth such a female answer represents. Does a woman feel she owes boundless subservience to a man who would confer the favor of his love on such a lowly creature, or does she see in the man's love for her an unerring token of his superiority? I've asked myself that question in passing, now and again, in life's quiet moments."

"Primal, classic questions you've touched on there, young man, with your apt little discourse on holy matters," Peeperkorn responded. "Desire intoxicates the male, the female demands and expects to be intoxicated by his desire. Which is the source of our duty to feel. And the source of the terrible disgrace when feeling is lacking, when there is an inability to awaken the female to desire. Will you drink a glass of red wine with me? I drink. I thirst. My loss of fluids today was considerable."

"Many thanks, Mynheer Peeperkorn. It's a little early yet for me, but I'm always willing to drink a sip to your health."

"Well then, help yourself to the wineglass. There's only one. I shall make do with the water tumbler. I'm sure this modest vintage will not be harmed if drunk from simpler vessels." He poured, though his trembling captain's hand required the assistance of his guest, and thirstily transferred red wine from the simple glass to his proletarian gullet, as if it were clearest water.

"That regales," he said. "Won't you have more? Then allow me to avail myself of—" He spilled a little wine as he poured himself another glass. The cover sheet of his comforter was splattered with dark red stains.

"I repeat," he said, raising a finger lance, while the wineglass continued to tremble in his other hand, "I repeat, that it is our duty, our *religious* duty to feel. Our feeling, you see, is our manly vigor, which awakens life. Life slumbers. It wants to be awakened, roused to drunken nuptials with divine feeling. Because feeling, young man, is divine. Man himself is divine in that he feels. He is the very feeling of God. God created him in order to feel through him. Man is nothing more than the organ by which God consummates His marriage with awakened and intoxicated life. And if man fails to feel, it is an eruption of divine disgrace, it is the defeat of God's manly vigor, a cosmic catastrophe, a horror that never leaves the mind—" He drank.

"Allow me to take your empty glass, Mynheer Peeperkorn," Hans Castorp said. "I find it most instructive to follow your train of thought. You have constructed a theological theory that ascribes to man an eminently honorable, if perhaps somewhat one-sided religious function. There is a rigor about your way of viewing things that, if I may say so, is also rather dispiriting—beg your pardon. All religious austerity is, of course, dispiriting for people of lesser stature. I would not think of wanting to correct you, but I would merely like to refer you back to your own comment about certain 'prejudices' that you say you have observed in Herr Settembrini's behavior toward Madame, your traveling companion. I have known Herr Settembrini for a long time, a very long time, not just for years, but for years and years now. And I can assure you that his prejudices, to the extent he has any, are in no way of a petty or philistine nature—it would be absurd even to think such a thing. With him, one can speak only of prejudices on a grand and therefore impersonal scale, of general pedagogic principles, upon which, I admit, given my status as a 'problem child of life,' Herr Settembrini has often insisted—but that would lead us too far afield. It is a very vast topic, which it would be impossible to address in a few words—"

"And you love Madame, do you not?" Mynheer suddenly asked, turning toward his guest a regal countenance with painfully ragged lips and pale little eyes under a brow full of arabesques.

In his shock, Hans Castorp stammered, "You asked if—that is—but of course I respect Frau Chauchat in her position as—"

"I beg you," Peeperkorn said, stretching out his hand in one of his restraining, cultured gestures. "Allow me," he continued, having now created a space to say what he had to say, "allow me to repeat that I am in no way reproaching this Italian gentleman for any lapse of courtesy that a cavalier—I reproach no one for such a lapse, no one. It merely occurs to me—that at the present moment I am enjoying—fine, young man. By all means—fine, lovely. I am delighted, let there be no doubt of that. It truly gives me great pleasure. And yet, I say to myself—to be brief, I say: your acquaintance with Madame is older than our own. You shared with her her previous sojourn here. She is, moreover, a lady of the most charming attributes, and I am but a sick old man. How does it happen that—since I am indisposed and she has gone down to the resort to do some shopping, quite alone, with no one to accompany her— nothing wrong with that, certainly not! And yet it would doubtless be— should I ascribe it to the influence, shall we say, to the pedagogic principles of Signor Settembrini that in regard to your own chivalrous impulses, you have—I beg you, please understand me when I say . . ."

"Oh, but I do, Mynheer Peeperkorn. Oh, no, that isn't it at all. I'm acting quite independently. On the contrary, Herr Settembrini has on occasion even—oh, I'm so sorry, I see some wine stains on your sheets, Mynheer Peeperkorn. Should we not—one usually sprinkles salt on them, at least if they're fresh—"

"That is unimportant," Peeperkorn said, keeping his gaze fixed firmly on his guest.

Hans Castorp blushed. "Things up here," he said with a forced smile, "are different from what is usual elsewhere. The spirit of the place, if I may put it that way, is not a conventional one. The patient has priority, whether man or woman. The rules of chivalry are of secondary importance. You are temporarily indisposed, Mynheer Peeperkorn—acutely indisposed, at this very moment. Your traveling companion is relatively healthy in comparison. And so I believe that I am acting as Madame would wish by serving as her representative here with you in her absence— to the extent one can speak of representing her, ha ha—instead of serving as your representative with her and offering to accompany her down into town. And why should I even think of forcing my chivalrous services upon your traveling companion? I have neither the right nor the authorization for that. I may say that I have a good sense of what is legitimate. In short, my situation is, I think, correct; it corresponds to the general state of affairs and in particular to my own sincere regard for your person, Mynheer Peeperkorn. And so in answer to your question—for you did ask a question of me—I believe I have given you a satisfactory answer."

"A very agreeable answer," Peeperkorn replied. "I listen with instinctive pleasure to your nimble little discourse, young man. It leaps over every hedge and ditch and rounds everything off agreeably. But satisfactory—no. Your answer does not quite satisfy me—forgive me if I disappoint you there. 'Rigor'—you used the word in regard to certain views I expressed just now. There is also a certain rigor in your remarks, a kind of stiffness, an austerity that does not seem consistent with your own nature, although I have noticed something of the sort in your behavior before. And I recognize it again now. It is the same stiffness you show toward Madame, and toward no one else in our group, during our strolls and outings. And you owe me an explanation—it is a debt, an obligation you owe me, young man. I am not mistaken in this. I have confirmed my observation too often, and it is not improbable that the same notion has occurred to the others—with one difference, that possibly, indeed probably, they know the explanation for this phenomenon."

Mynheer spoke in an unusually precise and compact style this afternoon, despite his fatigue from the malign attack of fever. There was almost nothing fragmented about it. Half sitting up in bed, with mighty shoulders and majestic head turned toward his visitor, he stretched one arm out across the bedclothes and held his freckled captain's hand erect at the end of the woolen sleeve, forming a precise ring of thumb and forefinger, thrusting the other finger lances in the air; and his mouth formed the words as sharply and exactly, as graphically in fact, as Herr Settembrini himself might have wished, and he added a throaty rolled *r* to words like "difference" and "occurred."

"You smile," he went on, "you blink and turn your head back and forth, endeavoring, it appears, to cogitate, but to no avail. And yet there can be no doubt that you know what I mean and what this is about. I do not claim that you do not occasionally address Madame, or that you fail to respond when the conversation happens to turn around the other way. But I repeat, it is done with a definite stiffness, or to be more precise—you are dodging, or avoiding something, and upon closer inspection, it turns out you are avoiding something specific. Indeed, one has the impression you have made a bet with Madame, a philopena, by the terms of which you are never to address her directly. You never say 'you' to her, never use the pronoun, formal or informal."

"But, Mynheer Peeperkorn. What sort of a bet would . . ."

"Surely I may call your attention to something of which you yourself cannot be unaware—indeed, you just turned very pale, even your lips."

Hans Castorp did not look up. He was bent over, engrossed in the problem of the red stains on the sheets. "It was bound to come to this," he thought. "That is what he was aiming for. I have even done my share, I'm afraid, to bring it to this. I've been plotting it to some extent, though that has only become clear to me at this moment. Am I really so pale? It may be—well, this is the critical moment. No way of knowing what will happen. Can I still lie? It probably wouldn't work—and I don't even want to. For now, I'll just stick with these bloodstains, red wine stains here on the sheet."

But no one spoke about them, either. The silence lasted for two or three minutes—revealing how even these smallest units of time can expand under such circumstances.

It was Pieter Peeperkorn who reopened the conversation. "It was on the evening when I had the privilege of first making your acquaintance," he began in a lilting tone, letting his voice fall at the end, as if this were the first sentence in a long story. "We had just celebrated a little feast, had enjoyed food and drink, and linking arms in an elevated mood, in a humanely re-laxed and adventurous spirit, we sought out our nocturnal couches in the small hours of the morning. And then it was, here at my door, as we took our leave of one another, that the inspiration came to me to invite you to place your lips upon the brow of the lady who had introduced you to me as a good friend from her previous stay here, leaving it then to her to respond in my presence to such a solemn, yet cheerful token of the advanced hour. You rejected my proposal outright, rejected it because you found it non-sensical to exchange kisses on the brow with my traveling companion. You will surely not dispute that was your explanation, which itself would have demanded an explanation—an explanation which you still owe me to this day. Are you willing to pay that debt now?"

"So he noticed that, too," Hans Castorp thought and bent down closer still to the wine stains, scratching at one of them with the tip of his curled middle finger. "The fact is, I had wanted him to notice, and remember, even then—otherwise I would not have said it. But what now? My heart's pounding fairly hard. Will there be a first-rate royal temper tantrum? It might be a good idea to look up to see if his fist is hovering just above my head. I find myself in a highly peculiar and extremely ticklish position."

Suddenly he felt his wrist, his right wrist, grasped by Peeperkorn's hand.

"Now he's grabbing my wrist," he thought. "Well, how ridiculous for me to sit here with my tail tucked between my legs. Have I wronged him in any way? Not in the least. Let the husband in Daghestan complain first. And then whoever after that. And then me. As far as I know, *he* has nothing at all to complain about. So why is my heart pounding like this? It's high time for me to sit up and look squarely, if respectfully, into that majestic countenance."

Which he did. The majestic countenance was yellow, with pale eyes gazing out from under the raised tracery of the brow; the expression on the ragged lips was bitter. Each read the other's eyes—the grand old man and the insignificant young man, the former still with a grasp on the latter's wrist.

At last Peeperkorn said softly: "You were Clavdia's lover during her previous stay here."

Hans Castorp let his head fall briefly, but then sat up straight again and took a deep breath. "Mynheer Peeperkorn," he said, "I would find it most repugnant to lie to you, and I am seeking some way to avoid doing so. It is not easy. I would be boasting if I were to confirm your observation, and I would be lying if I were to deny it. The matter should be seen as follows. For a long time, a very long time, I lived here at the Berghof with Clavdia—excuse me—with your current traveling companion without knowing her socially. Our relationship, or my relationship to her, precluded any social element; indeed I must say its beginnings lie in darkness. In my own mind, at least, I never addressed Clavdia except by that name and with informal pronouns—or indeed in reality, either. For the evening when I cast aside certain pedagogic fetters, of which we were just speaking, and approached her—under a pretense suggested to me by a past experience—was an evening of masks and disguises. It was Mardi Gras, an irresponsible evening, an evening of first names, in the course of which, in a manner both irresponsible and dreamlike, the use of informal pronouns achieved its full meaning. It was likewise the evening before Clavdia's departure."

"Its full meaning," Peeperkorn repeated. "Very delicately put." He let go of Hans Castorp and began to massage both sides of his face with the palms of his long-nailed captain's hands—the eye sockets, the cheeks, the chin. Then he folded his hands across the wine-stained sheets and laid his head down against his left shoulder, the shoulder nearer his guest, and it was the same as if he had turned his face away.

"I have answered your question as accurately as possible, Mynheer Peeperkorn," Hans Castorp said, "and have conscientiously tried to say neither too much nor too little. The main point was to allow you to see that it is more or less left to you whether or not you count that evening of farewell and meaningful informal pronouns—to allow you to see that it was an evening outside any schedule, almost outside the calendar, an hors d'oeuvre, so to speak, an extra evening, a leap-year evening, the twenty-ninth of February. And so it would have been only half a lie had I denied your observation."

Peeperkorn did not reply.

"I preferred," Hans Castorp began after another pause, "to tell you the truth even at the risk of losing your favor, which, to be frank, would have been a grievous loss for me—a blow, I can tell you, a real blow, that could only be compared to the blow I took when Frau Chauchat reappeared here, and not alone, but as your traveling companion. I was willing to take that risk because it has long been my wish that clarity should be established between us—between me and the man for whom I entertain such extraordinary respect. That course seemed finer and more humane—and I'm sure you know how Clavdia drawls the word out so charmingly in that magical, husky voice of hers—than silence and dissembling, and to that extent a weight was lifted from my heart, when you made your observation just now."

No answer.

"And there was one more reason, Mynheer Peeperkorn," Hans Castorp continued, "one more reason why I wanted to make a clean breast of things—and that is that I know from personal experience how annoying uncertainty can be in this area, when one is at the mercy of surmises and guesses. *You* now know who it was with whom Clavdia marked, spent, observed—yes, that's it—observed her twenty-ninth of February before the establishment of the present legitimate state of affairs, which it would be utter madness not to respect. I, for my part, was never able to attain such clarity, although it was clear to me that anyone who found himself in a situation where he must ponder such matters would have to assume certain precedents, or indeed predecessors—though I did know that Director Behrens, who as you are perhaps aware is an amateur painter in oils, had in the course of a great many sittings produced a magnificent portrait of her, with a lifelike mastery of the skin that, just between us, certainly takes one aback. It caused me a great deal of torment as I racked my brains over it, and does so even today."

"You still love her, do you?" Peeperkorn asked, without shifting position—his face still turned away. The large room sank more and more into twilight.

"Forgive me, Mynheer Peeperkorn," Hans Castorp replied, "but my sentiments toward you, sentiments of the greatest respect and admiration, would make it unseemly for me to say anything to you about my sentiments toward your traveling companion."

"And does she," Peeperkorn asked in a dull voice, "still share those sentiments even now?"

"I am not saying—" Hans Castorp responded, "I am not saying that she ever shared them. That is hardly credible. We touched on the matter theoretically a while ago when we spoke of woman's reactive nature. There is not much about me to love. What sort of stature do I have—judge for yourself. And even if a twenty-ninth of February did come to pass, that was solely because a woman can be lured on by the primary choice of the man—to which I may add that I find it rather boastful and tasteless of me to call myself 'the man,' although Clavdia to be sure is a woman."

"She followed her feelings," Peeperkorn muttered with ragged lips.

"As she did far more amenably in your case," Hans Castorp said, "and as she has done a good many times in all probability—that much must be clear to anyone who finds himself in the situation where . . ."

"Stop!" Peeperkorn said, still looking away, but gesturing with the palm of his hand to restrain his visitor. "Isn't it rather shabby of us to speak about her this way?"

"Surely not, Mynheer Peeperkorn. No, I think I can set your mind at ease there. We are speaking of human realities—and thus of matters 'humane,' in the sense of freedom and genius, if you will forgive me the somewhat stilted phraseology. But only recently I had occasion to make use of just such terms."

"Fine, continue," Peeperkorn commanded softly.

And Hans Castorp was speaking softly as well, and sitting on the edge of his chair next to the bed, hands between knees, bending forward toward the old monarch. "For she is a woman of genius," he said. "And her husband beyond the Caucasus has . . . granted her freedom to make use of her genius, either because he is very stupid or very intelligent, I cannot say, not knowing the fellow. In any case, it was wise of him, for it is her illness that confers such freedom on her, it is the genius of illness that she serves. And so anyone who finds himself in the same situation would do well to follow her husband's example and not complain, either about the past or the future."

"And so you have no complaints?" Peeperkorn asked, turning his countenance to him now—it looked ashen in the twilight. The eyes gazed out pale and dull from under the idol-like tracery of the brow; the large, ragged lips hung half-open, like the mouth on the mask of tragedy.

"I did not intend," Hans Castorp answered modestly, "to apply that to myself. My point was, rather, that *you* should not complain, Mynheer Peeperkorn, and so not withdraw your favor from me because of events that lie in the past. That is the essential issue for me here and now."

"Yet all the same, I must have unwittingly inflicted great pain upon you."

"If that is meant as a question," Hans Castorp replied, "and if I were to respond to it in the affirmative, that should in no way imply that I do not know how to value the enormous privilege of your acquaintance, for that privilege is inseparably bound up with the disappointment of which you speak."

"I thank you, young man, I thank you. I value the courtesy of your modest phrases. But setting our acquaintance aside—"

"It is difficult to set it aside," Hans Castorp said, "and indeed it would hardly be advisable for me to do so if I am to answer your question in the affirmative with no pretense. For the fact that Clavdia returned in the company of a personality of your stature could, of course, only increase and complicate the discomfort I would have felt in seeing her return in the company of any man. It certainly was hard for me to deal with, and still is, I cannot deny it. But I have intentionally held to the positives of the matter as best I could, that is, to my sincere feelings of respect for you, Mynheer Peeperkorn—which, by the by, also permitted me to needle your traveling companion just a little, since women do not particularly enjoy seeing their lovers getting along."

"Indeed—" Peeperkorn said, hiding a smile by brushing his cupped hand over mouth and chin, as if afraid Frau Chauchat might see him smiling. Even Hans Castorp smiled discreetly, and then they both nodded awhile in agreement.

"One should not begrudge me my little bit of revenge," Hans Castorp went on. "For if I matter here at all, I truly have some reason to complain—not about Clavdia and not about you, Mynheer Peeperkorn, but to complain in general, about my life and fate. And since I enjoy the honor of your confidence and this has turned out to be such a thoroughly exceptional twilight hour, I would like at least to attempt to indicate what I mean."

"Please do," Peeperkorn said politely.

And with that, Hans Castorp went on: "I have been up here for a long time, Mynheer Peeperkorn, for years and years—I don't precisely know how long now, but they are years of my life, which was why I spoke just now of 'life'—and I shall return to the matter of 'fate' at the appropriate moment. My cousin, whom I came here to visit, was a military man, an honest and good fellow, but that did not help him—he died here, leaving me behind, and here I am still. I was not a military man myself, I had chosen a civilian profession, as you have perhaps heard, a sturdy, reasonable profession, of which it is even said that it may bring nations closer together, but of which I was never particularly fond, I must admit. As to the reasons, I can only say that they lie in darkness, lie there together with the origins of my sentiments toward your traveling companion— and I expressly call her that to make clear that it would never occur to me to try to alter a legitimate state of affairs—with the origins of my sentiments toward Clavdia Chauchat and of my addressing her with only informal pronouns, a relationship that I never denied from the moment her eyes first met mine and fascinated me—fascinated me in the most irrational sense of the word, you understand. For the sake of her love and in spite of Herr Settembrini, I subordinated myself to the principle of irrationality, to the principle behind the genius of illness, to which, admittedly, I had long since, perhaps from the very start, submitted myself and to which I have remained true up here—for how long now, I no longer know, I have forgotten everything, broken off with everything, with my relatives and my profession in the flatlands, with all my prospects. And when Clavdia departed, I waited for her, just went on waiting up here, so that the flatlands is entirely lost to me now, and in its eyes I am as good as dead. That is what I meant when I spoke of 'fate,' and went so far as to suggest that I might possibly have cause to complain about my present situation. I once read a story—no, I saw it in the theater— about how a good-hearted young fellow, a military man like my cousin, by the way, gets involved with an enchanting Gypsy—and she was enchanting, with a flower behind her ear, a savage, mischievous creature, and he was so fascinated with her that he got completely off-track, sacrificed everything for her, deserted the colors, ran off with her to join a band of smugglers and disgraced himself in every way. And after he had done all that, she had enough of him, and came along with a matador, a compelling personality with a splendid baritone. It ended outside the bullring, with the little soldier, his face chalky white, his shirt unbuttoned, stabbing her with a knife, though you might say she as good as planned the whole thing herself. A rather pointless story, really, now that I think of it. But then, why did it occur to me?"

At the mention of the word "knife," Mynheer Peeperkorn had changed his sitting position in bed somewhat, suddenly edging away and turning his face to search his guest's eyes. Now he sat up more comfortably, propping himself on his elbows, and said, "Young man, I have heard, and I have the picture. And on the basis of what you have just said, permit me to make an honorable declaration of my own. Were my hair not white and were I not so debilitated by this malign fever, you would see me prepared to give you satisfaction, man to man, weapon in hand, for the injury I have unwittingly inflicted upon you, and for the additional injury caused by my traveling companion, for which I likewise must take responsibility. Agreed, my good sir. You would see me prepared. But as things stand, you will permit me to make another suggestion in lieu of that. It is as follows: I recall a sublime moment, at the very beginning of our acquaintance—I recall it, though I had copiously partaken of wine—a moment when, touched by your pleasant temperament, I was about to offer you the brotherhood of informal pronouns, but could not avoid the realization that such a step would have been overhasty. Fine, I refer today to that moment, I return to it now, I declare the postponement we agreed upon then to be at an end. Young man, we are brothers, I declare us to be such. You spoke of the use of informal pronouns in their full meaning—

and our use of them shall also be in the full meaning of a brotherhood of feeling. The satisfaction that old age and infirmity prevent me from offering you by means of weapons, I now offer you in this form; I offer it in the form of a bond of brotherhood, of the sort that is usually established against a third party, against the world, against someone else, but which we shall establish in our feelings for someone. Take up your wineglass, young man, while I reach yet again for my water tumbler—it will do this modest vintage no further harm—"

His captain's hand trembling slightly, he filled the glasses, with the assistance, offered in respectful bewilderment, of Hans Castorp.

"Take it," Peeperkorn repeated. "Link arms with me! And drink now thus. Drink it down!—Agreed, young man. Settled. Here, my hand on it. Are you satisfied, Hans Castorp?"

"That is, of course, no word for it, Mynheer Peeperkorn," said Hans Castorp, who had some difficulty downing the whole glass in one draft, and now took out his handkerchief to wipe the wine he had spilled on his knee. "What I mean is, I am terribly happy and still cannot grasp how this has so suddenly been bestowed on me—it is, I must admit, like a dream. It is an overwhelming honor for me—I don't know how I have earned it, at best in some passive way, certainly not in any other. And one should not be surprised if at first I shall find it rather daring to utter this new form of address and stumble in the attempt—particularly in the presence of Clavdia, who, being but a woman, may not be quite so pleased with this new arrangement."

"Leave that to me," Peeperkorn replied, "and the rest is merely a matter of practice and habit. And now go, young man. Leave me, my son. It is dark, night has fallen. Our beloved may return at any moment, and a meeting of us three would perhaps not be that convenient just now."

"Fare thee well, Pieter Peeperkorn," Hans Castorp said and stood up. "You see, I am overcoming my legitimate reserve and am already practicing this rash form of address. True, it has grown quite dark. I could easily imagine Herr Settembrini suddenly bursting in and turning on the light, so that reason and social order might hold sway—it's one of his weaknesses. Till tomorrow, then. I leave so pleased and proud, beyond my wildest dreams. Do get well. You'll have at least three days without fever now, and will be able to meet each day's demands. That delights me as much as if I were you. Good night."

Mynheer Peeperkorn (Conclusion)

A WATERFALL is always an inviting goal for an excursion, and we hardly know how to justify Hans Castorp's never having visited the picturesque cascade in the forests of the Flüela Valley, particularly since he had a special fondness for falling water. He may be excused for not having done so during the period he lived with Joachim, since his cousin had not been here for pleasure and as a man with a strict sense of duty had limited his field of vision to purposeful business in the immediate vicinity of the Berghof. And after his demise—well, even after that, Hans Castorp's relationship to the local landscape, if one ignores his ski outings, had maintained its conservative, monotone character, a trait that had held a certain special charm for the young man when he contrasted it with the range of his inner experiences and the duties involved in "playing king." All the same, he had eagerly seconded the plan for a pilgrimage to this highly recommended site when it was suggested within his little circle of seven friends (counting himself).

May had arrived—the merry month, if one believes the simple little ditties of the flatlands—but still quite fresh and with air somewhat less endearing up here, although the period of thaw could now be considered over. Snow had fallen in huge flakes several times over the last few days, but had not stuck and merely left the ground wet; the drifts of winter had melted, evaporated, and vanished, except for a few scattered remnants. The world's green accessibility seemed an invitation to the very spirit of enterprise.

As it was, for the last several weeks the group's social activities had been restricted by the poor health of their chief, the great Pieter Peeperkorn, whose malign memento of the tropics refused to respond to either the exceptional climate or the antidotes prescribed by as excellent a physician as Director Behrens. He was frequently confined to his bed, and not just on the days when his quartan fever went about its foul work. His spleen and liver were giving him trouble, too, or so the director indicated whenever he pulled aside those closest to the patient; nor was his stomach in classic condition. And Behrens did not neglect to note that, under such circumstances, one could not entirely dismiss the risk of chronic debilitation in even the most robust constitution.

Mynheer had presided over only one evening of eating and drinking in the previous week, and their walks together had likewise been limited to one abridged stroll. Just between us, by the way, Hans Castorp was relieved, in one regard at least, to see the bonds of the clique loosened somewhat, for he was having difficulty with the toast of brotherhood he had drunk with Frau Chauchat's traveling companion. In his public conversations with Peeperkorn, he displayed the same "stiffness," the same "dodging," the same "avoidance" evident in his dealings with Clavdia and based on a philopena, so to speak. When it came to the forms of address, he would substitute the oddest circumlocutions—that is, if he could not slur over them entirely. He was caught in the same dilemma— or better, its opposite—that governed his conversations with Clavdia when held in the presence of others, even if only before her lord and master; indeed, thanks to the satisfaction he had received from the latter, his dilemma had culminated in a formal double bind.

But the plan for an excursion to the waterfall was now on the agenda— Peeperkorn himself had selected the goal, and he felt up to the effort. It was the third day after a quartan attack; Mynheer let it be known he wished to take advantage of the fact. He had not appeared in the dining hall for the first meals of the day, but had taken them, as he often did of late, with Madame Chauchat in his parlor. Nevertheless, as Hans Castorp made his way to first breakfast, he was greeted by the limping concierge and told to be ready for a drive one hour after dinner; he was also to pass the order on to Herr Ferge and Herr Wehsal, likewise to notify Settembrini and Naphta that they would be picked up, and, finally, was given the task of ordering two landaus for three o'clock that afternoon.

At the appointed hour, then, they met at the portal of the Berghof. While Hans Castorp, Ferge, and Wehsal stood waiting for the residents of the royal suite, they talked and petted the horses, whose black, moist, clumsy lips took the sugar they offered on the palms of their hands. The traveling companions appeared at the top of the open stairway only a little later. Peeperkorn, whose regal head seemed to have grown smaller, stood there in his long, rather worn ulster with Clavdia at his side; he now doffed his soft, round hat, and his lips formed an inaudible, general word of greeting. Then he exchanged handshakes with each of the three gentlemen, who had moved toward the couple as they reached the bottom of the stairs.

"Young man," he said to Hans Castorp, laying his hand on the latter's shoulder. "How are you doing, my son?"

"Splendid, thanks. And that is mutual, I hope?" came the response.

The sun shone, it was a beautiful, bright day; but it had been a good idea to put on spring overcoats—the drive would be cool, no doubt. Madame Chauchat was also wearing a belted coat of some warm, fuzzy, large-checked fabric, and had even thrown a little fur over her shoulders. The brim of her felt hat was pulled down on one side by an olive-colored veil she had tied under her chin, in an effect so charming that it was almost painful for all present—except Ferge, the only man who was not in love with her. His impartiality meant that when they took their places in a temporary arrangement—until the nonresidents would join them—he was assigned a spot on the backseat of the first landau, across from Mynheer and Madame, while Hans Castorp climbed aboard the second carriage with Ferdinand Wehsal, though not without having first spotted a wry smile on Clavdia's face. The Malayan valet had joined them for the excursion; walking in his master's wake, his slight figure had appeared bearing an ample basket, from under whose lid the necks of two bottles of wine jutted up, which he then stored under the backseat of the first carriage. The moment he took his seat beside the coachman and crossed his arms, the horses were given the sign and the carriages moved off down the loop of the driveway, brakes set.

Wehsal had also noticed Frau Chauchat's smile, and with a display of rotting teeth, he mentioned it to his fellow excursionist. "Did you see," he asked, "how she was making fun of you, because you had to ride alone with me? Yes, yes, that's her way of adding insult to injury. Does it annoy and disgust you all that much to have to sit beside me?"

"Pull yourself together, Wehsal, and refrain from such ugly comments," Hans Castorp rebuked him. "Women smile on all sorts of occasions, just to smile. It is pointless to worry about it every time. Why are you forever cringing and writhing? Like all of us, you have your good points and your bad. For example, you play the music of *Summer Night's Dream* very prettily, and not everyone can do that. You must play it again soon."

"Yes, there you sit offering me your condescending advice," the wretched man replied, "and have no idea how much insult there is in your consolation, that you only humiliate me all the more with it. It's easy for you to offer comfort from your high horse, because even if you look rather silly at the moment, at least you had your chance once, and were in seventh heaven, good God, and felt her arms around your neck— good God, just to think of it burns at my gut and tears at my heart— and, then, knowing full well all that was granted you, you look down on me in my wretched torment . . ."

"You don't have a pretty way of expressing yourself, Wehsal. I find it really quite obnoxious—and I don't think I need to disguise the fact from you, since you've accused me of insulting you. I suppose you mean it to be repulsive, too; you quite deliberately attempt to make yourself disgusting, forever cringing and writhing. Are you really so terribly in love with her?"

"Horribly," Wehsal answered, shaking his head. "I can't tell you what I've had to endure—thirsting, craving for her. If only I could say it would kill me, but a man can't live with it or die from it. While she was gone, things began to get a little better, I was gradually forgetting her. But since she has returned and I see her every day, it's so bad sometimes that I bite my arm and flail my hands in the air and don't know what to do. It's a craving that shouldn't even exist, and yet you can't wish it didn't exist. Once it has hold of you, you can't wish it away, because you'd have to wish your life away, it's so bound up with it, and you can't do that— what good would dying do? Afterward—with pleasure. In her arms— only too gladly. But before? That's nonsense, because life is desire, and desire is life, and life can't be its own enemy. That is the damned hole I'm boxed into. And although I say 'damned,' it's just a turn of phrase; it's as if I were someone else—it can't apply to me. There are so many different tortures, Castorp, and if a man is subjected to one torture, all he wants is for it to end, that is his one and only goal. But you can be rid of the torture of fleshly desire by only one means, and under one condition—by its being satisfied. Otherwise—no, not for any price! It is an instrument of torture, and if it hasn't got hold of you, then you don't bother with it, but whoever it does get hold of soon gets to know our Lord Jesus Christ and the tears roll down his cheeks. Good God in heaven, what an instrument, what a piece of business it is. Flesh desires flesh, simply because it is not your own, but belongs to another soul— how strange and yet, when viewed in the right light, how unpretentious, how unabashedly benign. You could almost say: if that's all it wants, then in God's name, let it have it. What is it I want, Castorp? Do I want to murder her? Do I want to spill her blood? I just want to fondle her! Castorp, dear Castorp, forgive me for whimpering like this, but for God's sake she could comply with my wishes. And there's something higher, loftier about it, too. I'm not a beast, I'm a human being, too, after all. The desire of the flesh wanders here and there, it is not bound, not fixed, which is why we call it bestial. But once it is fixed on a given human being with a face, why then our mouths speak of love. You don't desire just her torso and the fleshly shell of her body; in fact, if her face were fashioned just a little differently, why, it's quite possible you wouldn't even want her whole body at all. Which only proves that I love her soul, and that I love her with my soul. Because to love the face is to love the soul."

"What is wrong with you, Wehsal? You're beside yourself, going on here in a vein that, God knows, is . . ."

"But that's just it, that's my misfortune," the poor wretch went on, "that she has a soul, that she is a human being made up of body and soul.

Because her soul wants nothing to do with my soul, and so her body wants nothing to do with mine. Oh, what rotten, beastly luck! And that is why my desires are condemned to disgrace, and my body can only writhe forever. Why doesn't she, body and soul, want to have anything to do with me, Castorp? And why is my desire for her such a horror? Am I not a man? Is a repulsive man not a man? I am a man to the nth degree, I swear it. I would outdo anything she has ever known if she would only admit me to the realm of bliss, open those arms whose beauty, like the beauty of her face, comes from her soul. I would inflict all the lusts of the world on her, Castorp, if it were merely a matter of bodies and not of faces, as well, if it were not for her cursed soul, which wants nothing to do with me, but without which I would not even desire her body—that's the devil's own hole I'm boxed into, damned to writhe there forever."

"Shh, Wehsal! Not so loud! The driver can understand you. He's not moving his head on purpose, but I can tell from his back that he's listening."

"He is listening and he understands—there you have it, Castorp! There you have the instrument, the piece of business in its full and unique character. If I were talking about metempsychosis or about . . . hydrostatics, he wouldn't understand, wouldn't have the vaguest, wouldn't even be interested. Because those aren't popular subjects. But the highest, final, and most horribly private piece of business, the business of the flesh and the soul—why, it's the most popular subject of all, and everyone understands it and can make fun of someone whom it has got hold of and whose days are tortured by desire and whose nights are the hell of disgrace. Castorp, dear Castorp, let me whimper a little—you don't know the nights I have. I dream of her every night—ah, what don't I dream about her! I can feel the burning in my throat and gut, just thinking about it. And it always ends with her slapping me, right across the face, sometimes even spitting, too—with her soul-filled face contorted in disgust, she spits at me. And then I wake up, bathed in sweat and shame and desire."

"Well, Wehsal, let's just be quiet for a while and resolve to say nothing until we've arrived at the grocer's and the others join us. That is my suggestion, those are my instructions. I don't wish to offend you, and I admit that you are caught up in an awful mess. But there was a story they used to tell at home about a girl whose punishment was that every time she opened her mouth, snakes and toads came out, snakes and toads with every word. The book didn't say what she did about it, but I've always assumed she probably ended up keeping her mouth shut."

"But it's an undeniable human urge," Wehsal said piteously, "a human necessity, dear Castorp, to speak, to ease your mind when you're in a mess like I'm in."

"It is even a human *right*, Wehsal, if you like. But in my opinion, under certain circumstances, there are rights one does not exercise for good reason."

And so, following Hans Castorp's instructions, they said no more; but the carriages quickly reached the grocer's little house entwined with wild grape, where they did not have to wait a moment. Naphta and Settembrini were already out on the street, the latter in his frayed beaver-trimmed jacket, the former in a spring overcoat, a quilted yellowish-white garment a dandy might wear. While waves and greetings were exchanged, the carriages were turned around, and the gentlemen climbed aboard. Naphta took the fourth seat in the first landau, next to Ferge; and Settembrini— in a splendid mood, bubbling over with lucid, witty remarks—joined Hans Castorp and Wehsal, who gave up his place on the backseat, which Herr Settembrini knew exactly how to use, assuming the careless pose of a gentleman of leisure out for a spin.

He praised the pleasures of riding, the way the body was moved along in comfortable repose past constantly changing scenery; he assumed an obliging, fatherly tone with Hans Castorp and even patted poor Wehsal's cheek, urging him to lose himself and his unattractive ego in admiration of this bright, shining world, to which he pointed in a broad gesture of his right hand, inside its shabby leather glove.

The drive was perfect. The horses, all four of them, were spirited, sturdy, smooth, and well fed, each with a blaze on its forehead, and their hooves banged out a steady rhythm against the road, a good surface, still without any dust. Here and there along its shoulders were piles of rock with grass and flowers sprouting from the cracks; telegraph poles hurried past and were left behind; mountain forests rose up; gentle curves loomed ahead and were taken, each arousing new expeditionary curiosity; and always in the sunny distance was a hint of mountains, some still snow- capped. They had left their own familiar valley behind, and the absence of everyday scenes refreshed them. Soon they stopped at the edge of a wood—they would have to continue their excursion from here on foot if they were to reach their goal, a goal with which they had been in contact for some time now. Without their even having realized it, their ears had picked it up, very tenuous at the start, but steadily increasing. They all heard the distant sound now that the carriages had stopped: a soft hiss, that at times slipped below the threshold of hearing, a trembling surge, to which each called the other's attention as they stood there rooted in place.

"It sounds timid enough now," Settembrini said, who had been here several times. "But once you're there, it is brutal at this time of year. Just be prepared—you won't be able to hear yourself think."

And so they headed into the woods, along a path of wet pine needles: at the head, Pieter Peeperkorn, his soft black hat pulled down over his brow, supported on the arm of his companion and lurching slightly with every step; directly behind them, Hans Castorp, bareheaded, like all the other gentlemen, hands in his pockets, head tilted to one side, whistling softly, looking about; then Naphta and Settembrini, then Ferge and Wehsal; and finally the solitary Malayan, the picnic basket on his arm. They spoke about the woods.

These woods were not like others, but offered views that were peculiarly picturesque, indeed exotic, eerie in fact. The woods teemed with a kind of mossy lichen, were laden with it, draped and wrapped in it; long, dingy, matted parasitic beards dangled from branches already cushioned and webbed with it. Hardly any needles were visible, just curtains of moss—a ponderous, bizarre, disfigured landscape cast under a sickly spell. These woods were not doing well, they were ill with this rank lichen that threatened to suffocate them. It was an impression they all shared as their little procession moved forward along the needle-strewn path, the sound of their goal growing louder in their ears as they neared it: a bumping and hissing, a gradually increasing rumble that promised to fulfill Settembrini's prediction.

A turn in the path revealed a bridge, a rocky forest ravine, and a waterfall leaping down it; as all this came into view, the audible effects reached their zenith—it was the pandemonium of hell. Masses of water plunged some twenty or twenty-five feet in a single vertical cascade of a width equally impressive, and then shot on ahead over boulders. Water plunged in a maddening cacophony of every conceivable noise and tone: thunders and hisses, howlings, boomings, tattoos, cracks, rattles, throbbings, and chimings—you truly could not hear yourself think. Scrambling over the slippery rocks, the visitors moved closer now, and stood there wet with spray, wrapped in misty vapor, their ears crammed and sated with noise; they exchanged glances and intimidated smiles; they shook their heads and watched the spectacle, this continuous catastrophe of hurling foam, with its deafening, insane, extravagant roar that frightened and confused them, baffled their ears. They thought they could hear—from behind, from above, from every side—menacing, threatening trumpet calls and brutal male voices.

Frau Chauchat and the five gentlemen clustered behind Mynheer Peeperkorn, and together they all stared at the surging waters. The others could not see Mynheer's face, but watched as he bared his head encircled with white flames and expanded his chest in the bracing air. They communicated by glances and signs, since words, even shouted directly into the ear, would presumably be lost in the thunder of the cascade. Their lips formed unsounded words of amazement and awe. Hans Castorp, Settembrini, and Ferge nodded their way to an agreement to scale the ravine on whose floor they stood, so that they could view the water from the platform up top. It was not overly difficult; a series of steep, narrow steps hewn into the rock led up to the next story of woods, so to speak. They climbed, one behind the other, walked out onto the bridge where it hovered just above the curl of the falls, stood at the railing, and waved to their friends below. They then crossed the bridge and, taking the more arduous descent on the other side, reemerged into view across the rapids, which were spanned at this point by a second bridge.

Their signs were now directed to the matter of teatime refreshments. It was indicated from several sides that they should withdraw a little from these noisy precincts for the purpose, so that they could enjoy their picnic relieved of this racket and not as deaf-mutes. But it was apparent that this was not Peeperkorn's pleasure. He shook his head, repeatedly thrusting one index finger at the ground, and his ragged lips parted with considerable effort to form the word "here!" What to do? In such matters of policy, he was master and commander in chief. The weight of his personality would have tipped the scales even had he not been, as always, the organizer and director of this enterprise. Stature has ever been tyrannical and autocratic, and always will be. Mynheer wished to take his tea in view of the falls, amid its thunder—that was his grand, stubborn decision, and whoever did not want to go hungry would have to stay. The majority were not happy. Herr Settembrini, who realized that all possibility of human exchange, of a democratic chat or perhaps even argument, had now been cut off, flung one hand above his head in his gesture of despair and resignation. The Malayan hurried to carry out his master's orders. There were two folding chairs, which the servant opened and set against the rocky wall for Mynheer and Madame. He then spread out the contents of the basket on a tablecloth laid at their feet: a coffee service and glasses, thermos bottles, pastries, and wine. They all pushed forward to help themselves. They then sat down on rocks, on the railing of the bridge. Coffee cups in hand, plates of cake on their knees, they silently picnicked in the tumult.

Peeperkorn sat with his coat collar turned up and his hat on the ground beside him, drinking port from a monogrammed silver goblet, which he emptied several times. And suddenly he began to speak. What a strange man! It was impossible for him to hear his own voice, let alone for anyone else to understand a single syllable of what he expressed without expressing it. Holding his goblet in his right hand, he lifted one forefinger, stretched his left arm out, the palm raised at an angle—and his mouth formed words that remained soundless, as if spoken in an airless room. They all assumed that he would immediately cease this pointless activity, to which they responded with disconcerted smiles; but he went on holding forth in the all-devouring din. His left hand made compelling, riveting, cultured gestures that demanded their attention; his little, weary, pale eyes were opened wide under the raised creases of his brow; and he directed his gaze now at one member of his audience, now at another, so that each of them was forced to nod with mouth open and eyebrows raised and to hold one hand up to an ear, as if that would somehow improve a hopeless situation. Now he even stood up! Goblet in hand, bareheaded, the collar of his wrinkled, almost floor-length overcoat turned up, his idol-like creased brow encircled by flames of white hair—there he stood beside a boulder, and his face grew more animated as he held the ring of thumb and forefinger up to it, finger lances jutting into the air, and lectured, punctuating his vague, inaudible toast with the spellbinding token of precision. They recognized the gestures and could read the individual words they were accustomed to hear from his lips: "Agreed" and "Settled"—but nothing more. They saw his head tilt to one side, saw the ragged bitterness on his lips, the image of the Man of Sorrows. And then they saw that luxurious little dimple blossom—sybaritic roguishness, a dancing hitch of the robes, the holy lewdness of the heathen priest. He lifted his glass, passed it in a semicircle before the eyes of his guests, and downed it in two, three gulps, to the last drop, the foot of the goblet upended in the air. Then he handed it with outstretched arm to the Malayan, who received the vessel, laying a hand across his chest. Mynheer Peeperkorn now gave the signal for departure.

They all bowed to thank him and made ready to obey his command. Those squatting on the ground sprang to their feet, those sitting on the bridge railing jumped down. The slight Javanese in his bowler and fur-collared coat gathered up the dishes and what was left of the meal. In the same tight order in which they had arrived, they now returned along the damp, needle-strewn path, and emerged from woods disfigured by lichen onto the road, where their carriages stood waiting.

This time Hans Castorp climbed in with the master and his companion, sitting across from the couple and beside good old Ferge, to whom all higher things were utterly foreign. Almost nothing was said during the ride home. Mynheer sat with his jaw slack, his hands palm down on the plaid traveling blanket spread over both his and Clavdia's knees. Settembrini and Naphta got out and said their good-byes before the carriages moved on across the tracks and the little brook. Wehsal rode alone in the second carriage as it wound its way up the looping drive to the portal of the Berghof, where they all parted.

Did Hans Castorp sleep more lightly, more fitfully that night because of some inner alertness of which his soul knew nothing? Certainly the slightest deviation from the Berghof's customary nocturnal peace, the tiniest muffled disturbance, even the barely perceptible sound of someone moving in the distance, was enough to bring him wide awake and make him sit up in bed. He had been awake for a good while when there was a knock at his door; it was shortly after two. He answered at once—energetic, fully alert, not drowsy in the least. It was the high, quavering voice of one of the nurses employed by the sanatorium, who asked that he come immediately to the second floor at Frau Chauchat's request. With even greater energy, he declared he would obey the call; he leapt out of bed, jumped into his clothes, brushed his hair from his brow with his fingers, and walked downstairs—not slowly, not quickly, uncertain less about what the hour would demand than how it would demand it.

He found the door to Peeperkorn's parlor open, as was the door to the Dutchman's bedroom, where all the lights were on. Both doctors, Head Nurse von Mylendonk, Madame Chauchat, and the valet were present. The Malayan was not dressed as usual, but was got up in a kind of Javanese folk costume—a shirtlike jacket with wide stripes and long, loose sleeves, a bright-colored skirt instead of trousers, a cone-shaped hat of yellow fabric atop his head, and a necklace of amulets across his chest; there he stood, arms folded, immobile, to the left of the head of the bed, where Pieter Peeperkorn lay on his back, his arms flung wide. Entering now, Hans Castorp turned pale as he took in the scene. Frau Chauchat had her back to him. She was sitting on a low chair at the foot of the bed, elbows propped on the quilt, chin in hand, fingers clutching her lower lip, eyes fixed on her traveling companion's face.

"Evenin', my boy," said Behrens, who had been engaged in a hushed conversation with Dr. Krokowski and the head nurse, and now greeted him with a melancholy nod and a skew of his little white moustache. He was wearing his clinical smock—a stethoscope stuck up out of the breast pocket—embroidered slippers, and no collar. "No go," he added in a whisper. "Job done. Step up closer. Cast him an expert eye. You'll have to admit it was beyond the reach of medical art."

Hans Castorp approached the bed on tiptoe. The Malayan watched his every move without turning his head, but the whites of his eyes were clearly visible. With a quick sidelong glance of his own, he discovered that Frau Chauchat was paying him no attention, and so he stood in his usual pose beside the bed—weight on one leg, hands clasped before the abdomen, head tilted to one side—gazing down in thoughtful reverence. Under the red silk quilt, Peeperkorn lay dressed in his woolen shirt, just as Hans Castorp had so often seen him. The hands had turned a blackish blue, as had parts of the face, resulting in considerable disfigurement, although the regal features were unaffected. The eyes were closed in peace, but the idol-like tracery of creases, four or five tense horizontal lines that turned down at right angles at the temples and had been formed by the habits of a lifetime, stood out in strong relief on the high brow encircled by white flames. The pained, ragged lips were slightly open. The blue coloration indicated sudden heart congestion, a convulsive and apoplectic arrest of all vital functions.

Hans Castorp stood there piously for a while, using the time to take in the situation, hesitating to change his pose, waiting for the "widow" to address him. But when she did not, he decided not to disturb her for now and looked back over his shoulder to the group of others in attendance. The director nodded his head toward the door to the parlor. Hans Castorp followed him out.

"Suicide?" he asked in a low, businesslike voice.

"You said it," Behrens replied with a dismissive gesture, and then added, "Top to bottom. Superlative job. Have you ever seen anything like this in the notions department?" he asked, reaching into his smock pocket and pulling out an oddly shaped etui, from which he extracted a small object that he now presented to the young man. "I never have. But it's worth a look. Never too old to learn. Whimsical and inventive. I took it from his hand. Careful. Just a drop on bare skin leaves blisters."

Hans Castorp turned the puzzling object between his fingers. It was made of steel, ivory, gold, and rubber—curious handiwork. It had two curved, shiny steel tines with extremely sharp points, between them a coiled segment of gold-inlaid ivory with tines of its own, which were more pliant or flexible to some degree and could be bent inward. The whole thing ended in a bulb of semihard black rubber. It was only a few inches long.

"What is it?" Hans Castorp asked.

"That," Behrens replied, "is a well-constructed hypodermic syringe. Or, to put it another way, a mechanical copy of the dentures of the spectacled cobra. Do you understand? You don't look as if you understand," he said, while Hans Castorp continued to stare in dazed amazement at the bizarre instrument. "Those are the fangs. They are not that massive, but they come equipped with a capillary, a very tiny channel, that emerges here, as you can clearly see, just above the tip. And of course, these channels have an opening at the root of the fang as well, which is connected to the rubber gland by a duct running through this ivory middle section. When the bite is made, the other teeth are pushed back a little, as you can clearly see, and exert pressure on the reservoir, pressing its contents into the channels, so that the moment the fangs enter the flesh, the dose is injected into the bloodstream. It's quite simple, once you can actually see it. Someone just has to come up with the idea. It was probably produced according to his own specifications."

"I'm sure it was," Hans Castorp said.

"The dose cannot have been all that large," the director went on. "But what is lacking in quantity, can be made up for in—"

"Dynamics," Hans Castorp finished the sentence for him.

"There you have it. What it was exactly, we'll have to investigate. I am looking forward to the results with some curiosity, there is doubtless much we shall learn. What do you want to bet that our exotic on guard duty in there—who just happened to don his best for tonight—could tell us exactly what's what? I assume what we have here is a mixture of animal and vegetable material—good stuff, indeed, the best, since it must pack one thundering wallop. By all indications, it must have taken his breath away at once, paralysis of the respiratory system, you know, rapid suffocation, presumably without great pain or agony."

"God grant it was so," Hans Castorp said piously, handing the eerie little implement back to the director with a sigh. He returned to the bedroom.

Only the Malayan and Madame Chauchat were there now. Clavdia raised her head this time as the young man approached the bed again.

"You had a right to be called," she said.

"Very kind of you," he said, adopting formal pronouns himself, "and it was the correct thing to do. He offered me the brotherhood of informal pronouns. I am so deeply ashamed now to say that I was embarrassed to acknowledge it in front of the others and used circumlocutions. Were you with him in the last moments?"

"His valet notified me after it was all over," she answered.

"He was a man of such stature," Hans Castorp began again, "that, for him, the failure of feeling in the face of life was a cosmic catastrophe, a divine disgrace. For you should know that he regarded himself as God's instrument of marriage. That was a bit of royal foolishness. But when one is deeply moved, one has the courage to say things that may sound crass and irreverent, but are more solemn than authorized words of piety."

"*C'est une abdication*," she said. "He knew of our folly, didn't he?"

"It was impossible for me to dispute it. He had guessed it from my refusal to kiss you on the brow in his presence. His presence is more symbolic than real at this moment, but will you permit me to do so now?"

She thrust her head slightly toward him, eyes closed, as if just blinking. He put his lips to her brow. The Malayan watched this little scene, rolling his brown animal eyes to one side until the whites showed.

The Great Stupor

YET ONCE MORE we hear Director Behrens's voice—let us listen closely. We are hearing it for perhaps the last time. At some point even this story will end; it has lasted quite a long time—or rather, its content-time is rolling along so fast that there is no stopping it now and even its musical time is running out. Perhaps there will be no further opportunity to lend an ear to the cheerful cadences of our idiomatic Rhadamanthus.

He said to Hans Castorp: "Castorp, old pal, you're bored. I see you every day pulling that long face, tedium written all over it. You're jaded, Castorp. You've been pampered with thrills, and if you don't get a first-class kick every day, you sulk and fret about in the doldrums. Am I right or wrong?"

Hans Castorp said nothing, and in doing so only revealed the gloom within.

"I'm right, as always," Behrens said, answering his own question. "And before you start spreading the poison of imperial tedium, my malcontent citizen, you're going to see that God and man have not deserted you and that medical authority has an eye on you, an unblinking eye, my good man, that its one ceaseless concern is your diversion. Old man Behrens is still here, after all. Well, all joking aside, my boy, I have an idea about your case. I've spent, God knows, sleepless nights coming up with it. You might even call it a revelation—and indeed I see my idea as holding great promise: no more and no less than an unexpectedly speedy detoxification and triumphant return home.

"My, what big eyes you have," he continued after a brief rhetorical pause, although Hans Castorp's eyes had not widened at all, but simply gazed at the director rather drowsily and absentmindedly, "and haven't the vaguest what old man Behrens might mean. I mean this: something's not quite right about your case, Castorp, that can't have escaped your keen powers of observation, either. Something's not quite right, because for some time now your symptoms of toxification have not squared with the undeniable improvement in your localized condition—and I didn't start meditating on that just yesterday, either. We have here your latest photo. Let us hold the wizardry up to the light. You see, even the worst grouser and crepehanger, as His Imperial Majesty likes to say, won't find much to object to there. A few foci have been fully reabsorbed, the pocket has grown smaller and is more sharply defined, which, being a well-informed patient, you know indicates healing. On the strength of these findings, then, one can come up with no real explanation for the waywardness of your body temperature. The physician sees himself compelled to explore new causes."

Hans Castorp's nod expressed no more than polite curiosity.

"And now, Castorp, you're saying to yourself: Old man Behrens is going to have to admit he botched the treatment. But you'd be barking up the wrong tree—wrong about the facts, wrong about old man Behrens, too. The treatment wasn't botched, its orientation was merely a bit one-sided, perhaps. I think it likely that from the very first your symptoms should not have been traced exclusively to tuberculosis, and I draw that conclusion from my presumption that they cannot be traced to it at all now. Some other source of disturbance must be present. In my opinion, you have a coccus infection.

"I am profoundly persuaded," the director reiterated more strongly upon observing the nods Hans Castorp offered in response, "that you have a strep infection—which is no immediate cause for alarm, by the way."

(There could be no question of alarm. The expression on Hans Castorp's face was, rather, more a sort of ironic acknowledgment—either of the brilliant conclusions reached or of the new worthy status hypothetically conferred upon him by the director.)

"No reason for panic," the latter said, varying his advice. "Everyone has cocci. Every ass has streptococci. You've nothing to boast of there. We have learned only recently that one can have streptococci in the blood and yet somehow not show any notable symptoms of infection. Though many of my colleagues do not yet know it, we are on the verge of discovering that one can also have tuberculosis in the blood with no consequences whatever. We aren't more than three steps away from seeing tuberculosis as a disease of the blood."

Hans Castorp found that quite remarkable.

"And so when I say 'strep,'" Behrens began anew, "you should not picture the standard severe symptoms, of course. We will have to do a bacteriological blood test to see if these poor things but thine own have even taken up residence. But the only way we can learn whether strep is the cause of your febrility—always assuming that it is present—is to observe the effects of a strepto-vaccine therapy that we shall likewise inaugurate. That is the path before us, my good friend, and I repeat, it holds promise of great, quite unanticipated results. Recovery from infections of this sort can be as rapid as the cure for tuberculosis is protracted. And if you respond to these injections at all, you will be in the pink of health within six weeks. What do you say now? Has old man Behrens been holding up his end or not?"

"It is only a hypothesis so far," Hans Castorp said languidly.

"A provable hypothesis. A highly fertile hypothesis," the director rejoined. "You will see just how fertile it is when the cocci start growing in our cultures. We'll tap your keg tomorrow afternoon, Castorp. We'll bleed a vein with all the style of the old village barber. It's all kinds of fun, and can have the most blessed effects on both body and soul."

Hans Castorp declared himself prepared to be diverted and thanked Behrens nicely for keeping such a steady eye out. His head tilted toward one shoulder, he watched the director row away. The boss's little speech had come at a critical moment. Rhadamanthus had been very close to the mark in interpreting his guest's expression and mood, and his new initiative was intended—expressly intended, he did not deny it at all—to help Hans Castorp move beyond the dead standstill at which he found himself of late, as was obvious in his body language, so clearly reminiscent of Joachim's in the days when certain wild, defiant decisions were forming inside him.

And we can say more. It seemed to Hans Castorp that not only he had come to this dead standstill, but that the world, all of it, the "whole thing," was in much the same state—or rather, he found it difficult up here to separate the particular from the general. Ever since the eccentric conclusion to his relationship with a certain personality and all the changes that conclusion had set into motion in the sanatorium; ever since Clavdia Chauchat's renewed departure from the society of those up here, including a respectful, considered farewell to her master's surviving "brother" exchanged beneath the shadow cast by the tragedy of a great failure—ever since that turning point, it had seemed to the young man as if there were something uncanny about the world and life, as if there were something peculiar, something increasingly askew and disquieting about it, as if a demon had seized power, an evil and crazed demon, who had long exercised considerable influence, but now declared his lordship with such unrestrained candor that he could instill in you secret terrors, even prompt you to think of fleeing. The demon's name was Stupor.

It will be said that the narrator is laying it on too thick, being too romantic in associating stupor with demonic forces, even ascribing to it some sort of mystic horror. And yet we are not fabricating tales here, but are keeping exactly to our prosaic hero's personal experience—knowledge of which has been granted to us in ways that, to be sure, elude all investigation, but that plainly prove that under certain circumstances stupor can take on such character and instill such feelings. Hans Castorp looked around him—and what he saw was indeed uncanny and malicious. And he knew what it was he saw: life without time, without care or hope, life as a stagnating hustle-bustle of depravity, dead life.

It was a busy world, with all sorts of activities taking place concurrently; and every now and then, one of them would become the rage, a mania that conquered all else. Amateur photography had always played an important role in the world of the Berghof; but twice now—and we have lingered up here long enough to experience periodic reoccurrences of such epidemics—it had become a passion that made fools of everyone for weeks and months. There was not a soul who at some point had not bent his head down over a camera wedged in the pit of his stomach, made a worried face, and snapped the shutter. There was no end of prints to be passed around at meals. Suddenly it was a matter of honor to do one's own developing. The darkrooms available did not come close to meeting the demand. The windows and balcony doors of rooms were hung with black curtains, and people dabbled with chemicals under red lights—until a fire broke out, and the Bulgarian student from the Good Russian table came within an inch of being reduced to ashes. A general prohibition decreed by sanatorium authorities followed. Simple snapshots were soon considered déclassé and color photography à la Lumière was the thing. They all reveled in pictures of people caught in the flash of magnesium, with vacant eyes staring dully from faces frozen in cramped expressions, as if the corpses of murder victims had been set up in chairs, eyes wide open. Even Hans Castorp kept a glass plate framed in cardboard, which, when held up to the light, showed him standing in a garish green woodland meadow, between Frau Stöhr and Fräulein Levi of the ivory complexion, the former in a sky-blue sweater, the latter in a blood-red one, his own face coppery against a field of pale yellow buttercups, one of which glowed in his buttonhole.

Then there was stamp collecting, which was always pursued by a few individuals, but occasionally ran rampant as a general obsession. Everyone pasted, haggled, traded. People subscribed to philatelic magazines, corresponded with special vendors, clubs, and private hobbyists, at home and abroad; and amazing sums were spent to purchase rare specimens, even by those whose budgets barely permitted them to stay at a deluxe sanatorium for months or years on end.

That would continue until the next fad took over—when, for instance, the collection and incessant consumption of chocolate in every conceivable form might become the fashion. Everyone had brown lips, and the most delicious productions of the Berghof kitchens were greeted by lethargic, carping gourmets, who had already stuffed and ruined their stomachs with Milka nougats, *chocolat à la crème d'amandes, Marquis napolitains,* and little "cat's tongues" sprinkled with gold.

Sketching pigs with one's eyes closed—introduced one long-ago Mardi Gras evening by a high-placed personage and enjoyed frequently since—had led to successive geometric teasers, which occasionally engaged the mental powers of all Berghof residents, even the last thoughts and energies of the moribund. Week after week, the sanatorium stood beneath the banner of an intricate figure composed of no less than eight large and small circles, plus several interlocked triangles. The task was to trace this polygram freehand, without ever lifting your pencil from the paper; the ultimate goal, however, was to accomplish this blindfolded—which in the end, apart from a few minor blemishes that were easily disregarded, was managed only by Prosecutor Paravant, the primary booster of such intellectual crazes.

We know that he studied mathematics—know it from the director himself—and recall the chaste motive behind his devotion to the discipline, whose cooling effects and ability to blunt the thorn in the flesh we have heard praised and whose more general rewards would probably have rendered unnecessary certain measures that the authorities had recently been forced to adopt. Chief among these had been the barricading of the passage from balcony to balcony—there where the milk-glass partitions did not quite reach the railing—with little doors that were locked at night by the bath attendant, amid general smirks and sniggers. Since then, demand had grown considerably for second-floor apartments, from where, after climbing over the railing, one could avoid the little doors and move from room to room by way of the projecting glass roof of the veranda below. These disciplinary reforms would certainly not have had to have been introduced on the prosecutor's account. The severe temptation that had coincided with the arrival of his Egyptian Fatima had long since been overcome, was indeed the last of its sort to tax Paravant's system. After that, he threw himself with redoubled fervor into the arms of the clear-eyed goddess, about whose soothing powers Director Behrens had so many virtuous things to say; and the problem that consumed his every thought day and night, to which he devoted all the persistence, all the sportsman's tenacity he had once brought to the conviction of poor sinners—back in the days before his frequently extended leave of absence, which now threatened to become permanent retirement—that problem was nothing less than the squaring of the circle.

In the course of his studies, this sidetracked civil servant had succeeded in convincing himself that the proofs science claimed substantiated the impossibility of this construction were invalid and that Providence had removed him, Paravant, from the world of the living below and brought him here, because it had chosen him to grab hold of that transcendent goal and drag it down into earthly realms of exact realization. That was what he was about. Wherever he went, he drew circles and made calculations, filled vast quantities of paper with figures, letters, numbers, and algebraic symbols; his tanned face, the face of an obviously unwell man, bore the visionary and mulish look of the monomaniac. He knew only one, dreadfully tedious topic of conversation: the ratio pi, that forlorn fraction, which a lesser genius of mental arithmetic named Zacharias Dase had once worked out to two hundred decimal places—a superfluous task, since even at two thousand places he would have had no greater prospect of approaching unattainable accuracy, indeed would not have been one whit closer to it. People fled before this tortured thinker, for whoever he managed to buttonhole was subjected to a passionate torrent of words intended to awaken a deeper sensitivity to the hopeless irrationality of this mystical ratio and to its shameful defilement of the human spirit. After pointlessly multiplying pi by diameter to find the circumference of innumerable circles, pi by the square of the radius to find their area, the prosecutor increasingly began to wonder if since the days of Archimedes humanity had not just been making the whole thing too complicated, if the solution to the problem was not childishly simple. What, you weren't supposed to be able to rectify circumference, or turn any given straight line into a circle? At times Paravant thought he was close to a revelation. Of an evening, he was often seen in the deserted and dimly lit dining hall, still sitting at his place, a piece of string carefully laid out in a circle on the bare tabletop; suddenly he would reach out in a surprise attack and pull it straight, only to hunch over again, prop himself on his elbows, and sink into bitter brooding. The director occasionally lent Paravant a hand in his melancholy puttering, even encouraged him in the fixation. In his suffering, the prosecutor brought his sweet anguish to Hans Castorp one day, and came back again and again, for in him he found a friend, someone with understanding and sympathy for the mystery of the circle. He illustrated the despairs of pi for the young man with a precise, painfully executed drawing of a circle trapped between two polygons, circumscribing one, circumscribed by the other, each with as many countless tiny sides as it was humanly possible to draw. The rest, however, the curvature that by some ethereal, spiritual means escaped the calculable embrace that could turn it into a rational number—that, said the prosecutor, his jaw trembling, that was pi! Sensitive as he was, however, Hans Castorp proved less susceptible to pi than Paravant. He called it smoke and mirrors, advised the prosecutor not to take this little game of tag so seriously, not to get so overheated, and spoke of the elastic turning points of which every circle consists, from its nonexistent beginning to its imaginary end, mentioning as well the mirthful melancholy of eternity, which has no permanent direction and keeps coming back onto itself—and spoke with such serene religiosity that it had a brief calming effect on the prosecutor.

Indeed, Hans Castorp's good nature destined him to be the confidant of more than one fellow resident obsessed with some idea and yet sadly unable to find a hearing among the easygoing majority. An erstwhile sculptor from the Austrian provinces, a handsome older gentleman with a white moustache, aquiline nose, and blue eyes, had come up with a project for raising public revenues, which he had written out in a fine hand, underlining the important points in sepia watercolor. The plan was that every newspaper subscriber would have to save his daily paper, weighing 1.4 ounces, which would then be collected on the first of each month, yielding approximately thirty pounds of used paper a year, no less than six hundred pounds in twenty years—at ten pfennigs a pound, that would come to sixty German marks. Five million subscribers, the memorandum continued, would therefore in the course of twenty years recycle newspaper worth the immense sum of three hundred million marks, two-thirds of which would be applied to renewing subscriptions, making them much cheaper, and one-third, around one hundred million marks, made available for humanitarian purposes—to finance tuberculosis sanatoriums for the general public, to subsidize struggling artists, and so forth. The plan was worked out in detail, down to a punch-holed form to be used as the receipt for reimbursements and a sketch of a sliding scale from which the department in charge of collection could figure the value of the quantity turned in each month. From any point of view, it was a solidly based, well-justified plan. Imprudent waste and destruction of newsprint, unwittingly flushed down the drain or sent up the chimney, was high treason, a crime against our forests and the nation's economy. Saving paper, conserving paper, meant saving and conserving cellulose, the forests themselves, and the human labor needed to produce cellulose and paper—both labor and capital. And since old newspaper would also be recycled as valuable packing paper and cardboard, which would then provide an important economic base for national and local taxation, the plan would also reduce the tax burden on newspaper subscribers. In short, it was a good plan, indeed incontrovertible; and if there seemed to be something uncanny and frivolous, sinister and mad about it, that was due simply to the skewed fanaticism with which the erstwhile artist pursued and advocated his one and only economic plan—which he evidently did not take seriously enough to make even the least attempt to put into action. Hans Castorp would tilt his head and nod as he listened to the man propagate his earth-saving ideas in flights of fevered eloquence, and all the while he would explore the nature of his own contempt and disdain that prevented him from joining the inventor in his battle against a thought-less world.

Several Berghof residents studied Esperanto and had learned enough to converse in the artificial lingo at meals. Hans Castorp cast them dark glances, and kept to himself the fact that he did not think them the worst of the lot. A group of English guests had recently introduced a parlor game that consisted of nothing more than the first person's turning to his neighbor in a circle and asking, "Did you ever see the Devil with a nightcap on?" to which that person replied, "No, I never saw the Devil with a nightcap on," and then passed the question along—and on it went, round and round. It was dreadful. But poor Hans Castorp grew even gloomier watching the solitaire players, who could be seen at work everywhere in the Berghof at all hours. For the passion for this pastime had so taken hold of late that the whole place was a den of iniquity; and Hans Castorp had all the more reason to feel gripped by horror, because he fell victim to the plague himself for a while—was indeed perhaps one of the most serious cases. He was afflicted by a game known as "elevens," in which a bridge deck is arranged in three rows of three cards each, and any two cards that add up to eleven, plus any of the three face cards when they turn up, are then covered anew, until, if fortune smiles, the game is won. One would not think it possible that such a simple game could be the source of such exquisite joy, to the point of sheer bewitchment. And yet Hans Castorp, like so many others, explored that possibility—explored it with a scowl, for debauchery is never cheerful. He was the plaything of the imp of the cards, a captive of the capricious whims of its favor, which would sometimes start things out on an easy wave of luck—all jacks, queens, kings, and sums of eleven—so that the game was over before the third time through (a fleeting triumph, which only pricked your nerves to try again); at other times the imp waited until the ninth and final card to deny any chance of its ever being covered or at the very last moment it abruptly blocked everything and cast an almost certain victory to the winds. Hans Castorp played solitaire everywhere, at any time of day—at night under the stars, in the morning in his pajamas, at meals, even in his dreams. He shuddered, but he played. Which was how Herr Settembrini found him one day when he stopped to visit, to "bother" him—as had been his mission from the very first.

"*Accidente!*" he said. "You're playing solitaire, my good engineer?"

"That's not quite it," Hans Castorp replied. "I'm just laying the cards out, wrestling with abstract chance. I'm intrigued by its fickle tricks, the way it can toady up to you and then turn incredibly obstinate. This morning I got out of bed and easily won three games, one after the other, once only twice through—a record for me. And would you believe that I've laid them out thirty-two times in a row now, without being able to get halfway through even once?"

Herr Settembrini gazed at him with sad black eyes, as so often in the course of these many little years. "At any rate, I find you preoccupied," he said. "It doesn't look as if this is where I shall find solace for my woes, balm for the inner conflict that torments me."

"Inner conflict?" Hans Castorp repeated, and laid out his cards.

"The world situation baffles me," the Freemason said. "The Balkan League will be formed, my good engineer, all my sources tell me so. Russia is working feverishly for it, and the arrow of the coalition is pointed at the Austro-Hungarian monarchy, without whose breakup Russia cannot accomplish a single one of its goals. Do you understand my scruples? I hate Vienna with all that is in me, as you know. But should I grant the support of my soul to Sarmatian despotism, when it is about to put the torch to our most noble continent? On the other hand, I would feel personally disgraced by diplomatic cooperation, even on a one-time ad hoc basis, between my own country and Austria. Those are questions of conscience that—"

"Seven and four," Hans Castorp said. "Eight and three. Jack, queen, king. It's going to work. You bring me luck, Herr Settembrini."

The Italian said nothing. Hans Castorp could feel those black eyes, that gaze of reason and morality, resting in deep mourning upon him, but went right on laying out his cards for a while, before he finally laid his cheek in one hand and stared up with a naughty child's sullen look of false innocence.

"Your eyes," his mentor said, "try in vain to conceal that you know how things stand with you."

"*Placet experiri,*" Hans Castorp had the impudence to reply, and Herr Settembrini departed—and then, to be sure, once left to his own devices, the young man did not lay out his cards again, but sat for a long time at the table in his white room, his head propped in his hand, brooding, gripped by the horror of the eerie and skewed state in which he saw the world entrapped, by the fear of the grinning demon and monkey-god in whose crazed and unrestrained power he now found himself—and whose name was "The Great Stupor."

A fearful, apocalyptic name, very much calculated to instill secret terrors. Hans Castorp sat and rubbed his brow and the area around his heart with the palms of his hands. He was afraid. It was as if "all this" could come to no good end, as if the end was surely a catastrophe, a rebellion of patient nature, a thunderstorm and a great cleansing wind that would break the spell cast over the world, wrench life from its "dead standstill," and overturn the "doldrums" in a terrible Last Judgment. He longed to flee, as noted—it was just lucky that medical authority had, as mentioned before, kept an "unblinking eye" on him, that it had known how to read the expression on his face and was intent on diverting him with new, fertile hypotheses.

In its fraternity jargon and cadence, medical authority had announced the true cause for the waywardness of Hans Castorp's body temperature and offered its scientific opinion that the cause would not be difficult to overcome and that a cure and authorized release back to the flatlands suddenly loomed ahead in the near future. Assailed by manifold sensations, the young man's heart pounded hard as he held out his arm to give blood, and he turned slightly pale as he admired the splendid ruby red of the sap of life rising to fill glass tubes. Assisted by Dr. Krokowski and a Sister of Mercy, the director himself performed this little operation with its far-reaching consequences. Then came a series of days that for Hans Castorp were dominated by one question: once outside his body, would what he had given pass the test under the eye of science?

Nothing had been able to grow as yet, of course, the director said at first. Unfortunately, nothing showed signs of wanting to grow, he said later. But then came a morning when he walked up to Hans Castorp during breakfast—seated nowadays at the upper end of the Good Russian table, where once had sat the great man with whom he had shared the bond of brotherhood—and, amid idiomatic congratulations, revealed to him that streptococci had been identified beyond a doubt in one of the prepared cultures. It was now a matter of probabilities: should the symptoms of toxicity be traced to the small tubercle bacillus, which was also present, or to strep, whose presence was quite modest? He, Behrens, would have to inspect the matter at length and more closely—the culture was not yet ripe. He showed it to Hans Castorp in the lab: a blood-red jelly with little gray dots here and there. Those were the cocci. (Every ass could have cocci, however, as well as tubercles; and if there had been no symptoms, these findings would have been of no further significance.)

Outside his body, under the eye of science, Hans Castorp's congealed blood continued to pass the test. There came a morning when the director in his spirited idiomatic phrases reported: Cocci had grown not just in one culture, but in all the rest now as well, and in great quantity. It was uncertain if they were all strep; it was more than likely, however, that the symptoms of toxicity came from them—though one could not be certain, of course, how many of those symptoms might be credited to unvanquished remnants of tuberculosis definitely present as well. And the conclusion to be drawn? Strepto-vaccine therapy! The prognosis? Extraordinarily good—particularly since the therapy carried no risk, and so could not hurt in any case. For the serum would be made from Hans Castorp's own blood, so that the injections could introduce no contagious matter into his body that was not already there. At worst, it would be useless, have no effect—but, then, could one call that a worst case, since the patient would be staying on at any rate.

Well, Hans Castorp was not willing to go quite that far. But he submitted to the therapy, though he found it ridiculous and disgraceful. These vaccinations of himself with himself could be no more than a disgustingly joyless diversion, a self-to-self incestuous abomination, an infertile, hopeless enterprise inside his own body. That was the voice of ignorant hypochondria, which proved correct only as to infertility—though, to be sure, completely correct in that one point. The diversion lasted several weeks. At times it seemed to make him ill—though, of course, he had to be in error about that—at times it seemed to help; but that turned out to be an error as well. The result was zero, though that was never expressly announced. The enterprise fizzled out, and Hans Castorp went on playing solitaire—eye to eye with the demon whose unrestrained power he could not help feeling was sure to come to some horrible end.

Fullness of Harmony

WHAT NEW ACQUISITION of the Berghof was it, then, that rescued our friend of many years from his mania for solitaire and led him into the arms of another, nobler, if ultimately no less strange passion? We are about to introduce it, since we ourselves are much taken by that mysterious object's secret charms and are honestly eager to share them.

In its never-resting concern for its guests, a thoughtful management

had decided to add another amusing gadget to the collection in the main
social room—purchased at a price we do not care to estimate, but that
must have been considerable, a handsome disbursement on the part of
the administration of this highly recommended institution. An ingenious
toy, then, on the line of the stereoscopic viewer, the tubelike kaleidoscope,
and the cinematographic drum? Yes indeed—and then again, not at all
like them. First, it was not an optical contrivance that the guests found
one evening in the music room—some of them greeting it by clasping
their hands over their heads, others by folding them reverently with heads
bowed—it was an acoustic instrument; and second, there was no comparison to those little mechanisms in value, status, and rank. This was no
childish, monotonous peep show, of which they were all tired and with
which no one bothered after his first three weeks here. It was an overflowing cornucopia of artistic pleasure, of delights for the soul from merry to
somber. It was a musical apparatus. It was a gramophone.

We are seriously concerned that the term may be misunderstood, be
associated with undignified and outdated notions, with an obsolete model
that in no way does justice to the reality we envision here, the product
of untiring advances in musical technology, developed to elegant perfection. My dear friends, this was no wretched crank-box, the old-fashioned
sort with a turntable and stylus on top, plus a misshapen, trumpetlike
brass appendage, the sort of thing you might have found at one time set
up on a tavern counter to fill unsophisticated ears with nasal braying.
This small cabinet, a little deeper than it was wide, was stained a dull
black, had a silky cord that led to an electrical wall outlet, and stood on
its special table in simple dignity—and bore no resemblance whatever to
such crude, antediluvian machines. When you lifted the gracefully beveled
lid, a well-secured brass rod raised automatically to hold it in place at a
protective angle, and inside you saw, set slightly lower, the turntable with
its green cloth cover and nickel rim, plus the nickel spindle that fitted
into the hole of the ebonite disks. At the front on the right was a device
like the dial on a clock for regulating the turntable's tempo, to its left,
the lever that started and stopped it; at the rear on the left, however, was
the sinuous, club-shaped nickel tube that had pliant, movable joints and
ended in a flat, round sound-box equipped with a screw into which the
needle was inserted. When you opened the double doors at the front, you
saw a diagonal pattern of wooden louvers stained black—nothing more.

"The newest model," said the director, who now entered the room.
"The latest achievement, children, top-notch, A-1, nothing better in the
warehouse." He said this last with an impossible, comic twist, the way
some poorly educated salesman might have praised the item. "This is no

apparatus, no machine," he went on, extracting a needle from one of the colorful tin boxes set out on the table and screwing it into place, "this is an instrument, this is a Stradivarius, a Guarneri—you'll hear resonances and vibrations of vintage *raffinemang*. It's a Polyhymnia, as we are informed here inside the lid. German-made, you see—we make far and away the best. Music most faithful, in its modern, mechanical form. The German soul, up-to-date. There's the library," he said and pointed toward a cupboard with rows of broad-backed albums. "I hereby entrust its magic to the public, to be enjoyed at leisure, though I likewise commend it to your tender care. Shall we give a disk a try, let her rip and roar?"

The patients implored him to do so, and Behrens pulled out one of the mute books laden with hidden magic, turned the heavy pages, the colorful titles visible through circular openings, extracted a disk from one of the pockets, and put it on. He flipped the switch that sent current to the turntable, waited two seconds until it had reached top speed, and carefully set the fine steel point down on the rim of the disk. A soft sound, like someone whetting a stone, was heard. He lowered the lid, and in the same moment from between the louvers at the open double doors—no, from the whole chest itself—a bustling, merry instrumental din burst forth, an insistent noisy melody, the first bars of a toe-tapping Offenbach overture.

They listened, mouths open and smiling. They could not believe their ears—how pure and natural the trills of the woodwinds sounded. A violin, in solo, offered a fanciful prelude. They could hear the bowing, the tremolo in the fingers as they slid sweetly from one position to the next and found their melody, a waltz, *"Ach, ich habe sie verloren."* The harmonies of the orchestra picked up the easy strains and bore them on—and it was simply ravishing the way the whole ensemble repeated it now in a sweeping tutti. Naturally it was not the same as if a real orchestra were giving a concert in the room. The body of sound, though not in any way distorted, had suffered a diminution in perspective; it was, if one may use a visual comparison for an audible phenomenon, as if one were gazing at a painting through the wrong end of opera glasses, so that it looked distant and small, but without forfeiting any definition of line or brilliance of color. The piece was clever, tight, tingly, and was reproduced here in all its witty, giddy invention. It came to a perfectly rollicking close, a droll galop that after a brief hesitation became a shameless cancan, evoking visions of top hats flung into the air, of flying skirts and bouncing knees, and its comic, triumphant ending seemed to have no end. Then the turntable stopped all on its own. It was over. Heartfelt applause.

They called for more and got it: a human voice came from the cabinet, a male voice, both gentle and forceful, accompanied by an orchestra, a celebrated Italian baritone—and now there could be no talk of any diminution or distancing. The splendid vocal organ swelled to its full natural range and power, and indeed if you walked into an adjoining room, leaving the doors open but staying out of the line of sight, it was exactly as if the artist were physically present, as if he were standing there in the salon singing, music in hand. He sang a showpiece aria in his own language— *eh, il barbiere. Di qualità, di qualità! Figaro qua, Figaro là, Figaro, Figaro, Figaro!* The audience almost died laughing at his *parlando falsetto*, at the contrast between this bear of a voice and his talent for tongue twisters. Ears more expert could follow and admire the art of his phrasing and his breathing technique. A master of the irresistible effect, a virtuoso in his native *aria da capo*, he held the penultimate note before the resolution— moving downstage now, or so it seemed, one hand thrust into the air— held it so long that they broke into polite bravos before he had finished. It was exquisite.

And there was more. A French horn executed lovely, discreet variations on a folk song. With the most charming, cool precision in her staccato, a soprano warbled and trilled an aria from *La Traviata*. The ghost of a world-famous violinist played as if behind veils, accompanied by a piano with the arid sound of a spinet—a romance by Rubinstein. From the gently simmering chest of wonders came the peal of bells, the glissando of harps, the blare of trumpets, the roll of drums. Finally, some dance records were put on. There were even copies of the latest imports— tangos, born in the dives of a port city and destined to turn the waltz into a dance for grandpas. Two couples who had learned the fashionable step now took to the carpet and showed it off for the others. After a final admonition to use each needle only once and to treat the disks "the way you would raw eggs," Behrens had retired for the evening. Hans Castorp now operated the machine.

And why him? He had managed it as follows. After the director had departed, a small group formed to take over the task of changing records and needles, of turning the switch off and on; he abruptly walked up to them, said, "Let me do that," in a subdued voice, and pushed them aside. They yielded, unruffled—first, because his expression seemed to say that he had years of experience at this, and second, because they were much less interested in occupying themselves at the source of this new pleasure than in letting someone serve it up to them in comfort, just so long as they didn't get bored.

Not so Hans Castorp. He had stood quietly in the background while the director demonstrated this new acquisition; and although he had not laughed or shouted bravo, he had followed the performances intently, twirling one eyebrow between two fingers, an occasional habit of late. There was something restless about the way he had changed position several times behind the others' backs, first walking into the library to listen from there, and then later stepping up to Behrens, his hands behind his back, a reserved look on his face, to take a closer look at the cabinet and ask about its basic functions. Somewhere inside him a voice said: "Wait! Look out! An epoch begins! For me!" He was filled with the very definite premonition of a new passion and enchantment, a new burden of love. What he felt was no different from what a lad in the flatlands feels when he casts that first glance at a girl and Cupid's barbed arrow unexpectedly pierces his heart. And suddenly there was jealousy in each of Hans Castorp's strides. Public property? Flaccid curiosity has no right to property, no strength for ownership. "Let me do that," he had said between clenched teeth, and they were quite content to let him. They danced a little longer to the casual pieces he played, and demanded another vocal number, an opera duet, the "Barcarole" from *The Tales of Hoffmann*, which sounded sweet enough to their ears. When he closed the lid, they departed for the peace of rest cure, chatting in fleeting excitement as they went. They left everything behind just as it was—the open box of needles, albums and disks strewn about. How like them. He pretended to join them, but quietly left the crowd on the stairs, came back to the music room, closed the doors, and stayed there half the night, hard at work.

He familiarized himself with the new acquisition; with no one to disturb him now, he examined the treasury of works that came with it, inspected the contents of the heavy albums. There were twelve in all, in two different formats, twelve records to each; and since many of the circular disks were minutely etched on both sides—not simply because many pieces required two sides, but also because a good number of them offered two different selections—it was difficult at first to get an overview of this confusing world of beautiful possibilities waiting to be conquered. Trying not to disturb the nighttime silence, he made use of certain needles that sat more lightly on the disks and thus dampened the sound. He played a good twenty-five disks, but that was barely an eighth of the temptations offered on all sides. Just a scan of the titles had to suffice for now, though from time to time he would select one at random and insert yet another example of these mute engravings into the cabinet and turn it into sound. The labels in the middle of the ebonite disks were different colors, but otherwise the eye could not differentiate them. Each looked like the other, each was filled to the center, or almost to the center, with a dense pattern of concentric circles; and yet this delicate tracery contained more sound than one could imagine, exquisite renditions of the happiest inspirations from every domain of the art of music.

There were a lot of overtures and single movements from the world of lofty symphonies, played by famous orchestras under well-known directors. He found a long list of lieder, too, sung to piano accompaniment by artists from the great opera houses—both those composed out of conscious, sublime, personal art, and simple folk songs, plus those that fell somewhere in the middle, as it were, which were products of the intellect and yet written with a genuinely profound, devout understanding of a given national spirit—artistic folk songs, if one may put it that way, with no implication of compromised sincerity in the word "artistic." There was one in particular that Hans Castorp had known since childhood, for which he now developed a mysterious, multifaceted love and of which we shall speak later. And what else was there, or better, what wasn't there? There was opera in every shape and form. To discreet orchestral accompaniment, a veritable international chorus of celebrated singers, male and female, put their highly trained, God-given talents to good use in arias, duets, ensemble scenes from all the many epochs and genres of musical theater: the Mediterranean bel canto, captivating in both its lighthearted and noble forms; a German world of folklore, rogues, and demons; French opera, grand and comic. And was that it, then? Oh, no. There was a chamber music series: quartets and trios; instrumental solos for violin, cello, and flute; concert pieces with violin or flute obligato; solo piano works. Not to mention simpler amusements—music-hall numbers, topical songs, melodies recorded by small dance orchestras that required a coarser needle to do them justice.

All alone and very busy, Hans Castorp sorted and arranged, surrendering a small number of the disks to the instrument, which awakened them to sonorous life. It was at about the same late hour as on that first night of revels with Pieter Peeperkorn of majestic, brotherly memory when he finally went to bed, his head hot and flushed; and from two to seven o'clock he dreamed of his magic box. In his dream he saw the turntable whirling around its spindle, so fast it became invisible, inaudible, not simply rotating wildly in place, but moving in a strange lateral undulation so that the arm beneath which it turned began to oscillate supplely, as if it were breathing—very useful, one might suppose, for the vibrato and portamento of strings and human voices. And yet in his dreams, no less than when he was awake, Hans Castorp was unable to comprehend it: how could these rich combinations of harmony now filling his sleeping ear be re-created simply by tracing a line, fine as a human hair, above an acoustic chamber, assisted only by the vibrating membrane in the sound-box?

He was back again in the salon early the next morning, before breakfast even; sitting down in an armchair and folding his hands in his lap, he let a splendid baritone sing to him from the cabinet: *"Blick' ich umher in diesem edlen Kreise."* And along with the swelling, breathing, articulating male voice, there came the natural sound of a harp accompaniment, absolutely authentic, not diminished in the least—perfectly amazing. And then Hans Castorp followed this with a duet from a modern Italian opera; and there could be nothing on earth more tender than the demure, intense mingling of emotions between a world-famous tenor, who was well represented in the albums, and a little soprano with a voice sweet and clear as glass—than his *"Da' mi il braccio, mia piccina,"* and her answering melodic phrase, so simple, sweet, and succinct.

Hans Castorp flinched as the door opened at his back. It was the director, who was checking on him; dressed in his clinical smock, a stethoscope peeking out of his breast pocket, Behrens stood there for a moment with one hand on the door handle and nodded to this new "lab assistant," who responded with a nod over his shoulder. The boss's purple-cheeked face and skewed moustache vanished as he pulled the door to behind him, and Hans Castorp turned back to his pair of invisible lyric lovers.

Later that day, after both the noon meal and supper, there were other listeners, a constantly changing audience—that is if you did not count Hans Castorp himself as part of the audience but as the dispenser of these pleasures. He was himself inclined to this latter view, and his fellow residents granted him as much, at least in the sense that, from the very beginning, they silently acquiesced in his determined self-appointment as administrator and custodian of this public facility. It cost them nothing; for apart from the superficial thrills of listening to their idolized tenor wallow in molten splendor, to a voice surging in a cantabile that blessed the world with the high arts of passion—apart from such thrills, they had no love for the instrument and were quite willing to let anyone who liked take care of it. It was Hans Castorp, then, who kept the treasured disks in order, writing the contents of each album on the inside of its cover so that every piece was immediately accessible upon request, and who operated the instrument itself—they soon noticed how deftly and gently he went about it once he had some practice. And how would the others have treated it? They would have ruined the records by playing them with used needles and leaving them lying around just anywhere on chairs, would have used the apparatus for stupid jokes like playing some sublime piece with the dial set at a speed of 110 or 0, yielding hysteric tweets or intermittent groans. They had already done it. They might be ill, but they were crude. And that was why within a very short time, Hans Castorp simply pocketed the key to the cupboard containing the albums and needles and had to be called if someone wanted to play records.

Late evening, after the social gathering, when the crowd had left, was his best time. Then he would stay behind alone in the salon or stealthily return to play music until well into the night. It turned out he had less reason to fear disturbing the peace than he had first thought, for he found that his ghostly music carried over only a limited range. The vibrations produced amazing effects near their source, but like all ghostly things, quickly languished with distance, grew feeble, their powers merely illusory. Within these four walls, Hans Castorp was alone with the wonders of his apparatus—with the lush achievements of this little truncated coffin of fiddlewood, this small, dull-black temple with its doors flung wide, before which he would sit in an armchair, hands folded, head on one shoulder, mouth open, letting the fullness of harmony spill over him.

The singers he listened to, but could not see, had bodies that resided in America, in Milan, in Vienna, in Saint Petersburg—and they could reside where they liked, because what he had was the best part of them, the voice, and he valued this purified form, this abstraction that still remained physical enough to allow him real human control, and yet excluded all the disadvantages of too close personal contact, particularly if they happened to be fellow countrymen, Germans. It was possible to identify an artist's nationality from pronunciation and dialect; the character of each voice said something about the individual's spiritual growth, and the level of intelligence was apparent in the way the possibilities of the mind were used or neglected in achieving certain effects. Hans Castorp was annoyed if intelligence was lacking. And he also suffered, bit his lip in shame, from the imperfections in technical reproduction; he sat on hot coals whenever he played some familiar record he knew contained a shrill or squawking tone—which could easily happen, especially with tricky female voices. But that was part of the bargain—love must suffer. Sometimes he would bend down over the spinning, breathing machinery as if it were a bouquet of lilacs, his head in a cloud of fragrant sound; he would stand in front of the open cabinet and savor the autocratic bliss of the orchestra conductor, raising a hand to signal a trumpet for its timely entry. He had favorites in his cupboard, several pieces of vocal and instrumental music he never tired of hearing. We cannot refrain from listing them.

One small group of records contained the closing scenes of a grandiose opera overflowing with melodic genius, written by one of Herr Settembrini's compatriots, an old Southern master of musical drama, who had composed it in the second half of the previous century on commission from an Oriental prince, as part of solemn ceremonies at the dedication of a work of technology that would bring nations closer together. Hans Castorp was more or less familiar with the plot, knew the rough outline of the tragic fate of Radames, Amneris, and Aida, who sang to him from the cabinet—an incomparable tenor, a stately mezzo with that splendid break in the middle of her register, and a silvery soprano. It was all in Italian, but he understood more or less what they sang—not every word, but enough here and there, given his knowledge of the plot and his sympathy for its situations, a personal empathy that had increased each time he played the four or five records, until it now became a genuine infatuation.

First came an argument between Radames and Amneris. The princess has him led before her in chains; she loves him and ardently longs to save him, even though he has cast aside his honor and his country for the sake of a barbarian slave girl—but to that accusation he replies, "In my thoughts my honor remained pure." This integrity of his inner soul, despite feelings of guilt, is of little help to him, however, since his crimes are all too obvious; he is brought before a court of priests with no sympathies for anything human, and they will make short work of him if he does not change his mind at the last moment—abandon his slave girl and throw himself into the arms of the stately mezzo with the break in her register, actions which, from a purely acoustic point of view, she fully deserves. Amneris fervently strives to convince the tenor to renounce his slave girl, tells him it will cost him his life, but in response to her desperate pleas, the tragically infatuated tenor, having already turned his back on life, can only reply: "I cannot!" and "In vain!" —"Once more, renounce her!" —"I cannot." —A blind rush toward death and the fiercest anguish of love unite in a duet of extraordinary beauty, but devoid of hope. Amneris's cries of agony accompany the priests' horrible formulaic response, which now rises muffled from the depths where a religious court is trying the unhappy Radames, who takes no part in the proceedings.

"Radames, Radames," the high priest sings urgently and makes it pointedly clear that he is to be charged with the crime of treason.

"Defend yourself!" the chorus of priests demands.

And when the high priest mentions that Radames has nothing to say, they unanimously agree he is guilty of treason.

"Radames, Radames," the chief judge begins again, "you deserted the field the day before the battle."

"Defend yourself!" the chorus cries out again.

"You see, he is silent," the totally biased judge notes for the second time.

And so this time, too, all voices unite in the verdict of "Treason!"

"Radames, Radames," his remorseless accuser says for the third time. "You were false to your country, your king, your honor."—The cry of "Defend yourself!" rings out anew. And finally, after once again being told that Radames has said not a single word, the priests announce their final, ominous verdict of "Treason!" And so the unavoidable cannot be avoided, and the chorus, their voices still in close harmonies, announce the sentence—his doom is sealed, he is to die the death of the damned, is to be buried alive in a grave beneath the temple of their angry god.

You had to use your own imagination for Amneris's outrage, since the music broke off here, and Hans Castorp had to change records. With downcast eyes, so to speak, he accomplished this with a few silent, deft movements; and when he sat down to listen again, it was the last scene of the melodrama that he heard: the final duet of Radames and Aida, sung at the bottom of their crypt, while above their heads bigoted, cruel priests, raising and spreading their hands in the ceremonies of their cult, lifted their voices in a dull murmur.

"*Tu—in questa tomba?*" The question rang out in the indescribably alluring voice of Radames, a tenor at once both sweet and heroic, horrified and ecstatic. Yes, his beloved has found her way to him, the woman for whom he forfeited honor and life; she has been waiting for him here, to be locked in the tomb with him, to die with him. But it was what they now sang to each other, or at times with one another, concerning this situation, interrupted now and then by the muffled tones of the ceremonies several stories above—it was this exchange of song that deeply stirred the soul of the lonely, nocturnal listener, both in regard to the situation and its musical expression. The words spoke of heaven, but the very music was heavenly, was sung in heavenly voices. The melodic line that Radames' and Aida's voices insatiably followed, first each alone and then together, its simple, blissful arc playing between tonic and dominant, suspended too long at the keynote, then ascending to a halftone below the octave, fleetingly brushing it, and returning to the fifth—that melody seemed to the listener the most radiant, most admirable music he had ever heard. And yet he would have been less in love with its sound had it not been for the underlying situation, which prepared him emotionally to hear the sweet music emerging from it. It was so beautiful, the way Aida had found her way to doomed Radames to share his fate in the crypt for all eternity. And the condemned man quite rightly protested her sacrificing her own dear life; and yet in his gentle, desperate, "*No, no! troppo sei bella,*" one could hear his true ecstasy in being united at last with the woman he had assumed he would never see again. It required no effort of imagination for Hans Castorp to share in the tenor's ecstasy and gratitude, but as he sat there with folded hands, staring at the little black louvers, from between whose slats this all burst forth, ultimately what he felt, understood, and relished was the victorious ideality of music, of art, of human emotions, their sublime and incontrovertible ability to gloss over the crude horrors of reality. You had only to picture coolly and calmly what was actually happening here. Two people were being buried alive; their lungs full of the gases of the crypt, cramped with hunger, they would perish together, or even worse, one after the other; and then decay would do its unspeakable work on their bodies, until two skeletons lay there under those vaults, each indifferent and insensitive to whether it lay there alone or with another set of bones. That was the real, factual side of the matter—a set of facts that stood all to itself, that had nothing whatever to do with the idealism of the heart, and that was triumphantly vanquished by the spirit of beauty and music. For the Radames and Aida of the opera, this factual future did not exist. They let their voices sweep in unison to the blessed sustained note of the octave, secure in the belief that heaven was opening before them, that their longings were bathed in the light of eternity. The consoling power of beauty to gloss things over did its listener a great deal of good and contributed much to his special fondness for this segment of his favorite concert.

It was his habit to relax from this terror and radiance by playing a second piece of brief, but concentrated charm—much more peaceful than the first, an idyll, but an exquisite idyll, painted and assembled with all the intricate economy of contemporary art. Purely instrumental, with no vocals, it was a symphonic prelude of French provenance, scored for a small ensemble, at least by modern standards, yet fitted out with all the tricks of modern tone coloring and cleverly calculated to set the soul spinning a web of dreams.

This was the dream that Hans Castorp dreamed: He was lying on his back on a meadow sparkling in the sun and strewn with colorful asters, a little mound of earth under his head, one leg pulled up slightly, the other laid across it—and, let it be noted, they were the legs of a goat. Just for the pure joy of it, since he was quite alone on the meadow, he let his fingers play at the stops of a woodwind he held to his lips, a clarinet or reed pipe, from which he coaxed gentle, nasal tones, one after the other, purely at random, and yet in a satisfying sequence that rose carelessly into the deep blue sky, beneath which the foliage of a few solitary birches and ashes flickered in the sun as the breeze brushed past. And yet his tranquil semi-melody, his impulsive doodlings, were not the only voice in the solitude for very long. Insects humming in the hot summer air above the grasses, the sunshine itself, the soft breeze, the rustling treetops, the flickering foliage—the whole gently swaying, peaceful, summery scene around him became a blend of sounds that gave ever-changing, constantly surprising harmonic meaning to his simple pipings. The symphonic accompaniment sometimes fell away into silence; but goat-footed Hans continued to blow his naive, monotonous air and lure exquisitely colored, magical tones from nature—until finally, after a long pause, a series of new instrumental voices entered, tumbling rapidly, each higher than the other, their timbres rising in self-surmounting sweetness, until every richness, every fullness held back up to now, was realized for one fleeting moment, which contained within it the perfect blissful pleasures of eternity. The young faun was very happy on his summer meadow. There was no "defend yourself" here, no responsibility, no war tribunal of priests judging someone who had forgotten his honor, lost it somehow. It was depravity with the best of consciences, the idealized apotheosis of a total refusal to obey Western demands for an active life. To our nocturnal musician's ears, this one piece's soothing effects made it worth many others.

And there was a third—made up of several records actually, three or four that belonged together and were to be played in sequence, since the tenor aria alone took up half of one disk of concentric rings. It was another French piece, an opera Hans Castorp knew well, one he had heard and seen repeatedly in the theater and to whose plot he had even alluded once in conversation—in a very crucial conversation. It was the music from the second act, in the Spanish tavern—a low dive, spacious, almost barn-like, with cloths on the tables and a kind of half-baked Moorish architecture. In a warm, slightly husky voice, both earthy and intriguing, Carmen declares she wants to dance with her corporal, and you can hear the castanets clattering now. At the same moment, however, trumpets—bugles—call from the distance, a repeated military signal that comes as no small shock to the little man. "Stop! Just a moment!" he cries and pricks up his ears like a horse. And when Carmen asks, "Why?" and wants to know what is going on, he cries, "Don't you hear?"—amazed that the message is not as clear to her as it is to him. Those were trumpets from his barracks, a bugle call. "They are sounding the retreat," he says operatically. But the Gypsy cannot understand and, more importantly, doesn't want to. All the better, she says, half out of stupidity, half out of impudence, now she won't need her castanets, heaven itself is sending her music to dance by and so—la la la la! He is beside himself. The pain of disappointment gives way to attempts to make clear to her what is happening and that no love affair in the world can prevail against this call. How is it possible, really, that she does not understand something so fundamental, so absolute? "I must return to camp, to quarters, for roll call," he cries in despair at an ingenuousness that only doubles the burden his heart already feels. But listen to Carmen now! She is furious, outraged to the depths of her soul; her voice is all betrayal and injured love—or she makes it sound that way. "Back to quarters, for roll call?" And what about her heart? Her good, tender heart that in its stupidity—yes, she admits it, in its stupidity—was prepared to amuse him with song and dance? "Ta ra ta ta!" and in savage mockery she holds a rolled hand to her mouth to imitate the bugle call. "Ta ra ta ta!" And that does it. The idiot leaps up—he is leaving. Fine then, run along! Here, here are his cap, his sword and knapsack! Clear out, clear out, run along, back to the barracks! He begs for mercy. But she keeps up her hot scorn, she imitates him, and pretends to lose her head at the sound of the trumpets. Ta ra ta ta, back to roll call! Merciful heavens, he's going to be late! Run along, there's the bugle call, and of course he starts acting the fool just when she, Carmen, was going to dance for him. That, that, that, is his love for her!

What an agonizing situation. She does not understand. This woman—this Gypsy—cannot, will not, understand. Does not want to—for without a doubt, her rage, her scorn, is not just for the moment, not merely personal, it is hatred, an ancient hostility to the principle behind those French bugles—or Spanish horns—that call her beloved little soldier back; and her highest ambition, both instinctive and impersonal, is to triumph over that principle. She uses a very simple means to get her way. She claims if he leaves, he does not love her; and that is precisely what José, there inside the cabinet, cannot bear. He implores her to let him speak. She refuses. Then he forces her to listen—a devilishly serious moment. Ominous sounds rose from the orchestra, a gloomy, threatening theme, which as Hans Castorp knew, moved through the whole opera until the catastrophic end, but here also served as the introduction to the little soldier's aria—the next record. And he put it on now.

"Through every long and lonely hour"—José sang it very beautifully; Hans Castorp often played this record by itself, removing it from its familiar context, and always listened in rapt sympathy. The content of the aria was not much, but the way it pleaded with such emotion touched him profoundly. The soldier sang about a flower that Carmen had tossed him when they first became acquainted and that had been his sole comfort in prison, where he had found himself on her account. In his inner turmoil, he admitted that there had been moments when he cursed fate for having placed Carmen in his path. But he had immediately repented of this blasphemy and on his knees begged God that he might see her again.

Then—and this "then" was the same high note with which he had just sung his "to see you, dear Carmen, again"—*then*—and now the instrumental accompaniment unleashed all its available magic to paint the little soldier's anguish and longing, his forlorn tenderness and sweet despair—*then* she had appeared in all her simple, fatal charm, and it had been perfectly clear to him that he was "lost" ("lost" with a great sobbing grace note preceding it), was lost for good and all. "Oh, my Carmen," he sang. "My being is yours," he sang in desperation, repeating the same anguished melodic phrase, which the orchestra also picked up again on its own, ascending two notes up from the dominant and with deepest fervor moving back to the fifth below. "My heart is yours," he assured her in trite, but tenderest excess, using that same melodic phrase again; now he moved up the scale to the sixth to add, "And I am eternally yours," then let his voice sink ten intervals and in great agitation confessed, "Carmen, I love you"—the last few notes agonizingly sustained above shifting harmonies, before the "you" with its grace note finally resolved the chord.

"Yes, yes," Hans Castorp said in somber gratitude, and put on the finale, where everyone congratulated young José for standing up to his officer and thus cutting off his retreat, so that he would now have to desert the colors, just as Carmen had demanded, to his horror, only moments before.

> Oh, follow to the mountains fair,
> The hills and crags and purest air,

the chorus sang—and you could understand the words quite clearly.

> To roam and walk with happy pride
> Your fatherland, the world so wide!
> You shall obey your will alone.
> A gift more rare than precious stone
> Is freedom, freedom, 'tis your own!

"Yes, yes," he said once more, and moved on to a fourth piece, something very fine and dear to him.

That it was yet another French work is not our fault, any more than is the fact that once again the prevailing mood was military. It was an intermezzo, a vocal solo, a "prayer" from Gounod's opera about Faust. Someone stepped forward, someone for whom he felt great sympathy, whose name was Valentin, but whom Hans Castorp called by another, more familiar name that carried great sadness with it and was identified in his mind with the person beginning to sing from the cabinet there, though the recorded voice was much more beautiful. It was a strong,

warm baritone, and its song was in three parts, consisting of a frame of
two closely related stanzas, quite religious in nature, almost in the style
of a Protestant chorale, and a middle stanza that had a gallant, chivalresque
spirit, warlike, lighthearted, but equally devout—which was what gave
it such a French military feel. The invisible person sang:

> And now since I must leave
> My homeland far behind—

and, given these circumstances, turned to the Lord of heaven, begging
him to protect the life of his dearest sister in the meantime. He was off
to war, the rhythms bounced about, grew bold and daring—to hell with
worry and care, he, the invisible singer, wanted to go where the battle
was the fiercest, the danger the greatest, to meet the foe gallantly and
devoutly, like a true Frenchman. But if God should call him to heaven,
he sang, then he would be looking down from there to protect "you."
And by "you" he meant his dear sister; but all the same it touched Hans
Castorp to the depths of his soul, and those emotions lasted to the very
end, when the brave fellow inside there sang above the massive chords of
a chorale:

> O Lord of heaven, hear my prayer,
> Take Marguerite into Thy tender care.

There was nothing else of importance about the record. We thought we
should mention it briefly because Hans Castorp liked it so very much,
and also because it will play a certain role later, on a rather strange
occasion. But now, we have arrived at the fifth and final work in the
group of real favorites—which, to be sure, was not another French piece,
but something particularly, indeed exemplarily German, and not from an
opera, either, but a song, one of those special lieder—simultaneously a
masterpiece and a folk song, and that simultaneity was what stamped it
with its particular intellectual and spiritual view of the world. But why
all the fuss? It was Schubert's *"Lindenbaum,"* none other than the old
familiar *"Am Brunnen vor dem Tore."*

Accompanied by a piano, it was sung by a tenor, a fellow with tact
and taste, who knew how to treat its simultaneously simple and sublime
material with a great deal of good sense, musical feeling, and narrative
restraint. We all know that there is a great difference between how this
splendid song sounds as an art song and as a tune in the mouths of children
and everyday folks. In the latter case, it is sung to the basic melody,
usually in simplified form, one stanza after the other; whereas here the
original melody is already varied in a minor key by the second of the

three eight-line stanzas, reemerges very beautifully in the major by the time the third stanza begins, is then dramatically abandoned in the "cold winds" that blow your hat from your head, and only finds its way back again in the last four lines of the stanza, where it is then repeated so that the song can be sung to an end. The most overpowering phrase of the melody occurs three times, always in its modulating second half—the third time, then, being in the reprise of the last half-stanza that begins "And many now the hours." This magical phrase, which we do not want to abuse with words, is found in the lines: "So many words of love," "As if they called to me," and "Since I have been away." And the warm, bright tenor voice, with its fine breath control and the hint of a restrained sob, sang it each time with such intelligent sensitivity for its beauty that it would grip the listener's heart unexpectedly, particularly since the artist knew how to heighten the effect with an extraordinarily intense head voice on the lines "It *al*ways drew me back" and "And *here* you'll find your rest." In the repetition of the last verse, however, where the line reads, "You *could* have found rest here," he sang "could have" the first time in full, yearning chest voice and only the second time in the gentlest of flute tones.

But enough of the song and this rendition of it. We would like to flatter ourselves that in our previous examples we succeeded in awakening in our listeners a general understanding of the intimate sympathy with which Hans Castorp approached his evening concerts. But it is, we must admit, a very tricky task to explain what this last work, this song, this old "linden tree," meant to him, and the greatest care must be given to nuance, if we are not to do more harm than good.

Let us put it this way: an object created by the human spirit and intellect, which means a significant object, is "significant" in that it points beyond itself, is an expression and exponent of a more universal spirit and intellect, of a whole world of feelings and ideas that have found a more or less perfect image of themselves in that object—by which the degree of its significance is then measured. Moreover, love for such an object is itself equally "significant." It says something about the person who feels it, it defines his relationship to the universe, to the world represented by the created object and, whether consciously or unconsciously, loved along with it.

Does anyone believe that our ordinary hero, after a certain number of years of hermetic and pedagogic enhancement, had penetrated deeply enough into the life of the intellect and the spirit for him to be *conscious* of the "significance" of this object and his love for it? We assert, we recount, that he had. The song meant a great deal to him, a whole world—

a world that he evidently must have loved, or otherwise he would not have been so infatuated with the image that represented it. We know what we are saying when we add—perhaps somewhat darkly—that his fate might have been different if his disposition had not been so highly susceptible to the charms of the emotional sphere, to the universal state of mind that this song epitomized so intensely, so mysteriously. But that same fate had brought with it enhancements, adventures, and insights, had stirred up inside him the problems that came with "playing king," all of which had matured him into an intuitive critic of this world, of this absolutely admirable image of it, of his love for it—had made him capable, that is, of observing all three with the scruples of conscience.

Anyone who would claim that such scruples are detrimental to love surely understands absolutely nothing about love. On the contrary, they are its very roots. They are what first add the prick of passion to love, so that one could define passion as scrupulous love. And what were Hans Castorp's scruples, what questions did he ask himself when "playing king," about the ultimate legitimacy of his love for this enchanting song and its world? What was this world that stood behind it, which his intuitive scruples told him was a world of forbidden love?

It was death.

But that is sheer madness! A beautiful, marvelous song like that? A pure masterpiece, born out of the profoundest, most sacred depths of a whole nation's emotions—its most precious possession, the archetype of genuine feeling, the very soul of human kindness? What hateful slander!

Oh my, oh my—that was all very pretty, was what any honest man would have to say. And yet behind this sweet, lovely, fair work of art stood death. It had special ties with death, ties one might indeed love, but not without first "playing king," not without intuitively taking into account a certain illegitimacy in such love. In its own original form, there may have been no sympathy with death, only something full of life and folk culture. But to feel spiritual and intellectual sympathy with it was to feel sympathy with death. In its beginnings, purest piety, the epitome of judicious concern—there should be no thought of contesting that. But in its train came the workings of darkness.

What was all this he had himself believing? He would not have let any of you talk him out of it. The workings of darkness. Dark workings. Torturers at work, misanthropy dressed in Spanish black with a starched ruff and with lust in place of love—the outcome of steadfast, pious devotion.

Settembrini, that old man of letters, was certainly not someone in whom he placed unqualified trust, but he recalled a certain lecture that his clear-minded mentor had once delivered, long ago, back at the start of his hermetic career—a lecture on "backsliding," on "intellectual backsliding" in certain spheres. And he found it useful to apply those teachings, with some caution, to the object at hand. Herr Settembrini had characterized the phenomenon of backsliding as a "sickness"—and from his pedagogic viewpoint, even the worldview, the intellectual epoch, toward which one "slid back" might appear "sick" as well. But what's this? Hans Castorp's sweet, lovely, fair song of nostalgia, the emotional world to which it belonged, his love for that world—they were supposed to be "sick"? Not at all. There was nothing more healthy, more genial on earth. Except that this was a fruit—a fresh, plump, healthy fruit, that was liable, extraordinarily liable, to begin to rot and decay at that very moment, or perhaps the next; and although it was purest regalement of the spirit when enjoyed at the right moment, only a moment later and it could spread rot and decay among those who partook of it. It was a fruit of life, sired by death and pregnant with death. It was a miracle of the soul—the ultimate miracle, perhaps, in the eyes of unscrupulous beauty, who gave it her blessing; yet it was regarded with mistrust, and for valid reasons, by the responsible eye of someone "playing king," who affirmed life and loved its organic wholeness. Both a miracle and, in response to the final compelling voice of conscience, the means by which he triumphed over himself.

Yes, triumph over self, that may well have been the essence of his triumph over this love—over this enchantment of the soul with dark consequences. In the solitude of night, Hans Castorp's thoughts, or intuitive half-thoughts, soared high as he sat before his truncated musical coffin . . . ah, they soared higher than his understanding, were thoughts enhanced, forced upward by alchemy. Oh, it was mighty, this enchantment of the soul. We were all its sons, and we could all do mighty things on earth by serving it. One need not be a genius, all one needed was a great deal more talent than the author of this little song about a linden tree to become an enchanter of souls, who would then give the song such vast dimensions that it would subjugate the world. One might even found whole empires upon it, earthly, all-too-earthly empires, very coarse, very progressive, and not in the least nostalgic . . . his truncated musical coffin, inside which the song decayed into some electrical gramophone music. But the song's best son may yet have been the young man who consumed his life in triumphing over himself and died, a new word on his lips, the word of love, which he did not yet know how to speak. It was truly worth dying for, this song of enchantment. But he who died for it was no longer really dying for this song and was a hero only because ultimately he died for something new—for the new word of love and for the future in his heart.

Those, then, were Hans Castorp's favorite recordings.

Highly Questionable

Edhin Krokowski's lectures had taken an unexpected turn after all these little years. His researches, dedicated to psychic dissection and the dream life of his patients, had always had a subterranean character, the whiff of the catacomb. Of late, however, although the transition had been so gradual his audience had scarcely noticed, his interests had moved in a new direction, toward magical, arcane matters; and his fortnightly lectures in the dining hall—the sanatorium's main attraction, the pride of its brochure—which were always delivered from behind a cloth-covered table in an exotic, drawling accent, to an immobile audience of Berghof residents and for which he always wore a frock coat and sandals, no longer dealt with masked forms of love in action or the transformation of illness back into conscious emotion, but with the abstruse oddities of hypnotism and somnambulism, the phenomena of telepathy, prophetic dreams, and second sight, the wonders of hysteria; and as he discussed these topics, philosophic horizons expanded until suddenly his audience beheld great riddles shimmering before their eyes, riddles about the relationship between matter and the psyche, indeed, the very riddle of life itself, which, so it appeared, might be more easily approached along very uncanny paths, the paths of illness, than by the direct road of health.

We say this, because we consider it our duty to shame irresponsible sorts who asserted that Dr. Krokowski had turned to arcane subjects in the hope of rescuing his lectures from what he feared was unmitigated monotony. His purposes, then, were purely emotional—or so said slanderous tongues, of which there is never a lack. It is true that during those Monday sessions, the gentlemen flicked their ears more vigorously to hear better and that Fräulein Levi looked even more than ever like a mechanically driven wax figure, if that was possible. But such effects were as legitimate as the changes that came with the evolution of the learned doctor's thought—an evolution he saw as not only consistent, but also inevitable. His field of study had always been concerned with those dark, vast regions of the human soul that are called the subconscious, although one would perhaps do better to speak of the superconscious, since there are occasions when the knowledge that rises up from those regions far exceeds an individual's conscious knowledge, suggesting that there may be connections and associations between the bottommost unlighted tracts of the individual soul and an omniscient universal soul. The realm of the subconscious, the "occult" realm in the etymological sense of the word, very quickly turns out to be occult in the narrower sense as well and forms one of the sources for phenomena that emerge from it and to which we apply that same makeshift term. That is not all. Any man who recognizes an organic symptom of illness to be the product of forbidden emotions that assume hysterical form in conscious psychic life also recognizes the creative power of the psyche in the material world—a power he is then forced to declare to be the second source of magical phenomena. As an idealist of the pathological, if not to say a pathological idealist, such a man will see himself at the starting point of a sequence of thought that very quickly flows into the problem of being-in-general—that is to say, into the problem of the relationship between mind and matter. The materialist, as the son of a philosophy of pure robust health, can never be argued out of his belief that the mind is a phosphorescent product of matter; whereas the idealist, who proceeds from the principle of creative hysteria, will tend to answer, indeed will very soon definitively answer the question of primacy in exactly opposite terms. All in all, this is nothing less than the old argument over which came first, the chicken or the egg, an argument that is so extraordinarily perplexing because of two facts: first, we cannot imagine an egg that has not been laid by a hen; and second, no hen exists that has not crept out of a postulated egg.

These were the issues, then, that Dr. Krokowski had been discussing in his recent lectures. He had come to them by organic, legitimate, logical means—we cannot emphasize that enough; and to go one step farther, we shall add that he had begun to discuss them long before Ellen Brand appeared on the scene and brought these matters to the stage of empirical experiment.

Who was Ellen Brand? We had almost forgotten that our audience does not know her, whereas the name is quite familiar to us. Who was she? Almost nobody at first glance. A sweet young thing of nineteen—everyone called her Elly—with flax-blond hair, a Danish girl, not even from Copenhagen, but from Odense on the island of Fyn, where her father owned a butter factory. She knew something about real life, had in fact spent a couple of years as a clerk in a provincial branch office of a national bank, sitting on a swivel stool, a sleeve-protector on her right arm, and staring at massive tomes—and had ended up with a fever. Her case was negligible, really more suspicion than fact, even though Elly was delicate, and obviously anemic, too—but definitely a likable girl, the sort you would have loved to pat on her flax-blond head, as the director did regularly whenever he spoke to her in the dining hall. There was an aura of Nordic coolness about her, a glasslike chasteness, a virginal, childish quality that was quite attractive, as were both the full, pure look in her blue, childlike eyes and her pointed, refined way of speaking, in a slightly broken German with the typical mispronunciations of Danes—like "fleck" for "flesh." There was nothing remarkable about her facial features. The chin was too small. She sat at the same table as Hermine Kleefeld, who mothered her.

This, then, was Fräulein Brand, Elly, the friendly little Danish girl, who rode a bike and used to sit on an office swivel stool—and there were things about her that no one would have even dreamed possible on first or second glance at that shining face, but that began to emerge within only a few weeks after her arrival up here and that Dr. Krokowski saw as his task to uncover in all their strangeness.

Some parlor games during an evening social were what first pulled the learned doctor up short. There had been all sorts of guessing games; then came the search for hidden objects, done with piano accompaniment, which would be played louder if the searcher got closer to the hiding-place, and softer if he or she wandered off track. This was followed by a game in which someone was sent out of the room, and when he came back had to guess the complicated task the others had decided he was to perform—exchanging the rings worn by two people, for example; or bowing three times in order to ask someone to dance; or fetching a particular book from the library and giving it to some particular person; and so on. It should be noted that games of this sort had not normally been played in Berghof society. Who had been the actual instigator could not be determined afterward. It had definitely not been Elly. But it was in her presence that they first took a fancy to such amusements.

The participants—almost all of them old acquaintances of ours, including Hans Castorp—showed some skill, to a greater or lesser degree, although a few of them were totally inept. Elly Brand's abilities turned out to be quite extraordinary, sensational, unseemly. Her resourcefulness in searching out hidden objects was greeted with much applause and admiring laughter, and that might have been the end of it; but when she began guessing her complicated task, people slowly fell silent. She accomplished everything they had secretly assigned her to do, carried it out the moment she entered the room, with a gentle smile, without hesitation, and without musical accompaniment, either. She fetched a pinch of salt from the dining hall and sprinkled it on Prosecutor Paravant's head, then took him by the hand, led him to the piano, and held his forefinger to plunk out the beginning of "Twinkle, Twinkle, Little Star." Then she brought him back to his seat, curtsied, pulled over a footstool, and sat down at his feet—exactly as they had racked their brains to devise.

She had been listening!

She blushed; and much relieved at seeing her embarrassment, they began to scold her in unison—until she assured them that no, no, no, they shouldn't think such a thing of her. She had not been listening, not outside, not at the door, truly she hadn't.

Not outside, not at the door?

"Oh, no." But she did apologize all the same—she had been listening here in the room, after she came in. She couldn't help that.

Could not help it? In the room?

It came in whispers. It was whispered to her what she had to do, very softly, but quite clearly and distinctly.

It was a confession, apparently. Elly felt guilty somehow, felt she had cheated. She should have told them she was not suited for such games, because everything was whispered to her. There is no earthly point in a contest where one of the competitors possesses supernatural powers. To use a term from sports, Ellen was suddenly disqualified, but in a way that made chills run up your spine when she confessed. Several voices immediately cried out for Dr. Krokowski. Someone ran to get him, and he came: he broke into a rugged, pithy smile once he had the picture, his very presence demanding their cheerful trust. They breathlessly reported this case of crass abnormality: an omniscient girl had appeared on the scene, a maiden who heard voices. —My, my, and what else? They should just calm down now. We would see. This was his native soil—marshy, soggy, unsteady footing for all, though he trod it with more steady assurance. He asked questions, heard them out. My, my, well, what had they here? "So that's how things are with you, my child, is it?" And he laid a hand on the young girl's head, the way everyone liked to do. Certainly something worthy of attention, but nothing to be frightened by in the least. He let his hand drift down from her head in a gentle stroke along her shoulder, to her arm, and fastening his exotic brown eyes on her bright blue ones, he submerged his gaze in hers. She returned it meekly, then more meekly still, that is, lowered her eyes more and more, as her head slipped slowly toward her chest and shoulder. When her eyes began to roll back, the physician passed his hand in a casual upward sweep in front of her face, declared everything perfectly in order, and sent the entire excited party off to evening rest cure—except for Elly Brand, with whom he said he wanted to "chat" a little.

Chat! They should have known. And yet no one felt all that easy about the word, even if it was a standard word for their cheerful comrade, Dr. Krokowski. Everyone felt the touch of an icy finger deep inside, even Hans Castorp, who was late in finding his way to his splendid lounge chair that evening; he stretched out and recalled how, as he watched Elly's unseemly achievements and listened to her embarrassed explanation, the ground had shifted under his feet, making him feel a little queasy and anxious all over, like a slight touch of seasickness. He had never been in an earthquake, but he told himself that it most probably evoked similar sensations of unmistakable terror—quite apart from the curiosity that Ellen Brand's disagreeable talents also awakened in him. It was a curiosity that bore within it a sense of its own ultimate hopelessness, that is, an awareness that there were regions to which his mind was forbidden the access it groped to find—giving rise to doubts whether it was simply idle, or perhaps sinful curiosity, which did not, however, prevent it from being what it was: curiosity. Like everyone else, over the course of his life Hans Castorp had heard one thing or another about arcane natural, or supernatural, phenomena—there has already been mention made of his clairvoyant great-aunt, whose melancholy story had been passed down to him. But never had that world, to which he would not have denied theoretical and unbiased recognition, pressed in hard upon him; he had no practical experience of it, and the aversion he felt to such experiences (an aversion based on good taste, an aesthetic aversion, an aversion that came with his pride as a human being—if we can apply such pretentious terms to our thoroughly unpretentious hero) was almost equal to the curiosity they aroused in him. He could sense in advance, quite clearly, quite definitely, that however such experiences might develop, they would never seem anything but preposterous, incomprehensible, and lacking in human value. And yet he burned to taste them. He understood that "idle or sinful"—which was bad enough as an alternative—was no alternative at all, that the two coincided, and that to say something was spiritually and intellectually "hopeless" was merely the amoral way of saying it was "forbidden." And yet the old *placet experiri,* planted in him by someone who would have most stoutly disapproved of any experiments of *this* sort, had taken firm root in Hans Castorp's mind. By now, his morality coincided with his curiosity, probably always had. It was the unconditional curiosity of the tourist thirsty for knowledge; a curiosity that, in having tasted the mystery of personality, had perhaps not been all that far from the realms emerging here; a curiosity that displayed something of a military character by not trying to evade something forbidden if it might offer itself. And so Hans Castorp decided to be on the alert and not to step aside if Ellen Brand should have further adventures.

Dr. Krokowski issued a strict prohibition against any more lay experiments with Fräulein Brand's hidden talents. He placed a scientific embargo on the child, held sessions with her in his analytical dungeon, and hypnotized her, so it was said, in an attempt to develop and train the possibilities slumbering inside her and to probe her previous psychic life. Hermine Kleefeld, as a motherly friend and benefactor, did the same, and learned a few things under the seal of secrecy, which under the same seal she then spread throughout the house, not excluding the concierge desk. She learned, for example, that the person or thing that had whispered things to the girl during the game was named Holger—it was a boy named Holger, a spirit, whom little Ellen knew quite well, a deceased, ethereal creature, something like her guardian angel. —And so he had blabbed the part about the pinch of salt and Paravant's forefinger? —Yes, his phantom lips caressing her ear, so close they tickled a little and made her smile, had whispered it all to her. —That must have been nice back in school to have had Holger whisper the answers when she hadn't done her homework. —Ellen had made no response. But later, she said that Holger probably was not allowed to do that. He was forbidden to get mixed up in serious matters, and besides, he probably had not known many answers to school questions.

It was learned, further, that since early childhood Ellen had experienced visions, although at wide intervals, both visible and invisible. What was that supposed to mean—invisible visions? Well, for example, at age sixteen she had been sitting alone in her parents' living room, at the round table, doing some needlework in the middle of the afternoon, and her father's Great Dane, a bitch named Freia, had been lying on the carpet beside her. The tablecloth was like a colorful Turkish shawl, the kind that old women wear folded in a triangle, its four corners hanging catercorner down over the edges. And suddenly Ellen had seen the corner closest to her roll up—watched it roll up, silently, carefully, evenly, almost to the middle of the table, so that when it stopped it made a fairly long tube; and while this was going on, Freia had first sat up ferociously, bracing herself against her front legs, hair standing on end, and then rising up full, had bolted into the adjoining room and hid under the sofa; and for a whole year you could not get her to go into the living room.

Had it been Holger, Fräulein Kleefeld asked, who had rolled up the shawl? Little Ellen Brand did not know. And what had she thought about the incident? Well, since it had been absolutely impossible to make anything of it, really, Elly had not given it much thought. And had she told her parents about it? No. That was odd, Fräulein Kleefeld remarked. Well, even though she had not given it much thought, Elly had the feeling that she should keep the event and others like it to herself—it was a strict secret, she felt bashful about it. Had that been a heavy burden to bear? No, not particularly. What was so burdensome about a tablecloth that rolled itself up? But there had been other things that were harder for her. For example:

The previous year she had been at her parents' house in Odense again, and very early one morning she left her room, which was on the ground floor, and was crossing the hall to climb the stairs to the dining room to make herself some coffee, as she normally did before her parents got up. She had almost reached the landing where the stairway turned, and there on the landing, right at the top of the stairs, she had seen her older sister Sophie, who was married and lived in America—it was her, really, physically her. She was wearing a white dress and, what seemed very strange, a wreath of marshy water lilies on her head; holding both hands clasped against one shoulder, her sister had nodded to her. "Why, Sophie—are you home?" Ellen had asked, rooted to the spot, half in terror, half in joy. Sophie had nodded once more and then vanished into thin air. First she became transparent, then visible only in the same way you see a current of hot air rising, and finally not at all—and the stairs were free again for Ellen to pass. It turned out that on that very same morning, in New Jersey, her sister Sophie had died of inflammation of the heart.

Well, Hans Castorp replied, when Fräulein Kleefeld told him all this, that made some sense, it sounded plausible. A vision here, a death there—at least you could see some sort of satisfactory connection. And he agreed to take part in a spiritualistic parlor game, a séance performed with a moving glass, that the others, having lost patience with Dr. Krokowski's jealous prohibitions concerning Ellen Brand, had decided to hold secretly behind his back.

Only a selected few were confidentially invited to this gathering, which was held in Hermine Kleefeld's room: besides the hostess, Hans Castorp, and little Ellen Brand, there were the ladies Stöhr and Levi, plus Herr Albin, the Czech gentleman called Wenzel, and Dr. Ting-Fu. One evening, at the stroke of ten, they quietly assembled, whispering and eyeing the arrangements Hermine had made, which consisted of a bare, round, medium-size table in the middle of the room; a wineglass placed upside down on it; and around the edge of the table, at regular intervals, little ivory squares, tokens from some game or other, on which twenty-five letters of the alphabet had been drawn in ink. Fräulein Kleefeld first served tea, which was greeted with thanks, particularly by the ladies Stöhr and Levi, who, despite the childish harmlessness of the occasion, complained of cold hands and palpitations. Once they had all warmed themselves, they sat down at the table, and by dim pinkish light—to enhance the mood, their hostess had extinguished the ceiling light and left only the red-shaded nightstand lamp burning—each of them placed one finger of his or her right hand gently on the upturned base of the glass. This was standard procedure. They waited for the glass to set itself in motion.

That could happen easily enough—it was a smooth tabletop, the edge of the glass was nicely ground, and the pressure exerted by their trembling fingers, light as it was, would of course be uneven, more vertical here, more from the side there, so that in time it would be quite sufficient to cause the glass to leave its middle position. At the periphery of its field of movement it would then chance upon letters of the alphabet, and if those toward which it moved formed words that made some sort of sense, it would be the result of a very complex phenomenon, almost impure in its intricacy, a blend of conscious, half-conscious, and subconscious elements—assisted and driven by the wishes of each person present, whether they admitted it to themselves or not—and of a secret sanction granted by unillumined layers within the souls of them all, a subterranean cooperation for strange ends, with each individual contributing more or less of his or her own darkness, the strongest contribution probably being that of sweet little Elly. Ultimately they all knew this before they sat down, and in his chatterbox way, Hans Castorp had even blurted it out as they waited with trembling fingers. Indeed it was the same realization that caused the ladies' cold hands and palpitations and the gentlemen's subdued mirth. They knew they had assembled in the still of the night for an impure game with their own natures, a test of unknown components of their inner selves, knew they were waiting, frightened and curious, for pseudo- or semi-realities that are called magical. It was almost merely for form's sake, a matter of convention, that the gathering presumed the ghosts of the departed would speak by means of a glass. Herr Albin was commissioned to act as their spokesperson and to negotiate with whatever presences might appear, since he had taken part in séances on a few occasions prior to this.

Twenty minutes passed, and more. They ran out of topics to whisper about, initial tensions eased. They supported their right elbows now with their left hands. Wenzel the Czech was about to nod off. Her dainty finger resting lightly on the glass, Ellen Brand focused her large, pure, childlike eyes beyond immediate matters and directed her gaze instead at the nightstand lamp.

Suddenly the glass tipped, gave a knock, and ran off from under their hands. They had trouble keeping their fingers on it. It slid to the edge of the table, moved along it a short distance, and then headed straight back to more or less the middle of the table. There it gave another knock and held its peace.

The start it gave them all was partly of fright, partly of joy. Frau Stöhr whimpered she wanted to stop, but it was made clear to her that she should have thought of that before and was to keep quiet. Things were under way now, or so it seemed. They stipulated that for a yes or no, the glass would not have to point to letters, but could simply reply with one or two knocks.

"Is there a spirit present?" Herr Albin inquired with a stern face, staring in the air above their heads. A hesitation—then the glass tipped and said yes.

"What is your name?" Herr Albin asked almost gruffly, reinforcing the energy of his voice with a shake of his head.

The glass stirred. It ran in a determined zigzag from token to token, but pulling back slightly toward the middle with each move; it ran to the H, to the O, to the L, after which it seemed to grow weary and confused, not to know what to do, but then it recovered, found the G, the E, and the R. Just as they thought! It was Holger in person, the spirit named Holger, the one who had known about the pinch of salt and all the rest, but who, of course, never got mixed up in any questions at school. He was there, floating in the breeze, hovering about their little circle. What should they do with him now? A certain reticence settled in. They consulted in whispers, behind their hands so to speak, about what it was they were eager to know. Herr Albin decided to ask what Holger's status and profession had been in life. He did it, as before, in the stern tone of a cross-examination, adding a scowl.

The glass was silent for a while. Then with a tip and a stumble it headed for the P, pulled away, and moved to the O. What was it going to spell? The tension was palpable. Dr. Ting-Fu giggled and said he feared Holger had been a policeman. Frau Stöhr was overcome with hysterical laughter, which did not stop the glass in its labors, however, and it hobbled, rattled, and slid its way to the T, but then—surely it must have left out something—it returned to the middle. It had spelled "pot."

What the—ah, so Holger had been a poet, was that it? And out of simple pride, it appeared, almost superfluously, the glass tipped and knocked once for yes. "A lyric poet?" Hermine Kleefeld asked, drawing out the first syllable till it sounded like "leer," as Hans Castorp automatically noted. Holger seemed reluctant about specificity. He gave no new answer. He quickly, confidently, clearly spelled out the same thing again, adding the E he had forgotten before.

Fine, fine, a poet then. The embarrassment grew—an odd embarrassment that was intended for manifestations in the uncontrolled regions of their own interiors, but, given the dissembling, semi-real quality of those manifestations, was directed instead to external reality. Someone wondered if Holger felt happy and content in his state. The glass dreamily tapped out the word "serene." Ah yes, so he felt "serene." Well, it was not a term they would have come up with on their own, but once the glass had spelled it out, they found it probable and nicely put. And how long had Holger been in this serene state? And now came something else no one would have hit upon, something dreamily self-revealing. It was: "Hastening while." Very good! It could just as easily have been "whiling haste," it was a bit of poetic ventriloquism from the beyond; Hans Castorp thought it splendid. For Holger, the element of time was a "hastening while"—but of course, he would have to deal with his questioners in a gnomic style, would surely have forgotten how to function with earthly words and exact measurements. And so what else did they want to know from him? Fräulein Levi admitted she was curious to know what Holger looked like, or if that didn't apply, had looked like. Had he been a handsome lad? She should ask him herself, demanded Herr Albin, who found the inquiry beneath his dignity. And so she asked him, using informal pronouns, if he had curly blond hair?

"Beautiful brown, brown locks," the glass traced out, twice spelling out the word "brown" in full. Mirth and delight reigned around the table. The ladies candidly announced they were in love. They blew kisses angled toward the ceiling. Dr. Ting-Fu suggested with a giggle that Mr. Holger was apparently rather vain.

The glass turned angry and frantic. It ran wildly about the table to no purpose, tipped furiously, fell over, and rolled into the lap of Fräulein Stöhr, who gazed down at it pale with horror, her arms spread wide. With many apologies, they carefully put it back in its proper place. The Chinese doctor was scolded. How dare he! Just look where such impudence got you! And what if Holger were to turn heel and run now, without saying another word? They coaxed and flattered their glass. Would he not like to recite a little poem? He had been a poet after all, before he started hovering and floating in the hastening while. Ah, how they all wanted to hear some of his poetry. They would enjoy it so much.

And look there, the good glass knocked once—"yes." There was really something kindhearted and forgiving in the way it did it. And then Holger the spirit began to recite poetry without hesitation, at great length and in immense detail, for who knew how long—it seemed as if they would never be able to silence him again. It was a thoroughly surprising poem that he offered in ventriloquist fashion, while those sitting around recited it aloud in admiration, a magical bit of reality, as limitless as the sea, which was its central theme. —Driftwood and tang flung in heaps along the narrow shore extending round the great arc of bay that rims the island's steep-duned coast. Oh look, its vast expanse is hovering, melting, dying green into eternity, where beneath broad misty veils of murky crimson and milk-soft sheen, the summer sun delays its setting. No lips can tell when or how that nimble silver mirror turned pure mother-of-pearl, became a play of colors beyond all naming, a pale, bright, opal luster of moonstone spread everywhere. Ah, as secretly as it came, the silent magic died. The sea passed into sleep. And yet soft traces of the sun's farewell linger beyond and above. Darkness does not fall till deep into the night. A phantom glow holds sway in piny woods along the crest of dunes and turns the pallid sand to snow. Illusive winter woods in silence, broken by the snap of heavy wings, an owl in flight. Stay and be our place of rest this hour. So soft each step, so high and mild the night. And far below, the sea is breathing in slow, protracted whispers as it dreams. Do you long to see it again? Then step up to the edge of these ashen glacial cliffs of dunes and climb, immerse yourself in softness that seeps cool into your shoes. The land falls steep with underbrush down to the rocky shore, and still the phantom scraps of day dart along the rim of that vanishing expanse. Lie down up here in the sand. How cool like death it feels, how soft like silk, like flour. You clench your hand, and it flows, a thin, colorless stream, to form a delicate mound beside you. Do you know that fine trickle? It is the soundless, slender rush through the straits of the hourglass, the stern and fragile device that adorns the hermit's cell. An open book, a skull, and in its light constructed frame, the double hollow of frail glass, and inside it, sand extracted from eternity, to tumble here as time in holy, terrifying stealth . . .

And so Holger the spirit's "leeric" improvisation followed its strange course, which led from the shores of home to a hermit and the object of his meditations, and to the boundless amazement of those around the table, wandered on, speaking in bold and dreamy phrases of things human and divine, spelling them out; and no sooner had they found a moment to express their delighted approval than it zigzagged off again into a thousand details that it seemed would never stop—and an hour later, there was still no end in sight, for the poem, which had dealt relentlessly with the pain of childbirth and a lover's first kiss, with the crown of suffering and God's strict, fatherly kindness, had plunged into the warp and woof of creation, into epochs and nations, had lost itself in the vastness of the stars, even mentioning the Chaldeans and the zodiac, and would most certainly have lasted on through the whole night, if the conjurers had not at last removed their fingers from the glass and with politest thanks declared to Holger that that had to be it for now. It had been marvelous beyond their fondest dreams and what a dreadful shame it was no one had written the poem down, so that it was doomed to be forgotten, for it had a quality about it that made it as hard to grasp hold of as a dream. The next time they would appoint someone to be secretary and then check how it sounded when you had it fixed in black and white and could read it as a whole; for the moment, however, and before Holger returned to the serenity of his hastening while, it would be much better, or in any event extraordinarily kind of him, if he would be willing perhaps to answer one or two practical questions the group still had for him—not that they had anything definite in mind, but, just on principle, would he be prepared in that case to do them this special favor?

"Yes," came the answer. But they now discovered the extent of their perplexity—what should they ask? It was like one of those fairy tales where the genie or fairy grants a wish and you risk wasting the opportunity on something useless. So many things in the present and future world seemed worth knowing, and you had to be responsible about choosing. And since no one else could decide, Hans Castorp rested his left cheek on his clenched fist and, one finger still on the glass, said he would like to know how long his stay up here was going to last yet, since he had originally come for only three weeks.

Fine, no one else had anything better, so let the spirit share this arbitrary item from the fullness of its knowledge. After a brief hesitation, the glass moved. It moved along a very peculiar path, a random pattern, so it appeared, in which no one saw rhyme or reason. It spelled out the word "go" and then "across," which no one could really make much of, and then it moved to say something about Hans Castorp's room, so that the laconic advice for the questioner read "go across his room." Across his room? Across room 34? What was that supposed to mean? And as they sat there, shaking their heads and discussing this, there was the sudden thump of a fist against the door.

They all froze. Was it a raid? Was Dr. Krokowski standing out there ready to break up their forbidden meeting? They stared at one another in chagrin, waiting for the outmaneuvered assistant to enter. But then came a bang from the middle of the table, another thump of a fist, as if to make clear that the first knock, too, had not come from the hall, but from inside the room.

It had been Herr Albin, one of his crude jokes! But he denied it, on his honor; and even had he not given them his word, they were all as good as certain that no one from their group had delivered the blow. So it had been Holger? They looked to Elly, whose total tranquility had suddenly become obvious to them all. She was sitting there with limp wrists, her fingertips barely touching the table's edge, her back against her chair, her head tilted to one shoulder; her eyebrows were raised, but her little mouth was smaller than ever, drawn downward, but with a hint of a smile that looked both innocent and sly; and her blue childlike eyes were gazing off into space, seeing nothing. They called to her, but not once did she show any sign of consciousness. In that same moment, the lamp on the nightstand went out.

Went out? There was no holding Frau Stöhr back now, she raised a hue and cry—she had heard the switch. The bulb had not burned out, it had been turned off, by a hand, which to describe as *strange* would be to put it mildly. Was it Holger's hand? He had been so gentle, so disciplined, and poetic up till then; but now he was degenerating into a low practical jokester. Who could guarantee that a hand that banged its fist against doors and furniture, that impishly switched off lights, might not also pack someone by the throat? Voices in the dark called out for matches, for flashlights. Fräulein Levi screeched that someone had pulled her hair. In her panic, Frau Stöhr was not ashamed of breaking into prayer. "Oh Lord, just this once!" she screamed and then whimpered for Him to be more merciful than just, even though they had been flirting with hell. It was Dr. Ting-Fu who came up with the sound idea of turning on the ceiling light—and at once the room was bathed in bright clarity. And while they established that the nightstand lamp had not burned out but had been turned off—it took only a very human flip of the switch to undo the covert maneuver and make it burn again—Hans Castorp quietly made a surprising discovery of his own, which might be seen as evidence that the childish dark powers manifesting themselves here had paid him particular attention. Across his knees was an object, the "souvenir" that had frightened his uncle the day he had picked it up off his nephew's chest of drawers: the glass negative that revealed the portrait of Clavdia Chauchat's interior and that he, Hans Castorp, had most definitely not brought into the room.

He put it in his pocket without any fuss. The others were busy with Ellen Brand, whose pose had not changed—she was still sitting in her chair, staring vacantly ahead, a strangely affected expression on her face. Herr Albin blew on her and imitated Dr. Krokowski's gesture, that casual upward fanning of the hand in front of her face, which roused her. She began—who knew why?—to weep softly. They petted her, comforted her, kissed her brow, and sent her to bed. Fräulein Levi declared she was willing to spend the night with Frau Stöhr, since that limited lady was so frightened that she did not know how she could ever go to sleep. Hans Castorp, his apported object in his breast pocket, had no objection to ending an evening gone awry over a cognac shared with the other gentlemen in Herr Albin's room, for he found that the effect of events like these was not as hard on his heart or mind as on his stomach—and the effect lasted, too, like that nauseating sway that seasick people claim they can still feel for hours after they have set foot on land.

His curiosity was satisfied for now. Holger's poem had really not been bad, but, as he had suspected, the hopelessness and preposterousness of the whole affair had borne down upon him so forcefully that even those few flakes of brimstone that had drifted his way were quite sufficient, he decided. When Hans Castorp told Herr Settembrini about his experiences, his mentor, as might be imagined, reinforced him in this resolve with might and main. "That," he cried, "was all you needed. Oh, calamity and desolation!" And on the spot he declared little Elly to be a cunning fraud.

His pupil did not say yes or no to that. He shrugged and observed that since reality could not be determined beyond the shadow of a doubt, neither, then, could fraud. Perhaps the boundaries were fluid. Perhaps there were transitional stages between the two, degrees of reality within nature, which, being mute, could not be evaluated and thus eluded a determination that, as he saw it, had something very moralistic about it. What did Herr Settembrini think of the term "illusion"—a state in which elements of dream and reality were blended in a way that was perhaps less foreign to nature than to our crude everyday thoughts? The secret of life was literally bottomless, and it was no wonder, then, that occasionally there rose up out of it illusions that—and so on and so forth, in our hero's amiably self-effacing and exceedingly easy manner.

Herr Settembrini hauled him over the coals quite properly and managed to firm up his conscience at least temporarily, extracting something like a promise never again to participate in such horrors. "Pay attention," he demanded, "to the human being inside you, my good engineer. Trust its clear and humane thoughts and abhor this wrenching of the brain, this intellectual swamp. Illusions? Secret of life? *Caro mio!* When the moral courage to decide and differentiate between fraud and reality begins to melt away, that marks the end of life itself, of formed opinions, of values, of any improving deed, and the corruptive process of moral skepticism begins its awful work." Man was the measure of all things, he added. Man had an inalienable right to make knowledgeable judgments about good and evil, about truth and the sham of lies, and woe to anyone who dared confound his fellowman's belief in that creative right. It would be better a millstone were hung about his neck and he were drowned in the deepest well.

Hans Castorp nodded in agreement and for a while did indeed keep his distance from such activities. He heard that Dr. Krokowski was holding sessions with Ellen Brand in his analytical basement, to which selected residents were invited. But he calmly refused to participate—though, of course, not without learning this and that from the attendees and from Dr. Krokowski himself. There had been fierce, involuntary manifestations of energy much like those that had occurred in Hermine Kleefeld's room; at such meetings, Comrade Krokowski would use his skill to hypnotize little Elly, putting her into a waking trance, and then, under all possible safeguards of authenticity, systematically obtain and cultivate phenomena: the turning on and off of lights, bangings on tables and walls, and much, much more. It had turned out that musical accompaniment facilitated these exercises, and so on such evenings the gramophone would be confiscated by this magical fellowship and moved from its usual place. But since Wenzel the Bohemian, a man of musical sensitivities, who would certainly never mishandle or damage the instrument, was in charge on these occasions, Hans Castorp could hand it over with reasonable equanimity. From the treasury of disks, he assembled a special album, a collection of light favorites, dances, short overtures, and other such folderol, which he made available to them and which admirably served the purpose, since Elly had no need of more sublime tones.

To these strains, then, or so Hans Castorp was told, a handkerchief had spontaneously sprung into action, or better, had risen from the floor, controlled by a "claw" hidden within its folds; the doctor's wastepaper basket had ascended to the ceiling and hovered there; the pendulum of a wall clock had been alternately held back by "no one" and then set in motion again; a serving bell had been "picked up" and rung—a whole series of these and other murky, trivial goings-on. The learned conductor of these experiments was put in the happy situation of supplying a Greek name, replete with scientific decorum, to these feats. They were, so he explained in lectures and private conversations, "telekinetic" events, movements of objects from place to place; the doctor included them in a range of phenomena that science had baptized with the name of "materialization," and it was to these events that all his aspirations were directed in his experiments with Ellen Brand.

In his jargon, they were dealing with biopsychic projections of subconscious complexes into the objective world, processes whose source one should attribute to the medium, a person whose constitution was in a somnambulant state; one might speak of such events as objectified dreams to the extent that they demonstrated an ideoplastic capability in nature— the capacity of thoughts, under certain conditions, to assume substance and thus reveal themselves in ephemeral reality. This substance could then stream from the medium and temporarily congeal outside his or her body to form biologically living organs, which served as grasping mechanisms, the hands that performed those astonishing trifles they had all witnessed in Dr. Krokowski's laboratory. Under some conditions, these mechanisms were visible and palpable, left their imprint in paraffin or plaster of Paris. Under certain other conditions, however, the formation of organs did not have to end there. Heads, individual human countenances, phantoms in full figure might materialize before the eyes of the experimenters, even engage in intercourse with them, within certain limits. But here Dr. Krokowski's teachings began to get blurry, a little cross-eyed, to take on an ambiguous, irresolute character that would have been suitable to his gushings on "love." For at this point he no longer spoke with a clearly scientific mien. It was no longer a simple case of lending assistance to the medium's subjectivity so that it might find a mirror in reality, but rather—at least partially, at least tentatively—certain "selves" from outside, from beyond, got mixed up in things; what they were dealing with—possibly, though never expressly admitted—were nonvital elements, entities that used the convoluted, furtive opportunity of the moment to return to matter and manifest themselves to whoever called them—in short, the spiritualistic conjuring of the dead.

Such were the results, then, that Comrade Krokowski worked hard to produce with the help of his followers. With a rugged, pithy smile he cheerfully bade them trust him as he strove to make them feel at home in these swampy, suspicious, and subhuman regions, enjoined them to see in his stout person a true leader, even for the timid and those dubious about such matters. And thanks to Ellen Brand's extraordinary talents, which he had made it his business to develop and cultivate, success smiled on him—to judge from everything Hans Castorp heard. Various participants had been touched by materialized hands. Prosecutor Paravant had been given a hefty slap on the cheek from the transcendent world, and had received it with scientific amusement, had even eagerly turned the other cheek—despite his being a cavalier, lawyer, and alumnus of a dueling fraternity, all of which would have demanded quite different conduct had the blow's origin been from the world of the living. A. K. Ferge, the simple martyr to whom all higher things were foreign, had held such a ghostly hand in his own hand one evening and had determined by touch that it was well formed and whole, whereupon, by some means he could not quite describe, it had withdrawn itself from his grip, which though hearty had been quite within the bounds of respect. It took a good while, some two and a half months, with two sittings per week, until a hand of otherworldly origins appeared for all to see, a young man's hand—or so it seemed under the reddish light of a ceiling lamp covered with red paper—that fingered its way across the tabletop and left traces in an earthen bowl of flour. But only eight days later, a group of Dr. Krokowski's assistants—Herr Albin, Frau Stöhr, Herr and Frau Magnus—appeared around midnight on Hans Castorp's balcony, where he had lain dozing in the biting chill; and with all the signs of distracted excitement and feverish delight, they told him in a hasty jumble of voices that Elly's Holger had let himself be seen, had shown his head above the shoulder of that somnambulant lady—and he really did have "beautiful brown, brown locks"—and had smiled an unforgettably gentle and melancholy smile before vanishing.

How did such noble sadness square with the rest of Holger's behavior, Hans Castorp wondered, with his unimaginative childish pranks and silly practical jokes, with that unmelancholy slap, for example, to which the prosecutor had been subjected? One apparently could not demand consistency and unity of character in this case. Perhaps they were dealing with a temperament similar to that of the miserable, hunchbacked man of the folk song, who in his wickedness begged for people's prayers. Holger's admirers seemed not to be troubled by any of it. What they cared about was convincing Hans Castorp to renounce his abstinence. He absolutely had to take part in the next session, now that everything was going so splendidly. For Elly had promised in her trance that next time she would produce any deceased person that the group might demand to see.

Any deceased person? Hans Castorp continued to hold back. Nevertheless, the idea that it could be any departed soul occupied his thoughts to such an extent that in the course of the next three days he came to the opposite conclusion. Or to be more precise, it did not take three days, but only a few minutes of one of them to accomplish this. His change of mind occurred while he was alone in the music room one evening, playing yet once again the recording stamped with the personality of Valentin, for whom he felt such great sympathy. He sat in his chair and listened to this good soldier pray as he answered the call to depart for the field of honor; he sang

> And if God takes me, should I die,
> I shall protect you from on high,
> O Marguerite.

And as always when Hans Castorp listened to this aria, deep emotions stirred within him, strengthened this time by certain possibilities that were compacted into a wish, and he thought, "Idle and sinful or not, it would certainly be wonderfully strange and a very special adventure. And knowing him as I do, if he has anything to do with this, he won't hold it against me." And he recalled the calm, generous reply of "Oh, please, go ahead and look," that he had once received out of the dark night of the X-ray laboratory, when he had thought it necessary to ask permission to commit certain optical indiscretions.

The next morning he announced he would take part in that evening's session, and half an hour after supper he joined the habitués of the uncanny as they made their way to the basement, chatting nonchalantly. They were all permanent residents, either firmly rooted or at least of very long standing, like Dr. Ting-Fu and Wenzel the Bohemian, whom he met on the stairs, and the group they greeted in Dr. Krokowski's office: Herr Ferge and Herr Wehsal for instance, the prosecutor, the ladies Levi and Kleefeld, not to mention those who had told him about the apparition of Holger's head, and, of course, the medium herself, Elly Brand.

As Hans Castorp passed through the door with the calling card tacked decoratively to it, he found the Nordic child already under the doctor's wing. Dressed in his black clinical smock, Krokowski was right beside her, one arm paternally flung over her shoulders; she stood waiting at the foot of the two steps that led from the basement down into the assistant's apartments, and the two of them together greeted arriving guests. These greetings were characterized by unhesitating, expansive cheerfulness on all sides. The intent, it appeared, was to keep the mood free of any constraining solemnity. They all talked at once in loud, jocular voices, gave one another encouraging pokes in the ribs, and made a point of showing just how at ease they were. Beneath Dr. Krokowski's beard, under that pithy expression that reassured and enjoined confidence, his yellow teeth were constantly in evidence as he repeated his "my d'gods" and were particularly visible as he welcomed Hans Castorp, who said nothing and looked unsure of himself. "Courage, my friend," his host seemed to say, tossing his head back with a little shake and pumping the young man's hand almost roughly, "why should anyone look down-in-the-mouth? No cant, no sticky-sweet piety here, just the manly cheerfulness of unbiased research!" But this pantomimed greeting did not make Hans Castorp feel any better. We noted that in coming to this decision, he had recalled his experience in the X-ray laboratory, and yet that association by no means suffices to describe his state of mind. Rather, it all evoked in him very lively memories of a unique and unforgettable hodgepodge of emotions—nervousness, playfulness, curiosity, disgust, and awe—that he had felt years before when, a little tipsy, he joined some pals and set out for the first time to visit a brothel in Sankt Pauli.

All invited guests were now present, and so Dr. Krokowski asked his two assistants—this time it was Frau Magnus and ivory-hued Fräulein Levi—to join him in the adjacent office for a physical examination of the medium, while Hans Castorp and the other nine participants waited in the consulting room for the completion of this standard procedure of scientific rigor, always conducted without any findings. Hans Castorp knew this room well, from the days when he had spent some hours chatting here with the psychoanalyst, behind Joachim's back. It was an ordinary doctor's waiting room like any other: back on the left, by the window, a desk with an armchair, plus an easy chair for the patient; a reference library on both sides of the door to the adjacent office; on the right at the rear, near the desk and chairs, but separated from them by a folding screen, a chaise longue set at an angle and covered in oilcloth; in the same corner, a glass cupboard filled with instruments, facing a bust of Hippocrates in the near corner; on the right wall, just above the gas fireplace, an engraving of Rembrandt's *Anatomy Lesson*; and a red carpet that covered almost the entire floor. And yet it was also obvious that certain alterations in the furnishings had been made for this special occasion. The round mahogany table, which one would normally have found surrounded by armchairs in the middle of the room under the electric chandelier, had been shoved into the near left corner, where the plaster bust stood; and set at an odd angle, closer to the fireplace, which gave off a dry heat, was a smaller table, with a skimpy cloth and a little red-shaded lamp, above which another lamp dangled from the ceiling, likewise with a red shade, its bulb, however, draped in black gauze. On, and beside, this little table were placed a few infamous items: the serving bell, in fact two different sorts of bells, one a handbell, the other a desk bell that you banged with your palm; the dish of flour; the wastepaper basket. Around the little table, about a dozen chairs and stools of various sorts had been placed in a semicircle, one end of which was near the foot of the chaise longue, the other almost in the exact middle of the room, just below the chandelier. And here, nearest the last chair, but about halfway to the door to the adjacent office, the gramophone cabinet had been set. The album of light favorites lay on a stool next to it. So much for the setup. The red lamps had not yet been lit. The chandelier supplied an abundance of white daylight. The window, the narrow end of the desk abutting it, had been covered with a black cloth, in front of which had been hung a cream-colored, open lacework curtain.

After ten minutes, the doctor returned with the three ladies from his inner office. Little Elly's external appearance had changed. She was no longer in street clothes, but in a kind of séance costume, a nightgown-like robe of white crêpe that left her slender arms bare and was gathered at the waist by a cincture or cord. Beneath it, her virginal breasts lay unencumbered and softly outlined—she was apparently wearing little else.

She was greeted enthusiastically. "Hello, Elly! Charming as ever! A perfect fairy! Good luck, my angel!" She smiled in response to the calls, fully aware that her outfit looked good on her. "Preparatory examination negative," Dr. Krokowski announced. "Let's get down to some hard work now, comrades!" he added, with only one of his palatalized, exotic tongue-tapping *r*'s. The others began to take their seats, hallooing, chatting, and clapping shoulders, and Hans Castorp, feeling put off by the tone of these opening remarks, was likewise moving to find a spot in the semicircle of chairs, when the doctor turned to address him personally.

"My friend," he said (my friend!), "since you are more or less a guest or novice in our midst this evening, I would like to single you out for a special honor. I charge you with the task of exercising scientific control over our medium. Which is done as follows." He directed the young man toward the end of the semicircle nearest the chaise longue and folding screen, where Elly had taken a seat on an ordinary cane chair, her face turned more to the entrance with its two steps than to the middle of the room; the doctor then sat down on a similar chair directly in front of her and grasped her hands, at the same time holding both her knees clamped between his own. "Do it in just the same way," he commanded, and signaled for Hans Castorp to replace him. "You will have to admit that her movements are totally restricted. But by way of redundancy, we shall have someone lend you support. My dear Fräulein Kleefeld, might I entreat you to assist?" And upon being summoned so politely and exotically, that lady joined the trio and clasped Elly's fragile wrists in both hands.

Hans Castorp could not avoid staring now and then straight into the face of the virginal child prodigy confined directly in front of him. Their eyes met, but Elly's slid down and off to one side in token of a modesty that was quite understandable given the situation; and she offered a little affected smile as well, tilting her head and pursing her lips slightly, just as she had recently at the séance with the glass. As a matter of fact, the sight of this demure affectation aroused another, more distant memory in her monitor—it reminded him more or less of the way Karen Karstedt had smiled as she had stood with him and Joachim beside her still-undug grave in the Dorf cemetery.

The semicircle had settled into place. They were thirteen in all, not including Wenzel the Bohemian, who kept himself available for tending to Polyhymnia's needs and, having now readied her for service, took a place on a stool toward the middle of the room behind the others. He also had his mandolin with him. After first flipping a switch that turned on both lamps that gave off reddish light and then flipping another that doused the white ceiling light, Dr. Krokowski took his seat under the chandelier, there where the arch of chairs came to an end. A gently glimmering darkness lay over the room, whose farther regions and corners were now totally inaccessible to their eyes. Actually, only the surface of the little table and its immediate environs were illumined in soft red light. For the first few minutes you could barely see your neighbor. Your eyes adjusted only slowly to the darkness and learned to make use of what light there was, which was augmented somewhat by the dancing flames in the fireplace.

The doctor devoted a few words to the illumination, apologizing for its scientific inadequacy. They should not, however, interpret it as mystification, as mere setting of the mood. Unfortunately, as much as he would like it otherwise, no additional light could be permitted for now. The nature of the forces they were about to study was such that they simply could not unfold in white light, could not become operative. That was a factual precondition to which they would have to reconcile themselves for now. Hans Castorp was content to do so—the darkness felt good, it minimized the peculiarity of the whole situation. Besides, this defense of darkness reminded him of the gloom in which they had gathered so piously in the X-ray room, and of how they had first had to let darkness wash over their daylight eyes before they could "see."

The medium, Dr. Krokowski noted, continuing an introduction evidently addressed in particular to Hans Castorp, no longer needed to be put into a trance by the attending physician. As the gentleman monitoring her would doubtless soon notice, she fell into that state all on her own, and once this occurred, her attendant spirit, known to them as Holger, would speak through her, and it was to him—and not to her—that one was to address one's wishes. It was a common error, by the way, an error that could even bring about failure, to believe one had to concentrate one's will and thoughts on the prospective phenomenon. On the contrary, it was best to diffuse one's attention somewhat, even quiet conversation was useful. Hans Castorp should, however, concentrate on keeping the medium's extremities under flawless control.

"The chain will now be formed," Dr. Krokowski concluded, and they proceeded to follow instructions, laughing when a neighbor's hand could not be immediately located in the darkness. Dr. Ting-Fu, sitting next to Hermine Kleefeld, placed his right hand on her shoulder and extended his left hand to Herr Wehsal, who came next. Beside the doctor sat Herr and then Frau Magnus, who joined hands with A. K. Ferge, who, if Hans Castorp was not mistaken, was linked to Fräulein Levi of the ivory complexion on his right—and so on. "Music!" Dr. Krokowski commanded; and the Czech, standing just behind the doctor and his nearest neighbor, turned the gramophone on and let the needle down. "Talk!" Krokowski commanded again at the sound of the first bars of an overture by Millöcker; and they obediently set to work to get a conversation going, about nothing, nothing at all—this winter's snowfall, the menu at supper, some new arrival, some wild or authorized departure. Half-drowned by the music, the talk would break off and start up again, its life sustained artificially. Several minutes passed.

The record had not yet come to an end, when Elly was seized by a violent spasm. A trembling passed through her body, her torso tipped forward until her brow was touching Hans Castorp's, and at the same time her arms began to make strange back-and-forth pumping motions, forcing her monitors' arms to do the same.

"Trance!" Fräulein Kleefeld announced knowingly. The music died away. The conversation broke off.

In the abrupt silence one could hear the doctor's soft, drawling baritone. "Is Holger present?" he asked.

Elly shuddered again. She swayed in her chair. Then Hans Castorp felt her give his hands a firm, brief squeeze.

"She squeezed my hands," he reported.

"He," the doctor corrected. "He squeezed your hands. He is present, then. Our d'gods, Holger," he said unctuously. Using informal pronouns, he now continued, "We welcome you most heartily, good fellow. And now, please recall how the last time you tarried here among us you promised to call up any person who has passed on and who might be named by our circle, be it brother or sister, and to make him or her visible to mortal eyes. Are you willing to do so now? Do you feel capable of honoring that promise today?"

Elly shuddered again. She sighed and delayed her answer. Slowly she lifted her hands, and those of the two guardians, to her brow, where she let them rest awhile. Then very close to Hans Castorp's ear, she whispered a fervent "Yes!"

The breath of speech directly on his ear caused our friend to experience that creeping epidermal phenomenon popularly known as "goose bumps," which the director had explained to him once long ago. We call it a creeping sensation in order to differentiate between its purely physical and its psychological aspects, since there was hardly any sense of horror involved. What he was thinking, more or less, was: "Well, she's certainly impudent enough!" But at the same time he was touched, indeed jolted, by a confused feeling born of his own confusion in hearing a sweet young thing, whose hand he was holding, whisper the word "yes" in his ear.

"He said yes," he reported, and felt embarrassed.

"Fine, then, Holger," Dr. Krokowski said. "We shall take you at your word. We are all confident that you will do your honest best. The name of the dear departed soul whose manifestation we desire will be given to you in a moment. Comrades," he said, turning to the group, "speak up! Who has a wish at the ready? Whom shall Friend Holger reveal to us?"

Silence followed. Everyone was waiting for someone else to say something. Over the last few days, each of them had probably scrutinized the direction of his own thoughts, asked himself to whom they reached out. And yet, the return of those who have died—or better, the desirability of such a return—is always a complicated, ticklish matter. Ultimately, to put it plainly, it does not exist, this desirability. It is a miscalculation; by the light of cold day, it is as impossible as the thing itself, which would be immediately evident if nature rescinded that impossibility even once; and what we call mourning is perhaps not so much the pain of the impossibility of ever seeing the dead return to life, as the pain of not being able to wish it.

They were all vaguely aware of this, and although they were not dealing here with a serious and authentic return to life, but a purely sentimental and theatrical performance, during which one would only *see* the departed person—nothing life-threatening, really—they nevertheless feared being confronted by whomever they had thought about, and each would have preferred to pass on to his neighbor the privilege of expressing such a wish. Even Hans Castorp, despite his having once heard that kind, generous "Oh, please, go ahead and look" emerge from the night, held back and at the last moment was quite prepared to let someone else go first. But it all seemed to be taking too long, and so turning his head to address the leader of the session, he said with a husky voice, "I would like to see my dead cousin, Joachim Ziemssen."

It was a great relief to everyone. Of all those present, only Dr. Ting-Fu, Wenzel the Czech, and the medium herself had not known the person now named. The rest of them—Ferge, Wehsal, Herr Albin, the prosecutor, Herr and Frau Magnus, the ladies Stöhr, Levi, and Kleefeld—loudly and happily expressed their approval, and even Dr. Krokowski himself nodded with satisfaction, although his relations with Joachim had always been cool, since the latter had proved less than obliging in the matter of analysis.

"Very good," the doctor said. "Did you hear, Holger? The gentleman named was a stranger to you in life. Do you know him in the world beyond, and are you prepared to bring him to us?"

High suspense. The sleeping woman swayed, sighed, and shuddered. She seemed to be searching and struggling as she slumped first to one side and then the other, whispering gibberish now in Hans Castorp's ear, now in Hermine Kleefeld's. Finally Hans Castorp felt the squeeze from both hands that meant "yes," which he duly reported.

"Fine, then!" Dr. Krokowski cried. "To work, Holger. Music!" he cried. "Talk!" And he repeated his injunction that there should be no strenuous concentration or forced visualization of their anticipated visitor—the only thing that helped was a casual, floating attentiveness.

And what followed now were the strangest hours our hero's young life had ever known until then; and although we are not completely sure as to his later fate, although we shall lose sight of him at a certain point in our story, we would like to think that they remained the strangest hours he would ever experience.

These were hours—more than two, we admit it straight out, including a brief pause in the "labor" that now began for Holger, or actually, for virginal Miss Elly—hours of labor that went on so dreadfully long that they all were close to despairing of any result, and indeed were often tempted out of pure pity to forgo the experience and cut this short, for it truly seemed unmercifully hard work, beyond the fragile strength of her of whom it was demanded. We men, if we do not shirk our own humanity, are aware of a certain moment in life when we feel this same unbearable pity—to which, absurd as it seems, no one responds, presumably because it is quite out of place—when we wrestle with a suppressed, outraged "Enough!" although we know it is not yet enough, cannot, dare not, be enough, and must go on and end one way or the other. It should be clear that we are speaking about a husband's, a father's pity, about the act of birth, which Elly's travails indeed so manifestly, so unmistakably resembled that even someone unfamiliar with birth would have had to have recognized it—someone like our young Hans Castorp, who, having never shirked life, now learned about that act of organic mysticism in this form. And what a form it was! And for what a purpose! And under what circumstances! Scandalous is the only word for the specific details of this animated maternity ward bathed in reddish light—from the virginal young lady in labor, with her flowing nightgown and frail, bare arms, to the incessant light favorites coming from the gramophone; to the artificial chatter that the semicircle attempted to keep going on doctor's orders; to the constant cheery cries of encouragement to the struggling girl—"Hello, Holger! Courage! Won't be long! Don't give up, Holger, just let it come, you'll do it!" And we are certainly not exempting from the scandal the person and circumstance of the "husband," either—if we may regard Hans Castorp as the husband in this case, since it had been his wish—the husband, then, who held the knees of the "mother" clamped between his own, her hands in his, hands as wet as little Leila's once had been, so that he constantly had to get a new grip to keep them from slipping away.

For the gas fireplace behind the semicircle was putting out heat.

A mystic consecration? Oh no, it was all too noisy, too preposterous there in the reddish darkness, to which their eyes had gradually become so accustomed that they could more or less take in the whole room. The music and their cries were reminiscent of a Salvation Army revival meeting, even for someone like Hans Castorp, who had never attended services held by those high-spirited enthusiasts. There was nothing ghostly about the scene, and if its effects were mystical and mysterious, if they aroused pious feelings in anyone, then it was only in a natural, organic sense—and we have already noted the more precise, intimate context involved. Elly's efforts came in waves, followed by pauses during which she would fall limply to one side of her chair, in a fully inaccessible state that Dr. Krokowski called "deep trance." Then she would straighten up and begin to moan; she tossed back and forth, pushed and wrestled with her monitors, whispered hot babble in their ears, made a series of sidelong whiplash movements as if trying to fling something out of her, gnashed her teeth, and once even bit Hans Castorp's sleeve.

This went on for an hour or more. Then the leader of the session found that it would be in the interest of all present to allow for a pause. Wenzel the Czech, who toward the end had provided a little change of pace by shutting off the gramophone and plunking his mandolin quite adeptly, now laid his instrument down. With a sigh, they all let go of one another's hands. Dr. Krokowski walked over to the wall to turn on the chandelier. There was a flare of blinding white, and all the night-eyes squinted stupidly. Elly went on slumbering; she was bent forward, her face almost in her lap. They noticed that she was busy doing something rather curious, an activity with which the others seemed familiar, but that caught Hans Castorp's attention, and he watched in amazement: for several minutes she reached out her cupped hand until it was at about her hip, then pulled it back—stretched it out and with a ladling or raking motion, pulled it back, as if she were collecting or gathering something. Then after a series of jerks she came to, blinked—her eyes, too, squinting stupidly into the light—and smiled.

She smiled, an affected and somewhat reserved smile. Their pity for her labors did indeed seem to have been wasted. She did not look particularly exhausted. Perhaps she did not even remember any of it. She sat in the chair reserved for patients at the back of the doctor's wide desk, near the window, between it and the folding screen arranged around the chaise longue; she had turned the chair enough so that she could brace one arm on the desktop and look out into the room. And there she sat, the object of sympathetic glances and occasional encouraging nods, and said not a word during the entire intermission, which lasted fifteen minutes.

It was a real intermission—everyone was relaxed and mildly satisfied with the work thus far accomplished. The gentlemen's cigarette cases clicked. People smoked with gusto and in scattered groups discussed how the session was going. They were a long way from feeling discouraged about it, from any sense that they might have to contemplate its ending in failure. There were sufficient signs to counter all such despondency. Those who had been sitting at the far end of the semicircle, near the doctor, all agreed that several times they had clearly felt the cool draft that regularly prepared the way for any phenomena and that originated with the medium herself, always streaming in one particular direction. Others claimed to have seen little flecks of white light, shifting points of concentrated energy that had appeared repeatedly along the folding screen. In short, no giving up! No faint hearts! Holger had given his word, and they had no right to doubt he would keep it.

Dr. Krokowski gave the signal for the session to resume. While the others took their seats again, he personally led Elly back to her chair of martyrdom, stroking her hair as she sat down. Everything went just as before; Hans Castorp asked to be relieved of his post as primary monitor, but was refused this request by their leader. It was important to him, the doctor said, that the person who had expressed the wish be afforded proof, by the direct evidence of the senses, that all fraudulent manipulation of the medium was out of the question. And so Hans Castorp resumed his peculiar position in front of Elly. The light was reduced to a dim red. The music started up again. Once more, there were several minutes of Elly's jerky spasms and pumping motions; but this time it was Hans Castorp who announced, "Trance!" The scandalous birthing proceeded.

But with what terrible difficulties! It did not seem to want to proceed at all—and how could it? What madness! What sort of motherhood was this? A delivery—how and from what? "Help, help," the child moaned, her labor pains threatening now to become a futile, dangerous constant cramp, known to obstetricians as eclampsia. She called for the doctor at one point, asked him to lay hands on her. Which he did, urging her on in pithy phrases. This magnetization, if that is what it was, gave her strength for further struggles.

And so the second hour passed. Eyes weaned from daylight again grew somewhat accustomed to the dim illumination; and the room was filled alternately with mandolin plunking and gramophone melodies from the album of light favorites. Then something happened—and Hans Castorp was the cause. He made a suggestion, expressed a wish, a thought, that he had been entertaining for some time, actually from the very start, and that quite possibly should have been offered before now. Elly was in her "deep trance," her face resting in her tightly held hands, and Herr Wenzel was about to change records or turn one over, when our friend began to say, with some determination, that he had a suggestion to make— insignificant, really, but then it might be useful, in his opinion. He had . . . that is, the house record library contained one particular piece, "Valentin's Prayer" from Gounod's *Faust*, baritone and orchestra, very attractive. He, Hans Castorp, suggested they might try playing it just once.

"And why is that?" the doctor asked from somewhere in the red darkness.

"A matter of mood, of an emotional state," the young man replied. The spirit of the piece was peculiar, quite special. He was merely suggesting they give it a try. It was not out of the question, in his view, that the spirit or character of the music might shorten the current proceedings.

"Is the recording here?" the doctor asked.

No, it wasn't. But Hans Castorp could fetch it right away.

"What are you thinking of!" Krokowski rejected the idea out of hand. What? Hans Castorp wanted to leave and come back, go fetch something and then have them pick up their labors where they had left off? That was inexperience speaking. No, it was absolutely impossible. It would ruin everything, they would have to begin all over again. And scientific accuracy likewise prohibited even thinking of engaging in any such arbitrary departure and return. The door was locked. He, the doctor, had the key in his pocket. And in short, if the record was not readily available, then they would have to—he was still speaking when the Czech interjected from beside the gramophone.

"The record is here."

"Here?" Hans Castorp asked.

Yes, here. *Faust*, "Valentin's Prayer." Here, he could see for himself. Somehow it had got put into the album of light favorites, rather than in the green album of arias, number two, where it properly belonged. How extraordinary, how fortunate, by accident or carelessness it had landed in the frothier stuff and only needed to be put on.

And what did Hans Castorp say to that? He said nothing. It was the doctor who said, "Well, then, all the better," and several people echoed him. The needle made its whetting sound, the cover was lowered. And to the chords of a chorale, a male voice began to sing, "And now since I must leave—"

No one spoke. They listened. The moment the music began, Elly took up her labors again. She started up in her chair, shuddered, groaned, pumped, and put her slippery wet hand to her brow. The record continued to play. It came to the middle section with the bouncing rhythm, the passage about battle and danger—gallant, devout, and French. Then it moved on to the finale, the reprise, with augmented orchestra swelling in massive tones: "O Lord of heaven, hear my prayer."

Hans Castorp was occupied with Elly. She reared back, drawing air in through her constricted throat, sank forward again with a long sigh, and crouched there without a sound. He was bending worriedly down over her, when he heard Frau Stöhr say in a whimpering peep: "Ziems—sen!"

He did not straighten up. There was a bitter taste in his mouth. He heard another cold, deep voice reply: "I've been watching him for some time now."

The record had come to an end, the last chords of brass had died away. But no one turned off the machine. The needle moved to the middle of the disk and scratched idly in the silence. Now Hans Castorp lifted his head, and without having to search, his eyes looked in the right direction.

There was one more person than before in the room. There, off to the side of the semicircle, in the background, where the red light was swallowed up in night that the eye could barely pierce, between the doctor's wide desk and the folding screen, there on the patient's chair turned toward the room, where Elly had sat during the pause—there sat Joachim. It was Joachim with the shadowy hollow cheeks and warrior's beard from his final days, with lips arched proud and full. He sat leaning back, one leg crossed over the other. Although whatever that was on his head cast a long shadow, his emaciated face visibly bore the stamp of suffering and the same austere, earnest expression that had made him look so manly. Two deep creases were engraved on his brow between the eyes, which had sunk deep into their bony sockets, although that did not distract from the tenderness of the gaze that came from those beautiful, large, dark eyes, directed in friendly silence at Hans Castorp, at him alone. His one minor sorrow of long ago, his protruding ears, was not noticeable under whatever that strange, unidentifiable thing was that he had on his head. Cousin Joachim was not in civvies; his saber appeared to be leaning against his crossed thigh and he held the hilt in both hands; also discernible, or so it seemed, was a holster attached to his belt. But this was no proper dress uniform he was wearing—no flash of color, no shiny buttons. It had a narrow tuniclike collar and side pockets, and a cross was dangling farther down. Joachim's feet seemed very large, his legs very thin—and they looked as if they had been wrapped, more for sport than for any military reason. And what *was* that thing on his head? It looked as if Joachim had plopped a bit of field gear, a cooking pot, down over his head and then fastened it under his chin with a strap. The effect was properly warlike, and yet it was like something out of the past, a sixteenth-century lansquenet perhaps—strange.

Hans Castorp could feel Ellen Brand's breath on his hands, could hear Hermine Kleefeld breathing rapidly next to him. Otherwise, there was no other sound except the incessant whetting scrape of the record still rotating beneath the needle that no one had bothered to lift. He did not look around to any of his fellow guests, did not want to see them, to know anything about them. Bending forward and leaning out to see past the hands and head on his knees, he stared into red darkness at the visitor in the chair. For a moment he thought he would throw up. His throat contracted and cramped in four or five fervent sobs. "Forgive me!" he whispered to himself, and then the tears came to his eyes and he saw nothing more.

He heard a voice murmur: "Speak to him." Dr. Krokowski's baritone called him calmly and solemnly by name and repeated his command. But instead of obeying it, he pulled his hands from under Elly's face and stood up.

Dr. Krokowski called out his name again, this time in a stern voice of warning. But with a few quick strides, Hans Castorp was already at the door; with a flick of his hand, he turned on the white light.

Ellen Brand had recoiled in shock, and now lay twitching in Fräulein Kleefeld's arms. The patient's chair was empty.

Hans Castorp walked over to Krokowski, who stood there protesting loudly, came up very close to him, tried to say something, but no words would come from his lips. With a brusque, demanding gesture he held out his hand. Taking the key, he nodded menacingly several times directly in the doctor's face, turned on his heels, and left the room.

The Great Petulance

AND AS ONE LITTLE YEAR succeeded another, a ghost began to walk the Berghof, one whom Hans Castorp suspected was a direct descendent of that demon we have already called by its malicious name.

With the irresponsible curiosity of the tourist thirsting for knowledge, he had studied that old demon, indeed had found potentialities within himself for lively participation in the monstrous acts of homage paid to it by the world all about him. Like the old demon, this new one had always been around, sprouting up here and there to hint at its presence, but as it spread now, it became clear that by temperament Hans Castorp was less suited for worship of this creature. All the same, the moment he let himself go the least little bit, he noted to his horror that his words, gestures, and expression, too, had succumbed to an infection no one in the place could escape.

What was it, then? What was in the air? A love of quarrels. Acute petulance. Nameless impatience. A universal penchant for nasty verbal exchanges and outbursts of rage, even for fisticuffs. Every day fierce arguments, out-of-control shouting-matches would erupt between individuals and among entire groups; but the distinguishing mark was that bystanders, instead of being disgusted by those caught up in it or trying to intervene, found their sympathies aroused and abandoned themselves emotionally to the frenzy. They turned pale and quivered. Eyes flashed insults, mouths wrenched with passion. They envied the active participants their right to use the occasion to shout. An aching lust to join them tormented both body and soul, and whoever lacked the strength to flee to solitude was drawn into the vortex, beyond all help. Frivolous conflicts multiplied throughout the Berghof, with recriminations exchanged right in front of the authorities, who attempted to arbitrate but could themselves lapse into bellowing abuse with frightful ease. And anyone who left the sanatorium with his soul more or less intact could never know in what condition he might return. Seated at the Good Russian table was a quite elegant provincial lady from Minsk, still young and only slightly ill—she had been sentenced to three months, no more—who one day went down into town to shop for French blouses. She got into such a wrangle with the saleswoman that she arrived home in a state of wild agitation, suffered a hemorrhage, and was soon diagnosed as incurable. Her husband was summoned and told that she would have to stay here now for good and all.

That is just one example of what was going around. We shall reluctantly supply others. Some readers will recall the student, or former student, with the thick circular glasses, who sat at Frau Salomon's table—the gaunt young lad who had the habit of chopping all the food on his plate into a hodgepodge, propping his elbows on the table, and wolfing it down, while occasionally pushing his napkin up behind his thick glasses. And he had sat there all this time, still a student or former student, wolfing down his food and wiping his eyes, without ever giving anyone cause to pay him more than fleeting attention. But now, one morning at first breakfast, quite surprisingly, out of the blue so to speak, he had a fit, a seizure, arousing general commotion and bringing the entire dining hall to its feet. It suddenly grew loud in that part of the hall—there he sat, pale and shouting—shouts directed at the dwarf, who was standing beside him. "You're lying!" he screamed, his voice cracking. "That tea is cold. The tea you brought me is ice-cold. I don't want it. Before you lie to me again, just see for yourself if it isn't lukewarm dishwater no respectable human being could possibly drink! How dare you bring me ice-cold tea! Where did you get the notion—what made you think you could serve me this tepid bilge with even a glimmer of hope I would drink it? I won't drink it! I will not!" he howled and began to drum both fists on the table, setting all the dishes rattling and dancing. "I want hot tea! Piping hot tea—before God and man, that is my right. I don't want this, I want it boiling hot. I'll die on the spot before I take one swallow of this—you damned cripple!" he suddenly shrieked, flinging off the last bit of self-control and breaking through to the madness of utter license. He raised a fist at Emerentia and literally bared his frothing teeth. Then he went on drumming, stamping his feet now, howling, "I won't. I will not!"—and the reaction in the hall was the usual. Tense and terrible sympathy went out to the raving boy. Some people had jumped up and were watching him, their fists doubled now, too, their teeth clenched, their eyes blazing. Others sat there pale, with downcast eyes, quivering. And they were still sitting like that long after the student had sunk back in exhaustion, gazing at his new cup of tea without taking a sip.

What *was* this?

A man joined the ranks of Berghof society, a thirty-year-old former businessman, who had wandered from sanatorium to sanatorium for years now with his fever. The man was an anti-Semite, on principle and as a matter of sport. His opposition to Jews was a cheerful obsession—this acquired hostility was the pride and content of his life. He had been a businessman, he was one no more, he was nothing in this world, but he had remained an anti-Semite. He was seriously ill, his cough sat heavy on him, and at times it sounded as if a lung were sneezing, a singular, high, brief, uncanny sound. But he was not a Jew, and that was the positive thing about him. His name was Wiedemann, a Christian name— nothing unclean about his name. He subscribed to a newspaper call *The Aryan Light*, and made speeches, as follows:

"I arrive at Sanatorium X in the town of Y. I decide I shall claim a spot in the common lounging area—and who is lying in the chair on my left? Why, Herr Hirsch! And on my right? Herr Wolf! But of course I departed immediately," and so forth.

"Serves you right," Hans Castorp thought with distaste.

Wiedemann had a quick, furtive glance. He truly looked as if a very real tassel were dangling just in front of his nose and he was constantly squinting at it, was unable to see beyond it. The erroneous belief that possessed him had become an itch of mistrust, a restless paranoia that drove him to pluck out any uncleanness that lay hidden or disguised in his vicinity, to hold it up to public disgrace. He taunted, he cast suspicions, he foamed at the mouth wherever he went. And in short, his days were filled with exposing to ridicule every form of life that did not possess the one merit he could call his own.

The emotional circumstances we have been describing exacerbated the man's illness beyond measure; and since he could not fail to encounter forms of life here that displayed the imperfection of which he, Wiedemann, was free, those same circumstances led to a dreadful scene that Hans Castorp witnessed and that shall have to serve as one more example of what we are describing.

For there was another man present—and there was nothing about him that needed unmasking, the case was clear. The man's name was Sonnenschein; and since one could not have a filthier name than that, from Wiedemann's very first day here Sonnenschein became the tassel in front of his nose, at which he squinted furtively and maliciously, batting at it with his hand, less to push it aside than to start it swinging so that it could annoy him all the more.

Sonnenschein, like Wiedemann a businessman born and bred, was also seriously ill and almost pathologically sensitive. A friendly man, certainly not stupid and even rather playful by nature, he hated Wiedemann for his taunts and the way he batted that tassel, until it was almost a sickness with him as well. One afternoon everyone gathered in the lobby because Wiedemann and Sonnenschein had run afoul of one another and were going at it like savage beasts.

What a horrible, wretched sight they were. They scuffled like little boys, but with the desperation of grown men who have come to such a pass. They clawed faces, pinched noses, clutched throats, all the while punching away at one another, grappling, rolling about on the floor in terribly dead earnest; they spat, kicked, grabbed, trounced, whacked, and frothed at the mouth. Clerks from the management office came running and with some difficulty separated the two bitten and scratched opponents. Drooling and bleeding, his face doltish with rage, Wiedemann stood there with his hair literally standing on end. Hans Castorp had never seen the phenomenon before, had never believed it could really occur—but Herr Wiedemann's hair stood up stiff and straight as nails. And he staggered away like that, while Herr Sonnenschein—with one eye turning black now and a bloody patch in the curly black hair that wreathed his head— was led away to the office, where he sat down, hid his face in his hands, and wept bitterly.

That was the Wiedemann-Sonnenschein affair. Everyone who witnessed it was still quivering hours later. In contrast to such misery, it is a comparative pleasure to tell about a genuine "affair of honor" that belongs to this same period and that definitely deserves the name, absurdly so, given the solemn formality with which it was carried out. Hans Castorp was not present at its various phases, but only learned about the complicated and dramatic course of events from documents, affidavits, and official minutes devoted to the affair, copies of which were circulated not only in the Berghof, not only in Davos, in the canton of Graubünden, in Switzerland, but also abroad, were sent as far as America, and were made available for study to persons who, one can be sure, would not and could not pay one whit of attention to the matter.

It was a Polish affair, a fracas of honor, which arose in the bosom of the Polish contingent that had recently found its way to the Berghof, a little colony that now occupied the Good Russian table. (Hans Castorp, we may interpose here, was no longer seated there, but had with time moved on to Hermine Kleefeld's table, from there to Frau Salomon's, then on to Fräulein Levi's.) This contingent was decked out so elegantly, so gallantly, that one could only raise one's eyebrows and prepare oneself for most any eventuality. It included one married couple, one young miss, who stood on cordial terms with one of the gentlemen, and then a whole group of cavaliers. Their names were von Zutawski, Cieszynski, von Rosinski, Michael Lodygowski, Leo von Asarapetian, and the like. Over champagne in the Berghof restaurant, a certain Japoll had, in the presence of two other cavaliers, made remarks, unrepeatable remarks, concerning both the wife of Herr von Zutawski and the young lady, whose name was Krylow and who was intimately associated with Herr Lodygowski. Measures were taken, certain formal actions resulted, all of which were contained in the written materials later distributed or sent by mail. Hans Castorp read:

"Affidavit, translated from the Polish original: On 27 March 19—, Herr Stanislaw von Zutawski approached Herr Dr. Anton Cieszynski and Herr Stefan von Rosinski with the request to call upon Herr Kasimir Japoll in his name and to demand satisfaction from same in the manner prescribed by the law of honor for 'gross insult and slander' inflicted by Herr Kasimir Japoll upon Herr von Zutawski's wife, Jadwiga von Zutawski, during a conversation with Herr Janusz Teofil Lenart and Herr Leo von Asarapetian.

"When only a few days ago, Herr von Zutawski learned of that aforesaid conversation, which took place toward the end of November, he promptly took timely steps to ascertain beyond doubt the full factual nature of the insult. Yesterday, 27 March 19—, the insult and slander were confirmed orally by Herr Leo von Asarapetian, a direct witness to said conversation, during the course of which those insulting words and insinuations were uttered; thereupon Herr Stanislaw von Zutawski felt constrained to apply without delay to the undersigned and authorize them to begin proceedings as prescribed by the law of honor against Herr Kasimir Japoll.

"The undersigned wish to make the following statement:

"1. On the basis of an affidavit prepared by one party on 9 April 19— summarizing the testimony given in Lemberg by Herr Zdzistaw Zygulski and Herr Tadeusz Kadyj concerning a suit brought by Herr Ladislaw Goduleczny against Herr Kasimir Japoll, and further on the basis of a decision rendered in that suit by the Court of Honor in Lemberg on 18 June 19—, both documents being in complete agreement in stating that Herr Kasimir Japoll 'cannot be regarded as a gentleman as a result of repeated conduct that is irreconcilable with the definition of honor,'

"2. the undersigned, drawing full consequences from the aforementioned documents, declare it impossible for Herr Kasimir Japoll ever to be capable of affording satisfaction.

"3. For their part, they likewise consider it inadmissible to pursue any affair of honor, or to mediate therein, with a man who stands outside the definition of honor.

"4. In consideration of these facts, the undersigned wish to inform Herr Stanislaw von Zutawski that it would be pointless to pursue a suit against Herr Kasimir Japoll before a court of honor, and suggest he prosecute the matter in the criminal courts in order to prevent further insult from a person who is so fully incapable of providing satisfaction."

—Dated and signed: Dr. Anton Cieszynski, Stefan von Rosinski."

Further, Hans Castorp read:

"Affidavit

"of witnesses concerning events transpiring between Herr Stanislaw von Zutawski and Herr Michael Lodygowski, parties of the first part,

"and Herr Kasimir Japoll and Herr Janusz Teofil Lenart, parties of the second part, in the bar of the Kurhaus in Davos, on 2 April 19—, between 7:30 and 7:45 p.m.

"Inasmuch as Herr Stanislaw von Zutawski, having received and duly considered the declaration pertaining to the matter of Herr Kasimir Japoll, dated 28 March 19— and signed by his representatives, Herr Dr. Anton Cieszynski and Stefan Rosinski, had come to the conclusion that the suggested pursuit of criminal prosecution of Herr Kasimir Japoll for 'gross insult and slander' of his wife, Jadwiga, would provide him no satisfaction,

"1. since there was legitimate reason to believe that Herr Kasimir Japoll would not appear in court and that, Herr Japoll being a citizen of Austria, any further pursuit would not only be made more difficult, but indeed almost impossible as well, and

"2. since no legal sentence imposed could compensate for the insult Herr Kasimir Japoll had slanderously brought upon the name and house of Herr Stanislaw von Zutawski and his wife, Jadwiga,

"Herr Stanislaw von Zutawski chose the shortest, and in his considered opinion most thorough and, given the circumstances, most appropriate course of action, after having been indirectly informed that Herr Kasimir Japoll intended to leave the aforementioned town the following day,

"and therefore on 2 April 19—, between 7:30 and 7:45 p.m., in the presence of his wife, Jadwiga, Herr Michael Lodygowski, and Herr Ignaz von Mellin, administered several slaps to the face of Herr Kasimir Japoll, who was sitting and drinking alcoholic spirits with Herr Janusz Teofil Lenart and two unidentified young women in the American Bar of the Kurhaus.

"Immediately thereafter, Herr Michael Lodygowski also slapped Herr Kasimir Japoll, stating that this was in payment for the gross insult rendered to Fräulein Krylow and himself.

"Herr Michael Lodygowski then promptly slapped Herr Janusz Teofil Lenart for the objectionable injury he had done to Herr and Frau von Zutawski, whereupon,

"without a moment lost, Herr Stanislaw von Zutawski repeatedly delivered a series of slaps to the face of Herr Janusz Teofil Lenart for the latter's slanderous defamation of both his wife, Jadwiga, and Fräulein Krylow.

"Herr Kasimir Japoll and Herr Janusz Teofil Lenart remained fully passive during the entire course of these events." —Dated and signed: Michael Lodygowski, Ign. v. Mellin."

Normally Hans Castorp would surely have laughed at this rapid-fire sequence of formal slaps, but his own inner state prevented that. He trembled as he read and was profoundly stirred by the rigid, but impressive antitheses so evident from the pages of these documents: impeccable deportment on the one side and rascally, disreputable laxness on the other. It was how they all felt. The Polish affair of honor was everywhere studied with great passion, and people clenched their teeth when they discussed

world toward him. Medical authority had ceased to invent diversions for him. Except for the question each morning whether he had slept "well," which, however, was purely rhetorical in nature and summarily posed, the director no longer addressed him all that often, and even Adriatica von Mylendonk (who had a sty ripe for lancing at the time of which we speak) did not speak to him for days at a time. Indeed, to be exact, they spoke seldom, almost never. People left him in peace—rather like a student who enjoys the peculiarly amusing situation of no longer being asked questions, of not having to do any work, because the decision has already been made to hold him back and so he is no longer in the running—an orgiastic sort of freedom, we may add, while asking ourselves whether there can be freedom of any other sort. In any case, here was a man whom medical authority no longer needed to keep under its watchful eye, because it was certain that no wild and defiant decisions would ever ripen in his breast—a dependable man, here for good and all, who had long since lost track of where else he might go, who was no longer even capable of forming the thought of a return to the flatlands. Did not the simple fact that he had been transferred to the Bad Russian table express a certain carelessness about his person? By which we do not mean to cast any aspersions whatever against the so-called Bad Russian table. There were no tangible advantages or disadvantages to one or another of the seven. It was a democracy of banquet tables, to put it bluntly. The same prodigious meals were also served at the so-called Bad Russian table; moving in rotation, even Rhadamanthus folded his gigantic hands before his plate there; and the people of several nations who dined at it were honorable members of humanity, even if they did not understand Latin and were not excessively dainty about their table manners.

Time—not the sort that train station clocks measure with a large hand that jerks forward every five minutes, but more like the time of a very small watch whose hands move without our being able to notice, or the time grass keeps as it grows without our eyes' catching its secret growth, until the day comes when the fact is undeniable—time, a line composed of elastic turning points (and here the late, ill-fated Naphta would presumably have asked how purely elastic points can ever begin to form a line), time, then, had continued to bring forth changes in its furtive, unobservable, secret, and yet bustling way. The boy named Teddy, to take just one example, was no longer a boy one day—though of course that did not happen "one day," but emerged out of some quite indefinite day. The ladies could no longer set him on their laps on those occasions when he left his bed, exchanged his pajamas for a sporty outfit, and came downstairs. The tables were turned, and no one had noticed. He now set them on his lap on such occasions, which both parties found just as delightful, even more so. He had—we won't say blossomed, but rather—sprouted into a young man. Hans Castorp had not seen it happen, but then he saw it. Time and sprouting, by the way, did not agree with the young man Teddy, he was not made for such things. Time proved no blessing—in his twenty-first year of life he died of the illness to which he had been susceptible. They fumigated his room. We can relate all this quite calmly, since there was no significant difference between his new condition and his previous one.

But more important deaths had occurred, deaths down in the flatlands, which were of greater concern to our hero, or would have been of greater concern at one time. We are thinking of the recent demise of old Consul Tienappel, Hans's great-uncle and foster father, of faded memory. He had most carefully avoided regions of unwholesome barometric pressure and had left it to Uncle James to make a fool of himself there; but in the long run, he had been unable to elude apoplexy; and one day news of his passing, in the form of a brief but delicately considerate telegram (delicate and considerate more in deference to the departed than to the receiver of the message), had reached Hans Castorp as he lay in his splendid lounge chair, whereupon he had purchased black-bordered stationery and written to his uncles or quasi cousins that having been orphaned twice, he now felt as if he had been orphaned yet a third time, and, still more distressing, was prevented, indeed prohibited, from interrupting his present sojourn to pay last respects to his great-uncle.

It would be disingenuous to speak of mourning, but all the same, for a while the expression in Hans Castorp's eyes was more pensive than usual. This death, which would never have been of great emotional consequence to Hans Castorp—and indeed after an estrangement of so many adventurous little years, all emotional content had been reduced to almost nothing—seemed to him nevertheless very like the breaking of yet another tie, a last connection, to the world below, bringing to perfection what he so rightly called his freedom. In truth, in the recent past of which we speak, there had been a total abrogation of every emotional bond between him and the flatlands. He wrote and received no letters. He no longer ordered his Maria Mancinis from there. He had found another brand up here, one that suited him and to which he was now as faithful as he had once been to his former girlfriend—a brand that would even have helped polar explorers get over their worst hardships in the ice and that when you smoked it made you feel as if you were lying on the beach and would be able to carry on. It had an especially well cured wrapper and was named Oath of Rütli; somewhat stubbier than Maria, mouse gray in color with a bluish band, it was very tractable and mild by nature; it had a snow-white durable ash that still showed the veins of the wrapper. It drew so evenly that it could easily have served as an hourglass for the man enjoying it, and indeed, given Hans Castorp's needs, did serve as such, for he no longer carried his pocket watch. It had stopped, having fallen from his nightstand one day, and he had refrained from having it put into measuring rotation again—for the same reasons he had long ago dispensed with calendars, whether the kind you tear off each day or the kind that provide an instructive preview of days and feasts, for reasons of "freedom," that is. It was his way of honoring the stroll by the shore, the abiding ever-and-always, the hermetic magic, to which, once with-drawn from the world, he had proved so susceptible—the magic that had been his soul's fundamental adventure, in which all the alchemistic adventures of that simple stuff had been played out.

And so there he lay, and once again, as the height of summer came round for the seventh time since his arrival—but he did not count—the year closed on itself.

Then came the rumble of thunder—

But modesty and reserve keep us from turning that thundering rumble into a blustering narrative. No bombast, no rodomontade, here. With appropriately lowered voice, we shall say that the thunderbolt itself (with which we are all familiar) was the deafening detonation of great destructive masses of accumulated stupor and petulance. It was, to speak in subdued, respectful tones, a historic thunderclap that shook the foundations of the earth; but for us it is the thunderbolt that bursts open the magic mountain and rudely sets its entranced sleeper outside the gates. There he sits in the grass, sheepishly rubbing his eyes, like a man who, despite many an admonition, has failed to read the daily papers.

His Mediterranean friend and mentor had constantly tried to rectify this situation somewhat and made a point of keeping his pedagogic prob-lem child roughly informed about events down below; but he had not been given much of a hearing by his pupil, who while "playing king" had let his mind turn the shadows of such things into one dream or another, but had never paid any attention to the things themselves, primarily out of an arrogant preference for seeing shadows as things, and things as mere shadows—for which one should not scold him too harshly, since that relationship has never been definitively decided.

Things were no longer as they had been once, when, after first establish-ing sudden clarity, Herr Settembrini would sit down at the bedside of a horizontal Hans Castorp and attempt to influence him by correcting his opinions about matters of life and death. It was the other way around

now; with hands tucked between his knees, the student now sat beside
the bed of the humanist in the little garret bedroom or next to the divan
in the cozy and private dormered studio, with its Carbonaro chairs and
water carafe, kept him company and listened politely to his presentations
of the world situation—for Herr Lodovico was seldom on his feet these
days. Naphta's crude end, that terrorist deed committed by a caustically
desperate antagonist, had been a terrible blow to his sensitive nature; he
had been unable to get over it, had been frail and subject to fainting spells
ever since. His contribution to *Sociological Pathology*, a lexicon of all the
works of literature with human suffering for their theme, had come to a
standstill, had stagnated, and the league waited in vain for that particular
volume of their encyclopedia. Herr Settembrini was forced to limit his
contribution to the Organization of Progress to oral reports, and he would
have had to have forgone even those had it not been for the opportunity
offered by Hans Castorp's friendly visits.

He spoke in a weak, but heartfelt voice, and he had much to say about
humanity's self-perfection by way of social reform. His discourses would
begin on dove's feet, but soon, when he turned to liberated peoples uniting
for universal happiness, there would come a sound as of the rushing
pinions of eagles—not that he wished it or even knew whence it came,
though doubtless it originated in the politics he had inherited from his
grandfather, which had then blended with the humanistic inheritance of
his father to create beautiful literature within him, Lodovico, just as humanity and politics were blended in the lofty idea of civilization, to which
he raised a toast, an idea full of the mildness of the dove and the boldness
of the eagle and awaiting its day, the dawn of the Day of Nations, when
the principle of obduracy would be defeated and a path opened for the
Holy Alliance of bourgeois democracy. In short, there were inconsisten-
cies here. Herr Settembrini was a humanitarian, and yet at the same time
and bound up with it, he was, as he half admitted, a man of war. He had
behaved very humanely in his duel with crude Naphta; but more generally,
whenever his enthusiasms blended humanity and politics for the ideal of
civilization's ultimate victory and dominion, whenever the citizen's pike
was consecrated on the altar of humanity, it became doubtful whether,
on a more impersonal level, he remained of a mind to hold back his sword
from shedding blood. Yes, Herr Settembrini's own inner state meant that
in his world of beautiful views, the element of the eagle's boldness prevailed more and more over the dove's mildness.

It was not unusual for him to be unsettled by his own scruples, to feel
divided and perplexed in his attitudes toward the world's larger constellations. Recently—a year and a half or two years before—the diplomatic

cooperation of his own country and Austria in Albania had troubled his discourse, a cooperation that both inspired him, since it was directed against demi-Asia with its lack of Latin, against knouts and Schlüsselburg prison, and tormented him as a misalliance with his country's sworn enemy, with the principle of obduracy and the bondage of nations. The previous autumn, the immense loan France had made to Russia for constructing railroads in Poland had awakened within him a similar conflict of feelings. For Herr Settembrini belonged to the Francophile party in his homeland, which was in no way astonishing when one recalls that his grandfather had equated the days of the July Revolution with the days of Creation; but a pact between that enlightened republic and Scythian Byzantium was a moral embarrassment to him—his chest felt constricted, but then, at the thought of the strategic significance of those railroads, it would try to expand and take in rapid breaths of hope and joy. Then came the murder of the archduke, which for everyone except our German sleeper served as a storm warning, a word to the wise, among whom we have good cause to count Herr Settembrini. Hans Castorp noticed how as a private, humane man, the Italian shuddered at the awful deed, but he also noticed how that chest rose at the thought that it was committed to free a nation, was directed against the citadel he hated—even though it could also be seen as the upshot of Moscow's schemes, which then constricted his breathing, and yet did not prevent him from characterizing the ultimatum presented by the Hapsburgs to Serbia only three weeks later as an insult to humanity and a ghastly crime, whose consequences he, as an initiate in such matters, clearly saw and greeted with quick, shallow breaths.

In short, Herr Settembrini's reactions were as complex as the cataclysm he saw gathering and to which he tried to open his pupil's eyes with veiled words; at the same time, however, a kind of patriotic courtesy and compassion kept him from opening up entirely on the matter. In the days of the first mobilization, of the first declarations of war, he got into the habit of reaching out both hands to his visitor and squeezing them in his own—which deeply touched the nincompoop's heart, if not his head. "My friend," the Italian said, "gunpowder, the printing press—yes, you undeniably invented those. But if you think that we would ever march against revolution—*caro* . . ."

During the days of stifling suspense, while Europe's nerves were stretched on the rack, Hans Castorp did not go to see Herr Settembrini. The wild headlines from below now found their way directly to his balcony door, they sent the Berghof into spasms, filled the dining hall with an odor of sulfur that constricted the chest, seeping even into the rooms of the bedridden and moribund. And it was during those same moments that our sleeper slowly began to sit up in the grass, not knowing what had happened, not rubbing his eyes yet . . . and let us draw the metaphor out in full, so that we may be just to the rush of his emotions. He drew his legs back under him, stood up, looked around. He saw that the enchantment was broken, that he was released, set free—not by his own actions, as he had to admit to his shame, but set free by elementary external forces, for whom his liberation was a very irrelevant matter. But even if his little fate shrank to nothing before universal destiny, was it not, all the same, an expression of some goodness and justice intended personally for him, and thus in some way divine? If life was to receive back her sinful problem child, it could not happen on the cheap, but only like this, in a serious, rigorous fashion, as a kind of ordeal, which in this case did not perhaps mean life so much as it meant three salvos fired in his, the sinner's, honor. And so he sank back down on his knees, his face and hands raised toward a heaven darkened by sulfurous fumes, but no longer the grotto ceiling in a sinful mountain of delight.

And it was in this position that Herr Settembrini found him—metaphorically speaking, of course; for in reality, as we know, our hero's cool, reserved manners excluded such theatrics. In cool reality, his mentor found him packing his bags—for since the moment of his awakening, Hans Castorp had been caught up in the turmoil and confusion of a wild departure, the result of that bursting thunderbolt in the valley. His "home" was now like an anthill in panic. The "people up here" were tumbling head over heels all five thousand feet down to the flatlands and its ordeal, were storming the little train, thronging its running boards— if need be, even without their baggage, which lay piled in rows on the platforms of the teeming little station, where even high in the mountains one could catch a whiff of the stifling smoke drifting up from below. And Hans tumbled with them. There in the tumult, Lodovico embraced him, literally took him in his arms and gave him a Mediterranean—or perhaps a Russian—kiss, a cause of no little embarrassment for our wild traveler, despite his own surge of emotion. And he almost lost his composure when at the last moment Herr Settembrini called him by his first name, said "Giovanni," and casting aside the forms appropriate to the educated West, let informal pronouns reign.

"*E così in giù,*" he said, "*—in giù finalmente! Addio, Giovanni mio!* I would have wished to see you go in some other way, but it doesn't matter. The gods have decreed it so, and not otherwise. I hoped to send you off to your work, and now you will be fighting alongside your fellows. My God, you are the one to go, and not our lieutenant. The tricks life plays. Fight bravely out there where blood joins men together. No one can do more than that now. Forgive me if I use what little energy I have left to rouse my own country to battle, on the side to which intellect and sacred egoism direct it. *Addio!*"

Hans Castorp forced his head out from among the ten others filling the little window. He waved above their heads. And Herr Settembrini waved with his right hand, too, while with the tip of the ring finger of his left hand he gently brushed the corner of one eye.

WHERE ARE WE? What is that? Where has our dream brought us? Dusk, rain, and mud, fire reddening a murky sky that bellows incessantly with dull thunder, the damp air rent by piercing, singsong whines and raging, onrushing, hellhound howls that end their arc in a splintering, spraying, fiery crash filled with groans and screams, with brass blaring, about to burst, and drumbeats urging onward, faster, faster. There is a wood spewing drab hordes that run, stumble, jump. There is a line of hills, dark against the distant conflagration whose glow sometimes gathers into fluttering flames. Around us is rolling farmland, gouged and battered to sludge. And there is a road covered with muck and splintered branches, much like the wood itself; branching off from the road, a country lane, a rutted quagmire, winds up the hill; tree trunks jut into the cold rain, naked and stripped of branches. Here is a signpost—no point in asking, the twilight would cloak its message even if it had not been riddled and ripped to jagged shreds. East or west? It is the flatlands—this is war. And we are reluctant shades by the roadside, ashamed of our own shadowy security and not in the least inclined to indulge in bombast and rodomontade; but, rather, the spirit of our story has led us here to watch these gray, running, stumbling troops as they swarm now from the woods, urged on by drums, and to gaze into the ordinary face of our companion of so many little years, that kindhearted sinner whose voice we have heard so often, to see him once more before he passes out of view.

They have been called up, these comrades here, for a final push in a battle that has lasted all day, to regain that hill position and the burning villages just beyond, which were lost to the enemy two days before. It is a regiment of volunteers, youngsters, students mostly, not long at the front. They were rousted out in the night, rode the train till morning, marched in the rain until afternoon, taking wretched roads, or, since the roads were already jammed, no roads at all, just field and moor. Seven hours in heavy, rain-sodden coats, with battle gear—this was no promenade. To keep from losing your boots, you had to bend down at almost every step and grab hold of the tongue with your fingers and tug your foot out of the squishy mire. It had taken one whole hour to cross a little meadow. And now here they are—youth has done it, their exhausted but excited bodies, tense with the last reserves of energy, have no need of the sleep and food they have been denied. Their flushed, wet faces, splattered with mud, are framed by chin straps and gray cloth-covered helmets worn askew; they are flushed with exertion and the sight of the casualties they took moving through the marshy wood. For the enemy, informed of their advance, had laid a barrage across their path, shrapnel and large-caliber grenades that burst into their ranks while they were still in the woods— a splintering, howling, spraying, flaming scourge across the wide, newly plowed fields.

They have to get through, these three thousand feverish lads; their bayonets have to provide the reinforcements that will decide the attack on the trenches dug before and behind the line of hills, that will help retake the burning villages, until they advance to a spot marked on the orders their leader carries in his pocket. There are three thousand of them, so that they can be two thousand when they reach the hills and the villages—that is the meaning of their numbers. They are a single body, so constructed that even after great losses it can act and triumph, even greet its victory with a thousand-voiced hurrah—despite those who are severed from it and fall away. Already in the course of their forced march, many a man has severed himself, has proved too young and too weak— turned pale and staggered, doggedly forced himself to be a man, only to fall back all the same in the end; he drags himself alongside the marching column for a while longer, as company after company passes by, and then he vanishes, lying down where it was not wise to lie down. And then comes the shattering wood. But they are still many now as they swarm out of it; an army of three thousand men can hemorrhage badly and still be a great teeming force. And they flood out over the scourged, rain-soaked land, the road, the country lane, the muddy fields; we shadows at the roadside watch from their midst. At the edge of the wood they are still fixing bayonets with well-drilled movements—the brass calls out urgently, the pounding and rolling drums sound out above deeper thunder. And they rush forward as best they can, with brash cries and night-marishly heavy feet, clods of earth clinging leadenly to crude boots.

They hurl themselves down before projectiles howling toward them, only to leap up and rush on, shouting courage in brash, young voices— they have not been hit. Then they are hit, they fall, flailing their arms, shot in the head, the heart, the gut. They lie with their faces in the mire and do not stir. They lie, arched over their knapsacks, the backs of their heads buried in the soft ground, their hands clutching at the air like talons. But the wood keeps sending new men, who hurl themselves down, leap up, and, with a shout or without a word, stagger forward among those who have already fallen.

Youngsters with their backpacks and bayoneted rifles, with their filthy coats and boots—and in watching, one might also see them with a humanistic, beatific eye, might dream of other scenes. One might imagine such a lad spurring a horse on or swimming in a bay, strolling along the shore with a girlfriend, his lips pressed to his gentle beloved's ear, or in happy friendship instructing another lad to string a bow. And instead, there they all lie, noses in the fiery filth. That they do it with joy, and also with boundless fear and an unutterable longing for home, is both shameful and sublime, but surely no reason to bring them here to this.

There is our friend, there is Hans Castorp! We recognized him a good distance off from that little beard he grew when he moved to the Bad Russian table. He is soaked through, his face is flushed, like all the others. He runs with feet weighed down by mud, his bayoneted rifle clutched in his hand and hanging at his side. Look, he is stepping on the hand of a fallen comrade—stepping on it with his hobnailed boots, pressing it deep into the soggy, branch-strewn earth. But it is him, all the same. What's this? He's singing? The way a man sings to himself in moments of dazed, thoughtless excitement, without even knowing—and he uses what tatters of breath he has left to sing to himself:

> Upon its bark I've ca-arved there
> So many words of love—

He stumbles. No, he has thrown himself on his stomach at the approach of a howling hound of hell, a large explosive shell, a hideous sugarloaf from the abyss. He lies there, face in the cool muck, legs spread, feet twisted until the heels press the earth. Laden with horror, this product of science gone berserk crosses thirty yards in front of him, buries itself in the ground, and explodes like the Devil himself, bursts inside the earth with ghastly superstrength and casts up a house-high fountain of soil, fire, iron, lead, and dismembered humanity. For two men had flung themselves down there beside one another—they were friends. Commingled now, they vanish.

Oh, how ashamed we feel in our shadowy security! We're leaving— we can't describe this! But was our friend hit, too? For a moment, he thought he was. A large clod of dirt struck his shin—it certainly hurt, but how silly, it was nothing. He gets up, he limps and stumbles forward on mud-laden feet, singing thoughtlessly:

> And all its branches ru-ustled,
> As if they called to me—

And so, in the tumult, in the rain, in the dusk, he disappears from sight.

Farewell, Hans Castorp, life's faithful problem child. Your story is over. We have told it to its end; it was neither short on diversion nor long on boredom—it was a hermetic story. We told it for its own sake, not yours, for you were a simple fellow. But it was your story at last, and since it happened to you, there surely must have been something to you; and we do not deny that in the course of telling it, we have taken a certain pedagogic liking to you, might be tempted gently to dab the corner of an eye with one fingertip at the thought that we shall neither see you nor hear from you in the future.

Farewell, Hans—whether you live or stay where you are! Your chances are not good. The wicked dance in which you are caught up will last many a little sinful year yet, and we would not wager much that you will come out whole. To be honest, we are not really bothered about leaving the question open. Adventures in the flesh and spirit, which enhanced and heightened your ordinariness, allowed you to survive in the spirit what you probably will not survive in the flesh. There were moments when, as you "played king," you saw the intimation of a dream of love rising up out of death and this carnal body. And out of this worldwide festival of death, this ugly rutting fever that inflames the rainy evening sky all round—will love someday rise up out of this, too?

FINIS OPERIS